# A Dash of Darcy and Companions Cottage Collection 2

# A Dash of Darcy and Companions Cottage Collection 2

5 Pride and Prejudice Novellas and 1 Novel

## LEENIE BROWN

LEENIE B BOOKS

HALIFAX

This book is a work of fiction. All names, events, and places are a product of this author's imagination. If any name, event and/or place did exist, it is purely by coincidence that it appears in this book.

Cover design by Leenie B Books. Images sourced from DepositPhotos and Period Images.



ISBNs: 978-1-989410-14-1 (ebook); 978-1-989410-24-0 (print)

# Contents


*Dear Reader,*  ix


*Unravelling Mr. Darcy*

Chapter 1  3

Chapter 2  11

Chapter 3  19

Chapter 4  29

Chapter 5  39

Chapter 6  53

Chapter 7  63

Chapter 8  73

Chapter 9  85

Chapter 10  95


*Becoming Entangled*

Chapter 1  105

Chapter 2  113

Chapter 3  127

Chapter 4  135

Chapter 5  147

Chapter 6  157

Chapter 7  171

Chapter 8  179

Chapter 9  191

Chapter 10  203


## Enticing Miss Darcy


Chapter 1  217

Chapter 2  231

Chapter 3  241

Chapter 4  249

Chapter 5  259

Chapter 6  269

Chapter 7  279

Chapter 8  289

Chapter 9  297

Chapter 10  307

Chapter 11  315

Chapter 12  325

Reclaiming Her Heart  331


## Mr. Darcy's Comfort


Chapter 1  357

Chapter 2   365

Chapter 3   375

Chapter 4   389

Chapter 5   399

Chapter 6   413

Chapter 7   427

Chapter 8   437

Chapter 9   449

Chapter 10   459

Chapter 11   469

## Master of Longbourn

Chapter 1   485

Chapter 2   495

Chapter 3   505

Chapter 4   515

Chapter 5   527

Chapter 6   537

Chapter 7   547

Chapter 8   561

Chapter 9   571

Chapter 10   579

Chapter 11   593

Chapter 12   601

Epilogue  609

## Assessing Mr. Darcy

Chapter 1  617

Chapter 2  629

Chapter 3  639

Chapter 4  649

Chapter 5  659

Chapter 6  667

Chapter 7  679

Chapter 8  687

Chapter 9  697

Chapter 10  707

Chapter 11  719

Chapter 12  731

Chapter 13  741

Chapter 14  753

Chapter 15  763

Chapter 16  775

*Before You Go*  783
*Excerpt from Choices*  784
*Other Books by Leenie*  788
*About the Author*  789
*Connect with Leenie*  790

# Dear Reader,

These five novellas and one novel are part of my *Dash of Darcy and Companions Collection*. These *Pride and Prejudice* inspired stories are quick, sweet reads designed to fit perfectly into a busy life.

*Dash of Darcy* titles in this collection answer the question "what if Darcy and Elizabeth's story took a different path to happily ever after?" Each of these stories departs from the original work, *Pride and Prejudice*, at some specific point in that story's timeline, and while some parts of the continuation may mirror the original, most do not because these tales are reimaginings and not retellings. This collection contains three of these titles.

Standing next to the *Dash of Darcy* titles are the *Dash of Darcy Companion Stories*. These stories are also quick, sweet reads, but they focus on characters other than Darcy and Elizabeth. Each of these titles is a sequel to a *Dash of Darcy* story. While not all *Dash of Darcy* stories have sequels, many do. There are three such sequels contained in this collection.

You will notice that included in this boxset is a bonus story found at the end of *Enticing Miss Darcy* called *Reclaiming Her Heart*. This short story helps one of the secondary characters in that story find her happily ever after, so it is like an epilogue but not for one of the main characters.

Happy Reading!

# Unravelling Mr. Darcy

*He's got one chance to claim his heart's desire, and he's holding nothing back.*

# Chapter 1

Fitzwilliam Darcy took one final lingering look at the lady who had stolen his heart, then crushed it beneath her dainty slippers. With some effort, he turned and willed himself to leave the parsonage even though his heart cried out for him to stay and plead his case. But what could he say? He had injured her sister in separating her from his friend. The injury was not intentionally done, but it was done nonetheless. And *he* had done it.

She was also correct in that he had been aloof, but was that not to be expected from one of his position? He had to think of his family when choosing a wife. Did she not realize the great difficulty he would likely face in presenting a lady of little means, with a family seemingly devoid of manners that would recommend them, to the highest circles in the ton?

What she was not correct about was Wickham. But how could he defend himself on that account without placing his sister's reputation in jeopardy? Why could she not see that Mr. Wickham was too charming to be trusted? She was not unintelligent. She was actually very clever and, yet, also very duped by a charismatic deceiver.

His shoulders sagged under the weight of such tormenting thoughts as he pulled open the door to the sitting room and prepared to leave his heart behind, laying at her feet, with no hope of it ever being restored.

His steps faltered just a bit as he stepped out into the passageway. He closed his eyes and whispered a plea that he not be sent away from her. With a sigh of resignation, he placed his hat on his head. He had hoped there would be an instant answer to his petition, but perchance he was to be punished for having harmed another by suffering the same fate of being separated from the person he loved.

"Wait. Do not go."

Darcy turned slowly toward the door to the sitting room. Was his mind playing a trick on him? Was it making him hear words that he wished to hear but were not actually spoken? He had already learned that the orb between his ears was not to be trusted in its contemplations of Miss Elizabeth Bennet. It had been certain she would welcome his addresses. It had fancied her in love with him, and it had been wrong — horribly, cruelly wrong!

"Do not go," Elizabeth said once again when he turned her direction. "Please."

"Are you certain?" Darcy asked as he came to the door of the sitting room.

Elizabeth nodded. "I should not have spoken as I did." She wrapped an arm around her abdomen and took a tentative seat on a chair. "I was abominably rude and have no excuse to plead, save my indisposition." She rubbed a small circular pattern on her forehead between her brows as if to still the throbbing that lay behind her fingers.

Darcy took in the prospect of the woman before him. Her cousin had said that she had not come to Rosings due to a headache, and it looked to be a genuine malady and not just a ploy to avoid his aunt or for him to be able to find her alone.

He deposited his hat and gloves on a small table near the window that faced the front garden and crossed the room to sit near her. "You are unwell," he said, and then he grimaced. Of course, she already knew she was unwell. He did not need to tell her.

She smiled at him and opened her mouth as if to speak but then closed it again before rising quickly, one arm still wrapped tightly around her middle. "Please wait. I shall not be long," she said and hurried from the room.

For several minutes, Darcy paced the small sitting room, pausing each time he passed the door to listen for footsteps in the hall.

Quite obviously Miss Elizabeth was unwell and had remained at the parsonage because of that reason, and for that reason alone. He shook his head. Such arrogance to think she was possibly providing him an opportunity to make his offer! She had not been expecting his addresses at all. It was a sobering thought.

All of the ladies of his acquaintance who were not married, as well as a few who were, constantly put themselves in his path in an attempt to snare him for one reason or another. But not Miss Elizabeth. She didn't fawn over him or promote herself to him. She was different — in a most agreeable way.

She was intelligent and lively. He sighed. And beautiful — not in the fashion of the day. He shook his head again. No, in this way she was also different. Her features, to look at them with a critical eye, as he had attempted to do, were not classically beautiful, but her eyes — how they danced and sparkled, capturing her every emotion. Her smile lit her face. She moved with grace, and her figure was exceedingly pleasing — slight but womanly.

He stopped once more near the door to the sitting room to listen for her approach, and hearing footsteps, he hurried to stand near the mantle. It would not do to be found wringing his hands and hovering at the door like some anxious nursemaid.

He did a fine job of playing the part of an unaffected gentleman for a full ten ticks of the clock before he was propelled to her side by the ashen hue of her face.

"You are ill," he said as he assisted her to her chair. "May I call for someone to come sit with you? Is there anything that you require? I could send for the apothecary if you would like. In fact, I could fetch him for you myself." The words fell from his lips as rapidly as his grandmother's did when she was concerned and on the verge of a nervous fit. He clamped his lips closed and sat beside Elizabeth.

"I require nothing but a few moments of quiet," Elizabeth said, placing a hand on his knee, stopping it from bouncing. "The tapping of your foot," she explained when he looked at her in surprise.

He grimaced. It was not like him to be so very agitated, but then the lady sitting next to him had been unsettling him from the moment he had met her.

"I should go. You are in need of rest, and I am keeping you from it."

His voice was as apologetic as his look. If he stayed, he was likely to cause her greater distress than he had already caused.

"Are you certain there is nothing I can get you to ease your discomfort?"

He could use a good swift ride and a large burning drink. His every fiber seemed on edge.

She bit back a smile and that tauntingly impertinent eyebrow raised as she glanced at his hands which were rubbing back and forth on his knees. Immediately, he stilled them and rose.

"Please stay. I assure you my affliction is nothing out of the ordinary."

"But you are ill. Your head hurts, and I assume your stomach is unsettled," he protested as he began pacing. "You are in need of care."

"Mr. Darcy, please sit down."

Her tone was curt, and he immediately complied with a wary look.

"Your pacing was making me feel quite faint," she explained. "It is easier at the moment to look at you when you are still." She sighed.

His brows drew together, creating a worried crease as he looked at her. How could she wish for him to stay and claim that she was not ill? He could plainly see her discomfort. Her skin was not so ashen as it had been, but she was paler than normal, and her eyes did not contain the same liveliness. Would it not be better for her to go to bed and rest? He should insist upon that very thing, and he would insist if he were not so drawn to remain here with her. He had willed himself out of the room once already, and it seemed his heart was not in a state to cooperate a second time.

"I do not wish to be indelicate, sir. I assure you I do know what is right and proper," she began, her cheeks flushing to a more normal colour and then to a deeper hue. "However, since you have a sister who is in your care, I will assume you are not completely ignorant of the fact that at certain times a lady suffers from a particular indisposition. For some fortunate souls, it is a trifling matter. Unfortunately, I am not among the fortunate. So, as you can see, there is no need  for concern."

Ah! He felt himself relax. This he both understood and knew how to assist.

"What you need," he said with a smile, "is a small glass of wine and a warming brick." He kept his tone soft and soothing. "Might I call for them?"

A small smile crept across her lips. "Your help would be most welcome."

He rose and, leaving the room, found the housekeeper and made his requests. Then, returning to the sitting room, he pulled a small footstool close to her chair for her use, took a small quilt that hung on the end of a chaise, and draped it over her legs.

"My sister, Georgiana, insists that warmth helps," he explained," unless it is summer; then warmth merely adds to her misery."

"You must be a good brother," Elizabeth said as she tucked the blanket around her waist.

"I wish I could say I am, but I fear I have failed her on more than one occasion." He walked to the door and stood looking down the passageway.

"Surely you are too hard on yourself."

"Do you think me incapable of failure?" His voice held a hint of anger. Her words accusing him of not being a gentleman still stung. He should likely not indulge that feeling at present, but the wound was too fresh to ignore. "I should think you would find me more than proficient in it."

She opened her mouth, and he expected a protest. However, no words fell from her lips before she closed them again. Her brows furrowed and her head tipped as she scrutinized him for a moment. Then with a bewildered look and a slight shake of her head, she again opened her mouth. This time the action was accompanied by words, but they were still not a protest.

"I fear I accused you unjustly," she said.

Darcy lifted an eyebrow and folded his arms across his chest as he leaned against the door frame, waiting for her to continue.

Her head bowed. "I should have asked you about my concerns rather than racing to unfounded conclusions."

There was contrition in her tone, and he longed to ease her discomfort just as he did when Georgiana used such a tone. But, he would not. He held his peace and allowed her to continue.

"I am ashamed to say at times such as these, my temper often gets the best of my tongue and together the two can cause much damage."

He pushed off the door frame and moved into the room as a servant arrived with the wine and warming brick. "Place the brick on the small of your back, if you can, and sip the wine slowly. I would lower the lights to ease the pain in your head, but for propriety's sake, I dare not. However, if you feel the need to close your eyes, I will understand."

She shook her head but did as he suggested. "You, sir, are an enigma," she said, situating the brick as he slipped a pillow behind her upper back. "I truly cannot make out your character. One moment you are lofty in manner, ordering and directing the lives of those around you, and the next, you are solicitous and gracious. You are a contradiction." She took a small sip of wine and then placed her glass on the table next to her chair.

# Chapter 2

"I do not see how that is an inconsistency in character," he said as he took a seat near her once again. "Does not everyone have two sides — the one which is for public display and duty and the one that is reserved for those closest to you? May not those two sides be complementary, each supporting and balancing the other?" He settled back into his chair. "Are you the same in all situations?" he added before falling silent, waiting for her reply.

Elizabeth took another small sip of her wine before responding. "I had not thought of it so, and therefore, I will grant that you might be correct in your assessment. However, I believe that the two need not, nor should they, be exclusive of each other."

"Perhaps you are correct." He drummed his fingers on the arm of the chair. "You may have uncovered yet another one of my faults, a failure to be all things to all people."

"I did not mean to ..." Her words dropped away as she saw the small smile which pulled up the corners of Darcy's mouth. She dropped her gaze to her glass. She had not thought him capable of teasing. Had Miss Bingley not insisted that Mr. Darcy was not to be teased? Did that not mean the gentleman did not approve of teasing at all? She felt her face flush as she thought it. Had she truly expected Miss Bingley to be forthcoming with information?

Foolish girl! She had told Jane not to trust Miss Bingley, yet here she sat, evaluating another based on that woman's words. She heard a soft chuckle beside her.

"Forgive me, I should not tease when you are unwell. Georgiana scolds me for doing so."

"You must love her very much," Elizabeth spoke softly. Perhaps Miss Darcy was not as Mr. Wickham had said. Mr. Darcy seemed to defy that man's every word with his graciousness to her after having been so abused by her mere moments ago. So many things suddenly appeared to be the opposite of what she had believed to be true. Oh, why must she come to these realizations at such a time as this! She blinked to keep from crying.

"I do." His voice was soft as was his smile when, upon finding his handkerchief pressed into her hand, she looked up at him. "She is all I have left of those who are dear to me, save for my cousin, his father, and the Dowager Countess."

"What is your sister like?" Elizabeth dabbed at her eyes.

As he spoke of Georgiana, suddenly, the man before Elizabeth — the gentleman who filled the room with his presence, who commanded respect from all whom he met — crumbled away, replaced by the image of...a person, and not all so different from herself. She saw not his wealth, nor his connections, nor his authority. She saw him — a son, a brother, a cousin, a nephew, and, yes, a master. All heavy responsibilities he shouldered by himself. Silently, she chided herself for not having taken the time to consider him as anything more than the dour and disapproving friend of Mr. Bingley.

He had paused. His eyes stared straight ahead, but she suspected his focus was not on the vase of flowers on the table or the chair that stood before the fireplace. Indeed, he seemed to be looking far off into the distance, and what he saw there caused his countenance to become drawn and pained.

"I nearly lost her last summer." His voice was barely above a whisper. "It was my own doing. Had I been more attentive, or had I been more willing to bear her displeasure, it would not have happened. But as I was both too willing to please and too occupied with my own concerns, she was nearly convinced to run away with a man with whom she fancied herself in love." He shook his head and turned his eyes back towards Elizabeth. "She had known him for years and trusted him because of her history with him. He was not, however, in love with her but with her money. He broke her heart, which in turn broke mine."

Elizabeth could not keep all the tears from falling. She wiped at them quickly. A niggling suspicion crept into her mind. Mr. Wickham had claimed to know the Darcy family for years. Such a disappointment to his fortunes must have left him bitter. "It is how he lost your good opinion forever." It was not a question, but a statement of understanding.

Darcy nodded.

"I shall not ask you about him again. I am ashamed I ever believed a word he said." She wiped again at her eyes. Oh, how her heart broke at the way she had accused him of treating Mr. Wickham poorly when, in fact, it was Mr. Wickham who had harmed Mr. Darcy. "I am so very sorry," she whispered.

Darcy grabbed the hand that was not wiping tears from her face and squeezed it firmly.

"He is a pretender, a liar, and a cheat. Many have been taken in by his tales. Please, do not berate yourself because of it."

She heard the concern in his voice and squeezed the hand that held hers. She wished with all her heart that she could ignore the pain her words and actions had caused her, but she could not. She would not. She had acted foolishly, and she must bear the consequences of such behaviour.

"Thank you, Mr. Darcy. But, I must allow myself to feel the full measure of my shame, so I might not be so easily led in the future."

He pressed her hand once more before releasing it. "I understand. I have carried my guilt with me for some time." He blew out a great burdened breath. "There is more I could tell you about that particular scoundrel, whom I once considered a friend."

"More?" she gasped. Was not the near ruin of a dear sister enough harm? What more could Mr. Wickham have done?

Darcy nodded slowly. "However, I am not presently capable of speaking of him with equanimity, and I do not wish to speak unfairly, although I would not refuse to speak to you of him in the future."

"You are too good, sir!" Did he still offer friendship by speaking of the future? She was uncertain why such a thought lifted her heart, but it did.

"No. I assure you I am not." His voice was hard. "I..." He paused. "I have done as he did. I have broken your heart by breaking the heart of your sister. Though my motives may have been different, the result is the same, and it is inexcusable." He bowed his head in shame.

"You are most heartily wrong!" How could he think himself the same as a man who would trick an innocent into an elopement?

His head snapped up, his eyes piercing hers with their intensity.

"Did you plan to take advantage of my sister's caring nature, sir?"

He blinked. "Of course not!"

"Did you think her irrevocably attached to your friend?" Charlotte's admonition for Jane to make her feelings more apparent played in Elizabeth's mind. Charlotte had been certain that Mr. Darcy admired Elizabeth, something that Elizabeth had protested — loudly — and yet, it seemed Charlotte had not been wrong. Perhaps she was also correct about Jane and Mr. Bingley.

"I did not."

So, she had been wrong, and Charlotte had been right.

"You feared his attachment was greater than hers?" she asked.

"I did."

At least, she had been correct about Mr. Bingley's loving Jane. So far tonight, that was the only thing about which she had been correct, and that knowledge stung. She had always prided herself on being correct in her assessments of people.

"Did you fear she saw only his wealth?" she asked.

"I could not do her such a disservice."

"But, my mother..." Elizabeth looked away, the tears were once again threatening. "She is indecorous at times."

He said nothing, his silence affirming her fears. Her family's improprieties were not only a hindrance to him in coming to the point of declaring himself to her, but they were also, as Colonel Fitzwilliam had said, a reason to advise Mr. Bingley not to return to Netherfield and pursue Jane. The gravity of what was lost due to the lack of restraint of both her mother and her sisters was nearly overwhelming.

"My father does little to curb her displays or those of my sisters.

What respectable man would wish his friend attached to such a family!" This was not the well-reasoned argument she had planned, and she fought to regain her composure. "Your actions in such a light do you more credit than harm."

"But they still did harm — far more grievous than one could imagine," he protested. "Not only have I deprived my friend of a worthy woman and, in so doing, broken the hearts of two ladies, but I find it has also resulted in the shattering of what remained of my own." He stood. "But it is no more than I deserve. I shall leave you now."

"No."

He turned to look at her.

"Please do not leave me so. I cannot bear being the source of such sorrow. Could we not try again?"

"Renew my addresses, so you can accept me out of pity? I think not." He shook his head but sat down once again.

"No, not pity." She shook her head in bewilderment. "I do not know what it is I feel, but it is not pity." She looked at him, confusion clearly etched on her face. "Until this moment, I did not know you. I thought I did, but I was wrong. I viewed you through my prejudice. I allowed my pride to skew every thought. Would you..." She placed her hand on his arm. "Would you allow me the opportunity to become acquainted with the Mr. Darcy you are instead of the one I have contrived?"

A mixture of hope and agony shone in his eyes. "Do I dare allow my heart to hope? My time at Rosings is at an end. How can you become acquainted with me if we are not together?"

"Oh." Her hand flew to her chest and rubbed softly at the tightness that had arisen there at being reminded of his departure.

"Are you well?"

"I do not know. I am oddly sad at the thought of your leaving Rosings. I suppose in all the events of this evening and the jumbled state of my mind, I had forgotten that it was to be so soon that we would lose your company."

He smiled knowingly at her — almost as if he knew what was causing her to feel as strange as she did.

"I shall give you all the time you need to become acquainted with me, Miss Bennet," he said. "You are to stay with your aunt and uncle for a time after you leave here, are you not?"

She nodded.

"May I call on you when you are in town?"

"I would like that very much." A smile crept to her lips as the pain in her chest vanished. What that meant, she would have to ponder later. For now, she would allow herself to feel this happiness.

He rose again to take his leave. "Do not rise to see me out," he said before she could move. "My cousin and I will call before we leave on the morrow. If there is anything you wish to send to your sister, we would be happy to deliver it." He gathered his hat and gloves from the table where he had left them. "Do you require anything?"

She shook her head. "Thank you, Mr. Darcy. Your assistance has already brought me much comfort."

"Very well, until tomorrow then." He bowed over her hand and gave it a kiss, causing her to suck in a quick breath. He tipped his hat as he once again left the room and her behind. However, this time as he stepped out of the sitting room and moved to exit the parsonage he was in a much happier frame of mind, and though his heart still lay at her feet, he had hope — hope that his heart would one day find its happy home in her possession and that she, in turn, would give him hers. *18*

# Chapter 3

"You seem rather morose about leaving Rosings," Colonel Richard Fitzwilliam said as he joined Darcy in the carriage the following day.

Darcy shrugged. He did not particularly wish to speak to his cousin about why he was not as pleased to leave Rosings as he normally was wont to be. On most trips to visit his aunt, Lady Catherine, leaving was the highlight of the visit, and his cousin knew it.

"You seemed to be dragging your feet to leave the parsonage just now."

Again Darcy shrugged.

"You have not developed an affinity for nonsensical ramblings and incessant effusions, have you?"

"No." Darcy pulled out a book of verses and opened it to the place that was marked, attempting to ignore Richard's raised brows and questioning look. The low chuckle from across the carriage, however, instinctively drew his eye.

"Aunt Catherine will not be best pleased." Richard smirked as he folded his arms across his chest and settled back into his seat.

Darcy's lips twitched. His aunt would be a great deal less than best pleased when she finally discovered that Darcy was attempting to win a lady who was not her daughter, Anne, as his wife. "When is she best pleased?"

"Oh ho!" Richard laughed. "Do tell what you have done."

"Who says I have done anything?" Darcy hedged.

"You." Richard extended his legs across the short span between the carriage benches and made certain to knock Darcy's leg in the process. "You are avoiding a topic, which is what you do rather than lie about whatever it is that you do not wish to reveal."

Darcy smiled and shrugged before turning his eyes to the words on the page before him.

"I'll have the truth," Richard said with a laugh. "You know I shall."

"Indeed, I do," Darcy replied. "But you enjoy the process of wheedling it out of me, and I should so hate to rob you of the pleasure." He closed his book and placed it on the bench next to him.

"Very well," Richard said with a grin, "I shall guess."

Darcy waved a hand to indicate to Richard that he had the floor.

"You have fallen in love with the lovely Miss Bennet."

Darcy picked up his book once again. "You have deciphered it, and now I shall return to my reading."

Richard snatched the book from his cousin's hands. "You have truly fallen in love?" There was no small amount of shock in his voice.

Darcy sighed. "Yes, I do believe that is what this foolishness is. At least, I do not suppose it is merely an infatuation that drives a man, despite rational argument and obligation to duty, to offer marriage to a lady."

Richard blinked, and his mouth dropped open.

Darcy watched as his cousin closed his mouth, opened it again, closed it once more, and then, with a shake of his head and a look of great perplexity, he finally spoke.

"You proposed?"

Darcy nodded.

"To Miss Bennet?"

Darcy nodded again.

"Miss Elizabeth Bennet?"

"That is the only Miss Bennet who was in residence at the parsonage." Darcy's lips curled up slightly. It was a rare sight for his cousin to be lost for words. Richard Fitzwilliam was not the sort of man to ever be caught unaware about much of anything.

"I knew you liked her, but marriage?"

"It seemed the thing to do."

Richard's brows drew together, creating a deep crease between them. "The thing to do? The thing to do?" He shook his head. "What has become of you?"

Darcy shrugged. "I honestly do not know, but if it will put your mind at ease, she refused me."

Richard scrubbed his face with his hands. "She refused you?"

Darcy reached across the carriage and reclaimed his book, which Richard had discarded on the seat. "You know, Cousin, you are usually the more loquacious between us," he taunted.

Richard's eyes narrowed, causing Darcy to grin broadly.

"Allow me to see if I have this startling news correct," Richard began. "You, the staid and steady, do only what is required and proper, Fitzwilliam Darcy, have actually fallen in love with a lady?"

Darcy nodded.

"And despite what I assume were sound arguments against making such a match, you have proposed to this lady?"

Again Darcy nodded.

"And this lady, whom I know to be intelligent, has refused you, your estate, and your income?"

"No, she refused me," Darcy responded. "Her rejection was clearly of me and nothing else." His brows drew together for a moment. "Do you think me vain and conceited?"

"She accused you of such?" Surprise coloured Richard's tone.

"Among other things," Darcy replied. "Do you think me arrogant?"

Still rather startled, Richard shook his head and shrugged. "You are aloof at times — so bent on presenting yourself in the best light that you do appear to look down your nose at others."

Darcy scowled. "Why did you not tell me I was being improperly proud?"

Richard laughed. "Would you have listened?"

Darcy shook his head. How had he allowed himself to become so proud? His parents had never taught him to be so, and he did not think himself unfeeling. How had he become so filled with who he was?

"I do not think you arrogant," Richard said. "You appear to be, but those of us who know you understand it is your unease. You do not fall into conversation easily unless you are at home among close friends and family. You are reserved and given to pondering and considering every option before making a decision. You have been given a great burden of responsibility in the care of Pemberley and your sister, and you fill the role of master credibly. None have suffered under your care."

Darcy shook his head. "Except my sister."

"The fault for Georgiana's pain lies with Wickham," Richard spat.

Darcy nodded. "I know, but I cannot help feeling my share of the guilt."

Richard blew out a breath. "Nor can I."

The two men rode along in silence for several minutes before Richard once again knocked Darcy's leg. "Tell me, if the lovely Miss Bennet, whom you claim to love, refused your offer of marriage, why are you delivering a letter to her sister and do not seem heartbroken?"

Darcy smiled. "Because although she refused my proposal, she has allowed me the privilege of calling on her in town."

Richard's eyes grew wide. "No, it cannot be."

"I assure you it is."

A grin split Richard's face. "And the letter gives you the opportunity to meet her uncle before you call on his niece. I had not thought you so sly."

Darcy laughed. "I am not. If her uncle is home when I deliver the letter, and I am able to meet him, it will be a happy coincidence. I offered to deliver the letter to her sister because it seems I have played a role in injuring her." He tipped his head, and his eyes narrowed. "About her sister. Perhaps you would care to tell me how Miss Bennet came to know that I played a part in separating Bingley from her sister."

Richard grimaced. "Miss Bennet's sister was Bingley's most recent angel?"

Darcy nodded.

Richard sighed and began his explanation.

~*~*~

Darcy grabbed Richard's arm as he moved to disembark the carriage in front of Darcy House. "Not a word about Miss Bennet to Georgiana or our grandmother."

"May I tell my father?" Richard asked with a smirk.

Darcy's eyes narrowed. "No. Allow me to clarify further. No one is to know about Miss Bennet until such time as I make it known. She may change her mind between today and when she arrives in town and refuse to see me." He hoped she would not, but it was entirely possible that her opinion, once Elizabeth had time to consider, might change.

No, he thought, it would not. She had blushed and smiled at him when he and Richard had called at the parsonage before they departed Kent. That was surely a good sign, was it not?

"You are doing it again," Richard said as he moved toward the open door.

"Doing what?" Darcy asked following behind his cousin.

"Imagining disaster." Richard straightened his coat and waited for Darcy to alight and stand next to him. "From what you have told me, until Lady Catherine discovers your defection, you have survived the worst of it." He chuckled. "And keeping this bit of news from our dear aunt will be easiest if not a word is ever shared."

He clapped Darcy on the shoulder. "When you deliver that letter, request that you be allowed to steal Miss Elizabeth away to Gretna Green. It would be easier to inform Lady Catherine once the union is irrevocable as there would be less chance she could interfere and all."

They walked up the steps to the door together.

"There will likely still be a fit of fury to be endured, but she would not be able to drive the poor young lady scurrying if she is already your wife."

Darcy shook his head. Leave it to his cousin to devise schemes and tactics to circumvent and outwit those who stood in the path of a desired result. Richard had always been that sort, however. Negotiating sticky situations seemed to be his greatest talent — if you did not consider the fact that many of the circumstances that needed evading were of his own creation.

"I only ask that you do not speak of this until I am prepared to answer to any and all on my own behalf as well as that of Miss Bennet," Darcy said as he handed his outerwear to a footman.

"And how do you plan to keep the fact that you are calling on a lady from your sister?" Richard followed Darcy down the hall to his study.

"I shan't. But there is no need to endure her questions or those of Lady Margaret until I have actually called on Miss Bennet and can answer with something more than hopes and wishes. And that is why you shall not say a word to Georgiana or your grand-mother."

He picked up and sorted through the stack of letters on his desk. He would not work on any business today, but he did wish to see what sort of things awaited his attention.

Richard flopped into a chair in front of Darcy's desk. "Grand-mother is curious, is she not?"

Darcy lifted his eyes from the letters in his hand. "Indeed, and observant."

The Dowager Countess of Matlock — or Lady Margaret as she insisted upon being called since dowager was, in Lady Margaret's unique sort of logic, a term for a frail old woman, and Lady Margaret, though not precisely young and robust, was not to be considered either old or frail — was keenly observant and ferociously curious. Not much escaped her notice, and she was nearly as relentless as Richard in finding out whatever bit of information she deemed she must know.

"I will not breathe a word of it," Richard assured.

"A word of what?" Georgiana asked from the doorway.

"Georgiana, you know you are not to be listening to other people's conversations," her brother scolded as he deposited all the letters on his desk and crossed the room to envelop her in a hug. "I have missed you."

"And I you, Brother," she replied. "How are Aunt Catherine and Anne?"

"They are as they always are," he replied as he released her from his embrace.

"So cantankerous and nearly invisible?" Georgiana asked, ignoring her brother's scowl and turning to give Richard a welcoming hug.

"It is not how you should speak of your relations," Richard chided, "but, yes. However, I do think Anne was even more withdrawn than she has been on previous visits."

"She is an heiress." Georgiana cocked her head to the side and fluttered her lashes at her cousin.

"I am not going to marry Anne," Richard said with a laugh. "I would prefer a heartier sort of wife." He held out his arm to her. "Shall we go call for some tea?"

"We absolutely must," she said as she took his arm. "Are you going to marry Anne, Brother?"

"You know I am not," Darcy replied as he followed them to the blue sitting room.

"And have you told Aunt Catherine?"

"No, I have not."

"You should."

"Yes, Darcy, you should," Richard said with a smirk.

Darcy shook his head. "You are both incorrigible — which I must tolerate from Richard but would rather not see in you, Georgiana." He was actually glad to see her smiling and teasing. She had spent so many months brooding over her near ruin and mending her broken heart that to have her tease, even if it bordered on being entirely too impertinent, was encouraging. He winked at her and received a smile in return.

"Once you tell Aunt Catherine, do you think she will allow Anne to come to town for a season?" Georgiana took a seat in what Darcy knew to be her favourite chair — the blue one near the window that overlooked the street.

"It would be Anne's best chance to find a husband," Richard answered, "but I am uncertain her health could endure a season."

Georgiana bit her lip. Darcy knew that look well.

"What are you thinking?" he asked.

"We should find her a husband."

Richard guffawed. "How do you intend to do this?"

Georgiana shrugged. "I do not know. I only wish Anne were not so lonely."

Darcy squeezed her shoulder. "You have a good heart, but I would prefer you not play at matchmaking for our cousin."

She sighed. It was a deeply sorrowful sound as if being denied a great adventure.

He smiled at her. "Tell me what you have been doing in my absence."

"And then will you tell me what Richard is not to breathe a word of?" she asked, as he removed his jacket before taking a seat.

"No." Darcy gave both her and Richard a stern look.

"Very well." Again, she sighed that deep sorrowful sigh, but a small smile touched her lips as she began to tell her brother and cousin all she had done in town while they were in Kent.

# Chapter 4

Elizabeth plucked a wildflower that grew along the path on which she walked. The sun was warm this morning, and the sky was nearly without a cloud. The ribbons of her bonnet fluttered ever so slightly in the breeze. All in all, it was a glorious morning — even if she had been required to endure her cousin's excessively long dissertation on what a privilege it had been for Elizabeth to visit Kent and, most especially, Rosings and the illustrious Lady Catherine.

Elizabeth's lips curled upwards as she remembered how her cousin had pressed upon both her and Maria, Mrs. Collins's sister, that one could not speak too highly of a patroness such as Lady Catherine. Indeed, one must not forget to mention her and her condescension to one and all when one returned to her home. Maria had nodded her head, very seriously considering all her brother-in-law's instructions and occasionally adding her own exclamation of delight of this or that thing about Rosings, which pleased Mr. Collins excessively. It also pleased Elizabeth, since it would mean the glory of all things Lady Catherine would be known to the neighborhood before Jane and Elizabeth returned. Therefore, Elizabeth would only have to answer questions about her visit.

She twirled the flower in her hand and bit her lip. She would also have to answer questions regarding the gentleman who called on her in town. Oh, she wished she had not been so open in her censure of Mr. Darcy. It would make it easier to reverse her opinion. But as it was, she found herself in a very difficult place. Even Aunt Gardiner had heard her condemnation of that gentleman.

She blew out a breath. It would be rather awkward to explain to her aunt and uncle, as well as Jane, that she wished to get to know Mr. Darcy now that she had the beginnings of a new understanding of him.

Once again, she replayed in her mind the events of his call at the parsonage — how he had approached her at first with such practised words, his damning explanation of his struggles, and then his anger and hurt at her response. She once again grimaced at the way in which she allowed herself to speak so freely and, worse, so spitefully.

She stopped and turned to look out at the vista of rolling hills. How he had been able to respond to her with anything less than hatred when she had called him back still amazed her. She knew if it had been she who had been treated as she treated him, she would not have done more than pretend a smile and accept her apology before hastening out the door.

She had spent the past week contemplating his graciousness in extending her another chance to decipher his character and learn about him — a man about whom she had apparently been entirely wrong. She touched the letter in her pocket. She likely should not have accepted it, but Mr. Darcy had been so insistent that she did on that morning when he took his leave of the parsonage.

"It seemed easier to do Mr. Wickham justice in writing than in speaking. You will find all my dealings with him in this account," he had said. "I wish for you to know exactly what his character is like."

"So that I might find yours better?" she had teased uneasily.

She sighed now, remembering the smile that touched his lips and the sparkle in his eye as he had replied, "I will not lie. I do hope it helps me in my quest."

If he had shown one morsel of that lighter side of his personality when he was in Hertfordshire, she was certain she never would have thought him capable of the things Mr. Wickham had claimed. Her shoulders rose high as she drew in a deep breath and then slowly lowered them as she released it. It was not true. If Mr. Darcy had been lighter in his tone, she would have likely thought he was ridiculing her. She had been so determined to dislike him. He had attempted levity a time or two when she was at Netherfield, and she had excused it away as arrogance and superiority.

A small flutter of eagerness had settled in her stomach this morning when she had awoken. One more day and she would be in town where she might see him again.

"Miss Bennet!"

Elizabeth turned toward the lane as Miss de Bourgh drew near in her phaeton.

"You must join me."

The ease and liveliness of Miss de Bourgh's tone and features startled Elizabeth. Until this moment, Miss de Bourgh had always looked serious and aloof, but presently, she seemed neither of those things.

"I am an excellent driver," Miss de Bourgh continued. She drew her horses to a stop beside Elizabeth. "Please, I have wished for an opportunity to speak with you, but between my mother and your cousin, I have not found a moment to do so. Please join me.”

There seemed no way of objecting without offending, and so, Elizabeth accepted and climbed into the carriage.

“Have you ever driven?”

“No, never.”

“Oh, my dear Miss Bennet, you must learn! It is the absolute best thing in the world to be trotting down the lane on your own — no maid, no footman, no mother.” She winked, shocking Elizabeth. “It is here that I am allowed to be me — just me.” She sighed. “You must understand the feeling. What with so many sisters and all.” She glanced at Elizabeth expectantly.

“Oh, I do,” Elizabeth agreed. “That is one reason I am so fond of walking.”

“I knew it!” Miss de Bourgh cried with a great deal of delight. “I should like to take a great many rambling walks just for the solidarity of them, but my health will not allow it. And so, I must find my pleasure in my phaeton.”

Elizabeth stole a sidelong glance at the lady beside her. This was not the Miss de Bourgh she had come to know.

“Do not worry, Miss Bennet — might I call you Elizabeth?”

Elizabeth nodded.

“Good.” A smile split Miss de Bourgh’s face. “And you must call me Anne. I think we will be good friends.” She turned her attention back to her well-trained horses.

Elizabeth suspected the creatures could traverse this road in the black of night and without a single command from their mistress.

“As I was saying, I have not lost my senses. I know I am usually quiet in company, but you have met my mother. Can you blame me for holding my tongue to avoid a lecture?"

Elizabeth joined her in a laugh. "Mothers can be a source of great distress for their daughters, can they not?"

"Oh, indeed!" Anne agreed. "And my mother will expect me to return in thirty minutes time and if I have not, she will send out half the household in search of me."

Elizabeth considered how trying it must be to have a mother who was so vigilant. Lady Catherine was nearly the opposite of Elizabeth's own mother. Mrs. Bennet was only attentive when it came to daughters whom she knew would marry well. Therefore, she had never been overly concerned with Elizabeth. Since Elizabeth had refused Mr. Collins's offer of marriage, Mrs. Bennet was even more certain that her second daughter would never marry.

"I have sought you out on purpose," Anne said in a hushed tone as if the trees near them might hear her and tell tales. "I have sent a letter to my cousin Mr. Darcy and asked him to call on you, and when he does, you must make him love you."

The horses' feet rose and fell four times before Elizabeth could find her voice, and as it was, all her mind was able to do was form a question. "I beg your pardon?"

Anne, who had watched Elizabeth's surprise with keen interest and obvious amusement, smiled broadly and repeated herself. "You must make my cousin fall in love with you, although I dare say it shall not be hard work. He seemed to pay an extraordinary amount of attention to you. I had half hoped he would declare his unwillingness to marry me on this visit, but he did not." She sighed. "It is a pity he did not. What a stir it would have caused!"

The excitement in Anne's voice reminded Elizabeth for a moment of her youngest sister, Lydia.

"You do not wish for him to marry you? I had heard you were betrothed," Elizabeth said cautiously.

She had assumed that bit of Mr. Wickham's tale had been untrue since Mr. Darcy had offered her marriage not even a week ago, but she had still intended to ask Mr. Darcy about it when she saw him in town, just to be certain. Apparently, she would not need to bother if Anne was, so to speak, tossing the gentleman at Elizabeth's feet.

"Oh dear, no! Darcy is so stodgy, so proper. I long to be free of the overbearing, not tie myself to it forever."

"Overbearing?" The word leapt from Elizabeth's lips. She had never once thought Mr. Darcy to be overbearing. Dull, perhaps. Arrogant, most assuredly. But not imperious. She paused. He had, however, been rather high-handed in his dealing with Mr. Bingley and Jane, so maybe it was possible that he could be overbearing? The idea was rather shocking.

Anne's eyes grew wide as she realized what she had said. "No, no, I do not think my cousin would be some sort of tyrant. It is just that he likes ceremony and schedules and rules." She shuddered at the word. "For all my life my mother has ordered me about and hired people to watch me. I am not sick nearly as often as she thinks I am sick. Oh, it is impossible to explain."

"Is it that your mother is demanding, and because your cousin is as serious and proper as your mother, you fear he will also be demanding?" Elizabeth asked it calmly, but her heart skittered and thudded at the thought. She did not wish for a demanding husband either.

Anne drew the horses to a stop on the side of the road and turned to face Elizabeth.

"Darcy is all that is kind. Truly he is, but he lacks..." Anne tapped her finger on her lip as she thought. "Humour — he lacks humour. He rarely smiles and never teases. He is serious to a fault."

Elizabeth shook her head. "I have seen him smile and even tease once or twice. I do not believe him to be without any humour at all. I will allow that he is rather grave, but might he not have reason?" She clamped her mouth shut. Why was she defending Mr. Darcy to his cousin? Was she attempting to persuade Anne to reconsider and marry the man?

"What reasons might he have for being so dour?"

Elizabeth thought for a moment. She did not really wish to justify Mr. Darcy's actions and risk Anne deciding that her cousin was whom she wanted to marry. However, she had begun the discussion and to end it abruptly would be rude.

"Where have you been in company with your cousin?" she finally asked.

"Why at Rosings, of course. Mother declared Pemberley too far for me to travel, so we always saw him here, save when his mother was ill at first and could still travel. Then we ventured to town when she had come to London to see various physicians."

"Then you have never seen him outside of your mother's influence?" Elizabeth remembered how ill-at-ease Darcy had appeared at the assembly in Meryton and again when Mrs. Bennet had called at Netherfield. She had assumed it was merely his haughty disdain for the people of Meryton, in general, and her family, in particular, that had caused him to behave so, but now, considering it in a new light, it might have just been an uncertainty of how to act and a wish to be proper.

"Could he not feel as intensely as you the strictures of your mother? Would that not make him less lively?"

Anne shrugged. "I will grant it might, but I should wish for a husband that will behave in a lively fashion no matter if my mother is present or not. I should fear that my cousin would wish to keep my mother too well-pleased, and in order for him to do so, my activities would be as curtailed as they are now. Do you know what it is like to be forbidden to wander the groves? Or to be allowed to dance only two sets with your instructor and never attend a ball because it might fatigue you? " She pinched her lips together tightly, her brows drawing together. "I wish to be fatigued. I wish to walk until I am tired and dance until I can no longer stand."

"And you fear your cousin would not allow such things?"

Anne nodded her head. "He will not treat you so because you are not sickly."

"I think any husband would care if his wife was risking her health," Elizabeth countered.

"Yes," Anne answered softly. "But I do not want him. He does not make my heart flutter. I do not feel any great joy when he arrives for a visit or sorrow when he leaves aside from missing the diversion that company brings." She grasped Elizabeth's hands. "Please, you must love him. He is handsome and rich as well as gentle and kind. He has always treated me with respect. But I cannot marry him."

"There is no betrothal to be broken?"

The flowers on Anne's bonnet fluttered as she shook her head. "He has never asked, and I would never accept."

Strangely, Elizabeth's heart rejoiced at Anne's reply. "If he calls on me, I will not turn him away. I cannot promise any further than that, for I, too, would wish for a husband that stirs my heart." To Elizabeth's surprise, she found herself wrapped in Anne's arms.

"Oh, you shall suit. I am certain of it. And then I shall be free to smile at Mr. Pratt when he accompanies his mother to visit my mother." She released Elizabeth and called to her horses to walk on. "She is Lady Metcalfe — the one who needed a governess and my mother recommended Miss Pope, Mrs. Jenkinson's niece. Do you remember?" She waited for only a moment, just long enough for Elizabeth to say yes, and then began describing in some detail the relationship between Lady Catherine and Lady Metcalfe, which in turn became a discussion of what it must be like to have a come out.

Elizabeth returned to the parsonage with weary ears and a very different view of the not so sickly or cross Miss de Bourgh and a slightly better understanding of Mr. Darcy.

# Chapter 5

"For you, sir," Mr. Kinney deposited a few envelopes in the tray on Darcy's desk.

"Thank you," Darcy said, glancing up from his account book. His brows furrowed as he saw the address on the top letter. Putting down his pencil, he picked up the curious missive. Why would Anne be writing to him? Hopefully, it was not some scheme of his aunt's to press the matter of his marrying her daughter. She had been more insistent than normal on this trip that the happy event was not far off. It made sense, he supposed, seeing how Anne would be twenty in a month — the same age both his mother and Lady Catherine had been when they married their husbands.

He broke the seal and unfolded the paper.

> *Dearest Cousin,*

His brows rose. Anne never referred to him as dearest anything.

> *As you know, I will be celebrating a very particular birthday next month, and I would request...*

Darcy groaned. It appeared this was exactly what he feared.

> *that you spend this month securing a bride and doing so with all*

*haste. If you are married before my birthday, I should be very grate-*
*ful.*

Darcy blinked and reread the letter from the beginning. No, he had not missed any words. Anne had just asked him to marry someone other than herself and to do it in quick order. He shook his head and continued on.

*I do not wish to injure your male sensibilities in any fashion, but I must be direct. I believe on the subject of our marriage, we are of one accord, for I do not wish to marry you, and I am certain that you do not wish to marry me. We would not suit. You are far too serious for a lady such as myself, and I do not think myself equal to the challenges of the cold in Derbyshire or the air in town. One or the other I might be able to endure, but to face both would be far too taxing.*

Too serious for Anne? The girl who cowered in the corner and never smiled? He shook his head again. This letter was befuddling and perhaps the longest single exchange of words he had ever received from his cousin.

*To help you in your quest to grant me my birthday wish, I would advise you to call directly on Miss Bennet. She is a lovely lady, full of vitality and of a hardy stock. She should weather well both your dour temperament and the conditions of Derbyshire and town. In addition to this, I believe you would suit eminently well, and I do believe you favour her.*

Not only was he too serious, but he was also dour? How else was he to be in the presence of Lady Catherine? Richard might not mind their aunt's reprimands, but Darcy did not relish to endure them. Anne was correct, at least, about his favouring Miss Bennet.

*You will be doing my heart a great service should you be successful in gaining her acceptance. I will do my part to keep my mother occupied, so that if even a whisper of your intentions reaches her ears, she will be unable to cause you any trouble.*

*Remember, you must be married in one month. Please, do not dawdle in doing your duty.*

*I shall be indebted to you forever.*

*Your grateful cousin,*

*Anne*

Darcy chuckled and shook his head in disbelief. How Anne intended to keep her mother from being able to interfere if word of his courting Elizabeth should reach her piqued his curiosity. He should very much like to hear of her plans, but he was not so curious as to write and ask. No, he would not write at all, for if he did, he knew his letter would pass through his aunt's hands before it ever reached Anne.

One month? He rubbed his chin as he studied the letter before him. He was not certain a month would be long enough, but he thought, as a smile crept to his lips, that it would be his pleasure to attempt such a feat.

He tucked the letter into the top drawer of his desk as he heard the soft tap at his study door, indicating it was time for him to accompany his sister to a few shops.

Three hours later, Georgiana had purchased perfume, gloves, and a fan. She had ordered two dresses, and she, along with her brother, had enjoyed a few sweets. Now, when all Darcy really wished to do was return home, Georgiana was asking to stop at yet another store.

"Please, Brother? If I am to spend the whole of tomorrow afternoon sitting with Grandmama, might I not have a bit of new ribbon or lace in my work basket." Georgiana peered out the window of the carriage as they travelled the streets of London. "It would make the task ever so much more enjoyable."

Darcy chuckled. "Spending time with Lady Margaret is hardly a thing to be endured." He noted the small pout that formed instinctively on his sister's lips. It was not an attempt to procure his favour, but rather a small twinge of disappointment which would soon be replaced by a smile and accompanied by a 'very well.'

"However," he continued, "if a bit of lace will make both you and her happy, we shall stop and procure the magical bit of froth."

A smile lit Georgiana's face. "Oh, thank you, Fitzwilliam! Lady Margaret loves a bit of finery with which to work." She looked out the window once more.

Darcy knew it to be true. His sister and their grandmother were a lot alike in that way. Both found great pleasure in adorning a hat or dress with a bit of finery. And as much as he wished to be home and did not relish the idea of having to give his opinion on which bit of lace would be best, he could not deny either his sister or his grandmother such a small pleasure when it was well within his power to do so. He sighed quietly. Perhaps he was too indulgent.

"That store. There." Georgiana pointed to a small establishment just up the street. "They have the best and finest selection."

Darcy frowned, just a bit. The storefront was neat in appearance, but it was small. "Are you sure you would not prefer a shop closer to home in a finer neighbourhood?"

She swatted his knee. "Do not be such a dolt, Brother. Ladies of quality frequent this store regularly, which is how I know about it. Many of my friends and their mothers have made mention of it." She turned pleading eyes upon him. "I have always longed to shop here."

He shook his head at how easily he was acquiescing to her request and tapped the roof of the carriage with his walking stick. "Very well. Though your language in reference to me leaves something to be desired." He raised a brow and affected a scolding look. "You shall have your wish today, Sweetling."

Her eyes narrowed at his use of his pet name for her.

As if reading her thoughts, he answered, "I know you are about to be presented to society and that you are indeed no longer a mere child. However, you are now and will always remain my baby sister — even when you are as old and hard of hearing and short of sight as Lady Margaret."

She giggled. "Lady Margaret would be shocked to hear you speak of her so. She is none of those things!"

"I know, but she is not young — no matter what she might claim — and therein lies my point."

Georgiana tipped her head, her smile was soft. "I love you, too, Brother."

He gave her knee a pat as the carriage drew to a stop. "How shall I ever give you away?" he asked. It was something he often found himself wondering. He could not imagine there was a man worthy of his sister, and he dreaded the day that she insisted there was.

"Once you do, you shall no longer have to accompany me to buy lace nor will the bills be yours to pay."

He chuckled. "Then find a suitable gentleman quickly," he teased as the door to the carriage was opened, and he climbed out before assisting her. "How much longer shall I have to play the part of the solicitous brother today? You do know these shops are not my favourite establishments."

She giggled. "I shall endeavour to make our foray amongst the frills and your discomfort as short as possible."

He carefully watched where her feet were stepping, guiding her safely to the door of the store. Stepping through the doorway, he took in his surroundings. It was indeed a shop of quality, well-kept and holding an air of dignity. He chuckled to himself. How could a store be dignified? Perhaps it was the elegant furnishings and the impeccably dressed assistants standing at the ready behind the counters along the artfully arranged displays evidencing the obvious care the shopkeeper gave to his establishment which lent to the atmosphere.

He turned to speak once more to his sister. "Where shall we begin, Sweet..." His words died on his lips as he beheld the lady standing behind his sister. "Miss Elizabeth." He bowed slightly.

Georgiana noted the slight flush to her brother's face and the smile he bestowed upon the lady named Miss Elizabeth. She looked at the young woman and noted a similar pink tinge to her cheeks. Elbowing her brother in the side, she waited for him to notice that there was anyone else within the store. She wanted to giggle at his startled expression as he turned to her. She tilted her head toward Miss Elizabeth and blinked at him, waiting for him to remember his duty in introducing her.

His brows drew together slightly as he looked at his sister before recognition dawned in his eyes. "Right," he muttered with a nod. "Miss Elizabeth, may I present my sister, Miss Darcy. Georgiana, this is Miss Elizabeth."

Georgiana extended her hand in greeting to the lady. "It is a pleasure to meet you."

"As it is likewise a pleasure for me. I have heard somewhat about you."

"You have?" Georgiana looked in confusion toward her brother. She had not heard of Miss Elizabeth.

"Indeed, I have, for your brother has spoken of you but not so much as either Lady Catherine or Miss Bingley. However, you may rest assured, they only speak of you in terms of highest praise." She studied the young girl before her. Wickham's description of Miss Darcy played in her mind. This was not a proud young lady. There was nothing cold in the way that Miss Darcy had greeted her, nor was there any air of pretension in Miss Darcy's manners.

Georgiana smiled at Miss Elizabeth and raised an eyebrow in her brother's direction. "You have met both my aunt and Miss Bingley?"

Elizabeth nodded. "I have just returned from a stay in Kent. My particular friend is married to my cousin, who happens to be your aunt's parson. It is through his position I met your aunt."

"And Miss Bingley?"

Elizabeth could not help feeling amused at how Miss Darcy avoided looking at her brother, who was scowling at her. "Mr. Bingley let the estate which neighbours my father's estate in Hertfordshire."

"You live near Netherfield?" This time Georgiana grimaced slightly as her brother cleared his throat.

It seemed to Elizabeth that Mr. Darcy was not without some experience when it came to curious younger sisters. "Indeed, I do," she replied. Then, noting how the young girl's brows drew together as she tried to reconcile some bit of information with another, Elizabeth added, "My aunt and uncle own this store and a few others. I am visiting them, along with my sister Jane, before we return to Longbourn."

"Oh." Georgiana brow remained furrowed for a moment longer before her features relaxed, and she regained her smile. "So you met my brother while he was at Netherfield with Mr. Bingley?"

"Georgiana," Darcy scolded softly.

"I do not mind," Elizabeth assured him with a smile.

"But I might," he said with a sheepish smile. "There are portions of my stay..." He found himself unable to complete his sentence as she raised a teasing brow, her eyes sparkling with impertinence. How her eyes captivated him. They were so expressive.

"We first met at an assembly," she said, turning her eyes back to Georgiana.

Georgiana's brows rose in surprise. "An assembly?"

Elizabeth nodded.

"Did my brother dance?"

Elizabeth laughed. "Only with Miss Bingley and Mrs. Hurst."

Georgiana's mouth dropped open for a brief moment before pursing her lips and directing a displeased look at her brother.

"Suffice it to say that our first meeting did not go well," Darcy replied hastily.

"And yet we are friends," Elizabeth added.

"Was there not a reason for coming into this store, Georgiana?" Darcy asked in hopes of changing the subject. "Did you not wish to find a bit of lace for Lady Margaret?"

"Mr. Darcy," Jane Bennet greeted as she joined her sister.

"Miss Bennet." Darcy bowed. "May I present my sister, Miss Darcy. Georgiana, this is Miss Bennet."

"My sister," Elizabeth added softly.

"It is a pleasure to meet you, Miss Bennet." As she spoke, Georgiana's eyes fell on the trim Jane held in her hands. Then, darting a look at her brother, whose eyes still remained fixed on Miss Elizabeth, she continued. "Miss Bennet, you have just the thing for which I am looking. That trim with a bit of lace is exactly what I need for my blue muslin. Would you mind showing me where you found it?"

Jane hesitated for a moment.

"I do not wish to inconvenience you, but it shall shorten my brother's torment if you were to assist me." Georgiana leaned forward and spoke softly as a customer brushed past her. "He is not fond of shopping in general and for lace in particular."

Jane smiled. "I imagine shopping for lace is not any gentleman's favourite pastime." She motioned toward the back of the store. "This is part of my uncle's newest shipment, so it is in the case back here. We will ask Mr. Greenwood to see the full tray. There are a few pieces that are similar to this and might interest you more."

Darcy watched as his sister followed Jane. "My sister wished for some trim to add to her work-basket when she goes to visit our grandmother tomorrow." He was not sure why he felt a need to explain his presence to Elizabeth. "She had heard of this establishment and had never been here before, so I indulged her."

"An indulgent brother?" Elizabeth teased.

"Perhaps too indulgent."

"I cannot believe it to be true," said Elizabeth firmly. "Your sister seems lovely and not at all spoilt as some do who are overly indulged. "

"True," Darcy agreed. "She is not like some I have seen."

"Such as my sisters," Elizabeth said.

"That is not what I meant." He shook his head at his own stupidity. "There are those of the ton…"

"It is true, and I am not offended," Elizabeth interrupted. "My youngest sisters are indulged and spoiled." She had considered his criticisms over the last week and had come to realize that, as much as it stung, he had been correct about her family.

"My uncle has a small sitting room over here." She motioned to an open door on her right. "There are those among his clientele who prefer to sit and read the paper while their wives shop. You may find it more pleasant to wait for your sister there. Jane will see that she is returned to you safely."

Darcy looked toward the door to the sitting room and then back to where his sister was exclaiming over some piece of material. "Will you join me as I wait, Miss Elizabeth?"

"I should like that very much."

He motioned for her to precede him into the unoccupied room and waited for her to be seated before taking a seat himself. The room was not large, but it was well laid out with three groups of two chairs with a table between them evenly spaced around the room. On each table, lay a neatly folded paper. Everything was bright and clean. It was a very relaxing environment. In fact, as he considered the lady next to him, his sister could shop at this store exclusively from now on if she wished.

"Did you have a pleasant trip?" he asked as he arranged himself in his chair.

"It was very pleasant, thank you. There was not a drop of rain to be seen anywhere along the journey and between Maria's constant chatter about Rosings and a book of poetry, I was well entertained for the entirety of the journey."

"Will you be staying in town for an extended time? Or is your sojourn only of a short duration?"

"I shall be here a fortnight, though my aunt has asked me to extend my stay."

"And will you?" He held his breath as he waited for her response. How he wished for her to stay, but if not, he would petition Bingley for the use of Netherfield if she would welcome him in Hertfordshire.

"I have been considering it." She averted her eyes, and her cheeks grew rosy. "There may be diversions in town to entice me to stay. However, Jane has been away from home for so long, and I must consider her wishes as well."

"My friend may call on her." Darcy offered. "Would she welcome such a diversion?"

Elizabeth smiled. "I believe she would, no matter how much she attempts to protest that she is no longer affected by him."

"I am sorry."

"For what?" Elizabeth asked in surprise.

"Have you forgotten the part I played in her sadness?" He settled more deeply in his chair but did not wait for her to respond.

"I have made Bingley aware of your sister's presence in town and confessed my stupidity. He left my house in quite a state."

Darcy straightened his sleeves. "This may be the only time you see me unscathed during your visit to town as I am to meet him tonight at our club for a bit of a joust."

Elizabeth could not hide her surprise. "And you are going to allow him to expend his anger upon your person?"

"I shall not have to allow it. He is, as my aunt would say, quite the proficient with sword and fist." He shrugged at her look of shock. "When you are trying to cross social boundaries, there is ample opportunity to practice defending yourself and any friend who might find himself at odds with his peers."

"He defended you?" Elizabeth was incredulous. "I should think, with your advantage in height and standing, it would be the reverse."

"Things are not always as they seem, Miss Elizabeth."

She stared at him for a moment, her brows drawn together. Would she ever have the full measure of the man in front of her? He knew first-hand the difficulties which might arise should she agree to marry him. There were those, perhaps even in his own family, who would react vehemently to any union which would bring direct ties to trade. Yet, he had chosen...her.

She shook her head and cursed her abominable pride which had kept her from seeing him for who he was, a man, who, in disposition and talents, would best suit her. But it was more than that. She knew it was. How often after he had left Netherfield had she replayed their exchanges in her mind. Oh, she had told herself it was to find fault and to prove that her assessments of him were correct. And when she had, on a few occasions, found her heart longing to sit with him and discuss various topics, she had assured herself it was to prove her superiority. How nonsensical she had been! Things most definitely were not as they first seemed. Even in her blindness, her heart had called out for him.

"Are you attempting to sketch my character again?" There was a look of amusement on his face.

She shook her head. "I have given up all hope of succeeding. You shall ever remain an enigma to me."

"Then why the scrutiny?"

She bit her lower lip unsure if she should ask. "You love me?" she whispered.

He nodded. "Most ardently." His voice was equally as soft.

"How?" There was so much she did not know about love. It was not something one could read about in books, and it was not a topic she wished to canvas with her mother — or her father. She and Jane had surmised many things about it and discussed it at length. Yet, she felt completely unprepared to understand such a subject.

He shrugged. "You may as well ask how one continues to draw breath. For just as surely as the Almighty places life in my body, he has placed a love for you in my heart which shall never be removed even after my last breath is drawn." He took both her hands in his. "Please, Elizabeth, tell me I might, in time, have some hope of success."

Happiness, deeper than any she had ever felt, fluttered in her heart, and joy suffused her features. Without thought, she lifted his hands to her lips and placed a small kiss on each of them. Then, with an impertinent grin and a raised eyebrow, she said three words which made his heart soar. "Perhaps you might."

# *Chapter 6*

*Perhaps you might.* Remembering Elizabeth's words from yesterday made Darcy smile as he accepted a cup of tea from his aunt, Lady Matlock. He shrugged in response to the questioning look Richard shot him and turned his attention to his tea.

"I hear Mrs. Anderson's daughter has refused another suitor," said Lady Matlock, peering over the teapot and looking at Darcy with a raised brow. "She is a pretty thing. Her taste in gowns is exquisite, and she dances very well."

Richard guffawed. "That is the fatal shot, Mother dear. Darcy does not care if a lady can dance well, for he intends not to dance more than absolutely required. "

His mother turned to him with a smile. "But *you* adore dancing, and she is generously dowered."

Darcy chuckled at the widening of Richard's eyes and slackening of his mouth.

"I do not adore dancing," he said stiffly. "I just tolerate it better than Darcy, and so it appears I adore it."

"Oh, for heaven's sake, Genevieve," said Lady Margaret, "it is rare to find a gentleman who is not a rake who adores dancing! Typically, a gentleman finds it a chore until he finds his hand in the hand of a particular someone and his eyes looking into the eyes of the lady across from him, a lady who for some reason holds his attention and stirs his desire as no other lady ever has." She shrugged. "It is the way it works, and you know it as well as I do."

"I know nothing of the sort," Lady Matlock protested. "Henry adores dancing."

"He does not," protested Richard. "Father would much rather sit in the card room."

"But when we were courting, and even before, he was always dancing and so gracefully." Lady Matlock sat on the edge of her chair and held her cup and saucer just below mouth level in front of her.

"Henry was not well-behaved," Lady Margaret countered. "Dancing was an allowable way for him to get his hands on the ladies and charm them into meeting him in less public locations."

Lady Matlock did not refute the statement. After all, it was a meeting in a not so public location that had led to her claiming the title of Lady Matlock.

"Darcy's father was all that was proper, and he enjoyed dancing," Lady Matlock said after taking a few quiet sips of her tea.

"Only with my mother," said Darcy.

Lady Matlock's brows drew together and her lips pursed in displeasure. "Sir Lewis. –"

"Couldn't keep time with a clock," Lady Margaret interrupted. "He may have loved dancing, but the toes of any lady he danced with disliked it immensely. You cannot count him. He also loved Catherine." The right corner of her lips turned up in a half smile as she took a sip of her tea. As everyone in the family knew, Lady Catherine and Lady Margaret disagreed with each other far more often than they ever agreed. It was likely due to each lady possessing a will of iron, but if asked, neither would ever admit to such. Each was far more likely to cite the interminable stubbornness of the other without so much as hinting that she was just as obstinate.

Possessing obstinacy rather than dancing, Darcy thought, would serve any lady better who dared to join the Fitzwilliam family. A wilting wallflower would likely spend too many days in tears and fits as she attempted to please a rather difficult to please lot of relations such as he possessed. Elizabeth would do well. The thought brought another smile to his lips.

"You are looking rather pleased this afternoon," Lady Matlock said rather tersely to Darcy. She was never one to feel her displeasure at being proven wrong graciously.

"I do apologize. I shall attempt to be sullen." Darcy tried to keep his expression blank, but he could not help a small smirk.

Lady Matlock gasped while both Lady Margaret and Richard dissolved into laughter. Georgiana lowered her head and attended most carefully to her stitching, though her shoulders shook, giving away the fact that she too had been shocked into silent giggles.

"Of all the insolent things to say! And from you! I should not expect it from you!"

No one could miss the irritation in Lady Matlock's tone or features.

"I do apologize," Darcy said once again, feeling just the tiniest twinge of guilt. However, he could not feel so remorseful as he likely should. He had felt rather light and not entirely himself since yesterday afternoon in that sitting room when Elizabeth had uttered those three words — *perhaps you might.*

Lady Matlock huffed. "It is all well and good that you do not wish to dance since you are unfit to be seen in company. How did you get that black eye?"

"Likely the same way he got the split lip," muttered Richard, earning him a glare from his mother. "Fisticuffs."

"It was just a bit of a joust with a friend," Darcy explained. Bingley was, thankfully, still Darcy's friend. He had vented his displeasure with Darcy's part in separating him from Miss Bennet, and then the two had retired to Darcy House to enjoy a couple of pints of fine ale while discussing their Bennet ladies.

"Why would a friend..." Lady Matlock's words died on her lips, and her eyes grew wide. "It was that tradesman's son."

"Indeed it was." Darcy rose and placed his empty cup on the tea table.

"That sweet boy?" asked Lady Margaret. It was how she often referred to Bingley. Her terms of endearment for Bingley's sisters were not so pleasant. She did not like Miss Bingley or Mrs. Hurst, but Bingley she adored. "Did you steal his angel?"

Darcy chuckled. "Not exactly but something along those lines."

Lady Margaret's eyes lit with curiosity. "Do tell," she said, patting on the seat of the blue tufted chair next to her. "And do not leave out any details."

Darcy took the seat indicated and, leaning close to his great aunt, whispered, "I thought the lady was indifferent to him and recommended he not return to his estate and call on her. However, it appears I was wrong, and he was not pleased to forgive me without sufficient repayment." He shrugged. "I do not blame him. I would likely do far worse to myself if I were in his position."

Lady Margaret's eyes twinkled. "Genevieve was not wrong in thinking you greatly altered today. I say, you seem as little concerned about your appearance as Richard is wont to be." She chuckled. "There must be a reason," she prodded. "What is her name?" she whispered, casting a wary glance at her daughter-in-law. "I promise I will not say a thing."

Darcy cocked a brow in disbelief. Lady Margaret was incapable of keeping such a promise.

Lady Margaret scowled. "But there is a lady?"

Darcy shrugged.

His great-aunt's eyes narrowed, and she turned to Georgiana. "There is a lady who is the cause of your brother's change in demeanor, is there not?" she asked, not bothering in her annoyed state to keep her voice lowered.

Georgiana bit her lip and cast an apologetic look in Darcy's direction, causing him to groan silently. "He has not told me," she replied, "but I believe there is."

Lady Matlock gasped. It was a delighted sound that made Darcy cringe.

"And does she like to dance?" Lady Matlock asked.

"Oh, he has never danced with her." Georgiana snapped her mouth closed.

"I thought we were not supposed to speak of her to Georgie," Richard said with a grin.

Darcy groaned aloud this time. There was little he would likely be able to conceal now that his aunt and grandmother were aware that both Georgiana and Richard knew about some lady who had caught Darcy's eye. However, he would do his best to keep as much of his intentions secret as he could for as long as he could.

"I did not speak to Georgiana about her," Darcy held Richard's gaze until he got a nod of understanding that Richard was still not to say a thing. Then turning to Georgiana, he said with a smile, "I did not dance with her at the assembly, but I did at Bingley's ball."

"Indeed?" Richard asked in surprise.

Darcy nodded.

"Might I ask one question?"

Again Darcy nodded in response to Richard's question. "You may if you feel you cannot wait until we are alone." From the flick of Richard's brows, there would be no deferring his curiosity until they were in private.

"If you did not speak to Georgiana about her," Richard asked, "then how does Georgiana know about her?"

"Oh, I met her," said Georgiana. "She is lovely." She turned with some excitement toward Lady Margaret. "We stopped at her uncle's shop. It is where we got this lovely lace." She picked up the piece of lace that lay on top of her grandmother's work basket.

"A tradesman's daughter?" Lady Matlock cried. "Oh, no, no, no. This cannot be."

"Her father is a gentleman," replied Georgiana. "Her uncle is a tradesman."

"A tie to trade is a tie to trade." Lady Matlock's brows rose as did her chin.

"It is not as if this family has not endured such denigration before," Lady Margaret's tone was sardonic. "Shall we start casting out everyone from the family who has such a connection?" She gave her daughter-in-law a pointed glare. "I do not think you are in a position to be so over particular, my dear."

Lady Matlock's father had been a distant cousin involved in manufacturing before he ascended to a title he had never expected to have, but illness, war, lack of issue of the right gender, and the like had designed that he should indeed be the person to keep the title from falling into extinction. His daughter had benefited greatly both from this change in status and the substantial dowry his years in trade had helped him amass. She had done her best to distance herself from anything that hinted at her former standing as a tradesman's daughter. However, Lady Margaret detested such arrogance, especially from one she considered an upstart who had trapped her son into marriage.

"She is very lovely," Georgiana repeated, looking from her grandmother to her aunt and finally to her brother with a look of concern.

Lady Margaret patted her hand reassuringly. "I would not expect your brother to become enamoured with anyone who was not delightful." She winked at Darcy. "Now, tell me, my dear, what is her name?"

"Miss Elizabeth Bennet," Darcy supplied. "I would thank you to not place my sister in the awkward position of speaking on my behalf."

Lady Margaret settled back in her chair and held her cup out to Richard, indicating she would like more tea. "I am listening."

Darcy drew a breath and released it slowly before beginning to share the news he knew his grandmother wished to hear. "Her father's estate is Longbourn in Hertfordshire. It is a modest estate, nothing grand."

"Hertfordshire?" Lady Margaret interrupted. "Is that not where Mr. Bingley was leasing an estate?"

Darcy nodded. "Yes, Netherfield is not but three miles from Longbourn."

Lady Margaret accepted her cup of tea from Richard. "Is that all you know of her?" she asked. Her tone was grave, but he could tell she was hiding a smile behind her cup by the way her eyes sparkled.

"No," Darcy said with a shake of his head. Lady Margaret could be as teasingly bothersome as Richard, and he loved her for it. She had always been the one he went to for advice regarding Georgiana after he had been left her guardian. He knew he would get sage advice that was logical. The other women in his family were, in his opinion, too flighty and given to airs and self-aggrandizement.

"Her eyes sparkle just as yours are now," he said softly. "I am certain you would like her."

"I shall like whomever you select as long as it is not that grasping harpy."

Darcy chuckled. "There is little danger of my ever choosing Miss Bingley."

"You are a man of sense," his grandmother commended him. "What is this Miss Elizabeth's fortune?"

"Minimal," Darcy replied, "but mine is substantial."

"And her family?"

Darcy grimaced. He did not wish to speak critically, nor did he wish to speak anything less than the truth. "She has four sisters. No brothers. The estate is entailed to a cousin."

"Are they a sensible sort of people?"

"Not all," he answered quietly. "But then what family does not contain some folly and foolishness?"

Lady Margaret's eyes grew wide. "You will not delineate their shortcomings? That is rather unlike you."

Darcy felt his cheeks grow warm. Normally, he would not hesitate to plainly state the deficiencies he saw in people. He shook his head. "I will not." He glanced at Richard. "It has been brought to my attention that doing so is not very gentlemanly and demonstrates a degree of arrogance."

His grandmother's lips twitched. "Yes, I do believe I have mentioned that on occasion. It is good you have finally found it to your liking to listen. You have always been one to be far too assured in your own opinion." There was a tenderness to her tone. "It is likely your only real flaw, but it is also your strength."

Darcy rubbed his swollen eye. "Bingley would agree," he said with a sheepish grin.

"So it was Bingley who taught you this?"

Darcy could tell by her tone of voice that she knew very well it was not Bingley, so he merely just shook his head in response.

"I think I should very much like to meet her." Lady Margaret placed her empty cup on the table next to her, spread the dress she was working on across her lap, and began pinning the lace from Mr. Gardiner's store onto it.

"I hope to present her to you eventually," Darcy admitted. "However, I have not properly called on her at home, so your introduction may have to wait for some time."

Lady Margaret looked up from her pinning. "I shall welcome her whenever you are ready."

Darcy muttered his thanks.

"Now, tell me of Bingley's angel."

"That would be Miss Elizabeth's sister," Richard supplied.

"Oh! The one I met at the shop?" Georgiana asked excitedly.

"Two ties to trade?" Lady Matlock muttered.

"Yes," Darcy answered to them both.

"Miss Bennet is so very nice," cooed Georgiana. "I am certain there is not a more pleasant lady in all of England — and so pretty! I described to her your dress, Grandmama, and she knew exactly what lace would be best. I had thought it would be one, but she insisted it would be another. And she was correct."

"Lace, Georgiana?" Darcy asked with a laugh. "Did I not suffer enough yesterday on our shopping trip? Must we speak of lace?"

"Make yourself scarce," retorted Lady Margaret. "We ladies enjoy a bit of banter about pretty things."

"As do we gentlemen." Richard laughed as he rose from his chair. "Come, Darcy, I will relieve your torment and find something with which we can amuse ourselves, and it shall not be lace."

Darcy rose to follow his cousin from the room. But on hearing Georgiana whisper that he had not looked all that tormented yesterday, he paused, turned toward her, and raised a brow. "Georgiana, I shall thank you to not make me the object of gossip."

"Oh, I would not dream of allowing something so horrid as that to happen," his grandmother assured him. "However, I do not believe it is gossip if she tells me of the shop where she purchased this fine bit of lace. That is simply relating an event."

Darcy's eyes narrowed, and he shook his head. "You are incorrigible," he muttered, earning him a broad grin in response.

"Yes, I am," Lady Margaret agreed. "Now make yourself scarce."

With a sigh, Darcy did just that, knowing full well, that every detail about Elizabeth which might be wrung from his sister would be.

# Chapter 7

Elizabeth placed her hand on Darcy's arm and allowed him to escort her from their supper box and toward one of the numerous paths in Vauxhall Gardens. The vast number of people that filled the supper boxes and paths was astonishing, and then when the torches were lit, and the orchestra was playing while waiters scurried back and forth making certain that all in attendance were happy, it was nearly overwhelming. She had heard stories of this place, but until now, she had never truly imagined its grandeur.

Darcy drew Elizabeth closer to his side as they strolled. "Are you enjoying yourself?"

"Immensely."

Darcy smiled at how the word was more breathed than spoken. "I had wondered. You have been rather quiet."

She looked up at him. "I am awestruck by my surroundings. There is nothing quite like this in Hertfordshire."

"Most assuredly," he agreed with a chuckle.

"I am surprised you would venture into this vast sea of humanity," she teased. "Our little assembly with its gathered throng was a great trial to you."

He saw her lips twitch, and he waited for her to complete her tease before he refuted her.

"Perhaps," she said, cocking a brow in a rather beguilingly impertinent fashion, "that is because the residents in the country are unwashed savages."

"Oh, indeed they are," he replied with a smile. "I have it on the greatest authority."

Her eyes grew wide. "Do tell," she prompted.

He leaned his head near her ear and whispered, "Miss Bingley."

Elizabeth laughed.

"I assure you it is true because her sister verified the fact and some rude man lent his voice to the assessment if I am not mistaken." He bent toward her ear once again. "You will forgive me for such ungentlemanly behaviour, will you not? I am attempting to improve my ways."

There was such contrition in his whispered words that she gave his arm a small squeeze and readily bestowed her pardon. Mr. Darcy had over the last four days been the perfect gentleman. Both her aunt and uncle had been duly impressed by his manners. According to Aunt Gardiner, there was nothing of grandeur about him, save for the way he carried himself when walking. However, it was not deemed arrogant but rather dignified. Aunt Gardiner had spoken at some length of how of anyone she had met, Mr. Darcy was justified in thinking of himself in lofty ideals since she had seen his estate and knew many of his tenants. The man was of no small fortune, and he was, to her knowledge, always just in his dealing with tradesmen in Lambton. Bills were not left unpaid, and even lowly delivery boys were given a nod when he saw that they were doing their work well.

Elizabeth had heard enough arguments in Darcy's favour to settle her more firmly in her new belief of his being among the best of men. Then, having observed him in her uncle's home as well as when she and Jane had gone to Darcy House to have tea with his grandmother and Georgiana, she was beyond convinced of her correctness in viewing him in such a light. So convinced was she of his noble character that she allowed her heart to be open to his declaration to her, and though it was little more than a fortnight since that horrid evening in the parsonage, she found herself quite certain that should he offer for her again, she would accept with alacrity. For her heart spoke of love, though her mind had yet to fully comprehend it.

Darcy stopped to greet an acquaintance and introduced Elizabeth to them as well as Bingley and Jane, who followed close behind.

"I say, Darcy," said Bingley before they began walking again, "it will likely be noted in the paper that you were seen in Vauxhall with a lady on your arm."

Darcy shrugged. "They had best describe her as beautiful," he said with a grin.

Bingley chortled. "I seem to have misplaced my friend whose greatest desire was to shun all of society."

"He is not misplaced." Darcy raised a brow at Bingley. "He has, it seems, found his good sense in a rather forceful fashion."

Bingley chuckled. "Yes, I dare say your appearance will also make the society page."

"Have you no pity for him at all?" Elizabeth asked in feigned disbelief.

"Not a jot," Bingley declared.

"Men are such strange creatures," Elizabeth stated with a laugh.

"It is a far better thing we do in settling our disagreements than what I have witnessed between my sisters," Bingley defended. "There would be days of tears and tantrums, and it is a wonder the door to Caroline's room never fell off its hinges."

"I agree," said Jane. "I would rather have Lydia and Kitty hit each other and be done."

"Jane!" Elizabeth cried. "How violent of you! I do believe your sojourn in town has corrupted you."

Darcy watched in amusement as Jane's eyes narrowed ever so slightly and her lips pursed while Elizabeth's twitched in an attempt not to smile.

"I believe it would be far better for you to remain in the country where such savagery is little known," Elizabeth continued.

"Little known?" exclaimed Jane. "How many times was the surgeon called to the Lucas's to stitch up one or the other of Charlotte's brothers after some fight?"

"And yet you would have him called to Longbourn to stitch up Kitty?" Elizabeth could not contain her smile any longer and let it spread across her face.

"Kitty?" Darcy asked in surprise.

"Oh, yes," Jane assured him. "If Lydia and Kitty were to fight — and I assure you they have — it would not be Kitty who would be victorious. Lydia, as you may well be aware, is a very determined sort of person."

Darcy chuckled. "I must be honest. I never thought much about what it would be like to live among so many sisters. It is very different from what my life has been like."

"Two sisters is more than enough," agreed Bingley. "I likely would not have survived if there had been more than Louisa and Caroline with whom to contend."

"Since your sister is much younger than you," Jane said to Darcy, "was your childhood quiet?"

Darcy shook his head. "At times it was, but Richard and his brother often visited and then there was Mr. Wickham." He flinched slightly as he said the name. "He was not always bad," he added softly. "At one time we rather enjoyed each other's company until differences in station were not so easily ignored."

Jane sighed. Darcy had given Elizabeth permission to share what she knew of Wickham with her sister.

"So you were betrayed by a friend?" Jane's question was little more than a whisper.

Darcy nodded. "Although it was not my first disappointment in him."

"You know," said Bingley in a light tone, "when your name appears in the paper tomorrow, my sister will be unbearable."

Darcy gave Bingley a grateful smile for turning the conversation. He did not wish to dwell on who Wickham had been or now was. The memories were not of a pleasant variety, and tonight, was to be an enjoyable outing.

"Might I take up a room at Darcy House?" Bingley continued.

This drew a general laugh from the group, and each couple settled back once again into their own space on the path, close to each other and yet quite distant.

They walked on in their private worlds of soft comments and smiles for some time and were just turning onto a path that would eventually lead them back to their supper boxes when Lord and Lady Matlock approached.

"There you are!" Lady Matlock cried. "We were concerned you

might have gotten lost on one of these paths. Not all of them are so well lit, you know."

Indeed, Darcy did know. In fact, he had considered taking such a path more than once. Such seclusion and shadows might have allowed him to press his suit with Elizabeth in a very pleasant fashion. However, he had no desire to have Elizabeth flee or worse be tied to him if they were discovered in some compromising position — whether real or imagined. This was not a courtship of the moment but a prelude to a lifetime, and as such, he would limit his kisses to her knuckles for now.

"If I had not been off visiting with a dear friend, I should not have allowed you to wander away without a chaperone," Lady Matlock continued. "One cannot be too careful with one's reputation."

"Indeed," Lord Matlock said with a smirk. "My wife knows all about dark corners, do you not, Genevieve?"

Lady Matlock's eyes grew wide. "I have both heard my share of stories and read about them in the paper."

"Yes," Lord Matlock's teasing smile stayed in place, "you have also been the subject of both. I do believe that is how you became my wife."

Lady Matlock gasped.

Her husband patted her arm. "Not every gentleman traipses down a dark path with wicked intentions or without a desire to be ensnared."

Darcy knew that though his aunt and uncle often seemed to be at odds with each other, they were not — or, at least, not completely. Theirs was, for the most part, a peaceful marriage. There were no loud rows and no scandal beyond the one played out in this very garden shortly before their marriage. There was the occasional disagreement that left a strained atmosphere, but, as far as Darcy could tell from other marriages he had observed, Lord and Lady Matlock's was among the exemplary ones.

"But, the Misses Bennets might not know of such things," Lady Matlock protested. "They are not of our circles. These things are very foreign to them, I would imagine."

"You believe compromises only occur in fine society?" Darcy could not keep the disdain from his voice. He had tolerated enough of his aunt's small gibes over the course of the past four days.

Georgiana had spent several afternoons with Lady Margaret, and Darcy had both seen her delivered to Matlock House and returned to Darcy House himself. Of course, he had been obliged each day to spend at least a few moments with Lady Margaret. Lady Matlock had made it a point of inquiring after *that tradesman's niece* each time he was there. He had been grateful that on the one day when Lady Margaret came for tea, she had not been accompanied by her daughter-in-law.

Lady Matlock laughed lightly. "Oh, I am certain there are many compromises that occur in the *lower* ranks. However, they are not as ruinous as they are in *our sphere*, for there are no titles or great fortunes to be squandered or tainted." There was no missing her snub by the tone of voice and the emphasis she placed on certain words accompanied by the looks she gave Elizabeth.

"That is not true," Elizabeth said with a smile, though inwardly she bristled. "Why just the other day, we heard of a merchant who was being forced to accept a ne'er-do-well as a son due to a compromise, and I assure you, the father's fortune, though not from land and merely in the form of pounds and shillings, is not insignificant. Indeed, his wealth had purchased his entrance into finer society."

"I do not wish to be disagreeable," Darcy began, giving Elizabeth a wink, "but I believe that that particular compromise was the fault of one of Lady Matlock's sphere, was it not? In fact, there might have been a lower title of some sort associated with the man."

Elizabeth tipped her head and for effect pretended to think for a moment. "I believe you are correct. The gentleman involved was a second son or some such thing — not directly in line to ascend, but close enough that a simple twist of fate might allow it."

Darcy nodded. "And not of a good character."

Lord Matlock chuckled. "Not of good character indeed! The man is as debauched as they come. The poor young girl who wandered into our elevated circles and found herself in that quagmire!"

Lady Matlock huffed softly.

It was evident to Darcy that she was not pleased with the turn of the conversation. He imagined that she had meant to denigrate the Misses Bennets and Mr. Bingley, not to have her own kind maligned.

"Is that not my point?" she asked sharply. "The girl was not prepared for our society. You cannot just wander into London from some hamlet and expect to comprehend the ways of the ton."

Her husband chuckled once again. "If you are attempting to say that the Misses Bennets are treading in dangerous territory, I must ask, my lady, what your opinion of our nephew is."

"I...that is not..." she stammered unable to form a good defense.

"I will have you know, my dear lady," he said, drawing her close to his side, "that our nephew *and* his friend are not the elements of the ton that Miss Bennet and Miss Elizabeth need fear. Darcy and Bingley are capable of seeing that no harm befalls their ladies."

"But there will be talk, and Mr. Gardiner is –"

"A fine upstanding man of good wealth and well respected," Lord Matlock interjected.

"But he..." she clamped her lips closed as her husband cleared his throat.

"Mr. Gardiner is in trade, as was my father," Bingley finished the thought that had been left hanging.

"As was your father, Aunt," Darcy said pointedly. "And yet, you have not only survived the worst of the ton, but you have succeeded in rising to its heights. I am certain it was not an easy thing to accomplish as many gentlemen and ladies of the ton can be vicious. Perhaps if your father had been a gentleman like Mr. Bennet, you would have found your acceptance less difficult."

Lord Matlock nodded. "Well said, Darcy." He turned to his wife. "I think, in the light of your experience, you would be more gracious and welcoming. I should hate to think you had become just like those who caused you so much pain."

Lady Matlock sucked in a breath and lifted her chin but spoke not a word.

"Come now, my dear. You have had your bit of fun and ruined these gentlemen's chances of sneaking off down some dark path and finding themselves as happily married as I am."

Lady Matlock gasped, and Elizabeth's cheeks grew warm.

"Not that they would or that their ladies would allow it," he added with a wink and a chuckle. "We should return before my

mother sets off in search of me since she knows I am precisely the
sort of gent to lead his lady down a shadowy path."

72

# Chapter 8

Elizabeth held her cousin Marianne Gardiner's sampler and looked at it while tipping her head and squinting her eyes. Marianne insisted that a completed project be examined carefully before it was ever pronounced acceptable, which, due to Marianne's attention to detail, it always was. In fact, Marianne's efforts were often far better than acceptable. Elizabeth suspected that besides her ten-year-old cousin's penchant for diligence, there was a small touch of genius in Marianne.

Having put in a good show of scrutiny, Elizabeth finally lowered the piece of stitching. "It is lovely."

Marianne bit her lip as she took her work back from Elizabeth. "Even this last row of flowers? I could not decide if they were large enough or not."

"They are perfect," Elizabeth replied with a smile. "They are half the size of your letters, which allows them to be part of the background decor rather than fighting for precedence with your verse."

A small smile tugged at Marianne's lips. "Do you mean it?"

Elizabeth wanted to chuckle at how her cousin had such a difficult time ever accepting the fact that what she created was indeed good. However, Elizabeth knew that a laugh — even a small one

— would not bolster the girl's confidence. In fact, it would likely drive her to question her work further, so Elizabeth simply smiled and answered, "yes."

The smile on Marianne's face grew wide. "Would you hang it in your room if it was placed in a frame?"

"Did you make it for me?" Elizabeth asked.

Marianne nodded. "But I am not supposed to say. It was to be a surprise."

"And it is. I am delighted and would love to hang it in my room. You do very good work. Far better than I could do when I was your age. In fact, I dare say your stitches are neater than mine are now!"

Marianne ran her hand over the sampler where it lay on her lap as a light pink stain of pleasure spread across her cheeks. "I am happy you like it. I should hate very much to give you something that you only displayed because you felt it your duty." She sighed contentedly and peeked up at Elizabeth. "Will you still hang it in your room once you live at Pemberley?"

It was Elizabeth's turn to wear rosy cheeks. "*If* I live at Pemberley, I will still proudly hang it on my wall."

"Oh, I know you will live there," Marianne said with the wistful confidence that was so easily possessed by a girl of Marianne's age and sensibilities. "Mr. Darcy has called every day that you have not seen him elsewhere."

"He has, but that does not mean –"

Elizabeth was unable to finish her thought as a commotion caught both her and her cousin's attention. Neither was left wondering about its source for any great amount of time, for within moments, the clamor had entered the sitting room. If there was one thing that was emphatically true about Elizabeth's mother, it was that Mrs. Bennet was not the sort of lady to be ignored — ever — even when it would be most acceptable to be overlooked.

"Mama," cried Jane rising from where she sat near the window. "Whatever brings you to town? Is Papa with you?"

Mrs. Bennet finished removing her hat and pelisse. "Your father insisted on seeing your uncle at his store." She waved a hand at the maid who stood, arms laden with outerwear. "My parcel." She turned back toward her daughters. "I found the most beautiful lace. It will be just the thing on your wedding dress, Jane." She waved her hand again in the poor maid's direction but this time added an impatient huff.

"Mama," Jane chided, "I do not have need of a wedding dress."

"Oh, but you will." Mrs. Bennet was busily untying the string that held the wrapping around the package the maid had given to her before scurrying away to deposit Mrs. Bennet's hat and coat in a room at the top of the stairs.

"When your uncle wrote to your father that the elusive Mr. Bingley had finally called on you, I knew that you would be betrothed before you returned to Longbourn." She proudly displayed the lace she had procured at Mr. Gardiner's shop. "Is it not fabulous?" She draped it over her arm as she took a seat.

"And I told your father that we must thank Mr. Darcy for helping Mr. Bingley find you. How he did not know your whereabouts is beyond me. It is not as if his sisters did not call on you here. However, it is good that Mr. Darcy knew where to find you."

Mrs. Gardiner took the lace from Mrs. Bennet and after an appropriate exclamation over the fineness of the piece, passed it on to Jane and rang for tea. "You will likely have your opportunity to thank Mr. Darcy soon, for he and Mr. Bingley will be arriving soon."

Mrs. Bennet's eyes grew wide, and she blinked. "Does Mr. Darcy still accompany Mr. Bingley?"

Mrs. Gardiner laughed. "No, Mr. Darcy has never accompanied Mr. Bingley, but Mr. Bingley always accompanies Mr. Darcy when he calls."

The room fell into silence for a time while Mrs. Bennet's mouth hung open and her brows furrowed. Finally, she snapped her mouth shut and then, with a deep crease still between her brows, turned to Jane. "I do not understand. Are both Mr. Darcy and Mr. Bingley calling on you? Mr. Darcy is wealthier, to be sure, but Mr. Bingley is so much more amiable. Can you not dissuade Mr. Darcy?"

Elizabeth sighed. Sense was not something her mother possessed in large amounts. "He is calling on me, Mama," Elizabeth said. "Mr. Darcy is calling on me, and I have no wish to dissuade him."

Her mother once again gaped and blinked wide eyes. "You? Mr. Darcy, who thought you unattractive, is calling on you?" She shook her head. "No, it cannot be."

"I assure you it is the truth," said Mrs. Gardiner. "And I dare say he does not find our Lizzy unattractive any longer — if he truly ever did. Did you not read the full letter my husband sent to yours?"

Mrs. Bennet shook her head. "I did not read a word. Thomas read it to me, and it said that Mr. Bingley with his friend Mr. Darcy had called on Jane and that apparently Mr. Bingley did not know Jane was in town until his friend told him."

"And you did not hear the rest?" Mrs. Gardiner asked, though the whole room knew that Fanny Bennet rarely listened to a full letter if there was a fascinating bit of information that caught her attention before the complete missive could be read.

"I do not recall anything further," Mrs. Bennet answered. She flopped back in her chair. "My Lizzy and Mr. Darcy," she muttered as if the idea was as odd as chickens that flew.

Mrs. Gardiner nodded and smiled. "Yes, our Lizzy and Mr. Darcy. In fact, it is likely from my observations that Mr. Darcy might offer before Mr. Bingley does." She sent a secret smile to Elizabeth, who had told her dearest aunt about the last evening she had spent with Mr. Darcy in Kent.

Mrs. Bennet's hand began to flutter in front of her face. "I might need a bit of a lie-down," she murmured before repeating, "my Lizzy and Mr. Darcy."

"Are you certain you cannot endure long enough to have a cup of tea and a little conversation with your future sons?"

Elizabeth shook her head when her aunt looked her direction. It would be so much better if her mother could be shuffled off to bed, and Darcy could be prepared in advance for the arrival of her mother. Her heart fluttered, and her stomach quivered. She knew his sentiments regarding her family, and though she knew that he had overcome them once to offer for her, he had done so while not in the presence of her mother.

~*~*~

"Will you wait much longer?" Bingley straightened his coat as Darcy exited the carriage.

"Wait much longer for what?" Darcy replied as he straightened his clothing as well

"As if you do not know!" Bingley checked his hat and stepped toward the Gardiner's front door. "How long until you offer for her?"

"I could ask you the same," Darcy replied with a flick of his brow.

"When she returns to Hertfordshire if not before," Bingley replied. He lifted and lowered the knocker before crossing his arms and smirking at his friend. "Now, what about you?"

Darcy shrugged. "I already did." He chuckled at Bingley's gaping expression. "And I was soundly refused."

"Refused?" Bingley repeated in surprise as the door to the Gardiner's home opened.

"And given a second chance," Darcy whispered as he moved past his friend and entered the house.

"A second chance?" Bingley asked softly as they gave their outerwear to a waiting servant.

"Yes," Darcy replied.

"Mr. Darcy," Marianne Gardiner stood up from the place where she sat on the stairs.

"Miss Gardiner." Darcy bowed. The girl before him smiled and curtseyed. He had been duly impressed with the fine behaviour of the Gardiner children. They seemed to have been taught all the proper graces for children of their age. "May I be of assistance?"

Marianne pulled her bottom lip between her teeth and glanced toward the sitting room door. "I am not supposed to be here. I am supposed to be in the nursery with my brothers and sister, but Lizzy looked so worried."

Darcy followed her gaze as she once again looked at the sitting room door. "Why is your cousin worried?"

"I think it is because her mother has arrived suddenly. It was quite a shock to see my aunt, you see."

Darcy waited patiently as the young girl ran the ribbon of her dress nervously through her fingers and looked as if she was deciding exactly how much to say.

"My aunt is not like Lizzy," she finally said, turning eyes up toward him that pled with him to understand her.

"I know," he replied. "I have met your aunt before."

Marianne sighed. "Then you know she can be..." She glanced once more at the sitting room door before whispering, "silly."

Darcy smiled. "I do, and might I tell you a secret?"

She nodded her head eagerly. "I am very good at keeping secrets."

"That is good to know, Miss Gardiner," Darcy replied. Then he crouched down to her level just as he used to do when Georgiana was younger and added in a whisper, "I have two aunts who are just as silly but perhaps not as loud as your aunt, although my aunt Catherine can be rather vocal."

He had expected her smile when he had told her his secret. However, the hand she placed on his shoulder and the understanding whisper of "aunts can be trying, but we must love them" that accompanied it came as a surprise.

"You are a very wise young lady," he said as he stood. "Thank you for telling me your cousin was worried."

Marianne dipped one last curtsey and scurried up the stairs before the gentlemen were announced.

"Mrs. Bennet is here?" Bingley asked with a sigh.

Darcy nodded as the door to the sitting room was opened. "She is worth it," Darcy whispered.

"Without a doubt," Bingley replied just before they entered the room.

Mrs. Bennet was indeed at the Gardiner residence, sitting in a chair next to Mrs. Gardiner and waving a handkerchief in front of her face until she saw the gentlemen appear. Then she straightened and tucked her handkerchief away.

"Mrs. Bennet," Darcy greeted. "It is good to see you. I trust your trip to town was pleasant."

He watched as her eyes shifted from Bingley to him and then to Elizabeth before returning to his face. Apparently, Mrs. Bennet knew that he was here to see her second daughter.

"Did you travel alone?" Bingley asked. "Or did Mr. Bennet and your daughters accompany you?"

Mrs. Bennet seemed to be recovering from whatever moment of nerves she had experienced that required a fanning. Her lips curled into a pleasant smile, and her eyes focused with more certainty on the gentlemen who stood just inside the sitting room door. "Oh, be seated, please," she cried. "You must not be so formal on my account. We are all good friends, are we not? You have dined at Longbourn, after all."

Darcy gave her a nod and took a seat next to Elizabeth, knowing full well that his every action was being examined closely. It was as if he was some sort of oddity that Mrs. Bennet had never before seen. He nearly chuckled at the thought.

Bingley, of course, had taken his place next to Jane and was repeating his inquiry about Mrs. Bennet's travels.

"Oh, yes," Mrs. Bennet replied as if startled from a reverie. Her head swung toward Bingley. "Mr. Bennet is with Mr. Gardiner, and Mary, Kitty, and Lydia are with my sister. Mary wished to stay at Longbourn, but I refused. It is not proper for a young lady to be on her own in such a fashion, I said. And Mary, being the good girl that she is, did not argue further. Lydia had hoped to stay with Mrs. Forester, but Mrs. Forester is just recently married, and it would not do to have Lydia getting in the way as Mrs. Forester is just getting her feet under her in her new position as mistress of her own home. Besides, Lydia will likely have the opportunity to be their guest once the militia removes to Brighton. Mr. Bennet has not yet agreed to it, but if I know my Lydia, he will."

Darcy glanced at Elizabeth, whose eyes had grown wide at her mother's words.

"Does the militia leave soon?" he asked.

"Oh, not for another two months, at least," said Mrs. Bennet, "and it is a good thing, too. They bring a festive air to things. Many a young lady swoons at the sight of a red coat, much as I did when I was but a girl." She sighed. "Oh, to be young once again."

"It has been my experience that not everyone in a village enjoys the presence of the militia," said Darcy.

Mrs. Bennet's brows rose. "I do remember you were not fond of some of the officers." There was a slight tone of accusation in her words.

"Darcy has the right of it," said Bingley. "There are dangers and difficulties associated with a group of men who are always shifting from camp to camp — especially the ones who are fond of drink, cards, and ladies. I believe it was that sort of officer of whom Darcy disapproves."

Mrs. Bennet huffed. "Mr. Wickham enjoys a game of cards, but surely he is not so bad as you suggest."

"I know him to be far worse," Darcy replied soberly. "Do not allow him to fool you with his pleasant manners and delightful tales." He accepted the cup of tea that Mrs. Gardiner handed him.

"Mama found the most beautiful piece of lace today," Jane said brightly. "Your sister will be sorry to know it has been purchased."

Darcy shook his head. "My sister and lace," he said with a chuckle, gratefully allowing Jane to turn the topic of conversation. He would speak to Mr. Bennet about Wickham later, and then, he might allow Bingley to share a quiet story or two with Mrs. Bennet about how Wickham had had a comfortable fortune and could have had more had he not squandered it.

"You have a sister?" Mrs. Bennet asked.

"You know he has a sister, Mama," chided Elizabeth.

Her mother shrugged. "I had forgotten."

"I doubt that very much," Elizabeth murmured.

Darcy bit back a grin. "You will get to meet her tomorrow," he said. "Since you are in town, I will finally have the opportunity to repay your hospitality. I have invited the Gardiners to dinner at Darcy House and would be delighted if you would join them."

"Do you know what you are asking?" Elizabeth whispered.

Darcy smiled at her and gave a slight nod of his head.

"I do not believe you do." Her reply was nearly lost in Mrs. Bennet's cries of delight.

And so, the conversation turned to entertaining and the many things Jane had done while in town. Darcy lent his voice to the discussion and even described in some detail the theatre where he had a box and expressed a desire to have Mrs. Bennet attend a play at some future time. Finally, the conversation dwindled and then lapsed into a pleasant silence.

Darcy was just handing his cup to Mrs. Gardiner in preparation of taking his leave, when Mrs. Bennet, who was once again looking at him as if he were a curiosity, blurted, "Whatever did you do to your eye?"

"That was my fault," Bingley answered before Darcy could. "We were having a bit of a joust and, well, I won."

Darcy was certain Mrs. Bennet's eyes could not grow any wider than they did at that moment. He was also positive that Bingley had just found himself to be a touch less amiable in Mrs. Bennet's perception.

"You hit him?"

Bingley nodded. "Several times. And he hit me as well. I just happened to land my punch better."

Mrs. Bennet gasped.

"They are boys," said Mrs. Gardiner, who knew exactly why Darcy's eye looked as it did. "It is how they settle things."

Mrs. Bennet gasped her displeasure once again, still unable to voice her disapproval.

"I deserved it," said Darcy as he rose to leave. "Will you walk with me?" he asked Elizabeth.

She took his hand and allowed him to lead her from the room.

"Are you well?" he asked as they stood in the passage.

Her brows furrowed as she nodded. He could see the question in her eyes. Her mother had been as silly as ever, and he suspected she feared he would be driven away by such things. He had, after all, listed her parent's failing in his poorly made proposal in Kent.

"I love you," he whispered. "Nothing and no one will change that. Not even your mother."

Her response was enchanting as a smile crept slowly across her face and settled in her eyes. He lifted her hand and kissed it. "You said I might dare to hope to one day win your affections." He paused and looked down at the hand he held in his. "I should like to speak to your father if you will allow it. He should know that we are courting and that I intend to marry you. It is only proper." He drew a deep breath. "May I speak to him?"

His heart beat wildly in his chest as a touch of panic rose in his mind, reminding him of the last time he had spoken to her about marriage.

"Yes."

Her response was barely above a whisper, but it shouted in his ears, swelled in his chest, and spread like sunshine across his face. "You would have me?"

She nodded, and he did something very much unlike anything he had ever done before. Without so much as a glance about him to see who might be watching, he pulled her into his arms and kissed her soundly.

# *Chapter 9*

Richard smirked behind his glass of wine while he stood near the fireplace at the far end of the drawing room at Darcy House.

"What has you looking so amused?" Bingley asked as he came to stand near Richard.

Richard shook his head. "Many things, but currently, it is the way Miss Elizabeth's father keeps watching Darcy and clearing his throat anytime Darcy moves closer to his daughter." He chuckled. "And you! I must say I have never seen a mother — especially one with marriage so foremost in her thoughts — watch you so warily."

It was true. Mr. Bennet had done an admirable job of acting the part of protective father for the past twenty minutes since the Bennets had arrived at Darcy House while Mrs. Bennet, after her initial exclamations of delight at her surroundings, had divided her time between repeating her pleasure at being in such a grand home and watching Bingley with a distrustful eye as if the man might at any moment spring upon her and do her harm.

Bingley shrugged. "Darcy did not tell you?" he asked.

"I did not see Darcy until just before the Bennets arrived." He turned so that his back was toward those seated in the drawing room, and he faced Bingley directly. "What should my cousin have told me?"

Bingley leaned to the side and looked around Richard's shoulder to where Darcy and his sister were entertaining the Bennets. "You promise not to draw any notice? No loud guffaws or exclamations?" Bingley asked. "For if you do attract attention, I shall leave you to explain yourself to Mrs. Bennet and face the wrath of your cousin as well as possibly Mr. Bennet by yourself."

Richard's head tipped as a grin split his face. "There may be just cause for Mrs. Bennet to think you untrustworthy."

Bingley smiled in response. "I am rather enjoying her distrust. She has done a great deal less fawning over me since she discovered I was the source of Darcy's injuries." He crossed his arms and lifted his chest proudly.

Richard shook his head. "Mrs. Bennet thinks you are violent? I do not see how that will help your cause if you are truly intent on marrying her daughter."

"I have five thousand a year," Bingley said with a shrug. "And I am, for the most part, likable, and it is not she but her husband who must give his consent." His smile grew. "Which he has already given."

Richard's eyes grew wide as he drained the last of his wine from his glass.

"To both me and Darcy," Bingley added just as Richard swallowed.

The gasp that accompanied the swallow caused Richard to start coughing.

Bingley bit back a grin and thumped him on the back. "He swallowed wrong," he explained to the rest of the room. "I am quite certain Mrs. Bennet thinks that this is somehow my doing," he whispered to Richard.

"It is," Richard sputtered between gasps. "Has no one told you that you should not share startling information when someone is in the middle of drinking?"

"Once or twice," Bingley said as he gave Richard's back one last resounding thump. "But I do appreciate the reminder."

"You and my cousin are betrothed?" Richard asked when he could once again speak without sputtering.

"Was that not the startling news that nearly caused you to expire just now?" Bingley asked with a laugh.

Richard growled, sobering Bingley somewhat. There were boundaries that one did not push. When Richard Fitzwilliam growled, no man or woman with a trifling amount of sense persisted in teasing.

"Yes," Bingley replied. "We are both to be married."

"When did this change in status occur?"

"Yesterday," Bingley replied somberly. "I accompanied Darcy into Mr. Gardiner's study, and once Mr. Bennet was done with Darcy, I figured it would perhaps help his cause — and my own, of course, — if I followed suit and asked permission to also marry one of Mr. Bennet's daughters. The eldest daughter that is. I did not just ask for any daughter. I did ask for a specific one," Bingley explained.

Richard nodded slowly as he processed this information. "What do you mean when Mr. Bennet was done with Darcy?"

Bingley smiled broadly. "He was not pleased to enter Mr. Gardiner's house and find Darcy kissing his daughter. There was a fair bit of stomping and snorting over the ordeal. It was actually rather surprising to me. Mr. Bennet has never appeared to be one to care overly much about his daughter's behavior, but then Miss Elizabeth is his favourite." He shrugged.

Richard turned, looked at his cousin, and then turned back to Bingley. "My cousin was kissing a lady in her uncle's house?"

"In the corridor near the entry," Bingley nodded as he assured Richard of the truth of the matter. "Now, if you will excuse me, I have a future mother-in-law to torment and her daughter to enjoy."

Richard grabbed Bingley's arm before he could make his exit. "What has become of him?"

"I beg your pardon?"

"Darcy. His behavior. It is...so...so unlike him."

Bingley shrugged. "It is something about not being thought proud or appearing to be due to his desire to appear proper to one and all."

Richard released Bingley's arm. "Does anyone besides those in Mr. Gardiner's study and the ladies involved know of this betrothal?'

Bingley shook his head. "I believe that will be shared at dinner."

Richard groaned. "My mother will be here."

Bingley smirked. "Yes, it should be entertaining."

"You are incorrigible," Richard chided as he followed Bingley to where the rest were assembled.

~*~*~

At precisely five minutes before dinner was to be served, Lady Matlock arrived, as she always did, with a flutter of activity and an apology for her tardiness. Perhaps the Bennets were fooled by her flushed appearance of hurry and her look of remorse, but no one

*88*

that had known her for any length of time believed a word of her apologies.

Lady Matlock enjoyed making somewhat of a scene upon her arrival. It offered her the attention she sought as most were too polite to point out her tendency toward fashionably late arrivals. Most were too polite, but Lady Margaret was not.

"My daughter does like to be noticed when arriving," she said as she greeted the Bennets.

"My Lydia is the same," Mrs. Bennet replied. "She does enjoy attention, and she is well-worthy of it. There is not a more lively and beautiful lady of her age in all of Hertfordshire. I am certain there are many who would rival her in town, but in Meryton, there is not a soul. Jane, of course, outshines her in beauty, but not in liveliness."

Elizabeth sighed. She had hoped her mother would be so impressed to be in the presence of Lord and Lady Matlock that she would be somewhat subdued. However, that did not appear to be the case.

"All will be well," Darcy whispered hopefully in her ear.

"I should like to believe that, but I cannot," Elizabeth replied.

Darcy wished to take her aside and assure her once again that nothing would change his love for her and that his relations were just as likely to be ill-behaved this evening, but he did not wish to draw Mr. Bennet's displeasure any more than he had yesterday. Nevertheless, if things became unbearable for Elizabeth, he would pull her aside and run the risk of having to wait six months to be wed.

"You do not mind if we rush you into dinner, do you?" he asked his aunt. "We were just about to go in."

"She does not mind in the least," Lady Margaret replied. "I am famished. Richard, your arm," she instructed. "Darcy, lead on."

And so the party was in short order ensconced within the dining room. Conversation flowed with some awkwardness around the table due in a large part to Lady Matlock's desire to point out the failings of the Bennets.

"I have heard your estate is not substantial?" Lady Matlock asked Mr. Bennet.

"It is modest," the gentleman replied.

"And Mr. Gardiner is your wife's brother?"

"Yes," Mr. Gardiner answered. "I have three sisters, who have all been well-settled. Mrs. Bennet, whom you have met, Mrs. Philips, whose husband is a solicitor in Meryton, and Mrs. Clark, who is settled in Sussex. Her husband is a parson."

"And you have no brothers?"

"Not any longer," Mr. Gardiner replied. "The sea can be cruel."

Lady Matlock's brows rose. "How dreadful!"

Mr. Gardiner shrugged. "It is the way of things in the navy, is it not? Some return with tales of glory while others remain behind and have their part of the glory in the details of the tale."

Lady Matlock fell silent.

Darcy knew that Mr. Gardiner had hit a chord with his aunt. She had never been one to disapprove of her son's choice of joining the military, but she was the reason he had settled on the militia rather than the regulars or the navy. Darcy knew that even with Richard not being called away to foreign soil, his aunt worried about him. Lady Matlock might be a lady who sought attention and the praise of her peers, but there was one place in her life where she had not striven to be as many of her station were. She had always been, and still was, greatly attached to her children.

"My brother did look smart in his uniform." There was a fondness in Mrs. Bennet's tone. She sighed. "There is something about a uniform," she added softly before turning her attention back to her food.

Darcy chuckled softly to himself as he watched her. "She is trying not to look at Richard," he whispered in answer to Elizabeth's questioning look.

Jane smiled. "That is because a colonel would be just the thing for one of her daughters."

"She is thinking of Lydia, no doubt," Elizabeth replied. "My youngest sister," she explained quietly to Richard, who was sitting across from her and next to Lady Margaret.

"The lively one?" asked Lady Margaret.

Elizabeth nodded.

"How old is your youngest sister?" Lady Margaret asked, with a sidelong, teasing look at Richard and curiosity suffusing her features.

"She is not yet sixteen," Jane replied.

Georgiana, who sat next to her great aunt, gasped.

"Are you well, my dear?" Lady Margaret turned toward Georgiana.

"Yes," Georgiana replied with a blush. "I was just startled that Miss Elizabeth's sister was my age and..." She pressed her lips together and glanced at her brother.

"What is it?" Lady Margaret pressed.

Georgiana shook her head.

"Whisper it in my ear. I must know." Lady Margaret bent her

head toward Georgiana, who complied, causing Lady Margaret to laugh. "I guess he is rather old compared to you," she said with a wink at Richard.

"I am not old," Richard retorted.

"You are to a girl of sixteen," said his great aunt.

"I should not like to see you attached to someone so young," Lady Margaret continued, raising an eyebrow imperiously at her grandson and giving him a stern look.

"There is no fear of that," Richard assured her.

"Not even if the young lady has a fortune?" His grandmother queried.

Richard shook his head. "I have more sense than you suppose."

She shrugged. "Perhaps you do. However, if such a young heiress of say eighteen or nineteen were to capture your attention and possessed sense as large as her fortune, I should not object. In fact, if she were penniless, sensible, and were to work her way into your affections, I would also not object. It is not as if you are without funds." She lifted a hand to prevent protest. "I know they are not what you would like them to be, but you are far from poor."

"I do not know why I bother attending these functions," Richard grumbled.

"Darcy's cook is excellent," Bingley said with a smirk.

"It was not a question," Richard muttered.

"We would miss you if you did not," Georgiana added with a smile.

Darcy agreed readily with his sister.

"All five out at once!"

The exclamation from Lady Matlock at the other end of the table drew the attention of the others.

To Elizabeth, the shock in Lady Matlock's tone sounded very familiar. It was very like how she had been questioned at Rosings, and she was both curious and anxious as to what her mother's reply would be. She glanced at Darcy, who was watching her with concern, and smiled reassuringly at him.

"You would miss all this entertainment if you were not here," she whispered across the table to Richard as Lord Matlock gently chided his wife for her outburst.

Richard lifted and lowered his shoulders and with a nod of his head said, "Mothers."

Elizabeth's smile grew at that one-word reply. It seemed not only daughters had mothers who could be trying.

"Do you have any daughters?" Mrs. Bennet countered at the opposite end of the table.

"We have three sons," Lady Matlock replied. "There is one younger than Richard who is studying the law."

"The law is a very good profession," Mr. Gardiner said.

"Indeed it is," Mrs. Bennet agreed. "And it is fortunate that a son can learn a profession and see to his own welfare. Such is not the case with a daughter. One must do her best to see her daughters well-settled." Mrs. Bennet lifted her chin and looked as if she was going to say more. However, a commotion in the corridor caught her attention, and whatever else she might have said was lost to the entrance of Lady Catherine.

# Chapter 10

Darcy rose as his aunt bustled into the room ahead of his frazzled butler.

"Is Anne here?" Lady Catherine demanded without so much as a word of greeting. She looked around the table. "Oh," she said, her shoulders sagging as her eyes completed the circuit of startled faces without seeing the one she sought.

"As you can see, Anne is not here," Darcy said.

"And who are these people?" Lady Catherine asked with a wave of her hand toward the Bennets.

"If you had entered as you were taught," Lady Margaret replied before Darcy could say a word, "you would know as introductions would have been made." She pushed herself out of her chair as if it was a great effort. "These are the Bennets and the Gardeners. This beautiful young woman is Miss Bennet, and I believe you already know Miss Elizabeth," Lady Margaret motioned to each person as she mentioned them. "This," she said to the room at large, "is my youngest daughter, Lady Catherine de Bourgh. Now, Catherine, please explain your rudeness so that I might eat my cake."

Dessert had only just arrived, and Darcy had been certain to request his grandmother's favourite, Apples à la Parisienne, be prepared for tonight's dinner. Lady Margaret would forgo nearly any part of a meal save dessert. It was her favourite course, and when it was a much-loved cake, she was even more determined to savour every morsel placed before her.

Lady Catherine lifted her chin and looked disapprovingly at the Bennets. "Perhaps it would be better if we discussed this without visitors present."

"They are not visitors," Darcy crossed his arm and smiled as her head snapped around towards him. "They are my soon-to-be relations."

A great gasp was heard from both Lady Matlock and Mrs. Bennet.

Mr. Bennet cleared his throat and rose. "We had thought to make our announcement at the end of the meal, but seeing as an explanation is needed...It is my joy to announce the betrothals of my eldest daughters."

"Betrothals?" Mrs. Bennet squealed and clapped her hands. "Oh, I knew you could not be so beautiful for nothing, Jane, and you, Lizzy..." she stopped as if uncertain what to say, but the pause was only momentary, for her delight would not be suppressed into silence. "Oh, I do not know what any man would see in you, Lizzy, but I am glad Mr. Darcy had the good sense to see it!"

"Darcy is betrothed to my daughter," Lady Catherine declared. "No matter what this...this..." she waved her hand in Elizabeth's direction, "daughter of yours has done to make Darcy forget himself and his duty."

"My daughter has not done anything untoward," Mrs. Bennet's tone was indignant. "Have you, Lizzy?" she added, ruining any argument she was attempting to make.

"Of course, she has," Lady Catherine refuted. "Darcy would

not neglect his duty if she had not. Does Anne know of this? Is that why she has run off?" Lady Catherine asked, turning back toward Darcy.

Darcy shook his head. "Two things," he said much more calmly than he thought was possible in his current state of displeasure. "First, I have never been betrothed to Anne, and second, Miss Elizabeth is all that is proper." He shook his head again. "No, not two things — there is more. I do not appreciate your disruption of my dinner, nor will I allow you to remain under my roof if you continue to be uncivil and unwelcoming to either Miss Elizabeth or her family."

Lady Catherine took a step back as if she had been slapped. "I had thought you better than this," her eyes slid from her nephew to Elizabeth and back.

"Madam," Darcy growled, "I would choose my words carefully if I were you. Now, state your business."

Lady Catherine's eyes narrowed at Darcy's terse command. "My daughter is missing." She drew a letter from her reticule. "Mrs. Jenkinson found this in Anne's room this morning."

Darcy crossed to his aunt and took the missive from her. Unfolding it, he read,

*Dear Mother,*

*Wish me happy. I am to marry and before I am one and twenty! Please have Sally pack my things so that when I return, they can be easily transported to my new home.*

*Anne*

"It seems she is to be married," Darcy said as he finished reading.

"Yes, I can read," Lady Catherine snapped as she snatched the missive back from Darcy. "But if she is not here, marrying you, then where can she be?"

"On the road to Scotland, no doubt," said Lady Margaret.

"Scotland!" Lady Catherine gasped. "But with whom?"

"Not Darcy," muttered Richard with a smirk, earning him a glare from his cousin. He pushed up from his chair. "How long has she been gone?"

Lady Catherine shook her head and slumped into the chair to which Darcy had led her.

"She retired to her room early last evening." She shrugged and, taking the handkerchief Darcy handed her, dabbed at her eyes. "That is the last I saw of her," she whispered.

At that moment, Elizabeth felt compassion for her and a greater love for the man who knelt beside his aunt, holding her hand. The woman might have moments ago riled him to anger, but now as she faced the loss of a child, he had moved from being affronted to being attentive. It reminded her of how he had appeared at the parsonage. He was such a mix of noble traits. Commanding in one instance. The embodiment of kindness in another. How she had ever thought it possible on short acquaintance to unravel the complexity of such a man was beyond her comprehension now. How foolish it had been to think him simple and easily deciphered. She smiled as she looked on as more questions were gently put to Lady Catherine. He would not forever remain an enigma to her as she had claimed. She knew precisely who he was. He was the best of men. And he was hers.

"Mr. Bennet," Mrs. Bennet had risen to her feet and was pacing the room, "you must do something."

"I do not see what I can do," Elizabeth's father responded.

Mrs. Bennet huffed. "A child is missing. You must help find her, for she has no father to defend her." She wrung her hands and, walking to the window, peered out into the night as if she might be able to discover something in the blackness.

"Very well," Mr. Bennet said. "Would you care to ride to Scotland with me, Gardiner?"

"It might be best if someone who knew what Anne looked like rode with you," said Lord Matlock.

"And what will you do when you find her?" Lady Matlock asked. "The damage is done."

"Why insure a marriage takes place!" cried Mrs. Bennet. "Unless he is, of course, completely unfit as a husband, then..." she tapped her lip, "you, my lady, might know of someone in need of a wife who would with a bit of persuasion be willing to marry a lady of means. I assume the niece of an earl would be a lady of means, would she not be?"

"Anne has a fortune," said Lady Margaret.

Mrs. Bennet gasped. "Oh, Mr. Bennet, you must not let him have her fortune if that is all he wishes!"

"No marriage papers have been signed," Lord Matlock assured her. "But your concern does you credit, madam." He went to the door of the dining room and requested a runner be sent to Matlock House to prepare his things for travelling.

Things were swiftly arranged. Lord Matlock would ride out along the north road with his youngest son, who was always looking for a bit of adventure, as he checked for evidence that Anne had indeed gone to Scotland. Mr. Bennet was happy to remain in town, and Mrs. Bennet was pleased to be thought of as a kindly sort of woman by one so distinguished as an earl.

Elizabeth was certain she would hear that story repeated often when they returned to Hertfordshire. It was, as Mrs. Bennet said at least twice, nearly as good as having been to St. James's.

When dessert had been cleared away, and the ladies left for the drawing room, Darcy slipped out into the corridor and took Elizabeth by the arm.

"Come," he said in a whisper.

Elizabeth followed him down the hall and into what appeared to be his study.

"Are you well?" he asked as he closed the door and turned the lock.

"Yes, I am perfectly well."

"My family," he began, "are ridiculous at times."

Elizabeth smiled. "Indeed, neither of us are without such relations."

"It illustrates how wrong I was to disparage your family." He could feel his ears warming with shame.

"You are forgiven," Elizabeth said, placing a hand on his cheek. "You have aunts and uncles of great standing who have made — and likely will continue to make — life challenging for you for having chosen me. You were not wrong to consider their reaction."

"You will marry me despite my trying family?" he asked.

"If you can tolerate my mother and sisters, I can abide your relations."

He drew her into his embrace. "I am not entirely certain how I was so fortunate as to win you."

She drew back from where she had lain her head against his chest and once again touched his face, running her finger along the yellowish bruise around his eye. "Does it still hurt?"

He shook his head. "Only if I rub it too hard in the morning. It itches a bit, however."

She ran her finger gently along his bruise once again. "I would have never thought to see the Mr. Darcy I first met with a cut lip and a blackened eye." She laughed lightly as she returned her head to resting above his heart. "But then you are not who I thought you were."

"I am not who I was," he said. "I have been working to untie the tightly woven mantle of duty and responsibility that presented itself in arrogance."

"Do not change," she said as she looked up at him.

"I am only amending the ungentlemanly parts," he replied with a smile.

She returned his smile. "I love you just as you are."

"And I you, my dearest Elizabeth," he dipped his head and kissed her briefly. "I was thinking," he said before kissing her again, "I have a fine travelling coach, and Scotland is not so very far away." He kissed her a third time.

"Mr. Darcy!"

"Fitzwilliam," he corrected.

"Fitzwilliam," she said shyly, "I am shocked that you have proposed an elopement. It is not a proper thing at all."

He found himself grinning with delight at the impertinent lift of her left brow. "If it would not distress your mother, I would steal you away this very night." He kissed her once again, but not lightly as he had done before. This was a long, lingering, delicious sort of kiss.

"Mr. Darcy," Mr. Bennet called through the door, "have you seen my daughter?"

Darcy smiled down at Elizabeth as he called back a "yes." Then he kissed Mr. Bennet's daughter once more as the doorknob rattled behind him. "You must work on him to allow us to marry soon," he said to Elizabeth. "Or we will be going to Scotland." He kissed her one last time before releasing her, turning to open the door and facing her father.

"You say you have a comfortable carriage?" Elizabeth blushed at the breathiness of her voice.

"Yes, it is well-sprung with plush seats." His hand rested on the doorknob.

"I will keep that in mind." She lifted onto her toes and pressed her lips against his. "If he will not agree to a month..." She left the rest of her consent to his plan unspoken.

The way her smile danced in her eyes held his gaze captive for a moment, and then, offering her his arm, he opened the door to face whatever might come — together.

# Becoming Entangled

Can Anne scheme her way out of one betrothal and into another?

# Chapter 1

Anne de Bourgh turned her phaeton from the well-travelled road on which she was travelling onto a less used avenue. Five large trees down the path was a small open area that was just the right size for a small carriage like hers. After drawing to a stop, Anne climbed down, secured her horses and, with a glance back at the avenue, scurried into the seclusion of the trees.

"You're late," a low voice rumbled, causing Anne to smile.

"It could not be helped," Anne replied, stepping closer to the source of the voice and enjoying the flutter his presence created in her chest. "I finally found Miss Bennet alone."

The gentleman pushed off from the tree against which he had been leaning and pulled Anne into his embrace as she continued, "She seems willing to take on my cousin."

"So you are free?" he asked hopefully.

Anne shook her head. "No, it is only a possibility, and there is still my mother. She will not give up her dreams so easily. If or, more likely when, she finds out that Darcy is courting Elizabeth, she will drag me to town and insist that he take me instead." She blew out a great breath. "I do not know why she insists on my marrying him."

"Because Darcy is wealthy, is her dearly-loved sister's son, and seems willing to please her, and I would venture a guess that the last item is doubtless her most compelling reason. Your mother does like to have her way." Alistair Pratt, Anne's long-time friend, placed a finger under her chin and, lifting it, brushed her lips with his. "She is almost as intolerable as my mother. It is no wonder they are such good friends," he said with a small laugh before turning serious. "Did you know that my mother has promised my attendance at a house party in Warwickshire?"

"She has not!" Anne had heard tell of house parties. They were nothing more than places to arrange matches in whatever way might be most effective. Why, just last year, her mother had told her of three young ladies who had been required to marry after attending such a function. It was the reason her mother assured her that she would never be required to attend such a dangerous event. A lady's reputation, after all, must be preserved. Besides, what purpose would there be in attending, her mother had asked, if Darcy was not there? It was not as if Anne needed to find a husband. No, she only needed to wait patiently until her cousin did his duty and claimed her. Duty! The word grated. What lady sincerely wished to be a duty that must be done?

"She has indeed." Alistair kissed Anne once more before pressing her head against his heart. "She has informed me that there are two candidates for Mrs. Pratt in attendance. Both are ladies of good standing and of whom she approves."

"And will you marry one of them?" Anne asked. There was absolutely no reason for her to ask such a thing except for a small jealous flutter in her chest. Alistair had assured her that his taste in ladies and that of his mother were two very different things. His mother, Lady Metcalfe, wished for a society darling to parade about the ton, but Alistair preferred a lady who was happy at home. Of course, he did not want a dowdy homebody since he longed for a bit of adventure and fun, but he also preferred staying at home and reading near the hearth to gadding about town.

"Not unless they are you," he replied, squeezing her tightly. "I am delaying my departure for as long as I can, though it is driving my mother to distraction. She thinks I need to be the first to arrive." He sighed. "I leave the day after tomorrow."

"So soon?" Anne's heart ached at the thought of being separated from him. It always did. She enjoyed spending a few stolen moments with him when it could be arranged, and his presence made a call from Lady Metcalfe so much more bearable when he could accompany his mother, for he would sit with Anne and over a cup of tea or a book of verses, share a limited but intimate conversation. Alistair did not treat her as some delicate flower about to wilt and be tossed out, nor did he think she was incapable of intelligent discussion. He treated her as she longed to be treated — as a friend, a very dear friend, and a bit more, a good bit more. This was not the first conversation the two had had about marriage. They had spoken of it often — nearly every visit — for the last six months.

"I am afraid it truly cannot be put off any longer than that." He released her and drew a small parcel of cloth out of his pocket. "I had hoped," he said, folding back the red material, "that you might accept this and me."

Anne gasped at the beautiful cross pendant composed of four rose cut diamonds set in silver with rubies interspersed that lay in his open palm. He was finally going to offer for her! She ran a finger over the shiny bauble as her heart beat a rhythm of delighted anticipation in her chest. "It is so beautiful. It must be of great value."

He lifted it from his hand and allowed it to dangle in front of her on its gold chain. "It is. It was left to me by my father's mother. I have always intended for my wife to wear it on the day of our marriage." He caught the twirling cross in his hand. "I wish for you to be my bride. I cannot abide sitting cautiously on the edge of a precipice waiting to know whether I will be hurled from it or pulled to safety any longer, and, therefore, I do not want to wait a moment more to settle things between us. I know we are not yet free to even make our courtship known, but surely, it will not be long before we can, will it? If your cousin truly loves Miss Elizabeth, as you suspect he does, he will not allow your mother to force him into marrying you, will he?"

Anne pulled a letter from her reticule. "I have written to Darcy, encouraging him to find a wife with all due haste, and I have made it abundantly clear that I do not wish to be that wife. If you will send this for me, then I shall consider myself free enough to accept your gift and bind myself to you with a promise." She smiled, both at the thought of being truly betrothed to a gentleman such as Alistair Pratt, who caused her heart to flutter, and at the way in which she had made her acceptance sound very much like a damsel in a fairy-tale.

"I will gladly deliver your missive," he replied with a beautiful smile that caused his eyes to sparkle. "Might I?" He unclasped the chain and held it out in an offer of placing it on her neck.

Anne nodded eagerly and turned so that he could fasten it at the back of her neck.

He lifted the necklace over her head and then made short work of securing it in place. He smoothed the chain against her neck and gave the place where the clasp lay a kiss. Then, turning her towards him, he continued smoothing the chain down toward the neckline of her gown, stopping short of reaching the edge of her garment. There he lifted the chain and allowed the cross to drop into hiding. A smile spread across his face as he watched the pendent slip from view. "The chain is the right length. I will replace it with a shorter chain once you are able to wear it for all to see." He lifted his eyes to hers as he grasped her hands and pulled her a step closer. "For now, only we will know what secret lies next to your heart."

"You must take a lock of my hair," Anne said. "I have nothing else to give you." She pulled her hands from his grasp and worked a tendril loose from behind her ear.

Alistair fished his knife out of his pocket and, unfolding it, cut the lock she held.

"Wait," she said before he could take the hair from her and tuck it into his pocket. "You must let me wrap it in my handkerchief. I embroidered the flowers on the corner along with my initials. It shall be something that will help you remember me while you are gone."

The precious item was quickly wrapped and tucked away with Alistair's knife.

"We have an understanding then?" Alistair asked. "You will be mine as soon as you are free?"

An impish smile played at her lips. "Before." She knew her mother would not give up Darcy easily, even if he were to engage himself to a lady within the month's time she had given him to do so in her letter — the one that was now safely in Alistair's care. She would make her escape well before the time was up.

"Before?" he repeated, a slight note of skepticism in his voice.

Anne nodded.

"How? You are not of age."

"One does not have to be of age in Scotland," Anne replied. Her heart swelled at the thought of the adventure that lay in stealing away from Rosings and flying to Scotland. Just the idea was enough to send her head spinning far more than dancing with her instructor had ever done.

Alistair shook his head. "An elopement is scandalous. My father would not approve."

"Neither would my mother," Anne replied cheerfully. "However, your father and mother wish for you to marry, do they not?"

"Of course. That is why I am being sent off to this party. But an elopement?"

Anne took his hand. He seemed to be slipping into an anxious temper as he was sometimes wont to do when his plans were upset. "I have heard your mother describe the sort of gentleman she wishes your sister to marry and the sort of lady she wishes for you to marry. I meet nearly all her qualifications. I have a fortune. My father was a baronet, and my uncle is an earl. My lineage and wealth are without fault for one who wishes to marry a lady of good social standing. I will allow that my standing within the ton is somewhat lacking, but that is only because I have never been to London for a season. I am certain that if I were to go, I would do well. My uncle, after all, is the Earl of Matlock, and with you as my husband — the next Lord Metcalfe — many would welcome me."

His brows furrowed. "The ton can be fickle."

"So I have heard," Anne assured him. "But that would be something with which we could deal after we are married. I do not even have to go to town for a full season. I would only wish to experience a few weeks of it — to dance, to visit the museum, and to drive in the park and to do it all with you. Oh, it would be delightful! I know it would be!"

"I have yet to find any of it truly delightful," Alistair muttered.

"But," Anne persisted, "that is because you must do it with the purpose of finding a bride. That will no longer be an issue, for you will have me, making you free of your mother's demands to visit this or that lady, and you would never again have to attend a house party." She lifted his hands and kissed his knuckles. "Please. We could both be free."

"But an elopement?" he said softly.

"Please," she pleaded again, this time with a small pout and flutter of lashes.

The right corner of his mouth tipped up. "I suppose you have a plan?"

A smile split Anne's face, and, lifting onto her toes, she gave his lips a quick kiss. "I had thought we would slip away together one night, but now, I shall have to reconsider how we might meet since you will not be here."

He wrapped her in his arms once again. "Do you desire so much to be my bride, or do you just desire to be free of your mother?"

"I do not wish to be free of my mother enough to marry my cousin," Anne replied. "He is not whom my heart desires. You are."

"Very well then. I shall send for you as soon as I have determined the best way to meet. Will that suffice?"

Anne's brows furrowed and her lips puckered as she considered it. Alistair was not a gentleman to go back on his word — at least, he had never done so with her. However, a small worry that he would attempt to avoid the scandal a clandestine meeting and elopement was sure to create would not be brushed away. "I will wait two weeks. If I have not heard from you in that time, I will find you on my own."

"You have never been further than London," he said, pulling back to look down at her.

"No, I have not, but I will not be put off. I will find you if you do not send for me. "

"There is no need to glare at me, my love," he said with a chuckle. "I am not going to leave you standing. I will claim you."

"I will be twenty in a month's time, and my mother will begin her campaign to see me married with fresh vigour. I know she will, for she wishes to see me married before I am one and twenty."

"I will not leave you standing," Alistair repeated. "Nor will I see you in the arms of another."

"You promise?" she asked.

"Yes," he answered. "You, Miss Anne de Bourgh, are mine." And then he spent several minutes proving his claim true with kisses and caresses before seeing her on her way back to Rosings.

# Chapter 2

Alistair extended his hands out in front of him, lacing his fingers together and pushing his palms toward the opposite side of the carriage. He lifted one leg, twirled his foot, and then lowered it before doing the same with his other leg. His limbs were stiff, and his journey had barely begun. Travelling was not something he enjoyed doing. Travelling from Kent to London was the extent of his tolerance for sitting idly in one spot while being jostled about over rutted roads.

He swung his hands out to each side before bringing them together behind his head and leaning back against the squabs for the last few minutes of his trip.

He would spend tonight in London with his good friend Jack Ralston before the two of them continued on to Stanton's house party in Warwickshire.

Alistair expelled a deep sigh. Warwickshire was such a long distance from Kent. If it were not for the fact that his mother had likely requested for Mrs. Stanton to write to her upon his arrival, Alistair would have been sorely tempted to remain in town for the month he was expected to be gone. As it was, even knowing how displeased his mother would be and the lecturing that would ensue, he was considering finding a place in town to while away his time. Undoubtedly, London was large enough that a lone gentleman might find somewhere to hide from family and responsibility.

The carriage drew to a stop in front of Albany where Ralston leased an apartment, and Alistair prepared to alight.

Responsibility was not something from which Alistair shrank as some gentlemen of his age and means did. He did not spend his money on copious quantities of coats and cravats. He did not cast away his inheritance at gaming tables or on other mindless pursuits. He found pleasure in studying and improving his mind — not that he allowed that fact to be widely known. He had endured enough teasing for such tendencies when young that he knew better than to broadcast them now. Once he had secured his wife and family, then, he might feel more at ease with being himself in front of one and all. He smiled. That time was soon. He patted the pocket where he carried Anne's lock of hair. He would tuck it into his trunk when he arrived in Warwickshire, but until that time, the precious packet would, for safety sake and his own comfort, travel on his person.

He stepped down from his carriage and made his way to Ralston's apartment. The door opened before Alistair could lift the knocker.

"Come in. Come in," Ralston greeted his friend.

Alistair handed his outerwear to the man standing at his post near the door that Ralston had thrown open.

"I know how you long for activity after being confined to a carriage. Therefore, even though I am certain you could defeat me in a match wearing your travelling clothes, you must change at once and accompany me to Angelo's." Ralston led his friend to the dressing room next to his bedchamber. "Do not wait for your trunk. I have had a set of clothes laid out for you."

"It is good to see you," Alistair said with a smile. He and Jack had been friends since Harrow. It was an odd mix. One being the studious sort of scholar who was often overlooked while the other was more of a sportsman and generally popular. "You know your clothes will not fit me."

Ralston nodded. "But Harold's will."

"Did you make a request to borrow these or a demand?" Alistair's brow cocked as he picked up the shirt that hung on the back of a chair. Harold was Jack's younger and slighter brother, and Jack at times forgot that they were no longer children instead of both grown men and resorted to requiring assistance from his brother rather than asking for it.

Ralston shrugged. "Does it matter?"

Alistair laughed as he pulled off his coat and began to remove his shirt. "You are very fortunate to have such an accommodating brother."

"So he has told me time and time again," Ralston said with a smirk. "Sit and extend your foot. I can remove your boots as easily as your man can, and I can do it in better time since his hands are occupied." He flicked his head toward a wardrobe on the not-so-far end of the small room. "There is room in there for what you will need," he said to Alistair's man, who was just entering with Jack's bag, followed closely by a pair of footmen carrying a trunk.

Alistair did as instructed, and as soon as he was free of his boots, he began working quickly on his breeches before his rather impatient friend decided to assist him with those as well. Alistair despised sitting idly for any length of time, but he was able to bear the inconvenience with a measure of aplomb. Jack, on the other hand, often wished things to be done before they could be started and thought it his duty to be the one to see them completed. It was not entirely unusual for him to become so engrossed in what needed to be done that he would act without thinking, and should there be a great deal of activity in the room to capture his attention or should there be a fascinating topic of discussion, the possibility of Jack's acting without thought increased.

"I thought you might need some sustenance before we go. There is a tray in the drawing room. Do not be long." Ralston gave a nod of his head and closed the door behind him.

"I do hope he leaves a few morsels for me," Alistair muttered to his man as the servant began gathering his master's discarded clothing.

~*~*~

A few minutes later, dressed in fresh, though borrowed, clothing, Alistair stepped into the drawing room to discover that there actually were a few morsels left for his consumption as well as a cup of tea — perfectly prepared. That was an uncanny thing about his friend. Jack might not be able to remember the words of a sonnet or the lines of a play, but he could always remember a name and a face as well as the preferences of his friends and other sundry facts about family, friends, and even mere acquaintances.

"My carriage will be waiting for us. I instructed them to have it sent around as soon as yours was brought in." He rose and walked to the window where he propped himself on the edge of a table and continued drinking his tea. "Was it a good trip?"

"As good as a few hours locked in a carriage can be," Alistair said with a smile.

Jack's lips curled into a smirk, and he turned his head once more to look out the window. "That depends on your company, or so I hear."

Alistair chuckled. "Conversation with one's self is not nearly so pleasant as with a friend."

"You are too proper," Ralston said with a laugh. "I was not speaking of conversation, and you know it." He drained the last few drops of tea from his cup and lifted his brows in question as he looked at his friend.

"I am almost finished," Alistair assured him.

Ralston nodded and returned his cup and saucer to the table in front of Alistair. "I feel almost ready to permanently name a lady to take the seat next to me in my carriage." He sighed. "It will mean giving up this," he said, indicating the apartment with a wave of his hand, "as I will have to find a larger dwelling. I should say a wife would not enjoy being told the cot in the dressing room is for her use."

Both men laughed at the thought.

"No," Alistair agreed, "I should say not." He placed his empty cup on the table, popped one last piece of cheese into his mouth, and stood to leave. "What has wrought this change in you? I thought you were determined to remain a bachelor."

Ralston led the way from the room. "Miss Georgiana Darcy."

Alistair's steps faltered. "I beg your pardon? Miss Georgiana Darcy? As in sister to Mr. Fitzwilliam Darcy?"

"One and the same." Ralston flashed Alistair a wide grin. "We shall be cousins."

Alistair shook his head in disagreement and disbelief. "She's not out yet," he cautioned.

"I know," Ralston said as he climbed into his carriage. "I have a year to wait, but Al, she's an angel."

"Her brother is protective, and you have a reputation of being... um... overly friendly."

"I have never ruined a lady," Ralston replied. "I do not even have a mistress as many do, nor do I keep company with lonely widows. I am friendly — as in cordial and obliging — but that is all." He shrugged. "A few stolen kisses in a garden are not ruinous or reason to call a chap out."

"Unless he gets caught kissing the lady and refuses to offer for her," Alistair mumbled.

"Which has never happened," Ralston retorted.

"And cannot happen for a full year if you are to be successful."

"Stop shaking your head. I can be perfectly chaste for a year. And lower that eyebrow. Honestly, Al, it is as if you have no faith in me at all."

"I trust you and your friendly manners more than I trust the ladies of the ton — several of whom will be at this house party."

Ignoring his friend, Ralston looked out the window and smiled. "Good," he said, clapping his hands together. "I do believe that is Darcy's carriage."

Alistair cocked his head, and his brows drew together. "At Angelo's?"

Ralston nodded. "I have a year to make a good impression on Miss Darcy's brother. I thought I would start tonight. You are as respectable as they come. Having you for a friend must count for something."

Alistair muttered his agreement, but as he was planning to

elope with Darcy's cousin and stir up a bit of a scandal, he was not certain being Jack's friend was going to benefit Jack very much.

~*~*~

"If you could allow me, perchance, to land a few points at the opening," Ralston said as the two friends entered the building. He waved to a friend or two and nodded to another. "What do you say, old chap? Help me appear better at this sport than I am."

Alistair chuckled. "You are better at all sports than I am. I shall not have to allow you to look so. It will just be so."

Ralston shrugged out of his coat and began preparing himself for their match. "No, that is not true. You often outdo me with foils. Your lunge is stealthy. I have yet to guess your tell."

"I have no tell," Alistair replied. "I simply react as the situation dictates."

"Yes, but others have a slight cock of their head or a shuffle of a foot — even a tensing of their frame can tell me about an opponent's strategy," he shook his head, "but not you. You keep to no set pattern, which I might point out is very unlike you in most things, for I dare say one could set his clock by when you do this or that on a normal day." He flicked his foil in the air and then sliced through it as if drawing a *z*.

Alistair readied himself. "I like structure." It was true. Alistair Pratt prized schedules and routines. He liked to rise at the same time each day, take an hour of exercise, and then have tea and toast with two eggs and an occasional piece of ham. He would then see to any tasks that needed to be done. His father always had a list of items that he expected Alistair to oversee as well as articles to read. It was his father's way of readying Alistair to take over the estate and preparing him to eventually take his seat in the House of Lords.

"Structure would include a routine method of defense." Ralston stepped into place and took his position. "If you could just structure your swordplay, it would be of benefit to me. That is all I am asking."

Alistair shook his head. "You would not be the first to request such. Do you not remember our master at school scolding me for not following their figures as he prescribed?"

Ralston broke out of his ready form and stood. "Indeed, I do. You were so diligent to follow the letter of the law in every other class. Why did you not when fencing?"

"It did not seem practical to broadcast to my opponent my every move, and I do like to be practical."

Ralston guffawed.

Alistair grinned at the response. His friend knew that Alistair rarely did things just for ceremony's sake if there was a more effective way of performing a task. It was what Jack claimed would one day lead Alistair to make a great discovery, for, according to Jack, it was the need to find a better method of doing something that led to all great inventions.

"Now, shall we?" Alistair sank into position, and the match began. Forward and back they shuffled, metal striking against metal and occasionally thwacking off cloth. Finally, after several minutes, the match was over, and the two men had joined a few others who were resting along the wall while the floor was occupied by others.

"So how did you leave your lady?" Ralston asked as he stretched out his legs and leaned back.

"She was not pleased to know why I was leaving," Alistair said, tipping his head toward the two men approaching them and giving his head a small shake. "No names," he whispered.

"Why?" Ralston whispered back.

"He is her cousin."

Ralston's eyes grew wide. "I apologize. I had forgotten. But was she in good spirits?"

A smile slid across Alistair's lips. "Very good. Perhaps better spirits than should be allowed. We have tentatively settled things between us."

"So soon?"

"We have been courting for some time. I would not say it was soon." He would say that the marriage would be soon — or rather sooner than it likely should be –, but he would not say he had come to the decision to marry Anne too quickly. They had known each other for years and had been secretly courting for many months.

"But you are only just finished school. You are in the prime of your maleness. Would you throw that away when the season has so many delightful debutants? Are you so certain of this one?"

Alistair folded his arms across his chest. "And I assume you have had ample time to consider and be in company with the lady for whom you claim you would give up your apartment at Albany?" He bit back a smile as Jack's eyes narrowed. Jack might have the physical advantage over Alistair in most sports; however, when it came to well-reasoned debates, there were few who could outwit Alistair when he was certain of his correctness on a matter. His father had trained him with debate after debate about nonsensical things as well as current issues in the news.

"I concede your point." There was very little joy, admiration, or anything that spoke of pleasant feelings in Ralston's tone. In fact, much to Alistair's delight, for it was enjoyable to disconcert his self-assured friend at times, Jack seemed rather put out. Of course, that might have been attributed more to the fact that Mr. Darcy and his friend Mr. Bingley had taken seats on Ralston's left, and one of those gentlemen was the very one Jack wished to impress.

"Mr. Darcy," Alistair greeted, leaning around his friend. "I trust you are well settled back into town after your sojourn in Kent." He blinked and attempted to school his features into not showing his surprise at the blackness of Mr. Darcy's eye.

"I am. Thank you," Darcy answered. "Did my aunt inform you of my stay or was it her parson?"

Alistair chuckled. "Neither. I saw you at church, and your cousin mentioned to me that you and Colonel Fitzwilliam had been to Rosings for a visit."

"Anne?" Darcy's brows rose.

"Yes, Miss de Bourgh. I accompany my mother often when she calls at Rosings, so Miss de Bourgh and I have become friends." They were, of course, more than just friends, but they were friends, so it was not a complete untruth, or so he told himself. He hoped that the warmth he felt creeping up his neck would be credited to the physical exercise he had just had and the temperature in the room and not to the discomfort he felt in trying to explain his relationship to Darcy's cousin.

"Ah, yes, the illustrious Lady Metcalfe," Darcy said with a smile. "My aunt often speaks of your mother."

"They are good friends of long standing," Alistair said.

"My aunt has assured me of that fact many times," Darcy replied.

"Do you know my friend?" Alistair asked in response to the nudge he felt to his foot.

Darcy cocked his head. "Ralston, is it not?"

"Yes, sir. Jack Ralston."

As much as Alistair wished to allow his friend to continue impressing the brother of a lady he fancied, Alistair was more eager to press his own suit in regards to his own lady's freedom from any possibility of being forced into marriage with Darcy. "Miss de Bourgh mentioned she had gained a new friend these last few weeks. I believe it was some relation of your aunt's parson?" The heat that had begun to slide back down his neck resumed it crawl up to his ears. He really must learn some technique to quell such a response when withholding information before he entered politics, for he was certain it would do him no good. It was a tell. And as he had told his friend earlier, tells, as much as routines in defense, were not practical.

"Miss Elizabeth Bennet."

Alistair could not keep his brows from raising slightly at the smile that spread across Darcy's face as he said the name. It seemed Anne had been correct in assessing the gentleman's feeling for Miss Elizabeth.

"Her cousin is Mr. Collins." Darcy tossed one leg over the other and seemed to relax into his chair.

The sight was startling. Alistair had never seen Darcy be anything but rigidly proper.

"You have a sister, do you not?" Darcy asked Alistair.

"Yes, Clarice."

"She is not out yet, is she?"

Alistair's brows drew together. These seemed odd questions for Darcy to be asking. "She is only thirteen."

"Right, that is why your mother needed my aunt's recommendation about Miss Pope. She is getting on well in her position is she not?"

"As far as I know, Miss Pope is an excellent governess, and my sister has not driven her to distraction. She reserves that for me."

"It is the way of younger sisters," Darcy agreed.

"Did you fall?" Alistair pointed his eye, indicating he was questioning Darcy about his bruise. This Mr. Darcy seemed far too relaxed and conversational to Alistair, and it was making him feel uneasy.

Darcy chuckled and rubbed his eye. "No, this is Bingley's handiwork. You both know Bingley, do you not?"

"By sight and name," Ralston said. "We have never officially met."

Darcy took a moment to apologize for the oversight in not making introductions and then allowed Bingley to introduce himself. This was followed, for a few moments, by a discussion between Ralston and Bingley about pugilism.

As Bingley and Ralston spoke of boxing, Darcy pulled his chair around to sit next to Alistair. "The reason I asked about your sister is that my sister insisted I stop at the best shop for lace and such fripperies today when we were in Cheapside, and I must agree that it is a very dignified store. I would not hesitate to recommend it to your mother or your sister when they are in town. It is owned by Miss Elizabeth's uncle, who from all appearances and the reports of his nieces, is a fine, reputable merchant. My sister was delighted with the few things she purchased."

"Oh," Alistair muttered. "Thank you, I shall tell my mother when she is in town. I should think Miss de Bourgh might enjoy such a place. She does like to stitch, or, at least, she is often working on some item of sewing when I visit."

Darcy shrugged. "She might, but she rarely comes to town."

"Yes," Alistair agreed. "But she is getting to an age where it might become necessary if she is to marry."

Darcy smiled. "This is true. There are not so many opportunities to find a husband in the country as there are in town — or so my aunt, Lady Matlock, and my grandmother, Lady Margaret, assure me. However, I think that perhaps the quality of selection rather than the quantity from which to choose is of more importance and that the country can be an excellent place to find a wife or husband."

"I would not disagree, no matter what my mother might say to the contrary," Alistair concurred. "We, Ralston and I, are on our way to a less than ideal place to find quality wives — a house party."

"A house party?" Bingley interjected. "Not even I enjoy those, and I do enjoy most places where I find myself."

"We intend to do our best to avoid any pitfalls while we are there," Ralston said. "I am of half a mind to not attend, but my mother is so insistent."

"As is mine," Alistair agreed. Then he tipped his head as an idea struck him. "Perhaps we could make an appearance — long enough for the hostess to not feel slighted and for her to inform my mother that I did arrive — and then we could find some excuse to leave early."

Bingley chuckled. "It would never work. If your mother and the hostess are friends, there will be a letter soon after your departure lamenting that your stay could not be longer and detailing the reason you gave for leaving. Females bent on marriage are of a devious nature whether they are looking to snare you as their husband or as their daughter's husband."

"Indeed," Darcy agreed with a laugh. "My advice is to find a lady who stirs your heart and remove her and yourself from the marriage mart as soon as you are able. It does not become more enjoyable or easier to endure as the years pass."

"Are you, gentlemen, intending to remove yourselves from the list of eligible bachelors?" Ralston asked.

Both Bingley and Darcy nodded.

"As soon as we are able," Darcy said.

"Your advice seems sound and most practical. There are duties to titles and estates to which we must see, after all," Alistair said.

"Practical," Ralston muttered with a shake of his head. "Al, taking a wife should likely be more than just a practicality of life."

"Oh, I intend to marry for love," Alistair admitted rather boldly. He knew that such sentiments were not shared by all of the ton, but having heard the way Bingley and Darcy had spoken, he suspected that they were two gentlemen who also intended to make a love match, and so he dared enough to be so bold. "I just find it practical to do so as soon as possible."

# Chapter 3

"As soon as possible?" Ralston wiped his mouth and reached for his glass of port. It was the third time he had attempted to broach the subject of Alistair's plans to marry since they had left Angelo's and the second since arriving for dinner at White's.

Again, Alistair shook his head in response and remained quiet. He did not wish to discuss his plans here where they could be overheard by eager ears.

"Pratt, Ralston," a gentleman in a blue coat and dark trousers greeted them as he brushed past their table.

"Conrad." Ralston acknowledged the man with a nod. "How is the new horse?" he asked and then turned to Alistair. "He bought a gorgeous hunter last week."

"We are getting along splendidly," Clifton Conrad replied with a smile as he took a seat at the neighboring table with three other gentlemen.

"And Miss Anson? Are you still getting along splendidly with her as well? My mother was saying a happy announcement was expected any day now," Ralston leaned back in his chair and continued to consume his port. "It was among the reasons she listed for me to go to this infernal house party Stanton's hosting."

Conrad laughed heartily. "You going to that, are you?"

"Indeed, we are," Ralston replied, indicating Pratt.

Conrad's brows rose, and he gave Alistair an assessing look. The two gentlemen were friends but just. They tolerated each other's presence with respectable indifference. Neither cared much for the other. Alistair did not approve of Conrad's less than honorable proclivities when it came to courting ladies, and Conrad disapproved of Alistair to the point of dislike or worse because Alistair had, at one time two years ago, mentioned the name of the lady he thought Conrad was courting to the lady Conrad was actually courting. It was a passing of information from one unknowing source to another, for Alistair was as much in the dark about the lady to whom he spoke being the true object of Conrad's matrimonial pursuits as the lady was about the existence of a rival. As events unfolded, it was discovered that Conrad was pursuing the charming woman to whom Alistair had spoken for her wealth and only for her wealth, and thanks to Alistair's interference, all hope of ever securing that substantial amount of money was quickly and wholly lost to Conrad. Conrad held the loss against Alistair, and Alistair felt no remorse for saving a young woman from certain misery.

"Looking for wives?" Conrad queried.

"No, appeasing our mothers," Ralston replied.

"Better you than me." Conrad picked up fork and knife and prepared to eat the meal that had been placed in front of him. "However, you might be as fortunate as I have been. Miss Anson is all a gentleman could wish for in a wife."

"Sizeable dowry?" Ralston asked with a chuckle.

"Among other things," one of the other men at Conrad's table called out, setting the whole group of Conrad's friends laughing.

"I had heard she was pretty," Ralston commented.

"Beauty, wealth, proper societal standing along with an understanding of how things work among the well-to-do," he said the last part with a significant look at Alistair.

Ralston shrugged. "That might be acceptable for some, but Al and I are planning to seek something a bit more consequential."

Alistair kicked Jack's ankle as Jack was draining the last drops of port from his glass. Conrad and his friends were not the sort with whom Alistair wished to discuss marrying for love.

"Indeed?" Conrad said with interest. "A love match is it then?"

"With any luck," Ralston replied.

Alistair sighed. Apparently, for Jack, a kick in the ankle was nothing of which to take note, and the subject was about to be canvassed unless Alistair could somehow turn the conversation.

"We have an early morning," he said to Jack, hoping that his friend would take the hint that they should leave.

Thankfully, he did and, after only a few more pleasantries between tables, rose to leave. "You'll tell me how you intend to secure Miss de Bourgh as soon as possible on our way home, will you not?" Ralston said as they moved away from their table.

"Yes, as soon as we are in the carriage," Alistair replied, casting a wary glance over his shoulder toward Conrad. He did not wish for that gentleman to know anything of his plans. Happily, Conrad was popping a forkful of meat into his mouth and did not appear to have noticed anything more than the fact that his goblet had been filled with port. However, looks can be deceiving, and as the two friends stepped out into the night, a bet which had nothing to do with the game of cards that was to follow Conrad's meal and everything to do with retribution was being placed at a particular table at White's.



"Now, tell me," Ralston demanded as the door to the carriage was closed. "It is not proper to speak of marrying with all haste and then leave the details hidden for two full hours. It is simply not right. I suppose if you were another who was given to rashness such a comment as you made could be overlooked, but you are not. You are a time for everything and everything in due time Alistair Pratt."

Alistair rolled his eyes. "Are you about through, or would you care to scold a bit longer? Honestly, Jack, there are times you sound very much like your mother." A grin spread across Alistair's face as Jack's eyes narrowed.

"I am her son," he defended. "It only stands to reason I might have inherited a few traits."

"Only a few," Alistair assured his friend with a chuckle. Alistair liked Jack's mother. She was doting and sweet, but she was also given to blathering on for an extended length of time when she got a bee in her bonnet. Likewise, irritation sometimes spilled out of Jack in a river of words. It did not happen often, and then only with those with whom he was intimately acquainted. "I do not intend to remain at Stanton's for the full duration of the house party. As soon as we arrive, I must investigate the best place and time for Anne to meet me before we continue on to Scotland."

Alistair crossed one leg over the other and peeked out the window. The sun had disappeared below the horizon, leaving only a few fingers of light in the sky. Lamps were being lit along the street and windows in homes were beginning to glow in a welcoming fashion. He smiled as he turned back to the silent interior of the carriage. "I do look forward to having Anne waiting for me behind the glowing windows of our home at the end of the day." A peace settled into his heart at the thought. Anne had always caused such a comforting feeling in him. It was as if with her his heart had found a home.

"You are eloping?" Ralston asked as he finally found his voice.

"It seemed the most practical course of action," Alistair replied.

Ralston shook his head as if trying to clear a fog from it. "How is an elopement ever practical?" he demanded. "It is always scandalous, but ... practical?" He shook his head again.

Alistair blew out a breath of air and settled back into his seat. "I need a wife. I love Anne. Anne needs to escape her mother." He held up a finger as he listed each point. "Added to that, there is the saving of the expense of a wedding breakfast. I suppose we will have some sort of dinner to celebrate when we return, but we should be able to keep it small and intimate as my mother will not be involved."

"Escape and saving money? These are your reasons for eloping?" Ralston was looking at Alistair as if Alistair would be a good candidate for a residency in Bedlam.

"Yes, as well as the need of a wife and the fact that I love her," Alistair added. "I did protest when she suggested the idea. I am not unaware of the scandal and possible displeasure this will bring. But, I cannot marry anyone else and neither can she." The sharpness of his words caused his friend to recoil a few inches from where he had been leaning forward.

"Possible displeasure? Possible displeasure? Have you considered the extent of the disapprobation you will face when you return? And not just from your mother, whom you are denying the privilege of seeing you leg-shackled by a parson, but what of Miss de Bourgh's mother?" He clasped the sides of his head with his hands. "And what of her uncle? Your father relies on the earl's support, does he not?"

Again, Alistair blew out a breath. "My father and Lord Matlock agree on most things. It is not as if Father must persuade Lord Matlock to vote in accordance with him on many issues. And I do not see how my marrying his niece would make Lord Matlock cut ties with my father. It is not as if I am some merchant's son without a penny to my name. My wealth is secure, and I shall, in the hopefully distant future, ascend to the title of Lord Metcalfe. A viscount is not so lofty as an earl or a duke, to be sure, but I do think it outranks a mere gentleman, even if that gentleman is Darcy."

"You are certain of this?" Ralston asked as they drew to a stop in front of his home. "You love her enough to face whatever consequences might come?"

Alistair nodded. "I would gladly face far greater scandal than an elopement will cause to see her by my side as my wife." He held his friend's gaze in the fading light as the shadows within the carriage lengthened and spread into blackness outside. If anyone knew how deep Alistair's aversion to scandal was, it was Ralston.

Ralston accepted the meaning and determination of his friend's words with a simple nod of his head as the carriage door opened. "Then, I will assist you," he said as he exited in front of his friend.

"And I will return the favour should it become necessary," Alistair assured him.

"I would expect nothing less." Ralston chuckled as he clapped his friend on the shoulder. "The place is looking positively brilliant, Mr. Patrick," Ralston called to the man climbing down a ladder which leaned against one of the lampposts in front of Albany.

"Just keepin' ye safe, Mr. Ralston. Don't need no low lives hiding out around here trying to snatch your pockets clean, nor do we need you stumbling unnecessarily over the path." The gentleman chuckled as he approached Ralston and Alistair. Placing his bucket on the ground, he doffed his cap. "Mr. Pratt, it's a pleasure to see you. What are you boys up to this fine evening? Are you off carousing?"

"Early to bed for us, I am afraid," Ralston replied. "There is a house party in Warwickshire which our mothers expect us to attend."

"Warwickshire," the gentleman said with a whistle. "That's a distance to drive."

"Indeed it is." Alistair's tone of agreement spoke of his dislike for travelling so far.

"Well, I will wish you well — whether that be that you find a wife or avoid such folly I will leave to you to decide." He doffed his hat once more.

"A bit of both," Ralston replied. "I hope to come home and secure a bride in town, but my friend here wishes to return with a bride in tow."

"May she be a blessing to you as my Molly is to me," said Mr. Patrick before moving on.

"Thank you," Alistair called after him. "I very much think she will be."

# Chapter 4

The next day as Alistair was dozing off while reading poetry shortly after they had stopped to change horses, Clifton Conrad was approaching the village of Westerham. His horse was fresh. He had changed mounts at Bromley and was determined to make an appearance in Hunsford. With any luck, he would find out something about what he needed to know.

Last evening, after Alistair had left White's, Conrad and his friends had set to finding out all they could about one Miss de Bourgh. It had required them to spend an extraordinary amount of time at the home of one of his friends instead of playing cards as they had intended. However, it had been well worth the effort, for they had discovered that the young lady was likely of no small fortune, being the only heir to her late father. The estate, it seemed, had not been entailed away from the females in the family, and as such, she was to come into ownership of it either when she came of age or married. In addition to her sizable fortune, she was also well connected, being the niece of Lord Matlock and cousin to Fitzwilliam Darcy, who, though not titled, was among the most respected gentlemen of the ton.

Conrad chuckled. It was amazing what information was held by some of the wags of the ton. A simple — "Pratt mentioned a

Miss de Bourgh, who is friends with his mother, Lady Metcalfe. I cannot say I recall the name de Bourgh." — had been enough to unveil all he needed to know.

According to his friend's mother, Conrad had discovered that Miss de Bourgh was a novice when it came to social matters in town, for she had never had a proper come out. However, his friend's mother was almost completely certain that Miss de Bourgh, who was nearly twenty, would make her debut on the arm of her cousin, Mr. Darcy, next season. After all, theirs was a long-standing arrangement, and since everyone knew that Darcy was not the sort to shirk his duty, Miss de Bourgh would soon be wed. To prove her point, she had pointed out how Darcy had been in town for several seasons and had not once singled out any lady in particular.

Conrad patted the side of his mount's neck. "To think Pratt was going to step between Darcy and duty." He chuckled again. "Pratt! Of all people! I should very much like to see that. He'd not have stood a chance." He chuckled again at the thought of the much smaller Pratt being called out and handily dispatched by the larger and more capable Darcy. "Perhaps that is how I should have allowed him to find his fate," he said as he patted his horse again. "Ah, but Pratt is no fool. He would not set himself up against such odds even if this Miss de Bourgh was Venus herself. Therefore, my four-legged friend, there must be some scheme afoot, and I intend to discover it."

And discover it he did by happy chance as he entered Hunsford.

"Good day," he said, tipping his hat to a pretty young lady in a curricle.

"Good day," she returned with a bright smile.

"I am certain you would not know where the best ale might be found, but could you direct me to where any ale, whether good or not, might be acquired?" An alehouse or tavern were often the best places to ferret out information.

The young lady straightened her posture and lifted her chin. "I happen to know both," she said, her eyes twinkling.

"Indeed?" Conrad replied in surprise. He had not expected any female to admit such a thing. He knew that not all ladies were ignorant of such topics, but most were not willing to admit to such intelligence.

"Oh, I do not speak from personal experience, of course."

The young lady's cheeks flushed a light shade of pink that added a vibrancy to her features that had to this point been lacking. She had been pretty before, but now — he noted with great pleasure — now she was rather beguiling despite her slight frame and angular features. There was life behind her proper exterior.

"Of course," he assured her.

"The knowledge has been shared with me by both a dear friend as well as my mother's parson."

A slow smile spread across Conrad's face. Her mother's parson? There was only one person in Hunsford who would be in the position to bestow a living. That much he knew from the ramblings of his friend's mother last evening. "Do tell," he said, encouraging the lady whom he suspected to be Miss de Bourgh to continue.

"Mr. Collins must indubitably be believed based on his profession, in which, I might add, he takes great pride."

"He is your mother's parson?" Conrad asked. This young lady

was pretty but also a bit of a rambler when she spoke. Hopefully, that would mean she was naïve and would be easily lead.

"Oh, yes," she replied with a laugh. "I often forget that not everyone knows Hunsford as well as I."

"And this Mr. Collins concurs with your friend about the ale at a particular house?" He asked, looking around to his left and then his right. "It is always good to have two opinions that agree," he added.

"Indeed it is, Mr.?" She fell silent and waited for him to introduce himself.

"My apologies, miss. Mr. Clifton Conrad, at your service."

Her lips twitched. "I do believe, Mr. Conrad, that at the moment I am at your service for you have no idea where the best ale can be found."

He chuckled. She was a saucy thing. He could understand why even a dullard such as Alistair Pratt would be charmed by such a lady. "And to whom do I owe my gratitude for such service as directing me to an alehouse?"

She dipped her head very prettily. "Miss Anne de Bourgh, at your service, Mr. Conrad."

"It is a pleasure to meet you, Miss de Bourgh." He had never spoken truer words in his life. He was more than pleased to have stumbled upon his prey so easily. "Now, Miss de Bourgh, if you could direct me to a source of refreshment, I will ever be in your debt."

"The Pig's Snout is just around that corner," she replied pointing in front of her and then to the left.

"And you say that your parson and a friend both recommend this establishment."

She nodded. "Yes, both Mr. Collins and Mr. Pratt declare it to be excellent, and neither gentleman is given to prevarications."

"Mr. Pratt?" Conrad mustered a great show of surprise to hear the name on her lips. "You could not possibly mean Alistair Pratt, could you?"

The lady's face lit with delight, and a pang of jealousy pierced Conrad's heart. He had never had a lady look so overjoyed simply to hear his name. Miss de Bourgh must actually love Pratt. While a small twinge of regret in having to break her heart passed quickly through his mind, a much greater thrill at the complete devastation he would inflict on Pratt overshadowed any momentary falter.

"Do you know him?" Anne asked.

"I do. We are friends." They were acquaintances, and acquaintances were a type of friend, were they not? Therefore, it was not a complete lie — not that Conrad felt any pang of conscience about lying, but should he need to defend his words later, it was good to make certain there was a small amount of room to twist one's self out of trouble.

"How delightful!" Anne cried. "And now we shall be friends. Alistair will be so surprised when he learns of it!"

Alistair? So, Miss de Bourgh and Pratt were so close then. "Indeed, he will be."

"He is not at home just now, however."

Miss de Bourgh's countenance fell. Yes, to separate two such lovers would repay Pratt for separating him from the fortune he had almost secured.

"Quite right. I had heard he was obliged to attend a house party."

Miss de Bourgh nodded slowly. "His mother insisted."

"Yes, that is what he said. I would love to continue our acquaintance, but I do find I am rather parched from my ride." And he had no great desire to discuss Alistair Pratt at the moment.

"And my mother will be expecting me home soon," Anne added.

"Might we meet tomorrow?" He did need to learn more about her if he was to devise an effective plan.

"Here?" Anne asked in surprise.

"I do not know where else," Conrad said with an apologetic shrug. "I am a mere traveller. Is there somewhere better? My only thought in choosing this location above some other is that this is a very public location which will lend it propriety."

Anne bit her lip and glanced back over her shoulder. "There is a small green just behind us. It is a lovely place for a respite. But if you are travelling, will you not be gone tomorrow?"

He shook his head. "I am in the area to see about a filly and will not return to London until the day after tomorrow."

"That is excellent! Then I shall be at the green at two o'clock tomorrow, just before I make my call at the parsonage as is my usual wont."

Conrad tipped his hat. "Until tomorrow Miss de Bourgh."

~*~*~

At a quarter to two the following day, Conrad found a bench under a sprawling ash tree and made himself comfortable to wait. However, his wait was shorter than expected, for Miss de Bourgh arrived a full ten minutes early. He shook his head. Of course, she was the sort to be early. Pratt would not approve of one who was tardy.

"Miss de Bourgh," he greeted as he approached to assist her from her carriage.

She hesitated for a moment before taking his hand.

"You do not distrust me, do you?" It would be a pity if she did.

"No, but meeting in a green without a chaperone is not exactly proper."

He helped her down from her perch. Though the layers of clothing she wore did not conceal the fact that she was a slip of a woman, she was still far lighter than any lady he had ever assisted before. In fact, if a strong wind were to come up suddenly, he was not altogether certain that she would not fly away on it.

"We are in a very open place. There is nothing to conceal us, and I am not the sort to seduce young ladies." In open fields, he added to himself with a silent chuckle. In more secluded areas, seduction was almost certainly guaranteed. But, Miss de Bourgh must not know that now, for at present he needed her to trust him completely.

Anne straightened her skirts and made certain her bonnet was securely attached to her head before she took a seat on the bench where Alistair's friend had been sitting. "Have you known Alistair for long?" she asked.

"For many years. We are members at the same club in town and circulate among the same set for the most parts." He lowered his voice the tiniest amount. "My father holds no title, so I do not know the members of the House of Lords in the same way that Pratt does." The eyes of the lady next to him lit with admiration once again.

"He will be excellent when he must finally take his place in parliament, do you not think? He is always keeping abreast of what is taking place in the world, and his knowledge of most things is extensive."

There was no small amount of pride in Miss de Bourgh's voice, and that fact made Conrad bristle as did the need to agree with her that Pratt was wonderful. But, pain him as it did, the smile she turned on him at his agreement let him know that he had managed to convince her that he too admired Pratt.

"You seem to admire my friend," he added to the end of his agreement. Her head lowered, but not before he saw a telling pink touch her cheeks and a secret smile creep to her lips. "I shall not tell him if you do," he whispered.

"Oh, he knows, but…"

She fell silent, rousing his curiosity. "But what?" he prompted.

She lifted her head and shook it slowly. "I cannot say."

"Very well," he said, leaning back and affecting a disinterested pose. "I hear he is expected to marry soon." Her head swung towards him. Were her eyes wide with interest, surprise, or trepidation? He could not quite tell. "That is why he has gone to this house party, is it not? His mother is hoping to see him settled soon."

Interesting. Her expression had relaxed. He must have hit on something with his mention of marrying soon.

"Just because a mother might wish something, does not mean it will occur, Mr. Conrad. My mother has been insistent since I was in leading strings that I will marry my cousin, but I assure you that I shall not."

"Indeed?" His brows rose. So the lady was refusing to marry Darcy and doing so in a very determined tone.

"Quite so," she said forcefully. "I shall marry whom I please."

Again, his brows rose. It appeared that inside the frail, pretty shell of Miss de Bourgh burned a fiery will. He would have to tread carefully.

"House parties are notorious for bringing about matches, even when a match is not desired," he said, reaching overhead to a low hanging branch and plucking a leaf. "Why, just last year, two friends, who intended to remain bachelors until they were at least thirty, married just three weeks after attending a house party. One of them had hoped to marry a lady he had left back home, but there was another lady at the party with a different plan." He twirled the stem of the leaf between his fingers as he peeked at her to see if his words were working as they ought. To his delight, she looked very uneasy. "An arranged meeting in a location not quite as innocent as where we are sitting, accompanied by a stumble requiring a gentleman to catch a lady can look rather improper if seen by the right people at the right time." He shook his head. "It is a pity that some ladies are so scheming, but there you have it."

He sat forward and propped his elbows on his knees. "I am certain nothing like that would happen to Pratt. He is far too level-headed to fall into a scheme, do you not think?"

Anne's head bobbed up and down uncertainly.

"Now, you must tell me something about you," Conrad said brightly. "I know that your mother's parson is Mr. Collins and that you are friends with Pratt, but I know very little about you beyond that."

"I do not know that there is much to tell. I am the daughter of Lady Catherine de Bourgh, and my home is Rosings Park. That is all there is to know about me."

"Oh, Miss de Bourgh, certainly you are wrong! You must have a favorite book or song, and there must be some activity that you enjoy above all else."

Anne shrugged. "I do enjoy driving, and embroidery is tolerable. However, I cannot choose a book or song because there are so many that I enjoy."

He watched her pull her lip between her teeth.

"I helped Cook bake a cake once. That was delightful. Oh! And I do enjoy playing chess and dancing, although I have never been to a ball."

"What? Never been to a ball?"

Anne shook her head. "No. My mother says my health will not allow it."

"Indeed?"

One of Anne's shoulders lifted and fell. "I do not think it would be too strenuous, but there is no convincing my mother."

"A real old dragon is she?" Conrad asked, causing Anne to laugh. It was a sweet musical sort of laugh, the kind that many in the ton tried to affect as it was the sort to capture a gentleman's attention and make him wish to hear it again.

"I believe a dragon would fear my mother, Mr. Conrad. She is quite simply impossible!"

"Then you must be stronger than a dragon." He smiled as he watched her lashes flutter and her brows draw together as she attempted to figure out why he should say such a thing. "You have said you are not going to marry your cousin despite what your mother wishes. If this is true, you must be far more fierce than any dragon that would cower before your mother. Indeed, I do not see how it could happen if you were not."

Her eyes sparkled, and she laughed that sweet laugh once again. "It is not so difficult, Mr. Conrad. I shall just marry before she can stop me."

# Chapter 5

Anne could not help but feel delighted at the startled expression Mr. Conrad wore at her words. It was perhaps not the wisest thing in the world to share such information on such short acquaintance, but since this man was Alistair's friend, there could be very little risk in trusting him with such information. Besides, she wished to go to Warwickshire, and Mr. Conrad might be just the person to help her get there. She glanced up at the clouds.

"My mother insists that I invite you to dinner if you are still to be in the area this evening." She turned wide questioning eyes to him. "You did say you were to be here until tomorrow, did you not?" His mouth was still hanging open just a bit, and his eyes were still rather large. Anne pursed her lips to keep from smiling in enjoyment of his expression. Surprising people really was entertaining. If only there were people around her on a regular basis that would allow such fun! Her mother would only scold, and Anne was not certain Miss Jenkinson knew how to laugh properly. Her companion's laugh was always creaky, like an old gate that was rarely used. Not at all pleasant.

"To Rosings, for supper?" Mr. Conrad stammered.

"You are not afraid of dragons, are you?" Anne asked with a laugh.

The gentleman next to her sat straighter at the challenge and assured her he was not. She had seen her maid Maggie use flattery and little challenges to get the footmen to do all sorts of things for her. Apparently, the same technique worked on gentlemen as well as footmen.

"I had to tell my mother of our meeting yesterday, you see. There are those in this village who love nothing better than to share tales in a most elaborate fashion. For the same reason, I also told her I was to meet you here on my way to the parsonage, and since she knew that you were a friend of Mr. Pratt, she insisted that I invite you to dinner. Mr. and Mrs. Collins will also be attending, so you have no reason to fear being lonely. It will be an entertaining little group. If Lady Metcalfe were not already gone to town, I am certain she would have joined us. But as it is, she is gone to enjoy the theater and such. Her husband is in the House of Lords, you know."

"Yes, yes, I did know that Lord Metcalfe was in Parliament." He shifted a bit uneasily on the bench.

"Alistair will be there one day, too," Anne added proudly. "You will come to dinner, will you not? You do not have other plans, do you?"

"I – I do not, so," he paused and his brow furrowed as if thinking, "yes, I would be honoured to come to dinner."

"Do you play chess?" Anne asked, excitedly.

"I do."

"Good. then we shall play, and if we are so fortunate, we might have a discussion about how you might help me with a niggling little problem."

Mr. Conrad blinked. "We have only met. How do you know

that I might be able to help you with anything?" His voice was filled with incredulity as she had hoped it would be.

"You are Alistair's friend, are you not?"

He nodded.

"And you do know the counties of England, do you not?"

Again, he nodded.

She stood. "Then you will be perfect." She paused, furrowed her brows, and pursed her lips as if uncertain about something. "Unless, of course, it is not something you are brave enough to do."

His brows flew halfway to his hairline. "Is it dangerous?"

A small smile played on her lips. "Not if we do it correctly. Now, if you would be so kind as to help me back into my curricle, I must be on my way to the parsonage. I do not wish to be late. Mrs. Collins will be waiting."

He was all that was gentlemanly as he helped her to climb up onto her perch. Once seated, she instructed him on how to get to Rosings and at what time he should call as she arranged the reins in her hand.

"Oh, there is one thing of which you must be aware. I will have to be on my best, most proper and reserved behavior this evening. My mother will insist on it." She smiled at the way his brow furrowed. "I did not wish for you to be startled if I am much different from the way I have been in our two meetings. I would not want to cause you any discomfort. You will also perform the part of gentleman admirably, will you not? Oh, listen to me. Of course, you will. You have been nothing but proper since we met. I just worry because of my mother, you see. She is very particular."

Conrad nodded. "That is understandable. It is her home, and I am a guest."

Anne was about to call to her horses to walk on, but just for fun, she thought she would make his eyes grow wide once more before she was away. "No, Mr. Conrad, you do not understand. She is particular about everyone, no matter where she is. If my mother were to visit the Prince Regent, she would likely insist that he sit where she said and do as she instructed."

There. That was the expression for which she had hoped. Now, she might be able to think on it and wear a pleasant expression while she listened to Mr. Collins tell her how wonderful it was that her mother deigned to invite him and his wife to dinner. It was amazing how that man found each and every occurrence of being invited to dinner at Rosings, though it happened once a week, to be worthy of such praise. She waved cheerily to Mr. Conrad as she reached the turn that would take her to the parsonage.

Tonight, if his answers to her mother's inquisition about his relationship with Mr. Pratt, as well as about his family and fortune and future plans, were appropriate, Mr. Conrad would become her escort to a house party in Warwickshire.

~*~*~

"What is your father, Mr. Conrad?" Lady Catherine asked as they sat down to dinner later that evening.

"He has an estate in Somerset," Conrad replied. Miss de Bourgh had not been wrong in warning him about her mother. The lady had a very demanding personality. She had insisted on rearranging the places where people were seated twice before she was satisfied that all were exactly where they should be for the best conversation. He also noted how her daughter was seated in the position farthest from her mother but closest to Mrs. Jenkinson, Miss de Bourgh's stern-looking companion. That woman was keeping an even closer eye on Conrad than Lady Catherine. It was most disturbing to be under such close and constant observation.

"Is it large?" Lady Catherine held up a hand forestalling his answer as she instructed a footman to see to it that the fire was lit properly in the green drawing room and not the blue as previously planned. "The air is rather damp and cool tonight, is it not?" She rested her spoon on her charger and nodded to another footman that she was finished with this course.

"Indeed, it is," Mr. Collins, who sat across from Conrad, unsurprisingly agreed with Lady Catherine.

Conrad had no doubt as to the reason Lady Catherine liked having her parson so close. The man agreed with her every word and praised her for the smallest suggestion, even if it was said in disparagement of something Mr. Collins himself had said or done. Ah, and now he was going to elaborate his agreement. Mr. Collins also had a fondness for hearing his own voice reverberate around the room. Conrad took a drink of his wine and waited for the conversation to come back to Lady Catherine's point. She did not seem the sort to be distracted from discovering the information she sought.

"I told Mrs. Collins," Mr. Collins said as he dabbed at his mouth, "that her warm pelisse would be just the thing tonight. The afternoon was warm, I told her, but the clouds were hanging low, which is a sure sign that the evening would be less than agreeable."

"Quite right," Lady Catherine agreed. "It was very good of you to think of your wife's health. There is nothing like damp to settle in the lungs and cause all sorts of discomforts."

"You are correct as always, my lady."

Conrad fought to keep his eyes from rolling at the clergyman's continued flattery. The man was all puffery.

"The green sitting room is so very cozy. There shall be no fear of anyone taking a chill in there," Mr. Collins added to his agreement. "A very wise choice, my lady. A very wise choice."

Lady Catherine gave him a nod and turned back to Conrad. "Tell me of your father's estate. Is it large?"

"It is not trifling, my lady."

"And his income?"

"Substantial. Five to six a year."

"And it is to be yours?"

"Yes." He had been questioned by many matrons of the ton regarding his future value, but he had to admit that none had been quite so direct in her questioning as Lady Catherine de Bourgh.

"Do you have any sisters or brothers?" she asked as a plate of pheasant and roast vegetables was placed before him.

"One sister. She is two years older than I."

"Is she married?"

"Yes, for several years now. Her husband is also a landowner, and they have two boys and a third child on the way," he answered, supplying the information he figured she would ask next, so that perhaps he would have a moment to chew and swallow a morsel of food between questions.

"That is very good. One should always attempt to have more than one child. Unfortunately, it is not always possible."

"Indeed," agreed Mr. Collins. "The good Lord blesses as He sees fit. Miss de Bourgh is such a fine young lady."

Lady Catherine cast a quick smile of approval in his direction before taking a sip of her wine and continuing her inquisition of her new acquaintance. "You are not yet married?"

"No," Conrad replied.

"My daughter is betrothed," Lady Catherine's look and words held a hint of warning.

Conrad looked down the table to where Miss de Bourgh sat, a forkful of food suspended before her mouth and her eyes wide. He smiled and, turning back to her mother, said, "So she has told me."

Out of the corner of his eye, he could see that Miss de Bourgh had continued eating and was looking pleased with his response. There were definitely secrets that the young lady was keeping from her mother.

"She has been betrothed for many years," Lady Catherine continued. "He is her cousin and of very good standing."

"For years?" Conrad repeated. "Is there something wrong with the gentleman that he has not claimed his bride? Does he have an aversion to the marital state?" He bit the side of his mouth as he saw Miss de Bourgh's fork stop in mid-air once again.

"There is nothing wrong with Darcy. Anne has simply not been ready to marry. She is only nineteen."

"Nineteen is not an uncommon age to marry. In fact, my sister married at eighteen," said Conrad. "I should think that any man who was betrothed to your fair daughter would be tripping over his feet in eagerness to have such a lovely wife." He took a bite of his pheasant and enjoyed watching Lady Catherine's features change from affronted to pleased.

"It is best not to rush into marriage," added Mr. Collins.

"I agree," said Conrad.

"There is much to consider when selecting a bride," Mr. Collins continued. "There is first and foremost her virtue. A wife must be a virtuous woman, circumspect in all things."

"Yes," Lady Catherine interrupted her parson. "There is much to consider, and you made a very wise choice. Mrs. Collins is everything someone of her position should be. And my Anne will be precisely what she is to be — the mistress of Pemberley."

Again, Conrad glanced down the table to Anne and smiled. "I am certain she shall be."

"My daughter tells me that you are friends with Mr. Pratt."

Conrad took his time chewing and swallowing the vegetables he had placed in his mouth just as Lady Catherine had asked her question. "I am," he answered simply.

"Lady Metcalfe is my particular friend."

"Yes, your daughter mentioned that to me. It is such a pleasure to share such a connection, your being Lady Metcalfe's friend and my being the friend of her son. I am sorry that Alistair is not here but in Warwickshire. It would have been much more enjoyable to call on a friend while about my business."

"And what business brings you to Kent?" Mrs. Collins asked.

"I am here to see about a filly. I have seen her and am considering if I shall take her or not. She has good breeding and should make a fine mare. I think I have set my mind on the purchase but did not wish to act with undue haste."

"That is wise," said Mr. Collins. "Thinking. Thinking should be done before any decision is made. I trust you will be happy with your new acquisition."

As he answered, Conrad could not help but allow his eyes to wander down the table once more to where the filly he was considering sat. "I am certain I will be."

# Chapter 6

Anne waited anxiously for the groom to make her phaeton ready. He had been a bit surprised that she requested it so early but not so shocked as to ask a great deal of questions. That was partly due, she supposed, to the fact that each morning for the past week, she had taken her morning drive earlier and earlier. She smiled and smoothed the covering of the basket she carried. Each day, she had taken this basket with her. The grooms thought it contained her breakfast and a book. She had insisted that a picnic first thing in the morning was just the thing. And, in fact, the basket had always contained her breakfast, but it had also contained some portion of the things she would need for travelling. She would not be able to take many things, but then Mr. Conrad had assured her that he would also gather a few things in town to add to her collection. It had not been too challenging to gain his assistance. There was a side of Mr. Conrad that seemed to enjoy an adventure as much as Anne did. He and his friend were very different in that respect. Alistair was more cautious.

"All is ready, miss. May I tie your basket on the back?"

"No," Anne replied with a shake of her head. "I prefer it to be on the floor near my feet. However, a blanket would be nice. I find the air a bit crisp this morning, and the dew is heavy. I should hate to sit on the ground and soil my dress."

The groom scurried off to retrieve a blanket while Anne stashed her basket and climbed into the phaeton unassisted. She had worn two dresses again today and did not wish for a groom to discover such information when helping her into the carriage. She needed all to proceed smoothly without anyone cottoning on to her plan.

"Thank you very much," she said as the groom tucked a blanket in next to her basket. Then, with a wave and a *walk on*, she was on her way. First, she would stop at the tree where she and Alistair always met. Her things were waiting for her there in a small trunk. She giggled to herself at how she had been able to convince Mr. Conrad to leave that trunk for her.

Then, after collecting her trunk, she would continue on to the inn at Bromley, where a proper carriage and Mr. Conrad waited to take her to Warwickshire.

And just as promised, Conrad was eagerly awaiting Miss de Bourgh's arrival at the inn in Bromley, and after a time of refreshment and tea, they began their journey just as a message was being delivered to Mr. Pratt in Warwickshire.

~*~*~

Alistair took the letter from the tray and broke the seal as he walked to the far end of the drawing room where everyone was gathered to hear about today's activities. He hoped that by some stroke of luck this missive would call him away from the planned picnic near the folly. Two young ladies, Miss Hewitt and Miss Northrup, had decided he would be an excellent prize, and no matter how he tried to dissuade them, they would not leave him be. In fact, their attentions had only increased with each attempt at discouragement, and each one seemed willing to do the other harm in order to be the lady who successfully snared him.

Anne's plan of escape was seeming a welcome idea at present. In fact, he would write to her later today with instructions about where to meet him. Perhaps he could slip away a day or so early and be waiting for her away from these scheming debutantes and their chaperones, who, in Alistair's opinion, seemed to be extremely inattentive to the way their charges' appeared to skirt the edge of propriety. House parties were a bane to the happy existence of a bachelor who did not wish to be trapped.

"Who is it from?" Jack asked, coming to peek over Alistair's shoulder.

"Perhaps if you would allow me to read it, I might be able to tell you," Alistair replied as he unfolded the sheet of paper.

*Pratt,*

*I have made a lovely new acquaintance when I travelled to Kent. It is no wonder you have been keeping her a secret from the rest of us. Miss de Bourgh is a pretty thing — and so lively! We have become good friends in a very short time. As you read this, know that I am bringing her to you. We will be alone on the road for two days. I will allow her, of course, to choose who she prefers when we arrive at Stanton's. That is if you still want her in the state in which I plan to deliver her to you. Or perhaps, if I find her to my liking, we shall continue on to Scotland ourselves without stopping in War-wickshire.*

*An eye for an eye, an heiress for an heiress, is that not how it goes?*

C.C.

"That blackguard," Alistair spat as he crushed the letter in his hand.

"Who?" Jack asked.

"Conrad," Alistair said, pressing the wadded up paper against Jack's chest as he turned to leave. "I will be gone within the hour." He would be gone sooner if he could manage it. He had been so certain when leaving White's with Jack that Conrad had not heard Anne's name.

His legs propelled him through the drawing room, up the grand staircase, and all the way to his bedchamber before they began to waver. When had that letter been written? How long had they been on the road? Would they arrive after he had left? So many questions raced through his mind, spinning and chasing after each other as he tossed his bag on the bed and began stuffing his things inside it.

Two questions kept attempting to push their way to the fore, and although Alistair tried not to entertain them for more than a brief moment, they soon drowned out all the others and would not be ignored. He dropped onto the edge of the bed and answered them. He would marry her even if she was ruined as long as she would still have him.

Despite his answer, the question of Anne still having him would not be silenced. She had accepted him, he reasoned. She would still accept him, would she not? Surely Conrad was not so silver-tongued as to have convinced Anne that she could do better than Alistair, was he? She would not believe that Conrad was the better choice, would she? But if Conrad had seduced her, would she feel bound to the scoundrel do to the possible conse-quences of their intimacies?

Alistair closed his eyes and swallowed against the bile that rose in his throat at the thought of Anne in the arms and bed of another. However, swallowing did not have the desired effect. Such revulsion could not be repressed, and Alistair rushed around the bed, grabbing the chamber pot just as the contents of his stomach made a reappearance.

"Come," he called between wretches. One more heave and he was able to sit on the edge of the bed.

"I am going with you," Jack said as he handed his friend a towel to dry his mouth. "You might need a second."

Alistair accepted the glass of water Jack had poured for him, sipping a bit and spitting it into the chamber pot before taking a swallow and hoping to retain it within his quivering innards.

Jack took a place on the bed next to his friend. "I do not know your Anne," he began, "but if you love her, she must be intelligent enough to see through Conrad's lies. Perhaps not at first — I will allow you that worry — but he is not a good liar. You know this. How many times has he lost at the tables in White's because he becomes confident in his ability to win? He has his tells. She'll not fall for him."

Alistair wished with all his heart that what Jack was saying was true, but he could not wholly accept it. "She is so trusting," he whispered. A sad smile tipped the corners of his mouth as he thought about how her eyes would grow large with amazement at the stories he would tell about the soirees he had attended in Lon-don. "She has never had a season. She knows little of the dark and dangerous underbelly of the ton where the vipers and riffraff meet to plot the downfall of innocents."

"From what you have told me, your Anne is not without the ability to scheme herself. She might not see him for what he is at first, but she will see the truth."

"But before he has ruined her?"

"That I cannot promise," Jack said grimly. "However, you can run him through if he has. He is terrible with a sword." Jack had left his seat next to Alistair and was packing Alistair's bags. "I've set my man on getting my things ready and have sent for yours to see to it that the carriage is ready. I figured there was no need for him to come in here and see the mess you were making of his work." He looked up from his work of smoothing a jacket in Alistair's trunk. "Do we head toward London or Scotland? That letter sounded very self-assured."

Alistair nodded his understanding. "And that self-assuredness is his tell that he will become careless," he said thoughtfully.

"Indubitably," Jack replied. "So London?"

Again Alistair nodded. "I do not think him smart enough to send the letter after they had left Kent. Do you have it? We could check the postmark."

Jack grinned. "I already have, and you are correct, as always." He looked at the empty wardrobe and then at Alistair. "Is there anything else, sir?"

Alistair could not help but smile at Jack's words. He was a very fortunate fellow to have such a friend. He rubbed his abdomen. "Perhaps some tea and a biscuit or two."

Jack snapped the lid of Alistair's trunk closed. "It will be awaiting us in the carriage." He waved to the door. "Shall we make our excuses and be gone?"

Alistair straightened his jacket. "Indeed we should."

~*~*~

Anne rubbed her neck. Sleeping with one's head tipped back and to the side made for a very stiff neck.

"Your neck would not hurt if you had allowed me to provide you with a shoulder on which to sleep."

Anne lifted her chin. "It would not be proper."

Conrad's responding chuckle was deep and not altogether friendly. "I do think we left propriety behind when we climbed into this carriage at Bromley. It really would not be so bad a thing if I sat beside you and allowed you to rest your pretty head on my shoulder. Who would know? There is no one here but us, and I can jump back to my respectable seat when we stop. None would be the wiser."

Anne shook her head. "No. I would know."

Conrad moved so that his leg brushed against hers.

"Do not touch me," she said, pulling her leg away. "It is not proper." The gentleman across from her was not as pleasant as the fellow she had met on the green in Hunsford or the one that had dined at Rosings.

"I apologize. I am not fond of being confined to a carriage." He turned and looked out the window. "We will be stopping soon for fresh horses."

Anne studied his face. He seemed rather bored. Travelling was not all that exciting after the first few hours. "Will we be stopping for very long?" she asked. "I admit I have never been in a carriage for this long before." London had been the extent of her previous travels, and they had passed town not long before she had fallen asleep. Rising early was not something of which she planned to make a habit. It was tiring.

"A few minutes or half an hour if you wish to take a turn or two of the courtyard and refresh yourself. A glass of wine and a bit of food might not be unwelcome."

As if it was listening, Anne's stomach rumbled its agreement.

"A light meal it will be," Conrad said with a smile much more like the ones he had worn when she had first met him.

~*~*~

Some cold meat and cheese along with a warm and fluffy roll accompanied by what passed for tea at the establishment at which they stopped seemed to do the trick for both Anne and her companion. Her stomach was pleasantly satisfied, which in turn made her mind happier as well. The same seemed to be true of Mr. Conrad. He had settled into his seat in the carriage without even making an attempt to coerce her to sit beside him. It was the first stop they had made today where he had not endeavoured to see her seated on the bench next to him.

As pleasant as it was to not be put upon in such a fashion, it was also a trifle annoying. It seemed almost as if he had lost interest in her altogether. Anne knew she did not seek his attentions, but to have them withdrawn was — well, it was just disappointing. There was a touch of a thrill that came from denying a gentleman what he wished.

She pulled out her book and opened it to where she had left off reading.

It was probably best not to indulge such delectable feelings as thwarting a gentleman in his pursuit stirred, for they were likely the sign of being a wanton, and Anne was not unprincipled. She knew how a proper young woman was to act. She just found it added a bit of liveliness to an otherwise dull existence when one pushed against the bounds of propriety.

"What are you reading?" Conrad inquired, looking up from the packet of papers through which he was shuffling.

"Folktales," she replied, opening the book to the first page.

"You enjoy fanciful tales, do you?" Conrad placed one envelope on the bench next to him and, placing the other papers back in the packet, propped the bag between himself and the carriage wall.

"Indeed I do. I just finished reading *Histories* by Monsieur Perrault. They were very good."

"You read French?" Conrad asked as he picked up his letter and broke the seal.

"And why should I not? I am the daughter of a baronet and the niece of an earl. My education has been excellent."

"Of course," he muttered.

An irritating smile played at his mouth. Did he not believe her? "I assure you that I can both read and speak French."

He peeked up at her from his letter. "I do not doubt you."

"You do not look as if you believe me."

"My apologies," he said with a bow of his head.

Anne straightened her skirt and then lifted her book. "I read a translation, but I could read the French if I had a copy of it to read."

Conrad chuckled.

"It would be wrong of me to allow you to think I had read the French when I had not. Integrity is of great value, do you not think?"

"It has its place, I suppose."

Anne placed her book on her lap. "You suppose?"

"Yes."

"Honor and uprightness are not things to be picked up and worn for a mere moment. They must be a constant adoration!"

"You may be correct."

That irritating smile was back, and it made Anne bristle. "I am correct," she said, lifting her book and beginning to read the tale of Bonny Jane. This one always made her skin tingle with expectant dread.

"And you think a gentleman or lady must always be either all virtue or all reproach?"

Anne sighed and lowered her book again. "Yes."

"Is that so?" He folded his arms across his chest and smiled at her, his letter discarded on his lap. "And which does that make you? You speak of propriety, yet you would hide your actions and fly to Scotland to marry without approval."

Anne huffed.

"It appears to me that you have indeed laid your integrity aside to achieve a noble goal."

Anne's lips pursed.

"You do not have to admit that I am correct. I can allow you to hold to your belief, no matter how flawed it might be."

"My belief is not flawed," Anne grumbled, returning to her book. The story did not seem nearly so tantalizing now as it had a few moments ago.

"Do you believe Pratt to be all virtue?"

"I do."

"And you think he is true to you at every turn?"

Anne slowly lowered her book. "I do," she said hesitantly.

Conrad lifted one brow in question. "I do not think any man can be completely noble. There are moments of weakness, shall we say. I do not believe we are capable of devotion in the same way that a lady is. It is not in our framework."

"Nonsense!"

"I fear it is not," Conrad replied grimly. "Have you received a letter from Pratt since he has been gone?"

"It is too early for a letter."

"I have a letter," he held up the missive in his hand. "Not from Pratt but from another chap who is also at Stanton's."

"You are gentlemen. Sending letters to one another is not something that is suspect. Alistair could not send me a letter without it causing a stir. Therefore, we must be circumspect in how it arrives as well as with the frequency with which we correspond. The postmaster is not above gossip."

"I will allow you that." He paused, his brows furrowed as if he were considering something. "My friend, Grenville, mentions Pratt."

Anne leaned forward eagerly. "He does? What does he say?"

"I am not certain you wish for me to prove you wrong once again."

Anne leaned back and placed her book to the side. "What do you mean, prove me wrong?"

Conrad smiled sadly at her. "Pratt may not be as true as he appears."

Anne gasped. It had to be a lie.

Conrad lifted the paper he held and read,

*There have been no interesting compromises or instances of near disaster yet, so I do find myself somewhat bored. The ladies will come around eventually, I suppose. However, there is one matter of interest. It seems our friend Pratt might not retain his bachelorhood for much longer. He has shown a preference for Miss Northrup, which has ruffled Miss Hewitt's feathers as she has likewise set her cap at him. He pretends to be brothered —*

"Pardon me," Conrad muttered. "He forms his letters very ill at times."

*He pretends to be bothered by the attention, but he has not attempted to dissuade them.*

"Alistair is polite," Anne refuted both his friend's accusations and her heart's disquiet. Alistair had promised himself to her. All would be well.

Conrad shrugged. "You are correct. Pratt is polite, and perhaps that is all it is. I just hope it does not lead to his downfall."

Anne picked up her book again and attempted to apply herself to the words. However, worry made her reread each line twice over. Finally, with a shake of her head, she closed the book. How could she enjoy reading when it was interrupted by thoughts of other ladies fawning over her betrothed? She fingered the chain that hung around her neck.

Conrad crossed the carriage to sit beside her. "I have upset you," he said apologetically as he slipped his arm around her shoulders in a comforting fashion.

"He is polite," she repeated.

"Yes," Conrad agreed as he tugged her closer to his side. "Pratt is very polite. I am certain that is all it is, and my disquiet is for naught."

"You should be on your side of the carriage, Mr. Conrad."

"May I not comfort a friend in her distress? Do you trust me so little?"

Anne bit her lip. The way he was holding her was soothing. "You may stay as you are for a moment, but only for a moment."

"As you wish, Miss de Bourgh. Just tell me when I should release you, and I will."

Anne nodded and rested her head against his shoulder as he reached around her to where her book lay on the bench. With a gasp, she pulled away from him a little.

"Pardon me. I was not kissing you. I was merely retrieving your book, so that I might read it to you."

It was possible, she supposed, that his lips had brushed her forehead by accident. Anne studied his face for a moment. He seemed sincere, and so she returned her head to his shoulder. As she sought a comfortable place to rest her head, he cleared his throat and began reading.

> *Loud roars the north round Bothwell's hall,*
>
> *And fast descends the pattering rain:*
>
> *But streams of tears still faster fall*
>
> *From thy blue eyes, oh! bonny Jane!*[1]

---

1. *Bothwell's Bonny Jane by M.G. Lewis*

# Chapter 7

Conrad tucked Anne's hand in the crook of his elbow as he led her from the carriage to the inn where they would stop for the night. "Are you hungry?"

Anne giggled. "My stomach has been rumbling loudly enough that I am certain you know the answer to your question."

"I would not be so indelicate as to mention such noises," Conrad teased. As much as he knew this was a mission of revenge, he was finding it hard to remain completely untouched by Miss de Bourgh. There was something about the mixture of her delicate frame and strong determination that was a trifle beguiling. "We shall have to play the part of a married couple," he whispered near her ear. "To protect your reputation," he added in reply to her questioning look. "Now, do you wish to eat first or get settled into your room?"

Anne ran her free hand over the wrinkles of her skirt.

"Your room it shall be," Conrad said with a smile. "You will enjoy your dinner much more after being able to wash away the dust of travel."

"Thank you," Anne said as they stepped into the inn.

"Wait here," Conrad said, leading her to a table and pulling out the chair for her to be seated. "I shall see to our accommodations."

It would be much easier to arrange things as he wished without her there to scold him and make a muddle of his plans.

Anne took in her surroundings. There certainly were a lot of people. Nearly every table was filled with people hurriedly eating. The din of the room was more than she had ever experienced before, but it was not unpleasant. This was life. This was what lay beyond the walls of Rosings and the roads of Hunsford. Here, there were masses of people from various walks of life. Some sat nobly as if presiding over the others who scurried and hurried. There were men in fine coats and children in dusty jackets and ragged hats. A cat wrapped itself around one of her legs, and she leaned down to scratch its ear.

She jumped as a horn sounded, and the throng of people in the coffee room surged to its feet and pressed toward the door.

"Stay close," a mother called to her son. "Put the biscuit in your pocket, Rose," she instructed her daughter. "We must go."

"Yes, Mama," said a little girl with golden curls as she slipped her hand into her brother's and followed behind her mother. Anne watched them until they were lost in the group of people clamouring around the stagecoach.

It was not long until the clamour subsided and the room in which Anne sat slipped into a near peaceful existence. There were still a few who remained, but they dotted the room. Two maids worked quickly clearing away cups and plates, while a hostler entered and, after having a few words with one of the maids, made his way toward the door at the far end of the room.

"I have our key." Conrad looked around the room. "There is a private dining room in the back. We will eat there."

Anne nodded and stood. She would have gladly eaten in the

hustle and bustle of this room, but she supposed a private dining room would be more pleasant. She followed Conrad up the stairs and down a hall to a door that stood open. A servant was just exiting as they arrived.

"Everything is here?" Conrad said as he handed the man a coin.

"Yes, sir," the servant replied.

Conrad gave the man a nod of dismissal. "Our chamber, my lady," he said to Anne with a sweeping motion toward the door.

Anne's feet would not move. "Our room?" she squeaked.

He nudged her toward the door. "Yes, our room. The inn is full, and not all the patrons are of the trustworthy nature. There were not two rooms together, and I will be dashed to bits on the cliffs and cast into the sea if I am going to leave Pratt's betrothed unprotected."

Anne entered the room slowly and took in the furnishings. "There is only one bed," she said.

"Yes, but it is large enough for two to sleep in it quite comfortably."

"We are not sharing a bed!"

He tossed his hat on the table near the door and began shrugging out of his coat. "I shall sleep on my side, and you shall sleep on yours. There is no one here to say a word about our sleeping arrangements. All will be well."

Anne folded her arms and glared at him as he began to untie his cravat.

"I do not wish to get it wet when I wash my face." He flicked the piece of cloth over the back of the chair on which he had hung his jacket and began to unbutton his shirt. He chuckled as she gasped and turned away from him. "There is a screen in the corner. If you wish to refresh yourself behind it, I will bring the water over to you."

Anne hurried to hide herself behind the screen.

"It is not improper to remove your hat," he called after her in a teasing fashion.

Anne's fingers fumbled with the ribbons to her bonnet. She had not expected to be in a room with a gentleman. This was an incredibly vexing development. She peeked out from behind the screen at the bed. Good heavens! He had removed his shirt. She screwed her eyes shut and pulled her head back around the screen. Perhaps there was a way for her to remain here, all night. She blew out a breath and placed a hand on her rapidly beating heart. This was not good. Not good at all.

"Your water, my lady."

Anne gasped and closed her eyes once again. "Go away," she said, waving her hand at him. "You are not dressed."

Chuckling, Conrad placed the water on the floor at the edge of the screen and moved away. "I will keep my nakedness on the far side of the room."

"And under a shirt," she chided.

Conrad continued to chuckle as he pulled his shirt back over his head. Miss de Bourgh had to be the most innocent lady he had ever met. Many would blush and be horrified as she had been when seeing him without his shirt, but not many would clamp their eyes shut so securely. Most would only feign closing their eyes and would peek under their lashes. A seduction might not be possible. He tipped his chin up as he tied his cravat. The hint of a possible assignation would likely be enough to anger Pratt, but it would not make tonight so pleasurable as he had hoped.

"I am fully clothed," he called to her as he stretched out on the bed to wait. Her wine glass had not been refilled at any point during their meal at Rosings. Perhaps a bit more wine than normal would make his advances more acceptable. He blew out a breath. With or without wine he would have to proceed cautiously with this skittish filly.

"Why are you lying on the bed?"

A smile spread across his face at her accusatory tone. "My body is tired. Care to join me?"

"I most certainly do not!"

She was replacing her bonnet.

"You do not need to wear that to dinner," he said, pushing up on his elbows.

Her lips pursed and her brows drew together, and he expected her to ignore him. However, to his delight, she did not. She removed her bonnet. He sat up and swung his legs off the bed. "You will be happy to know that this inn has very soft beds." He crossed to the door. The way her cheeks grew rosy at the mention of that piece of furniture was entertaining.

Opening the door, he extended his arm to her. "May I escort you to dinner?" His arm hung in the air for nearly a full minute before she stepped forward and took it. "You have nothing to fear," he assured her. "I will keep you as safe as Pratt would keep my betrothed if I had a betrothed and I needed him to do so."

That seemed to be the words he needed to say, for her hand rested more firmly on his arm as they proceeded down the steps to the dining room.

Conrad congratulated himself on the success of their dinner. Miss de Bourgh had remained relaxed, and he had been able to keep both the conversation as well as the wine flowing. By the time they were returning to their room, Miss de Bourgh was giggling at the smallest things and needed help to navigate the stairs. Her cheeks wore a rosy hue, her eyes sparkled with playfulness, and Conrad doubted there would be any difficulty in getting her to climb into bed next to him.

He was correct.

Anne's head felt light and her eyes tired. The pillows and blankets of the bed called out to her. Her body craved rest.

"What has you looking so sour?"

"I had not considered how I was to dress or undress without my maid." She rubbed her head. "I cannot think how I am going to prepare for bed."

"Turn around," Conrad instructed, taking her by the shoulders and turning her. "I can manage a few fastenings."

"It is not proper," she slurred.

"I will not tell," he whispered next to her ear, allowing his lips to nearly touch her. She flinched but did not scold him. He saw her eyes flutter before he pulled back to continue his work of helping her undress. Completing the task he had begun, he kissed her gently on the nape of her neck.

She gasped but again did not scold. Slowly, she stepped behind her screen. "My trunk, please," she called.

Conrad obliged and carried the small trunk behind the screen.

"Put it down right there."

Conrad pulled his eyes away from her. The wine had most certainly had a desirable effect on her, for she stood before him in only her chemise, stays, and petticoat.

"I need help with this," she turned her back to him. "I should have worn the other one," she muttered as he began to untie her. "The other one ties in the front," she said over her shoulder to him. "This is not at all proper," she added.

"No," he leaned toward her ear, "but I'll not tell," he whispered. This time, he allowed his lips to brush her ear lightly.

Anne gasped. "You must stop doing that," she scolded.

"Whispering?"

"No, kissing me," she said, turning towards him. She was not very sure on her feet, however, and the quick movement added to the dizziness she already felt propelled her into his arms.

"One kiss of thanks for my assistance," he asked, looking down at her nearly exposed bosom.

Her lips parted, and her eyes grew wide. "I am sorry," she said, trying to escape his embrace.

"One kiss?" he asked again. Then, before she could answer him in either the affirmative or the negative, he pressed his lips against hers.

"Now that was not so bad, was it?" he asked with a smile as he released her. Her right hand covered her mouth, and she said nothing in reply which was just as he had hoped. He took one more sweeping look at her and left her to finish preparing for bed. With any luck, that kiss would not be his last tonight.

Anne's hands trembled as she finished removing her stays and then her petticoat. She searched through her trunk. There was a comfortable day dress in there if her foggy brain was remembering correctly. That, rather than a nightrail, would be best for sleeping so close to a man that seemed very good at unfastening dresses and stays and whose lips were so very soft.

Conrad sighed and laced his fingers behind his head as he lay in bed waiting for the nearly fully clothed lady next to him, on the other side of a blanket dividing wall she had created, to fall asleep. The kiss had perhaps been too much. He should have waited until she was nearly sleeping to attempt anything.

Now, he would only be able to arrange the covers and himself in such a fashion that when she awakened, she might believe that more had happened than was true. Her displeasure would likely be as intense as her headache in the morning, but for now, as her breathing became deep and even, he would enjoy drawing her to his side and running his hands over her slight but womanly form. If Pratt refused her, he would not be opposed to taking her for a wife. She was an heiress after all.

# Chapter 8

Anne pushed Mr. Conrad's arm off of her and sat up as the door to their room opened. Why was he once again not wearing a shirt? She scooted away from him and clutched the blanket to her chest.

"Uncle!" she cried as Lord Matlock, followed by her cousin Edward Fitzwilliam entered the room. Anne slipped out of bed and straightened her dress as best she could.

"Anne de Bourgh," her uncle rumbled.

Anne clutched her head. "Not so loud," she begged. Her stomach roiled, and she sought the chamber pot.

"Out of bed," Lord Matlock ordered as he flicked the covers off of Conrad.

Conrad scrambled to get up.

Edward tossed him his shirt.

"Who are you?" Lord Matlock demanded.

"Conrad," Edward supplied. "Clifton Conrad."

"Fitzwilliam," Conrad acknowledged the younger man with a nod of his head. "Lord Matlock." He bowed.

"You," Lord Matlock barked at Anne, "put on your shoes and come with me."

"My hair..."

"Is fine," her uncle growled.

Anne huffed and crossed her arms.

"Bring what you need if you must," he added.

"You," he said, turning to Conrad, "dress and meet us in the dining room. Edward, see that he gets there in a timely fashion." He turned back to Anne, who was just slipping her feet into her slippers. "Come along."

Anne grabbed a small mirror and brush as well as a few ribbons from her trunk and scurried after her uncle. "It is not what it seems," she said as they descended the stairs.

"No one is to disturb us," Lord Matlock said to the innkeeper, who nodded readily.

"It seems," said Lord Matlock, as he closed the door behind him, "that you are on your way to Scotland and could not wait until after you said your vows before the blacksmith."

Anne's eyes grew wide, and she pulled herself up to her full height. "I am on my way to Warwickshire." She lifted her chin and glared at her uncle.

"You were in bed with a half-dressed gentleman — if he deserves to be called that," Lord Matlock fumed.

"I was fully clothed," Anne countered.

Her uncle shook his head. "Your stays were draped over your trunk."

Anne blushed. What else did one do when your uncle spoke about your undergarments? However, despite her mortification, she raised her brows and challenged him with a glare she hoped was equal to one of her mother's. "Have you ever slept in stays? They are most uncomfortable."

Her uncle's lips twitched but only briefly. "No, I have never slept in stays. However, I know that they are not easily removed by one's self."

Anne walked over to a chair and blew out a breath as she rubbed her head. "I may have had help," she said as she sat down, "I vaguely remember help. I think I was foxed."

Her uncle blinked and then looked at her closely. "You were drinking?"

She nodded. "I had wine with my supper." She closed her eyes and rubbed her head again. "Could you please lecture me less loudly, and would it be too much to ask for the window to be opened?"

Lord Matlock crossed the room and opened a window near her. "Move your chair closer to the air," he instructed before going to the door and asking for some tea and toast to be brought. Then, he drew a chair near her. "Now, tell me your tale. I will not lecture in anything louder than a whisper until that blackguard appears. Then, I will have to roar. It is required," he added with a small smile. "Where is Pratt?" he asked softly.

Her lips trembled. "In Warwickshire. I was on my way to meet him," she whispered. "You know about Alistair?"

Her uncle nodded. "You mentioned him to Miss Elizabeth, and Darcy knew that Pratt was at Stanton's. I was on my way to Warwickshire when I happened upon this establishment and asked if they had seen you and Pratt. I expected to find you with him, not what's his name."

"Mr. Conrad," Anne supplied. "He is Alistair's friend and was helping me find Warwickshire." She sighed as tea and toast were placed before her. "It was foolish."

Her uncle nodded in agreement. "Darcy is marrying Miss Elizabeth. You would have been free to marry another."

She nodded. "I know, but I want to marry Alistair, and he is at a party with ladies who are trying to take him away from me."

"Why would you think that?" her uncle said in surprise.

"Mother has always told me how horrid house parties are, and then, Mr. Conrad told me how someone he knew ended up married to a lady he did not wish to marry after attending a party last year. And then, he had a letter from his friend that said Alistair was being pursued by two ladies." She lifted a shoulder and lowered it in a sad shrug. "I may already be too late."

"My dear niece," her uncle's voice was soft and understanding, "things are never as bad as your mother says. She has always had a flare for the dramatic. And as far as Mr. Conrad's tale about his unhappily married friend is concerned, well, his story might be true, but that is one gentleman out of hundreds. It does not happen to us all. Even I could have avoided being forced to marry my wife if I had wished to do so." He winked at her. "Truth be told, I did not wish to avoid marrying her. I had every intention of making her my bride. However, your grandmother did not like Genevieve all that much, so I had to be subversive to secure my love." He placed a hand on his niece's knee. "Much like you felt you had to scheme to avoid your mother's plans."

Anne gave him a sad smile.

"We shall sort out this Mr. Pratt," he added. "Ladies may pursue, but that does not mean they will be successful. However," he said, becoming more businesslike and serious, "you were found in bed with another gentleman. It matters not that you were fully clothed and only sleeping?" He raised a questioning brow.

Anne's face flushed bright red as she nodded as vigorously as her sore head would allow.

"Your reputation is likely ruined. I doubt we can keep this completely quiet." He leaned back in his chair. "If your Mr. Pratt will have you, then all will be well. However, if he refuses, then you will have to choose to either marry this Mr. Conrad or retire to Rosings with your mother."

Anne's eyes filled with tears. "Do you think he will refuse me?"

"You love him so much?"

Anne nodded as the tears that had gathered began to spill down her cheeks.

"And does he love you?"

"He said he did."

"Then I dare say he will not desert you. A man will overlook many things when he is in love." He took her cup from her and placed it on the table, then, he drew her up and into his embrace. "I cannot say all will be well because I do not know that it will be, but I can promise you I will do all that is in my power to make it so." He released her and fished his handkerchief out of his pocket to dry her tears.

The door opened behind them, and Edward shoved Conrad into the room.

"I'll try not to growl too loudly," Lord Matlock said to Anne before turning to Conrad and ordering him to be seated on the other side of the room.

"My niece assures me nothing of a permanent nature occurred last night," he began. "However, her mind seems to be somewhat foggy, so I would like to hear confirmation from your mouth."

"She is correct," Conrad answered quickly.

Lord Matlock took a chair from next to the table and turning it around, straddled it as he sat facing Conrad. "How much wine did you allow her to drink?" His voice was low and dangerous.

Conrad shook his head and shrugged. "A few glasses," he replied.

"And what was your intent in getting her drunk?"

Conrad swallowed. "I did not intend to get her drunk."

"Come now," Lord Matlock cajoled. "Do you believe him, Edward?"

"No, I do not."

"And what do you think his intent was?" Lord Matlock asked his son.

"To lower her inhibitions and make her more pliable."

"That is my hypothesis as well." He glanced at Conrad. "What do you say we do with him?"

"He shall have to marry Anne," Edward replied just as the door to the room flew open.

"The devil he will!" It took very few steps for Alistair to cross the room. The small moment of relief he had felt on learning that Conrad was indeed at this inn had vanished with Edward Fitzwilliam's words. In its place surged nearly overwhelming anger. "You steaming pile of refuse." He yanked Conrad out of his chair. "I ought to run you through, you piece of filth." He pressed him against the wall. "What did you do to her?"

"Nothing," Conrad said with a small smirk.

Alistair leaned closer and lowered his voice while he placed his forearm across Conrad's neck. "I swear, Conrad, if you laid so much as one finger on her, I will call you out no matter what the laws say."

"Anne," Alistair called.

"Yes," she replied from beside him, causing him to start.

"Did he harm you?"

"No."

"Did he touch you in any way that was not proper?"

"Will you still have me if he did?"

Alistair growled and pressed his arm against Conrad's throat more firmly.

"Will you?" Anne asked.

"Yes, no matter how he has touched you."

"He kissed me," she said. "When he was helping me out of my stays."

"When he was what?" Alistair nearly shouted, turning to look at her.

"I could not untie them myself," Anne explained.

"Is that all?"

Anne grimaced as Conrad made a gasping sound as if breathing was becoming difficult.

"His arm was across me when I woke."

"You shared a bed?"

Anne nodded. "To sleep. Only to sleep. I swear it, Alistair."

Alistair pressed down once more on Conrad's neck as he leaned close. "Angelo's. I will meet you at Angelo's in two day's time."

"Before we go to Scotland?" Anne asked in a whisper.

"We are not going to Scotland," Alistair said as he released Conrad. "I will marry you properly, no matter how long it takes to convince your mother and mine to allow it." He shook his head. "Of all the feather-brained things to do, Anne. Why would you run off with him?" He waved his hand at Conrad.

Anne lifted her chin indignantly. "He is your friend and knew where Warwickshire was."

Ralston, who had been standing at the ready in case Alistair needed his assistance, snorted. "Conrad is no friend of Al's."

Anne's head swung towards Ralston.

"Jack Ralston," he said by way of introduction. "Alistair's actual friend."

Anne folded her arms across her chest. "Who are Miss Northrup and Miss Hewitt?"

Ralston smiled. "A couple of ladies who will be excessively jealous of you. Those two would not leave Al alone no matter how much he tried to dissuade them."

"You attempted to dissuade them?" Anne asked Alistair, who nodded. "But Mr. Conrad's friend Mr. Grenville said you did not."

"Grenville?" Ralston repeated with a laugh. "Grenville was not at Stanton's."

Anne's brows furrowed. "He was not?" she asked Alistair.

"No."

Anne lifted her hands in exasperation. "Then how did Mr. Conrad get a letter from him that told about Miss Hewitt and Miss Northrup?" Her eyes grew wide, and she gasped as the truth dawned on her.

"You lied," she said to Conrad. "Did your friend send you that letter?" she asked as she advanced on him.

"No," he said backing away. "I wrote that letter to make you distrust Pratt. He ruined my chances last year," he spat. "He deserved to have his own ruined."

Anne took a step closer to him. The sound of her hand connecting with his cheek echoed through the room. "You lied to me, and you lied about Alistair. Why, I ought to run you through!"

"Anne," Alistair cautioned.

Anne leaned forward, mere inches from where Conrad rubbed his smarting cheek. "Angelo's. I will see you at Angelo's."

"Anne," Alistair cautioned again.

"What?" she asked with wide eyes.

"You cannot meet him at Angelo's."

Anne looked passed him to her cousin. "Edward, did you or did you not mention that Angelo's allows ladies to join?"

Edward swallowed and looked apologetically at his father and Alistair. "I did, but it is not a good idea."

"Then I shall call him out to that," she waved her hand, "field about which you told me."

"Duels are against the law," Edward replied.

Anne lifted her chin. "Then, it would be best if you allowed me to meet him at Angelo's, would it not?"

Lord Matlock chuckled. "You are every inch as determined as your mother with all the wit of your father." He rose and clapped Alistair on the shoulder. "A force with which to be reckoned and one that could bring mighty change if directed properly. Are you certain you are up for such a challenge?"

Alistair smiled. "I am."

"Well, then, let's get you all back to London where I will help you obtain a license as quickly as possible," said Lord Matlock. "And I will make certain you are allowed in Angelo's, at least once," he added. "If you need some instruction, Edward, Richard, or Darcy would be happy to assist you."

"She needs no instruction," Alistair said with a grin. "Just please allow me to have first go at him? I should hate to be denied my chance to avenge my love's honour if she has already dispatched the scoundrel."

"You fence?" her uncle asked.

"Alistair taught me," Anne said proudly. "We got bored with chess," she added as an explanation, "and there is only so much one can talk about when she meets her beau in the grove." She pressed her lips closed in response to Alistair's clearing his throat.

"Is that so?" Lord Matlock asked with a chuckle. "And Pratt is a good teacher?"

Anne nodded but said nothing.

"Al is hard to beat when it comes to sword play," said Ralston proudly. "When I win, it is never done easily."

"Then I suggest you never spar with Anne," Alistair said. "You remember the bruise on my arm last summer?"

Ralston's eyes grew wide.

Alistair nodded. "Anne learns quickly. I find it challenging to beat her."

Anne's face was once again flushed, but this time it was not from embarrassment or anger. This time it was from the pleasure one feels when the gentleman she loves praises her for her abilities, even if they are not proper accomplishments.

"You will have to tell me how you do it," Ralston said to Anne. "He has no tell."

Anne smiled. "Yes, he does."

"I do?" Alistair asked in surprise. "Our fencing master scolded me incessantly for not following patterns."

Anne wrapped her arms around Alistair's and laid her throbbing head on his shoulder. "It is not found in a pattern," she said. "It is –"

"Do not tell him," Alistair interrupted. "Fencing is one of the few sports at which I can outdo Jack." He patted her hand. "But you can tell me later so that I might overcome such a weakness as having a tell."

"Only if you still allow me to win occasionally," she said as she smiled up at him, her eyes capturing his perfect sapphire blue eyes. Those eyes that told her everything: the ones that lay his heart before her, that shone with pride when she won a game of chess, that flashed with passion when he debated a point in a discussion, and that flicked in the direction in which he was going to move immediately before he would lunge forward in a thrust.

# Chapter 9

Anne snuggled into the corner of the carriage, a blanket wrapped around her and another folded to use as a pillow as she leaned against the wall of the vehicle. Her head throbbed, her stomach was only slightly settled from the toast and tea, and it felt as if someone were wiggling a feather inside her throat. Therefore, although she longed to sit and talk with Alistair and his interesting friend, sleep would be a welcome way to spend the trip to London. She would likely need to feel more lively and less like a wrung out old rag when facing her mother. She shook her head. If only there were some way to avoid her mother.

"Are you comfortable?" Alistair asked.

Anne smiled at him. "As comfortable as one can be sleeping in a carriage."

"You could put your feet up. I am certain Al would not be opposed to allowing them to rest on his legs," Ralston suggested from the other side of the carriage.

Anne raised a disapproving brow. "It would not be proper. I promise you, Mr. Ralston, that I do know how to behave appropriately." Her lips twitched as she lifted her feet and placed them on Alistair's legs. "However, I do not always choose to do as I should."

Ralston chuckled. "So it would seem, and please call me Jack. We shall nearly be related, after all. Alistair and I are as close as brothers."

"You do not mind?" Anne questioned Alistair as he placed a hand on her lower leg.

He shook his head. "Not at all."

Anne turned back to Jack. "If I had a sister, you could marry her and then you would be brothers." She straightened her blankets and gave a little cough.

"Are you well?" There was concern in Alistair's voice.

"I am just in need of some rest," Anne assured him as she settled back and closed her eyes. It was lovely to be travelling with Alistair. Sitting in a carriage with Mr. Conrad had not been so pleasant and relaxing as it was with Alistair and his friend. It was too bad she did not have a sister. Jack seemed to be a fine fellow to whom she would not be opposed to being related. Her eyes popped open. "I have a cousin."

"I beg your pardon?" Jack looked up from the paper he had acquired at the inn.

"Georgiana Darcy," Anne clarified. "She is nearly old enough to court. You could marry her, and then, you and Alistair could be cousins. It might not be as good as being brothers, but it would be something."

"That," said Jack with a pleased smile, "is a very good idea. I think I shall take you up on it."

Alistair shook his head and rolled his eyes at his friend as Anne, seemingly satisfied and rather pleased with herself from the look on her face, closed her eyes once again. He had not considered what might happen once Anne and Jack met. Anne was full of ideas and desire to see them completed, and Jack was full of energy and all too eager to take on a task — any task that might prove profitable and diverting. Alistair ran his hand up and down Anne's leg from knee to ankle and back. He suspected that from henceforth his life would be anything but dull.

Anne slept for the entirety of the journey to town. She stirred slightly when they had stopped for the horses but had not woken. She had coughed three times, however, causing Alistair to become concerned that there was an issue brewing that would require more than a few hours of sleep in a carriage to cure. Anne's constitution was not so robust as some, and when she became ill, it always started with a cough that would often settle for some time in her lungs.

"How do you feel?" he asked as the carriage slowed and Anne stretched and yawn while waking.

"I –" she squeaked, her hand flying to her throat. "My throat is sore." It took a great deal of effort to force the whispered words out of her mouth. "My voice –"

"Shhh," Alistair said. "Does anything else hurt?"

Anne shook her head.

"No aching muscles? No headache?"

Again, she shook her head.

"Lean toward me," he instructed. He placed his lips lightly on her forehead. "You are warmer than you should be. Have you been out in the damp air?"

Anne bit her lip and nodded. "Mornings," she whispered.

He sighed and shook his head. "Part of your plan, no doubt."

She nodded.

"You know that damp air is not good for you, Anne," Alistair scolded gently.

Ralston chuckled. "If I did not know better, I would think the two of you were already an old married couple."

"Keep the blanket wrapped around you," Alistair instructed, ignoring his friend's comment. "There is no use having you get chilled again," he added as the carriage door opened.

Anne did keep the blanket wrapped around her shoulders as best she could while descending from the carriage. However, as her feet touched the ground, Alistair pulled the blanket more snugly around her and then scooped her into his arms.

"I can walk," she whispered.

"And I have wanted you in my arms since I saw you at the inn," he whispered back before placing a chaste kiss on her forehead. "Do not protest, and allow me to keep you here for a little while."

She smiled and nestled her head into his shoulder.

"Is Anne ill?" Lord Matlock, whose carriage had arrived just before Alistair's, approached them.

"She has been coughing, her throat hurts, she has little voice, and she feels as if she may be developing a fever," Alistair replied.

"Do you require assistance?"

"No, my lord, I can manage."

Lord Matlock smiled slyly. "It is so much more pleasant to provide a heroic service to your lady than to call for a footman to see to it, is it not?"

"Indeed," Alistair agreed. He had met Lord Matlock several times over the years, but he had never before seen this almost rakish side of the man. An image of Lord Matlock and Alistair's father standing at the edges of a ballroom assessing the ladies came to mind. Alistair's father had declared many times that they had been an odd pair of friends — one of a more serious nature while the other was more devil-may-care — but until this moment, Alistair had never seen how that could be possible. Lord Matlock had always been gregarious, but he had also always been as proper as Alistair's father.

"Now, Mr. Pratt, I am going to allow you to carry her to her bedroom and might even allow a moment or two for you to take your leave in private. However, I do not think I can save you from the questions of my sister," Lord Matlock cautioned.

"I can speak to Mother," Anne whispered.

"You can barely speak and need to be in bed," Alistair replied. "I will speak to your mother," he sighed and added, "and mine," as he saw the third coach that stood in front of Matlock House. There were two other carriages as well, but he was uncertain as to whom they belonged since all he could manage was a quick glance at them as he followed behind Lord Matlock.

~*~*~

"You are very good to her," Lord Matlock said as Alistair stepped out of Anne's room.

"Thank you, my lord," Alistair replied to the man who was waiting for him in the hallway.

It was better, Lord Matlock had said, for them to meet with Lady Catherine in the sitting room and for Anne to get settled before her mother accosted her with questions. Therefore, Anne's uncle had insisted on standing guard in the hall while Alistair settled Anne into a chair in her room where she was to wait for her maid to come get her ready for bed.

"Anne said you had told her that you love her," Lord Matlock said as they walked side by side toward the grand staircase.

"I do, sir."

"I can tell, and I am happy for it." Lord Matlock stopped three steps into his descent and turned to Alistair. "Do not misunderstand me. I know her mother loves her, but my sister is not good at showing her love as most mothers might. She attempts to coddle and cosset, but I fear it appears more like orders and directives — and insufferable restrictions."

Alistair nodded. "I know, my lord. I have spent a great deal of time at Rosings with my mother and Lady Catherine. I know her strictures are not meant to smother even if those are the results."

Lord Matlock clapped Alistair on the shoulder and shook his head as a smile spread across his face, crinkling the corners of his eyes and causing them to sparkle with delight. "I had it figured that we might find a gentleman to love and care for Anne once Darcy finally declared his intentions not to marry her, but I feared we would never find a gentleman who could both love Anne and tolerate, let alone understand, her mother. There are many in this family who do not understand Catherine as you have just explained her." He chuckled. "It should not surprise me, I suppose. You are your father's son, and he has always been able to tolerate Catherine's friendship with your mother."

"It was he who first explained to me how such overprotection was a sign of great care," Alistair said as they resumed their descent.

Lord Matlock chuckled again. "And then, I imagine, he went on to tell you that while it demonstrated affection, it was also a weakness."

Alistair nodded. "Which in turn became a lesson on carefully guarding your strengths so that they do not become weaknesses when left to run rampant."

"That does sound like your father. He is a good man and a good friend. From what I have seen of you, you are the same. I am happy to give my blessing to you and Anne and will welcome you to our clan with open arms."

"Thank you, my lord."

"You could dispense with the my lord and call me Uncle as all my nieces and nephews do," Lord Matlock suggested as they reached the landing.

"Thank you, my lord," Alistair replied with a smile. "Perhaps after Anne and I are married. Change is not always easy for me to accept."

Lord Matlock clapped him on the shoulder once again. "Very like your father," he declared. "Now, are you ready to enter the din?"

The sound of voices wafted from the drawing room door and down the hall to where they stood.

"No, my lord, I am not certain I am, but it must be done."

"Ah, honesty. It is not always so easily found." Lord Matlock chuckled. "To be truthful, I would rather avoid this as well, but as you said, it must be done. Tomorrow, I shall see to a license, although I do suppose a wedding will need to be put off until Anne is well."

She would get well and soon. A physician would give Anne a few tinctures and with rest and time, she would recover. Or so Alistair told himself to calm one set of fears as he followed Lord Matlock into the drawing room to face another.

The room was full and filled with laughter and talking, or at least, it was until he stepped inside the doors and the din faded to silence. Darcy, his friend Bingley, Miss Elizabeth, a pretty young woman who bore a resemblance to Miss Elizabeth, Miss Darcy, Colonel Fitzwilliam, Lady Margaret, Lady Matlock, his mother and his father, as well as Jack, all stopped talking and turned to look at him. Alistair, in turn, looked at Lord Matlock, hoping that the gentleman would begin this discussion.

With a wink and an understanding smile, Lord Matlock did just that. "Anne is being tucked into bed, and I have sent a man to get Mr. Bishop. She is only a little ill, Catherine," he said as Lady Catherine began to rise from her chair. "It is only a small cough and sore throat accompanied by what might be a fever."

"There is never a trifling illness where Anne is concerned," Lady Catherine retorted.

"There is nothing you can do that is not already being done for her. Sit down."

Alistair's eyes grew wide at the sharp tone Lord Matlock used. However, it was impressive how quickly Lady Catherine capitulated to his direction.

"You will only make it difficult for her to rest if you go up there," Lord Matlock added more gently. "She cannot talk to you. Her voice is weak. It would only weaken further if she were to speak to you, and you know she would. That is why it is for her best that you remain right here."

Lady Catherine's chin raised as did her brows. "In light of such information, I would agree."

"Besides, I believe Mr. Pratt has something he wishes to say."

*Wishes* was not precisely the word that Alistair would have used. If he had a wish, it was for a chair in which to sit since his legs felt a bit wobbly. However, since Lord Matlock still stood next to him, Alistair remained standing and drew a breath, hoping the action would stop his heart from trying to beat its way out of his chest. "Miss de Bourgh and I wish to marry." There, that should cut to the chase and help this ordeal to be concluded most expeditiously.

"You and Anne?" Lady Metcalfe asked in surprise.

"Yes," he replied.

His mother pulled her head back as she often did when not entirely certain if something was a good idea or not. "She is not particularly robust," she said softly as if saying it in a lower voice would lessen the insult he was certain Lady Catherine would hear in his mother's words.

"There is nothing deficient in my daughter!"

He had not been wrong.

Lord Matlock tapped his shoulder. "Come. Sit."

Alistair followed him and took a seat next to him. There was no way he was moving far from the side of an earl who had given his approval of the marriage.

"She is not so strong as some." Lady Margaret's countering her daughter's statement came as a surprise to Alistair. "She is more like my Anne."

"She is not deficient," Lady Catherine repeated.

"I did not mean to say she is lacking," said Lady Metcalfe, "but there are certain duties to a title..."

"My dear," Lord Metcalfe interrupted, "this might not be the best time and place to discuss such things."

"It must be considered," Lady Metcalfe argued.

"I shall marry no one else," Alistair said before his mother could begin her standard lengthy discourse on what a proper viscountess should be.

"You must marry," his mother insisted.

He nodded. "I am well aware of that fact, Mother, and I will marry — Anne, and no other."

Her lips pursed and her brows drew together in a look of displeasure with which he was familiar and, he knew, would only give a moment's reprieve before she attempted once again to prove to him that she was indeed correct and he was in error. That was not going to happen.

He folded his arms and leaned back in his chair. "This — your unwillingness to see things as I do — is why I had agreed to Anne's plan to elope."

Again the room, which a moment ago at his declaration of not marrying any other had begun to hum with whispers, fell silent.

"You were going to elope?"

"Yes, Father, we were. I need a wife and do not wish to marry for anything but love. However, I knew that Mother would protest that I could find a better choice, just as she has, and Anne knew that Lady Catherine would also protest that Anne was already betrothed." He glanced quickly at Darcy. "Therefore, it seemed the practical thing to do to elope and secure a wife while avoiding wasting time in debate over the matter." He shifted forward in his chair. "However, no matter how much Anne might enjoy the excitement and scandal an elopement would bring, she deserves to be wed properly."

Lady Margaret rose from her chair and crossed to where a

decanter stood on a table. "Did you come to this conclusion before or after my son intercepted you?"

Alistair's eyes narrowed. Did that small smile mean she already knew that it was not he and Anne who had run off together? "Did not Ralston tell you?"

"Tell me what?" Lady Margaret's smile remained in place, and her eyes did not widen naturally in question but more as if the expression was forced.

Alistair looked at Jack, who shook his head.

"Anne was not in my company when her uncle found her," Alistair said. "She was on her way to meet me — not that I knew of her plans until Conrad's letter arrived at Stanton's."

"I think you might want to start this tale at the beginning." Lady Margaret took her seat, a full glass of sherry in her hand.

"Very well," said Alistair, giving her a pointed look. If he was guessing correctly, she was throwing down a challenge of sorts to see if he would try to avoid the telling of the full story. He would not. He would give her the entertainment she sought, but not without tossing out a small challenge of his own. "Might I have a bit of something to refresh my voice as I tell it?"

Lady Margaret raised her glass in salute. "Genevieve, Mr. Pratt needs some port," she instructed.

Lady Matlock's brows furrowed, but she rose and procured the drink while Alistair began to tell his tale, calling on Jack and Lord Matlock to corroborate facts where needed.

# Chapter 10

"Did you win?" Anne asked Alistair as she sat beside him in her uncle's barouche a week after having arrived in town.

She had been disappointed to have not been able to go to Angelo's with Alistair, but she had been confined to bed for three days after arriving in town. It was only after her fever subsided that she was allowed out of bed, and then, for the next two days, it was only for meals or to be measured for wedding clothes.

Then, yesterday, her mother had declared her well enough to go shopping, and when Anne had awoken this morning feeling better and not worse for the exertion of the previous day, Lady Catherine had been convinced that receiving callers would be acceptable. However, her uncle — wonderful, understanding man that he was — had declared sunshine and a change of scenery would be a far better elixir. So it was that, after a short argument between Lord Matlock and his sister, Anne had been instructed by Lady Margaret to change into walking clothes and was allowed to go for a drive and a possible walk in the park with Alistair.

"We have not met," Alistair said with a sly grin. Tomorrow, Anne and he would leave London for Kent. Their wedding would follow in a day — it was rather impressive how quickly a license and marriage papers could be acquired by someone of Lord Matlock's standing. However, before they left town and took up their life together as husband and wife, there was one small gift which Alistair had been able to arrange for Anne.

Anne sighed a small disappointed sigh.

Alistair placed an arm around her shoulders and drew her closer to his side. "I could not dispatch of the blackguard without you."

Anne gasped, and a smile spread across her face. "Me?" she squealed delightedly. She leaned forward and peered out around the side of the canopy. "Are we going to Angelo's and not the park?"

"Indeed we are," Alistair replied, pulling her back to his side and kissing her gloved fingers. "We can still visit the park after we have concluded our business with Mr. Conrad if you wish. I do not wish to fatigue you, but I know how you have always desired to drive through the park. I shall leave it up to you completely. However, I would remind you that should you become ill, we will have to postpone our wedding, and I would rather not wait any longer." He kissed her fingers once again.

Anne smiled, and proper or not, she rested her head against his shoulder. "Might I decide after we have been to Angelo's?"

"Of course."

Anne sighed contentedly and, peeking up at him, said, "I love you."

"And I you," he replied, punctuating his words with a kiss to her forehead. "Now, tell me all about your shopping trip yester-day."

And she did. For the rest of the trip through the streets to Angelo's and even as they exited the carriage and entered the club, she told him of the ribbons, lace, and gloves she had purchased to go with this dress or that hat. However, her rambling tale of just how lovely a store Miss Elizabeth's uncle had stopped mid-sentence when she stepped through the door to Angelo's.

She wrinkled her nose. The air was rather pungent with the aroma of gentlemen who had been exercising. She did not mind the smell of Alistair after a match in the grove, but here, where there were no fresh breezes and there was more than one gentleman wiping his brow, the smell was not so pleasant. She leaned toward Alistair. "I do believe I shall need an airing after this."

Alistair chuckled. "We can leave now if you wish."

She shook her head as her eyes fell on Conrad standing in his shirt sleeves near the wall. "Not until we have accomplished what we came to do."

"Very well, my dear, then, come with me. Jack has all the equipment waiting for us." He led her to where his friend was waiting.

"I must admit that after having listened to Al tell me about your skills for the last few days, I am rather excited to watch you, Miss de Bourgh."

Anne laughed nervously. "I hope I do not disappoint," she said, looking around nervously. "I have never had an audience that was not comprised of trees and woodland creatures."

"Just focus on Conrad," Alistair instructed. He placed his hands on her shoulders and looked her in the eyes. "The others are but squawking crows to be ignored."

She smiled and nodded as she repeated, "squawking crows."

"Now, be a good girl and sit with Jack while I defend your honour."

Anne giggled and raising up on her toes, placed a kiss on his cheek much as she imagined a princess might do before sending her knight into a battle for her hand. The action brought a few calls from the gentlemen who had begun to gather and a pleased grin from Alistair.

"It seems we are drawing a crowd." Alistair lowered his mask into place but not before he had shot a pointed look at his friend.

"I might have mentioned the match to a few people," Jack replied.

"Right, a few," Alistair's tone was skeptical. If he knew Jack, every person in the club had heard about this match. He shook his head and stepped up to greet Conrad.

Anne tipped her head and studied Mr. Conrad. "Alistair is very good."

"He is," Jack agreed.

"Mr. Conrad knows it," she added.

"I imagine he does. It is no secret. But how do you know he knows?"

"His feet are shifting."

"He is just getting set to begin," Jack countered.

"No," Anne replied. "One does not shift his feet when he assumes the ready position unless he is uncertain of his abilities."

Jack chuckled. "Alistair has taught you well."

Pride filled Anne's chest. "He has. He is very good."

"He is," Jack agreed once more as the match before them began.

Anne perched on the edge of her chair and watched in rapt silence. The excitement of the event caused her heart to race and her muscles to long to be used. She wished to only watch Alistair as he lunged and dodged, for he did cut a fine figure; however, knowing that she would face the same opponent next, she forced herself to study the way Conrad's foot lifted and his weight shifted a moment before he attacked. It was no wonder Alistair could beat him so handily. Conrad performed the figures in the book she had read just as they were drawn and with only a modicum of finesse.

When the match had concluded, and as expected, Alistair had landed the most touches, he extended his hand to Conrad. Then, he turned to her and made a sweeping bow.

She stood and replied to his gesture with a small curtsey and a nod of her head.

"Your turn, my dear," he said, taking her hand and lifting it to his lips to the sounds of cheers. Angelo's had never been quite so raucous as it was at the moment. He held her sparkling eyes with his. He loved how vibrantly those eyes shone when there was a battle to be won. It mattered not if it was a game of chess, a joust, or a scheme to free herself from her mother's plans for her. Her determination and enthusiasm was palpable. "Squawking crows," he said to her before moving aside and allowing her to take her place.

"Do you wish for a moment of refreshment before we begin?" she asked Mr. Conrad when he bowed to her. "I should hate to have these observers think I had only outdone you because you were fatigued."

A ripple of laughter circled the room.

"Is that Anne?" Darcy asked as he came to take a place next to Alistair.

"It is. Fitzwilliam arranged it," Alistair replied.

"Why?" Bingley asked.

"Conrad lied to her," Jack answered.

"And Fitzwilliam had once upon a time mentioned to Anne that ladies were allowed at Angelo's," Alistair added.

"So she called him out," Jack added proudly. "And since she can beat Al, it should be an interesting pairing."

"Anne knows how to fence?" Darcy asked in surprise.

"As you can see," Alistair muttered with a nod toward where Anne was just engaging Conrad. He sucked in a breath and held it. Anne had beaten him several times, but she had never gone against anyone else. He was proud of her for even wishing to attempt it, but he had to admit that he was also nervous that she would get injured or worse, lose.

His fears were soon allayed as Anne neatly dodged a few thrusts and landed several hits. A victory was well within her reach.

"Ow!"

He caught his breath once more as Anne failed to successfully dodge a lunge, and for a moment, he worried that she would get injured. However, his concern was quickly turned to amusement as he recognized Anne's small growl of annoyance and knew that with that hit, Conrad had sealed his fate.

"She disarmed him," Jack said with no small amount of awe.

Alistair nodded. "Yes, yes, she did, just as I taught her."

"You taught her to fence?" Darcy asked.

Alistair nodded as he stood and joined the others, who were clapping enthusiastically.

Anne tipped her head and curtsied quickly before retrieving Conrad's foil. "You will not lie to me in the future nor will you say anything against my husband." She held his foil out to him but did not release it until she had received his agreement. Leaving him, she returned to where Alistair and the other stood.

"Do you wish for a match?" she asked.

"He wishes for a kiss," someone called from the wall to her left. "Do you?"

Alistair smiled and shrugged.

Anne raised a brow. "Then earn it," she said, slicing the air with her foil, once again sending a ripple of laughter around the room.

Alistair shook his head and, picking up his mask, followed her to the mat. "Win or lose, I will claim my prize."

"Oh, no, Mr. Pratt," Anne teased, "a prize is only awarded to a winner. Therefore, when I win, I shall claim my prize."

Alistair had thought Angelo's raucous when Anne had kissed his cheek and then taken her turn against Conrad, but that was nothing compared to the cheer that greeted Anne's comments as well as the one that accompanied her win. And he was certain that Angelo's had never before and would never again hear a roar like the one that arose when Anne tossed aside her mask and foil and, pressing herself and her lips firmly against Alistair, claimed her prize.

~*~*~

Two days later, as Anne stood before her mirror, she carefully positioned her sleeve and gloves so that her mother would not see the bruise on her arm. It was not a large bruise, but Anne knew that it was large enough to cause her mother to inquire after it. She had sworn her cousin and his friend Mr. Bingley as well as Jack to silence about the joust at Angelo's, and she had been careful to keep the paper from her mother's notice both yesterday and today. She knew that her appearance at Angelo's would not go unmentioned, especially after the display she had put on following her defeat of Alistair. Her cheeks flushed. It was rather exhilarating to behave so brazenly, but it was not something she planned to repeat or publish any further than it had already been circulated.

"Anne Catherine de Bourgh!" Lady Catherine said as she threw open the door to her daughter's room.

Anne cringed at the tone of her mother's voice.

"Lady Metcalfe has just made me aware of a rather shocking story."

Drat! She had forgotten that Alistair's mother might see the paper and share the story with her mother.

"What were you thinking? Going to a gentleman's club and behaving like a…" she waved the paper she held in the air as she sought for the right word, though none seemed to come to her.

As Anne stood before her mirror, a smile spread across her face. She could not remember a single time in her life when her mother had been at a loss for words until now. There was a strange feeling of satisfaction that accompanied the knowledge.

"It was inappropriate," Anne offered. "And I shall not do it again. Now, if you will excuse me, I have a wedding to attend."

"Inappropriate does not begin to describe what you did, young lady," Anne's mother, having found her voice again, continued as she followed her daughter down the stairs.

"Edward told me that Angelo's accepts ladies," Anne said as she reached the bottom of the stairs. "So going to the club was actually not all that inappropriate."

Lady Catherine gasped. "Whether they accept ladies or not, you should not have been there!"

Anne shrugged. "I disagree."

Lady Margaret chuckled as she joined them. "It is not the first scandalous story this family has had in the paper, is it, Genevieve?"

"Mother," Lord Matlock cautioned. "Not today. I could find no better wife, and I was quite happy to have captured her."

Lady Margaret patted his arm and whispered. "I know, but a mother must roar."

"Not today," he replied before turning to his niece. "Anne, you are a vision. Are you ready to go claim your husband at the church?"

Her husband. Pleasant prickles raced up her limbs and settling in her stomach. "I am," she said with a smile.

Lord Matlock extended his arm to Anne as he addressed her mother. "Catherine, are you ready to give your daughter away and in so doing, claim a son?"

"Must I?" she replied.

"I am afraid you must," he assured his sister. "There is no break-ing this engagement after that piece in the paper."

Lady Catherine's shoulders drooped. "I thought I had one more year before this day would come."

Anne blinked as she saw Lady Margaret wrap her arm around her daughter's. "Trust me, Catherine. Even with another year to prepare yourself, you would still face this day with a mix of joy and sorrow. However, you must lift your chin, set your smile, and enjoy this day. Lead on, Henry."

And so, Anne exited her childhood home for the last time as Miss de Bourgh and climbed into her uncle's carriage to be taken to the church to become Mrs. Pratt.

~*~*~

At the church, Alistair waited with Jack at his side. The day had finally arrived. He would no longer be sent to house parties or expected to attend soirees while his heart, his Anne, stayed at Rosings unable to openly stand at his side.

"They have arrived," Darcy said as he approached the front of the church.

Darcy, Georgiana, and Elizabeth had arrived ahead of the others from Rosings. Anne had insisted that Elizabeth be the one to stand up with her at her wedding since it was Elizabeth's willingness to marry Darcy that had given Anne her freedom to marry where she chose. It was a pile of rubbish, as far as Alistair was concerned. Anne would have married where she chose even if Darcy were still unattached.  His Anne was a determined sort of lady.

Finally, the doors to the church opened and Anne, on her uncle's arm, joined Alistair before Mr. Collins and the ceremony began. It was not a long ceremony — they never were, even when the parson was as given to rambling as Mr. Collins was.

Having taken their vows and placed their names in the register, Anne and Alistair climbed into her curricle to return to Rosings for the wedding breakfast. A feast had been arranged in the dining room and Miss Jenkinson along with her niece, Miss Pope, had been engaged to play several dances on the piano and violin.

Just before the dancing was to begin, Alistair drew Anne aside and out to the garden.

"Are you well?" he asked.

"I have never been better," she replied. "I rested as much as I could yesterday, just as you suggested."

"Then, you are ready to make your debut at a ball?"

"Oh, I am. I so very much am," she cried. "Thank you for insisting on dancing. I know my mother would not have agreed to it if you had not been so unrelenting."

He drew her into his embrace. "You may dance as many dances as you wish as long as you promise you will not make yourself ill in doing so. I do not wish to spend my wedding night alone."

Anne blushed. "I shall only dance two sets. Both with you."

He tipped her chin up and kissed her lightly. "There will be other balls. I promise." He kissed her once more. "Now, Mrs. Pratt, shall we return to our guests?"

She shook her head and pressed her lips against his once more for a longer, more intimate kiss than the two he had given her. Then, with a whispered "I love you," she allowed him to lead her into the ballroom and into a future that would be filled with laughter and dancing, rides in the park and walks in the grove, as well as the arrival of children and the occasional family row. And while her happily ever after might not be the sort she would find in her book of fairy tales, it would be everything Anne had ever dreamed it would be. For how can such a life be anything less than fulfilling and blessed when a lady's heart and that of her gentleman have become so very entangled with love.

# Enticing Miss Darcy

*He's determined to win her, but first, she'll need to learn to trust her heart.*

# Chapter 1

Jack Ralston straightened the sleeves of his jacket and affected a relaxed pose, leaning against one of the two pillars which flanked one entrance to the Winsleys' ballroom. Debutantes and their chaperones picked their way along the edges, not wishing to ruin the chalk drawing on the floor before the dancing began. The room was about half-filled if Jack were guessing correctly.

The Winsleys always drew a large crowd. Lady Winsley, a particular friend of Jack's mother, was perhaps the foremost hostess in the ton this year. No one else's soirees had graced the pages of the Times with more flowery descriptions than the ones that had been hosted here in this house. First, there had been an elegant dinner party with many notable members of the ton in attendance. Then, there had been an evening of Shakespeare — complete with costumes and masks. And just two weeks ago, there had been a musicale. Each and every event had been lauded. Tonight would likely be no different. Jack only hoped that tonight he would be more successful than he had been at each of the previous soirees held in this home.

Not once had he been able to capture the interest of the enticing Miss Darcy for longer than a few moments. He could not understand it. He had spent nearly a year attempting to win her approval — he paused to reflect on when he had met her — yes, it would be a year next month — and he thought he had had it. She always welcomed him with a lovely smile when they met and never shied away from conversing with him as he had seen her do with others she met while visiting this or that venue with her grandmother, Lady Margaret, and sister, Mrs. Darcy.

However, as soon as she had been presented at her first official soiree, he had become just one of her entourage of companions, relegated to the uncomfortable position of trusted friend. He rolled his eyes and shook his head. Friends!

He pulled out his watch. She would be here soon. She always arrived about a quarter of an hour early. He blew out a breath. Friends was, at least, a start. But it was nowhere near what he wished to be.

"Jack!"

With a smile, Jack swung away from his scrutiny of the ballroom and toward the voice the he had come to know well. "Mrs. Pratt," he said, giving her a bow.

Anne waved his words away. "It is Anne," she chided, releasing her grip on her husband, Alistair's, arm and leaning forward to give Jack a hug. It was not so easily accomplished these days with her ever-growing belly in the way.

"I should think a ball would not be good for you in your condition," Jack said with a wink. "Your husband is not shirking his duties and allowing you to run amuck and harm his heir, now is he?"

"No, he is not," Alistair replied. "She is not to dance."

Anne scrunched up her nose, clearly not pleased with the pronouncement and yet unwilling to defy it. But that was how it was with Anne and Alistair. She would push, and he would push back. And, more often than not, Anne would capitulate. Alistair was nearly the only one to whom the daughter of Lady Catherine would defer.

"My condolences," Jack said with a smile which was readily returned. "Will we be playing cards this evening?"

Anne's smile spread, and the familiar twinkle of mischief sparkled in her eyes as she shook her head. "I have read no announcement in the paper."

Alistair sighed. "My wife has decided you need help — again."

Jack laughed. "I do not wish to find myself the main topic of conversation tomorrow morning as I did the last time you helped."

Anne shook her head and gave him a scolding look as if he should not be concerned about such a thing. "Who was to know that that lonely looking tabby would jump from your arms and attack Mrs. Hollingsworth? It truly looked as if it was in need of assistance, and it would have been a very impressive act of kindness had the cat cooperated."

"The good news is that Lady Winsley's cats are much better behaved than most strays," Alistair said dryly.

The incident had happened on a walk in Hunsford during the summer. The Darcys had been visiting Lady Catherine, and Jack had, at Anne's invitation, been visiting the Pratts. Such a visit would allow Jack ample time to be in company with Georgiana, Anne had assured him. After all, had not both she and her cousin, Fitzwilliam Darcy, found the groves at Rosings to be the ideal place to court their loves?

Jack should have known, with such logic and the information

that Darcy had been soundly refused by Elizabeth while in Kent, that it was not the best-laid plan. However, he could not resist the opportunity to spend a full three weeks with Georgiana Darcy.

They had met on several walks, and they had had many wonderful discussions. In fact, it was on one of these not-so-chance meetings when Anne had spotted the tabby tangled in some bramble, and while Darcy spoke to Mrs. Hollingsworth, who was out for a drive, Anne had whispered to Jack that helping a poor defenseless creature would appear quite romantic to any lady. Therefore, without much thought, Jack sprung into action.

He had pulled the cat from the bushes and was petting it gently as they walked over to where Georgiana stood near Mrs. Hollingsworth's curricle. All had been going as planned — the cat was safe, Georgiana was smiling, and then, Mrs. Hollingsworth's pug had started barking. The cat hissed, and instead of leaping from Jack's arms and running away as any cat with a modicum of sense would, this feline leapt toward the dog and onto Mrs. Hollingsworth's lap. The resulting cry of surprise and the flicking of the ribbons had sent the horses trotting down the lane.

"That incident has been the source of many minutes of conversation, has it not?" Anne asked hopefully.

Jack shook his head. "Not in a pleasant sort of way," he assured her. "I would rather not be the source of a good laugh."

"But every lady likes to laugh," Anne insisted.

"Not every gentleman wishes to be laughed at," Jack replied. "He would like his wit to be the source of a few giggles but not his pride."

"She shall not forget you," said Anne.

"Ah, but will she think of him as he wishes her to think of him?" Alistair asked.

Anne's lips pursed and her brows drew together. "Perhaps not," she admitted. "But I will maintain that it is good to be memorable and pleasantly so. A small folly is a far better thing for which to be remembered than some nefarious scheme or hateful gossip. "

"I will allow that to be true," Jack said, "but it also still stands that I would not like to be remembered twice for some folly, whether small or large." He raised his brows and gave her a pointed look.

"Take me around the ballroom. Alistair can hold up that pillar just as well as you can."

"Would you not rather take a turn of the room with your husband?" Jack asked.

"No, he already knows my plan," Anne replied. "And he agrees it might work."

Jack looked at his staid and steady friend, Alistair Pratt. "You approve?"

Alistair nodded. "I do." He shrugged. "It is not without its risks, but it is unlikely to end with your name in the paper should things go sour."

"That is not reassuring. What do you see going wrong?"

Alistair was a contemplative sort of fellow, well-versed in logic and reasoning, and able to see problems before they appeared. Therefore, if Alistair saw a reason for caution, Jack wished to know about it.

Alistair shook his head and smiled. "I have been promised a most pleasant reward if I allow Anne to explain her plan before I begin casting aspersions about."

Jack shook his head. He could just imagine what sort of reward the blushing Mrs. Pratt had promised her husband to make him agree to hold his tongue. "Very well, Mrs. Pratt, shall we take a turn about the room?"

Anne placed her hand on his arm but turned to her husband before beginning their walk. "When Georgiana arrives, you must claim two dances for Mr. Ralston."

Jack chuckled at the look of dismay on Alistair's face.

"I shall not hear it, Mr. Pratt," Anne said with a laugh. "He is doing you a favour by taking your wife for a walk around the ballroom, so you are being gracious and making his request for him — which he will be most grateful for when he returns. I walk more slowly these days, so he feared he would not be back in time to ask Georgie for those dances, and you were noble enough to offer to do it for him."

Alistair sighed and shook his head, but Jack could see the admiration in the man's eyes at his wife's cleverness.

"She's very creative," Jack said with a laugh.

"That she is," Alistair answered. "She has taken up writing," he added.

"Have you indeed?" Jack asked as he and Anne began a slow circuit of the ballroom.

"Oh, I have — but not horrid novels — I do not like gruesome stories. I did at one time, but no longer. I prefer happier tales. However, that is not why we are here. I shall allow you to read my stories when you visit. For now, we must discuss how you are going to persuade Miss Darcy to marry you."

"This plan of yours does not involve a flight to Gretna Green does it?" Jack asked as they began their slow trek around the ballroom. "Mrs. Armstrong, Miss Armstrong," he said with a polite nod of his head as they passed a matron who was smiling in his direction. This was Miss Armstrong's second season, and she had not been at all subtle in her hopes that he would pay her more attention than he did. She was a lovely girl, but she was no Georgiana Darcy.

"No, we will save Scotland for later if it is needed," Anne replied.

Jack's head snapped around to look at the lady beside him instead of the others in the room. She was smiling widely, and he shook his head. She enjoyed a scandal far too much!

"Seriously," she added, "if it is needed, we will spirit her away, but it would do you far more good to secure her without a scandal. Darcy is not the sort of man to approve of a scandal, and you do not wish to have him displeased with you for the remainder of your life and beyond."

Jack chuckled. "I do not believe Mr. Darcy is quite as dreadful as your words and tone imply, but I will agree that I would rather not begin my life as his brother-in-law with his being unhappy with me."

"Oh, he is dour," Anne assured Jack. "Perhaps not so much as he used to be before he married, but he is a Fitzwilliam, and as such, Fitzwilliam Darcy has an unyielding temper." She shook her head. "He's very much like my mother in that regard."

"I will allow he is serious, but I cannot agree that he is as recalcitrant as your mother." Lady Catherine, Jack had learned, was twice as obstinate as Alistair's mother, and Jack had always considered Lady Metcalfe to be excessively stubborn. That was perhaps why the two ladies, Lady Catherine and Lady Metcalfe, had been able to tolerate each other for so many years.

Anne shrugged. "Perhaps."

Jack raised a quizzical brow at her.

"Very well, no one is so unyielding as my mother."

"Except perhaps for her daughter?" Jack asked with a playful grin.

"I will not protest that," Anne replied with a laugh. "One must learn to be assertive if she is to survive as the daughter of Lady Catherine."

Jack patted her hand where it lay on his arm. "You are more sensible than your mother — most times."

She laughed again. It was a delightful sound that was filled with enjoyment. Jack admired that about his friend's wife. She never did anything by halves. She threw herself into an activity or plan wholeheartedly, or she did not begin it. There were no in-betweens with Anne Pratt. In that, she and he were rather alike, for Jack also enjoyed entering into projects in which he could immerse himself.

"Mr. Henson, Miss Henson," he greeted as Anne and he attempted to slide between where Mr. Henson and his sister stood and the wall without causing a scene.

Anne pulled him ahead. "Stop talking to all the debutantes," she chided. "They will expect you to ask them for a dance."

"Am I not supposed to dance with them?"

"Not until you have secured your two with Georgiana." She huffed. "What if we enter into a conversation where you feel obliged to ask for a dance, and then, upon returning to Alistair we discover you have just given away one of your two dances with Georgie?"

"I see your point," he conceded. "Now, perhaps you could share your plan with me?"

Anne leaned a little heavier on his arm so that she could whisper to him from a safer distance. "You are to be her friend. Treat her well. Make her laugh. Find ways to help her."

"I think I already do that," Jack replied.

"You do," Anne answered. "However, you do it with such an air of desperation, as if she were the sun, the moon, and the stars all wrapped into one, and you would be lost without her."

"She is, and I will be," Jack replied. He knew that his heart would never recover from the blow of not winning Georgiana Darcy's hand. The happiness of his life would be at an end if she were to become someone else's. When he met her, he had thought it was merely because she was beautiful and all that a young woman should be — demure, polite, well-spoken, amiable. However, having spent the past year in her presence as much as he had, thanks to the connection his best friend Alistair now had with the family, Jack had discovered that Georgiana Darcy was as lively as she was beautiful and that her beauty extended deep into her very being, and, as a result, he had fallen from infatuation into love — painful, unrequited love.

"But you are not to let her know that," Anne chided. "There must be a coolness about you. You like her as a dear friend but not as a possible wife. You must appear to be looking elsewhere to find a Mrs. Ralston. You will dance with her twice at each ball for a time and then, you will dance with her once, and then not at all.

You will call on her, daily, if you wish, for a time, but then sporadically and finally, you will not call at all."

An uneasy, fluttering sort of dread settled in around Jack's heart. "I do not like this plan. I do not see the point of it at all other than to allow her to spend more time with other gentlemen and possibly lose her to one of them."

Anne sighed. "You sound very much like Alistair."

"Those were his objections?"

She nodded.

"So, then, what is the point of this charade?" They had almost completed their circuit, and Jack could see Alistair was writing on Georgiana's dance card.

"To make her miss you," Anne said with a smile. "She enjoys your company. She has said she does, but she does not see you as someone she must have in her life. She has only just had her come out and is enamored with the newness of the season — first soirees, new dresses, new beaus — it is all quite distracting and alluring, I assure you. But she will tire of it all and come to realize that you are better than all the other gentlemen who come to call. There is nothing more enticing than the gentleman who used to be in your pocket but treats you coolly now."

Jack looked at Anne skeptically. "Are you certain?"

"No," Anne replied honestly, "but I imagine it to be true, and you have been attempting to court her and gotten nowhere. And do not forget that there is always Gretna Green if we must rescue her from making a match that is not you."

Jack grimaced and shook his head. "I do not know if this is wise."

"Try it your way, if you wish, but..." She shrugged. "I have read no announcements in the paper."

"I will consider it, but I will not commit to anything just yet."

"That is understandable," Anne assured him. "But do not wait too long. The season does not last forever, and I shall be unable to help you in a month." She placed a hand on her belly. "If Alistair does not confine me to our townhouse before that."

"He only wishes to see you healthy and happy," Jack said softly.

Anne smiled. "I know, and it is sweet." She patted his arm. "One day soon it will be you tucking your wife away to ensure her and her baby's safety." Her lips pursed, and she cocked her left brow. "If you follow my plan, it might be even sooner."

Jack chuckled. "I have promised to consider it."

Anne sighed. "Very well. Now, take me back to my husband. The dancing will commence soon, and if Georgiana is not your first partner, you will need to procure one."

"Do you have a card?" Jack asked as they returned to where Alistair stood with the Darcys.

"No," Anne replied.

Jack's brows drew together as if concerned. "Well, dance card or no dance card, I will spend the third set with you in the card room."

Anne giggled behind her fan. "Did you bring enough money with you to lose tonight, Mr. Ralston?"

He nodded. "I brought it especially for your entertainment."

Alistair shook his head. "You are a horrid influence on her, you know?"

"I had thought it the other way around," Jack quipped in return. "Mr. Darcy, it is a pleasure to see you. Mrs. Darcy, Miss Darcy, you are both looking well this evening. It certainly looks as if Lady Winsley has outdone herself again tonight." He made a sweeping motion toward the ballroom. "Mrs. Pratt and I have made a thorough inspection, and all looks to be in order." He winked at Anne, who once again giggled behind her fan. "Miss Darcy, did Mr. Pratt make my request of you?"

Georgiana turned her smiling face from regarding her cousin Anne to Jack. "He did. We have the first and the dinner set. He thought it would be best for me to begin and dine with a friend whom I know well."

"That is Pratt for you. Always thinking and always practical," Jack replied lightly. Friends. There was that word again. He would have to give Anne's plan careful consideration. Perhaps if Georgiana Darcy were to miss him, it might shift him out of that spot as her friend and into a place more amenable to his desires. He offered her his hand. "Shall we take our place then?"

"I have never seen my cousin so happy," Georgiana said as they made their way onto the dance floor.

"Alistair has never been a dreary sort of person, but there is a rather pleasant aura of happiness about him that was never there before he married," Alistair returned. "They are good for each other."

Georgiana took her place across from him. "They are, but Mr. Pratt is not the only reason for my cousin's happiness."

"He is not?" Jack said in surprise as the musicians played the first notes, and he bowed.

"No," she replied with a smile upon rising from her curtsey and crossed behind him. "She is fortunate to have you for a friend. Not everyone can abide my cousin's exuberance with such aplomb as you do." They joined hands and made their way down the line. "Of course, none of us knew she possessed such liveliness until last spring."

"I find her charming," Jack replied as they turned and moved back to their place before separating.

Their conversation regarding Anne continued in snatches — a word here, a comment there, as they crossed and returned, joined hands, circled and changed places.

"I had worried she would always be lonely," Georgiana said as the dance concluded. "I am so happy she has found friends."

Jack inclined his head. "I am delighted to have met her acquaintance, and might I say your tender heart does you great credit? For it does."

Her eyes danced with pleasure, and she darted a look toward the edge of the ballroom.

"Is she still standing there watching?" Jack followed her gaze and saw that Anne was indeed standing almost precisely where they had left her. He took Georgiana's hand and circled around the others as they took their place for the second dance. "Alistair is no doubt attempting to convince her that she should take a seat."

"He does worry about her."

The expression in Georgiana's eyes softened and took on a wistful complexion. Yes, Anne's advice about continuing to provide concerned care for Miss Darcy would likely grant him a place of some sort in her heart. He only hoped that it would be the place he desired.

"He does dote on her," Jack agreed as the next dance began. "I only hope to be so fortunate as my friend."

"I am quite certain you will be," Georgiana replied.

"From your lips to God's ears," Jack replied with a wink before they were separated, and their conversation was once again relegated to bits and pieces woven between and around their companions.

# Chapter 2

Georgiana stretched and sighed as her maid, Alice, drew the curtains open, allowing the sunlight to flood the room.

"Do you want the blue dress or the green today, miss?" Alice asked as she crossed the room to stoke the fire.

"The blue?"

"'Tis not my choice, miss, but you do look lovely in the blue."

"Then the blue it is," Georgiana said as she sat up in bed and pushed the blankets off her legs so that she could climb out.

"It will likely be a busy day of callers since your dance card was full last night," Alice said with a smile.

"I hope it is not too busy." Georgiana slipped her feet into her slippers and made her way to the dressing room. "I enjoy the soirees to a point, but the calls..." she sighed. "I find them to be a trifle taxing."

"You will do well," her maid assured her.

Georgiana knew that many ladies of her rank in society did not enter into conversations with their servants. However, Alice had been with Georgiana since before her father died and was very dear to her, for the woman had never once said a word about Georgiana needing to dry her tears. She had not even lifted a disapproving brow. Instead, Alice had provided Georgiana with fresh handkerchiefs and an ear to listen to things that were not possible for Georgiana to say to her brother. In fact, it was Alice who had helped Georgiana learn about the changes that occur for a girl as she becomes a lady. Fitzwilliam was understanding of her misery and provided what comfort he could, but he was not able to help her as Alice was. So, it was that Alice and her mistress often started their day with a little tete-a-tete.

"Tell me about the ball. Was it all that you expected?"

"Oh, it was beautiful! The Winsleys' ballroom is about the size of three of our green drawing rooms."

"A good size for forming sets then." Alice poured warm water into the basin and placed a fresh towel on the hook on the side of the washstand.

"Oh, it is," Georgiana agreed, slipping out of her nightgown and taking up the soap. "And it was so well arranged and lit! Everything fairly sparkled."

"Did the light catch your earbobs as you had hoped?"

"I could not see them, but Elizabeth assures me it did."

Alice draped stockings over her arm and reached for a clean chemise. "And did you dance every dance?"

"I did." Georgiana's feet were still well aware of the fact that she had danced every set, but it was a satisfying sort of discomfort. "I danced every set with a new partner save for the two sets Mr. Ralston claimed." She splashed water on her face and after drying it, reached for the cloth to remove the rest of the soap she had rubbed onto her person. "Actually, it was Mr. Pratt who claimed the dances for his friend as Mr. Ralston was taking a turn around the ballroom with Anne."

"He is a fine young man," Alice said as she waited for Georgiana to finish the last bits of her ablution.

Georgiana had to agree. Jack Ralston was everything a young man should be — sensible, good-humoured, lively, and in possession of happy manners as well as a healthy fortune. He was also rather handsome — tall with a muscular build, wavy hair the colour of a good cup of tea with just a splash of cream and eyes the colour of chocolate. Added to this, he was so good to Anne, teasing her, prodding her on, and yet watching out that all was well with her. It was endearing really. He would make someone a fine husband one day. The idea of him having his own lady for whom to care made her sigh and smile. Some lady would be very happy.

Her brows furrowed as she held her stays in place over her chemise. Perhaps she could help Jack find a lady who was worthy of him. From what she had been told by her aunt and grandmother, ladies of quality were not easy to come by in the ton. Many appeared to be all that was proper. They smiled and spoke softly as they ducked their heads demurely, but, according to her grandmother, it was often a ploy. Georgiana was not certain if it was true or not, but, based on what she knew of Caroline Bingley and Caroline's sister Louisa Hurst, Georgiana found it challenging to refute the fact that Lady Margaret's words might be true. And if they were true, Georgiana would be greatly saddened to learn that a gentleman as worthy as Jack Ralston had been taken in by such a lady.

Georgiana stuffed her arms into her sleeves and helped Alice straighten and smooth them.

"Did any of the young men catch your fancy?" Alice asked as she finished the last of the fastenings of Georgiana's dress.

Georgiana shook her head as she smoothed her skirts and turned this way and that in front of the mirror before sitting to allow Alice to work on her hair. "There were several who seemed nice."

"Nice?" Alice looked at her mistress in the mirror and raised a brow.

Georgiana shrugged. "Handsome, polite, able to carry on a conversation with great civility."

"But none who caught your eye in any special way?"

"No." Georgiana sighed. She had not met one gentleman yet who had caused her to hope for a second dance or to wait with anticipation to see if he would call.

"They are not all hiding a deceitful heart," Alice said softly. "There will be one who will wish to court and marry you for you and not your fortune."

Georgiana's reflection in the mirror smiled sadly back at her and her maid. "I know it is true, but…"

"It is hard to trust."

"Precisely so," Georgiana agreed. She had once allowed her heart to be fooled by Mr. Wickham, a handsome man with pleasing manners, and had nearly been consigned to a life of misery. As it turned out, Mr. Wickham had not been in love with Georgiana as he had declared. He had been in love with her money and the pain he could cause her brother by marrying her, for he was a former friend of Fitzwilliam's, who felt he had been wronged and was justified in seeking revenge for being treated ill. However, Mr. Wickham had not been treated poorly. He had refused the living set aside for him by Georgiana's father and had accepted a sum of money in its place. It was not wrong of Fitzwilliam to refuse to grant the living to Mr. Wickham when it fell open, even if Mr. Wickham had squandered all of his money and was in a dire state of existence. It was this event of being duped by Mr. Wickham which had caused Georgiana to be less trusting and always wary of gentlemen. And it was this guardedness that Georgiana now feared would make it impossible for her to find a husband.

"You will learn to trust again," Alice assured her. "There are good men out there like your brother and Mr. Pratt as well as his friend Mr. Ralston." She placed her hands on Georgiana's shoulders. "If you are uncertain, they can guide you."

Georgiana smiled and nodded. "Of course. Although I dare say, my brother will be hard pressed to think any of them worthy of me."

"Aye, that may be. So, it might be best to consult Mr. Pratt or your uncle. Lord Matlock is as fine as they come."

Georgiana rose from her bench, and though she knew that many would frown on her for such an action, she hugged her maid. "Thank you," she said. "You always know what to say to make me see reason."

"Go on with you," her maid said. "Mrs. Darcy and Miss Annesley could have told you the same."

Georgiana's lips curled into a smile. "That may be, but they are never in here helping me into my stays and stockings, and it is in these moments when I need the encouragement."

Alice shook her head and chuckled as she set to tidying the room while Georgiana left to make her way to the breakfast room.

After having eaten a good breakfast and spending time practising a particularly challenging piece of music, Georgiana settled into a chair near the window to work on some stitching and to wait to see if anyone would call.

"Are you as nervous as I am?" Elizabeth whispered.

Georgiana looked up from her stitching. "You are nervous?"

Elizabeth nodded. "Every day. I know I will become used to being Mrs. Darcy and eventually forget that people are scrutinizing me and hoping I will misstep, but that day has not yet arrived."

"But you have been married for nearly a year." Georgiana could not help but be startled that Elizabeth, who carried herself with such confidence and always seemed to know what to say, would be apprehensive about callers. "I have not noticed you being uneasy."

"Then, I must hide it well," Elizabeth replied with a smile. "Finding one's way in a new society is not easily done — at least not by me."

"I do not believe it," Georgiana protested. "I cannot believe it. Calls make you uneasy?"

Elizabeth nodded. "I have never had a season."

"Oh."

"We had assemblies in Meryton, and there were small soirees, but I knew everyone who would call. It was not so grand a society as here in town. Even when I would come to town and stay at Aunt Gardiner's, the callers were always the same familiar faces."

Georgiana pushed her needle through the fabric she held, drew the thread through, and repeated. "Then we shall be nervous together." She took one more stitch before looking up at Elizabeth and smiling. "At least you do not have to entertain gentlemen while considering if they will make good husbands."

"No," Elizabeth agreed with a laugh. "I do not need to do that for myself, but I do hope to help you with that very thing. It took a great deal of convincing to keep your brother from sitting here with us. So, I do not want to fail you or him." Elizabeth crossed to the window and looked out at the street. "You know I have not always been so good at judging character as I had hoped I was."

Georgiana smiled. "My brother is at least partially at fault for that."

Georgiana's brother was known for being aloof at times, especially when in a new or uncomfortable situation. He had not made a good first impression on Elizabeth and had then proceeded to misread her at every turn. It had ended in a refused offer of marriage as well as a dramatic shift in her brother's behavior as he attempted to unwind his tightly bound pride and sense of duty. For that, Georgiana would forever be indebted to Elizabeth. She knew that her debut and first season would be immeasurably easier now that her brother had his wife to help him remain relatively calm.

"I do not need an introduction." A voice carried into the room from the hall.

"I hear your grandmother has arrived," Elizabeth said as she returned to her seat. "Do you suppose she has come to call or to chaperone?" she added in a whisper.

"Chaperone, no doubt," Georgiana replied.

"Two of my favourite grandchildren," Lady Margaret said as she entered the room. "You both look fetching." She tilted her head and looked closely at Elizabeth. A brow raised. "Any news? Am I to be a great grandmother?'

"Grandmother!" Georgiana exclaimed.

"Do not scold. I am old and will not be kept in suspense. My heart will not tolerate it."

"Your heart is as strong as many younger than you, Grandmother," Georgiana chided but looked expectantly at Elizabeth for an answer.

Elizabeth's cheeks were rosy. "It is too early to say." She skewered both of them with a sharp look. "I have not even mentioned the possibility to Fitzwilliam. It could be nothing more than a miscalculation of days."

"And do miscalculations often happen for you?" asked Lady Margaret, earning another shocked "Grandmother!" from Georgiana.

"No," Elizabeth replied simply. "But that does not leave it outside the realm of possibilities."

"Have you felt ill?"

Elizabeth shrugged. "Tired but the season is taxing."

"And so is becoming a mother," Lady Margaret said with a smile. "If you find yourself feeling less than well, I would be delighted to stand at Georgiana's side at a soiree as long as it is not a musicale. There are so many young ladies who think they can play an instrument and sing but clearly cannot. What remains of my life is not long enough to have to endure such torture willingly."

Georgiana covered a giggle with her hand.

"Now, tell me, Georgiana. Do I have a hope of seeing you married before I perish?"

"Lady Margaret," Elizabeth scolded with a laugh. "You are far from perishing."

Lady Margaret smiled, and her left brow flicked up. "One never knows." She reached into the bag she had brought with her and, placing her spectacles on her nose, took up her knitting, and cast a glance at Georgiana. "I am waiting, my dear."

"I have not met any gentlemen whom I wish to marry," Georgiana replied. "But then, I suppose one cannot know if she wishes to marry a man based on a few moments of conversation between performances or in snatches while they dance."

"It is entirely possible to know if one wishes to know if she wants to find out more about a gentleman after such conversations," Lady Margaret replied. "There are none who have interested you so much as make you wish to know more about them?"

Georgiana shook her head. "Not yet."

"Well, perhaps I can find one or two today whom I think might fit the role of grandson." She waggled her eyebrows and smiled mischievously. "I have not felt this much excitement in ages. It has likely been since your mother had her debut. Your mother was so much easier to sit beside and guide than Catherine." She shook her head. "Catherine was always her own person and such a challenging one! I heard Anne was in attendance at the ball last night."

"She was," Georgiana replied, "but she did not dance. Alistair would not allow it."

"He is a good husband for her," Lady Margaret said.

"He is," Georgiana agreed. "She watched the dancing, strolled around the room a time or two, and, as I understand it because I did not witness it, won a great deal of money while playing cards."

Lady Margaret chuckled. "Her mother would be shocked to hear that her daughter was playing cards at a ball."

There was a decided gleefulness to both her grandmother's chuckle and words that made Georgiana shake her head.

"Did Mr. Ralston attend?"

"Yes, he danced the first and supper sets with Georgiana," Elizabeth answered.

"Oh, good. Then he will call. I confess I was hoping he would." She peered over her spectacles at Georgiana. "He would make an excellent grandson."

"He's Jack," Georgiana replied. "You might as well push my cousin Edward in my direction. It would be the same."

Lady Margaret's brows furrowed, and her lips pinched together in displeasure. "A grandmother can dream," she muttered. "He is such a nice boy." She turned to Elizabeth. "Speaking of nice young men, how are Mr. Bingley and his wife?"

"They are well. Jane says the twins are growing stronger and more challenging each day, as is my mother. Charles is considering giving up Netherfield and looking elsewhere for an estate to purchase."

"One should always have at least a half day's journey between oneself and a challenging relation," Lady Margaret agreed. "Ah, there he is, the very gentleman we had hoped would call. Is that not right, Georgiana?" Lady Margaret said as Mr. Kinney announced Mr. Ralston and the tea service was brought in. "And just in time for tea."

# Chapter 3

"I am expected?" Jack asked with a surreptitious glance toward Georgiana.

"Not so much expected as hoped for," Lady Margaret said with a smile. "Now, come sit here, my boy." She motioned to a chair that was between her and her granddaughter.

"We are always pleased to have you call, Mr. Ralston," Elizabeth said as she rose to pour the tea.

Jack did not miss the relieved look that passed between Georgiana and Mrs. Darcy. Perhaps not everyone was hoping to see him as much as Lady Margaret implied.

"I am always delighted to be accepted into your drawing room," he replied. "It is the expected thing for a gentleman to call upon a lady after a soiree, is it not? They have not changed the rules of propriety and politeness on me since last season, have they?"

Lady Margaret chuckled. "They have not."

"It is lovely of you to have called," Georgiana added. "Did you enjoy the ball last evening?"

Jack inclined his head indicating that he had enjoyed himself. Calls, even when made at the home of someone whom you knew, were not particularly enjoyable. The conversation was always so stilted – for propriety's sake and all that nonsense.

"It was a very enjoyable evening, although I did leave with emptier pockets than when I arrived." His lips quirked up into a half smirk. "Not that I minded so much. I had every intention of leaving my money with Mrs. Pratt."

"Did you let her win?"

Jack enjoyed how Georgiana's eyes danced with delight as her brows rose and a smile graced her lips. He shook his head and affected a somber expression. "She would not allow that. Mrs. Pratt is no fool."

Georgiana shook her head. "I am not certain I believe you."

Jack shrugged. "I might have paid less attention to my cards than I should have, but your cousin is very entertaining, which makes it a struggle."

"You did not wish to win." Georgiana's lips pursed as she attempted to hold back a grin.

"No, I did not."

"You spoil her." Lady Margaret shook her head and peered over her glasses at Jack. "As does that husband of hers," she added with a wink.

"It is so delightful to watch Mrs. Pratt's enjoyment," Jack explained. "Might I inquire as to what you are making?" There were rows and rows of neat yellow stitches spread across Lady Margaret's lap.

"I have a great-grandchild arriving soon, and he or she will need something to keep him warm."

"It is a blanket, then?"

"It is indeed."

Conversation lapsed into silence for a moment. This was the part of calling that drove Jack mad. It was worse than sitting for a quarter of an hour without moving. There was no purpose to the silence, and Jack did not care for doing things that served no purpose. He was also aware that he was wasting precious time, for, at any moment, they could be joined by some other swain who wished to steal Georgiana away from him. And yet, he could not think of a thing to say – he, Jack Ralston, who was not generally at a loss for words – ever – had not a thing to say.

"The weather is better today than yesterday," he finally said. It was not the most sparkling bit of conversation, but it did fill the silence. "The park will likely be crowded later."

"Are you going driving or riding?" Lady Margaret asked.

"I hadn't thought to do either. I just imagined that the fine weather would bring out one and all. One must not miss an opportunity to display one's self if one is fond of such things."

"And is one fond of such things?" Georgiana asked with a giggle.

"Not particularly. I enjoy watching others parade about, and I am not opposed to the conversations that often occur when so many are out, but I have no particular desire to be seen by one and all – not that I dread it, either. And you, Miss Darcy, is it something of which you are fond?" He knew the answer, but he wished to hear her say it both because he liked listening to her and because he dreaded the silence that might once again descend upon them.

"No, I do not like being on display."

"However, it is something which is hard to avoid during the season," Elizabeth added.

Again, Jack noticed the silent communication that passed between the two ladies. Women were so good at that — conversing without saying a word. If he were to guess the meaning of the two looks he had seen so far today, he would have to guess that Georgiana was neither eager to see him nor was she all that comfortable with her position of sought-after debutante.

"It is indeed," he agreed. "We could have the knocker removed. You would get far fewer callers if it was not in place. But alas, it was not removed soon enough to avoid my intrusion." He smiled at her as he said it.

"You are not an intrusion!" Georgiana exclaimed.

"But he is," Jack muttered as the door opened and another gentleman, a Mr. Allerton, was announced. He watched as Georgiana's posture straightened as she greeted him. She was clearly not at ease with her position of sought-after debutante.

"Allerton," Jack said with a nod of his head. "You may have my chair."

"You are leaving?" Georgiana asked in surprise.

"I do not wish to overstay my welcome, and I promised Mrs. Pratt I would take tea with her."

Georgiana smiled. "You are very good to her."

"Thank you," Jack said with a grin. "I find it best to stay on the good side of one who can wield a foil as skillfully as your cousin."

It was more than that, of course, and from the rise of Georgiana's brow, he suspected she knew it. However, he hoped she would not press the matter further. Allerton did not need to know about how Mrs. Pratt had become something of a sister to him. Allerton was a fine enough fellow, but he was known to embellish tales at times. Jack had no desire to have it spread about the ton that he was infatuated with his friend's wife – he wasn't, but it was likely what would become of the tale once Allerton had put a polish on it.

Mr. Allerton was settling into the chair Jack had vacated as the drawing room door closed. Georgiana was smiling at him just as she smiled at everyone. Jack gathered his hat and coat from Mr. Kinney and exited Darcy House with his brain all in a muddle. She had not been eager to see him. She had smiled at both him and Allerton with very little difference between the two smiles. However, there had been a sadness in her eyes when he had told her he was leaving.

He turned and looked at Darcy House's closed door before climbing into his carriage. A year! It would be a year next month, and he had made little, if any, progress in securing Georgiana Darcy's interest, let alone her heart. He entered his carriage just as another was drawing to a stop behind his to deliver, no doubt, another caller for Miss Darcy. He shook his head as he settled into his seat and the door was closed. This would not do. He had never struggled to make an impression on a lady before this. His most significant difficulty had always been keeping the ladies from becoming too attached to him.

He had money, he was handsome with a certain prowess about him, and he was charming. There was, in his mind, very little to keep a lady from admiring him, save for an attachment to another. But — Georgiana had no suitor. If she did, Anne would have certainly told him. There must be some other reason for her rejection of his attentions.

"You are a friend," Anne said later when Jack had aired his consternation with her. "Georgiana does not see you as others do. Did I not already canvas this when we discussed my plan?" She picked up her cup of tea and took a sip before discarding it in favour of a sandwich. "I swear I have never been so hungry so often in my entire life."

"I, on the other hand, have always been this hungry this often for my entire life."

Anne giggled, and Jack sighed.

"I see the point of your plan more clearly now. I cannot continue as I have been. I must either change my tactics or give her up completely." He took a slow sip of his tea as he considered giving Georgiana Darcy up in favour of someone who readily fell for his charm. The thought settled in like a crushing weight.

"You must do as I say. Make her miss you." Anne gave him a stern look. "I *will* have you for a cousin."

"That is not for us to determine." Moroseness, an unusual state of mind for Jack, wrapped itself around him like a scratchy barn blanket which one only used when the air was too cold to refuse it. He placed his still half-filled cup on the table. "I shall not call on her again."

"Not at all?" Anne's eyes were wide with surprise.

"Not at all."

"Will you not take her for a drive?"

He shrugged and shook his head. "I may dance with her, but never the first dance and never more than one." It stung just to say such things, but he knew he must make a marked change in his behaviour. "I will still play the part of a friend." How he was growing to hate that word! He drew a breath and blew it out slowly. "And if she falls for another, I will wish her happy and be on my way."

"You cannot mean it!"

He shook his head. "You must believe me when I say I do not want to mean it, but I will not force myself upon a lady who is determined to refuse me. I could not bear to see her unhappy."

Anne's mouth hung open.

"It is your plan," he added. "I will play the part of a friend but appear to be looking elsewhere for a Mrs. Ralston."

Anne snapped her mouth closed. "You are taking the plan too far! I had intended for you to tease and taunt not desert her."

Again, Jack drew in a deep breath and blew it out slowly. "I am not deserting her. I am allowing her to choose."

Anne's left eyebrow rose as she scowled at him.

"It is how I wish to parry."

Anne shook her head. "One does not win a match by dropping his sword." She rolled her eyes and huffed. "Very well. I suppose you will not be moved on this?"

"I am resolved." The left side of his mouth tipped upward in a half-smile. "I shall not distance myself so far that she will forget me. I said I would still play the part of charming, devil-may-care friend. It is your plan," he repeated.

"It is not," Anne refuted.

"Yes, I believe it is. Did you not tell me to stop calling on her, stop dancing with her, and seek another?"

"I said eventually – as in a gradual withdrawal of affections, not an abrupt reversal."

"Would you care for another sandwich?" Jack moved the plate towards her.

"That is it? You will discuss this no further?"

"There is nothing left to discuss." Anne could argue her points over and over again, and he could refute them just as many times.

Nothing would change. He had played the part of smitten swain for nearly a year and made not an inch of progress. He would not continue down a losing path.

Anne selected a sandwich from the plate, and Jack did the same.

"You will, of course, warn me if your cousin has lost her heart to another, so that I might be prepared for any announcement?" He would need time to find somewhere to be, so that his mourning could be done in private, for he knew that even to hear of her being given to another would crush his heart and to have to witness it without a time to harden himself to it would be unbearable.

"I should not," Anne grumbled, "but I will."

# Chapter 4

One week later, throngs of people moved from their carriages on Bow Street, up the steps, between the columns, and through the doors of the theatre while Comedy and Tragedy kept watch. Tonight, Comedy would shine from the stage while Tragedy waited his turn to play another day. But neither moved a stony lip in protest of not being adored by this mass of people, for they knew that soon, the fickle amusement seekers of London would shift their allegiance from one to the other for the few hours they would spend within these great stone walls.

Just beyond where Tragedy and Comedy stood watch and through those great doors, gentlemen and ladies mingled in the vestibule, greeting one another and surveying each other – some with covert glances and other's raised brows and lifted chins peering down their noses at nearly everyone. In the midst of this crowd and for the first time ever when attending a play, Georgiana placed her hand on the arm of a gentleman who was neither her brother or cousin.

Mr. Bernard Tibbett smiled down at her and then, covering her hand with his free one, led her to the grand staircase as they followed Darcy and Elizabeth up to the landing and on into the saloon leading to the private boxes.

Georgiana's stomach fluttered. She had spoken with gentlemen at soirees and danced with them at balls, but until this moment, she had not spent a full evening in the presence of one – just one — gentleman. However, while on a drive through the park when Mr. Tibbett had asked her to accompany him to the play this evening, she had been unable to formulate a good reason to refuse. She enjoyed the gentleman's company, and, while her stomach might be nervously fluttering now, it was not because he caused her to be uneasy. He put her at ease nearly as readily as her brother, her uncle, her cousin, Mr. Pratt, or Jack did. There was no nagging sense of distrust.

That last bit made her stomach do an extra tumble. While she might trust the man beside her, she was not certain she trusted her ability to choose who should or should not be trusted. That mechanism of her mind had betrayed her once already. So, while she was excited to be taking a seat next to Mr. Tibbett this evening and speaking with Elizabeth later of him in terms of a possible match, she was only tentatively excited. She would not allow herself to give her emotions full reign. She would be cautious.

Mr. Tibbett waited for Georgiana to be seated before he took his place next to her. "Have you ever seen *As You Like It*?"

"No, but I have read it."

"Which character do you prefer?" He smoothed his jacket by giving its hem a firm tug.

"Orlando," she replied with a smile.

"Not the heroine, Rosalind?"

Georgiana shook her head. "No, I do like Rosalind, but Orlando is so noble and kind. What he does for the old man and even his brother is endearing."

"Might I do well to be jealous of this fictitious gentleman?" Mr. Tibbett asked with a chuckle.

Georgiana raised a brow and gave him a slightly imperious, though playful, look. "No more so than any other gentleman be he real or imagined."

"Is that so?" Mr. Tibbett shifted slightly, so that he was closer to her and could speak in lower tones. "Are there any particular non-fictitious chaps of whom I should be aware?"

Georgiana blinked. She was not comfortable with such a forward question even if it was said lightly. Flirting was not what she preferred. She would rather that a gentleman just be himself and speak to her as a friend would. However, it seemed flirting was part of the game that was played during the season, for the only gentleman who had come to call on her who did speak to her as a friend was Jack. She sighed. He had not been to see her in a week, so she had been subjected to far more flirting without a reprieve than she would have liked.

"Just my brother," she replied with a smile, causing the gentleman next to her to straighten. "The rest you shall have to ferret out on your own."

"The rest?" he asked in surprise.

There were no others, but Mr. Tibbett did not need to know that. So, Georgiana merely shrugged and looked at the boxes across from them and then to the left and right as far as she could see without leaning forward. "It is a full house tonight, is it not?"

"It seems to be," her brother replied. "But the crush is not so oppressive when one has his own place."

"Indeed!" Elizabeth replied with a laugh. "If only assemblies had boxes where one could hide away from the masses."

Georgiana smiled as her brother lifted Elizabeth's hand and kissed his wife's knuckles, and she was reminded that teasing and flirting were not always unpleasant nor were they something confined to the participants of the season. However, it was so much more delightful to watch two people so completely in love tease and flirt than it was to bear what felt like the practiced role of a gentleman when he called on or danced with her.

"I see Anne has managed to get Alistair to take her to the theater." Elizabeth nodded toward a box across and to the left of them. "She was hoping he would allow her to attend when she called two days ago."

"Anne – Mrs. Pratt – is my cousin," Georgiana explained to Mr. Tibbett.

"Ah, I know of Pratt and his wife," Mr. Tibbett said. "I did not, however, recognize Mrs. Pratt's Christian name, so I thank you for the clarification." He looked across the expanse of the theater. "It seems Mr. Ralston has joined them."

"He is their particular friend," Georgiana said, looking again at Pratt's box. "Oh," she said in surprise. "Who is that with him?" A pretty looking blonde was giggling behind her fan while Jack was no doubt sharing some delightful tale.

"I will be of no help," said Elizabeth. "I am still learning who is who."

Mr. Tibbett squinted as he looked in the direction of the lady in question. Then, his eyes grew wide, and he blinked. "It appears to be Miss Parkes. Hmm, I did not know she enjoyed the theater. I thought she said she found it a bore." He shrugged. "Perhaps Mr. Ralston's presence makes it more enjoyable." He leaned back in his seat.

"You know her, then?" Georgiana asked.

He nodded. "Yes, Miss Hazel Parkes, third daughter of Mr. Geoffery Parkes of Warwickshire. This is her second season."

"Warwickshire?" Georgiana asked in interest. Jack had attended a house party in Warwickshire with Alistair last year.

"Have you ever been there?" Mr. Tibbett asked.

"No, but Mr. Pratt and Mr. Ralston attended a house party there shortly before my cousin and Mr. Pratt married."

Mr. Tibbett's head bobbed up and down slowly. "At Stanton's," he said. "I was there as was Miss Parkes."

"Oh." Georgiana tipped her head and studied what she could make out of the lady sitting next to Jack. "Is she nice?"

"Miss Parkes?"

"Yes."

Mr. Tibbett shrugged. "I suppose so, yes."

Georgiana wished to know if the lady put on airs and pretended to be what she was not, for she did not wish for Jack to tie himself to someone who would not care for him as he deserved. However, she would not ask such a thing. For if she did, Mr. Tibbett might think that Jack was one of the gentlemen of whom he should be jealous, but he was not. He was Jack — kind, considerate, funny, endearing Jack. She sighed as the noise in the theater faded into silence, and the play began. She cast one more glance at Jack and Miss Parkes. Jack was leaning toward Anne and whispering something to her that caused her to swat him with her fan and Alistair to laugh. He really was charming, she told herself, and for a moment, she wished that she was sitting comfortably next to the charming Jack instead of here with Mr. Tibbett. Then, after one last look at her cousin's box, she turned her attention to the stage and allowed herself to be swept away by the equally as charming Orlando.

~*~*~

"We must go see Anne," Elizabeth said at the beginning of the intermission. "And personally, I would find a walk to be lovely after sitting for so long. What say you, Georgiana?"

"Hmm?" Georgiana slowly turned her head toward Elizabeth. Her mind was still on the empty stage, contemplating the latest scene.

"I said that it would be a fine thing to take a walk and visit with Anne."

Georgiana smiled slowly. "Oh, of course. We must, or Anne will feel ignored."

"And we do not want that," Darcy muttered.

Georgiana raised a brow at the comment.

"She will make certain she is not ignored," Darcy explained. "She is Aunt Catherine's daughter."

"She allowed us to ignore her for years," Georgiana replied.

"Yes, but she has decided that she will no longer be over-looked," Darcy refuted, "and once she has made a decision, there is little which seems able to stop her."

"Except her husband," Elizabeth said with a smile. "Mr. Tibbett, you do not mind accompanying us to Mr. Pratt's box, do you?"

"Oh, not at all." Mr. Tibbett stood and offered Georgiana his hand in assistance in rising. "A walk would be most welcome, and it is not as if any but Mrs. Pratt are strangers to me."

So it was, that not many minutes later, the group of four stood inside Mr. Pratt's box, doubling its number of occupants.

"Oh, I had hoped you would visit," Anne cried in delight. "I

~254~

was just telling Alistair that we should make our way around to you, but he would not hear of it." Her lips pursed, and a brow rose. "He thinks I am too fragile for such an excursion." Her lips slid into a small smile as she spoke, letting one and all know that she was not truly put out with her husband.

"It would have involved a lot of jostling and bumping," Alistair inserted.

"And I, for one, would find such treatment ghastly difficult to abide." Jack placed his hand over his heart with a flourish. "So, it was not a limiting of his wife's activity, but an act of utmost sympathy for a friend."

This comment, of course, drew giggles from both Mrs. Pratt and Miss Parkes as well as Georgiana and Elizabeth. The gentlemen of the party were by varying amounts less amused. Darcy chuckled softly. Mr. Tibbett made no sound of enjoyment at all, and Alistair shook his head and apologized for his friend.

"I am afraid a trip to the theatre always has an unhinging effect on Jack," Alistair said. "He will for the next day and a half fancy himself an actor."

Jack raised a hand in protest. "Have you not attended the script, my friend?"

"As carefully as the next person," Alistair replied flatly.

"I fear you have not," Jack countered.

Alistair shook his head once again, this time with a great sigh. "I should not say this, but please explain."

"Oh, yes, do!" Anne added.

Jack straightened, cleared his throat, and in dramatic fashion said, "Has the bard not said all the world's a stage, my friend?" He placed a hand on Alistair's shoulder. "And all the men," he motioned to himself, "and women," he motioned to Miss Parkes, "merely players. They have their exits and their entrances." He placed his hand on his heart again with a flourish. "And one man in his time plays many parts."

"Bravo!" cried Miss Parkes. "That was very well done, Mr. Ralston."

Jack smiled and took as sweeping a bow as he could in such close quarters.

"Really, Jack, you are too much at times," Alistair muttered.

"It is the theatre," Jack countered. "If there is anywhere in all the world where one might be too much, it is here. Are not the players hired because they excel at too much?"

"You have a point," Darcy agreed.

"Thank you, sir," Jack said with a small bow.

"Might it be possible that you return to just enough?" Alistair asked.

There was such a look of pleading in the poor man's eyes that it caused Georgiana to press her lips together to keep from laughing.

Jack acquiesced, and introductions were then made.

"How are you finding the play?" Elizabeth asked Anne and Miss Parkes.

"Delightful," said Miss Parkes and Anne agreed.

"I thought you had mentioned not enjoying the theatre," said Mr. Tibbett, whose posture, Georgiana noticed, was more rigid than it had been all evening.

Miss Parkes tipped her head and gave him a smile much as a governess might a poor confused child. "I believe what I said was that the theatre is too full of tragedy for my liking, and I am certain you would not see me here if this play were a tragedy. There is far too much worry and woe in the world. I have no need to come to the theater to be reminded of that. Comedies, however, I adore. I do not think one could keep me away from the theatre if there was the opportunity to laugh and feel one's heart lighten."

"I see," said Mr. Tibbett before falling silent.

"I admit I also prefer comedies to tragedies," Georgiana said to fill the void. "However, it is the ability of the players to transport me to a different time and place that truly captures my mind and spirit. I fear I could never be an actress." She glanced at her brother who had raised an eyebrow at the comment. "Not that I ever would be," she added with a small smile. "I do not have the ability of Mr. Ralston to affect airs."

"Ah, with practice, one might be surprised," Jack interjected.

"No," Georgiana insisted. "I am certain I would never feel at ease on the stage."

"Nor would I," said Miss Parkes, laying a hand on Georgiana's arm. "So many eyes! Singing at a musicale is trying enough, and there are never the masses of people in attendance there that there are here."

"That is so true," Georgiana agreed. "I do not sing, however."

"You may not sing, but you play the piano better than anyone I know," said Miss Parkes.

"Thank you." Georgiana attempted to keep the confusion she felt from showing in her expression.

"I attended the musicale at Winsley House, although I did not exhibit. I had a sore throat," Miss Parkes explained.

"I should like to hear you sing."

"Her voice is divine," said Jack, causing Miss Parkes to blush.

"She sang at several musicales last year, and there was a bit of singing at Stanton's."

"There was?" Mr. Tibbett's features registered his surprise.

"On a walk around the garden. Miss Parkes and a couple of other ladies were singing as they went," Jack explained.

"Oh," Mr. Tibbett replied.

Then, Mr. Tibbett once again lapsed into silence, which was odd. He had always been a great conversationalist on every other occasion in which he had been in company with Georgiana. She would like to ask him about it, but she thought it too great an impertinence, so she did not. Thankfully, none of the others in the group were so lacking in words as Mr. Tibbett, and conversation about the décor, the weather, and a few other sundry and mundane topics was had.

"You will all come to tea tomorrow, will you not?" Anne asked Elizabeth and Georgiana as Darcy began to mention the need to return to their box. "Miss Parkes has already agreed to come. I think we shall all be great friends."

"I would like that," Georgiana replied.

"Am I invited?" Jack asked in teasing tone.

"No," Alistair replied. "You and I are going to Angelo's so that you can attempt once again to discover my tell."

"If you would allow your wife to tell me," Jack replied.

Alistair shook his head. "She has not even told me."

"I prefer winning far too much," Anne said with a giggle. "Not that he allows me near a foil at present," she added.

"As he should not," said Jack.

"Thank you," said Alistair.

"Come," said Darcy. "We really must return to our box."

# Chapter 5

The shouts of soldiers taking part in a drill greeted Georgiana and her friends as they entered Hyde Park.

"Is this not exciting?" Anne asked. "Not only will we have a refreshing walk but also a show."

"We are not walking far," Alistair cautioned. "I cannot believe I allowed you to talk me into letting you out of the carriage."

Anne smiled sweetly at him and fluttered her lashes. "You are the very best husband."

"Indeed, I am," he muttered, "or perhaps the daftest."

"I cast my vote for the second option," said Jack with a grin, earning himself a glare from his friend. "We promise only to walk to those trees." He pointed to a group not far off. "Then, I shall spread out the blanket and your wife may take her ease as we listen to the goings on."

"It is a lovely day," said Miss Parkes. "I had feared the fog would never lift, but it has."

"There is nothing so gloomy as a foggy day when one wishes to be in the sunshine," Anne agreed.

Georgiana could not agree more. Foggy days were delightful when spent reading or playing the piano, but they were dreadful for trips to the park. Not only did they obscure the beauty that could be found here, but they also wreaked havoc on a lady's coiffeur. She was particularly glad that the fine weather would not reduce her hair to the appearance of a shabby old mop since she was not just strolling on the arm of her brother but that of a suitor – or so Mr. Tibbett appeared to be. He had not officially spoken to her on the subject, but he had called every day since their trip to the theatre four days ago.

"Do you wish to stay here with your cousin, or would you prefer to walk a distance further?" Mr. Tibbett asked as Jack unfurled the blanket and Alistair caught the end to lower it onto the ground.

"I suppose a short distance further would not be unthinkable, especially if we are within sight of the others." Her pulse had quickened at his suggestion. Ever since her ordeal in Ramsgate, she had been hesitant to be alone with a gentleman anywhere. However, if they were within sight of others, then nothing untoward could happen or be said to have happened.

"We shall stay close," he assured her.

"I have not taken a walk with a gentleman alone," she explained.

"We are not alone," he assured her, waving a hand at the numerous people who filled the park.

She giggled. "I know there are others here, but which of them is a gossip? Who will delight in crafting an exceptional tale of impropriety? Will it be that gentleman with the walking stick over by the flowers or the lady on his arm?"

"Or neither," Mr. Tibbett said. "I think we are safe as long as we just stroll." He smiled at her. "However, a well-crafted tale would not be such a horrid thing. I am beginning to believe I would not be opposed at all to being tied to you." He patted her hand. "Not at all."

"Oh." It was all that she could think of to say at such an almost, but not quite, declaration of admiration. Her brows knit together. Strange. Her heart did not feel fluttery. There was no warmth of delight spreading through her limbs and onto her face. Perhaps this was how one felt when she was properly and sincerely in love instead of merely swept away by the charming words of a handsome scoundrel. It was somewhat disappointing, but she was sure she would get used to it. She would have to ask either Anne or Elizabeth about this later.

They came to a stop a good fifty feet from where the others were seated on the blanket and delving into the basket of treats Anne had insisted upon bringing. "I see Ralston is being his excessively entertaining self," Mr. Tibbett commented as the ladies and even Alistair laughed.

"He is amusing," Georgiana said with a smile.

Mr. Tibbett made a little, disgruntled sound. "Annoyingly so," he muttered.

"Do you not like him?" Georgiana asked in surprise. How could anyone not like Jack Ralston? He was perhaps the friendliest person in all of London.

"Only his airs," Mr. Tibbett replied. "As a person, he is a fine gentleman – all that is proper and charming, but those airs." He shook his head.

Georgiana's brows knit once again. Airs? Jack? "You do not think him sincere?"

"No, it is not that," Mr. Tibbett replied. "He is, I am sure, a very sincere person. He is just silly."

"I find nothing absurd about Mr. Ralston." How could he speak of an endearing person like Jack in such a fashion? Her heart felt the slight most severely.

"It is nothing to fret about, my dear. It is just a difference of opinion about the sort of person we prefer. I prefer Pratt to his friend. Pratt is a serious sort of fellow."

Georgiana did not respond, for she was unsure of what she wished to say. She liked both Alistair and Jack. She did not prefer one over the other.

"I see by your silence I have offended you. I must apologize. That was not my intent."

"Of course," Georgiana replied with a small smile.

"Come," Mr. Tibbett said. "We will return, and all will be well. It is not that I do not like Ralston, you see. I am willing to be in his company and endure his teasing, even if it is not what I prefer."

"That is good," Georgiana muttered. As they walked toward where Anne was seated, a troubling thought gripped Georgiana. "Do you expect your wife to prefer the same sorts of people you prefer?" she asked, bringing him to a stop.

"Does not every gentleman?"

"I had not thought they did. At least, that is not how my brother sees things." Fitzwilliam had at one time been more particular in his choices and on insisting that they were the only correct way to view things, but since he had met Elizabeth, he had changed. He was now quite accepting of a variety of opinions. Even if he did still prefer to have his acknowledged as correct, he always considered the views of others.

"Your brother has married well. He and Mrs. Darcy seem to suit each other perfectly."

"But they did not when they met."

"She came to see things as he did, as it should be."

Georgiana shook her head. "No, it was quite the opposite."

Mr. Tibbett's brows shot up. "That is most unusual."

Her brother and Elizabeth were not the only people she knew who had married and were happy despite being more different than alike. "Mr. Pratt and my cousin Anne have very different personalities, and yet they get on very well together."

"Yes, but she seems to mind his suggestions."

"As she should?" Georgiana asked sharply. This was an altogether shocking side of Mr. Tibbett that she had not yet seen, and she did not like it one bit. In fact, at the moment, it was making her wish to bid him a curt good day and be on her way. However, she would not be so rude.

"Is that not what proper young ladies are taught?" He wore a look of complete and utter confusion.

Georgiana shook her head. "I should like to have an almond cake if there are any remaining."

"Have I offended again?" he asked.

Georgiana raised one brow.

"I have?"

"Do you truly not know how?" She could not keep the incredulity she felt from either her voice or her features. How could he not realize that such an autocratic attitude was offensive? Had she not already said that his views were counter to those of her brother? And if she had not been taught to believe as he did, then, did not his question about proper young ladies imply that she was somehow not proper?

"No. I plead ignorance."

He had that correct! "It matters not. We are not betrothed or even courting, so there is no need to have a discussion such as we are having."

"But we might be," he said with what almost sounded like desperation in his voice. "Mightn't we? Eventually? Do we not rub together well?"

Georgiana shrugged. "I thought we did, but now, I am not entirely certain." She pursed her lips and glanced at her friends. "Both Alistair and Mr. Ralston are my friends, and I would wish to keep them – always."

His eyes lit with understanding. "Of course, I would not restrict your seeing your friends."

"Even if they are silly?" she pressed.

"Even if they are silly," he agreed.

"And what if I found a new friend who was not up to your standards? Would I be allowed to keep that friend as well?" She very much doubted it.

He paused. "It is perhaps not ideal, but permissible, I suppose."

She shook her head. "I am still unsure we would suit."

This was something else about which she would have to speak to Elizabeth or Anne. She knew that many ladies did bow completely to their husband's wishes and desire. They even bowed to the opinion of each gentleman with whom they danced in an effort to secure a husband, but Georgiana had always thought that she would meet someone who would love her as she was and not wish to change her. However, that was before Mr. Wickham. Perhaps what she sought was not reality. Perhaps that was as fanciful a dream as the idea of warming pleasure sweeping over your person when a gentleman declared he would like to have you as a wife. Perhaps young ladies who married as happily as Elizabeth and Anne had were among the fortunate few. She hoped it was not true, but perhaps it was. The thought was very unsettling.

"We have known one another such a short time," Mr. Tibbett soothed. "There is yet time to discover all we need to know and to grow in our fondness for each other, is there not?"

Fondness? At this moment, Georgiana felt little fondness for the gentleman, but then, one did not always feel as one should when she was put out. "I am certain you are correct," she replied with as pleasant a tone of voice as she could muster.

"I believe you wished for an almond cake, did you not?"

He was looking hopefully at her, but there was something in his expression that seemed too confident for her liking at present. It was almost as if he thought he had swayed her opinion to agree with him. She attempted to check her displeasure but could not quite accomplish it. Removing her hand from his arm, she smiled sweetly. "They are my favourites, but I do not know what Anne has had her cook prepare. I might find something I prefer more." Then, she left him standing though it was only for a moment before he recovered from his shock and caught up with her.

"Is all well?" Jack asked a short time later as he presented her with a tin of sweets.

"Of course, all is well," Georgiana replied. It was not, but Jack was not the person with whom she needed to speak about the thoughts which were troubling her. "I am merely being pensive. It happens occasionally," she added with a smile.

"If you insist," he muttered.

From the look on his face, she knew that he did not believe her. He seemed to know her well. Much better than Mr. Tibbett did!

"I do."

"Then I shall ask no more," he returned. "We are all allowed to have our own thoughts and opinions. It would be a rather dull world if we did not."

Dull. That was it! That is how she felt about Mr. Tibbett and his view of what a proper lady should be. "It most certainly would be a colourless existence if we were all alike in every detail and thought."

Jack glanced at Mr. Tibbett, who was now attending their conversation most carefully. "What say you, Tibbett? Do you prefer everyone agree with you, or do you enjoy a good verbal joust?"

"Oh, a joust!" Anne cried.

Georgiana giggled, and Alistair whispered to his wife that she was not the person to whom the question was addressed.

Mr. Tibbett cast a wary glance at Georgiana. "To be completely candid, I prefer harmony."

Miss Parkes snorted softly.

"It is the truth." Mr. Tibbett gave the lady a stern look.

Her eyes sparkled with impertinence. "As long as that harmony is to your liking," she said with a laugh.

"I do not see why it is wrong to wish others to agree with you," he argued in return.

One of Miss Parkes' eyebrows rose. "Let me put a question to you, Mr. Pratt and Mr. Ralston, as I already know Mr. Tibbett's response since he explained it to me so well at Stanton's. Do you or did you while circulating among the debutantes of the season prefer that they all agree with everything you say to them as they are taught? Or would you rather the young lady possesses her own opinions and not be afraid to voice them for fear of rejection?"

"I beg your pardon?" Anne asked in surprise. "Young ladies – all young ladies – are taught to simply agree with gentlemen? On everything?"

"Some are," Georgiana answered.

"Indeed? Huh." She shook her head. "I thought that was just some preposterous idea my mother and Mrs. Jenkinson had concocted to make me hold my tongue."

Alistair laughed. "It would be something your mother might do, but I fear she was not scheming when she told you that." He lifted her hand to his lips. "And I am glad you were not the sort to blindly follow. I enjoy hearing your true thoughts." He looked to Miss Parkes. "How could I love my wife as I do if she were pretending to be something she is not?"

Miss Parkes smiled.

"Here! Here!" Jack agreed heartily. "A lady should be in possession of a good mind and be able to speak it fittingly." He chuckled. "I would not wish for a nagging harridan any more than I would wish for a milquetoast maiden."

Mr. Tibbett said nothing. He just glowered at Miss Parkes, who smiled in a most satisfied fashion.

# *Chapter 6*

"She's watching you," Anne hissed in Jack's ear before easing into a chair with his assistance. She sighed in relief as she wiggled her feet and then added, "Go ask her to dance."

Jack casually glanced over his shoulder in Georgiana's direction. "Do you think it best?"

Anne sighed in exasperation. "Yes. Did I not just minutes ago explain to you how she needs to be reminded that you exist and are a wonderful person – far more wonderful than that Mr. Tibbett who keeps calling on her."

Jack could hear the irritation in Anne's voice. She had had several things to say about *that Mr. Tibbett* as they drove home from the park yesterday. He had thought Miss Parkes was going to expire from giggling. His lips tipped up in a small amused smile. Miss Parkes had added her own disparaging comments as well. He shook his head slightly. And to think that Miss Parkes actually thought that Tibbett could be and should be brought up to scratch. Ah well, love, much like beauty, was in the eye of the beholder. Who was he to discourage Miss Parkes from attempting to win Mr. Tibbett's heart, especially if it meant keeping the gentleman from marrying Georgiana?

"I had thought she would send him packing after whatever it

was at the park." Jack gave his sleeves a tug and then affected a position of nonchalance against the wall next to where Anne was seated.

"She's a Darcy," Anne grumbled.

"Why does your husband allow you to attend these things?" Lady Margaret interrupted Anne before she could launch into what Jack knew would be a commentary on the interminable patience of her Darcy cousins.

"To keep you company was tonight's reason," Anne replied with a smile as her grandmother settled into the chair beside her. "And I will have you know, just as I did him, that I can sit around here just as readily as I can at home."

Lady Margaret leaned closer to her granddaughter. "There is a certain exhilarating something about just being here, is there not?"

"Indeed," Jack muttered, giving Lady Margaret a wink and a mischievous grin when she looked his direction. "Such strategies and posturing! It is almost as entertaining as a play."

Lady Margaret shook her head. "I am afraid you are wrong, Mr. Ralston. This soiree is much more entertaining than a play, for there is no scripted ending. No one knows the outcome of tonight's story. Anything could happen."

Jack inclined his head in acceptance of her statement and then added, "not all unscripted endings are happy, however."

"Indeed, they are not! Some are magnificent tragedies." She smirked. "Such as why you are not yet my grandson."

Jack blinked, and his indifferent expression slipped for a moment. He raised a brow in question at Anne, who shook her head.

"You have not called at Darcy House in two weeks as of tomorrow." Lady Margaret gave him a disapproving look.

"I have no intention of calling." He turned his attention back to the dancing. Georgiana was so light on her feet.

"Are you set on that Parkes girl then?" Lady Margaret asked.

"No." He spared her a brief look – long enough to see that her expression had not softened. "There is nothing to fear," he added.

She continued to look at him with that stern expression for a full minute before turning to Anne. "Where is your husband?"

"Speaking with Darcy."

She huffed. "He should be here. With you. I feel a need for Mr. Ralston to take me for a turn around the garden, but we cannot leave you unattended."

"I will be required to claim my partner as soon as this set is finished," Jack said.

"Then sit here," Lady Margaret demanded, motioning to the chair next to her with her head.

Jack remained where he was until she lifted a brow and her scowl deepened. Then, with a sigh, he acquiesced and sat.

"I like very much that you do not bow to my every whim," she began, "but know that there is a limit, Mr. Ralston."

"I will make a note of that," he replied.

"You do not wish to marry Miss Parkes?" she asked.

He shook his head.

"And my granddaughter ?"

Jack drew and released a breath.

"I will take that as an affirmative."

Jack nodded.

"Then why have you not called?"

Jack looked around her to Anne. "That is per your other grand-daughter's suggestion."

Lady Margaret looked at Anne in surprise.

"He is not following the plan as I prescribed," Anne muttered behind her fan.

"Someone needs to explain to me why I must spend my few remaining days fretting that my youngest granddaughter will marry that..." she clamped her lips closed as if she had reconsidered what she was about to say and deemed it not appropriate. Lifting her chin, she concluded, "Mr. Tibbett."

"If you call on me tomorrow, I can explain," Anne assured her.

"I would rather be at Darcy House entertaining Mr. Ralston." She shot Jack a displeased look and shook her head. "She has not told me a thing, but she is not happy."

Jack held up his hands in a plea of innocence as she skewered him again with a most severe look.

"Please tell me you are at least going to dance with her?" Lady Margaret whispered as the music faded to a close.

"The next set," he said with a smile.

"You did not tell me!" Anne cried.

If she were not smiling, he might have thought her truly cross, but her delight was evident in both her smile and the sparkle in her eye. "It is such a treat to surprise you, Mrs. Pratt. How could I tell you and miss out on such pleasure?" He rose and straightened his jacket. "I will make my way across to where she is standing with her brother and his wife if that is acceptable to you ladies, and I will do my part to let her know she should consider me along with Mr. Tibbett." He gave them a small bow and took his leave.

"I do love a bit of a scamp." He heard Lady Margaret say as he walked away.

The appellation brought a smile to his lips. His mother had used that word to describe him since he was in leading strings. His curiosity and love for adventure had helped him earn the title of mischief-making scamp, and he had missed the exhilaration that came from teasing and charming – which is what his mischief-making had grown into as he aged. He had spent much of every season, up until last year, laughing and having a grand time at these soirees. He was not a rake. However, he did like to see a lady smile and giggle, and he was not above sneaking a quick kiss in a dark corner should the opportunity arise. However, that is where his fun stopped. He had no desire to be forced into marriage until he was well and truly besotted with the lady. He sighed. Much as he was with Miss Georgiana Darcy. However, he would not compromise her for all the gold in England. It was his desire to be allowed to court her, which had led him to put away his less serious nature. He smiled. Well as much as such a nature could be put away. It was always there. Lying just below the surface with a ready quip. But he had attempted to act the part of a properly proper gent to win Mr. Darcy's approval.

Now, having given up his plan to win Georgiana through being ever present, he had slipped quite handily back into his playfulness. Miss Parkes had suggested it. She had mentioned how he had been quite irresistible to many young debutantes for the very reason that he was always ready with a smile and a laugh. Surely, Miss Darcy was not so different from the other ladies that wore debutante white and hoped to be courted by a winsome gentleman, she had said. She had also assured him that it would make

Miss Darcy miss him more if he were not so dull as every other gentleman who was attempting to be a proper suitor.

"Miss Darcy," he said with a bow. "I do believe the next set is ours. Mr. Darcy, Mrs. Darcy," he acknowledged each of them with a bow of his head.

"I have not had you in my drawing room in some time," Elizabeth said with a smile.

He chuckled. "Do you miss me?"

"You are far more entertaining than some of the callers we have had." Elizabeth laughed lightly.

"Ah, the court jester." Jack placed his hand on his heart as if wounded and sighed, causing Elizabeth to continue laughing.

"I assure you, you are missed," she replied. "It is always pleasant to have a call from a friend."

"Indeed, it is," Georgiana agreed.

Friend. There was that word again.

"Ah," Jack replied, "but is it not better to have chairs available to those who might be more than friends? Is that not the purpose of the season?"

Darcy chuckled. "I would rather that all the chairs be filled with horrible old matrons rather than young hopeful swains, but your presence I might not abhor."

"Unless I was a young hopeful swain?" Jack knew it was rather bold to ask it, but he did wish to know Mr. Darcy's opinion of him.

The man tipped his head and rubbed his chin as he considered Jack. He shook his head and then with a shrug and a look of surprise said, "No, you, I could tolerate even as a young hopeful swain."

"I shall keep that in mind," Jack assured him. There was something interesting about the way Mr. Darcy's lips curved up slightly into a contained smile. Did the man suspect more than Jack thought?

The musicians had taken up their instruments, and couples were gathering on the floor.

"We should take our places." He extended his arm to Georgiana and gave a parting bow of his head to her brother and his wife.

"I should like it if you called," Georgiana said as they made their way to where the others were lining up.

"As a friend or a suitor?"

Georgiana blinked, and her steps faltered. "I am not certain I understand your question."

"Your sister wishes me to call as a friend, and your brother has given me leave to call as a suitor. I was just wondering which you would prefer."

She blinked again, and her brows drew together as she took her place across from him. "Would you call as either?" Her voice was filled with incredulity as if the concept of him as a suitor was a completely new thought to her.

"I would prefer one over the other," he said as the music began. "However," he said as they touched hands and began their figures, "it is not my preference that matters."

Georgiana's mouth formed an *o*, and her eyes widened the tiniest amount. Anne and Lady Margaret would be pleased to know he had presented himself as an option and so boldly.

He and Georgiana wove their way in, out, and around the other dancers as well as down and back up the line but spoke not a word. Jack enjoyed watching the various perplexed expressions that crossed Georgiana's face each time they joined hands.

Finally, the music faded, the steps had all been completed, and it was time to form the next line.

"What of Miss Parkes?" Georgiana asked in a whisper.

"She is a friend," he answered.

"Are you not courting her?"

"No," he replied honestly.

Again, her lovely lips formed an *o* while her brows drew together. "Does she know?" The question was asked almost too softly to be heard, and the look of agony on Georgiana's face which accompanied it was nearly his undoing.

"Of course," he replied quickly as the music began. Thankfully, her expression relaxed, though her brows remained drawn together slightly until the dancing had begun in earnest. He could not watch her contemplations without his heart pinching. It was perhaps the longest dance he had ever endured.

Finally, after what had felt like an interminably long period of time, they stopped, clapped, bowed, and curtsied.

"Are you certain she knows?" Georgiana asked as she placed her hand on his arm.

"Yes."

They took three silent steps toward the edge of the ballroom.

"Do you think me a cad?" Jack asked in a whisper. There could be no other reason for her questioning. She must think him capable of playing with the affections of a lady. The thought not only stung, it angered him. He thought that she would know him better than that. Had he not shown himself to be anything other than a true friend for the entirety of their acquaintance?

"I do not know what to think. I have..." her voice trailed off, and she shook her head. "No, of course, you are not."

She was forcing a smile to her lips, but it was not reaching her eyes. Jack expelled a breath in a whoosh. She did not trust him. "It is perhaps better if I do not call then," he murmured as they drew near to where her brother and Mrs. Darcy were standing. "I thank you for the dance," he said a bit more loudly. "I will not importune you again," he added in a whisper. Then with a quick bow to both her and her family, he turned and left her, the room, and the building, for a gentleman should not be in company when his heart was breaking.

# Chapter 7

"What have you done to our poor Mr. Ralston?" Elizabeth asked as they watched him make his way with a fair bit of haste toward the exit. He paused to speak with Miss Parkes and only waved to Alistair but did not join his friend.

Georgiana shook her head. "I do not know." She bit her lip to keep it from trembling. The ache in her heart as she watched the now empty doorway where he had been just a moment before was threatening to come spilling out of her eyes. She did not know precisely how she had done it, but she knew that whatever she had said or done had hurt Jack. "I would like to visit the retiring room. Brother, would you inform Mr. Tibbett that I will return? He was to have the next set."

She needed a moment to collect herself if she was going to be able to speak with Mr. Tibbett and smile as she danced, although she was not even certain that it was possible to pretend such lightness when one's heart hurt as hers did. Her brother was looking at her in that wary fashion that always meant he was not sure she was telling him everything he wished to know, but at present, there was no more she could say to him without becoming a watering pot and creating a scene. "Please?" she whispered.

"Are you well?" Darcy asked equally as quietly. "We can leave if you are not."

Georgiana shook her head. "I do not need to leave." She wanted to leave — to run from the room, down the steps, and out into the coolness of the night to catch Jack and apologize for whatever it was she had done to injure him.

"Your brother will be disappointed," Elizabeth whispered as she put her arm around Georgiana's shoulders. "He would love nothing better than to have an excuse to escape."

Georgiana giggled in spite of the ache in her heart.

"Come. We will both refresh ourselves." Elizabeth linked her arm with Georgiana's. "And you can tell me why you look on the verge of tears." She leaned her head closer. "But only if it will not cause you to cry. We do not wish for red eyes and a swollen nose."

Georgiana gave Elizabeth's arm a grateful squeeze. They walked quietly down the hall, past the open door to the card room, and finally, after passing a sofa which stood across the hall from a narrow table laden with flowers beneath a large gilded mirror, they turned into the room that had been designated for the use of the ladies.

The whole time they walked, Georgiana replayed her conversation with Jack. He had teased about wishing to court her. She had asked about Miss Parkes, and then... Oh, that must be it! His question about her thinking him a cad and the pain that had been in his tone when he asked it repeated itself. Why had she questioned whether he was telling her the truth or not? He was Jack. He was not Mr. Wickham.

"How will I ever learn to trust a gentleman?" There were three other ladies in the room, and Georgiana did not wish for them all to hear her, so she kept her voice pitched low.

Elizabeth sighed. "He duped me as well," she said.

"But not as he did me." Georgiana slipped behind a screen that had been set up for privacy.

Elizabeth stood just out of Georgiana's view. "No," she said, "but he nearly broke my heart, though I did not know it. Can you believe I listened to his stories about your brother?"

Georgiana did not reply. She had heard the full tale of how Elizabeth had listened to Mr. Wickham's tales of woe which painted Fitzwilliam in such a poor light that it had been part of why Elizabeth had refused Fitzwilliam's first offer of marriage. Georgiana knew how convincing Mr. Wickham could be with his words. It was strangely comforting to know that she was not alone in having been tricked by him.

Elizabeth stopped Georgiana as she came out from behind the screen. "What he did – who he is – is reprehensible."

"He is," Georgiana agreed.

"Not all men are like him," Elizabeth added before slipping behind the screen to take her turn.

Georgiana knew Elizabeth was right. Not all men, especially Jack, were like Mr. Wickham. Georgiana turned to see who was left in the room. Two ladies were just making one final appraisal of their hair and preparing to leave. The third lady who had been in the room was already gone. However, as the door opened to allow the two remaining ladies to leave, a new one entered.

"Miss Darcy, are you enjoying your night?" Miss Parkes crossed the room to greet her.

Georgiana bit her lip and nodded her head.

"That is not the expression of one who is truly enjoying herself," Miss Parkes said with a laugh. "Mrs. Darcy," she greeted as Elizabeth joined them. "I stepped on my hem and tore a hole in my dress, as you can see." She lifted her skirt so that they could see a small hole near the bottom on the right side. Then, she sat on a bench near them and took a small kit containing a needle and thread from her reticule. "I am forever causing some damage to my dresses, so it is best to be prepared to fix it," she explained as she prepared to repair her hem. "Thankfully, my partner for the next set has bowed out of his place, and I have time to put myself to right." She slipped off her shoes and wiggled her toes. "My feet will be glad for the reprieve. Sit with me," she offered.

Ah, that is why Jack had stopped to speak with Miss Parkes. Georgiana felt a pang of guilt at having caused Miss Parkes to miss out on a dance, no matter how much that lady might claim her feet would be appreciative of the rest. "Mr. Tibbett will be waiting," Georgiana said. She had no desire to return to the ballroom, but she was uncertain she wished to stay here and have a chat either. She genuinely wanted to go home.

"It will do him good to wait," Miss Parkes assured her. "That gentleman needs to learn his place."

Georgiana blinked at the sharpness in her tone.

"It is a sad tale, but I am happy to tell it if you wish to listen."

"I should go," Georgiana said as she sank down onto the bench next to Miss Parkes.

"I will be happy for the few moments of repose," said Elizabeth, drawing a chair near. "However, your brother will not be entirely pleased." Her tone held a caution.

"I will speak fast," Miss Parkes assured her. "I know I do not like it when my brother is cross."

"Nor do I," Georgiana admitted. "Most times," she added with a small smile.

"There are moments, are there not?" Miss Parkes asked with a laugh. Then as she began the job of repairing her dress, she launched into her story. "As I am certain you could tell from our discussion at the park yesterday, Mr. Tibbett and I have known each other for some time – since we were children really. Our parents are friends of long standing, you see."

Georgiana nodded when Miss Parkes looked up from her stitching.

"I had thought I had him secured. He seemed to have returned from school a proper young gentleman. The ideal husband." She shook her head. "He has always been opinionated but..." She blew out an exasperated breath. "His head had swollen to twice its normal girth!" She once again shook her head. "Did you know, one time when he and my brother were out riding with me..." Her brow scrunched. "I believe I was twelve or so. His family had come for a visit that summer." She glanced up from her stitching again. "On that ride, he actually told my brother, while they were having one of their ridiculous conversations about what made a proper wife, that he wished for a wife with whom he could discuss the classics. A sharing of opinions was deemed a right proper thing – and he did not mean that the lady must hold to the same opinions as he did." She gave a sharp nod of her head in agreement with Georgiana's startled look. "I know it is shocking after how he was yesterday, is it not?"

"Indeed," Georgiana said.

"You think you know a person and then without warning, he shifts and changes, and no matter how you attempt to forget him and find another to take his place in your heart, the blasted man will not be displaced." She tied off her string and snipped it off soundly with her scissors. "We had a difference of opinions over reading material, of all things!" She returned her sewing things to the little case.

"It is apparently a travesty of epic proportions for a wife to read a novel – and nearly worthy of a trip to the Tower should that novel be one that her husband has not provided for her." Bitterness mingled with anger dripped from her tone. "I, knowing his previous thoughts on wishing for a wife with whom to discuss the classics, was shocked and asked, in a fit of pique, if it were acceptable to read a novel if the lady had received it from her mother. You see, I was reading a novel that had been given to me by my mother when he came upon me in the garden. Perhaps if it had been some classic tale by Shakespeare instead of one of those horrid things by Mrs. Radcliffe, I might have never known his opinion on such things until we were married." She shook her head. "He replied that any lady who would give her daughter a novel without first making sure it was by an author the husband approved was not a fit mother, and her daughter was not the sort of lady he would wish to marry." She shrugged. "Any possibility of rational discussion dissolved rather quickly, and the meeting ended with my turning him away most severely." She grimaced. "My tongue can get the best of me at times."

Elizabeth laughed lightly. "I believe I understand that."

This comment was followed by a short discussion between Elizabeth and Miss Parkes about the dangers of a loose tongue, but

Georgiana only heard a word here and there. She was still considering Miss Parkes' tale.

"You love Mr. Tibbett?" she asked when the conversation drew to a close.

"Sadly, yes, and despite his despotic ideals."

"How?" Georgiana asked. "He is not what you thought he was."

Miss Parkes shook her head. "I do not know. I guess I believe he is still what he was. He just has become so focused on becoming the perfect gentleman that he has forgotten. At least, that is what I hope. He has always wished to be..." She paused as she sought for the right word. "Oh, I do not know how to say it – accepted? Right?"

"Without fault and attending to duty in the way he thinks is expected?" Elizabeth supplied.

"Precisely!" Miss Parkes cried. "But he is not viewing things rationally." She sighed. "I thought my walking away might shake him from it, but it has not." She rose and smoothed her skirt. "So, I have been attempting to sway him with jealousy."

"You have?" Georgiana asked.

Miss Parkes drew a deep breath and released it. "I fear you will think me horrid and no longer wish to be my friend, but I persuaded Mr. Ralston to play the role of suitor to see if it would spur Mr. Tibbett to view me in a different light. You know — as a woman worthy of an offer. However, it seems it is not working."

Georgiana gaped at her. Miss Parkes had persuaded Jack to pretend to court her? Miss Parkes did know that Jack was nothing more than a friend, and he had been completely honest in his replies just as she had suspected and should have known. Her heart sank. There was no denying what had hurt Jack. It was her inability to know whom to trust because he knew she did not trust him.

"Perhaps I should not confess it, but Mr. Ralston wished me to be successful." Miss Parkes continued, her eyes focused on the toes of her shoes.

"Why?" Georgiana asked softly.

"His affections lie elsewhere." Miss Parkes looked up at Georgiana. "Mr. Tibbett's returning to me would protect the lady who holds Mr. Ralston's heart from marrying before she could see him as more than a friend."

Georgiana plopped down on the bench. "He loves me? Jack loves me?" Tears gathered in her eyes. He had left her in such a way just now that she could not doubt he thought he had no chance with her. But then, she had not known she wanted him to have a chance with her. In fact, even now, she was not completely certain what she wanted other than what she had known since yesterday – she did not want to be Mrs. Tibbett.

"He does." Miss Parkes sat down beside Georgiana. "Are you well? Have I shared too much?"

Georgiana made an uncertain sound and shrugged as she wiped a tear from her eye. "I do not know."

"I do," said Elizabeth. "You are not well. Miss Parkes has perhaps shared just enough, and your brother will be pleased to take you home."

"He mustn't know!" Georgiana cried as she brushed frantically at her tears.

"About what?" Elizabeth asked. "That Mr. Ralston is enamoured with you?"

Georgiana nodded.

"My dear," Elizabeth took Georgiana's arm and helped her rise, "your brother already suspects as much. I did not until he told me, but it took very little argument to convince me of the veracity of the situation."

"Fitzwilliam knows?"

Elizabeth nodded. "Apparently, some gentlemen think that not-so-accidental meetings in the grove at Rosings and friendly calls made on a lady with no overtures of expectation are to be understood by we ladies as indications of affection."

"It is amazing our country runs as well as it does with such foolish creatures at the helm," Miss Parkes said with a laugh.

"Oh, they do eventually cotton on," Elizabeth assured her, "or, at least, the ones that matter do. Now, if I am going to abscond with Mr. Tibbett's partner for this set, could I prevail upon you, Miss Parkes, to take Georgie's place?"

"I would be delighted to be of service as long as I can be assured that I am not harming Miss Darcy in doing so."

"Oh, no!" Georgiana cried. "I had determined yesterday that he was not the husband for whom I wished, but I was not certain if I should trust myself with such a decision until I had pondered it for some time. I have been wrong before."

Miss Parkes wrapped her arm around Georgiana's arm which was not being held by Elizabeth. "Then, I will happily stand in for you, Miss Darcy."

"That is very good news," said Elizabeth as they moved to the exit. "After all, I hear tell that often dancing is a good way to encourage affection."

# Chapter 8

"Wait here." Elizabeth, Georgiana, and Miss Parkes had passed one set of doors into the ballroom, and there was a small alcove under the stairs where two chairs flanked a table. "You do not mind sitting here for a moment with her, do you?" she asked Miss Parkes.

"No, I do not mind at all." Miss Parkes took a seat.

"I will get Lady Margaret," Elizabeth said to Georgiana, "and then we will find my husband and your dance partner," she said to Miss Parkes.

Georgiana watched Elizabeth scurry into the ballroom. She willed her tears to stay dried and not gather for a flood as they threatened to do. She had not cried over a gentleman this much since Ramsgate. She rolled her eyes toward the ceiling, hoping that it would be impossible to shed tears when one's eyes were open so wide. If it had not been so painful to refrain from blinking and to hold them in such a position, it might have worked. However, it was painful, and blinking could not be put off forever. So, she dabbed her eyes with her handkerchief and smiled apologetically at Miss Parkes. "I am not normally a watering pot."

"Neither am I," said Miss Parkes, "but I can assure you that I cried for days after that house party in Warwickshire." She scooted to the edge of her chair and turned toward Georgiana. "I was so distraught at the thought of losing him to some silly notion about the superiority of men in all things." She paused. "I will grant them superiority in many things, but not all," she said seriously. "I am not a complete revolutionary." She gave Georgiana a crooked smile. "Not that Mr. Tibbett would agree."

"Indeed," Georgiana said with a small laugh. "Do you really think he can be brought up to scratch?"

"I do." Miss Parkes looked down at her hands, and, for the first time in their short acquaintance, Georgiana saw her blush. "He once told me he loved me. It was on the day before he left for school. He even kissed me, and then he wrote me a letter on my birthday each year he was away." She peeked up at Georgiana. "I cannot believe a gentleman would forget a love such as that so easily. I have seen how he glares when I am laughing at something Mr. Ralston has said. Jealousy beats in his heart. I am almost certain of it."

"I wish you well," Georgiana said. "I wish I could feel so certain of any man."

Miss Parkes reached over, placed a hand on Georgiana's hand, and lowered her voice to a whisper as Lady Margaret approached. "You will. Do consider Jack."

Georgiana nodded but did not say a word for she could not if she were to keep from shedding more than one or two tears. Considering Jack was all she had done since he walked out of the ballroom door.

"My dear girl," said Lady Margaret. "What have you done to yourself? Elizabeth says you are not feeling quite the thing, and from the looks of you, I would have to say I agree."

"Will you see her to the carriage while I find her brother?" Elizabeth asked.

"I most certainly will," Lady Margaret said.

Georgiana rose to leave. "Thank you for sitting with me," she said to Miss Parkes.

"Well, seeing as I was part of the reason for your tears, it really was the least I could do."

"No," Georgiana assured her. "I am the reason for my tears. I..." she shrugged as she could not continue to admit her guilt without those tears falling again.

"We should go find Mr. Tibbett," Elizabeth interrupted.

"One moment, Miss Parkes," Lady Margaret said before Elizabeth and Miss Parkes could leave.

"Yes, my lady," Miss Parkes responded with a curtsey.

"My granddaughter, Mrs. Pratt, informs me that you, for some unknown and inexplicable reason, wish to capture Mr. Tibbett."

"I do." Miss Parkes voice was all earnestness.

"Then get on with it. There was a loose stone on the paved path to the right in the garden the last time I was here. Perhaps it has not yet been repaired and could cause a lady to lose her footing." Lady Margaret's eyebrow and tone of voice both lifted in an indication that she was not merely warning Miss Parkes of a possible hazard.

"Grandmother!" Georgiana gasped.

Lady Margaret looked at Georgiana and smiled but made no attempt to excuse herself for suggesting a compromise.

"I shall bear that in mind," Miss Parkes said before joining Elizabeth and returning to the ballroom.

"Games," Lady Margaret huffed. "As entertaining as they might be to watch, I do not like how they can get so turned about that my granddaughter is in tears." She took Georgiana by the arm and together, they went to retrieve their wraps.

"Now," Lady Margaret said as they descended the steps and began their walk down the carriage line to their vehicle, "tell me what has you in tears. Is this Mr. Ralston's doing? I shall not abide a gentleman who causes my Georgiana to cry, even if I do enjoy his company as much as I do Mr. Ralston's."

"Oh, Grandmother, it is not his doing. It is mine. Entirely mine." She waited while her grandmother was handed into the carriage and then she herself was assisted before continuing. "Not a one of these tears are for me," she said as she settled onto the bench next to Lady Margaret. "They are for Mr. Ralston, but not because of him."

"You will have to explain that to me."

"While we were dancing, he asked me if I would consider him as a suitor."

"And this did not meet with your approval?"

"Oh, no, I mean, yes." Georgiana blew out a breath. Her mind was so jumbled. "I was shocked. I had never considered him as anyone who would be interested in me or as someone whom I would wish to have court me, although I do not know why." She fell silent for a moment.

Why had she never considered Jack as a possible suitor? She liked him very much. He was so pleasant and always put her at ease. He was handsome, there was no denying that. In fact, as she considered him now, there was absolutely no reason for her to have not considered him before this.

"One does not always recognize the value of the plate from

which she eats every day, until there is no plate from which to eat," said her grandmother.

Georgiana nodded. That was it. She had never seen him as anything but a friend.

"But that cannot be what has led to your tears," her grandmother prompted.

It was not. Her tears... Georgiana thought for a moment about their cause, listening again in her mind to the tone of Jack's voice and watching him leave. "I hurt him," she blurted. "I questioned him about Miss Parkes and did not readily accept his answers. He left because I was unable to trust him." She shook her head. That was not true. "No, it was not that I could not trust him; it was that I could not trust myself to trust him." She turned on the seat and grasped her grandmother's hands. "I knew he would not lie to me, but I hesitated."

"He was playing a part," Lady Margaret said. "He was not truly courting Miss Parkes."

Georgiana smiled. "Yes, yes, I know. He told me, and he would never lie to me." It was as if a torch had been lit in her heart, and she could see into the dark shadows where she had feared hurt and shame lay waiting for her. "He would never hurt me, Grandmother." She once again blinked against tears but not tears of sorrow. These were tears of happy realization.

"And why is that, my dear?" her grandmother prompted.

Georgiana's smile grew. "For the same reason you or Fitzwilliam would not hurt me. You love me."

"Ah, but your brother or I might cause you pain at some point."

Georgiana shook her head. "Not purposefully. You would not purposefully dupe me, and neither would Jack. He loves me." She flopped back against the bench and clapped her hands. "He loves me," she said with a sigh. It was a wonderful feeling to know that a gentleman such as Jack Ralston loved her.

"I am glad you have finally figured that out."

Georgiana sat up and looked at her grandmother, who was smirking very much like her cousin Richard did when he felt as if he had outsmarted Fitzwilliam. "You knew?"

"Yes. I've known from the moment he walked into Matlock House when Alistair returned with Anne."

"How?"

"There is no denying the look of a man who is completely smitten when he sees the object of his affection, and Mr. Ralston had that look when he saw you."

"Does everyone know?" Georgiana felt somewhat embarrassed at being so blind.

Her grandmother shrugged. "Most likely."

"And you did not tell me?"

"Why should I tell you?"

"So, I would know!"

Lady Margaret shook her head and chuckled. "It is better to discover these things on one's own than to be told."

Georgiana was not at all certain that her grandmother was right. She would have rather known for the past year that the gentleman who was walking with her, calling on her, and dancing with her loved her and was not just playing the part of a kind friend.

"And what of you? How do you feel about Mr. Ralston?"

Lady Margaret's question was to go unanswered for the present for at that moment, the door to the carriage opened, and Elizabeth entered, followed by Darcy.

"That smile does not look like tears," Darcy said as he took his seat. "But we are not returning to the ballroom."

Georgiana could see his relief in being away from the ball and not finding his sister in tears by the way he settled back against the squabs.

"There were tears," his grandmother assured him. "Many tears. However, I am nearly certain we are through with them until she realizes that she may have lost the gentleman she loves."

Georgiana gasped. "Do I love him?"

"I would like to answer no," Darcy said, "for I do not think I am prepared for you to love any gentleman, but, I would not be doing my duty in seeing you happy if I did. Therefore, I will suggest you spend some time considering life without Mr. Ralston. I have found it to be a very clarifying exercise. If the thought of life without Mr. Ralston does not darken your horizon and colour your existence with a bleakness that feels as if it will crush you, then, you do not love him. However, if such contemplation does cause such thoughts of desolation, then you may assume you love the chap."

Lady Margaret laughed. "That is perhaps a bit extreme," she said, "but Fitzwilliam has a point. You should take some time to consider carefully how you feel about Mr. Ralston. Marriages are not things which can or should be undone."

Oh! The thought of such serious contemplation made Georgiana's heart quiver. Until just now, she had very much doubted her heart to inform her correctly about anything. Be that as it may, she would at least attempt to do as her brother suggested. "May I apologize to him before I have finished thinking?"

"Apologize?" Darcy asked.

"I fear I have hurt him," Georgiana explained.

"Yes," Elizabeth responded, taking her husband's hand. "It is quite acceptable to apologize to a gentleman you have hurt even if you do not know whether or not you love him."

Darcy lifted his wife's fingers to his lips. "Quite right, my love."

"Tonight?" Georgiana asked.

"No," her brother responded. "I suspect Mr. Ralston will not be fit for company at present. Maybe tomorrow."

# Chapter 9

Jack flopped into his favourite chair near the hearth in his sitting room. With it turned just as it was just now, he could view the blackness of the night outside his window, and tonight that darkness felt like a welcome friend who could understand the bleakness of his life.

He sighed and wrapped the blanket he had brought with him around his legs. He was heart-sick and exhausted, but he had no desire to find comfort in his bed or to lose himself in sleep, nor did he wish to numb his pain with drink. He did not wish to find comfort.

He wanted to stew in his misery, to allow it to engulf him, and play itself out. Tomorrow, after a night of feeling each acute pang of rejection, he would pack his things and travel to his father's hunting lodge. Then, he would allow himself to seek succor for his soul in peace and quiet while tromping about the woods, riding for hours, and collapsing from fatigue into what he hoped would be dreamless sleep.

"You have a caller, sir," his butler stood at the door to the sitting room. "Are you home?"

A caller at this hour? Jack had no desire to see anyone, but he could not just send whomever it was away. It could be important.

"Who is it?" He moved only his head to look in his servant's direction.

"Mr. Darcy, sir."

Jack scrubbed his face and blew out a breath. He most certainly did not wish to see the brother of the lady who had just rejected him. "I am not fit for company."

"Yes, sir," his butler replied. "That is what Mr. Darcy said. He is most apologetic about calling at this hour but said it was necessary."

Jack could not imagine what would be so necessary to require a call now rather than waiting until a proper time tomorrow, but he did not wish to offend the gentleman, and he was curious.

"Very well. Show him in." As his butler left the room, Jack considered tossing off his blanket and attempting to make himself presentable, but he could not bother himself to do it. What did it matter what the man thought of him now anyway? It was not as if he needed to win Darcy's opinion to be allowed to marry Georgiana since she did not seem desirous of considering Jack as a suitor.

"Thank you for seeing me," Darcy said as he entered. A small smile tipped his lips as he sat down across from Jack. "You look no worse than I imagined you would."

Jack inclined his head in acceptance of the strange compliment.

"My sister," Darcy began uneasily, "explained to me what happened tonight, or at least, what she thinks happened."

"I was tired of dancing and left," Jack lied.

Darcy's left eyebrow rose, and he wore a look of disbelief. "I have no doubt you were fatigued, but I highly doubt it was from dancing. You see, I have worn the same expression you did when you parted ways with Georgiana, and, had Elizabeth not stopped me from leaving the parsonage at Hunsford, I would have likely found myself wallowing in grief, just as you are now. However," he glanced around, "I am certain, I would have been keeping company with a bottle of port or some such thing, but I see you are alone."

Jack shifted to sit up a bit straighter. So, Darcy did know that he cared for Georgiana as more than a friend — a great deal more.

"I prefer to experience the agony unaided." He shrugged. "I hope in doing so, it will run its course more quickly."

Darcy chuckled and shook his head. "I very much doubt the misery will leave you any faster if you are sober rather than properly foxed. However, I'm not here to talk you into dousing your feelings with alcohol or any such thing. I have just left my distressed sister in the care of my wife and have come to share a tale with you."

Jack was sitting full upright and on the edge of his chair now. "Distressed? Did something happen to Miss Darcy?"

"You left."

Jack blinked and shook his head. "I beg your pardon. I do not see how my leaving could be the cause of her distress."

Darcy sighed. "Neither did she, although I do believe she is coming to realize its cause." Darcy shifted in his seat but did not bother to explain himself further. Instead, he launched into his tale. "Two years ago, my sister imagined herself in love..."

Jack listened most intently to Darcy's story about how Georgiana had narrowly escaped a life of misery at the hand of a practiced liar and former family friend. His breathing became laboured as he imagined her pain at finding out the scoundrel had only wished for her money and had no care for her at all. "And this Wickham still lives?" the question was nearly a growl.

Darcy nodded. "He does."

"How?" Jack was utterly lost for comprehension of how a brother could allow a man such as Wickham to retain his life after having dealt so cruelly with the heart of an innocent young lady, especially one as precious as Georgiana's.

"There are laws," Darcy began, "and had he been lucky enough to fire the first shot, I could not and would not leave my sister alone in this world. Trust me, when I say I wanted nothing more than to run him through. But I could not."

Jack's head bobbed up and down slowly. He understood that. There were times when honor was not found in defending it, but rather in seeing to the care of those whom one's heart loved far more than it desired vengeance.

"Georgiana has recovered well from her ordeal, but it has not left her heart without a scar." Darcy leaned forward. "Do not leave town."

"It is what I would do," he explained in response to Jack's look of surprise.

He rose to leave. "Go to bed. Get some sleep, and when you see my sister tomorrow, so that she might explain to you about the scar Wickham left, be gentle. Her intent was not to reject you, but I will allow her to explain that." He placed the hat he held on his head. "There is just one more thing you should know before tomorrow."

"What might that be?" Jack had risen to see his guest to the door.

"I would not be opposed to calling you brother." He clapped

Jack on the shoulder. "Sleep well, and remember that there are no laws against my humiliating you at Angelo's."

Jack bid him goodnight before returning to the sitting room to gather his blanket. Sleep well? Jack shook his head. He was certain he would sleep less now than he would have half an hour ago, but at least, now, he would not be spending a sleepless night in agony but instead in hopeful anticipation. He blew out a great breath and, with a spring in his step, took himself off to bed.

~*~*~

Georgiana had tossed and turned all night. Try as she might, she could not find a position that was comfortable enough for her mind to stop its incessant consideration of Jack Ralston. She had risen twice, lit a candle, and attempted to commit her admission of guilt to paper just to have it out of her mind. Each attempt was now ashes.

Therefore, when the first pale light of dawn began to lift the blackness of the night to usher in the day, she greeted it with happy relief. Piling her pillows behind her back, she sat up, and, pulling her blankets up, tucked them under her arms. The fire had died to embers, and the morning air was cool. She would call for her maid and get dressed, but she did not wish to wake Alice any earlier than necessary. Even if she were dressed, it was not as if there was anything she could do to hurry the day ahead to the time when she could call on Mr. Ralston and make her apology.

She tapped her fingers on the blankets. Waiting, whether done while staring up into the dark all night or sitting watching the shadows flee the light of the sun, was difficult. She let out a sigh and scooted over to the edge of her bed. She had left her small writing case on the bedside table after her last attempt to write

301

to Jack. Perhaps she could try once again. She arranged herself so that she could write without damaging the coverlet, and, just to be certain she would not leave a horrid and permanent stain on the sprigged material of her quilt, she chose a pencil from the case's contents rather than a pen. Surely, Jack would not be offended if she did not use ink.

*Dearest Jack,*
She paused and smiled at the words. He was a dear man.

*I have spent a good portion of the night attempting to commit to paper my failing, and as the morning dawns, I find I am still at a loss for how to tell you all that is in my heart. Perhaps such things should not be consigned to paper. They are, perchance, better spoken face to face.*

Yes, she nodded in agreement with herself, it would be so much better to speak to him than to write. She was about to crumple her paper when a thought of a different nature struck her. Seeing one's failings recorded on a page might be disturbing; however, seeing one's praises was something entirely different. She smoothed the paper on the top of her case and picked up her pencil once again.

*Since I am at a loss as to how to adequately describe my sorrow in causing you pain, I will turn my pencil and my mind to more pleasant contemplations.*

*There are few to whom I would write and address them as informally as I have you. All of those whom I do not address as Miss or*

*Mr. are far too dear to me to be held at such a distance as such titles give, for they are all, every one of them, people whom I love.*

Georgiana bit her lip and reread the words. Then, with a shake of her head, she crumpled the paper and put it aside. Just like admitting one's faults, declaring one's love for a gentleman should be done in person, not in a letter. She put her writing case away. Then, she rose, crossed the room to toss this final attempt at a letter into what remained of her fire, and rang for Alice before returning to the comfort of her bed to wait and once again contemplate Jack.

"Good morning, miss," Alice greeted as she slipped into the room.

"I am sorry to call you so early," Georgiana apologized, "but I cannot stay in this room any longer."

Alice tipped her head and looked at her mistress. "You do not look rested."

"I am as rested as is possible."

"A difficult night?"

"Yes," she replied from inside her nightgown as she pulled it over her head and prepared to make use of the warm water Alice had added to the wash basin before scurrying off to pull a dress from the wardrobe. There was no need to tell Alice what had kept her awake, for Georgiana, as she had prepared for bed, had shared with her maid all about what had happened with Jack at the ball.

"Yellow or pink?" Alice called.

Yellow was cheerful, but pink was better for hiding the effects of a poor night's sleep since it complimented her complexion better than yellow. "Pink."

The requested dress was draped over the screen behind which

Georgiana stood, and she could hear Alice gathering all the other pieces of clothing that would be needed. She finished her ablutions and slipped into the fresh chemise which Alice had left hanging on the hook on the right side of the mirror above the washstand.

"He's a fine young man." Alice tied Georgiana's stays. "He'll not disappoint you." She picked up their conversation from last night as if only a few moments and not a full night had passed.

How Georgiana hoped what Alice said was true! "But I did not trust him. That is not an easy thing to overcome."

Alice clucked and shook her head as she shook out her mistress's petticoat while Georgiana put on her stockings. "You did not trust *you*. There is a difference." Once again, she clucked and shook her head at Georgiana's look of partial belief. "Mr. Ralston is no fool. He will understand." Alice gave a displeased huff. "What that scoundrel did to you at Ramsgate was unthinkable! Damaging a tender heart such as yours! You have done well to recover as you have. There are far weaker ladies who would take to their beds and nearly die from neglecting their health. But not my Miss Darcy." She winked as she prepared to help Georgiana into her petticoat. "My Miss Darcy is made of sterner stuff. She's brave; she is. And she can, and will, make a wonderful Mrs. Ralston. Mark my words, miss. He'll offer for you."

Georgiana's heart skittered at the thought. Was she ready to become a Mrs. Anybody? She had only just made her debut. She held her dress in place while Alice made quick work of the fastenings. Then, she took her place at her dressing table.

Alice reached over Georgiana's shoulder to get some pins and the brush before she began her work. "Trust your heart," she whispered near her mistress's ear. "It will not steer you into a gale this time. No," she continued with a shake of her head while she began pulling the brush through Georgiana's hair, "it has learned how to bring you into a safe harbour." She paused and looked at Georgiana in the mirror. "And you know your brother approves of Mr. Ralston as does Lady Margaret. He's high quality; he is." She returned to her work and, much to Georgiana's amusement, continued to mutter her approbations as she worked.

By the time, Georgiana was ready to go downstairs, she was as confident as she had ever been that her heart was indeed guiding her in the correct direction, which, she suspected from the pleased smile on her maid's face, was precisely Alice's intent.

# Chapter 10

Jack stretched and squinted at the sun that shone through the window as the drapes were drawn open.

"There is a letter for you," his man said with a nod toward the bedside table.

Jack rubbed his eyes, pushed himself up to a sitting position, and took up the missive. Breaking the seal, he read:

*Jack*

*I expect you to call – early. Proper hours are for acquaintances, not for future cousins. I shall send Alistair in search of you should you not arrive before eleven only because he will not let me leave the house today. In fact, I shall do well to be allowed to move from my chair. He is a dear though, is he not?*

*Anne*

Jack rolled his eyes and shook his head as he chuckled at Anne's message, then he read what his friend had added at the bottom.

*She's had very little sleep because she was worried about you, and I refused to rouse you in the middle of the night. Do come soon.*

*A-*

The words brought a smile to Jack's lips. His friend was such a doting husband! That the staid and steady, practical Alistair Pratt had become such a gentleman was no surprise. The man had a heart capable of profound and enduring compassion. Jack knew that to find a place within the confines of close friendship with Alistair Pratt was to find a welcome of the most lasting kind – even if a person were to be a bit of a trial to the man's patience, as Jack had been more than once over the years of their acquaintance. Alistair's wife seemed to be cut from the same cloth, for Anne had accepted Jack as if he were a brother from the moment they had met.

Jack looked at the clock. Nine! Already? He would have to hurry. He had no desire to have Alistair sent out looking for him simply because he had not fallen asleep until the sun was rising and had, therefore, slept later than was his regular wont. Thankfully, he was not unaccustomed to preparing for his day with a bit of haste. He was not the sort of chap to linger at his toilette or retie his cravat multiple times. He liked to be quick about his business.

However, there was one thing for which he always paused not matter how quick he might need to be in the morning. He would not, even for Alistair's wife, leave his house without a proper cup of tea and several morsels of food. He knew that tea would most certainly be served by Anne, but, considering how loudly his stomach rumbled from the moment his eyes opened until he had taken his first bite of food, tea and a few sweets or sandwiches would not be enough to ward off his hunger. It was better for him to spend the time necessary to break his fast at home and arrive for his call with a full stomach and a pleasant countenance even if it did delay him a few minutes longer than he would wish. For, he thought to himself, a hungry Jack was never as pleasant a Jack as a sated Jack.

He popped the last of his breakfast into his mouth, chased it down with what remained of his tea, and taking up his hat, bid a cheery farewell to his butler.

It was a glorious day, and Jack drank in every bit of its delights as he rode the few blocks from his apartment to the Pratt's townhouse.

True it was not the pleasantest of days. The wind today was a bit brisker than normal, and people scurried before it with collars pulled up and hats secured tightly by ribbons or hands, but, the sun was shining, no rain was falling, and Georgiana Darcy had not rejected Jack. That last fact could have turned even the darkest, most bitter, sleet and ice-filled day of winter into a glorious day for Jack, for that is what hope could do when allowed to fester all night in the mind of a besotted gent.

He swung down from his mount and tossed the reins to a groom before bounding up the steps and tapping a short pattern on the door with the knocker.

"Good morning," he said as he placed his hat on the long narrow table that stood next to and to the right of the door in the Pratt's sitting room.

Alistair rose from his seat and tossed his own hat and coat, which he had draped across his lap, to the side. Evidently, he had been just waiting for his wife to give him his orders to go fetch Jack.

Jack followed Alistair's pointed look at the clock. It was not yet eleven, but it was closing in on the hour. "I had to eat before I came," Jack explained, "and, I had to stop for these." He handed a bouquet of spring flowers to Anne.

"Oh, they are lovely." Anne promptly brought them to her nose to breathe in their sweet fragrance. Then, as Jack took a seat, she placed the flowers on the table next to her. "You do not look at all distraught." Her tone was slightly accusatory and disappointed.

"I am not," he replied with a grin and then said no more. It was fun to watch her brows furrow and her lips purse with displeasure when he did not immediately impart all the information she wished to hear.

"Why?" Anne demanded. "You looked distraught when you left the ball last night, and then Georgiana had to be taken home because she was unwell, and Mr. Tibbett was forced to dance with Miss Parkes. It was quite a to-do, I assure you. And I wish to know the particulars." She folded her arms across the top of her belly which, to Jack, seemed to grow rounder and rounder each day.

"There is not much for me to tell." Jack rested his left arm on the arm of the settee, extended his right one along the back of the piece of furniture, and stretched his legs out in front of him, crossing them at the ankles. "I presented myself to Miss Darcy as a possible suitor, and she did not readily accept," he summarized.

Anne's eyes narrowed. "You are not telling me all."

"I swear that is what happened," he protested and then elaborated on his summary. "I presented myself as a possible suitor. Miss Darcy asked about Miss Parkes. I told her we were nothing more than friends. She did not seem to believe me. I asked her if she thought me a cad, and she hesitated before assuring me that she did not consider me as such. Then, I bid her farewell and went home to wallow in my misery before fleeing town today."

Anne's brows furrowed. "I do not understand. Were you hoping Georgiana thought you a cad?"

Alistair chuckled. "No, my dear, I believe it was the fact that Georgiana had to consider whether he was or was not a cad before replying which caused the distress."

"Exactly!" Jack agreed. "What gentleman wishes to have the lady he loves question his gentlemanliness?"

"A lady should be given a moment to think," Anne muttered. "Ooo." She grimaced and placed a hand on her swollen abdomen.

"Are you well?" Alistair asked.

"I think it was just the little one stretching as he is sometimes wont to do," she replied. "Ooo," she said once again as she rubbed her abdomen.

"You should lie down," Alistair suggested.

"Yes, you should," Jack agreed.

"Not until I know why you are no longer distressed," Anne replied, her hand still rubbing her stomach as she continued to grimace.

"Very quickly then." Jack sat forward. He was not at all certain that Anne was indeed well, and the thought that he might be the reason was most unsettling. "I went home prepared to grieve my loss of Miss Darcy, and I was well into my painful reverie when her brother called on me. He explained a few things about his sister to me, assured me that Miss Darcy had not meant to refuse me, and then told me that he would not be opposed to having me as a brother." A grin split Jack's face. "I have done it, Al. I have won Mr. Darcy's approval just as I set out to do last year. And," he held up a finger to punctuate his point, "I have not lost Miss Darcy."

Anne leaned forward, her face still wore a pained expression. "I am so pleased," she managed to say between clenched teeth.

"You must go to bed." Alistair was at her side in an instant, helping her to her feet. "Jack, help me get her to her room."

Jack took a place on the other side of Anne and offered her his arm. "Do not be afraid to lean on me heavily," he said softly.

Slowly, they made their way up the stairs and to Anne's room.

"Shall I fetch the doctor?" Jack asked as Anne pushed herself up onto the bed, insisting she would rather sit than lie down despite Alistair's protests that lying might be best.

"Please," Alistair said as he removed his wife's slippers.

"A servant can go," said Anne.

"No," Jack said, placing a hand on hers, "I will feel better if I have something more to do than pace below, wondering what is taking the man so long."

"Thank you," she whispered.

"Rest," Jack encouraged. Then, he placed a hand on Alistair's shoulder, looked his friend in the eye, and said softly, "I will be a quick as I can be. All will be well."

As he hurried from the room, he hoped that it was true. It was too early for the baby to come. There was yet a month before the child was expected.

Taking the stairs two at a time, he told a maid, who was in the hall, to have the flowers Anne had left in the sitting room put into a vase and taken to Mrs. Pratt. Then he informed the butler that he would return soon with the doctor, and, snatching his hat from the table in the sitting room, he left.

~*~*~

Georgiana yawned and rested her head against the back of her chair. Her eyes were too tired to continue the stitching she was attempting to do. She would rest them for a few moments.

Sometime later, a hand gently shook her shoulder. "Good morning, my dear," said Lady Margaret as Georgiana's eyes opened. "I take it you did not sleep well?"

Georgiana shook her head. "I slept very little, if at all." She tipped her head to the side, and her brows drew together. Why was her grandmother here? "I had thought you were not coming today. Were you not to visit Anne?"

Lady Margaret settled into a chair, and her maid arranged a basket of knitting supplies at her feet before scurrying off at the wave of Lady Margaret's hand. "That was the plan before your brother's note arrived insisting I come sit with you today in case you have callers."

How long had she been asleep? Apparently, it had been at least long enough for her brother to send a note and for Lady Margaret to arrive. Georgiana shook her head in an attempt to clear the fogginess that seemed to reside within it. She still could not figure out why her grandmother was sitting with her rather than Elizabeth.

"Elizabeth is ill."

"I beg your pardon?" Georgiana sat forward, eyes wide.

"It is nothing about which to fret," Lady Margaret replied with a small knowing smile. "The doctor has arrived, and your brother will be put at ease shortly."

"I do not understand."

"My guess is that you will be an aunt in the not too distant future. Many ladies feel unwell at the beginning. I know I did." She shook her head. There was a faraway look in her eyes and a small smile on her lips. "I could only eat dry toast and weak tea for breakfast for several weeks and only broth with bread for many dinners." Her eyes came to rest on Georgiana. "Your grandfather was so solicitous and understanding."

Georgiana loved how her grandmother's face always shone with such fondness when she spoke of her late husband. "Do you really think Elizabeth is with child?"

Lady Margaret nodded. "I do indeed. Now, tell me, are you expecting any callers today?"

"There may be a few," Georgiana replied. "However, I had hoped to call on Jack, but if Fitzwilliam is otherwise occupied..."

"I have a carriage," Lady Margaret interjected, "so if your brother is not able to escort you to make your apology, I will." She straightened in her chair and tipped her head toward the door where the butler stood. "It seems we will have at least one caller today."

"Mr. Tibbett to see Miss Darcy," said Mr. Kinney.

Lady Margaret shook her head. "Blast," she muttered.

Georgiana giggled softly before greeting their visitor.

# Chapter 11

"I am delighted to see you are well, Miss Darcy," Mr. Tibbett said as he took a seat. "I was quite concerned after you left last night. Miss Parkes assured me it was nothing more than fatigue and a headache, but my mind would not rest easy until this moment when I could see for myself that you were indeed well."

"My head has cleared, and all is beginning to be put to right." Georgiana stole a secret glance towards her grandmother.

Mr. Tibbett shifted in his seat and rubbed his hands on his knees. "I had hoped to find your brother at home to callers, but your butler informed me that he was unavailable."

Georgiana's eyes grew wide. "Indeed?"

Oh, this was not good!

"Was there a particular reason?" Her heart raced, and she felt as if she might cast up her accounts.

It was a most shocking reaction to have to the news that a gentleman who had been calling on her regularly for two weeks wished to speak to her brother, but there it was. Fear, anxiety, panic, and the desire to flee warred within her. If she had not already determined that she loved Jack and that Mr. Tibbett was not whom she wished to marry, such an acute reaction as she was currently experiencing would have left no doubt in her mind that she did not love the gentleman before her.

For though she had been confused for the past two years about what did or did not constitute how a lady should feel about the gentleman she wished to marry, she knew that wanting to push him out of the room and throw the bolt on the door behind him was not an indication of affection.

"I had hoped to ask him for permission to seek your hand." He swallowed, cast a wary look at Lady Margaret, and once again wiped his hands on his pants.

The action made Georgiana wish to giggle. It appeared as if his considering marrying her was causing him a great deal of pain, perhaps even as much as his proposing the idea was causing her.

"Why would you do that?" It was rather obvious he did not honestly wish it.

He blinked. "I thought we got on well."

"Oh," was all Georgiana said in response. It was not a ridiculous reason. Getting on well together was often the only requirement beyond wealth and standing spoken about by some – many in society.

"Do we not?" He was wiping his hands on his pants again.

A deep crease formed in Georgiana's brow as she considered his question. They had enjoyed themselves on drives and at the theatre, but that was not enough for two people to marry, was it?

"Do you love her?" Lady Margaret asked before Georgiana could admit that yes, they did get on well.

Georgiana silently sighed in relief that she would not have to broach the subject of love with Mr. Tibbett. She was not at all certain he would consider her opinion as valid, but the opinion of the Dowager Countess of Matlock should hold some sway.

"I... I... intend to," Mr. Tibbett stammered.

"So, you do not love my granddaughter?"

"I am fond of her."

"But fondness is not love," said Lady Margaret.

"But it can become love," he refuted.

"Fondness is not enough for me," Georgiana said. "I wish to be loved."

"You will be," he insisted.

"But I wish to be loved now, though not by you," Georgiana declared, causing the poor gentleman in front of her to gape. She was not even certain that he knew what love was, not that his knowledge or lack thereof would sway her in the least, but it was important to the happiness of a friend.

"And what of Miss Parkes?" Georgiana asked on behalf of that friend.

He blinked. "Pardon me?"

"Did you not, at one time, tell her that you loved her?"

"Is that what she has told you?"

Georgiana could see his ire rising in the way his eyes narrowed. "Did you tell her that you loved her?" Georgiana repeated.

He pressed his lips together into a displeased frown before eventually answering, "Yes, but it was years ago."

"Was it a lie?"

His eyes grew wide. "No."

"Then you still love her?"

"I... I... We do not suit."

He would seek her hand when he loved another? Georgiana

shook her head. Her own displeasure was mounting on Miss Parkes' behalf.

"Do you know, Mr. Tibbett that I, too, enjoy reading novels and intend to continue to do so after I am married." She held up a hand to stop him from speaking. "And I expect to be trusted by my husband enough to select them for myself without his prior approval?" She smiled at her grandmother. "Revolutionary, is it not?"

"But a lady does not know what is best," Mr. Tibbett protested.

"I beg to differ," said Lady Margaret. "A lady who is as well-bred as my granddaughter, and I would venture to add Miss Parkes, knows very well what is best. They are ladies of high calibre, young man. They are not the sort of ladies to go cavorting or to throw caution to the wind at the smallest inclination of securing a bit of drivel to read. If you do not have enough respect for the lady whom you wish to take for a wife to trust her choices in reading material, how shall you ever trust her with your children or the household accounts?" Lady Margaret tipped her head and gave him a pointed look that said she expected a reply to her question. However, Mr. Tibbett seemed to be either unwilling or unable to formulate such a thing at present.

"I once had a gentleman tell me he loved me and then withdrew his words as you have done to Miss Parkes. I will not tie myself to such a man," Georgiana said quietly.

"I did not withdraw my words," Mr. Tibbett protested.

"Perhaps not in words but in action. A gentleman, who loves a lady and declares such to her, does not court or make offers to other ladies." Georgiana shook her head. "She still loves you."

She waved her hand from the top of his head to the bottom

of his boots, indicating his person. "Not this gentleman, who is attempting to check off some list of what makes him the perfect husband with the perfect wife, but you. The you she knew for all those years before you became this." Once again, she used her hand to indicate his person.

She paused as his mouth opened to make some retort but then closed again. With any luck, he was considering his actions in regard to Miss Parkes, though Georgiana was not entirely certain he was. It was more likely that he was formulating some way to renew his address. However, no matter how many times or in what fashion he attempted to press his suit, the answer would remain the same. He was not Jack.

"I should like very much to have you sit at my table someday for dinner with your wife and my friend at your side." Georgina said, "I hold no ill will for you, Mr. Tibbett. Indeed, I wish you happy; however, I do not wish to marry you."

Presently, the gentleman looked as far from happy as was possible. He had folded his arms across his chest and was scowling.

"It's that Ralston," he grumbled. "Not a serious bone in the man's body and yet, he turns every female's head."

"Not Miss Parkes' head," Georgiana said.

Mr. Tibbett snorted.

"I assure you it is true," Georgiana continued.

"But you? He has turned your head has he not? I saw how you looked at him last night while you were dancing."

Georgiana shook her head and smiled. "No, Mr. Tibbett, Mr. Ralston has not merely caught my attention. He has captured my heart. I adore his lightness, but there is a depth to him, sir, that is..." she shook her head again as she attempted to order her thoughts, "remarkable. He is steady and true. He does not say one thing and do another. He is loyal and caring. He is..." she shrugged, and her smile grew, "everything for which I could hope to find in a husband, and I love him."

Jack steps faltered as he followed Mr. Kinney past the sitting room door. Georgiana loved someone? His heart did not know whether to sink or take flight. Could he be the gentleman of whom she spoke?

"Mr. Ralston," said the butler, who was several steps ahead of him.

"I will wait here for the doctor," Jack replied. "You were correct, I do not need to accompany you."

"Do you wish to be announced?" Mr. Kinney's lips twitched slightly in amusement.

Jack shook his head. "No, I will make myself known."

"Very good, sir. I will inform the doctor that the matter is of an urgent nature."

"Thank you," Jack replied before turning toward the sitting room and pushing the door open. She was wearing such a lovely pink gown that perfected her in a way Jack found quite captivating.

"Who?" he asked from the doorway. "Who is this fortunate fellow that Miss Darcy loves? Tibbett?" He looked at the gentleman in surprise. He had not realized that Georgiana had a caller.

Mr. Tibbett shook his head and rose. "No, it is not I."

"That is fortunate for Miss Parkes," said Jack. "She had hoped she had not lost you."

Mr. Tibbett's brows drew together.

"She is rather set on securing you," Jack added.

"So I have been told." Mr. Tibbett bowed. "Good day, ladies. Ralston."

Jack watched the man leave the room. "He does not seem happy," he muttered.

"No man is when an offer has been refused." Lady Margaret's lips twitched, and her eyes sparkled.

"He offered for you?" Jack could not contain his surprise as he turned to Georgiana, who nodded in answer. "Oh." His heart both rejoiced that she had refused Tibbett and drummed loudly its fear at having come so very close to having lost her to the man.

"I should check on Elizabeth." Lady Margaret tucked her knitting into her basket and rose.

"I had heard Mrs. Darcy is unwell," Jack said. "That is why I am here, I was looking for Mr. Bishop."

Lady Margaret paused at the door to the sitting room. "Why?"

"Anne is having some pains." He blew out a breath. "And it is too early for that," he added softly.

"I see," said Lady Margaret. "Then, I shall go up and hurry the doctor along." She nodded toward Georgiana and whispered "get on with it" before she left, making certain to close the door firmly behind her.

"It is not Mr. Tibbett whom you love?" Jack crossed the room to sit where Lady Margaret had been sitting at Georgiana's side.

Once again, Georgiana found her heart racing and her being filled with flutters of nerves. However, this time there was no thought of fear nor even the smallest bit of panic. There was only joyful anticipation. "No, it is not Mr. Tibbett."

"Then who?" he prodded hopefully.

"Before I answer," she said, "I must apologize for my words last night. I know that you would never be untruthful with me. It was not that I did not trust you. I did not trust *me*." She blew out a breath. Admitting one's failing in person was just as difficult as committing it to paper. But it had to be done.

"I do not understand."

"I once thought I was in love, but I was not. However, my heart had led me to believe it was true, and I nearly consigned myself to a life of misery and heartbreak." She looked down at her clenched hands in her lap. "Since that time, I have had a great deal of difficulty knowing if I should listen to what my heart was telling me or not. It told me I could trust you, but I was not certain I could trust what my heart said since it had deceived me before." Oh, how did one explain something like this?

Jack covered her hands with one of his. "No, your heart did not deceive you. *It* was deceived by a scoundrel – a good-for-nothing charlatan. You were not at fault."

She peeked up at him. "You know about... Mr. Wickham?"

Jack nodded.

"How?"

"Your brother came to see me last night. I believe he wanted to make certain I did not leave town."

She gasped. "You were going to leave?" How close had she been to losing him altogether?

He nodded. "I could not stay here and see you courted by another. Watching you these last weeks as you danced or went for a drive or attended the theater with this gentleman and that ..." He shook his head. "Until last night, I had hope that you would eventually notice me, miss me even. While I harboured that hope, I could endure the discomfort, but without it, I could not."

"Oh, Jack," she cried. "Can you ever forgive me for causing you such pain? It was not intentionally done." Tears gathered at the thought of having hurt him so severely.

"Tell me who you love," he said quietly.

She blinked against her tears and smiled. "You. Only and always you."

His eyes closed as he exhaled. She loved him.

She wiggled one of her hands out from under his and placed it on his cheek. "I do not know what I was thinking. How could I doubt that you would ever bring me anything but joy? I have watched you with my cousin and Alistair. You do not prevaricate, nor do you love by halves." She smiled. "You even braved scratches to rescue a cat."

He chuckled. "Anne thought it might impress you."

"You wished even then for my good opinion?"

"Since the day I saw you in Gunter's last year." He leaned his cheek into her hand. "Will you marry me?"

"Why?" She needed to know it was because he loved her and not just because they got on well.

"Because I will cease to exist if you do not, and my heart shall shrivel into nothingness without you, for I love you with all that I am."

A watery smile suffused her face. That was the answer for which she hoped a gentleman who proposed marriage would give as his reason for doing so. "And I can read whatever I wish?"

He brushed a tear from her cheek as he nodded.

"And may I complete my season before we marry?"

"Whatever you ask is yours as long as you, Georgiana, are mine."

She stroked his cheek with her thumb. "Then, yes, I will most happily marry you."

Again, he closed his eyes and exhaled, enjoying her caress and allowing himself to savour the peace and joy her answer brought.

"You will not think me wanton if I ask you to kiss me, will you?" Georgiana whispered.

"Not at all," Jack replied with a laugh. Then, drawing her to her feet, he granted her wish.

# Chapter 12

Georgiana leaned her head against the back of the chair in which she sat and, closing her eyes, drew a deep breath. She was tired, but far too happy to fall asleep. Her heart had never felt so – oh what was the word? Safe? Content? Treasured. Perhaps that was it. To know that a gentleman such as Jack Ralston loved you as he did – placing his whole happy existence in the return of that love — was ... well, it was just too wonderful for words. That was likely why she could not think of the correct word for how she was feeling.

"About what are you smiling?" Anne lay on her side on her bed with her arm propped under her pillow so that her head was raised a bit higher in order to see her cousin better.

Georgiana's eyes popped open. "I thought you were sleeping."

"I was, and now, I am not," Anne grinned at her. "Tell me about the smile."

"I will, but, first, you must tell me how you are feeling," Georgiana insisted.

"Rested and uncomfortable – who would not be with a belly this big?"

"Any pains?" Georgiana questioned.

"Not a one," said Anne. "I am certain I will be ready to take a ride in the park by tomorrow."

Georgiana shook her head. The doctor had declared Anne's pains to be a false alarm, and the baby's way of announcing that his arrival would be sooner rather than later. He had also instructed that Anne was to stay in bed except for the occasional half hour in the sitting room or a short drive to take some air. Alistair had taken the doctor's orders to heart, and Georgiana knew that Anne would be following them to the minutest detail. The thought of how much Alistair cared for his wife warmed Georgiana's heart.

"You will not be going to the park for some time, I should think," she said to Anne. "Your husband is very concerned about you and the baby."

Anne smiled. "I know, but I do enjoy how he insists on cosseting me." She pushed up to a seated position. "Now, tell me what has you smiling."

Georgiana had arrived with her grandmother and the doctor and had, only a quarter of an hour ago, crept in to take her turn sitting next to Anne's bed so that Anne would not lack for entertainment if she awoke.

"I was thinking of a particular gentleman," Georgiana replied coyly.

"Not Mr. Tibbett. Please say it was not Mr. Tibbett."

Georgiana laughed at the look of dread which matched the tone of her cousin's voice. "Do you not like him?" she teased.

"Not for you," Anne retorted.

"And who would you match me with if not Mr. Tibbett?" Georgiana asked. She knew the answer to that. Jack had already shared with her about his and Anne's plan.

Anne huffed as if Georgiana had asked the most ridiculous of questions. "Why Jack, of course!"

"Jack?" Georgiana feigned shock.

Anne's eyes narrowed. "You do not fool me," she said.

Georgiana laughed. "I should not tease." She was given a teasing smile in reply.

"No, you should not," Anne assured her. "I am an invalid, after all, and teasing an invalid is very improper."

"Indeed, it is," Georgiana agreed with exaggerated solemnity. "Have I told you how much more I prefer the Anne you are now over the quiet Anne we visited at Rosings?"

Anne nodded. "You have. Many times, but I do not mind hearing it over and over. Now, tell me. Were you thinking about Jack?"

Georgiana nodded. "We are betrothed."

Anne squealed and clapped her hands. "Oh, I knew you'd make a good match!" she cried. "Where is he? I must wish him joy!"

"He is downstairs with Grandmother and Alistair."

"Send for him." Anne ran a hand over her hair and then smoothed the blankets in preparation for company as Georgiana did as instructed.

"Is Darcy here?" Anne asked.

Georgiana shook her head as she returned to her chair. "Elizabeth was not feeling well."

Anne's eyes grew wide. "Why are you smiling about that?" she demanded.

"Because I am to be an aunt," Georgiana replied.

Once again, Anne squealed with delight and clapped her

hands. "Cousins so close together in age will be wonderful!" Her lips pursed, and her eyes sparkled with merriment. "Do you think if I have a son, and Elizabeth has a daughter, I should petition your brother about a betrothal?" She covered her mouth with her hand to contain her laughter.

Anne was not the only one to laugh at the idea. "Do not let your mother hear you," Georgiana cautioned.

"Oh, never," Anne agreed. "Betrothals should not be arranged. They should be chosen." She held a hand out to Georgiana, who grasped it. "I am so very happy for you. There is nothing better than finding the one whom your heart loves and joining with him in marriage."

"Elizabeth said something very similar, as did my brother." The door to Anne's room opened as she spoke.

"You wished to see me," Jack said as he stepped into the room.

"Come here and let me kiss your cheek," Anne ordered.

Jack did as instructed. "Has Georgiana shared our news then?"

"She has indeed," Anne replied, "and I wanted to wish you joy." She clasped his hand in hers. "You must wait to marry until I can dance."

He chuckled. "I must apologize since we are sneaking off to Gretna Green tonight."

"You are not," Anne released his hand and swatted his arm.

"You are correct," he replied. "Georgiana wishes to finish her season before we wed, and I am loath to deny her anything she wishes." He moved to stand near Georgiana, and she took his hand.

How she liked the comfort that had always settled in around

her when he was near. She was still uncertain how she had not recognized before now that he was what her heart craved.

Anne smiled approvingly. "That is a good plan, and not just because I will be able to dance by the end of the season. You will also need to dispose of your apartment and find a proper house in town." She waved away what he was about to say. "I know you have an estate, but we shall gather in town often, shall we not?" She bit her lip, which had begun to quiver. "I will miss you."

Jack chuckled. "My estate is not far from yours. A day's drive. And yes, we shall gather together often," he assured her. "I would not miss out on spoiling my cousin's children."

Georgiana pressed her lips together as she saw a familiar mischievous look return to Anne's eyes.

"Perhaps our children will marry," Anne said, barely containing a laugh as she said it.

Jack shook his head as he, too, laughed. "There will be no matchmaking between our children."

Georgiana smiled up at him. Their children. What a lovely thought. "Our children shall choose," she said, returning her gaze to Anne, "for love. Just as we did."

Jack pulled Georgiana to her feet and, much to Anne's delight, wrapped her in his embrace and kissed her quite thoroughly. "I will send you your husband," he said as he released Georgiana and placed her hand on his arm, "in exchange for my betrothed." He led Georgiana out of the room. Slowly, they descended the stairs and walked down the hall to the library. "Your wife is awake," Jack said to Alistair.

"And delighted, no doubt, to hear your news?"

"Quite," Jack replied with a grin. "I told her you would go up to see her."

And Alistair did go up to see his wife while Jack and Georgiana slipped out into the garden and Lady Margaret continued working on the blanket she knew was going to be needed soon for her first great-grandson. Several more blankets would follow that first one in fairly quick succession. Darcy and Elizabeth would have a daughter before Christmas, and Georgiana and Jack would eventually, in the summer after Georgiana's second season, add a daughter of their own to the growing brood.

Easters, summers, Yuletides, and sundry other occasions during the years would find the cousins gathering either in town or country where houses would ring with love and laughter. And Anne would look upon the group with pride, claiming credit for both Jack's and Darcy's happy marriages as well as her own. Alistair would attempt to correct her by reminding her that Darcy was determined to win Elizabeth well before Anne's letter reached him and that her plan to help Jack snare Georgiana had almost ended in disaster. Anne would smile obligingly, pat his hand, and declare it had all worked out just as it should, a fact with which no one could argue. For despite one refused proposal, one misguided trip to Scotland, and one failed attempt at enticing Miss Darcy, they had all claimed their loves and found their own happily ever afters.

And Miss Parkes and Mr. Tibbett? What became of them? Well, that's another tale, and a glimpse at their futures can be found on the next page

# Reclaiming Her Heart

A Short Story Sequel to Enticing Miss Darcy

"A moment, please." Mr. Jones, the Parkes' butler, motioned to a chair that stood in the entrance hall and then strolled down the corridor, past the morning room on the left and the sitting room on the right, beyond the curved stairs, and to the door that was tucked just behind them.

Mr. Bernard Tibbett took a seat on the straight-backed chair and tapped his foot as he scowled at the flowers on the table across from him. Ralston! He shook his head and muttered the name. Of all the gentlemen to be bested by, it had to be Ralston – quip-filled, always pleasant, rarely somber, Jack Ralston! He blew out a great, distressed breath and shook his head. Miss Darcy had seemed like such a good choice. She was quiet, decorous, and indeed, all that he thought a young lady should be to make a proper, amiable wife. She reminded him so much of Mrs. Bell. How could she be like... He rose as the door to the right of the table containing the bouquet of flowers opened and revealed the person whose name completed his thoughts.

"Mr. Tibbett." Hazel Parkes spared him only a small nod. "Have you come to share your joyous news?"

"I know not of what you speak," he replied.

"Come now, Mr. Tibbett. I know I am a female, but I am not devoid of every mental faculty. I heard you speaking to Harold about your hopeful little appointment when I was waiting for my next partner after our dance. You do remember that dance, do you not? It was the one Miss Darcy was to have, but she had gone home with a headache."

Hazel clasped her hands firmly in front of her and arched an imperious brow at him.

"Eavesdropping is not becoming," he muttered.

Her eyes grew wide, and her nostrils flared as she sucked in a breath.

"Neither is..." She clamped her mouth closed. As long as the sun still shone from morning until evening, she would not admit to him that she still remembered his declaration of love for her — a declaration which had proven to be false. Instead, she schooled her features into a placating smile and said, "it was not intentionally done." Then, she dipped a small curtsey. "I will wish you joy and be on with my day."

Before he could say anything, she turned and hurried to the stairs. She could not stand there speaking with him and retain her composure. Anger and hurt warred within her, each threatening to spill out of her. Either she would dissolve into tears without explanation, or she would provide him with a harridan-worthy explanation about curs such as he before becoming a watery puddle of misery. As it was, she would do well to reach her room before such a calamity befell her.

Bernard watched her nearly run up the stairs to be away from him. She had seemed welcoming last evening. She had flirted and smiled while they danced. Not once had she been disagreeable, which had been a pleasant change from how she always greeted him since that house party last spring.

However, this morning, her goodwill seemed to have evaporated, and she, along with everyone else on whom he had called, was not pleased to see him. In fact, she had never looked at him with so much disdain. And her tone! It was perhaps sharper than it had been at Stanton's when she had told him in unequivocal words that he was the last gentleman on earth whom she would agree to marry.

He pasted a less perplexed and more pleasant look on his face as Mr. Jones returned to direct him into the study, where he could find Hazel's brother.

Harold Parkes closed the account book he had been attempting to reconcile and rose to greet his friend. "I had not expected to see you so early."

"I had hoped to be sitting in a different study," Bernard replied.

Harold motioned to the chairs near the hearth.

Bernard sank into the well-worn, mossy green, softness.

"I take it that your offer was not met with exuberance?" Harold scrubbed his face as he extended his legs and crossed his ankles.

"No. It was refused."

"Out of hand?" Harold asked with surprise.

"Not without explanation." Bernard rested his head against the back of the chair and looked up at the ceiling. "Apparently, your sister has bent Miss Darcy's ear about our misunderstanding at Stanton's last spring."

Harold guffawed. "Misunderstanding?" He shook his head.

"Disagreement," Bernard clarified.

"Are you still holding to that ridiculous ideology?"

"It is not ridiculous. Dr. Bell is happily married and has been for years, and his wife is precisely what a wife should be." Unlike his parents who constantly argued – not that many knew. His mother knew how to keep up appearances in public, but at home, whatever his father said, his mother refuted.

Harold blew out a breath. "Mrs. Bell is lovely, but she is not..." he paused and grimaced. "She has feathers for brains."

"She is sweet and obliging," Bernard countered, although he had to admit she was not the most astute lady with whom he had ever spoken. In fact, she was a trifle dull when left to herself to carry a conversation. However, a dull woman was better than a quarrelsome one.

"I will grant you that." Harold shifted in his chair. "So, tell me, was that the full extent of Miss Darcy's reason for refusing you?"

"No."

Being called out on his opinions by a lady he thought would make an excellent wife and then reprimanded by her grandmother, who was none other than the Dowager Countess of Matlock, would have been enough of a blow to bear, but it was not the thing that stung the most.

Bernard's upper lip curled in disgust. "Ralston," he fairly snarled the name.

"I beg your pardon?"

"It seems Miss Darcy also prefers Ralston to me."

What was it with that man? Jack Ralston was no better looking than he was, nor did the man possess a title or greater wealth than Bernard did.

A slow smile spread across Harold's face.

"This makes you happy?" Was everyone going to treat him oddly today?

Harold shrugged. "Perhaps."

How could everyone be so blasted pleased with Jack Ralston? Bernard crossed his arms and glared at his life-long friend. "Explain."

"I am not supposed to say a word."

"Then say several," Bernard ground out.

Harold's face pinched in a pained expression, and he shook his head. "Hazel."

It was only one word, but it said a great deal. Harold and his sister were closer than many siblings. They rarely kept any secret from each other. Bernard knew this. He also knew that he would be hard-pressed to extract from his friend a secret that his sister had shared with him.

"Both Miss Darcy and Ralston said she was set on snaring me."

"Ralston? Was he there when you made your offer?" Harold asked in surprise.

"No, he arrived after Miss Darcy had finished declaring her love for the sapskull. I imagine they are happily betrothed by now from the way he was looking at her all last night and again today. Besotted fool."

"Besotted he may be, but he's no fool. Alistair Pratt would not abide him if he were."

Bernard blew out a frustrated breath. "Do not defend him to me. I am in no mind to hear any further accolades about the incomparable Jack Ralston."

"I was not praising him. I was merely pointing out your error,"

Harold shot back. "He loves her, and according to you, she loves him. I wish them well."

Bernard rolled his eyes and then, grasping the arms of the chair, pushed to his feet. "I am not fit for company," he said.

"Or, at least, you are not fit for company who will not allow you to wallow in self-pity." Harold moved not a muscle other than those required for speaking and containing a smile.

"I am not wallowing! I was refused – again – over stupid books!" Bernard paced to the window and back. "They are books! Who refuses a man over the choice of a novel?" He shook his head. "This is precisely why a lady needs guidance because, without it, she will throw away a perfectly good offer for a stack of paper and ink! Books!" He made a full circuit of the small room and was halfway into a second before his friend broke the heavy silence.

"It is not books." Harold's voice was calm, measured, and a trifle dangerous, just the sort a gentleman might use before coolly calling for your execution.

Bernard spun toward him.

"I have told you before. Hazel did not refuse you because you did not approve of her reading material – which, I will add, was given to her by our mother, whom you unwittingly insulted in your tyrannical diatribe." He shook his head. "My father, my mother, and even I have always trusted Hazel to make informed and rational decisions, and at one time, you even wished to hear her opinions yourself. Yet, now, you would throw away a perfectly good match – my sister – over books! It is not Hazel who needs guidance."

Blowing out a breath, Harold rose. "Until last night, I did not know about your declaration to her before you left for school.

However, the whole ugly affair came pouring out of her after she heard you tell me of your desire to call on Mr. Darcy, leaving me with a weeping mess to console until Mother had found all the necessary tea and potions to help Hazel sleep."

Bernard gaped at his friend. "Hazel?"

"I know. It is hard to believe that a girl as seemingly sturdy and full of boldness as Hazel would melt into a pool of tears, but she is still a female." He rubbed his face. "It is the second time you have been the cause. She was in shambles for at least a fortnight after your *misunderstanding* last year. I understand that much better now." He shook his head. "I would have never expected you to be a cad."

"I am not." Was he?

"Perhaps you are not. Perhaps you did not realize that you would not suit until after you had declared yourself. I suppose it could be attributed to youthful ignorance."

Bernard swallowed. "Are you cutting ties with me?"

"I should, but I am not. However, it would be best if we kept our meetings to more public locales for a time." He exhaled loudly and shook his head. "For one, I am, despite my present appearance of relative calm, greatly offended by you on my sister's behalf. Also, and most importantly, it would not be best for Hazel to have you about, you see." He tipped his head back and forth from side to side as if measuring some thought. "Last night, my mother heard about your declaration," he said after a minute of contemplation, "and the full extent of your disagreement at Stanton's. She is less than pleased." He gave his friend a pointed look. "She is not home at present, so you are, for the time being, safe."

Mrs. Parkes was angry with him as well? Was there anyone left in London who was not? And why? Because he preferred people to agree with him?

"She's calling on your mother," Harold added.

There was another person who would be displeased with him. "Maybe I should call it a season and return to the country."

"It might be best. Then, Hazel can get on with finding a proper husband who will respect her for the person she is." Harold's tone was severe.

"You hate me."

"A bit," he admitted. "You broke my sister's heart – repeatedly. How can I not despise you at least somewhat, no matter our history?"

Bernard nodded solemnly. "I can understand that."

Harold exhaled deeply once again as if the topic was one that took a great deal of effort to canvas. "If I suspected it was intentionally done, I would have dragged you from your home last night and demanded satisfaction. However, I know that you can be a bit of an idiot, so, I did not."

An idiot? Harold thought of him in such a fashion? That news shocked him. "I thank you then for seeing me, and I will not importune you at home again."

Harold inclined his head in acceptance of Bernard's words. "I will likely see you at some soiree or another. Give it a few months. After Hazel has found a good match, then come around again. There is nothing like her children being happy to make my mother most welcoming. Until then, I will call on you or meet you at our club, unless Father is with me." He gave Bernard a wry smile. "When Mother is unhappy, so is Father."

"Again, I thank you for seeing me today."

"Better I than Hazel."

Bernard winced.

"She saw you?"

He nodded.

Harold sighed, and his shoulders drooped. "Then, you will understand if I do not show you out but go see to her?"

Was Hazel really so distraught? "She truly still loved me after she turned me away so harshly?"

To Bernard, 'How I could have even thought myself in love with a person like you is beyond my understanding' did not speak of lasting affection.

"Apparently, yes." Harold opened the door to the study. "Mother will be expected shortly. You should make your escape, though I do not envy what you will likely face when you arrive home."

Bernard bid his friend farewell. He knew his mother would not hide her displeasure. She had, for years, been hinting at a possible match between him and Hazel, and he had considered the idea a good one. He had always liked Hazel — quite a bit actually. She was spirited, bright, and pleasant – exactly the sort of lady he had always thought would best suit him until another lady who was also spirited, bright, and pleasant and whom he loved dearly, his mother, had begun arguing with his father at every turn and demanding a separate living establishment. Then, he was not entirely certain he was right, but by then, his heart had latched unto Hazel and would not let her go. So, he had pushed his doubt aside and told her that he loved her.

As he thought on the disharmony in his parent's marriage while he was at school and compared it to the marriage of Dr. Bell, the rector of the parish he attended during those years, he had come to the conclusion that a proper wife would be one who was quiet and demure, nearly mousy. He had held out hope that Hazel had matured into such a woman. Her letters to him were always proper. She spoke of nothing untoward. But then, when he had approached her last season at Stanton's, any hope of ever having a happy, peaceful marriage with Hazel Parkes had been dashed to bits by a blasted book! A book! If she would argue with him over one of Mrs. Radcliffe's concoctions, there was little promise that she would be the one to help him create the serene family for which he wished.

He climbed into his carriage. If only his head and his heart could agree upon the same thing! His head had led him to court and offer for Miss Darcy, who, despite appearing to be an ideal choice, had been just as disagreeable – though far less scathing – in her refusal. His heart, on the other hand, had shouted to him that offering for anyone who was not Hazel Parkes was folly of the greatest kind. And now, that heart was bleeding both for the pain that he knew he had caused Hazel and because it knew it would never have what it desired. Hazel would not suddenly become the quiet and demure wife for which he wished. In fact, she would become someone else's wife, and for the first time since that moment in the Stanton's garden, his head was not certain it had been right in allowing her to walk away.

~*~*~

"Parkes."

"Fitzwilliam," Harold replied with a nod.

Hazel pulled her eyes away from those gathered in the Armstrong's music room to see who had approached.

Edward Fitzwilliam, handsomely attired in a jacket of blue that made his eyes seem even closer to the colour of a midnight sky, stood next to her brother. "Miss Parkes," he addressed her with a smile, "you are looking fetching this evening."

"Thank you, Mr. Fitzwilliam. You are looking rather dashing yourself," Hazel replied.

"I do cut a fine figure, do I not?" A grin split his face as he puffed out his chest. "All we Fitzwilliam men do, you know."

Edward Fitzwilliam, the third son of the Earl of Matlock, had always been a bit of a saucy fellow. He was not at all full of himself, as his words might imply, but he could not resist the opportunity to respond with affected arrogance whenever the opportunity arose, especially if by doing so, he might also draw a smile from a pretty lady.

And draw a smile he did, as well as a satisfying giggle.

"Your cousin has mentioned that you and your brothers are quite handsome." Hazel felt a lightness she had not felt in three days lifting her chin and prodding her to be a trifle forward. "She truly cannot imagine why none – not one — of you has yet married."

Edward shook his head. "That does sound like Anne. Wait, it was Anne, of whom you spoke was it not? I do have other cousins. It could have just as easily been Georgiana." He shook his head again. "No, it had to have been Anne."

Again, Hazel giggled. "It was indeed Mrs. Pratt."

The gentleman next to her brother blew out a breath. "Between her and my grandmother, we shall all be married by summer." He shrugged. "The viscount is on the precipice, Darcy has already succumbed, and even sweet little Georgie is swiftly following suit. That leaves just the colonel and me as holdouts."

"Well, marriage is nothing into which one should run headlong," Harold said.

"Indeed, it is not!" Hazel agreed emphatically.

"You are not looking to marry this season?"

"No," both Parkes siblings replied.

"My cousin was hoping one of you might be on the happy path to matrimony."

Hazel pressed her lips together. Her heart hurt less each day, but her anger had yet to abate. That was why she was here tonight. She would share her distress with the people who were gathered, and then, she would reclaim the heart she had given Bernard Tibbett and find a far worthier gentleman to whom to give it.

"Until last week, I had hoped the same," she replied matter-of-factly. "However, not every gentleman can be brought up to scratch." Until last week, she had thought that they could, but Mr. Tibbett had certainly proven that wrong.

"Nor should they be," Harold muttered, earning him a grateful smile from his sister.

"My condolences to you on having run across a gentleman of impeccably poor taste." Edward shrugged in response to her furrowed brow. "He would have to have less than adequate mental abilities if he were to refuse you. I was not lying when I said you were fetching; however, I may have understated my approval to avoid looking like a green schoolboy."

The furrow became a scowl, and Edward put up a hand in protest. "I would pledge my oath at Old Bailey that it is true."

"You do look beautiful," Harold whispered. "I told you as much before we left home."

"But you are my brother," Hazel replied. "You are supposed to say such things to please me."

"And when have I ever said anything just to please you?" Harold asked with a laugh.

Hazel shrugged. "Very well, I shall believe you both."

"That is very good news," Edward said. "I should hate for you to hold firmly to a lie." He smiled at her skeptical look. "Now, if you do not already have a place to sit, might I suggest we find a place for three so that I might join you?"

"Do you truly wish to?" Hazel asked in surprise. She was still not certain she trusted his smooth words and pleasing manners, no matter how much she desired them to be true.

Edward's mouth curved up in a half grin. "Yes, I honestly do, but since I am under oath, I must inform you that my cousin would be greatly displeased if I did not at least attempt to sit with you."

Apparently, he was the truthful sort and not just a flatterer, for what gentleman would admit to such a thing unless he were being completely candid.

"Then, I shall secure us some seats," Harold said.

"Miss Parkes? Shall we follow?"

Hazel placed her hand on Edward's arm.

"Anne has also instructed me to tell you that she requires a call. She realizes that you have not been feeling quite the thing lately, but that is no reason to avoid all your friends." He shrugged as Hazel turned startled eyes toward him. "I am only repeating verbatim what she instructed me to say." His eyes sparkled. "She says tomorrow would be ideal, and she expects you for tea. However, do not be surprised if you must take it in her room as Alistair is being such a dear about following the doctor's orders to the letter."

"The doctor's orders?" Hazel repeated.

Edward nodded. "She has been having some pains, and so she is confined to bed with only short periods of time when she is allowed up and about."

"I wish I had known!" Hazel's brow furrowed. "Wait. How did she know I was not feeling well?"

Edward shook his head. "That I could not tell you." He smiled mischievously at her as she took a seat. "I suppose you will have to call on her to find out?"

"I suppose I shall," she agreed as he settled into the seat beside her.

Leaning toward her, Edward asked, "Are you performing?"

She nodded. It was the only reason she had ventured forth tonight instead of staying ensconced in her room with a book, a cup of chocolate, three quilts, and just as many cats — each demanding her attention and showering her with affection when she granted it. If only some men could be as responsive as cats!

"You have no music."

"I need none," Hazel returned with a smile. "I have chosen to do a piece that is very familiar to me." She could not have attempted anything new. Her mind had not been in the best form for practising the past three days. However, this song, which she had learned from her governess years ago, seemed to complement her melancholy brokenness quite well.

"You are very sure of yourself then?"

"Hazel is always sure of herself," Harold interjected into the conversation.

"Not any longer," Hazel muttered.

"He's a cad," her brother grumbled.

"Ah, I shall ask no further," said Edward. And he did not, he instead commented on the proportion of the windows, the fact that the drapery was not quite the shade of blue he preferred, and how a violin was not nearly so pleasing to the ear as its larger cousin, the violoncello. This led to a discussion of the piano versus the harp. As it turned out, Edward was unable to pick a favourite between those two instruments, leaving his opinion simply as it really depended upon who was playing. "I prefer a song be presented with emotion," he concluded.

"Then, you will enjoy my sister's performance." There was an ample amount of pride in Harold's voice.

Hazel patted his hand. Hopefully, she would not put so much feeling into her song tonight that it leaked out her eyes. However, she had a handkerchief at the ready just to be safe.

"I shall await it with great anticipation," Edward assured them both.

And from his open expression, Hazel believed he would. She watched him surreptitiously as the performances began.

Piano would be first, harp next, sundry other instruments, including one violoncello would follow, and then to close out the night, there would be voice.

Mr. Fitzwilliam applauded each performance, even the ones during which he grimaced. Bernard would not have done so. He would have only applauded those he enjoyed, and he would not have confined his displeasure to a grimace. He would have muttered about whatever it was he found wrong. Now that she was considering him through different eyes – ones that were no longer clouded by infatuation – she could see that he was excessively particular! How had she not seen that before? It was not as if he had ever hidden his opinions. Still, her heart ached at the thought of never being good enough for him, and that was very vexing. She should not care, but she did.

Finally, it was her turn.

Edward rose to allow her to exit their row and whispered his best wishes for her success as she passed him.

Her confidence buoyed by his words, she lifted her chin and approached the piano. Her singing instructor had already taken his place at the instrument. She gave him a welcoming smile and turned to face her audience. The room seemed even more crowded from this vantage point, but crowds had rarely daunted her before, and she was determined that they would not tonight either.

Her breath caught as she saw Bernard leaning against the wall at the back of the room. He was here and apparently alone. She allowed her eyes to focus on him only for a moment before seeking out her brother and Mr. Fitzwilliam. Then, she gave a nod of her head, her teacher began to play, and drawing a breath, she plunged into her song, releasing every ounce of her misery into the words.

> *As I walked forth one summer's day,*
> *To view the meadows green and gay*
> *A pleasant bower I espied*
> *Standing fast by the river side,*

*And in't a maiden I heard cry:*
*Alas! alas! there's none e'er loved as I.*[1]

Her voice and passion were captivating, and Edward followed her gaze as she sang. She scanned the room as if speaking to each person. However, her eyes often stopped for the briefest of moments on some object near the door. Although he had no desire to watch anything other than the enchanting songstress before him, his old friend Curiosity, begged him to see what or whom stood near the door.

Ah! It was as Anne had said. Miss Parkes had been jilted by Mr. Tibbett, and, from the way the lady was singing – as if her soul was being cleansed and she was laying a dear friend to rest – Miss Hazel Parkes would not be jilted by that fellow again. Surprisingly, the thought pleased him.

He returned to his attention to the pretty lady at the front of the room. She was just finishing her song and dabbing her eyes. As the last note faded, the room remained solemnly silent for three heartbeats before Edward stood and began applauding. Others soon followed his example.

Hazel graced him with a dazzling smile and made her way back to her seat.

"Magnificent," Edward said as Hazel once again took her seat. "You were correct, Parkes," he said to Harold. "I enjoyed that thoroughly."

"There is not another with her talent," boasted Harold.

"I would readily agree." Edward enjoyed how Hazel's cheeks grew rosy and how she attempted to hide a pleased smile.

---

1. *from* As I Walked Forth *by Robert Johnson*

There were yet three unfortunate ladies to sing. They were unfortunate because they had to follow Hazel's performance, and Edward was certain there was not another lady in all of England, whether on stage or beside a hearth, who could have followed Hazel and not suffered for it.

He attempted to pay attention to each performance and greet its ending with enthusiasm, but he could not.

He had been to many such soirees as this at his grandmother's request. At each one, he would smile and bow as required. He would congratulate and commend young ladies to earn a giggle or a blush. And each time he would return home to give a report to his grandmother about the number in attendance and which lady had piqued his interest. It was normally some young debutante that had seemed the prettiest and most amusing, but never had one of them caused him to feel so distracted as the lady beside him. It was a most unusual but not wholly unpleasant feeling – unsettling, perhaps, disquieting, most assuredly, but not distressing. In fact, it was in a way, extremely alluring.

After the last lady took her seat and their hostess once again thanked them for their attendance, Edward found himself not wanting to make a hasty exit. He wished to stay right here with Miss Parkes. The evening had consisted of a song and a smile mingled with a few words of conversation, but for him, it had been the most enjoyable evening of any season in which he had participated. As people began to make their way to the door, he reluctantly rose from his seat.

"Will you be calling on my cousin tomorrow?" he asked, offering an arm to Hazel to escort her from the room.

"I must. I am sorry I have not done so already."

"Then, you will not be home to callers tomorrow?" He cast a look over his shoulder at her brother.

The gentleman smiled and nodded his assent to the silent request to call on his sister.

"No, I will not be, but then, I do not expect any callers."

"None? After that performance?"

Hazel laughed. "I do not expect any." Her left brow rose. "Should I expect anyone?"

She did not dip her head or flutter her lashes. Her expression was open. This was not an attempt to tease or flirt. She seemed genuinely interested in his answer. "Not if you are at my cousin's," he replied. "However, my cousin may be in need of entertainment, so perhaps I will call on her as well."

"I am certain she would appreciate that."

"I have a meeting with a friend tomorrow and had planned to use the carriage," Harold interjected. "If Fitzwilliam is going to Mrs. Pratt's and so are you, why do you not share a carriage? You have a gig, do you not, Fitzwilliam?"

"I do."

"Then it is settled," said Harold.

"Since when do you have an appointment tomorrow?" Hazel questioned her brother.

He smiled and shrugged. "Since this moment."

Her mouth dropped open. "Are you attempting to play match-maker?"

The shock and displeasure in her voice caused Edward to chuckle. Most ladies would not remonstrate their brothers in pub-lic. Hazel Parkes was perhaps the most interesting woman of the ton he had ever met. "I certainly hope so," he replied before Harold could do more than stammer a couple of times.

"You do?" Hazel turned wide eyes toward him.

"I do," he replied. To his delight, she did not turn away or shrink from his unwavering gaze. She was no milquetoast maiden.

Her head tipped to the side as she studied him. Patiently, he waited for her reply.

"What do you think of the writings of Mrs. Radcliffe?"

He blinked at the unusual question. "They are delightfully horrid novels."

"You have read them?"

"One or two. Have you? For if you have not, I would recommend *The Romance of the Forest.*"

"Indeed?" she asked in surprise as a smile spread across her face.

"Most certainly. It is highly diverting."

"Yes, I thought so, too. As did my mother, who gave it to me as a gift."

"A book is a thoughtful gift. Your mother is wise."

"You do not condemn her for giving me a novel?"

Again, he blinked. "Why should I? She is a woman of sense, is she not? She is capable of making rational decisions?"

"She most certainly is," said Harold with some force.

There was obviously something important about this discussion that Edward had not yet figured out. "Then why should I question her choice of novel for either herself or her daughter?"

"Some would say that only a gentleman knows what is best for a lady," Hazel answered.

Ah! If he were a betting man, and occasionally he was, Edward would say this had something to do with Mr. Tibbett. "I do not hold to such ideals." The lady beside him expelled a soft breath of relief.

"Then, my brother may play matchmaker to his heart's content."

To his delight, her eyes held his with unflinching intensity.

"May I then accompany you to Anne's house tomorrow?" he asked.

"You may."

The crowd near the door had dwindled, so they moved forward.

"Have you ever read a law book?" Edward asked as they reached the steps of the Armstrong's home.

"No, never," Hazel replied. "Why would I?"

"There are tales in them that would put even Mrs. Radcliffe's imaginings to shame."

"Do you think I should read one?" she asked in surprise.

He shook his head as he shrugged. "If you wish. But I would warn you that the stories are not made up."

"You would really allow me to read one?"

"You are a rational being, are you not?"

"Most days," Harold muttered, earning him a glare from his sister.

"Then I do not see why you could not be trusted to decide if you wished to read it or not."

"Huh."

The sparkling, witty Miss Hazel Parkes seemed to be lost for words for a moment. Then, as they were approaching their carriage, she said, "I think I would need to read one account or a portion of one before deciding if I should like to read further."

Edward smiled. "I shall deliver one such portion to you on the morrow when I arrive to take you to my cousin's home."

"It is fine to read it, is it not?" she asked her brother.

He nodded. "You will judge wisely."

"Thank you," she said both to her brother and Edward. "I should like to read it."

"Until tomorrow." Edward handed her into her carriage and kept to his spot on the walk until the Parkes' carriage was lost in traffic. Then, with a whistle on his lips, he turned to make his way home and tell his grandmother about the enchanting Hazel Parkes.

~*~*~

As Bernard Tibbett watched Hazel enter her carriage, his heart sank. She was gone. He had no doubt after her performance tonight, and the way she and Fitzwilliam had been conversing while a very satisfied looking Harold oversaw the whole thing, that he had thrown away any chance he would ever have with the lady who had first captured his heart. He sighed. "Books," he muttered as he made his way to the carriage that would, tomorrow, carry him home to his father's estate.

There was a young lady, two estates over, who had never once been to town for a season, though she was old enough to have done so twice over. She seemed the quiet, demure sort. He would pay her a visit.

He sighed heavily once more, resigning himself to his fate. The peace such a match would bring would surely outweigh the heaviness he felt at present. Would it not?

It would, but not immediately.

While others might have looked upon Mr. Tibbett's life as dull, he himself did not find it so. He occasionally regretted Hazel Parkes, but with each passing month the regret became less and less, and he grew to love his quiet wife and reveled in his peaceful country life.

Hazel read several of Edward's law books. Each one made her shudder and demand that something be done to not allow such things to happen again. Edward would simply smile at his beautiful, opinionated, spirited wife and assure her that he was doing his best. Did he not hold a seat in parliament? And did not his wife arrange the best soirees — soirees at which she won more than one fellow Member of the House to his position?

Hazel always answered the same way – with a kiss and a reminder of just how fortunate he was to have her. England would surely devolve into anarchy without women such as she.

Edward would wrap his arms around her and laugh as he replied, "I could not agree more."

What often followed such a declaration cannot be shared on these pages as it is much too improper for a book such as this. However, about ten months after such a discussion, it was not unusual for a new Fitzwilliam to be added to Lady Margaret's growing brood of well-loved great-grandchildren.

Such a happy life was as apt an ending as any playwright might pen. For what had begun for Miss Parkes as a tragedy had, in the third act, shifted to something altogether different when Hazel gathered her fortitude, attended a musicale, and presented a song that led her to Edward Fitzwilliam and reclaiming her heart.

# Mr. Darcy's Comfort

*Sometimes the deepest sorrow can bring the greatest joy*

# Chapter 1

Fitzwilliam Darcy lifted his pen and paused while he carefully considered his words. As he did so, he allowed himself to watch the enchanting Miss Elizabeth Bennet smile at something she was reading. For a moment, his thoughts were captivated by what it might be which had caused her amusement rather than how he should broach the next topic in the letter he was attempting to write to his cousin Colonel Richard Fitzwilliam.

So far, Darcy had inquired after his sister and had commented on the general news of the area and the more specific details concerning his friend Charles Bingley and Netherfield, the estate where he was now ensconced. Whether that ensconcing was more of Darcy's free will or a sense of duty was debatable. Helping his friend was no burden. However, abiding the man's sisters was a bit of a task and trying to Darcy's patience. He should just tell Caroline Bingley of his engagement. Perhaps then she would stop fawning over him at every turn, but he could not do that.

His betrothal, though well-known within the family and amongst the small circle of friends his aunt entertained at Rosings, was not something he wished to have published far and wide. Nor was it something which had ever been verified by him. In fact, he had yet to admit to the reality of such an arrangement in which he found himself to more than his younger sister, his cousin to whom he now wrote, and, of course, to his betrothed. He had not even confirmed its veracity with his aunt, Lady Catherine de Bourgh, even though it was her daughter, Anne, whom he was expected to soon marry.

Anne had insisted that he not publicly tie himself to such an arrangement until it was well and truly a thing which must be. She had held out hope that she would find another to care for her, but she had not. And then, she had insisted that her health be stronger than it was before being required to perform the duties of a wife. However, she had not grown stronger. Now, as she approached her twenty-third birthday, it was no longer avoidable, and Anne had, on Darcy's last trip to Rosings in the spring, agreed that come the new year, they would marry.

Darcy had willingly agreed. He saw no need to delay further. He and Anne had always gotten on well together. There was no reason for him to believe that they would be anything other than happy, save for the nagging worry that he always carried with him regarding her health. He cared for Anne, and he knew that the intimacy that marriage would bring would likely also bring a new, more profound, and enduring sort of love. The fact that she shared a constitution that was as weak as his mother's drew him to morose thoughts and reflections on the pain he had experienced first with his mother's passing and then again when his father died. To lose a well-loved parent was gut-wrenching, but to lose a wife...

He sighed. He was not certain he could survive it half as well as his father had.

A chuckle from the lady reading the book across from where he wrote drew him back from his reverie. She was why he was writing.

"Mr. Darcy," Mr. Sedlow, Netherfield's butler stood at Darcy's side, speaking in a low, discreet tone, "there is a gentleman here to see you, but he requests that you speak to him in the study."

"Who is it?" Darcy inquired as he tucked his pen away and folded his letter.

"A Colonel Fitzwilliam, sir. He says it is of great importance and privacy is required."

Darcy's brow furrowed. It was extremely unusual that his cousin did not enter the library and make his presence known to one and all. Richard was fond of attention and more at ease in company than tucked away in a room with a book for any length of time.

Bingley looked up from where he was conversing with Miss Bennet near the fire and gave Darcy a quizzical look as Darcy rose to leave the room. Darcy shrugged in response. He knew little more than Bingley did about why he, and only he, was being summoned. It could not be about his sister Georgiana for Richard had not been in town. He had been to Brighton with his father.

Darcy stopped mid-stride as he entered the study. Richard was standing at the window gazing out over a barren field. His shoulders drooped, and, on his arm, he wore a band of black.

"What has happened?" Darcy crossed to where Richard was.

"I could not allow an express rider to deliver this to you," he held out a letter edged with black.

Taking the letter, Darcy broke the seal.

*Darcy,*

Darcy stumbled toward a chair. His legs were not going to hold him upright much longer. The words of the letter swam before him.

"She died quickly," Richard whispered. "She was coming down to tea and missed a step or caught her toe in her hem or something. She was gone before any of us could reach her."

Tears slid silently down Darcy's cheeks. "My Anne is dead?" His voice was barely a whisper.

Richard nodded. "She will be interned next Thursday. My father knew you would wish to attend."

"Of course," Darcy muttered. He did not wish to stand beside yet another grave filled with the remains of someone he held dear, but he needed to see her, to send her on her way. "Do you wish to leave now?"

"Morning will be soon enough," Richard replied. "There is little you can do. Father has likely seen to everything by now. He had begun even before he wrote that letter to you."

"And Aunt Catherine?"

"The laudanum in her wine is helping. Father is insisting that she join him at Matlock until he is needed in town."

"I could stay with her at Rosings," Darcy offered.

Richard shook his head. "No, Father will not hear of it. You have given your word to Bingley, and since you no longer have a betrothed, Father would like to remind you of your duty to Pemberley." Richard smiled wryly. "He apologizes for being so direct."

Darcy's head bobbed up and down slowly as if he understood what was being said to him, but in truth, he found his thinking muddled.

He needed to be outside, away from the walls of this study which seemed to draw closer with each breath. He loosened his cravat as he rose. "I am going for a ride," he said, brushing tears from his cheeks with the palm of his hand.

"I will ride with you."

Darcy pressed his lips together and shook his head. He did not wish for anyone to witness the completeness of his grief. He wanted to weep in private.

"You should not be alone," Richard insisted. "It is part of the reason I insisted on delivering this news to you myself."

"Please." The word was difficult to form and get out. As it was, it came out as little more than a weak plea.

"I will keep my distance," Richard replied. "I soiled many handkerchiefs yesterday as well as a few on my ride today, and I was not promised to her." He placed a hand on his cousin's shoulder. "You will eventually need to ask questions. You are Fitzwilliam Darcy, after all."

Darcy nodded as he brushed away more tears. It was impossible for him to voice any argument, whether strong or weak, that he should be allowed to mourn in private. His voice failed him, and his mind was suddenly so very weary.

"Since I am still dressed for riding, I shall inform our host of my arrival and your plans to travel," Richard said as they stepped into the corridor. He grasped Darcy by the shoulders and turned him about. "Use the servants' stairs," he ordered. "Miss Bingley will not look for you there." He gave him a push in that direction. "Send word when you are on your way to the stables."

For once, Darcy was glad for his cousin's decisive manners and ability to see problems before they could present themselves. He had no desire to see anyone, let alone, Miss Bingley. So, he did as instructed and hurried to the servants' stairs, pausing for a moment to inform a man that his horse would be required before taking the flight two steps at a time.

"Mr. Darcy," Elizabeth said in surprise as he stepped into the hall.

"Miss Elizabeth," he nodded his head in greeting. Blast! She was seeing her sister to her room. He had hoped everyone would still be in the library, but of course, Miss Bennet was not well enough to remain in company for long. Even now, he could see the tiredness in her posture and eyes.

"Are you well, sir?" Elizabeth asked.

"I have had some unsettling news," he answered.

"I am sorry to hear it."

"Thank you." He made to move past her, but for some reason, he could not do so without explaining himself further. "My cousin Anne has died," he put it as starkly as he could. He did not wish to couch the news with anything which would make it sound any less harsh than it was. "We were to be married," he added.

Jane gasped. "Oh, how tragic," she whispered.

"Colonel Fitzwilliam, another one of my cousins, just brought me the news. I will leave in the morning." He gave them a small bow. "I shall wish you a quick recovery, Miss Bennet, as I am uncertain if I will see you before I leave."

"You will return, will you not?" Jane asked.

Darcy nodded. "I have given my word to Bingley." He could feel his throat tightening once again, and he ignored a wayward tear which slid down his cheek. He needed to be in his room. "Miss Elizabeth." He bowed once more and turned to leave them. However, a hand on his arm kept him from making his escape. He looked first at the small hand and then lifted his eyes to Elizabeth's face.

She said not a word. She only squeezed his arm and gave him a small smile before turning back to her sister. It was a little gesture, but one which was filled with great compassion. She did not try to offer some platitude or trite word of comfort. Her eyes conveyed her understanding, and her silence allowed for his grief to be acceptable.

He watched her pull her sister close as they continued on their way to Jane's room and was struck once again by how different she was from most of the ladies of his acquaintance. Her manners fascinated him. He closed his eyes and turned away. How could he be thinking of Miss Elizabeth in such terms at a time like this?

While his mind reproved him, Darcy's feet carried him to his room where his man waited to make him ready for riding. Darcy smiled to himself, knowing there was only one way his man knew to be awaiting him. Richard had likely sent him before going to the library to share his news with Bingley. Richard was much like his father in that regard. Lord Matlock was known for how readily he could formulate and execute a plan. He had an eye for detail and all the charm of a rake intent on seducing a maiden when it was needed to persuade someone to his cause. While Darcy was proficient at noting details and constructing plans, he lacked the finesse his uncle and cousin possessed.

He sighed. Lacking charismatic adeptness was much less of an issue when running an estate than it was when finding a mistress for that estate.

He thanked his man and pocketed the extra handkerchiefs that had been laid out for him on his bed as the weight of his loss settled in around him once again, causing him to pause before leaving his room. "Anne," he whispered, "how will I ever happily manage my responsibilities without you?" He lifted his eyes toward the ceiling. "I cannot do this on my own," he prayed. Then, he pulled the door open, looked up and down the hall, and, seeing as no one, save a maid, was about, hurried toward the servants' stairs and his escape into the countryside of Hertfordshire.

# Chapter 2

"Good morning." Elizabeth kept her voice low as she entered the breakfast room where Darcy sat cradling a cup of tea. The man looked dreadful, but that was to be expected from one who was grieving. Had not Mr. Goodwin looked positively ghastly after Mrs. Goodwin and Celia died? Grief was a taxing master.

"Did you sleep at all?" she asked. From the bags under his eyes, she doubted it.

He shook his head. "Only a little."

The words came out in a raspy whisper, causing Elizabeth to stop in her tracks and turn toward him instead of continuing on to procure a bit of food from the sideboard. "Are you planning to leave early?" She watched him grimace as he swallowed the sip of tea he had just taken before she inquired.

"Yes," he managed a whisper.

Her brow furrowed. "I do not think it is wise."

His eyes grew wide, and his jaw did that thing it did when Miss Bingley was beginning to annoy him.

"Pray..." he turned his head and coughed lightly "...tell why."

Elizabeth poured a cup of tea and then took a seat near him. "You are ill."

"It is nothing," he retorted.

"Your throat hurts, you are coughing, and I would dare to venture that you have a fever."

He shrugged and took a sip of his tea, grimacing once again as he swallowed. "I must go."

She nodded. "You must, I agree, but you need not go today."

"I must."

Elizabeth drew a breath and released it slowly. There were feelings that one did not just forget and that often renewed their acquaintance with a person when witnessed in the mien of another. "I can imagine how much you must long to be near her, even if she is no longer here, but you cannot travel when you are so ill. If you rest for a day or two, the fever will likely break, just as it did for Jane, and then you may venture forth. You will still arrive with time to do and say all that you feel you must."

Darcy shook his head. "You cannot know."

Elizabeth took a deliberately slow sip of her tea. "You cannot know that I cannot."

The way his brow furrowed was gratifying to a degree because it meant he was considering what she had said, but it also worried her since, to this point, he had not been slow with a rejoinder during any of the discussions they had had where their opinions had not immediately agreed.

"You are not the only person to have suffered loss," she explained softly.

"I apologize."

"You are unwell, so you are forgiven," she replied with a small smile. "Now, to the issue at hand..." She paused to greet Colonel Fitzwilliam as he entered. "You must not focus solely on your desires," she continued as the colonel began gathering his breakfast. "You have a sister, do you not?"

Darcy's brows remained furrowed as he nodded.

"To whom will you leave her when your fever becomes rampant, and you expire and all from a want of patience?" It was harsh, but he seemed the stubborn sort, whose brain was currently addled by illness and who needed an argument to be laid before him in indisputable terms.

"It is but a chill."

Elizabeth wanted to roll her eyes. He was perhaps more stubborn than Lydia!

"You are ill?" Richard asked as he took his seat.

"He is," Elizabeth answered. "You can hear it in his voice and, if you watch, even tea hurts his throat." Her words matched Darcy's grimace perfectly as he swallowed. "And he has not refuted my claim that he likely has a fever."

Richard chuckled. "You are as devious as the nursemaid I had when I was a boy. She always knew what ailed me before I ever admitted to it."

Elizabeth hid a small smile behind her cup as she took a sip of her tea. "It is beneficial to know the signs of illness if one wishes to cover them and avoid the apothecary's concoctions." She placed her cup on the table.

Again, Richard chuckled. "I wish I had been that clever."

Elizabeth inclined her head in acceptance of the compliment. "He should not travel," Elizabeth said before taking another sip of her tea.

"I would agree," said Richard. "I can send a message to Father letting him know we will arrive later than expected."

"I must go," Darcy insisted.

Elizabeth raised a brow and looked at Richard.

"Not if you have a fever," Richard said.

Darcy cast a displeased look at Elizabeth.

"I must go check on Jane," she said. "I think she is planning to spend a bit longer in company today. We may even be able to return home soon if she keeps progressing." She paused. "If going home were as necessary for Jane as your trip is for you, Mr. Darcy, she would be well enough to travel already – not that my mother would hear of it — but in my estimation, she would be. And it has only been two days. Be patient."

Her plea was met with a resigned sigh and a shrug, but it was progress.

"Broth and tea," she said as she dipped a curtsey. "And sleep," she added as she left the room.

"I can send for the apothecary." She heard the colonel suggesting.

She could only imagine the refusal with which such a suggestion must have been met. Mr. Darcy did not strike her as the sort that wished to be coddled and fed potions. In that way, they were much the same. Elizabeth disliked being wrapped in over many blankets with a poultice around her throat and a horrid tasting draught to take. However, there were times when even she had to admit that it was necessary.

She climbed the stairs and slowly wandered down the hall toward Jane's room. She ran her finger along the smooth mahogany top of a table which stood in the hall and smiled at the chair with its leafy brocade standing dutifully beside it. It was strange to be wandering these halls once again after so many years. Parts of it felt very familiar, yet none of it felt as welcoming and happy as it once had when Celia slept in the room Jane now used.

Elizabeth tapped lightly on Jane's door before opening it. "How are you this morning?" she asked as she crossed to take a seat next to the bed where Jane was propped up with a tray, bearing tea and dry toast as well as an egg, sitting next to her.

Jane's smile was relaxed and natural, a sure sign that she was indeed recovering. "Not even the toast hurts this morning, and my stomach actually rumbled."

Elizabeth placed a hand on her sister's forehead. "You are still delightfully cool, but not chilled?"

Jane shook her head. "No, not at all. I shall be well enough to go home very soon." She leaned toward where her sister sat. "Though I must admit I would rather stay."

"And why is that?" Elizabeth already knew the answer but would not stop her sister from voicing it. Jane's happiness was always contagious, and, at the moment, Elizabeth felt as if she could use a bit of cheering up.

Jane's eyes sparkled and, after coughing softly into her handkerchief, she picked up her cup of tea and sighed. "Mr. Bingley."

"You truly like him?"

Jane nodded. "Very much." She sighed once again. "I would almost dare to say I love him, but it is too soon for such things. I have had so very little time in company with him that I am certain it is only presently infatuation. However, I am certain, and nearly set on the idea, that I could very easily come to love him with a slightly longer acquaintance."

Elizabeth pulled her feet up and tucked them under her dress. "Even with sisters such as he has?"

The teacup that was just about to touch Jane's lips lowered, and she gave Elizabeth a serious look. "It is not *his* sisters who I fear will cause me heartache. You do remember Lydia and Kitty, do you not?"

Elizabeth sighed. "And Mary."

Jane shook her head as she swallowed. "Mary knows how to hold her tongue and does not flaunt herself as Lydia and Kitty do. If any of our sisters are to drive away possible matches, it is those two."

"If our mother does not do it first."

The comment was met with a small sigh of resigned agreement. "If he were to ask," Jane's eyes studied the content of her cup carefully as she spoke, "I would accept even though I do not, as of yet, love him."

"You would consider marriage without love?" Elizabeth asked in surprise.

"I do not think it would remain so," Jane answered. "Mr. Bingley is kind. He has been very respectful and solicitous. I would not fear being treated ill. And he is not poor. I would want for nothing." She paused as she ate a small bite of egg. "I am not getting any younger. Gentlemen such as Mr. Bingley do not arrive in Hertfordshire daily, and our sisters are not growing less silly. I fear they and our mother will drive away all the sensible men. Therefore, if a sensible and amiable gentleman such as Mr. Bingley were to offer, I would accept with alacrity."

Elizabeth traced the outline of a flower on the arm of her chair. What Jane said made sense. "Do you think there will ever be another such gentleman who might take on your slightly less pretty, decidedly less patient sister?"

"Oh, Lizzy!" Jane cried. "I shall see to it that you are presented with the best gentlemen in all of England when I am married. You shall be only slightly less happy than I." She winked as she took a sip from her cup.

Elizabeth shook her head and chuckled, but she knew it was true. Jane would do whatever she could to see that Elizabeth was happy. She always had. Nurturing was just part of who Jane was.

"There is Mr. Darcy." Jane brushed a few wayward crumbs from her toast off the blanket. "He is no longer betrothed."

Elizabeth's eyes grew wide. "Jane!"

"In time. Not now." She took a sip of her tea. "I think you would suit."

"No, we would not."

Jane shrugged. "I think you would. He is intelligent and well-read. He does not shy away from a debate – that is what you said, is it not?"

Elizabeth nodded slowly. She had not shared that fact with Jane to recommend Mr. Darcy as a candidate for marriage. She had said it because she had found it delightful to torment both him and Miss Bingley by refusing to agree with him on all points.

"He is wealthy, and from how he spoke of his cousin, he is a man capable of deep attachment."

"He might wish for a handsome wife," Elizabeth protested. She found it particularly annoying when Jane was being sensible about something with which she herself did not agree. Arguing was enjoyable. Losing an argument was far less so.

"You are handsome," Jane retorted. "He said not handsome *enough*, and that does not mean you are not handsome."

"He said I was tolerable. Tolerable."

"He was betrothed. He was not supposed to find you anything more than tolerable."

Oh, Jane was impossible at times!

"But he is no longer betrothed, and in time, when he is ready to begin his search for a wife anew, he will find you more than tolerable because he can," Jane continued.

Elizabeth rolled her eyes. "You are as bad as Mama!" she scolded.

"No," Jane replied with an impertinent grin. "Mama would never think a gentleman could find you and your love of books to be anything more than merely tolerable." Jane reached over and placed a hand on Elizabeth's knee. "Just one of her many foolish notions," she added softly. "You are handsome and intelligent. Precisely the sort of lady I could see someone like Mr. Darcy finding irresistible."

"Jane!"

"And now you know how I feel when Mama begins praising me."

"You poor dear."

"Precisely," Jane replied. "It shall be a relief when I am finally married and can no longer be pushed forward at every gentleman to whom we are introduced."

The room fell silent for a few moments as Jane finished eating her breakfast, allowing Elizabeth's mind to wander back to the gentleman in the breakfast room, whom, though she would never admit such to her sister, she found to be nearly as fascinating as he was disagreeable.

"He is ill," she blurted.

"Who is ill?" Jane asked.

"Mr. Darcy. I saw him in the breakfast room before I came to see you. Colonel Fitzwilliam was there, too. Not at first, but before I left."

Jane tilted her head and studied Elizabeth in a way that made Elizabeth feel uneasy.

"You will like Colonel Fitzwilliam," Elizabeth continued. "I met him last night after you had gone to sleep."

"Is he handsome?"

Elizabeth shrugged. "I suppose he is, though not so pleasing to look at as Mr. Bingley, nor so tall as Mr. Darcy. He is, however, the second son of an earl."

"An earl?" Jane repeated. There was a bit too much eagerness in Jane's tone. It reminded Elizabeth a bit of her mother when it came to prospects of worthy gentlemen.

"Lord Matlock is Mr. Darcy's uncle and Colonel Fitzwilliam's father."

"A colonel would not be a bad match," she gave Elizabeth a pointed look as she said it.

"Jane!"

"What?"

"You are as bad as Mama!"

"I only wish to see you well-settled."

Both girls dissolved into laughter as each knew that Jane's response was precisely what Mrs. Bennet's argument would have been.

"Perhaps I am a bit too much like her," Jane said once they had sobered. "Now, tell me about Mr. Darcy being ill."

"He has a fever, a cough, and a sore throat. There is not much else to tell." She leaned her head back on the chair and allowed her eyes to follow the bit of carved trim that ran around the edge of the ceiling for as far as she could see it without turning her head. "He will not be leaving today." Her eyes filled with tears as she thought about him being confined to Netherfield instead of travelling as she knew he wished to do.

"What is wrong?" Jane asked.

Elizabeth shook her head. "I was merely thinking about Celia and being at Aunt Gardiner's."

Jane once again reached over and laid a hand on her sister's knee. "You would not have been allowed to attend the funeral."

"I know, but I wish I had been near."

"We will visit the churchyard as soon as I am able," Jane assured her.

Elizabeth nodded and brushed a tear from her cheek. "It is odd being here. Even after all this time, I still expect to see her."

"She is here," Jane replied. "In your memories, she is here and always will be. We must remember the past as it gives us pleasure. Celia would not wish for it any other way."

Elizabeth brushed another tear from her cheek. "I know, and I shall try. I truly shall."

# Chapter 3

For the fifth time in fewer than twenty minutes, Darcy bemoaned having to lie in bed when he should be halfway to Kent. He had never liked lying about doing nothing, and presently, he disliked, even more, the way such idleness gave time for reflection upon morose things.

He pushed back the blankets and swung his feet over the edge of the bed and into his slippers. He paused a moment to allow the room to stop spinning before he rose like a creaky old man with rheumatism. It took him a full minute to decide if pulling on enough clothing to be proper and escaping the confines of this room was worth the whole-being aching effort it would likely be. Finally, as his legs began to protest that they must either find rest or movement, he pulled on his breeches and tied a robe snugly around himself, making sure that the collar was pulled up his neck as high as it could go. There was no way he was going to make an effort to don a cravat. Frankly, he did not care if someone saw his bare neck as long as he could find a chair in the library in which to sit and read, but, despite his rather apathetic attitude, he would attempt to keep himself covered.

"Where are you going?"

Darcy groaned as Richard met him in the hallway before he could reach the servants' stairs. "To the library."

Richard crossed his arms and stood in his path.

"I cannot stay in bed."

Richard remained stoically blocking his path.

"I will not stay in bed," Darcy amended.

"There is a chair near the hearth in your room. You may sit in that."

"I do not want to remain in my room."

"You sound very much like a recalcitrant child." Richard smiled as Darcy growled and then coughed.

"There is too much to think about in there." If he were in the library, there would be numerous books through which he could page as he attempted not to think of how his future had changed so drastically from what it was to what it was now to be.

"There will be too much to think about in every room of this house, as well as every acre of its fields and surrounding park." Richard grasped him by the shoulders and spun him toward his room. "You shall keep your diseased person to your room."

There was not enough strength left in Darcy's diseased person to protest, and so, he dutifully allowed himself to be directed back to his room.

"I shall go to the library and procure you a stack of distraction. Miss Elizabeth," he said as Elizabeth stepped into the hall, "do you have a maid with you?"

"There is one in Jane's room," she answered in confusion. "Does Mr. Darcy need something?"

"Yes," Richard replied with a grin, "he needs someone to ensure he stays in his room until I return."

"Would not a footman be better than a maid?"

"The maid is not for Darcy," Richard replied. "The maid is for you. He will stay put much better if a lady such as yourself is watching rather than a footman whom he can order about."

"I would not..." Darcy began only to be cut off by his cousin.

"You have already attempted an escape. I will not risk a further attempt." Richard turned back toward Miss Elizabeth. "You proved yourself adept at being cunning this morning in the breakfast room. He shall have to work hard to outwit you, especially with his fever-addled brain."

Elizabeth looked from the colonel to his cousin and back as she shook her head. "I am certain it is not proper. I may not be from town, but even here in the wilds of Hertfordshire there are rules of propriety which must be followed, and entering a gentleman's bedchamber, even accompanied by a maid, is not on the list of acceptable activities."

"I will leave the door open, and I promise I will not be long. Your reputation will not be damaged. You may simply stand at the door. My cousin is going to sit near the hearth and attempt to be patient while I fetch him a book."

"And where are Miss Bingley and Mrs. Hurst?" Elizabeth asked as she followed Richard toward Darcy's room.

"Your maid," Richard said with a tilt of his head back toward Jane's room.

"Right." Elizabeth turned, hurried back to Jane's room, and popped her head inside to call the maid.

"Good," Richard declared as he saw the maid approaching with Elizabeth. "Miss Bingley and Mrs. Hurst are gossiping in the sitting room. I think you will be safe from them." He followed Darcy into his room and, taking a blanket from the bed, draped it across his cousin when Darcy sat down. "Now," he said turning to the maid, "I have asked Miss Elizabeth to ensure that Mr. Darcy is well while I dash down to the library and fetch a few books."

"I could go to the library," Elizabeth offered.

Richard shook his head. "I know which books he will find most distracting."

Elizabeth's brows furrowed.

"Truly, I would send you if I were certain you would bring what he needs..."

Elizabeth's mouth dropped open, and a small huff escaped her cutting off his words.

"It is not that I do not find you clever –"

She crossed her arms and leveled a stern glare at him, which seemed to fluster him quite a bit.

"I am not wearing a dress and can go faster."

She bit back a laugh. "I think you would find yourself mistaken if we were to put that to the test, but I will allow it to remain unproven."

Laughter followed by coughing erupted from the room.

"I shall bring some port," Richard added with a smug look.

"I would have chosen brandy," Elizabeth replied with a lift of her chin.

Richard shook his head and chuckled. "Not just clever," he muttered as he turned to leave, "you are also indomitable."

"Do not forget it," she called after him. Then, she took a position leaning against the doorframe.

"He is not easily flustered," Darcy said to her. "I must thank you for the entertainment."

Elizabeth curtseyed.

"I will remain right here until he returns. You do not have to stand guard."

Elizabeth shook her head. "And allow your cousin to think I am incapable of doing as instructed? I think not, sir."

Darcy grinned. Miss Elizabeth was delightfully refreshing compared to the ladies of the ton. Not one of them would have protested being asked to attend him to his room, where, after his cousin had vacated the hall, they would have sent the maid scurrying and affected a compromise. But Miss Elizabeth would not. She would stand just there at the door, keeping watch.

"Have you slept yet?" she asked.

He shook his head. "I have tried."

Elizabeth nodded. "You see her face when you close your eyes."

"How do you know?"

"How much do you know about the owner of this estate, Mr. Darcy?"

Her response caused him to pull back in surprise. "I know his family has owned it for many years. It is not entailed, and he has no male heir. However, he does have a daughter who is married, and he would rather spend his days near her than here."

"He is a widower."

"Yes, I had heard that."

"He used to have two daughters. Ava is the one who is married. She is six and twenty. Celia would have been twenty last month on the twenty-third, but she died with her mother in a carriage accident five years ago."

He watched her close her eyes and shake her head as if not wishing to continue. "She was your friend?" he asked softly.

Her head bobbed up and down slowly. "I was visiting my Aunt Gardiner in town when the accident happened. I was not allowed to come home." She brushed a tear from her cheek. "That is why you must rest, for you must go to your –"

"Anne," he supplied when she looked to him.

"As soon as you can."

"I am sorry you did not get to come home."

She shrugged a shoulder and dashed away another tear. "Thank you." She attempted to smile at him, but the gesture wavered. "Brandy helps. It is what my aunt gave me to make me sleep after I heard the news. That is why I would have chosen brandy."

He returned her smile with a wavering one of his own as tears clung to his lashes. "Then, I will insist upon a glass when Richard returns. Now that you have mentioned it, I believe that is what Mrs. Reynolds gave my sister after my mother died. Just a sip or two. She was very young."

"So much loss," he heard her whisper as he turned his eyes to watch the low flames dance and the sparks jump behind the fireplace screen.

"How does one bear it?" she asked softly.

He shook his head. He was not certain he could bear it. "A little at a time, I suppose."

"One foot in front of the other," she agreed.

He looked at her again. "Indeed."

"But one need not bear it alone," she added.

His cousin must be returning for she looked toward the servants' stairs.

"If you need anything, Mr. Darcy... if there is anything I can do to help you bear this burden..." she shrugged as if she thought it was impossible that she should be able to provide any help, "you need only ask."

"Will you tell me about your friend sometime?"

She nodded. "If you will tell me about your Anne." She held up a finger. "But not until you have recovered and have gone to see her. When you return will be soon enough."

"When I return," he repeated. "Miss Elizabeth," he called as she turned to leave.

"Yes."

"Thank you. You have already been a great comfort."

She dipped a curtsey. "I am glad," she said and then took her leave.

"You look far less agitated than you did when I left you here." Richard placed a stack of four books on a small table and pulled it closer to where Darcy sat.

"Did you bring port?" Darcy replied.

Richard shook his head and lowered his voice. "No, brandy, but do not tell her."

Darcy chuckled. "As long as you pour me a generous serving."

"I am surprised she recommended it."

"Why?" Darcy picked up a book and began paging through it.

"I do not know, really. I suppose I did not expect her to know one drink from the next. She is surprising." He brought a glass of caramel coloured liquid to Darcy and then lowered into a chair with his own glass. "I rather like her."

Darcy's left brow rose as he looked up from his book. "Do you?"

Richard nodded. "I do. Do you not find her interesting?"

The right corner of Darcy's mouth tipped up as he gave a small shrug. "I suppose," he prevaricated. He found her too interesting was the problem. No, he realized as soon as he had thought it, it was no longer an issue.

"Does she come from money?"

A frown creased Darcy's brow. "You find her that interesting?"

Richard swallowed the gulp of brandy he had taken and nodded. "I could if she had money."

"That is rather mercenary of you," Darcy muttered.

"I am not wealthy like you," Richard argued. "I must consider such things. You have never complained about such comments before."

"I find it unsettling when it is about a friend." He took a swallow of brandy and found an odd sense of pleasure in the pain it caused. Just as it cleaned a wound, the burning liquid should help his raw throat to heal. He shook his head. "I understand she has very little to recommend her other than her looks and personality. I am afraid you will have to remain only mildly interested." If at all, he added to himself.

He allowed the brandy to burn his throat once more as he imagined her standing at the door telling him about her friend. She was a lady who deserved to have someone care for her tender heart without thought of how much money she had or did not have or even without a thought about how bewitching her eyes could be.

Richard sighed. "That is too bad. It is dashed hard to find a lady as interesting as Miss Elizabeth. The ton is riddled with proper, never-say-what-you mean beauties, but I would prefer a lady of substance."

"That is understandable."

Richard stood and placed his glass on the mantle. "You will now have to find such a lady as well." His tone was as gentle as Darcy had ever heard it. "You do not need a lady of means," he added before pacing to the window and looking out.

Richard was as unable to remain still as Darcy was. No, that was not true. He was likely worse. The man was perpetually in motion. In that way, he was a bit like Bingley.

"Allow me to at least see Anne buried before you remind me of my duty," Darcy replied.

"I did not mean to be heartless."

"I know." Darcy swirled his drink, then put it aside instead of taking another swallow.

"Did you love her?" Richard came back to sit on the edge of his chair.

"I did. How could I not? She was my cousin, and we were good friends."

"And expected to marry."

Darcy nodded. "Yes, and expected to marry."

Richard shifted backward in his chair. "Did you love her as a man loves a woman or just as a friend loves a friend?"

"Must we speak of this?" Darcy wanted to lose himself and his thoughts in a book. He did not want to contemplate the things that had both kept him awake and appeared to be those that his cousin seemed bent on discussing.

"I think we must." Richard shrugged. "I have always found it best when faced with a tragedy to dissect it and see it for what it is."

"I do not."

"No," Richard agreed, "you brood and grow sullen and disagreeable until finally there is no other option but to face what is."

"I think my method is acceptable."

Richard shook his head. "I would normally leave you to yourself, but I fear you will be too long in coming to the point."

"What does it matter how long it takes me to grieve the loss of Anne?"

Richard blew out a breath. "Have you met our aunt's new parson?"

Darcy shook his head. "No, why would I have met him?"

"No reason, I suppose, but it would make it easier for you to understand what I am about to say if you knew how ridiculous the man is." Richard shook his head. "So many words! He uses twenty when five would do!"

"He is a parson."

"No," Richard replied with a firm shake of his head, "it is more than that. He is pretentious and stodgy." He pressed his lips together into a frown for a moment and then continued. "He is young but attempts to present himself as wise beyond his years. He is about my height but somewhat rounder in the middle than I am. He possesses very little grace in his movements, and he continually bows deeply to our aunt as he praises her for her benevolence."

"He does sound ridiculous," Darcy agreed.

"Oh, he is!"

"However, I do not see what he has to do with my method of grieving."

"He was supposed to have travelled to Hertfordshire, but Anne's death prevented it." Richard stood and retrieved his brandy. "His purpose coming to Hertfordshire was to find a wife among his cousins."

"He has relations in Hertfordshire?"

Richard nodded. "At Longbourn."

"I beg your pardon?" Longbourn? The Bennets were relations of Lady Catherine's parson?

"As I understand it, there was a breach in the family some time ago. Longbourn is entailed to this Mr. Collins, and he and our aunt think it will mend the rift if he were to make one of his cousins mistress of Longbourn by marrying her."

"Oh."

"Indeed. As I see it, Bingley is smitten with the eldest Bennet, whom I have yet to meet."

Darcy nodded. "Not without reason. She is beautiful."

Richard grinned. "I would expect nothing less of a lady who had captured Bingley's attention."

It was true. Bingley had a discerning eye when it came to finding the most beautiful lady in any room, and he was proficient in making such a lady notice him. However, this time, with Jane Bennet, it seemed Bingley was more than just enjoying a small flirtation. He seemed genuinely enamoured.

"Does Miss Bennet return his admiration?" Richard asked.

Darcy shrugged. "I have not noticed such."

Richard's brow furrowed. "Why do I ask you? You are dreadful at reading such things. I will watch for myself." He waved the topic away with his hand. "For now, I will assume that the attraction is mutual. It is Bingley of whom we speak, after all. So, when this Collins comes to call, Miss Bennet will likely not be among the options. I understand there are five daughters so her removal will leave four. If I am guessing his tactics correctly, he will think it unseemly for a younger daughter to be married before an elder one, and so he will select the next in line as his wife. It really is too bad that Miss Elizabeth does not have more money. I would willingly save her from him if she did, but alas, I cannot." He finished what remained of his brandy. "Longbourn is not a prosperous estate? Mr. Collins made it sound as if it were quite promising, but then, he does tend to be overly ambitious with his praise of most things of which he thinks our aunt will approve."

"Longbourn is a modest estate," Darcy murmured.

"Allow me to repeat my question from before. Did you love Anne as a man loves a woman or as a friend loves a friend?"

Darcy scowled. "I have been considering that very thought for days," he admitted.

"For days? Even before I arrived?"

Darcy could feel the shame of his contemplations over the past few days rising from his unsettled stomach, past his rapidly beating heart, and up his neck as it sought to burn upon his cheeks. "Yes."

"Why?"

Darcy scrubbed his face with his hands. "Miss Elizabeth," he whispered as his heart ached at having been contemplating another lady when he was betrothed to Anne. He should never have let his desires sway his sense of duty.

"You like her?"

"I was writing to you about her when you arrived. I did not know what to do. I found myself attracted to her as I have never felt before, but I was promised to Anne. And for the first time in my life, I wished I was not."

Richard leaned forward and placed a hand on Darcy's arm where it rested on the arm of the chair. "Anne would have never held you to your understanding if she knew another had touched your heart. It is why she insisted on waiting so long. She knew you loved her as a cousin, and she knew you would care for her as well as any man could. However, she also wished for your heart to be happy, and she feared she would never provide that happiness."

"How do you know?" Darcy whispered as tears slid freely down his cheeks.

"She told me. When we were at Rosings for Easter. Right before she promised you that she would make your betrothal known and would marry you in the new year. She would have gladly broken your betrothal to see you happy. Just as you would have denied your heart to see to her care. You were alike in that way." He rose and removed the blanket from Darcy's lap. "You must get in bed."

Darcy allowed his cousin to help him out of his robe and breeches and into bed.

"She would want you to be happy," Richard repeated. "When we return to Netherfield after we have said our farewells to our cousin, seek out Miss Elizabeth. I think you would suit, and I am certain Anne would grant you her blessing." He crossed the room to sit once again near the hearth as Darcy turned onto his side and, amid many tears, finally fell asleep.

# Chapter 4

Two days later, just as Elizabeth had predicted, Darcy's fever broke, and Richard called for the carriage to be readied. Within an hour, Darcy had been bundled into it with more blankets and foot warmers than he thought he required, but since he was just thankful to be on his way, he kept his complaints to himself.

The journey proved to be more trying than he expected, and, on Richard's insistence, he was allowed only to make a quick appearance to his aunt and uncle before being once again ensconced in bed. To be honest, he was grateful for Richard's interference and found that sleep, which he feared might have remained at Netherfield rather than following him to Rosings, had not deserted him. He slept from his arrival until the next morning, although he did find himself waking before the sun had risen.

He rolled over, attempting to find the source of the snoring he heard. Richard was draped face first over a cot that had been placed near the fire. Darcy shook his head and smiled. It was comforting to have someone care so much for him as to forego the comfort of a bed to keep watch over him.

Richard snorted and shifted. Then, with a curse, he tugged the blanket that had dropped onto the floor back up and tossed it over his legs, only for it to drop once again to the floor.

"You can go to your own room," Darcy said.

"You're awake."

"Yes."

Richard rubbed the corner of his eye with a knuckle as he sat up. "How do you feel?" He teetered sluggishly and then shook his head.

"I am well."

Richard's brows furrowed. "You are not well. You are improving. Now, tell me what is indeed improving and what is still needing improvement." He pushed to his feet and padded across to the bed so that he could lay a hand on Darcy's forehead. "Cool," he declared as if Darcy did not know that his fever had not returned.

"Your throat, how is it?"

"It only hurts a bit, but that is likely because I am thirsty."

Immediately, Richard crossed the room and filled a tumbler with a small amount of port. His lips curled up on one side when Darcy raised a brow as Richard handed him the glass. "I thought brandy might be too much so early in the day, and I think even Miss Elizabeth would agree with that."

Darcy shook his head and took a swallow of his drink. It did not burn at all.

"No wincing. You must be telling the truth."

Darcy scowled.

"You are known to hide what truly ails you," Richard replied to the unspoken accusation. "Now, tell me. How is your head?"

"I am well."

"That is not what I asked."

"My fever is gone, and neither my throat nor my head hurt as they did. Aside from some stiffness in my back and legs, my body does not ache."

Richard looked him up and down as he tilted his head to one side and then the other.

"You would make a good nursemaid," Darcy muttered.

"You need one when you are ill, and it is better I fill the role than allowing Aunt Catherine to see to it."

Darcy could not argue that point. His aunt was overly zealous in her attendance to any malady. He was surprised that her physician and the apothecary had not visited him. But then, she might not be able, at present, to worry about him. "How is she?" he asked.

"Father convinced her that you were not on death's doorstep and that no concoctions needed to be made."

Apparently, even when grief-stricken, his aunt was able to rally enough to worry about the health of another.

"I will allow you to rise."

"I had planned to do so whether you granted me permission or not," Darcy replied.

Richard shrugged. "I know. However, this way, I feel as if I had some say in the matter."

Darcy chuckled. Richard did like to be in command. He had always been that way; it was not his current occupation that had caused him to be so, though it was a disposition such as he possessed that lent itself well to Richard's rank.

"How is your heart?" Richard asked as Darcy threw back the covers and swung his legs over the edge of the bed.

"It aches a great deal more than the rest of me."

"Will you sit watch?"

Darcy nodded. "I should like to. Will Aunt Catherine allow it? I am not female."

"She has allowed Father, so I am certain she will allow you to take a turn as well." Richard rang for Darcy's man as Darcy made use of the chamber pot before finding his robe and taking a seat near the fire to enjoy another small amount of port. "However, you have been ill, and we would not wish for you to become so again, so your activity might be limited. Do not push yourself beyond what you are able."

Darcy heard the worry that lay beneath the slightly severe tone Richard used. "I will do my best," he agreed.

Richard smiled. "I shall see that you do." He nodded to Darcy's man and made his way to the door. "I shall see you in the breakfast room. You must eat." He stood at the door and waited until Darcy had given his agreement that he would eat before leaving the room.

~*~*~

After having eaten, Darcy made his way to Anne's small sitting room. He paused outside the door for a moment, blew out a breath, drew another, and though his heart would not remain beating at the pace he wished it would but instead insisted on increasing its rhythm, he stepped into the room. Anne lay peacefully at one end. She looked no less fragile in death than she had in life.

"Aunt Catherine," he said softly. He knew that though Anne looked as if she were sleeping, she was not, but still, he kept his voice low as speaking any louder seemed wrong.

His aunt looked up from her work of tying black ribbons around small packages. "I have one for you, Darcy." She searched her basket and pulled out a larger item. It was wrapped in lavender cloth and tied with the same black ribbon she was using on her current project. "I selected a few items for you that I know she cherished." She held the gift out to him. "She is still beautiful, is she not?"

Darcy turned his head to look once again at Anne. "Yes," he answered. Anne's was not a classical beauty but one of delicacy like a fine piece of china. "I have come to spend some time with her."

Lady Catherine rose from her chair. "You would have been good to her." She placed a hand on his arm. "And she would have made you happy. I know it."

Darcy smiled. "I believe you are right."

She sighed loudly as if lifting some heavy object. "You shall never be my son." She patted his arm. "It is a pity."

"Indeed, it is," Darcy agreed. It would not have been an easy task being her son, but he could have managed. "Mother would be disappointed, would she not?"

Lady Catherine patted his arm again and nodded. Her lips were firmly pressed together, and her eyes were watery. He knew she was not the sort of lady to allow her emotions to be aired before others. Therefore, he respectfully looked away.

"Mother has likely met her, and they are having tea while Mother shares stories about you."

To his surprise, he found himself wrapped in his aunt's arms. It was something that had not happened since just after his mother had died.

He squeezed her tightly. "I may never be your son, but I shall always care for you," he whispered. "I promised Mother I would."

"You are a good boy," she replied. Then, she straightened herself, gathered her basket, and left him alone in the room.

Darcy walked over to where Anne lay and studied her face. "Your mother is going to miss you. She already does." He and Anne had spoken about how Lady Catherine would adjust to Anne's being in Derbyshire after they married. They knew that, eventually, Lady Catherine would come to live with them. Darcy had planned to have Richard see to Rosings until it might be needed for a second son of his and Anne's to manage it. But now? He blew out a breath. Things were different now that Anne was gone. The fate of Rosings would lie in the hands of his uncle, Lord Matlock, according to the provision in Anne's father's will. However, there was time for all that to be decided.

"Your mother can still live with me if she so chooses," he assured Anne. "I will not cast her aside unless she becomes too demanding. Then there is that cottage we had discussed as being perfect for her." He smiled down at Anne. "What shall I do without you? I am not good at conversing with ladies. How shall I ever convince someone to take me on?" Pulling a chair close to where she lay, he continued, "There is someone who caught my eye. I was writing to Richard about her when I learned of your accident." He closed his eyes as feelings of betrayal washed over him.

"I did not know what to do. I had promised both you and Mother that I would marry you, and yet, my heart was beginning to question if I should keep such promises. Was it better to honour my word despite my heart being engaged elsewhere? Or was it better to break my word and follow my heart?" He shook his head. "No, I do not think I could have done that. I would have eventually forgotten her and been quite content with you." Again, he shook his head.

"You deserved to be loved better than that." He looked at her closed eyes, imagining the blue that lay beneath the lids. "You see the quandary in which I found myself?"

He crossed the room and retrieved the package his aunt had given him. Pulling the ribbon, he unwrapped what lay inside.

"Your mother has given me your diary. I do hope there are no horrid secrets in it. Shall I read it?" he asked her.

He might, just to hear her voice once again.

There was also a miniature of Anne and a ring — a golden band engraved with Anne Sophia de Bourgh and a small rose on a field of black enamel. "She must have had this commissioned quickly," he muttered. He had expected some sort of mourning item to be given him, but he had not expected it so soon. He placed the ring on his finger. It fit well enough.

"I could never forget you, even without these things," he said to Anne. "You will always be in my heart. I may not have loved you as well as I should have, but I did love you."

He flipped open the diary, read a few lines on the first page, then paged through to the end. She had begun keeping this journal several years ago. The entries were sporadic and not daily. They appeared to chronicle his visits along with the comings and goings of notable people in the household and village. He stopped a few pages from the end of the book. It was dated June of this year.

He caught his breath. She mentioned the letter he had written to her about Georgiana's ordeal at Ramsgate.

*I hope I will be able to help guide her after we marry, but I fear I do not have the right sort of experience to do so. I have never been to London for a season. I cannot know what she will need. It is times like this when I feel unequal to the task of being Mrs. Darcy.*

He had never considered how Anne might feel being asked not only to take on an estate but also a young lady not many years her junior.

"You would have done well," he murmured. "You knew how to listen to and care for others. You were quiet, but you were not without intelligence about life and people. I would have helped you." He sighed. "It is a nearly overwhelming task to care for Georgiana. I have done my best, but I feel as if I have failed her in some ways. If I had married you earlier, perhaps I would have done better."

He flipped one page and then another.

*I fear I will not satisfy his heart as it should be satisfied. He loves me. I know this, but it is not as an ardent lover. I have spoken to Richard about such things, and he assures me that all will be well. I should dislike very much to be what stands between Fitzwilliam and the love he deserves to receive. I shall love him as best I can, but will it be enough? I would not hold him to his promise if I knew another had captured his heart, but none has. So I will marry him in the new year and pray I can fulfill my role as his wife.*

He read that paragraph again. "I knew you were uneasy about our marriage, but..." His voice trailed off. He had no idea she had been so uncertain. Perhaps Richard was correct. Anne would give him her blessing to marry where his heart led.

He stood, laying the journal aside. Then, taking the ring from his finger, he placed it on top of her hand and covered it with his own.  "I am so grateful to you for having been willing to marry me despite your misgivings," he began, "and in honour of your heart's desire, I pledge to you that I shall only marry a lady who has captured my heart, and I will wear this ring in recognition of this promise until such time as I have fulfilled it."  Then, he kissed his fingers and placed them on her cheek.  "To you, I pledge my troth in this matter," he whispered as he slipped the ring back on his finger.

# Chapter 5

"How are you?"

Darcy turned his head away from looking at the prospect outside the window and toward his uncle who had come to stand near him.

"She liked seeing the sheep in the fields."

A hand grasped Darcy's shoulder firmly. "We will all miss her, but yours was of a particular relationship, and what I wish to know is how you are doing? And I do not mean are you well." Lord Matlock nodded toward the chairs at the end of the room not next to where Anne presently lay. "Come. There is a window over here where we can overlook nature as we speak."

Darcy followed his uncle to the other side of the small room.

"Someone will be here to relieve you soon," Lord Matlock added. "Then we can retire to your room where you can rest. I would not have you relapsing."

Darcy fought to hide a yawn. He was tired, and his body ached. A rest would be most welcome. The discussion he would have to have with his uncle was perhaps not as welcome. However, it could not be put off. A betrothal had come to an end. Rosings' future had to be decided as did his own. He shook his head.

"It is too much," he muttered.

His uncle's replying smile was understanding. "There is time to deal with all that needs doing." His brows flicked upward. "Most is done." He sank into a chair while Darcy stood near the window. "I had a great deal of time to do some arranging and to write to Sir Louis's solicitor. I expect his response soon. But we can discuss that later. I first would like to know how you are accepting your new-found freedom."

Darcy sighed. Freedom?

"You were bound by duty, and now you are not," his uncle added in response to Darcy's sigh. "You are now free to choose a bride. How does that sit with you?"

"I do not know." Darcy turned to look at Anne. "She would have released me from my promise."

"I know. Richard told me."

"Yes, he told me, too. As did her journal."

"And you would have stood by your promise come hell or high water."

Darcy shrugged.

"You were both nearly too noble at times."

Darcy turned startled eyes to his uncle.

"There are times when denying one's wishes and desires is not best, such as when pledging yourself to another in marriage when your heart is engaged elsewhere. I know it is perhaps not the most popular belief of my peers, but I do think each gentleman and lady should strive to find felicity in marriage if possible. And happiness cannot truly be achieved when there is regret standing in the way." Lord Matlock blew out a breath and dug out his handkerchief. "You fulfilled your promise to your mother and to Anne.

She knew love. You loved her well, just as your mother wished. And you were faithful to Anne until death parted you."

No, he had not been truly faithful. He had considered Elizabeth before Anne had died.

"I know about the young lady in Hertfordshire."

"You do?"

His uncle nodded. "A pretty young lady with a will of iron and a keen mind but with little money and a few ties to trade."

His uncle, much like Richard, was not one to mince words. Darcy appreciated that about Lord Matlock. "Then you know I was writing to Richard when he arrived?"

"Yes. You were conflicted. You had a duty to complete, and yet your heart betrayed you and made you question." He rose as a maid entered. "Come. Anne will be watched over."

Darcy nodded but, instead of following his uncle out of the room immediately, he first crossed to Anne and told her softly that he would return at least once more before they must part forever. Then, he followed his uncle from the room.

"It seems as if you loved her more than you perhaps thought."

"As a dear friend," Darcy replied. "As I do you or Richard or Georgiana."

"But not as one might a wife?"

"No." Darcy's heart was heavy with grief, and he doubted his ability to continue on without Anne, but it was not because his life had been ripped from him as he had seen in his father's eyes when his mother died. He doubted his ability to continue on because he doubted his ability to find a wife.

"My lord." Rosings' butler approached them. "Mr. Collins has arrived, and my lady is above resting."

"Collins, you say?" Lord Matlock turned from the stairs and toward the drawing room.

"Yes, sir," the butler replied.

Darcy did not think he had ever heard such an exasperated sigh as the one that his uncle blew out. Richard had said that this Collins was trying, but he had thought that Richard might have exaggerated the man's annoyance. However, after hearing the sound that his uncle made at the mere mention of the name, it seemed Richard's account was accurate.

His uncle turned to him. "Go on up to your room, Darcy. I will deal with this and visit with you later." Turning back to the butler he clarified, "He is in the drawing room?"

"Yes, sir, the blue one."

"The blue one," Lord Matlock repeated, his tone fraught with unwilling resignation to the task before him.

Darcy followed behind his uncle.

"Are you not going up to rest?" Lord Matlock said with a glance over his shoulder.

Darcy shook his head. "Richard has told me somewhat about Mr. Collins, and I admit to being curious."

"He will drive you to distraction," his uncle cautioned.

"I accept the danger."

"If I could go up and rest rather than sit in this room with that man, I would," said Lord Matlock as the butler opened the drawing room door. He shook his head, blew out one more breath, and entered the room with Darcy close behind.

"Mr. Collins," Lord Matlock greeted a slightly large and clumsy-looking fellow. He was not an ill-looking gentleman, but he the manner in which he carried himself was awkward.

The man moved forward in a hunched fashion and bowed low before Lord Matlock.

"My lord," the man said, "I do not mean to inconvenience, but I thought it my duty to ensure that all is as well as can be expected here at Rosings. Not that all is ever well when one has sustained such a grievous loss as you have."

His head hung in a bowed fashion and his hands were clasped tightly together in front of him.

"My sister is resting –"

"Oh, that is good, very good. It can be so challenging to find proper rest when tragedy befalls one." Mr. Collins clamped his lips closed when Lord Matlock cleared his throat. "I should hate to see her take ill," he added as if the words could not be contained despite his best efforts to remain silent.

"It is very good that Lady Catherine is resting," Lord Matlock said as he motioned to the group of chairs where Richard was sitting. "It is why I will not allow her to be disturbed at present."

"Wise, so wise," Mr. Collins muttered as he took his seat.

"I trust all is ready for the service?"

"Oh, yes, my lord, everything is perfectly ready, not a thing has been ignored. I would not wish to disrespect such a fine young woman as Miss de Bourgh, nor would I have the community think ill of my lady or you, my lord. All is in readiness."

Darcy looked at Richard and raised a brow to which Richard gave a small nod. The man had said yes using far more words than necessary and in such a repetitive fashion.

"And all is well at the parsonage?" Lord Matlock continued.

"Oh, indeed! A finer house could not be found in all of England for the likes of me. I am quite content there." His eyes shifted from Lord Matlock to Darcy and back.

"Forgive me, I have forgotten myself, Mr. Collins," Lord Matlock said. "This is my nephew, Fitzwilliam Darcy of Pemberley. Darcy, Mr. Collins, Catherine's parson."

"A pleasure to meet you, Mr. Collins," Darcy said. It was the polite thing to say. The truth of the statement remained to be discovered. So far, the gentleman was entertaining, though Darcy could see how his excessive fondness for speaking could wear on a person, especially a person such as Darcy, who enjoyed quiet.

"The pleasure is all mine," Mr. Collins replied. "I understand you have been ill, so I must say that I am excessively pleased to see you are improved enough to be out of bed and in company. I had feared your journey would set you back. It can, you know. However, it has not been tremendously cold, nor have we had rain in nearly a week, so I would say you had the best sort of weather for travelling if one must travel at all while ill. And, of course, it was necessary."

"Indeed, it was," Darcy muttered.

"You were in Hertfordshire, were you not?"

"I was."

Collins shifted in his seat and sat a bit straighter. "I have relations in Hertfordshire, a distant cousin and his family, though I have never met them."

Darcy expected him to continue on speaking, but to Darcy's surprise, Collins did not ramble on about his family. Instead, he looked to Darcy as if expecting him to show keen interest and question him on his good fortune of having relations in an area of the world in which Darcy had been. Darcy glanced at Richard, who was reclined in his chair and wearing an amused smirk.

"What is their name?" Darcy held Richard's gaze as he asked the question. It was satisfying to see his cousin's eyes grow wide in surprise.

"Bennet," Collins replied, "of Longbourn. Mr. Bennet is my cousin, and I am his heir."

"Indeed?" Darcy responded with feigned surprise. He had already received such intelligence from his cousin, but Mr. Collins did not need to know that.

"I declare it is the very truth. The estate is entailed, and since my cousin has failed to produce a son and has only daughters, Longbourn will fall to me upon his demise."

"And you have not seen the estate?" Richard queried.

"That is correct. There is a familial breach of long-standing that has kept me from visiting. However, I have of late written to my cousin and been accepted as a guest. I was to have already arrived at Longbourn, but the Lord has delayed my journey." He turned toward Lord Matlock with a very concerned look on his face. "I do not regret that it has been delayed. I am certain the Lord has a very good reason for such a pause in the plans of man. Not that the passing of dear Miss de Bourgh is good. It is just that even such a calamitous occurrence can be used in the hand of God to produce good. Take Joseph for instance, –"

"I understand," Lord Matlock interrupted.

Collins nodded and remained silent for a full half minute. "Have you met my relations?" he asked Darcy. "I admit to being curious about them."

"I have. They seem a respectable family, well-liked in the community, that sort of thing."

"And the daughters? Are they..." He flushed and fell silent.

"They are lovely young ladies," Darcy assured him.

"Your aunt, my lady, has suggested that I consider marrying one of them to mend the breach, as an olive branch of good will, to let them know that what has passed before has been forgotten and that they shall not be ill-treated when the time comes for me to claim my inheritance, you see. I am not an unreasonable person."

"It is good to be reasonable," Darcy muttered, though he doubted just how practical a man of so many useless words could be.

"I should not have to care for all of the daughters, should I? You did say they were lovely, so am I to assume that they will be able to find husbands?"

"I should think so," Darcy replied. "However, I am not the best judge of such things."

"But you have seen them and have not found anything lacking in their looks?"

Darcy shook his head. "No, they are all pretty. Miss Bennet is perhaps the most beautiful, but the others are equally as attractive in their own ways. They seem to take after their mother in that regard, for Mrs. Bennet is still a handsome woman."

Collins's smile was tight. "Yes, I had heard from my father that she was pretty in her youth, and I had hoped that perhaps the daughters would have taken after their mother in that way. It is perhaps the best she could give them if my father is to be believed."

Darcy's brows rose. "How do you mean the best she could give them?"

"Mrs. Bennet's father was in trade – a merchant with warehouses in Cheapside or some such place. Not at all the sort of lady a gentleman should consider. Her education would be lacking, and as such, how would she teach her children? I suppose a governess could be employed. Indeed, one should be employed if one wishes for his children to excel. You do not know if they had a governess, do you?"

Darcy shook his head. "I am afraid I never inquired after such a thing. However, Miss Bennet and Miss Elizabeth do not lack for intelligence. They are the two daughters in whose presence I have spent the most time."

Collins leaned forward eagerly. "Are they refined in their accomplishments?"

"I cannot say. What I may find adequate or even exceptional, you might not."

"But you do find them adequate?"

"Yes, I do."

"And Miss Bennet is beautiful?"

Darcy nodded but did not get to answer as Richard was quicker to respond.

"Quite, but you shall have to look elsewhere as I believe there may be a happy announcement in her future."

"She has a suitor, then?"

"One could say that," Darcy replied. "However, nothing official has been proclaimed and to speak about it further would tread along the very edge of gossip, would it not?" He did not wish to divulge anything of Bingley's affairs as he did not know for sure

if Bingley were indeed planning to offer for Miss Bennet. He suspected it to be the truth, but he had not had such intelligence
from Bingley on the subject.

Collins's brow furrowed. "Then, tell me about her next
younger sister."

"Miss Elizabeth?" Darcy asked in surprise, glancing at Richard,
who was looking rather self-satisfied. He had said Collins would
select Elizabeth if Jane were not an option. It was rather annoying
how his cousin could rightly discern the character and habits of
an individual so often.

"Yes, I believe that is what you said her name was."

"She would not do for you," Darcy replied.

"She would not?" Richard asked.

Darcy glared at his cousin. Richard knew very well that Elizabeth would not suit this Mr. Collins. He had been the one to
declare it to Darcy. He was playing a game and leading the conversation where he wished it to go. However, Darcy would curtail
his fun.

"No, she would make a deplorable parson's wife," he said. "She
is a lovely young woman, do not misunderstand me. She is handsome – tempting even – and possesses a quick wit. However, she is
– how shall I say this?" He paused and found himself smiling as he
recounted the debates he had participated in with Elizabeth. She
needed a husband who would appreciate such skill just as he did.
His left brow rose as the thought hung in his mind for a moment
before he tucked it away to consider later. "She is not retiring. If
she holds an opinion on a topic, she feels no compulsion to keep
it to herself."

"She is forward?" Mr. Collins's eyebrows had disappeared beneath the shock of hair which hung down on his forehead.

"No, that is perhaps not the best word," Darcy replied. "I think headstrong might be better." Strong, determined, and beautiful might be better words, but headstrong seemed the best choice to dissuade Collins in his quest. Whether he could or should consider her as a choice for himself or not, Darcy would not see her tied to the likes of Collins. "She just simply would not make a good parson's wife. That is all. Why, imagine if she should disagree with you on some point in front of your patroness?"

Lord Matlock was suddenly taken in a fit of coughing and excused himself to the far side of the room.

"I do hope my lord is well and has not contracted your illness," Collins said to Darcy, casting a worried glance toward where Lord Matlock stood with his back to them.

"I am certain he is well," Darcy assured Collins. In fact, Darcy was certain that his uncle was not coughing at all but rather laughing from the way the man's shoulder shook.

Collins looked once more at Lord Matlock and then turned his attention back to Darcy. "And who is after Miss Elizabeth?"

Darcy smiled. He had succeeded. Elizabeth would not be considered by Collins. "Miss Mary is next, then Miss Kitty, and, lastly, Miss Lydia." He twisted Anne's ring on his finger as he listed off the remaining Bennet sisters. "However, it might be best if you wait until you have arrived in Hertfordshire before selecting one or another to pursue. I have not spent much time in company with the younger Bennets, and I am loath to make faulty recommendations."

None of the younger sisters had made a favourable impression on him, but he was not about to say such a thing and perhaps put Elizabeth back into the mind of Mr. Collins. Besides, he had been in a foul mood for much of his stay thus far in Hertfordshire, and therefore, had likely not been capable of considering them as anything other than silly and indecorous. Had he not rejected Elizabeth out of hand? And yet, upon closer inspection, he found her fascinating and refreshing – not at all like how he had first perceived her.

Collins's brow furrowed deeply once again as he nodded slowly. "I can see the wisdom in such a statement," he admitted.

Darcy pushed up from his chair. "I find I am growing excessively weary. I am perhaps not so improved as I had thought."

He also wished for a solitary place in which to ponder what his heart was attempting to tell him about the enchanting Elizabeth Bennet. He had promised Anne he would follow his heart, but he could not follow what he could not clearly understand, could he? He spun the ring on his finger once again.

"Oh, one must be cautious," Mr. Collins said emphatically. "It is a dreadful thing to be out of bed too soon after an ailment. The return of a sickness can be worse than the initial malady. Why, that was just the case with my father. He thought he was well, so he went out shooting, only to be laid up a few days later and expired inside a month."

"I am certain I only require rest." And a quiet place to think. His heart was demanding he consider Elizabeth and only Elizabeth as a possible wife he could love, and the room was growing rather warm at such a thought. He needed to escape.

"Yes, yes, most likely," said Mr. Collins, though there was a hint of skepticism in his voice and a wary look in his eyes.

"Mr. Collins," Darcy said before moving to the door of the room, "you will still be travelling to Longbourn, will you not?"

"Most certainly. At the beginning of the new week, I shall be on my way. My cousin has graciously accepted my petition to arrive at a more distant time to what was originally agreed upon."

"That is very good," Darcy interrupted when the man stopped to draw a breath. "Do you have a curricle or cart?"

"No, no, not yet, though I do intend to acquire some form of vehicle after I marry. I have been laying by a sum for years with just such a purpose in mind. I am very frugal, you see. My lady has commended me on my economy."

Darcy smiled at how the man stuck his chest out just a bit. "Then, you must allow me to offer you a place in my carriage. Colonel Fitzwilliam and I will be returning to Hertfordshire on Monday next."

The man's eyes grew wide, and he bowed himself forward. "You do me a great service, sir. I am most honoured."

"It is but a little thing," Darcy assured him. "And," he added as he stood at the door looking down the hall toward Anne's sitting room and considering once again his promise to her, "it stands to reason that I should care for my aunt's parson when I can and in such a manner as is available to me. Besides, it is not unreasonable to think we might at some future time be related." He looked past Collins to Richard and smiled. "There are four Bennet ladies who, as of yet, have not been claimed."

And with that declaration, as Richard snapped his mouth closed and Lord Matlock once again dissolved into coughing, Darcy exited the room and walked down the corridor to the stairs, pausing for a moment before Anne's door as he twisted her ring on his finger. He was certain she would have liked Elizabeth. Blowing out a great breath, he silently vowed to Anne once again that he would marry the one lady who had, without his knowing it, captured his heart. Then, with a slightly lightened, comforted heart, he continued on to his room.

# Chapter 6

For four days Elizabeth had been confined to the house as rain, often falling in torrents, had created small rivulets in the garden and great puddles on the roads. Not a soul could travel about without running the risk of either getting stuck in the mud or drenched to the bone and catching a chill. November rains were not warm, after all. And though Elizabeth did not mind getting wet in a summer rain shower, the thought of a teeth-chattering soaking in November had been enough to keep her indoors despite her youngest sister's boisterous displeasure both about Mr. Bingley's ball being postponed and the rain keeping the officers away.

Elizabeth could not say she was sorry the officers had been kept away. While she would have enjoyed the diversion they would bring, there was one amongst them about whom she felt very uncertain. Mr. Wickham was handsome and charming and had caught Elizabeth's interest when she and her sisters had happened to meet him and a few of his fellow officers in Meryton. She would not deny that his features drew her to look at him with admiration, nor would she deny that he was a most pleasant conversation partner. He had kept her well entertained while they played cards at her Aunt Philips's house.

"What are you pondering as you look out on the muddy fields?" Jane asked as she wrapped an arm around Elizabeth's shoulders.

Elizabeth smiled at her sister and wrapped her own arm around Jane's waist. She was delighted that her sister was nearly entirely well. There was only a small cough that remained, and it expressed itself very rarely. "Officers."

"Officers?" Jane said in surprise. "All of them, or one in particular?"

Elizabeth laughed. "You know me well. I am pondering a particular lieutenant."

"A handsome lieutenant," Jane amended.

"He is that," Elizabeth agreed.

"But you are not considering his looks, are you?"

Elizabeth shook her head and moved away from the window to sit on her bed. "He is everything charming, but there is something amiss. I cannot say what, but I feel there is."

She had not had such a feeling of unexplained unease in some time. The last time she had felt as she did now, it had been proven just, for the man her father had hired to help with the harvest and who had caused Elizabeth to feel ill at ease had been found not only being entirely too friendly with a tenant's daughter but had also been caught poaching eggs from the same tenant's chickens. She doubted that Mr. Wickham was the sort to steal into chicken coops and pilfer eggs, but she would not trust him to be alone with herself or her sisters. He was excessively agreeable and seemed willing to become intimate in conversation on a very short acquaintance.

Elizabeth pulled her feet up under her and scooted to the top of the bed where she propped a pillow behind her back, so she would have something on which to lean. "I was also thinking of Mr. Darcy."

Elizabeth huffed softly and rolled her eyes as Jane, wearing a delighted smile, joined her on the bed. Jane had been bringing Mr. Darcy's name up in their private conversations since the day he had left Netherfield.

"Mr. Wickham painted him as cold and aloof," Elizabeth continued.

"I know, you have told me."

"And I, myself, have found him both arrogant and disdainful."

"You have," Jane agreed.

"And I do not think I am wrong in saying that he has behaved in such a fashion."

"But?" Jane prompted.

Elizabeth's lips pursed as her brow furrowed. Mr. Darcy seemed a complex puzzle whom she had yet to figure out. "I cannot believe that he is wholly without feelings as I once did. He was so...shaken by his cousin's death."

Silence reigned for a full minute before Elizabeth continued. "And if what you said about it being odd for Mr. Wickham to be so eager to share information about an acquaintance without much provocation and to someone he had only known for a day, there must be a reason for such odd and improper behaviour."

"That seems likely," Jane agreed.

"And since Mr. Wickham's description of Mr. Darcy was not at all flattering, I must assume Mr. Wickham wishes me to think ill of Mr. Darcy." She turned and looked at her sister. "But why? That I cannot reconcile."

"A disagreement perhaps? Or jealousy?"

Elizabeth nodded. She had considered both of those as reasons. "Do you suppose it is true that Mr. Darcy denied Mr. Wickham the inheritance he was supposed to receive?"

"I could not say with any degree of accuracy," Jane replied, "but I should think that it is true, though it might only be true in part. There may have been circumstances that made it impossible for Mr. Darcy to bestow the living, and Mr. Wickham is unwilling to accept the loss as anything less than completely Mr. Darcy's doing."

"Perhaps," Elizabeth muttered.

"Come, we must prepare for callers. It has not rained in a day, and the roads are surely dry enough for some brave soul to venture forth."

"And by some brave soul you mean Mr. Bingley," Elizabeth said with a laugh.

"Indeed, I do." Jane's face lit with a beautiful smile.

"He shall offer for you, and if he does not, I shall declare him to one and all to be the daftest gentleman to have ever walked the earth."

"Oh, Lizzy, do be serious!"

Elizabeth scrambled off the bed. "I am perfectly serious. I can see how much you admire him, and how could any gentleman not fall in love with you? You are perfection in human form."

"I am not," Jane retorted. "And you may ask several near suitors why they never pursued me beyond a call or two. I have not remained unmarried because I have refused any offers." She stood at the door with her hand on the knob. "Why are you putting on your boots and not your slippers."

"Mr. Bingley is not calling for me."

"But he may be accompanied."

"Yes, by his charming sisters." Elizabeth looked up and rolled her eyes at Jane. "I shall be devastated to have missed a chance to visit with them, but it is a risk I am willing to take in favour of fresh air."

"Mr. Darcy might be with them."

"Why would he be?" Elizabeth asked as she donned her bonnet. "If he has returned, I would not expect a man in grieving to call on neighbours whom he has made clear are beneath him."

"And what if you are wrong? What if he does call, and he does so to see you?"

Elizabeth laughed heartily at the questions as she fastened her pelisse. "Then you may tell him I have gone to Oakham Mount, and he may find me there, although you might wish to warn him that I will look a fright as I suspect my skirts shall not stay pristine."

"Mama will scold," Jane warned.

"Undoubtedly," Elizabeth agreed. Coming to stand next to Jane at the door, she added, "I do not wish to encounter a particular handsome lieutenant, and if the roads are dry enough for Mr. Bingley to call, I dare say, after the way Lydia and Kitty were flirting with the officers when last we saw them, there will be more than one red-coated gentleman in our sitting room."

Her comments were met by silent protest in the form of a scowl. In fact, to show the depth of her displeasure, Jane remained silent as they descended the stairs.

"You are not going out." Mrs. Bennet stood at the bottom of the stairs. "You will return to your room and make yourself presentable for guests. Oh, my!" She waved her handkerchief with one hand and placed the back of her other hand on her forehead. "How I shall abide it, I do not know. Now, turn yourself about, and do as you have been told! I will not tolerate a word of argument, Elizabeth."

Her mother rarely used that harsh tone. Something was not right. "What is it, Mama?" Elizabeth asked as she began to unfasten her pelisse.

"Mr. Collins." Her mother visibly shuddered as she said the name. "He will arrive this afternoon. I just know I shall despise him, and yet, I must pretend I do not." Her handkerchief fluttered again. "I do not think I am equal to it."

"Oh, Mama! How dreadful!" Jane's voice was filled with understanding. "But I have seen you rise to many other unpleasant occasions with aplomb. Did you not take tea with Mrs. Goulding the day after you heard her gossiping about how dreadfully lacking she thought your garden was? And did you not convince everyone there that there was not a thing out of the ordinary? You performed that display very well. So well, in fact, that Lady Lucas still whispers about Mrs. Goulding and her lack of taste."

"Well, yes," Mrs. Bennet conceded weakly, "but Mrs. Goulding will not be tossing me into the hedgerows upon Mr. Bennet's demise."

Jane placed an arm around her mother's shoulders. "And neither will Mr. Collins, for I shall do my best to snare Mr. Bingley, and then, I shall place my sisters in the way of many handsome and rich gentlemen, and you shall have your choice of fine estates at which to make your residence."

Her mother looked almost convinced that she should be ecstatic instead of despondent but then... "Even Mary and Lizzy?"

"Especially Lizzy and Mary," Jane replied. "I shall see to them first."

Mrs. Bennet pondered that for a moment and then smiled before turning to Elizabeth. "Why are you still standing there? Be quick. We have a very important guest to entertain. I will have you all looking your best." She clapped her hands. "Oh, Mr. Collins is not married. He might do very well for Lizzy."

Elizabeth shook her head. "No, Mama. You know I am not the tractable sort that a parson would need for a wife."

Mrs. Bennet huffed. "Not being tractable is why you shall never marry," her mother scolded. "Now, go make yourself presentable." She turned to Jane. "Mary knows more scripture than our parson, and he gives the sermons every week. Perhaps she would be appropriate. I would not mind seeing her as mistress of Longbourn. She would keep it in good order."

Jane guided her mother toward the sitting room. "Indeed, she would, Mama, but perhaps we should let Mr. Collins and Mary decide if the match is a good idea before we begin to plan their future."

~*~*~

Darcy blew out a breath of relief as Mr. Collins exited the carriage in front of Longbourn.

"It was your invitation," Richard grumbled. "He did not have to travel with us."

Darcy grimaced. "I know. He talked more than I had thought possible." He glanced out to where Collins was overseeing the removal of his trunk. The man pulled at his cravat and straightened his coat three times in the space of two minutes. "Nerves."

"I beg your pardon?"

Darcy turned back to his cousin. "We must go in."

"Must we?" Richard asked with a smirk.

"Yes, and not for the reason you think," Darcy retorted. "At least, not entirely for the reason you think." He moved to the door. While it was true that he wished to see Elizabeth, he was possibly more curious to see how Collins behaved when presented with the three remaining Bennet sisters. Whichever Bennet caused Collins to pull at his sleeves or adjust some other item of his clothing or caused him to bubble over with a litany of words would be the Bennet they would have to ensure he attained. He had been observing Collins for the entirety of their trip and had just now sorted out what he thought was the source of the man's odd behavior

Richard climbed out of the carriage. "What other reason is there?" he whispered near Darcy's ear.

Darcy simply shook his head and waved his hand for Collins to precede them to the door. This was his family's home even if the man had been estranged from them for his entire life, and he should be the one to enter first.

Collins arrived at the door to Longbourn before Darcy but then fell back. "I cannot," he muttered.

"You must," Darcy encouraged. Had he actually seen the man tremble?

Collins shook his head.

"Very well. I know them, I will do the introductions if you prefer," Darcy offered.

Collins's head bobbed up and down mutely. Mutely. Darcy chuckled softly. That was not a word he expected to use about the loquacious Mr. Collins. Darcy spoke to Mr. Hill when he opened the door and then led his cousin and Mr. Collins to the sitting room.

"Mr. Darcy!" Mrs. Bennet cried in surprise, covering over the other names Mr. Hill announced. "Oh, we are honored that you would call at such a time as this." She bit her lip as compassion filled her eyes. "It is never easy," she muttered.

"No," Darcy agreed. "It never is."

"Please be seated. Hill, see that tea is brought quickly. Have you just arrived back in Hertfordshire?" As she spoke, she flitted across the room and prepared a table he suspected would be used for the tea service.

"Yes, I thought since my cousin and I were travelling this direction, we could deliver your cousin to you."

There was a momentary look of displeasure that crossed the lady's face before it was swiftly tucked away.

"Allow me to present to you my cousin, The Right Honorable Colonel Richard Fitzwilliam, and your cousin, Mr. Collins."

"Right Honorable," Mrs. Bennet murmured, dropping into her chair as if overcome by the appellation.

"Yes, my father is Lord Matlock," Richard said.

"Lord Matlock," the words were more breathed reverently than spoken.

Darcy wondered for a moment if the woman was going to swoon.

"I am a poor soldier, ma'am. Nothing more," Richard assured her as he took a seat as Jane was indicating he should.

"Mama," Jane said softly. "You have not introduced us to our guests."

Mrs. Bennet gave her head a shake. "Forgive me. I must say I have never had the relation of a lord, a real lord, in my sitting room." She paused. "No, that is not true. I have never had the son of a lord in my sitting room. I have entertained his nephew and done so admirably. There is no want of hospitality to be found here, I can assure you."

"I would not dare to even consider that there was," Richard replied with a smile.

Of course, Richard would find Mrs. Bennet entertaining rather than vexatious. Darcy supposed he should likely adopt the same point of view if he were to become part of her family.

"Colonel, Mr. Collins," Mrs. Bennet rose from her chair and crossed to where her eldest daughters were standing. "This is my eldest daughter, Jane, and my second eldest, Elizabeth. Next to her is Mary." She cleared her throat almost imperceptibly and glared at Mary, who tucked her book behind her and followed her sisters in dipping a curtsy.

Darcy watched Collins. He was obviously not unable to notice beauty when it stood before him. There was a bit of redness creeping up the man's neck as he greeted each daughter as she was introduced. But he kept his greetings short, his hands were still, and his bow only what was necessary.

"And next to me," Mrs. Bennet had crossed to her chair once again, "is Catherine, though we call her Kitty, and then my youngest, Lydia. I am certain Mr. Bennet will be along soon to greet you as well. He has been out with Sir William doing who knows what today, but he expects you, Mr. Collins, and he will be delighted to meet you, Colonel."

Darcy took note of how Collins stumbled over the name Catherine and tugged at his cravat before bowing low. Miss Kitty.

She would be the one. That settled, he relaxed into his chair and allowed the conversation to flow about him as he considered Collins and Miss Kitty until Elizabeth interrupted his reverie.

"I had not expected to see you so soon," she said.

"I did not wish to be rude and deposit your cousin at your door without calling for a few moments myself."

She blinked. "You did not?" Her eyes grew wide and her cheeks flushed.

"I can understand why you would wonder. I have not been the friendliest sort of fellow during my stay with Bingley, have I?"

She grimaced and gave a small shake of her head in reply.

"I must apologize for that and attempt to amend my ways." He smiled at her and spun the ring on his finger.

"You are well?" Jane asked.

"I am. Not even a lingering cough. And you? The last I saw you, you were not well."

"I am not quite so fortunate. My cough has not left me so quickly as yours has you. But, I am well."

"I am relieved to hear it." He glanced surreptitiously at Mrs. Bennet and lowered his voice. "Has my friend called to inquire after your health?"

Miss Bennet blushed prettily and ducked her head as her sister laughed softly.

"You surprise me with such a forward question, sir," Elizabeth said.

"Do I indeed?" he asked without giving an explanation for his action.

"Yes, you do, and I am certain you wish to draw me out, so that I will impertinently inquire after your reason for such uncharacter-istic behaviour, revealing me to be less proper than I should be."

"I assure you that is not the reason at all," Darcy replied. "I had hoped to inquire if his sisters have attended him."

"Oh," Elizabeth blinked. "They called once since Jane arrived home, but then it rained for four days, so we have not seen them since."

"I had noticed the roads were showing signs of rain. And how were his sisters?"

Her brows furrowed. "The same as always."

"This will sound very arrogant, but did Miss Bingley mention me?"

Jane nodded. "Yes, but not any more than she normally would."

"And she was just as civil and polite as she always is," Elizabeth added.

Darcy bit back a laugh at the sardonic tone Elizabeth used. "I am relieved. I feared she might have redoubled her efforts to snare me. Bingley had to explain a bit about my betrothal when request-ing that the ball be postponed."

"She did not know of it before?" Elizabeth asked in surprise.

Darcy shook his head. "Very few knew of it. Anne had only recently agreed to make our arrangement public knowledge."

"Oh," Elizabeth said once again but this time fell silent.

"I should like to explain that arrangement to you sometime. I cannot now, of course."

Elizabeth nodded.

"And you did promise to tell me of your friend. I admit I am curious to learn of her... and you."

Just then, their conversation was interrupted by the serving of tea, and it was not afterwards possible to return to in the same fashion. However, Darcy felt he had accomplished his purpose in speaking with Elizabeth, for she was eyeing him curiously.

In truth, his comments had found their mark, for Elizabeth found herself considering him even after he had departed as she wandered up to her room while Mr. Collins babbled on about some gardening fact with her mother and Kitty.

# Chapter 7

Two days later, as the sun climbed to its peak in the sky, Elizabeth and Mary climbed the path to Oakham Mount. She had finally been able to escape from the confines of Longbourn without all of her sisters and Mr. Collins in attendance. That man spoke so much and so pointlessly! She supposed it was good that he had taken orders, for a love of speaking was an asset for a parson. She was equally as glad that his sermons were prepared beforehand, as that must decrease the likelihood of his rambling off after some lost rabbit in the midst of delivering his sermon.

Elizabeth paused to watch a pair of riders in the distance. They raced along the field and then turned toward her. She stood where she was until she could make out who they were. Then, she lifted a hand and waved.

Colonel Fitzwilliam waved in return before saying something to his cousin and pointing to where she and Mary stood.

"Is that Mr. Darcy?" Mary asked.

"And his cousin." Elizabeth waved again as Darcy looked her direction. She had not seen either gentleman since the day they had deposited Mr. Collins at her door.

"You seem rather eager to see them." Mary gave Elizabeth a questioning look.

"I suppose I am," was Elizabeth's only reply.

"Why?" Mary prodded.

Elizabeth shrugged. She did not wish to tell Mary that she suspected she liked Mr. Darcy and not just as a friend. How he had managed to worm his way into her good graces with a hasty apology for his behaviour the other day, she was uncertain. No, she thought as the riders approached. It was more than that apology. It was seeing him as a gentleman capable of great depths of emotion that had first endeared him to her. And then, with every disparagement she had heard fall from Mr. Wickham's lips and replayed in her mind as she lay in bed thinking before drifting off to sleep each night, her esteem of Mr. Darcy had grown. She had determined that her feeling of unease about Mr. Wickham must be accepted as a warning and every word he said scrutinized and doubted.

"Do you like him?" Mary continued.

Elizabeth sighed. "I might," she whispered. "But please do not tell anyone, especially Mama," she begged.

"Why should I do that?" Mary asked in surprise. "I hear enough about Mr. Bingley and Jane, and then there is Mama attempting to push me towards Mr. Collins." She shook her head. "I do not wish to hear any more talk about matches!" She bit her lip and ducked her head. "I can tell you a secret in return that should Mama hear of it, I would be doomed."

"Indeed?" Elizabeth pulled her eyes away from the approaching gentlemen and turned them toward her sister. "Do tell."

"You may tell Jane but no one else." Mary's tone demanded compliance, and Elizabeth readily gave her assent.

Leaning a bit closer to Elizabeth, Mary whispered, "Mr. Lucas has been sending me letters and intends to speak to Papa when he has completed his studies."

"Mr. Lucas?" Elizabeth repeated in surprise.

Mary's head bobbed up and down. "When he is home, we often talk at church, and he is one of the few who asks me to dance at assemblies. He has approached me in town now and then when I am on an errand and he is home. But we have spoken of many things by way of letter, so I am certain we will get on quite well together."

"How have you received letters without Mama knowing?" Elizabeth could not contain her surprise. Mary was so proper. Mary reprimanded anyone who was improper. And yet, Mary was carrying on a secret correspondence with a gentleman?

"If one appears excessively dull and proper, Mama will leave her alone."

"But even Mama would know about your receiving letters and would not remain quiet."

Mary shrugged. "Not if they are delivered by Maria instead of Hill."

Elizabeth's mouth dropped open.

"You will not tell," she repeated.

"Of course, I will not, but do be cautious, and consider Mr. Lucas when he returns before you accept any offer."

"I am not so silly as Papa believes," Mary said with a sly grin. "I will not tie myself to anyone unless I am certain of their constancy and respect."

"And love?" Elizabeth asked.

"Yes, of course," Mary replied. "Without love, how would a gentleman be able to remain constant?"

"Why, his honour would demand it!"

Mary shook her head. "Honour has its limits, but love endures always." She looked past her startled sister and extended her greetings to the gentlemen who had finally reached them.

"Are you well?" Darcy asked Elizabeth after the pleasantries of meeting had been performed, and he and Elizabeth were walking ahead of Richard and Mary.

"Quite well," Elizabeth replied.

"You looked a bit out of sorts when we rode up."

"My sister," she said with a shake of her head. "I cannot tell you what she said, but you must believe me that it was shocking. It is nothing which warrants your concern, however, for it is nothing dreadful. It was just so different from what I ever expected from her."

"Sisters can surprise us," Darcy agreed.

"Has your sister surprised you?" Elizabeth asked.

Darcy wore a grim expression as he nodded. "I fear her surprise was not as innocent as your sister's appears to be, but like you, I do not feel at liberty to speak of it at present. She is well, so do not fret on that account. Not uninjured," he added, "but well."

"I am pleased she is well." Elizabeth was not sure what else to say. Her curiosity was aroused, but she would not pry into something that was so obviously grave a subject. Perhaps with time, he would share his secrets with her. They did seem to be becoming friends, so it could happen, could it not?

Of course, Elizabeth's curiosity would not leave the topic alone, and as they walked on in silence, Elizabeth pondered her sister's revelation and then Mr. Darcy's comments.

Had Miss Darcy hidden something from her brother? It seemed

most likely. She wondered what Miss Darcy was really like? Was she serious like Mary or lively like Lydia? Perhaps she was more like Miss Bingley. If Mr. Wickham's words were correct, Miss Bingley was who Miss Darcy would most likely resemble. Elizabeth's steps faltered. However, if Mr. Wickham's words about Miss Darcy being cold and proud were wrong, was it because he had been spurned by her? Could he have been the surprise she had kept from her brother?

"Are you well?" Darcy asked as he caught hold of Elizabeth's elbow, as once again she stumbled as she realized just why Mr. Wickham might despise Mr. Darcy.

"I was too engrossed in my thoughts," Elizabeth explained.

"Do you often stumble when your thoughts are so encompassing?" Darcy tucked her hand into the crook of his arm. "I should not wish for you to fall," he said with a smile in response to her raised eyebrow.

"I am usually very sure on my feet," she assured him.

"I am glad to hear that."

Something in his tone had shifted from one of ease to one tinged with sorrow.

"Are you well?" she whispered.

"Anne died when she fell," he explained and then looked away to somewhere far off in front of them.

"Tell me about your Anne," Elizabeth offered. She recognized the look he was wearing. His Anne was in his thoughts, and Elizabeth knew that often speaking of Celia had helped ease the pain that mere thinking had brought.

"You do not mind?" he asked.

"I am willing to listen if you are able to share."

"Anne is...was...the daughter and only child of my mother's sister, Lady Catherine de Bourgh."

"Your poor aunt," the words escaped Elizabeth before she could catch them.

"Indeed," Darcy replied. "She has lost both her husband and now her daughter."

Elizabeth blinked against the tears that sprang unbidden to her eyes.

"My mother and her sister were not only sisters but also dear friends. Correspondence flew from Pemberley to Rosings and back on a regular basis."

He was smiling softly and looking into the distance as he spoke. Elizabeth was struck with a sense of grief for Lady Catherine once again as she recalled that Darcy's mother had also died.

"Lady Catherine is not an easy person to love." He glanced down at Elizabeth. "She is demanding and particular, but my mother was an angel who could soothe a dragon's anger with a smile."

Elizabeth could not help smiling at the sweet way he spoke of his mother.

"When Anne was born, my mother was as delighted as could be, but then, Anne became ill and grew weak. She never fully recovered. The weakness remained, and my mother, as well as Lady Catherine, feared for her as she grew older. How would such a lady find a husband who would treat her well? How would she endure a season, so that she might find a husband? But then, my mother landed on the perfect solution. Me." He drew a breath. "Anne and I have...had...always been great friends, so when my mother approached me with the idea, I was not entirely against it. Then, when my mother became so ill that she could not write her own letters and could not leave her bed, she called me in and made me promise to marry Anne and to love her as she deserved to be loved." He shrugged. "How could I refuse my mother what became her last request of me?"

"Oh, how sad," Elizabeth murmured.

He shook his head. "Not entirely. That promise saved me from bothering to put forth effort in learning to flirt and converse with ladies. I had no need to win a wife, for I already had one waiting for me. However, Anne knew that I did not love her as a man loves a wife."

"You did not love her?" Elizabeth asked in surprise.

"No, no, I loved her, deeply, just as I had my mother and my father and as I do my cousin Richard and my sister, but not as a man loves his wife."

They had come to a lovely little green area, and she saw him look at his cousin and nod toward a large rock to their left. Richard replied with a nod of his own and led Mary in the opposite direction.

"I have experienced the heart-wrenching agony of losing my parents and now my Anne," he continued as they approached the rock. "However, when my mother died, I witnessed the agony of a man who has lost his very reason for living. While my love for Anne was deep, it was not the sort that joined soul to soul or begged me to wish for children who resembled her. I longed to care for her, of course, and knew that we would have children and in so doing, would delight Lady Catherine, but..." his voice trailed off. "It is hard to explain, but it is different."

"I saw Mr. Goodwin after his wife and daughter died. I believe

I understand somewhat," Elizabeth said as she took a seat on the rock. Mr. Goodwin had sat staring at Mrs. Goodwin's portrait for days before deciding that he could not remain at Netherfield and had moved to town, to a rented house that had never been Mrs. Goodwin's home.

Darcy smiled as he sat down. "I knew you would, or at least, I thought you might."

"You did?"

He nodded. "You knew exactly what I needed when I was sick and at Netherfield. The brandy helped."

"I am glad."

"I will miss Anne for as long as I live." He had turned to look in the direction Mary and Richard had gone. "But my heart is not shattered as my father's was." He looked at her quickly. "That does not sound heartless does it?"

Elizabeth shook her head. "No."

He looked out at the prospect. "I made her a promise."

He glanced in her direction again. "I was given her journal. She did not love me any more greatly than I loved her. She had put off announcing our engagement for years and had hoped that I would find someone who would capture my heart just as she wished to find someone for herself." He watched as he spun his ring. "It was just this spring when she agreed that come the new year, we would finally marry. However, she would have released me from our arrangement even after we had announced it if I had found someone. I did not know that until Richard told me, and then I read it in her journal." He drew in a deep breath and released it. "That is why I promised her that in honour of her, I would pursue my heart and only marry for the deepest of affection."

Elizabeth did not know how to respond to such a tale. It was so intimate a story that every response seemed trite in her mind.

Darcy remained looking at his hands and spinning his ring. "I should like to call on you," he said with a quick and uneasy glance at her, "if you would allow it. I know my behaviour has not been what it should be, but I would like the opportunity to prove to you that I am not unworthy of you. Would you grant me permission to call on you?"

Elizbeth's eyes grew wide, and her lips parted. Mr. Darcy wished to court her? He had declared he would only pursue his heart, and then he had asked her if he could pursue her?

"You cannot," she replied. "You are in mourning."

"We could meet as friends for now, and once the period of mourning for my cousin has passed, I could speak to your father if you wish, and if you do not, I will return to town and not press my suit any further."

There was a note of desperation in his voice. She shook her head. "It is the grief speaking."

"No, I assure you it is not."

Again, she shook her head. She had no desire to be a substitute for the lady who had been lost. "We can be friends," she replied, "but I fear we cannot be anything more. You do not think it is the grief, but I am not convinced. You found me only tolerable when we first met, and we have done little else besides argue in the entirety of our acquaintance until your Anne died. I have provided comfort, nothing more." Her heart broke as she witnessed the pain in his eyes before he turned his face away from her.

"You are wrong," he said softly. "I loved you before Richard arrived. However, I will agree to meet as friends and nothing more until I can prove to you that you are wrong." He stood and offered her his hand.

"I am sorry," she whispered as she placed her hand in his. How her heart longed for him to prove her wrong. However, grief was a tricky fellow, and she had no desire to be an instrument in grief's deception.

"No more than I am," he replied. "Now that I have told you of my Anne, I think we should walk here again tomorrow, so that you can tell me about your friend."

She studied his face. "I am only agreeing because I promised I would tell you about Celia."

He nodded and smiled. "As long as you are agreeing, I do not care your reason."

"Mr. Darcy," she chided.

He shook his head. "You are wrong."

"I am not," she retorted. "And it is very wrong of you to make me argue with you over such a thing. It is not proper at all that I should speak so disagreeably to one who is in mourning."

He smiled. "Then, do not disagree."

"Oh," she cried in exasperation, "you are a very determined and annoying fellow!"

"I have made a promise," he replied, "and when I make a promise, my will to see it fulfilled is implacable."

"As implacable as your temper?" she questioned, her mouth dropping open at the self-satisfied smile he turned on her.

"More," he replied.

# Chapter 8

As luck would have it, the following day was dotted with intermittent sputterings of rain, and a walk to Oakham Mount was not possible.  Elizabeth rose from her chair in the sitting room and paced to the window for the fourth time in the last half hour.

"Go walk in the garden," her mother chided. "I will not confine you to the house when all you are going to do is cause my nerves to flutter each time you pace across the room. I do not know why you are so eager to have callers. It is not as if any are calling to see you."

Mary peeked up from her book and smiled quickly at Elizabeth.

"I should have thought you could have snared Mr. Wickham," said Mrs. Bennet, "if you had been more pleasant. He seemed to have taken to you quite nicely, and he seems to have promise. I should imagine he will not remain a lieutenant for long."

"She shall not have him," said Lydia, "for I shall. I do so admire a man in a red coat."

Elizabeth sighed and returned to her chair. She was not entirely certain that Lydia should be so eager to snare a man like Mr. Wickham, but to protest would only deepen Lydia's determination. Therefore, she only said, "A uniform is very becoming, but I do not think I would make a good wife for a soldier. All that moving about!" She shook her head. "It is not for me. I prefer to settle into a neighbourhood and surround myself with friends."

"I should very much enjoy meeting new friends everywhere!" Lydia cried.

Elizabeth shook her head at Lydia's stubbornness and tried to turn her focus back to the needlework she had been doing. However, creating rosettes was not so satisfying as watching to see if Mr. Darcy would keep his promise and call on her even though they could not walk to Oakham Mount. And more frustrating than keeping her stitches neat and the thread from knotting was the thought that she very much wanted him to keep his promise because she longed to see him. She blew out a frustrated breath.

"Do go take a turn of the garden," her mother snapped.

"Come," Jane whispered. "We will see if anyone calls."

"Do not go far, Jane. I would not have Mr. Bingley kept waiting," her mother chided as she saw Jane rise to leave with Elizabeth. "Do not damage your sister's chances, Elizabeth."

"I would not dream of doing so, Mama. We will keep a close eye on the drive."

"See that you do," Mrs. Bennet replied.

"Your attendance to your daughter's marital prospects does you great credit," Mr. Collins said.

"I have five. I must be vigilant." Mrs. Bennet turned a cunning smile on the man. "We may expect a happy announcement for Jane at any time, but she has four sisters, Mr. Collins, and you are in need of a wife. Mary, why do you not read to us from the Psalms. It will help us pass the time so agreeably, and Mr. Collins can expound upon them if he wishes."

"I do not wish to read," Mary replied.

"You are reading now," her mother retorted.

"But not the Psalms, and I do not wish to read aloud or hear Mr. Collins expound on anything."

Mrs. Bennet huffed. "When did you become so incorrigible?"

"About the time Mama began pushing her in front of Mr. Collins," Jane whispered as she closed the door to the sitting room behind them.

Elizabeth laughed softly. "Mary has her eye on someone else entirely," she whispered as she took Jane's arm to go up and get their outerwear.

"Does she indeed?" Jane asked curiously.

"I am allowed to tell you and only you. No one else is allowed to know." They climbed the stairs slowly, heads bent together. How she would miss these moments of sharing secrets when Jane married and moved from Longbourn. Her heart pinched at the thought of losing one so dear. She knew that Jane would not be lost forever, but she would be so removed, and her attentions would naturally shift to her husband and children.

"I will not tell a soul," Jane assured her.

"She has been corresponding with Mr. Lucas. Maria sends and delivers the letters."

Jane gasped. "Our Mary?"

Elizabeth nodded. "Shocking, is it not?"

"It most certainly is!" Jane agreed.

They had reached their room, and each sought her coat and bonnet.

"Why did Mary tell you such a secret?"

Elizabeth applied herself to her fastenings. "We were just talking on our walk yesterday."

Jane stilled Elizabeth's hands. "I will not believe that! Mary would not share such a secret without reason."

Elizabeth blew out a breath and pulled her hands away from Jane. It was nearly impossible to keep a secret from Jane unless one simply did not say anything. "Mary asked if I liked Mr. Darcy, and I said I did."

Jane squealed softly and wrapped Elizabeth in her embrace. "Oh, I knew you would make a good match. We shall be always in each other's company if you marry him, for Mr. Bingley is his dearest friend."

Elizabeth shook her head. "You really are as bad as Mama," she chided. "And I am not marrying him." She wanted to add he has made no offer, but she could not say that without lying.

"But you might. Mary said he and the colonel walked with you yesterday. I do believe he likes you."

"Yes, so I have heard, repeatedly." She raised a brow and gave Jane a stern look before opening the door.

"If you were not so stubborn, Lizzy, you would listen to me and attempt to draw him along."

Again, Elizabeth shook her head. There was no need to draw him along, but there was also no need to share that information with Jane.

"You would do so well together," Jane whispered as they descended the stairs, "I know you would." She stopped halfway down as a maid went scurrying past, followed by Mr. Hill running in the opposite direction and then calling for a footman.

Elizabeth dropped Jane's arm and raced down the stairs and in the direction in which Mr. Hill had gone. She stopped at the door to her father's study, her hand on her mouth, her eyes wide, and a sob catching in her chest. Her father sat in his chair, his head leaned back and his face white as any piece of linen she had seen drying on a bright summer day. A footman pushed past her.

"Is he..." she tried to form the word dead, but her mouth would not cooperate.

"He is breathing, but barely," Mr. Hill replied. He placed his ear against her father's chest. "There is a low beating."

"I will send someone for the apothecary," Elizabeth offered.

Mr. Hill nodded as he and the footman began attempting to move Mr. Bennet from his chair.

Elizabeth turned and rushed toward the door, tears blurring her eyes. He could not die. He just could not. How would she live without him now, and then, Jane when she married? She would be alone. Completely alone.

"Mrs. Hill," she called, turning in a confused circle in the entry way. "Mrs. Hill, we need Mr. Jones. With all haste." She shook her head and covered her face with her hands, turning back toward the stairs and bumping into someone who wrapped his arms around her. Someone who smelled a lot like cedar and cinnamon just as Mr. Darcy did.

"What has happened?" Darcy asked.

It was him. Comfort warmed her heart even as the tears spilled down her cheek. "Papa...is...ill," she managed to get out. Where was Jane? "I need...to tell...Jane."

"She knows," Darcy replied. "She is here with us."

"And Mama...we must..." She could not say the rest. Her mother would be beside herself with fright and anguish. How could she be the one to tell her mother something like this? She could not.

"Is there somewhere we can sit?" Darcy asked as he held her. "You need to sit and recover before you tell anyone anything."

"This way, sir." Mrs. Hill led them to the small drawing room that was just beyond Mr. Bennet's study. Elizabeth allowed Darcy to guide her, and Bingley and Jane followed close behind.

"Mama will worry," Elizabeth muttered. "There is so much commotion; she will worry."

Darcy tucked her into a chair and knelt before her. "Allow me to look in on your father and see what is being done, and then I will send your mother to you here." He pressed his handkerchief into her hand and waited until he had received a nod of her head in agreement. Then, he disappeared to see what needed to be done.

~*~*~

Darcy found Mrs. Bennet outside her husband's room with Kitty at her side and Lydia pacing the hall. Mary, he had met on the stairs and sent to Elizabeth.

"Miss Bennet and Miss Elizabeth are in the drawing room by the study waiting for me to return with news of their father." He kept his voice low and calm. "You might be more comfortable there with them. I promise if you are needed, I will come and get you myself."

Mrs. Bennet blinked at him, her eyes not focusing completely. Then, she shook her head. "No, I will not leave him. Oh, what is to be come of us?"

"Become of you? Whatever do you mean?" Mr. Collins had made his way up the stairs and down the hall to where they stood outside Mr. Bennet's door.

Darcy rolled his eyes at Collins's inability to catch the woman's meaning. "The estate is entailed," he whispered.

"Yes, I know," Collins replied. "But I do not see why that is of such great concern."

"We will be tossed into the hedgerows," Mrs. Bennet wailed.

"Who would do that?" Collins asked in surprise. "It is not in Mr. Bennet's will that you be thrown out of your house, is it?"

Darcy wondered at the look of utter confusion mixed with indignation that Collins wore. Did he not realize that the woman feared he would throw them out? Even as Darcy was thinking it and searching for a way to divert the conversation, Mrs. Bennet removed all doubt with a cry of...

"You! You only came to snatch my home from me and my daughters."

Collins stepped back two paces. "Me?" He pointed to himself and looked from Mrs. Bennet and Kitty to Darcy and back. "Me?" he repeated.

"Oh, it is too much!" Mrs. Bennet buried her head on Kitty's shoulder and wailed.

"I would never do such a thing!" Collins continued. "I am not my father."

Kitty wrapped her arms around her mother as Lydia took up the fight, and Darcy longed to enter Mr. Bennet's room so that he might learn of the man's condition and report it to Miss Elizabeth. However, he was loath to leave what appeared to be brewing into an unpleasant situation.

"Are you not going to take possession of Longbourn if Papa is..." Lydia clamped her teeth together and pulled herself straight, obviously struggling to contain her emotions. "Unable to continue being its master," she concluded.

"I must but..."

"Then we shall have no place to live," Lydia interrupted.

Collins's brows drew together, and he seemed to shrink before Darcy's eyes transforming from the self-assured gentleman he attempted to portray into a softer, gentler parson. He shook his head. "You are mistaken. There shall be rooms here for you for as long as you need them. There is no need for you to leave your home until you marry." He sighed. "My father was a hard man and even cruel. I am not unfamiliar with his fits of anger and his irrational disposition. However, I am not he." He shook his head again. "Come, Mrs. Bennet. You will only do yourself harm if you remain here in your condition. You must find somewhere to rest while you wait. You cannot care for Mr. Bennet as he needs if you yourself are ill."

Darcy watched in amazement as Kitty smiled, offered her thanks, and allowed Collins to help her take her mother to her room. He had not thought the man capable of being so rational. He waited until the hall was clear before rapping softly on the door to the master's bedroom and waiting for it to be opened.

"May I be of service?" he asked Mr. Hill. "It would take time, but I could send for my physician if need be."

Mr. Hill shook his head. "I do not think he would arrive in time," he whispered softly.

"Does he still live?" Darcy asked.

Mr. Hill nodded slowly. "For now, but his heart is weak, and I am uncertain how long it will last."

Darcy blew out a breath as the words of a physician standing in the master's room at Pemberley replayed themselves in Mr. Hill's comments. He, at least, had known such a time was coming, for his father had been weak for several months before the end. Elizabeth and her family had been taken unawares by this turn of events. Having just experienced a loss of a shocking nature, Darcy could well imagine the fear and sorrow that tore through each lady and servant. "If he survives the night and has grown no weaker, I will send for my physician. He cared for my father when his heart began to decline. He may have some answer."

Mr. Hill thanked him and allowed him to leave.

There was nothing Darcy could do that the apothecary was not already doing. He would be of greater service below in the drawing room where he had left Elizbeth and Jane with Bingley. Hopefully, Bingley's sisters had remained in the sitting room and had not imposed their presence upon the others. His wish was not to be granted, however, for Louisa was seated beside Jane, and Caroline had pulled a chair over near Elizabeth. Bingley hovered between the two Bennets and Hurst had ensconced himself in a far corner.

As Darcy entered, Caroline grasped Elizabeth's hand and turned troubled eyes at Darcy. "I do hope you have brought us good news and not ill."

Darcy shared a look with Bingley. Both knew that Caroline was playing a part. She was not cold-hearted. She was not hoping for the worst, but her being at Elizabeth's side and offering comfort was most likely a ploy to garner his approval. She could have just as easily sat with Jane.

Darcy looked past her to the lady whom he wished to speak to alone. "He still lives, but his heart is weak."

"He may die?" Mary asked pointedly.

Darcy drew a breath. "It is a possibility. I have offered to send for my physician should he be needed. He cared for my father when his heart was weak." He shook his head. "I would like to say all will be well, but I cannot."

"Mama?" Elizabeth asked.

"She knows your father is ill and has retired to her room. Miss Kitty and Miss Lydia as well as Mr. Collins were attending her, though I expect Mr. Collins has since gone to see your father." He cared not what Miss Bingley or anyone else in the room thought. He would be near Elizabeth as he spoke of such things, so he knelt before her.

"Mama will be so worried." She shook her head and motioned to the room.

"Collins has assured her that he has no intention of turning anyone out," Darcy whispered.

"He does not?"

"No. Your home is safe should the worst befall your father." Not that Darcy would have allowed her to be put out. He would have insisted on making some sort of arrangement for her and her family, for they would eventually be his family, too, whether Elizabeth was willing to admit that now or not.

"Thank you," she whispered, her voice catching as emotion once again threatened to overcome her.

"It was not I," he replied.

She shook her head. "Not for my home being secured, for knowing what I needed to hear and speaking so plainly."

"It is what I would have wanted."

She smiled softly at him but said not a word. However, it was enough. He knew that even though she was in pain, he had provided her with a small amount of comfort. He pushed to his feet.

"I am staying the night," he declared to Bingley. "Since I have offered to send for my physician, I wish to remain here to save time. I will send for my things and a man to be ready at any hour to ride off."

"I shall see my sisters home and return with all that you need," Bingley replied. And with a final word of parting to Miss Bennet, he gathered his sisters and Hurst and was off.

Darcy sighed and sank down into the chair Caroline had vacated and took up Elizabeth's hand. "I will make certain you get to see him soon," he whispered. Then, he rested his head against the back of his chair and closed his eyes while continuing to hold her hand.

# Chapter 9

Darcy stretched and rubbed his eyes as he looked out the window of the guest room he had been given for his use for as long as he might wish to use it. He had thanked both Mrs. Bennet and Mr. Collins for the offer, but he knew that no matter how much he might wish to stay so close to Elizabeth, he should not. The house was unsettled enough as it was with the master being ill. It did not need to see to an extra guest, especially when that guest had accommodations just three miles away. He sighed. He knew that even if Netherfield came equipped with a lady desperate to impress him with her skills, he should return to it rather than staying here.

"Come," he called in response to the knock at his door.

"I beg your pardon, Mr. Darcy," Mr. Hill said as he stood just inside the room. "But the master is no worse nor is he much improved. If..." The man shifted uneasily. "If..."

"I shall send for my physician straight away. It is not an imposition," he assured the man.

The senior servant visibly relaxed and thanked him before ducking out of the room with instructions to send the man Darcy had told to be ready. Darcy straightened his cravat as he checked his appearance one last time before exiting the room himself.

"Good morning," Kitty greeted him with a smile as she came up the stairs and proceeded on to her room.

When she was not flitting about an assembly room or giggling over something with her younger sister, Miss Kitty seemed to be as sweet and long-suffering as her eldest sister, Miss Bennet. Darcy shook his head. He needed to do a more thorough assessment of people before making judgments about them. Had he not considered Collins a bit of a pompous fool at their first meeting? And yet, having observed him on his arrival at Longbourn and in the hallway yesterday, the man had not been arrogant but rather anxious to please and very compassionate.

"Mr. Darcy, I trust you slept well." Mr. Collins rose from his place at the table as Darcy entered, nearly spilling his tea in his haste to show deference.

"As well as one might in such circumstances as these."

"Right, right. That was perhaps silly of me to say. I should have considered..." his voice trailed off.

"Did you sleep well?" Darcy asked, earning him a look of surprise that was soon replaced with a more relaxed expression.

"As well as might be expected." A small smile played at Collins's lips. He returned to his tea, and the room fell silent for a moment before Mr. Collins cleared his throat and whispered. "I did not offend with my inquiry then?"

Darcy shook his head. "I have been known to say things in a fashion or at a time when it is," he tipped his head and smiled wryly, "well, when it is most inadvisable. I struggle in company," he added simply. "Among friends or with my tenants and staff, I have little trouble, but..." he ended the thought with a shrug.

"But you are Mr. Darcy," the man across from him said in surprise.

"Yes, and that does make it worse, I assure you. I am supposed to be at ease, always dignified, and all that." He was not entirely certain why he was sharing so much of himself with this awkward man whom he had only known for a short time.

"You are very candid," Mr. Collins replied.

"I was thinking the same thing." Darcy lifted his cup. "I suspect the death of my cousin has had somewhat of an altering effect on me."

"As it might," Collins agreed. "One does not know how the changes death brings will affect one until he has passed through the trial and emerged on the other side. Some become bitter and resentful, taking out their displeasure on any poor creature who might come across their path."

He leaned back in his chair and folded his hands across his abdomen, looking very much like a particular professor Darcy had sat under during his years at school. That instructor always reclined backwards and folded his hands when he was about to launch into a lengthy subject or make a point that he knew would make his students ponder and would raise debate. Darcy wondered which Collins was about to do, though he hoped it would not be a long sermon.

"Then others wallow in grief," Collins continued, "dredging it up and wrapping it about their lives like a heavy mantle until all is consumed with melancholy and the light of a summer's day with all its intensity cannot penetrate the gloomy fortresses they have created."

Darcy returned his cup to the table and turned his attention to his plate while Collins spoke.

"The happy few are invigorated upon exiting their trial. The sanctity and blessing of life has been realized with new purpose, and they attack each day as if it were their last. For, when death has left its calling card, we all find ourselves reminded of the words of the apostle James, 'For what is your life? It is even a vapour, that appeareth for a little time, and then vanisheth away.' None of us are guaranteed a moment, let alone a day."

Satisfied with his proclamation, the man leaned forward and took up his cup once again. "I think, the last response is the best," he declared before taking a sip of his tea. "Good morning." His teacup clattered as it was hastily returned to its saucer, so that he could rise.

Darcy followed suit, though a bit less frantically.

"Did you sleep?" he asked Elizabeth as she took her seat next to Jane and across from Mary.

She nodded. "The brandy helped."

He had requested that she be sent a small amount of the relaxing elixir before he retired last night and was happy to hear it had been beneficial.

"You will eat?" He eyed the solitary cup before her.

Her lips curled up into a small smile. "After I have seen Papa."

"My man has gone to town," he replied.

"It is a most generous thing you do," Mr. Collins interjected, his tone reverting from the capable lecturer of a moment ago to the one of a man still seeking his place and stepping carefully to avoid any unpleasantness that might lie on the path.

"I could not do otherwise," Darcy assured him. "I am returning to Netherfield, but I had hoped to look in on your father before I left if you do not think he would mind the intrusion."

It was agreed that Darcy would accompany Elizabeth to Mr. Bennet's room as soon as Elizabeth had finished her tea.

~*~*~

"Papa," Elizabeth said softly as she perched on the edge of his bed and took his hand. He looked so frail, though she thought his cheeks held more colour than they had last night.

Mr. Bennet's eyes opened, and he smiled. "My Lizzy," he said. "What brings you to see me this morning? Are there no meadows to roam?"

"Oh, Papa, how can I wander the countryside when you are not well. We have been worried." She did not wish to be out of his sight, let alone some great distance from the house rambling through the countryside when he was lying in bed, so ill. Time with him was too precious. Hills and trees could wait. He could not.

"There is naught about which to worry my child. It is how life goes."

"Papa," she whispered softly and fought to keep her tears in check. She knew it was true, but she did not wish to hear it.

"Now, do not be missish, my dear," he replied with a wink, "or I shall surely mistake you for one of your younger sisters." He chuckled softly at her huff. Then his eyes moved beyond her to the gentleman standing at the door.

"Mr. Darcy wished to look in on you," Elizabeth explained.

"He is here very early."

"He did not leave yesterday," Elizabeth replied. He had been so solicitous.

Darcy moved forward. "I wished to be near in case I could be of service in any way," he explained.

Mr. Bennet's eyes grew wide.

"I know I have not been the most amiable of neighbours," Darcy continued. "For that I should like to ask your forgiveness."

She could feel his presence casting a shadow on her from behind. It was oddly comforting having him so close that she could lean back and rest on him if she so chose. Quickly, she tucked such startling thoughts away.

Mr. Bennet looked from Darcy to his daughter and back. "We are all disagreeable at times," he said. "I should hope we are all able to overlook a shortcoming or two. You are indeed forgiven, sir."

"Thank you."

"I must extend my condolences on the passing of your cousin. My Lizzy has told me that you were close."

Though her father's heart was weak, his mind was not. Elizabeth could see it in the way his eyes twinkled faintly. His curiosity was nearly as great as her own. However, a small conversation about Mr. Darcy's cousin would likely quell it.

"We were betrothed," Darcy answered plainly.

Again, Mr. Bennet's eyes grew wide. "Indeed?"

No, Elizabeth thought, his curiosity was not going to be suppressed by statements such as that!

"The result of a promise made to my mother before she passed."

"Not a love match then?"

Darcy shook his head. "Not on either side, but we were companionable and great friends."

Elizabeth allowed her eyes to follow the pattern from one block to the next on her father's quilt. Why her father chose this moment to become more like her mother, she did not know. However, if she were to remain quiet, perhaps the conversation would turn to more mundane things like the weather or crops.

"And what shall you do now?" Mr. Bennet asked. "An estate needs a mistress."

Elizabeth closed her eyes and groaned silently. Having one parent embarrass you in front of a handsome gentleman was enough. Why must her father insist upon joining her mother in such an activity?

Darcy shrugged. "Persuade another to take me on, I suppose."

A faint pink stained Elizabeth's cheeks, for she knew precisely whom he wished to persuade, but he was a reserved man. Surely, he would not say more.

"Pull that chair over," Mr. Bennet said. "There is no need for you to stand for this interview. I am quite enjoying getting to know you."

Darcy did as instructed.

"Will you seek a love match this time?" Mr. Bennet attempted to push up in his bed, and Elizabeth helped him while scolding softly that he should not ask such things. "What have I to do with my time, save discover a few things of interest," he protested.

"I could read to you," Elizabeth offered.

"I intend to marry for love," Darcy replied.

Apparently, the reserved Mr. Darcy was intent upon continuing this conversation!

"I have four daughters," Mr. Bennet said.

"Papa!" Elizabeth cried.

"He has twice the consequence of Mr. Bingley," Mr. Bennet

retorted. "I must at least attempt to provide for you in my final hours."

"Papa!" Elizabeth said once more, dread washing over her at his words.

"Mr. Bingley holds some promise," Mr. Bennet continued, causing Elizabeth to gasp in exasperation.

There was little disguise to such a statement! At least her mother couched her inquiries in a more guarded fashion.

Darcy chuckled. "I would agree. My friend seems genuinely smitten; however, I do not know Miss Bennet's sentiments on the arrangement."

Elizabeth shook her head. Mr. Darcy was engaging in gossip with her father about her sister and his friend? Things were not right.

"I would venture her heart is engaged." Mr. Bennet looked at Elizabeth, who had once again gasped softly. "If this conversation is going to be too shocking for you, my dear, you do not need to remain. I intend to talk about you next."

Elizabeth darted wide eyes at Darcy, who was looking rather amused.

"I had hoped," Darcy began.

Elizabeth's breath caught. No, he was not going to speak about her, was he?

"To speak to you about Miss Elizabeth at some point," he continued. "However, she has not given me permission to do so."

Elizabeth wished to snatch a blanket from her father's bed and toss it over her head with a hope that it would magically cause her to fade away, so that she could not hear this conversation or see the all too pleased look on her father's face. However, none of those things were possible, so the best course of action seemed to be to take part in the discussion.

"It does not look at all like it will rain today," she said.

Her father chuckled. "Well," Mr. Bennet said, ignoring Elizabeth's attempt to turn the conversation, "if she has not given you permission to speak to me, then I suppose I should not ask you about your intentions."

"Indeed, you should not," Darcy agreed. "Though I do assure you they are honorable."

"I would not doubt it," her father replied more seriously. "I look forward to when she does give you permission to speak to me."

Darcy accepted Mr. Bennet's words with a small incline of his head.

Indignation at being spoken of so freely without so much as a care for how she might feel rose within her and could not be contained. "She is not ever going to give you permission to speak to him," she snapped. They were impossible. "Teasing at a time like this?"

She pushed off the bed. "I will return later when the room is not so crowded," she said to her father before fleeing the room.

# Chapter 10

Darcy watched her leave, and, while he wished to jump from his chair and chase after her to apologize, her father's words stopped him.

"You love her?"

Darcy nodded. "I do."

"And you have told her?"

Again, Darcy nodded.

Mr. Bennet shifted in his bed and pushed a pillow further in behind his back. "She wrestles with things. She always has." He smoothed his blankets. "While the other girls accept things readily, Lizzy questions, which is not so bad a thing." He blew out a shallow breath and winced as he did so. "Why did she refuse you?"

"She thinks I am mistaken because of my grief. She offered me comfort and understanding and thinks I have confused that with love."

"That is not an argument without grounds." Mr. Bennet replied. "It can happen."

Darcy drew and released a breath. "If my feelings for her had begun after I learned of Anne's death, I might consider her argument to plausibly be valid." Guilt roiled in his stomach.

"Anne was an easy solution to my need for a wife until I met your daughter. Then, my duty to Anne began to feel just like that – a duty." His heart ached to admit such things, but even if he had tried, he could not have contained his thoughts, for in his current state of mind, he needed to be counselled by someone who might guide him. He shook his head. "I did not know what to do. I was writing to my cousin Colonel Fitzwilliam to ask his advice when he arrived with the news of Anne's accident."

"Hits you in the gut, does it not? You wish to be free from an obligation and then it appears most unexpectedly, and you begin to wonder if it was in some way brought on by your desires."

Darcy stared at Mr. Bennet. How did the man know that?

Mr. Bennet shrugged. "You are not the first gentleman to find himself in such a situation. When I was young – much younger than you even. I longed to be free of my father. I wished to pursue a career in education." A smile played at the gentleman's mouth as he stared at the wall across the room. What he saw there in his memories, Darcy did not know.

"My father wished for me to become a parson. He had connections and could have gotten me a good living, or so he said." His accompanying sigh was as weary and worn a sound as Darcy had ever heard.

"He would have had me near home. He always wanted his children gathered where he could direct their comings and goings. I was intent on my dream and argued my position vehemently. I did not wish to instruct only as prescribed by the church. I wished to explore science, to discover things, to read great lengthy tomes and expound upon them. My father, of course, threatened to cut me off, and so I acquiesced. I studied what he told me as well as a few things he did not, chafing the whole time and wishing to be free of him."

He turned his gaze to Darcy. "His heart stopped working one day, and my brother came into his inheritance. I continued my studies in preparation for taking orders. I could have studied whatever I wished, but the weight of having wished to be free of my father and his demands hung heavily on me."

"You were going to be a clergyman?" Darcy asked in surprise.

"I was until my brother succumbed to a fever, and I was left with this." He spread his arms wide, indicating the estate. "Just months before I took orders and while I was betrothed to a pretty young merchant's daughter." He shook his head. "Had I been a compliant son with a happy disposition, my father still would have died. Just because I wished to be free of him at the same time he died does not mean that one precipitated the other. The same is true for you. Your desires had no part in the death of your betrothed. Such things leave us with some unsettled matters, however."

Darcy nodded. "Anne would have released me from my duty, but I could not have been released from my promise to my mother." He smiled wryly. "My uncle assures me I have fulfilled it, but there is a twinge now and again because I had considered not keeping that promise."

"You love my Lizzy so much that you considered disappointing your mother?"

Darcy blew out a breath and nodded. "I do. I do not know how it happened, but she holds my heart."

Mr. Bennet chuckled weakly. "I believe that is the way every gentleman who has married for love has felt. It creeps up on you, ensnaring you while you are unaware. I do not know you as well as I would like, Mr. Darcy, but I believe you would do well with my Lizzy. If I do not survive long enough for her to come to her senses, know that you have my blessing. I have heard tell of your fortune, so I know she will want for nothing in this physical world, but more importantly, I know she will be loved."

"Most ardently," Darcy agreed.

Mr. Bennet shifted again in his bed. "Now, about your friend and my Jane."

Darcy chuckled. "Shall I send him to see you?"

"Aye, if he loves her." He stifled a yawn.

"I have overstayed my time," Darcy said, moving to rise. "And have kept you from your rest."

"I have enjoyed your visit, and," Mr. Bennet said. "I have no desire to rest, young man. However, it seems I have no choice."

Darcy smiled. "I have sent for my physician. He treated my father."

Mr. Bennet cocked his head to the side. "I thank you, and I will gladly see him." His brows drew together. "I fear there is little he can do, but I will see him." He winced and rubbed his chest. "If you would be so kind, would you seek out my Lizzy and send her to me. I must make things right with her, or she will be left with a terrible weight should my time be shorter than even I realize."

"I will see that she comes to see you," Darcy assured him. Then he ducked out of the room and went in search of Elizabeth. Her father was not the only one who needed to apologize.

~*~*~

Darcy's search was not long in duration, for he had the good fortune of coming upon Mr. Collins as he was descending the stairs.

"Ah, Mr. Darcy, have you been with Mr. Bennet this whole time?"

"I have been. It seems we had a great deal about which to speak."

"Good. Good," Collins said as he stepped up one step most likely on his way to see Mr. Bennet or to retire to his room.

"Have you see Miss Elizabeth?" Darcy asked.

Mr. Collins returned to his lower position on the stairs. "I did see her. She was dressed for a walk, but she assured me she is only going as far as the edge of the garden and did not need a chaperone. If she should be needed, she said she could easily be found." The man moved up a step once again but then turning back a second time, he lowered his voice and added, "This episode with her father is unsettling for us all, and she appeared overcome with emotion. I tell you this," he looked up the stairs and then down, "so that you might be prepared. I have an extra handkerchief if you should need one."

"I am well-supplied, but I thank you for your offer. It was most generous," Darcy said.

Collins seemed delighted with such a compliment, but before he could elaborate beyond an acceptance of Darcy's gratitude, Darcy continued his descent of the stairs. The garden. The edge of the garden. That is where he needed to be. Not standing on the stairs listening to Mr. Collins.

Elizabeth was right where she said she would be, pacing along the low border at the back of the garden, pausing when she came to the opening that led to a path which would take one to the wilderness beyond. He suspected she would dearly love to take that path, for he knew how much she loved to walk.

"Miss Elizabeth," he said as he approached.

She stopped but did not turn toward him.

"Your father sent me to find you."

She wiped at her cheeks with one gloved hand and nodded mutely, but still she did not turn toward him.

He took a step toward her. "I would have come to find you even without his request."

He watched her brush her cheeks once again, and fishing his handkerchief from his pocket, he began moving forward but while being careful to stay behind her. He did not wish to intrude when she most likely longed to express her grief in private. Extending his hand around her side, he offered his handkerchief silently.

"Thank you," she whispered as she took it.

He stepped back one step, no more. He did not even wish to be that far from her. He longed to embrace her, to allow her to weep on his shoulder, to hold her and soothe her, but it was not his place. Therefore, it was best if he remained at least a small distance from her.

"I must apologize," he began. "I should not have mentioned anything about my desires."

She nodded as she dried her eyes and drew a shuddering breath.

"Your father wishes to see you," Darcy said softly. "Do not wait too long before returning to him."

She turned toward him, her eyes still filled with tears. "He is dying."

Darcy nodded. "He is."

"And you were talking about matchmaking and marrying?" She shook her head as if it was a thought that could not be accepted because it was too reprehensible.

Darcy swallowed. "We were."

"Why?" she demanded.

Darcy blew out a breath and, turning to his right, looked out into the wilderness beyond the garden. "You were going to tell me of your friend," he said, "and one day, I would still like to know about her, but do you remember how you felt about life when she died?" He glanced at her, and she nodded.

"It seemed shorter somehow, did it not?" he asked.

"Immeasurably."

"When my mother died, life grew shorter. I felt vulnerable and less protected, but life proceeded without much change on my part. Then, my father died, and I took on the responsibilities of an estate and a sister." He sighed. "I have done better with Pemberley than I have with my sister."

Turning back toward the garden, he faced her. "Once again, with my father's death, life grew shorter. There was one fewer person between me and death." He shook his head and looked at the sky just above her, willing his own emotions to remain under regulation. "But life continued on, weightier than it had been, but it continued. Responsibilities arose and were tended to. Months and years passed, just as they always had. And then Anne died." He drew and released a deep breath. "She was so young."

He turned toward the wilderness again. "It is not as if I had not heard of a young person dying. I have attended funerals for infants and sent my condolences to husbands who have lost wives." Had he not, just three weeks ago, sent such a letter to one of his tenants after receiving news from his steward about the man's wife dying while birthing their third child?

He turned toward her and offered his arm. "But Anne...Anne was mine, and then she was gone. And as much as it pains me to think it, life will go on without her."

They began pacing toward the far end of the border. "However, this time, I cannot allow life to remain the same."

The garden was silent save for the sounds of boots on dormant grass for a short time until Darcy broke the silence. "I intend to embrace life before it is lost to me, and that is why I was speaking of marriage and matchmaking with your father."

He stopped as they reached the end of their path and lifting her hand from his arm, he turned toward her without releasing it.

"I will not remind him of the brevity of his life. If he wishes to discuss your sister and my friend in the privacy of his room, I will do it. And when I saw the opportunity to discover if I would have his blessing to court you should I ever be fortunate enough to secure your approval, I took it. It was perhaps not done as it should have been, but I did not want to always wonder." He squeezed her hand. "Can you forgive me?"

He held his breath as he waited for her to ponder his words. Finally, her head bobbed slowly up and down, and he released his breath.

"Your father wishes to see you," he repeated.

Her lips curved up slightly.

"May I see you to the house, Miss Elizabeth?"

"Yes, Mr. Darcy, you may."

He wrapped her hand around his arm and escorted her to the house.

"Miss Elizabeth," he said as they were about to part ways. He would see that his carriage and things were removed from the house while she would go see her father. He longed to stay but knew he could not.

"Yes," she replied, turning away from the staircase and back toward where he stood in the entry.

"I am only at Netherfield. If anything changes, if you find you are in need of anything, anything at all, please send for me."

"I will."

She turned toward the stairs but only took two steps toward them before turning back. "Mr. Darcy," she called and then waited until he had finished telling Mr. Hill what he needed.

"Yes, Miss Elizabeth?"

"I should like it if you would call." She ducked her head in such a fashion that, Darcy suspected, had her cheeks not already been rosy from the coolness of the day, they would have been tinged with pink.

"You would?" He could not keep the smile from his lips.

"I would," she replied, lifting her eyes to him. "And," she added as her lips curled into a small smile, "you may bring your friend if you want. I am certain my sister would be delighted to see him."

Darcy's smile grew, and he arched a brow. "At a time like this?" he questioned softly.

Her head turned just a touch in the direction of the stairs, and her eyes lifted as if she were looking at the floor above. She nodded. "Yes, I think now would be perfect."

"Are you certain you wish for me to call on you?"

Again, she nodded and took a step closer to him, so that she could speak in a softer tone. "I am not agreeing to a courtship."

There was a note of caution in her voice. "I am still not convinced that you are not pursuing me due to grief, nor am I convinced it is not anxiety making me accept you. However, I should like to discover the truth," again, her eyes lifted toward the ceiling, "before it is too late."

Darcy rejoiced at the hope her words brought. "I shall return this afternoon with my friend — if that would be acceptable." He was certain he had never seen such a sweet welcoming smile as the one she wore as she assured him it was indeed acceptable. Then with a parting curtsey and a final look over her shoulder at him from part way up the stairs, she was gone, and Darcy departed Longbourn with a comforting new joy in his heart.

# Chapter 11

For two days, Darcy and Bingley were the only callers admitted to the house while Mr. Bennet convalesced. Each afternoon, they sat in the sitting room with their ladies before being sent up to Mr. Bennet's room where he told them tales of his daughters when they were young and listened to exploits from the gentlemen as well.

On the third day after falling ill, Mr. Bennet had had enough of his frailty and insisted upon being taken to his book room, and callers were once again accepted beyond the two men he knew would be his sons if he should survive long enough to witness it.

It was on this day that Darcy was greeted by a most unwelcome sight upon entering the sitting room at Longbourn, for reclining in a chair near Elizabeth was...

"Wickham." He attempted to keep his tone flat, but from the way Elizabeth's eyes grew just a tiny bit larger, he knew he had failed to keep all of his displeasure from his tone.

"Darcy," Wickham responded with what was not quite his normal amount of ease. That was good. He should feel a trifle uneasy. In fact, he should feel extremely uneasy.

"Of all the vermin..." Richard muttered as he entered behind Darcy.

That was the moment when Wickham's slight disquiet turned to obvious anxiety as he stood.

"Colonel Fitzwilliam," he said with a bow. "I had not thought to see you. I had heard Darcy was at Netherfield, but I heard no word of your arrival."

"Did you not?" Richard crossed the room. "The room seems rather full."

"Indeed, it does," Wickham agreed without moving from his place.

Richard's eyes narrowed. He looked to Wickham's left where Lydia sat and then toward Darcy before procuring a chair from the far corner of the room and wedging it between Wickham and the youngest Miss Bennet.

Lydia huffed.

"He is not for you," Richard explained.

Lydia's mouth gaped open for a half minute before she snapped it closed and folding her arms, glared at Richard. "That is not for you to decide," she snapped.

"Very well," Richard replied. "Do you have a fortune?"

Lydia blinked and stammered a no.

"Then, as I said, he is not for you. The last young lady he importuned was an heiress – more his type. He has no land and quite likely not many pounds to his name. Are you willing to be impoverished?"

Darcy chuckled softly to himself at the look of utter loathing Lydia leveled at Richard, not that Richard would be perturbed by such.

"Miss Elizabeth," Darcy said while his resolute cousin continued to stare down the immovable Lydia Bennet, "I had hoped to take a walk in the garden. The sun is bright."

She smiled at him and held out her hand, which he took readily and drew her to her feet.

Wickham's brows rose. "So that is how it is, is it?"

Darcy did not appreciate the note of laughter in the man's voice, but rather than succumb to the urge to flatten him, he tucked Elizabeth's hand in the crook of his arm and replied with a simple yes, followed by an offer to join them if he wished.

"I should like to take a walk," Lydia said, popping out of her chair.

"So would I," said Richard, rising and placing himself between her and Wickham.

"Not with you," Lydia retorted.

"I am not allowing you to walk with him," Richard tipped his head toward Wickham.

"You have no say." Lydia took a step closer to him, her nostrils flaring.

"Lydia," Mrs. Bennet scolded. "He is a colonel."

"He is rude."

Mrs. Bennet nodded. "His approach is unconventional," she admitted, "but he is a colonel, and his father is an earl. Go get your things and walk with him."

"You cannot mean it." Lydia's voice was tinged with horror.

"Oh, but I do. Mr. Wickham can walk with..." Mrs. Bennet looked around the room, her eyes falling on Kitty.

"No," Richard snapped, drawing the woman's attention.

"I beg your pardon?" Mrs. Bennet's eyes were wide, and her handkerchief fluttered.

"Collins needs a partner," Bingley interjected.

"I...I... do not need to walk," Collins stammered.

"What? The heir must rusticate while everyone else enjoys the fresh air?" Darcy inserted.

Mrs. Bennet gasped. "You are right, of course, Mr. Darcy. Mr. Collins should join you, but Mary is not here. She is with Hill. I could go get her."

"There is no need to bother yourself," Darcy said calmly. "I am certain Miss Kitty could tolerate a turn of the garden with Mr. Collins. Could you not?"

Kitty bit her lip and looked first at Darcy and then Lydia, who was now glaring at her. If Darcy was not mistaken, Miss Lydia would rather see Wickham left standing than to see her sister on his arm.

"I am certain I could," Kitty replied.

"But Mr. Wickham..." Mrs. Bennet muttered.

"You could join us, Mrs. Bennet," Darcy offered.

"Me? On the arm of a young man in my garden?" The thought seemed nearly too strange for the woman to grasp, but then her look of perplexity slid into a smile. "It's just the thing!" she cried. "I should hate for Mr. Wickham to go away without seeing the garden. He has not yet seen it, you know." She scampered away, calling for her daughters to follow and make haste in retrieving their things.

Wickham shifted uneasily as the ladies, and Mr. Collins left the room.

"Five hundred pounds," Darcy said, turning to face his former friend.

"For what?" Richard asked.

"For Wickham to find some other sitting room to frequent," Darcy replied.

"Five hundred pounds," Wickham scoffed. "This sitting room is worth more than that."

"Five hundred pounds and your life," Richard muttered.

Wickham's eyes grew wide.

Darcy raised a brow at his cousin in response.

Richard shrugged. "It was a pleasant thought."

Darcy shook his head.

"One thousand," Bingley offered. "I can spare five hundred. Caroline has not been to a shop in two weeks."

"He deserves nothing," Richard grumbled, "at least nothing so pleasant as you offer."

"One turn of the garden with Mrs. Bennet," Darcy said, ignoring Richard, "and then you take your leave and do not return."

"And you will give me five hundred pounds?" Wickham said incredulously.

Darcy nodded. "Call on me in a month's time, and I will give you five hundred pounds as long as you have not returned to Longbourn or been found with any of its residents of the female variety."

"I was not serious about Miss Lydia," Wickham said with a smirk. "Now, Miss Elizabeth..."

"Is mine," Darcy growled, stepping within inches of Wickham, his jaw clenching, and his fists balling.

Wickham swallowed and retreated a step. "Five hundred from you both." He looked around Darcy to Bingley.

"In one month's time," Bingley agreed.

Wickham shrugged. "Very well. It is perhaps the easiest thousand I shall ever earn."

"One moment," Richard said before everyone left the sitting room to greet the ladies they could hear on the stairs. "You're agreeing to stay away from them always."

"I cannot help it if I see them in town or at a soiree," Wickham retorted.

"You will be civil but not excessively charming," Richard explained. "I am certain you understand my meaning." He threw an arm around Wickham's shoulders and pulled him close to his side as they crossed to the sitting room door. "You do understand, do you not?"

Again, Wickham swallowed hard and agreed to the terms. Then, when Colonel Fitzwilliam released him, he smiled and offered Mrs. Bennet his arm.

~*~*~

"Miss Elizabeth." Tugging along a recalcitrant Lydia, Richard hurried after Darcy and Elizabeth on the garden path.

"If I must walk with you," Lydia complained, "I should like to walk and not scamper."

"I do apologize, Miss Lydia." Richard glanced at her briefly and slowed his pace. "Is that better?"

"Perhaps," Lydia replied with a lift of her chin and a small huff.

Richard chuckled, which only served to draw another huff from his partner.

"Miss Elizabeth." Richard pulled some folded pieces of paper from his pocket and handed them to her. "I had hoped to give these to you in private, but..." He glanced back to where Wickham was walking with Mrs. Bennet, "but my plans did not include him."

"Why do you hate Mr. Wickham?" Lydia demanded. "I think he is a very friendly sort of person, unlike some." Her eyes raked up the colonel's person while her lips curled in contempt.

Darcy saw Richard's eyes narrow. It was a sign that his cousin's limit of tolerance was nearing an end, which was not surprising since Wickham's presence tended to have that effect on him.

"I would rather walk with Mr. Collins than you," Lydia continued. "He is ridiculous, but at least he is nice."

"Those papers should help you in making your decision," Richard said to Elizabeth as she turned the letters he had given her over in her hand. "One was intended to be sent to me, and the other I procured from Darcy's sister, Georgiana, while in town."

Elizabeth shook her head. "I do not understand. My decision? About what?"

"About whom," Richard replied with a tip of his head toward Darcy. "I would prefer if the whom did not know I had given those to you, but, well, plans changed."

Elizabeth darted a look toward Darcy. "This has been a most unusual afternoon."

First, Mr. Darcy had seemed angry to see Mr. Wickham, and then Colonel Fitzwilliam had all but thrown the man from the room. And now, she had letters in her hand that were supposed to help her decide something about Mr. Darcy?

Richard blew out a breath, pulled Lydia in front of him, and then covered her ears with his hands, ignoring her protests. "Darcy loved you before Anne died." He nodded toward the letters. "Those are my proof. He would never share anything like this with you. He would simply continue to be gallant and attentive with the hope that eventually, you would be won over. However," he blew out another breath, "I fear there is not enough time for such maneuvers."

He released Lydia.

"You are horrid," she cried.

"Lydia," Elizabeth chided.

"He is very high-handed." She stood cross-armed, glaring at Richard. "And he was very rude to Mr. Wickham and has yet to explain himself."

"Lydia, it is not polite to ask him to explain himself."

Lydia's glare shifted to her sister. "I do not see why I have to be polite when he is not."

"Lydia, please," Elizabeth begged.

"Mr. Wickham is not to be trusted," Darcy interjected. "There was a young lady of our acquaintance who was led to believe by his charming manners and pretty words that he loved her and she him." He paused. "As I understand it, he had even convinced this young lady to elope with him."

Lydia's eyes grew wide, and she gasped.

"The young lady's family did not approve of him, you see." His brows furrowed. "Not because of his station as a steward's son, but because of his proclivities, which I fear, for delicacy's sake, I cannot mention beyond what I have said. It would be most improper."

A startled squeak escaped Lydia, and her hand flew to cover her mouth.

"As it turned out, the scheme was discovered, and it was brought to light that Wickham had no feelings for the young lady.

His intention was only to acquire her fortune. The young lady, of course, was heartbroken."

Lydia had spun around, so that she was watching Wickham. "This is true?" she asked.

"I am afraid it is," Darcy replied. "She was your age." He nodded in reply to her wide-eyed look. "He only appears to be charming."

"But I have no fortune," Lydia replied.

"He was playing with your heart nonetheless," Darcy assured her.

"But why?" Her lashes fluttered.

"His proclivities would favour your...beauty," Richard replied

"Oh!" Lydia squeaked as her hand once again flew to her mouth.

"You cannot repeat this, Lydia," Elizabeth cautioned. "Such a tale could cause this other young lady great sorrow if it were known." She glanced at Mr. Darcy, who nodded.

"Oh, I shall not tell a soul," she pulled her bottom lip between her teeth, "except, maybe Kitty?"

"You may tell your sister," Darcy assured her.

"If you had but explained that to me from the beginning," Lydia said, taking the arm Richard offered her, "I should not have been half so cross with you."

"I could not just march into a room and expound such a tale," Richard said as they began to walk away.

"You think I'm beautiful?"

Elizabeth laughed and shook her head. Of course, that would be the one thing Lydia would fixate upon. "I believe your cousin has found himself in a most uncomfortable position," she said to Darcy.

"It would not be the first time," Darcy admitted. "Richard can be a trifle too direct at times."

"I think it is endearing that he should put himself in such a place for my sister's safety." Elizabeth turned the letters over in her hand once again. "It seems it is not grief which has caused you to think well of me." She smiled sheepishly at him. "Which I believe you have already told me."

"You have not read those letters. It could be a ploy," Darcy said as he and Elizabeth began walking side by side down the path.

"He placed himself between my sister and Mr. Wickham."

Darcy nodded. "He did."

"I doubt these are a ploy. Do you wish me to read them?" Elizabeth had to admit to herself that she was curious about the contents of the letters.

"I do not mind if you do."

Elizabeth turned the letters over once more and then unfolded the first. It was a partial letter. She held it out so that he could see it.

"I was writing that one when Richard arrived to tell me about Anne. The first part is just news of the area. It is likely the last few lines he wishes for you to see."

Elizabeth scanned down to the bottom of the writing.

*I find myself in need of advice. I have promised myself to Anne, and in a few week's time, our betrothal will be announced. However, I find myself captivated by another. I have attempted these past weeks to dissuade my heart from longing to see her eyes sparkle with amusement or to hear her engage in debate. Her laughter is intoxicating. Her mind is sharp and quick. She is ...*

That was where it ended. There was no more.

"I found I could not keep my heart from desiring you," Darcy said as she began refolding the paper. "But I was betrothed. Not officially, but in word. I found that as time passed, I could not reconcile myself to either breaking my promise or being parted from you."

"You would have kept your promise," Elizabeth said softly. There was not one thing she had witnessed in her acquaintance with Fitzwilliam Darcy that said he was anything less than constant. He might have been dour and disapproving and even rude, but he was not capricious.

"I would have," he admitted, "but I did not want to."

She turned and held out the letters to him.

"Do you not wish to see what I told my sister about you?"

She shook her head. "No, I want to go to my father."

"Very well, I shall not detain you," he said, taking the letters from her and stuffing them into his pocket.

"I want you to go with me."

"You do?"

"Yes," she replied, a smile spreading across her face. "I am a lady of my word, and three days ago, I told him that I would never give you permission to speak to him. Therefore, I find I must speak to him on your behalf. I only need to know what you would like me to ask him."

His eyelids fluttered. His mouth dropped open and then snapped closed. "Would you ..." He shook his head as a pleased, yet perplexed look crept across his face. "You do not mean..."

"But I do," she assured him. "Grief has not clouded your mind, and it no longer clouds mine. I should like very much to marry you if you will but ask me."

"You will marry me?"

Oh, his smile was beautiful.

"Yes, most happily."

"Truly?"

She had barely gotten the word "yes" out of her mouth before she found herself wrapped in his embrace. "We must go see my father," she urged him. "He must know of my happiness."

"Of course, of course, he must know." Darcy agreed.

And he would.

In just a short time, Mr. Bennet would have the pleasure of giving his daughter a knowing smirk as he kissed her cheek and congratulated Darcy on being more determined than his most obstinate daughter. Elizabeth would protest, and Mr. Bennet would chuckle and kiss her once again as he assured her of both is love and happiness. But that would come later. First, there was something that Darcy needed to do, and so he did not release her and go with her immediately to her father's side.

Instead, he placed a hand on her cheek as she looked up at him and said, "He will know, I promise you that, but first..." He smiled as he brushed her lower lip with his thumb. "First, I must kiss you. I truly must."

And he did.

Gently, reverently, as if she was the most precious thing in the world, his lips brushed hers and then pressed against them more urgently, and as he did, Elizabeth wound her arms around him with a sigh of contentment as a feeling of perfect well-being washed over and around her. No matter what sorrows lay ahead or what memories of griefs long past would arise, she knew that she would always wish to be right here, in his arms, surrounded by Mr. Darcy's comfort.

# Master of Longbourn

*From awkward and unlovable to handsome and loved.*

# Chapter 1

William Collins pushed back the shock of golden brown hair that always fell across his forehead and studied his face.

It was not angular. There were no high cheekbones nor was there a prominent chin.

His eyes were evenly spaced but not of any particularly intense colour. In fact, they reflected the colour of his hair, which meant there was nothing to set them apart as an admirable feature.

His nose was good. It was straight and not too large. There was no hook at the end, nor were any distracting hairs protruding from it. One thing. One solitary thing that was good about his face was not enough.

He looked at his mouth. Not large, nor small. Merely regular.

He allowed the hair to flop down onto his forehead once again as he pulled at what he considered a definite imperfection. His jowl was far too soft and fleshy to be attractive.

Blowing out a great breath, he began stuffing his shirt tails into his breeches. How was he to persuade Miss Kitty to consider him if he had no particularly handsome features to recommend him?

It was as his father had said. He would be the last in their family to be master of Longbourn because ladies did not marry lumpy puddings such as he.

He plopped down onto his bed and pulled on his boots, which, though freshly polished, were old and well-worn as well as still rather dull. Much like the rest of him.

Until now, he had not thought himself so lacking as his father had proclaimed him to be. He had excelled in his studies far more than his father would ever have thought possible, and despite his father's assurance that he would not, he had made some friends — even a few who were important enough to help him acquire a valuable living. True, none of them wished to visit, but they did correspond, and that was something, was it not?

And yet, here he sat in what would soon be one of the rooms of his estate, having to face the prospect that he might grow old and lonely just as his father said simply because he was dashed ordinary. It was not being ordinary, however, that grated the most. No, what stirred his spirit and caused him to scowl was the fact that in this, he feared he could not prove his father wrong.

The sigh which escaped him surely could have moved the heavy green drapes that hung on either side of the window had he been close enough. He fell backward onto his bed and stared at the canopy above him. All his striving was to come to naught and simply because he was not handsome enough to persuade Kitty Bennet to look at him as Miss Elizabeth looked at Mr. Darcy or Miss Bennet looked at Mr. Bingley. Miss Kitty did not even look at him with that transient fondness of a flirt like Miss Lydia looked at every officer who came within her line of vision.

He could not charm Miss Kitty into liking him, for he had less charm than he had becoming features. All was lost.

If it were not for the man lying close to heaven's gates in the room just down the hall, Collins would take himself back to Kent and throw himself into his preaching with such fervour that some pious young girl might come to admire him for his oratory skills. Those he had – when he was in the pulpit.

"Surely, there must be a way to sway her. Mustn't there be?"

The empty room had no response to such a question, and neither did his mind. However, there was a duty to be done. He was the heir apparent, and with Mr. Bennet incapacitated, it fell upon him to see that all was well within the house and regarding his family.

He smiled at that.

Family. No matter if he married or not, he had a family. And it was one which seemed to tolerate him far better than his own father ever had.

Bolstered by the thought, he pushed up to a sitting position and then rose from the bed. Pulling on his waistcoat and jacket, he wondered if the funds at Longbourn would allow for him to have a man to help him with these things.

His father had thought it an extravagance, which was likely because it would have taken from the funds he needed to chase every new scheme that was placed before him. There were several hundred if not thousands of pounds which were planted with hopes of heavy returns. Sadly, his father was as wise as he was kind, and his fortune dwindled steadily. Collins had not been left penniless when his father died, but along with what remained of his inheritance, he had also been bequeathed a fine array of bills. Therefore, his coffers were neither empty nor well-filled.

He straightened his cravat, gave his sleeves one more tug, and exited his room.

"Good morning, Mr. Collins," Kitty greeted as he began his descent of the stairs.

Ah, it was a good morning, indeed, if Kitty's smiling face was the first he had the pleasure of seeing. However, it would be a better morning if he could remember to speak instead of just staring when she spoke to him.

"Good...morning," he finally stammered to her retreating form. Yes, that would impress her. He shook his head and hurried down the stairs to the breakfast room.

Thankfully, the breakfast room was pleasantly empty when he entered. He would have a few moments to gather his thoughts and recover from his embarrassment before having to speak to anyone.

"Good morning."

Tea sloshed over the side of the cup into which Collins was pouring.

"I did not mean to startle you."

"Think nothing of it, Miss Elizabeth. I was merely too immersed in my thoughts to pay proper attention to my surroundings." He glanced at her as he mopped up the tea his saucer had not caught.

"I am afraid it is a horrid fault which I must own." His hand stilled. Had she actually smiled at him? And not in a what a fool fashion? Hmm. That was unexpected.

"I believe there are several of us in this house who fall prey to such things on a regular basis," Elizabeth replied as she brought him a fresh cloth before taking her seat. "I have been known to wander for hours, lost to time, while pondering. And it is best to make some small sound before speaking to either Jane or Kitty when they are intent upon their stitching, or one might be the cause of a pricked finger."

"I shall endeavour to remember that, and I thank you for alerting me to the danger." He sat down and began eating his egg. "The eggs are good."

"They are," Elizabeth agreed. "Have you been to see the outbuildings at all?"

Collins shook his head. "None but the stable."

"Then, on a fine day, Mr. Darcy and I shall have to take you on a tour." She pulled in a deep breath. "They will be yours eventually."

"Ours. They will be ours," he corrected with a small smile. He knew the blessing he would receive through the inheritance of Longbourn. Without it, he would likely have always remained a parson. Not that that was so bad a thing, but to be the master of one's own estate? Ah, that...that was success. That was position. That was more than his father had ever had.

"Thank you," Elizabeth said softly. "You have been most gracious with my mother." She took a sip of her tea.

"How could I be otherwise?" Collins asked in surprise, but then his brows drew together as a thought struck him. "I never knew your father, and he never knew me. He only ever knew my father, and if one were to describe my father to me, I would fear such a person." He shrugged. "I did."

"You feared your own father?" Elizabeth's hand covered her mouth, and her eyes were wide.

"No need to apologize. It is hard to imagine when one has been in possession of a father who is what a father should be – indulgent, kind, not overly serious, nor one to raise his voice." Again, he shrugged. "At least, that is how I imagine a good father should be."

The hours he had spent locked in his room for some small indiscretion which had sent his father on a screaming rampage which ended in a bruise or two and a hungry night had given him plenty of time to imagine what a proper father should be – the sort of father he hoped to be.

Elizabeth tipped her head and looked at him for a long while as he finished his egg and spread jam on his toast. Finally, she smiled and returned to her tea.

"Then, I hope you will have a long time to spend with my father."

There were tears in her eyes, and he looked steadfastly at his toast until his own tears were forced to retreat. It was another failing on his part. He was too soft. The mere appearance of tears in the eyes of a lady should not cause him to become weepy, but, much to his shame, it did. "That would be my prayer as well, Miss Elizabeth."

"Elizabeth."

He lifted startled eyes to her.

"We are cousins. You may call me Elizabeth."

"Are you certain?" He had never called any lady by her Christian name.

"Yes."

"Very well, Elizabeth." The word felt so strange on his tongue as if it was missing an article of clothing to make it complete.

"Do you have any brothers or sisters?"

"N...no. My mother died at my birth, and my father never

remarried." Which was likely good for the ladies of the land, since none had to be tied to such an ogre as his father.

"How sad."

He nodded. "I often wished for a sibling and, of course, my mother, but that is not what God had designed for me to have. And knowing such, I attempted to be content."

"Do you have any other cousins?"

He shook his head. "None of whom I know. Your father was the only one whom my father ever mentioned." If there were others, they must not have had money, for money, land, or possessions of any value were what made relations and acquaintances important to his father.

"So, we are it? We are your family?"

"As the good Lord reigns above."

Elizabeth fell silent and once again studied him as she ate.

He would dearly like to know what was going through her head, and a longing to fill the silence with some sound nearly overwhelmed him. Sitting in silence, being scrutinized, while still feeling out of place in a new surrounding, begged him to release some of his anxiety in the form of words.

"It is a beautiful day."

The words would not stay contained, no matter how he tried.

"It might be a good day for a walk to Oakham Mount. That is what it is called, is it not? That hill to which you like to walk." He clamped his lips closed. When the words started, they often just spilled out in great torrents.

Elizabeth chuckled. "Yes, that is what it is called, but I should like to confine myself to the garden and the wilderness just beyond."

Dunderhead. Her father was ill. Of course, she did not want to be far from home.

"I was not thinking," he muttered. "It would be best to stay close. I should have thought of that."

"Things are out of the ordinary, and you have just gained a family."

She was one of the kindest and most understanding ladies he had met.

"You are very gracious," he said. "Not at all obstinate," he muttered and then froze with his tea lifted halfway to his mouth.

Carefully, he moved just his eyes to see if Elizabeth had heard him. From the way her eyebrow arched, she must have.

"I do apologize. I am sure Mr. Darcy meant it in the most flattering way. He is quite taken with you."

He shrank into himself as he saw her expression change from one of curiosity to unpleasant surprise.

"My thoughts do not always stay where they should," he said before clamping his lips closed.

"Mr. Darcy said I was obstinate?"

"Oh," Collins groaned.

He had hoped Mr. Darcy would one day be his friend, and it had appeared like the man was becoming such. However, now, he doubted greatly that such a thing should ever happen.

"I asked him about my cousins when we were at Rosings. My lady, Lady Catherine, that is, had suggested I consider marrying one of you."

He swallowed. This was going from bad to worse. Her look of surprise was not receding.

"I had to consider it. It seemed a good plan to mend the breach my father had caused in our family." He pulled at his cravat. "I thought it most proper to inquire after the eldest, but I was assured Miss Bennet expected to have a happy announcement shortly. Naturally, I then inquired after the next in line." He made a small gesture towards her with his hand. "You. And Mr. Darcy immediately told me that you would not make a proper parson's wife at all. He was quite adamant. However, having met you, I do not know why he would disparage one so lovely as yourself."

His brows furrowed. "Why are you so pleased?" Her look of surprise was completely gone.

Her head dipped, and a faint blush stained her cheeks.

"Because I think I know why he said what he did, and," she looked up at him, "he is not wrong. I can be entirely too stubborn at times, and I would make a deplorable parson's wife. I do not possess the nature that is necessary for such a role."

"I apologize. I should not have said anything."

"No," Elizabeth replied firmly. "I am pleased you did."

"But Mr. Darcy will be angry."

Elizabeth chuckled. "I very much doubt that. He is not so dour and disapproving as I once thought."

"Disapproving?" Collins's eyes were large, and his lashes fluttered twice at the thought. "Mr. Darcy is all that is good."

"Oh, I agree," she replied quickly. "However, he can be disapproving. You may ask him about that some time. I will not mind at all if you do." Her lips had quirked up into a teasing smile.

She was so obviously in love with Mr. Darcy.

"Wait." He returned his last piece of toast to his plate without taking a bite. "You thought Mr. Darcy was disagreeable?"

She nodded.

"And yet, you are betrothed to him?"

Again, she nodded. "Astonishing, is it not?"

Indeed!

"I admit to being somewhat flabbergasted," he admitted aloud while inwardly he rejoiced. If Mr. Darcy could persuade a lady who thought him disagreeable to marry him, was it not also possible that Mr. Darcy could help a gentleman, hoping to do the same thing, on to success?

# Chapter 2

Collins glanced up from the book he was reading as Kitty entered the sitting room. Her dress reminded him of the sunshine as it bathed a meadow in its warm glow. He startled and cleared his throat while turning his eyes back to his book as a sigh attempted to escape the confines of his mind. He peeked up. It did not appear that she had noticed his moment of discomposure. For that, he sent up a small prayer of gratitude.

"Are you still reading sermons?" Mrs. Bennet inquired as she took a seat near him.

She was a nice enough lady, if a bit scattered at times, but he did not particularly relish a conversation with her just now. He wanted to pretend to be reading while in truth he observed the fair maiden near the window whose hair was shining like spun gold.

"My Mary has read many sermons," Mrs. Bennet continued.

"That is very good," Collins muttered as his eyes shifted to where Mary sat, glaring at him as she always did. Did her mother genuinely think that a daughter so obviously against a match could be swayed from her position by the commonality of reading materials?

"Oh, she is a very good girl."

Mrs. Bennet's look of reproof for that very good girl was in stark contrast to her tone of praise. Did the woman think him so simple as to be easily led? Did she think this way of all gentlemen or was it him in particular?

He closed his book and tapped his finger on its cover as he thought.

"You look very serious, Mr. Collins. I do hope you are contemplating some happy event."

Only his training from the tutor under whom he studied kept him from shaking his head at her pathetic attempt to sway him with her tone and a quick glance toward her daughter.

"No, it was neither happy nor sad," he replied with what he hoped was a pleasant expression. "I find I tire of reading sermons. It is delightful to indulge in a bit of poetry on occasion. The way some men can convey the beauty of the Almighty's creation in so few words is one of the great mysteries. A true gift from God it is." He clamped his lips closed before he babbled further. If *she* were not looking up at him from her stitching, perhaps he would not feel this infernal need to speak so strongly. *She* made his heart and mind race so much faster than it normally did when uncomfortable. But, it was an agony he would willingly endure to be near her. He turned his mind to what Mrs. Bennet was saying.

"I had not thought it possible for a man such as yourself to grow weary of sermons. It is most remarkable."

"A parson is merely a man, Mrs. Bennet," he replied, stretching out his legs and folding his arms across his abdomen in a most comfortable fashion. "We are educated, of course, in the things of God and the church, but we are at the center of our very being merely men. While learning the things which we must to fulfill our role as guide and instructor is an honour and one of great import, we find all manner of common things to be of interest and even a source of pleasure. My tutor, Mr. James, for instance, liked nothing better than a good long ramble in the fields and forest as well as a hunt. We must be complete, he would say. Being of only one focus is not very useful to anyone, he would also say. A parishioner should feel at ease in your presence. That was another of his sayings. It makes one more interesting as a conversationalist when one breaks bread with his patron or patroness as well as other members of his parish."

"Indeed!" That one word seemed to be the only thought Mrs. Bennet could form on such a surprising revelation.

"I am not a great hunter." Collins bowed his head humbly. "But if one wishes to eat pheasant, one must learn to make a tolerable attempt at the sport."

"Oh," Mrs. Bennet gasped.

Mary snickered and bent her head closer to her book.

"I quite enjoy pheasant," Kitty said. "Although I do not like the idea of having to shoot one. In fact, I should not be able to eat it if I did."

"A tender heart is a welcome thing in a lady such as yourself," Collins assured her. "I am certain that is why hunting is left to the gentlemen. Our sensibilities are not so easily engaged."

"I should not mind shooting a pheasant and then eating it," Lydia declared with a pointed look for her sister and one of disdain for Mr. Collins.

No matter how many times he had assured Miss Lydia that he was not going to remove them from their home when he claimed his inheritance, she did not seem willing to believe him. There was a scoffing, suspicious sharpness to her personality. However, that could be due to the fact that he was a stranger and her father was gravely ill.

"Then bravo for you," he commented. He would not succumb to her taunts. The scripture did say that a soft answer turns away wrath, so he would endeavour to be kind and compassionate.

Lydia blinked. "You are not going to say it is not fitting for a lady?"

"No." He opened his book. He knew ladies who accompanied their husbands on hunts. He did not care for such a wife himself, however.

"You are not going to say a thing?" Lydia pursued.

Collins shook his head and shrugged. "I see no need to say anything further."

Her brows furrowed. "Not a thing?"

Again, he shook his head and added a smile.

"Lydia, do be polite," Kitty scolded softly.

The reprimand was met with a decidedly annoyed huff.

"I thought you tired of sermons." Elizabeth held out a book to him. "It is *Lyrical Ballads*. I thought you might enjoy Wordsworth's writings."

Collins snapped his book of sermons closed and took the book from Elizabeth. "Oh, I do. He is quite delightful."

"He is," Elizabeth agreed. "Mr. Darcy recommended this particular volume to me."

The bookplate was inscribed with "Fitzwilliam Darcy."

"Oh, I could not take his book from you." Collins held it out to her.

"I have read it," she assured him, "and Mr. Darcy would be pleased to be able to do you this small service."

"You are very kind and so is Mr. Darcy." Collins opened the book. Mr. Darcy liked poetry just as he did? This was good.

"You might be able to join him and Mr. Bingley for a hunt," she offered. "I shall mention it to him."

"That would be most pleasurable," Collins replied.

A friend. He had a friend. A true friend. Miss Elizabeth would not lend him such a precious book and take up his cause by presenting him to Mr. Darcy if she were not a friend.

Mrs. Bennet found her voice with a quick gasp of realization. "Poetry is just the thing. Do read a few lines to us. Would that not be delightful, Mary?" She cast a glance at Mary, who, instead of glaring, completely ignored her mother's attempts to engage her in the conversation.

"I think poetry would make sewing so much more pleasant," Kitty said, filling the brief moment of silence that Mary's lack of response created.

"If you would find it gratifying," he looked first at Kitty then her mother so as not to make his intentions too obvious.

"Oh, we would," Mrs. Bennet assured him.

Kitty merely smiled softly and nodded before returning to her work.

But it was enough. He would climb a Hawthorne tree if Miss Kitty asked him to do so. Therefore, he would read until he was told to stop or until Mr. Darcy arrived, whichever came first. So, without a further moment of hesitation, he began...

*"Why, William, on that old grey stone,*

He had gotten as far as "The Last of the Flock" before he was forced to cease reading. Taking his marker from his book of sermons, he placed it instead in the book of verse. He had read those sermons numerous times. It was entirely likely that he would remember the exact page. He put the books to the side and rose to greet their guests. Again, he had to stifle a sigh as he watched Darcy lift Elizabeth's hand to his lips in greeting. That was for what he longed, someone to be so pleased to see him. No, not someone. His eyes wandered to Kitty once again. It had been challenging to keep his eyes anywhere but where she was.

"Mr. Collins, it is a pleasure to see you."

Collins swung his head toward Mr. Bingley, who had drawn Miss Bennet across the room toward where Collins sat. "I... I believe the pleasure is mutual," he stammered. Believe? Such a poor choice of words.

"Mr. Collins has been reading to us," Jane said as she took a seat.

"Indeed?" Bingley looked curiously toward Collins.

"Miss Elizabeth lent me *Lyrical Ballads*." His sleeves felt out of place, so he pulled on them. Ah, better. "She assured me that Mr. Darcy would not be offended if I read it."

"Darcy?" Bingley chuckled. "No, he is forever lending this or that book to me in hopes that I might one day enjoy the activity. However, so far, he has been utterly unsuccessful, though I did

---

1. *from Postulation and Reply by William Wordworth*

read a couple of verses in that book before returning it to the shelf." Bingley settled easily into his chair.

How did he do that? He made it look so simple to enter a room and be at ease. His clothing did not demand readjusting, and his actions were so fluid and smooth. It was an enviable trait.

"I am not a great reader," Bingley continued. "I do not despise the pursuit of knowledge, but to sit for hours to do anything is, in my way of thinking, dreadful. Darcy is not so content to be at leisure as he appears either."

"It is more gratifying to be employed than idle, I will grant you that," Collins replied, "but I must admit that being employed in the enterprise of reading, especially something as beautiful as the words of a poet, is one of the greatest pleasures in life."

Bingley chuckled once again. "I wish I had your love for such things. It would make a rainy evening or a carriage ride much more pleasant." He looked around Jane to where Kitty sat quietly pulling her needle through her fabric. "What say you about reading, Miss Kitty? Are you a proponent for reading or are you against it?"

Kitty put her work in her lap and cast a quick glance at Lydia, who answered for her. "Kitty enjoys novels."

"And poetry," Kitty added. "I also like poetry."

"But not as much as a truly horrid novel." Lydia's look in Collins's direction taunted him to reply severely. "Do you read novels, Mr. Collins?"

"I cannot say that I find an excess of pleasure in them, for I often find myself wishing to instruct the characters on proper behaviour." His brows drew together. "There are some that are not so very bad, but then there are others that are most improper.

However, I suppose if I were to think on it a great deal as your question is now prompting me to do, I must admit that there is also poetry which is not fit for everyone's consumption." He nodded. "Yes, yes, I do believe you are right, Miss Lydia. A novel might be preferred over poetry at times, but the reverse must also be acknowledged. It is not the form but the substance which makes a piece worthy of the time employed in reading it. There are even portions of the newspaper that are perhaps better left unread – indeed unprinted! For instance, gossip is gossip whether whispered behind a fan or scrawled in black and white for all to read." He stopped speaking as he realized that Miss Lydia was staring at him with her mouth hanging slightly agape. "Yes, I read novels, but not often," he said in conclusion.

"I have never read an entire novel," Bingley inserted. "However, I have read portions of them to my sisters on a winter's evening."

"You just abandon the story?" Kitty's eyes were wide with disbelief. "Are you not curious to know how it ends?"

Bingley's lips curled into a smile, and he winked. "I always know how it ends. One does not need to read the full book to know that."

"Whatever do you mean?"

The look of utter confusion on Kitty's face was charming. Collins would happily study it for hours.

"I believe he means he reads the ending," Jane said softly.

"Precisely!" Bingley declared.

"Without reading the rest?"

From her tone of voice, there was no denying the fact that Kitty found such an action to be an atrocity of the greatest sort.

"Yes," Bingley replied simply.

"I fear I cannot approve of such an action." There was a stern, almost governess-like, tone to her words.

Bingley merely shrugged. "If the ending were enticing enough to excite my curiosity to discover the rest of the tale, I might read the remainder. Perhaps I am reading the wrong books, but none have excited my curiosity in such a fashion, and I am an admittedly curious person."

Collins's brow furrowed. He would never have possessed enough courage to admit such a thing as not finding any novel the least bit interesting. Even if he did find all novels dull, which he did not, Collins would not have been so ready and nonchalant in admitting to it. How did Mr. Bingley proceed as if he did not care what any of the Bennet ladies thought of him?

"We cannot all enjoy reading," Jane said to her sister.

And Miss Bennet seemed not to be put off by such an admission? Collins looked between her and Mr. Bingley before glancing across the room to Mr. Darcy. If he could learn Mr. Darcy's strategies to draw a lady into liking a gentleman, then he might also be able to learn to be as affable as Mr. Bingley, might he not? He pursed his lips. He would need to find a time to approach each of them, and, seeing the way in which Kitty greeted Captains Denny and Saunders as they entered the drawing room just then, the sooner the better.

# Chapter 3

Collins peeked out of his bedchamber's door, looking up and down the hall. Mr. Bennet had not gone below to his study today, and Bingley and Darcy had been in the master's chamber for three-quarters of an hour.

He tucked his watch back into his pocket, silently closed the door, and placed his ear against it, listening for the telltale click of a door latch and voices breaking the quiet of the corridor. Kitty had spared him a glance or two after the officers arrived, but no more than two. He could not wait any longer to seek help in swaying her opinion. He had been at Longbourn for a week and one day complete, and while she had grown friendlier toward him on the day her father was taken ill and he had offered comfort, she had not increased her attentions to him in the days following. He did not possess the skills needed to win her good opinion. He needed help. He needed...

Finally! There were the sounds for which he waited.

Closer. Louder. Collins threw his door open and stepped into the hall in front of Bingley and Darcy.

"Come." He motioned frantically toward his room as he once again looked up and down the hall to see if anyone else had entered it. "Please," he begged the startled men. "I am in desperate need of advice."

The two men shared a look, Bingley shrugged, and they turned into his room.

Collins expelled a great breath, straightened his sleeves, took note of the empty hall once again, and then joined the gentlemen in his room. "Please be seated."

He had arranged the two chairs that were in the room so that they faced his bed. As his guests sat themselves in those chairs, he himself took up his position on the edge of the bed and prayed he did not make an utter fool of himself — or worse — offend with wayward words. He blew out a breath again and fiddled with his sleeves. He could do this. He had practiced the words for half an hour. He was merely speaking to his reflection in his mirror or parishioners in pews.

He smiled tightly and muttered his thanks for their acquiescence in attending him in his room. "How is the master today?"

He would have to broach his subject eventually but perhaps a few moments of small talk would be useful in slowing his racing heart.

"He seems no better nor any worse," Darcy replied.

"Good, good."

"He insists that I continue with my plans for the ball I promised Miss Lydia I would host," Bingley added.

Collins's brows rose. "He does not plan to attend, does he? I should think such a thing would be far too great an exertion for one whose heart is weak."

Darcy was smiling at him and not in the most pleasant fashion.

"No, of course, he does not," Collins said in reply to his own question. "It was a foolish thing to think." He sighed. "My tongue runs away with me at times."

"We are not offended," said Bingley. "But, I know I, at least, am curious to know with what we may help you."

"Yes, yes. Of course, you are. It is not the usual way of things for a gentleman to usher you into his room for a secret meeting."

"It is if the gentleman is my cousin," Darcy replied with a smirk.

"Colonel Fitzwilliam?" Did the man have any other cousins? Surely, he must. Colonel Fitzwilliam was a colonel, after all, and not the heir to Lord Matlock.

"Yes." Darcy's lips were twitching as if he wished to chuckle.

Embarrassing himself, seemed to Collins to be well underway. Hopefully, he could refrain from offending. Then, he might be able to consider this meeting a success.

"I," he began and then rose from the bed before continuing. He rubbed his hands on his trousers. "I will one day be the master of this estate. I do not wish for it to be soon. How could I? The loss of a father as wonderful as Mr. Bennet will cause my cousins," he blew out a breath and shook his head instead of finishing his thought. He paced to the wardrobe and back. "Be that as it may, it does appear that God has deigned I become Master of Longbourn far sooner than anyone would wish."

"It does indeed look that way," Darcy replied solemnly. "Bingley and I would be most pleased to help you find your feet in such a position."

A smile, a real, relaxed, non-forced smile curled Collins's lips, and he nearly placed his hand on them to feel the surprising expression. He had not thought to be able to smile or feel anything akin to relaxation during this discussion. "I would be forever grateful, and I know I will need assistance. However, there is a matter of estate management with which I could use your aid even before I am officially installed in the capacity of the master."

He tugged at his sleeves and drew a calming breath.

"Whatever you need," Bingley assured him.

Collins grimaced. "Do not pledge yourself until I have requested in full, for you may not indeed be able to help one such as myself." He glanced in the mirror. No. He shook his head. He would rise above his father's words. He would not be the last of the family to be master of Longbourn. "You, Mr. Darcy, are happily betrothed, and you, Mr. Bingley, seem to nearly be so."

The men before him nodded and shared a knowing smile which caused Collins to pause as his brows furrowed in contemplation of such a response.

"You love Miss Kitty," Bingley blurted.

Collins did not think his eyes could grow any wider. "You... you... know... that?" he managed to stammer after the first moment of initial shock wore off.

"You are far more uneasy around her than you are around any other member of this family," Darcy explained.

"Yes... Yes... I am." Collins plopped down on the bed. If they had noticed, did that mean everyone else had as well? Did Kitty know? He pulled at his cravat.

Darcy chuckled. "I do not think anyone else has been watching for such signs. I am the one who informed Bingley of your preference. It was noticeable from your first meeting when we arrived."

"And I know I would not be at ease if Miss Bennet greeted a red-coated gentleman as her younger sisters did," Bingley added.

"Then you see my quandary. I am no competition to such men."

He waved a hand, indicating his person. "However, Mr. Darcy, I know that you were not well thought of by Miss Elizabeth, and yet, she very much approves of you now."

"Did Miss Elizabeth tell you as much?"

Collins's head bobbed up and down emphatically. "She did, and she said that I had permission to say as much to you."

Darcy smiled and shook his head. "She is correct. I slighted her before we had even met."

"Indeed?" Collins attempted to pull his brows back down from his hairline, but they would not obey. His surprise was too great.

"Indeed," Darcy assured him.

"Then, how did you convince her to consider you?"

Darcy shrugged. "It was not I but divine intervention. She was allowed a glimpse of a different man after I learned of Anne's death and before I travelled to Rosings."

"That will not work," Collins muttered. Then, he brightened. "You have since grown in her favour, have you not?"

"Yes."

"Then you could perchance assist me in how to woo Miss Kitty, could you not?"

"I –"

Collins's excitement could not be contained, and he turned to Bingley without as much as a moment's pause to allow Darcy to reply. "And you could teach me to be at ease, could you not? And then." A smile much larger than he thought he was capable of smiling split his face. "We shall be brothers, and I shall have a mistress for Longbourn. And we shall have a son, and I will not be the last master of Longbourn as my father insisted." Yes, yes, this plan would work brilliantly.

Bingley laughed heartily. "You would like us to –"

"Be my tutors," Collins pled. "I shall die a lonely old man as my father said if you do not."

"We cannot promise success," Darcy cautioned.

"No, no, I do not expect you to perform miracles, of course." His smile faded. Perhaps the plan would not work as brilliantly as he imagined.

"As long as you realize that our help may not sway her from another, we will help you," Darcy assured him.

Bingley rose from his chair and crossed to the wardrobe. "Do you have a man?" he asked as he pulled the doors open.

"No, I cannot justify such a luxury."

"You will need one," Bingley said as he looked through Collins's possessions. "However, we will have to make do for now. I know a thing or two." He turned and looked at Collins with a grimace. "I think it would be best if my man had a go at your hair and taught you a few more knots." He pointed to his own cravat. "A lady does like a well-turned-out gentleman."

Collins nodded.

"How will we arrange such a meeting?" Darcy asked. "To bring your man here would give rise to suspicion. And to have Collins appear at Netherfield for such an appointment would set your sisters on the trail of something about which to gossip."

Bingley pursed his lips. "You are right. I shall ask my man for his opinion and then relay the information to you myself."

Again, Collins nodded his approval. "Whatever help you can provide, I will appreciate most highly."

"She likes novels," Bingley add. "Are there any which you might read here?"

Collins blinked. "I do not know. I could ask Miss Lydia, I suppose."

"That should shock her appropriately," Bingley said with a smirk.

Darcy shook his head. "No, ask Miss Kitty which is her favourite, and then read that."

"Miss Kitty?" The racing was beginning again in his chest as he considered such a thing. Asking Miss Lydia would be much easier than asking Kitty!

"You will have to learn to speak to her if you ever wish to marry her," Darcy said.

"Right. Right. Yes. Of course."

Darcy's answering smile was sympathetic. "It gets easier," he assured. "Trust me. I know that feeling of dread that has settled into your belly. It will lessen with each time you practice speaking to her, even if it is about foolishly mundane things."

Collins sighed. "You are certain?"

Darcy nodded.

Collins rose from where he sat and gave his sleeves a tug. "Then, I will do it."

"Brave man!" Bingley said as he clapped him on the shoulder. "We brothers must band together."

Collins smiled at first at the appellation of brother, but then his brows furrowed. "You would truly welcome me as a brother?" He had never thought to be anyone's brother. A friend perhaps. A cousin most definitely, but not a brother. A brother was something far more important than mere friend or cousin.

The half-minute pause which followed his question was nearly unbearable.

"We would," Darcy said as Bingley nodded his agreement. "I have been preparing myself for just such a thing since we met in Kent. Do you not remember?"

"Oh, I do. I do." He had only considered Darcy's comment in the sitting room at Rosings as a pleasant and proper thing to say. He had never dreamt he could actually be a brother to a man such as Fitzwilliam Darcy! His father would likely say it was yet impossible. After all, it did require him persuading a lady to accept him.

Darcy rose to leave, but pausing before moving toward the door, he tipped his head and looked very seriously at Collins. "Was your father cruel?"

Collins swallowed. "Yes."

"He did not treat you well?" Darcy's eyes seemed to be searching Collins's very soul, or so it felt.

Collins shook his head. "He would have been happier without me." Oh, it still stung to admit such a humiliating thing, but these men had pledged him their help and brotherhood. There was no need to hide his shame from them.

Darcy shook his head slowly, sadly. There were understanding and disgust for such treatment in the small movement. "That is in the past."

His words were quiet but burgeoning with meaning and comfort. It was nearly too much to be borne in a proper gentlemanly fashion. Collins swallowed and whispered his thanks.

"Until tomorrow," Bingley said, leading the way to the door. "I expect to see a novel in your hand," he added with a pointed look. "I do not care if you read it. I only care that one — you demonstrate an interest in things she enjoys — and two — you have talked to her."

Collins nodded. "I will have a novel." He would have anything either gentleman asked him to have as long as they continued to be willing to help him.

He expelled a great breath of relief as the door closed. He could and would persuade Kitty to consider him. He would.

"Yes," he said to his reflection in the mirror. "I will win her. I cannot fail with two such capable tutors." His face scrunched as his brows furrowed, and his lips pursed much like they would after eating something unpleasant. He swallowed. "But first, I must acquire a novel."

# Chapter 4

Kitty tapped lightly at her father's door and then smoothed her skirts and fixed her fichu as she waited for the door to be open. Her father had asked that they all visit him at least once per day, and so she had presented herself at his side just as was requested.

She had only just finished straightening her sleeve when Elizabeth opened the door and with a smile invited her to join them. Jane sat in one chair repairing the hem of a petticoat. Elizabeth had abandoned a book on her chair, so she had likely been reading.

"Are your other sisters with you?" Mr. Bennet asked.

"No, sir. Mary is in the garden with Maria, and Lydia is still standing at the window watching the officers leave." She shifted uneasily from one foot to another. The sight of her father propped up by pillows in his bed was becoming more familiar, but it still unsettled her. "How are you feeling?" she asked as he motioned for her to come forward.

"No better, no worse," he replied with a smile. "And it is dreadfully boring to be confined to one's room."

Kitty could well imagine that it was. There was so little to do and see when one was in bed.

"Tell me the news of the village."

"I have not been to Meryton in days," Kitty replied as she sat on the edge of the bed near him.

"But you have had visitors. Surely, the officers brought some news of interest with them, did they not? And if Maria is here, then Lady Lucas must also be visiting your mother."

Kitty nodded. "Lady Lucas is here. However, I did not get an opportunity to listen to her tales." She slipped off her slippers and drew her legs up and to her left, positioning herself comfortably as she had always done as a little girl. "Captain Denny said that Mr. Davison's cow escaped again and that Tommy Archer has been tormenting the cats at the inn again. This time, he tied their tails together, and Mrs. Bateson chased him off with a broom. And Captain Saunders told Lydia that the milliner has just received a new shipment of ribbons."

"Is he planning on decorating his cap?" Mr. Bennet said with a chuckle.

Kitty smiled and shook her head. "No, he just happened to hear that when two maids were awaiting their orders at the butchers. I suppose they were taking such information home to their mistresses."

"Quite likely," Mr. Bennet agreed. His head cocked to the side. "Do you favour either of the captains?"

Kitty shrugged one shoulder. "They are handsome." Very handsome, truth be told. But then, a smart redcoat added a dash of allurement to even the most common of gentlemen. And there was something in the way in which an officer carried himself that begged attention and admiration.

"One more so than the other?"

She frowned as she thought. Captain Saunders was the taller of the two, but Captain Denny's shoulders were broader. Both had pleasant countenances. She shook her head. "No," she replied.

He patted her hand. "Then you have not lost your heart to either?"

She tipped her head to the side, the small pensive frown returning. Both officers were excellent conversationalists, and she enjoyed their company, but... She shrugged. It did not feel as if she had lost any of her heart, not even a morsel.

Again, her father patted her hand. "You will know when your heart is engaged. You will not need to wonder – at least, not for long. The feeling might confuse you at first, but it will not remain hidden. That is how it is. Is it not, Jane?"

Kitty turned toward her sister expectantly. Jane was smiling, and her cheeks were rosy, but she did not seem at all put out by the question.

"I believe I came to the realization that my heart was engaged far more easily than some," she replied with a pointed look at Elizabeth.

"But how do you know such a thing?" Kitty asked. She was seventeen. These were things she needed to know.

"I am not certain I can explain it," Jane replied. "I just know that should Mr. Bingley offer for me, I will accept, and we will be happy."

Mr. Bennet chuckled, which was followed by a cough. "Should he offer?" He handed the cup of water back to Elizabeth. "Mark my words, Jane, he will offer soon. He seemed nearly ready to come to the point today."

"Is that why you have been talking with Mr. Bingley and Mr.

Darcy so much?" Kitty asked. "To persuade them to make an offer?"

Mr. Bennet shook his head. "No, my dear. I do not need to persuade them. I just wish to know them better. I want to know my girls are well-cared-for before –"

"Do not say it," Kitty whispered.

"Whether I say it or not, does not mean it will not happen," her father replied.

Kitty lifted her chin but did not lift her eyes from their study of his coverlet. "I prefer not to speak of it. That is all." If she did speak of him dying, she would dissolve into tears just as she did each night before she fell asleep.

"Very well," her father agreed. "We shall not speak of my demise."

"Thank you," she whispered.

"Mr. Collins has promised me that you and your mother shall always have a home," he added.

"We are not speaking of it," Kitty scolded.

"I was not," he retorted. "I was going to say that Collins surprises me. He is not at all like his father."

"I fear his father was not kind to him," Elizabeth added. Her book lay open on her lap.

"Why do you think that?" Mr. Bennet asked.

"Because of something he said about you," she replied with a smile and turned back to her book.

She was not reading. Kitty could tell by the way her lips twitched. It was a game Elizabeth often played with their father. There would be some tantalizing tidbit of news that Elizabeth had heard which she would present but only just barely. She would leave out details just to get him to ask. Kitty wished she had such skill, but she did not like to tease her father, no matter how he might tease her. Teasing was not a strong suit for Kitty. Everyone, even Jane and Mary, was better at teasing than she was.

"You will not tell me?" her father said with a small laugh. "I should refrain from asking so that you will have to keep the information contained." He waggled his eyebrows. "But I will not. I must know what he said about me."

Elizabeth laughed and closed her book. "He thinks you are the picture of perfection for fathers."

"I am that," their father replied with a wink and a chuckle.

The three girls joined him in laughing.

"He said he feared his father," Elizabeth continued after they sobered. "He did not say more, but he did not have to."

"Oh, how dreadful!" Kitty cried. She had not been so close to her father as Elizabeth or Jane had been, and her father did tease her, at times, to the point of causing her pain – though she never told anyone such a thing –, but she had never feared him. Not even when he was terribly angry with her for disobeying and ruining his favourite book when she was ten.

Elizabeth nodded her agreement. "He seems like a very nice gentleman, if a bit odd."

"He does speak excessively at times," Kitty agreed. "But…"

She had been watching Mr. Collins since his arrival, and she thought she had discovered something about him. However, she was not certain she should say. If Lydia were to know that she was even contemplating the man, life would become nearly unbearable. Lydia did not like Mr. Collins. She thought him a bore and was certain that as soon as he was in charge of Longbourn, all forms of fun would cease. She would be made to read scripture and sermons and would not be allowed to dance or flirt. Kitty did not agree, of course, but once Lydia had an idea in her head, it was difficult to remove.

"But what?" Jane prompted.

Kitty drew her lip between her teeth and shook her head. "It is nothing."

"Nothing?" Her father's tone did not hide his disbelief.

"I should not say. It is just a thought and not a word of it would hold any truth. I am certain it would be wrong for me to share such a thing."

Her father arched a brow. "Are you becoming Mary?"

"No, no. I just do not wish to treat Mr. Collins poorly. He does seem like a very nice gentleman, just as Elizabeth said."

"As nice as the officers?" Her father's smile was teasing.

"He is not as handsome," Kitty replied. If he were to wear a red coat and walk smartly, he might come close. He was tall, his shoulders were broad, and he was not the sort of gentleman to blow over in a gale. She felt her cheeks grow warm at the thought of finding Mr. Collins even marginally handsome. "He is more patient, I believe."

"How so?" her father asked. "I really do need to ask him to visit me more. There are things I need to tell him about the estate."

"Papa," Kitty scolded. "We are not talking about that."

He patted her hand. "Forgive me. I had forgotten. Now, tell me what makes you think of Mr. Collins as patient."

Kitty shifted on the bed and sat a bit straighter. "Well, for one, he knows Mary does not wish to be pushed at him, and so he attempts to divert Mama. But he will not be rude about it. Even if Mary is at times."

"My daughter is being rude?" Mr. Bennet said in surprise.

Kitty grimaced and nodded.

"I shall have to speak to her," her father muttered. "Continue."

Kitty pulled herself up from the deflated position his question about Mary had caused. "Secondly, Lydia has attempted to provoke him, and he has replied with such grace." She smiled. "It has Lydia beyond vexed."

It was a comment that caused not only Mr. Bennet to chuckle but also Jane and Elizabeth.

"Then," Mr. Bennet said, "he is made of some pretty stern stuff if he can abide your mother's machinations and Lydia's temper."

Kitty nodded. "He is. I honestly think he is. However..." She shook her head. "No, I should not say."

"Are you certain?"

"Yes, Papa, I am."

Just then, there was a tapping at the door and, at her father's call, the door pushed open.

"Oh, I do not mean to intrude." Collins's words turned to chaff in his mouth as he took in how Kitty was so charmingly perched on her father's bed.

"You are not an intrusion," Jane said. "Please, come in."

Collins closed the door and crossed the room. "I had meant to inquire if it would be acceptable for me to peruse the books in your study to add variety to my reading repertoire. I have a book of sermons and a lovely book of poems thanks to Mr. Darcy and Miss Elizabeth's generosity, but I thought that there might also be some books in your possession which I might use to gain further knowledge on some subject."

"You are a man of learning then, are you?" Mr. Bennet asked.

"I do enjoy it, yes."

Mr. Bennet looked at Elizabeth; then after a moment of pause and some sort of silent communication which Kitty could not quite see, he turned to her. "Would you, my Kitty, be willing to escort Mr. Collins to the study and help him find what he seeks?"

"Oh, I am not certain I am the best person to do so, but I will." She would not deny her father such a simple request even if it did puzzle her that he was not sending Elizabeth.

"I did not mean to take any of your daughters from you. I am certain I could find what I need on my own."

"Kitty will help you this time, and then the next time you wish for a book, you need not even ask. Just avail yourself of them as it brings you pleasure. I would never deny a man of learning the opportunity to discover something new." He sighed. "There is nothing quite like that feeling."

Kitty smiled at the faraway look in her father's eyes. He often wore that sort of expression when he started speaking of books and learning.

She rose from the bed and slipped her feet into her slippers, before bending to kiss her father's cheek and whisper an *I love you*. Since he had fallen ill, she had promised herself that she would tell him that every time she parted from him.

Mr. Collins opened the door for her and then after closing it, scurried to walk next to her.

"I must apologize for taking you away from your father."

"I am happy to be of service," Kitty replied with a smile she hoped would help him feel more at ease.

However, it seemed to have the opposite effect on him as he started straightening his coat. He was such a nervous gentleman. But then, if his father had been unkind, how else might he be?

Her brows furrowed at the thought. The cats at the inn had grown less friendly and slightly mean since Tommy Archer had begun tormenting them. Recalling one particular little tomcat, however, caused her expression to smooth. Not all of them were so unfriendly. That one timid little tomcat, who was not yet a half year old, was just as gentle as ever when you could find him. He spent much of his time tucked into some shadow as if he were afraid to be seen. In fact, Shadow is what she had begun calling him when she saw him prowling the streets.

"What sort of book do you wish to read?" Kitty asked as they descended the steps.

The gentleman near her stumbled but caught himself. "I.. I.. am not certain. I will know when I see it, I suppose. I am uncertain what sorts of books your father has."

Kitty stepped down the two steps to join him at the bottom of the stairs. He really was a very tall gentleman.

He pushed back the hair that fell forward on his forehead. It was a lovely shade of brown. Not dark, but not too light either. In her opinion, it suited his colouring quite well.

"Are there any topics in particular which you enjoy studying?" Kitty asked as they walked down the short hallway to her father's study. For a talkative fellow, he currently seemed to need a great deal of prompting to speak.

"I would rather not say."

Kitty's eyebrows rose, and she looked at him curiously. What topic was so dreadful that he could not share it?

"It is not an inappropriate subject. No, no. It is not that at all."

It was, however, a subject that stirred the man's nerves from the way words were falling from his mouth in explanation.

"How could the subject of a book cause offense to me?" she asked, interrupting his litany of words.

"No, no. I did not say that properly. It is not that it will cause offense. It is rather that the topic is about a subject that might stir emotions."

Kitty's brow furrowed. "It would be far easier for me to help you if you told me what the subject was."

A severely pained expression crossed his face as he whispered, "Estate management. Perhaps something on agriculture."

"Oh." Now, she understood. He did not wish to bring up the fact that her father was gravely ill. It was awkwardly endearing. "I understand. You studied to be a parson, not the master of an estate."

He nodded. "I took some classes because I knew one day I might need them. But, I thought I had years to learn from watching parishioners and spending quiet evenings reading."

The image of this large yet gentle man sitting before a fire on a winter's evening with a book in his lap and a mug of something warm at his side reminded her of her father and wrapped her heart with comfort. It was good to know that her home would be left to such a man.

"I think Papa keeps those books on these shelves." She led him to a bookcase just to the left of her father's desk and opened the doors.

"Thank you," Collins said, stooping down to look inside. "Ah, this might be a good place to begin," he said as he pulled out a large tome.

"You should take a moment or two to look around, so that if you come down in the middle of the night with just a candle, you will be able to find what you seek."

"An excellent idea," he mumbled.

She watched him walk around the room, stopping now and again to peer at some title or another.

"Are there any novels?" he asked.

"I did not think you enjoyed novels." Had he not said so this afternoon?

"I do not on most occasions, but I have been considering your sister's words and find that I cannot appropriately evaluate my like or dislike if I do not read some novels."

She tipped her head and looked at him curiously. "You would read a novel to please my sister?"

He nodded. "She is not the only one who admitted to liking them."

"Do you mean you would read one for me?" She could not contain her surprise.

"Should I not discover the things that my cousins enjoy?"

He was looking a bit like he was going to sink into a shadow just as Shadow did when there was a loud noise.

"Why, yes, of course." Her brows furrowed. "Should I then read a book of sermons?"

She blinked. His smile when he was not in company with her sisters and mother was rather attractive.

"Only if you wish, Miss Kitty. You need only ask, and I shall lend you one of mine. However, you may find it dull, and I would not wish to task you with something arduous."

Kitty returned his smile. "That is very kind." She waved a hand to a shelf next to the door. "Papa keeps the novels near the door with the poetry books, so that I do not need to disturb him when I wish to return one and get another."

"How wise," Collins said crossing to the shelf. Then, turning to her, he said, "No, I shall not select it. I shall trust you to choose one for me that will please both yourself and your sister."

"You are certain?" she asked as she began looking through the books on the shelf, trying to determine which novel might suit a man such as Mr. Collins. "Oh," she said as her eyes fell on a book she felt was perfect for him. "*Evelina*," she said, handing him the book. "There is a parson in it." A very kind parson, much like she imagined he would be.

"Indeed?" He took the book from her and tipped it this way and that as if it were some sort of oddity.

She nodded when he looked her direction.

"How interesting," he muttered as he paged through the book, looking rather pleased.

That look of pleasure, for some reason, made Kitty inexplicably happy, and as they parted ways — he to find a place to read, and she to return to her father to let him know that she had completed her task — she sincerely hoped Mr. Collins would enjoy the novel and not just suffer through it on either Lydia's or her account.

/ Chapter 5

"Is this a favourite novel?" Bingley asked the next day as he sat in Collins's room waiting for the man to don the clothes he had laid out on the bed.

Collins shot him a wary look as he tucked in his shirt tails. "I do not know, but she selected it for me because she thought I might enjoy it. Does it qualify? Have I completed my task?"

Bingley chuckled and turned the book over in his hand. "Yes, it qualifies. Did she say why she thought this book would appeal to you?"

"Yes, yes." Collins's head bobbing up and down vigorously. "She said there is a parson in it."

"Just that it had a parson? No other reason?"

"Just the parson."

Bingley shrugged. "That is enough I suppose."

Collins took his waistcoat from Darcy. "You truly think this waistcoat with these breeches is good?"

"Yes," Bingley said from behind the open book he held. "Not every piece of clothing must be of identical colour."

"Are you certain?" Collins looked at his breeches and the tan of the waistcoat he was buttoning. To him, tan was worn with brown, not black, breeches.

"Does Darcy wear all one colour?" Bingley asked, snapping the book closed and tossing it on the bed as he crossed to where Collins stood before the mirror. "She selected a good book. You might enjoy it."

"You have read it then?" Collins tilted his head up while peering down his nose into the mirror, attempting to watch Bingley begin tying his cravat.

"Portions. It's not dull." Bingley's brows furrowed and one eye closed. "No, that is not right." He untied the neckcloth and began again. This time, he wore a pleased smile upon completion. "Not so good as my man does, but presentable." He stepped back. "What do you think?"

Collins leaned toward the mirror. The knot was not so very different from how he usually tied it, but it was more pronounced with a bit more fluff. "It seems fitting."

"Do you have a pin?" Bingley asked.

"I am a simple man. I fear I do not."

His eyes grew wide as he saw Darcy produce a pin from his pocket. It was not ornate or bejewelled, but merely golden in tone with a knot at the top.

"I could not," Collins protested with a shake of his head.

Bingley raised one brow and gave Collins a disapproving look that made him wish to slip into the shadows.

"Stand up straight, man," Bingley commanded.

Collins's eyes grew wide, and he did as instructed. Where was the pleasant fellow who flopped easily into armchairs?

"This knot looks even better when the tails are pinned...just..." Bingley pushed the pin through the fabric, "so." He gave a sharp nod of his head and smiled. "Much better. She will be impressed."

Collins had to agree. The pin did add a dash of something to the cravat. It was rather flattering. But...

"I feel foolish," he muttered. "I am not..." He stopped short as Bingley once again leveled a disapproving look at him.

"You are," Bingley said with some force, "the master of Longbourn – not officially, of course, and we are not wishing that to happen any time soon. However, you must believe it, for it is your future. You are the master of Longbourn. The heir apparent."

Collins swallowed and nodded.

"And the master of an estate must look the part," Bingley added.

Again, Collins nodded. He was not confident it was entirely necessary that he be dressed so finely, but he was not about to say that to Bingley and earn yet another look of displeasure.

Darcy chuckled. "You will have to forgive my friend. He is nearly as bad as his sister when it comes to fashion. Not quite a dandy, but..."

Bingley scowled. "Appearance is important for one attempting to shift his position."

"I will not deny the fact," Darcy agreed. "However, one does not need to be quite so militant about it." He turned to Collins. "The knot would be just as appropriate without the stickpin, but we are on a mission to turn at least one head, are we not?" He lowered his voice, "And amongst the three of us, Bingley is the expert at turning heads."

Bingley laughed. "No, that would be your fortune," he retorted. "If one cannot be the most smartly turned out chap in the room then he should follow Darcy's example and be the richest." He smirked. "Especially since he is no longer the tallest."

Bingley folded his arms and gave Collins one final scrutinizing look. "You are at least two inches taller than Darcy when you stand straight. Do not hunch. Broad shoulders and ample height should be displayed. Carry yourself with authority."

"Can I not just wear these colours and a pin?" Collins pled. "I am not equal to the task of total reform in one evening."

Bingley shrugged. "It is a start. But, you have to admit there is something in an officer's carriage that demands attention."

Collins nodded and drew his shoulders back some. This was perhaps going to be harder than he had thought. For so long he had been attempting to hide his size and indeed his presence by becoming small. Standing so boldly felt not only awkward but a trifle dangerous.

"One thing at a time," Darcy assured him. "You must become the best you that you can be. No one," he shot a look at Bingley, "expects you to become what you are not."

"Right, right," Bingley muttered. "I do have a tendency to throw myself into a project wholeheartedly. I shall endeavour to keep my enthusiasm in regulation." He shook his head. "But, there is potential here."

"Potential?" Collins questioned. "Potential for what?"

Darcy nodded. "He is right. You are not an unattractive gentleman."

Collins shook his head. It could not be true. How often had he been teased for being too large and too awkward? He was nothing more than a lumpy pudding, was he not? He looked from one gentleman to the other, who nodded in response to the question he felt in his heart and was clearly written on his face.

"I have written to my uncle regarding my betrothal and the state of Mr. Bennet's health," Darcy said as they moved to the door to exit the room to make their way to the sitting room where they would wait until dinner was ready. "He is settling matters regarding Rosings and will likely need to consider what to do with the living you now hold once..." He said no more as he pulled the door open.

Collins blew out a breath. "I know it is a blessing," he whispered as they entered the hallway, "but I cannot help feeling..." He shrugged. It felt utterly wrong to be grateful to be gaining something at the expense of the loss of a man like Mr. Bennet.

Darcy clapped him on the shoulder. "Both Bingley and I know how painful such a blessing can be. You are not alone."

*Not alone* were very comforting, but rather strange words, to Collins. He had not been alone all his life. He had been surrounded by people, but he had rarely felt the acceptance that was being offered to him now. Other than Miss Lydia and Miss Mary, the Bennet family, as well as these two gentlemen, had been very accepting of him.

Would that not just make his father beside himself with amazement?

The thought of his father spitting and sputtering over such a thing as his son being welcomed into a family made the right side of Collins's lips lift into a small smirk.

"Oh, Mr. Collins!" Mrs. Bennet cried as he entered the sitting room. "You look very handsome this evening, does he not, Mary?"

At such a welcome, Collins felt as if he should back out of the room, but he did not. Nor did he allow himself to curl inward for Bingley's brow was slightly raised, and he had no desire to disappoint his tutor. He had always wished to do his best with every lesson – not that his best was always as good as what was expected.

Mary shot an angry glare at Kitty and then, forcing a smile, replied. "As handsome as always, do you not think so, Lydia?"

Mrs. Bennet gasped and glared at her middle daughter who was batting her eyes innocently and smiling a saccharinely sweet smile.

He should perhaps relieve the young woman's apprehension and tell her that he had no desire to marry her. Of course, he should not do that now. Her mother would not appreciate such at thing being canvassed openly. But perhaps later, he could find a time to speak to Mary in confidence. For now, he simply muttered his thanks and quickly found a chair in which to sit so that he could feel less conspicuous without angering Bingley. He could also feel the need to speak rising within him, and he was not certain what exactly would come out of his mouth if he should open it.

Lydia tossed her head. "He looks as if he is trying to be something he is not."

Mrs. Bennet gasped once again and then made a pretty excuse to extract herself along with Mary and Lydia from the room.

"I have never seen Mama look so displeased," Kitty whispered to Elizabeth once the door to the room had closed.

"Nor have I," Elizabeth replied, "and I have tested her patience many times." Her lips curled upward slightly.

Apparently, his cousin Elizabeth was not entirely penitent for having caused her mother some consternation.

"I must apologize for my sisters," Kitty said, turning to Collins. "It is as my mother said. You do look handsome."

Such a compliment was just what was needed to make him feel as if all the work and awkwardness might be worth it. Unfortunately, it was also all that was required to set the words to flowing.

"Thank you. You are very kind as are Mr. Darcy and Mr. Bingley. It is their doing that I am dressed as I am. I am afraid that I am a rather simple man and not so familiar with what is considered fashionable or unfashionable. As a parson, I saw no need to be intimately acquainted with such things. As long as my clothes were well-fitted and not overly worn..." He clamped his lips closed at the sound of Bingley's soft cough. "I merely wished to say I am appreciative of both your compliment and the help I have received." He again pressed his lips together before they could run away with some other thought.

"I had not thought that gentleman discussed fashion," Kitty said, turning her lovely eyes away from Collins and looking to her older sisters in confusion.

"We do," Bingley answered. "Perhaps, however, not so much as ladies do."

"It is not just your valet who dresses you? You decide what you like and do not like?"

Collins could not help smiling at the innocence in her voice. It was as if she had never considered what topics of conversation gentlemen might discuss.

"A good man is indispensable," Bingley replied. "They are a great source of knowledge, of course, but they do look for guidance from the gentleman they serve, much as my sister's maid does for my sister."

"Oh."

Her lips were such a lovely shade of pink and formed an *o* so sweetly. And her eyes, her clear blue as a deep lake on sunny day eyes, were delightfully wide. Collins was certain there was no expression or countenance that could be found to be more perfectly beautiful than hers.

"I have begun reading *Evelina*," Collins said, turning the conversation and, thankfully, her eyes back to him.

"And do you like it?" she asked eagerly.

"I have only read the first correspondence, and I must say I am intrigued to see what the response to such a request will be."

"Then, you have not met Mr. Villars yet? He is the parson."

The animation that claimed her features as she spoke of the novel was enough to sway his opinion about them altogether. He could read such works and discuss them with her to see her eyes light as they were now and to watch her bite back a smile by tucking her lower lip between her teeth. It really mattered not if they were dull or entertaining. He could and would read them.

He shook his head. "I have not met him yet."

"I just know you will like him. He is all that is good. He truly is." Her lips pursed, and her brows furrowed. "There is deception in the story, and I know that is not a proper thing."

Collins nodded in agreement. Deception was not a virtue to be sure. "Does the deception persist?"

"Oh, no. Everything turns out just as it should," Kitty assured him. "I was just concerned that you would see the deception and..."

"Condemn the book as a whole?"

Collins's question was met with a small nod, which caused him to smile and relax into his chair as his arms folded across his abdomen.

"What did the serpent do in the garden? Did he not deceive Eve? And then later, did not Jacob deceive his father at his mother's request? If deception is in the scriptures, can it be wrong to have it in a novel?" He shrugged. "Perhaps so, and perhaps not. It depends, I believe, on the way in which it is presented. If it is lifted up as a thing to be desired or a path to be followed, then the author of the book is in great error, for he or she is leading readers astray. However, if an author shows deception for what it is – an offense against man and God – then I see no wrong in its inclusion in a novel, for the writer is in such a case presenting it as he or she should. Using it even as a warning about the ills of society. Was it not Sir Phillip Sidney who proclaimed that poesy can encourage us, the readers, to virtue and good deeds?" He paused for a moment, brows furrowing as he thought. "Yes, yes, I do believe it was Sidney who wrote *The Defense of Poesy*, was it not?" He looked at her, but seeing her wide eyes, he then turned to Darcy. Surely, a man such as Mr. Darcy would know such a thing.

"It was," Darcy assured him.

Relief washed over Collins. He would have hated to have gotten that fact wrong, for up until then his speech was rather well-done – logical and not rambling. Surely, she would be impressed by such a thing, would she not?

"So, you see, it is not just I who thinks such things," he ended with a nod.

"Indeed," Kitty replied. "I have not thought about such things." She looked at Elizabeth. "Do we have this *Defense of* what was it?"

"*Poesy*," Collins replied.

"I have not read it," Elizabeth replied. "But Papa would know."

"If he does not have it, I do," Darcy interjected. "I can send for it."

"Would you?"

Even Darcy smiled at the excitement in her voice. "I apologize. I had not thought you such a great reader, Miss Kitty."

"Oh, I am not unless it is a novel or some lovely verses. I find most other things dreadfully dull, but I should like to see this *Defense of Poesy*."

"It is not so entertaining as a novel," Darcy cautioned.

Her lips pursed for a moment, and Collins thought perhaps she would decide not to read it. But then, she shook her head and smiled. "It is at least worth an attempt, is it not? How else shall I know if I approve of it or not if I do not try it? Is that not so, Mr. Collins?"

Collins blinked. She had nearly quoted, word for word, his explanation of why he would read a novel. "Yes, yes," he agreed, grimacing inwardly at his tone of utter surprise. However, from how her smile stayed affixed to her face, it seemed she did not mind. "Indeed," he added, "one does not know unless one tries."

# Chapter 6

Collins entered the dining room with Mrs. Bennet as instructed, fully intending to sit next to her at the foot of the table as he had always done. However, tonight things were not going to be as they had been.

"Come sit next to me," Mr. Bennet instructed.

"It is very good to see you at the table, sir," Collins said as he claimed the chair on Mr. Bennet's right.

"I tire of my room," the man replied with a smile. "I should like to enjoy at least a few more meals at this table, and Darcy's physician has told me that I may attempt half of whatever I feel I can do. Therefore, I shall eat at least one of my meals each day at this table."

"I am glad to hear it, sir."

"As am I," added Elizabeth, who was seated next to Darcy and across from Collins.

"Ah, my wayward offspring," Mr. Bennet muttered as Lydia and Mary entered the room. He lifted a hand and waved them to his side. "You have something to say before we begin, do you not?"

To Collins, it did not look as if either daughter had anything they wished to say, but their heads bowed, and each muttered an apology.

"Not so well done as I would have hoped," said Mr. Bennet, "but it will do. You may take your seats next to your sister." He turned to Collins. "I have instructed my wife that should you desire to find a wife amongst my remaining daughters, it is to be of your choosing and not hers. And as for my daughters," he raised a brow and gave Mary and Lydia a pointed look, "I will expect them to look to their sister Jane and follow her example in how to comport themselves appropriately." He sighed. "It is in the shadows of life when one realizes his folly and fears it shall leave ruin in its wake."

Collins wished to turn his head to see what effect such words might have on Mr. Bennet's daughters, but he did not want to appear indecorous. So, he kept his eyes firmly fixed on the plate before him.

"I hear you have selected some reading material for pleasure and business," Mr. Bennet continued. "I am pleased to know you take the role set before you so seriously. It does my heart good to think both this estate and my family will be left in capable hands."

"Papa," Kitty said softly.

"Yes, my dear, I know. I shall speak of my demise only a small portion more, and then I shall not return to the topic. Potatoes?" Mr. Bennet said, passing a dish to Collins.

"A favourite," Collins muttered as he accepted the dish.

A few other items passed before him, and as soon as his plate was filled, and he was about ready to begin eating, Mr. Bennet raised his glass.

"I have some most excellent news," he began before pausing to cough. "Our Jane is to be married."

The announcement was met with a delighted squeal from Mrs.

Bennet and an eruption of questions from both her and Jane's sisters.

Collins waited patiently as the excitement dwindled. Despite the small jibes and occasional harsh looks they gave one another on occasion, it was evident that the sisters did care for each other.

Kitty smiled nearly as much about the news as Jane did. Elizabeth's knowing smile told him that she had already been made aware of the betrothal. Mary extended her happiness in a prim sort of fashion, although a secret smile played at her lips. Poor Miss Lydia with her sharp edges exuded with delight before any save her mother had voiced her raptures, but then returned her eyes to her plate, and her smile slipped into a sullen expression, though only for a moment. Mr. Bennet chuckled with delight, coughed, chuckled some more and then as the noise retreated, lifted his glass once more and toasted the happy couple.

"I am not through with my news," he said, as he returned his glass to the table. "As we are all aware, my heart is not strong. Therefore, I have come to a conclusion, that I should like to take my ease and pass along the daily comings and goings of Longbourn." He pushed to his feet with some effort.

"Papa," Kitty whispered.

"I shall be well," he assured her before continuing with his speech. "My cousin, Mr. Collins's father, was a hard man and not a very astute one. I would have been hard-pressed to find any pleasure in leaving my home to such a man. However, I find that his son resembles him in no way. I have found our Mr. Collins to be a most gracious and kind gentleman, eager to learn, and attentive to detail." He smiled at Collins. "He will care for Longbourn as it deserves. Perhaps even better than I cared for it myself. Therefore,

I propose that from this moment forward, Mr. Collins take up the reins of management while I am still capable of assisting him in learning what is needed."

Collins shook his head. "I am not ready."

Mr. Bennet placed a hand on his shoulder. "We are never truly ready for such responsibility until it is thrust upon us. You, however, will benefit from my guidance for now, and you will do well."

"But what of Hunsford?" He looked from Mr. Bennet to Darcy and back.

"If you remember, I wrote to my uncle," Darcy replied.

"And you may return to Kent as planned to say your farewells and see that all is properly transported to your new home, of course," Mr. Bennet added before sinking into his chair. "I am not going to grow any stronger. I may tarry for some time in my current condition, but I shall not improve."

Collins nodded his understanding. It was a nearly overwhelming thing that was being asked of him, and to be completely truthful with himself, he feared not only his ability to capably run an estate, he also disliked how some, such as Miss Lydia, would receive him. He had only just begun to be accepted by this family, save for Lydia and Mary, of course. But he was working on how to win them over. This would likely set that progress back a pace or two if not further. However, seeing the strained and weary look in Mr. Bennet's eyes, he knew he could not refuse him. To have an inept usurper, as he might likely be viewed, as head of an estate was better than to press Mr. Bennet into an earlier grave than was probable.

"Will you do this for me?" Mr. Bennet asked. "Will you allow me to see you well-situated before I leave?"

Collins looked down the table and then back up. All eyes, some hopeful, others suspicious, and most startled, were turned on him, waiting for his reply. He swallowed, licked his lips, which was of little use since his tongue felt as dry as his lips, and replied, "I would not deny you such a request. In truth, I could not and have a clear conscience. But, I must admit to feeling unequal to it."

"I think you more than equal to it," Mr. Bennet replied.

"Then, let it be as you say. I shall stand in your place," Collins replied. His mouth still felt dry, and his stomach was twisting with the words while his heart raced along at an excited yet hopeful pace.

"Very good," Mr. Bennet leaned back in his chair and smiled broadly. "Tomorrow, bring the account books to my room, and we shall begin your instruction."

~*~*~

Not just the next day but for three days – two before Sunday and one after, Collins carried books to the master's chamber and learned as much as his mind would allow him to absorb.

Then, each evening after dinner had concluded, he would retire to his room, sit before his mirror, and relate to himself what he had heard. Inevitably, he would stumble on some fact and have to jot it down so that he could ask to have that portion of Mr. Bennet's instruction repeated to him.

So devoted was he to learning as much as he could in as short a period of time as was possible for a man such as he who loved learning, yet did not excel at it, that he had very little time for anything else. Or that is, he had very little time for anything else other than reading a bit of *Evelina*. The task of reading that novel was nearly as important as learning estate management. In fact, if he wished to secure his desired mistress of Longbourn, it was likely even more important than figures regarding crops and goods.

He tapped his thumb and second finger together as he descended the stairs on the fourth morning after he had agreed to take on the role of master in waiting. "There is a wall in need of repair in the spring." He stopped on a step about two-thirds of the way to the bottom and continued tapping his fingers as he thought. "Was it below the road or above? Below or above, below or above?" His brow rose, and he smiled. "Below, definitely below."

"What is below?"

Collins startled and turned to see Kitty just behind him on the stairs. "Oh, my apologies. I was lost in thought."

Kitty smiled. "Yes, I can see that. But I am curious to know what is below." She joined him on the step on which he stood and placed her hand on his arm, which had offered itself to her without so much as asking his permission.

"There is a wall in need of repair. It is not severely damaged, but it is showing wear and will with a winter or two more of rain and ice be so much worse for the wear if it is not attended to directly when the weather allows in the spring. It is better, you see, to attend to such things while they are small matters. For if it is left to fester and grow, the matter will soon become one of great expense rather than a small expense. And one must be careful with one's funds. God has not given privilege to a man just to see him squander it, though I will admit that I have seen many who have done just that. Great sums of money thrown away on pleasure and never recovered! Estates that have been sold off in pieces or borrowed against in the most grievous fashion for want of caution." He clamped his lips closed as he saw the small amused smile playing at her lips. He wished, of course, to see her smile, but not at his expense.

"You seem very dedicated to being successful."

He sighed and nodded. "I am."

She left her hand on his arm despite being at the bottom of the stairs. "Are you taking those books to the study?"

He nodded. "That is where they belong, so I thought it fitting to return them to their proper place." He pressed his lips together again. She was smiling at him in that amused fashion once again.

"May I walk with you?"

He blinked. "To the study?"

She nodded.

His brow furrowed, his lips pursed, and he shrugged. "I see no reason why you may not."

"We have not seen much of you in days. If it had not been for meals as well as services on Sunday, we might have forgotten you were here at all," she said as they walked the short distance down the hall. "Have you been studying these books all that time?"

"I am not a fast learner," he admitted as he crossed the room to where the books belonged. He had even spent a good deal of time on Sunday reviewing the things learned on the two days prior. Things needed several repetitions before they became ingrained in his mind.

"Nor am I," she replied. "Lizzy and Mary are very quick, Jane and Lydia a bit less so, and then there is me."

He spun toward her. "No, it cannot be. You seem very capable to me."

"And you seem very capable to me."

That small amused smile was on her lips again, but when coupled with the kindness he found in her eyes, he could only be glad to be the cause of her enjoyment.

"So, we are alike," he said.

She nodded. "In that way, yes." She took a seat in front of her father's desk as he returned to placing the books where they belonged and gathering two others. "I should like to know if there are any other ways in which we are alike."

His hand froze on the book he was about to pull from the shelf. She wished to know about him?

He glanced at her surreptitiously. She was still smiling that pleasantly pleased smile. It did not appear as if she was making sport of him, not that he thought her capable of such a thing. Miss Lydia was perhaps capable. He shook his head and pulled his mind back to the topic before him. "There is likely little else we share."

She was tipping her head and looking at him very closely when he turned around.

"I believe you are wrong, for it seems we both wish to please my father," she said.

He smiled. "That is true." He sat down in Mr. Bennet's chair and then immediately popped up.

"You may sit there. It is your place," she said softly.

He turned and looked at the chair. "It does not seem right," he muttered.

"But it is," she insisted. "Papa would wish for you to sit there."

"Are you certain?"

She nodded, and he sat, tentatively, just on the edge of the chair.

"You have met my father." She looked down at her hands as if uncertain whether she should continue. Then, having seemingly reached a conclusion in the half minute that silence reigned in the room, she looked up and continued. "I doubt from what Papa has said that I should like to meet your father, but I would like to know about him."

Collins shook his head. "No, you would not." A gently bred lady with a tender heart such as hers did not need to know about the wounds both visible and invisible that his father had inflicted.

"He was so bad then?"

Collins inhaled deeply and released the breath slowly. "He was unkind, ill-tempered, and a man who cared only for himself."

Her head tipped once again, and her eyes grew sad. "That is most unfortunate," she said softly.

Indeed, having a father such as his was unfortunate. He rose from his place and picked up his books.

"My father teases me," she said as she followed him in rising. "He says Mary, Lydia, and I are the silliest girls in all of England."

Collins stopped his progress to the door and turned toward her. "But you are not."

She shrugged. "Perhaps."

"No," he took one step closer to her. "You are not." She was kind and beautiful and perfect. There was not a single thing about her that was silly.

Again, she shrugged.

"Fathers can say things that are not true." He ran the hand that was not holding the books through his hair. He struggled to reconcile a father who said such things about his daughter with the man who lay in bed in the master's chamber. "My father said many things that were not true of me. I know that they are not true because I have proven them false." He shook his head. "I cannot imagine your father treating you cruelly." Before he could help himself, he reached out and cupped her cheek.

She smiled and pressed her cheek into his hand. "Papa is not cruel. He teases, I know. And it hurts sometimes, but his intention is not cruel. Please, do not think ill of him." Her eyes were filled with tears.

"I will not." He brushed one wayward tear away with his thumb and then realizing what he was doing, snatched his hand away from her face with a muttered apology.

She reached out and took his hand. "We are alike in that we have fathers who have said things about us that are not true." She released his hand and wrapped her arm around his as they walked the three steps to the door. "Are you going to be studying those all evening?"

"No," he replied. "I shall be spending some of my time with Evelina's dear Mr. Villars."

"Oh," she cried. "Do you like him?"

He chuckled at her exuberance as they exited the study. "Yes, he seems to be a very good man."

She sighed. "I knew you would like him. I just knew it."

# Chapter 7

Collins sucked in a long draught of cool, crisp air. Clouds hung low in the sky, and he suspected with the bite that was in the air, there might be snow rather than rain in the great grey puffs above him. He pulled his collar up and squaring his shoulders, entered the milliner's shop. Shopping was not something he did often, and when he did feel he must purchase some item, it was rarely obtained at a milliner's shop.

The store was not crowded. There were only a few patrons making selections at the various counters. He would need to find the ribbons. The right side of his mouth tipped up in a small smirk. Who would have thought he would find himself shopping for ribbons?

He paused at a case to admire the gloves. Those might do. He bent to inspect them more closely. Yes, the ones with the floral stitching. Mrs. Bennet so enjoyed her garden. Surely, she would appreciate the pattern on these gloves. He summoned the clerk and had the gloves wrapped and put aside.

Ribbons were next.

Lydia preferred dark colours at this time of year, did she not? He scrunched up his face as he thought. Yes, yes, dark in the winter to compliment the lack of sun or some such thing.

What would Mary prefer? He tipped his head to one side and then the other as he considered her. A bit of lace? Some of that frilly blue stuff? He sighed. She wore very few embellishments.

The lace would suit Jane, and the yellow ribbon would – no, it would not. Elizabeth wore green more than any other colour. The green ribbon would do for her.

Back to Mary.

"Have you seen her?" One young man said to another in a hushed tone.

Collins moved forward a step so as not to be able to listen to the conversation the young men behind him were having. Unfortunately, they moved with him.

"Not yet," said the other young man. "I have come home a day early. She will not expect me."

"Her father is ill."

Collins paused in his deliberation between the blue frill or the plainer blue ribbon. Were they speaking of Mr. Bennet?

"Yes, she wrote to me about it," the second young man replied. "She said her mother was attempting to push her in front of some large oaf of a cousin, so that she could be mistress of Longbourn upon her father's demise."

They were speaking of Mr. Bennet and Mary... and, he frowned, him. It was not the first time someone had called him a name such as an oaf, but it was not exactly something one got used to hearing and accepted without some amount of displeasure.

The first young man chuckled. "Just like Mrs. Bennet, is it not?"

"Indeed," the second young man agreed with a laugh. "Although my mother is just as bad."

"You have the right of that. I have been invited to dinner three times in the past month."

"Let me guess. She sat you next to Charlotte and not Maria?"

"Between them, but then she directed the conversation so that I had to ignore your younger sister in favour of your elder sister."

"Charlotte is not getting any younger."

"That may be, but I am not marrying her. I prefer my ladies to be younger and how shall I say it? More willing to laugh at my jokes even when they are droll."

"Maria does enjoy a good laugh, does she not?"

Collins motioned to the clerk. He wished to have this purchase over with as soon as possible so that he did not have to listen to any more of the conversation behind him.

"This lace, the blue ribbon as well as the green, the purple – no the darker one – and..." He smiled. "The pink with the gold thread running through it." That would look very well in Kitty's hair or on her bonnet.

"And do not forget the gloves," he added.

"On which account shall I place these?" the clerk asked.

Collins leaned forward. "Bennet of Longbourn," he whispered.

"I beg your pardon?"

"Send the bill to Longbourn," he repeated in a slightly louder voice.

"Longbourn?" The clerk repeated.

"Yes, yes, that is it," Collins stammered as he glanced over his shoulder.

"You must be Mr. Bennet's cousin. I had heard you were visiting." The clerk looked down at the receipt she was writing. "Or were visiting before the master fell ill. Will you be remaining?"

Collins nodded. "I will be except for perhaps a small journey to collect my things in Kent."

"It is good that you are here. I have heard nothing but good things about you from the ladies that frequent my shop."

"I am glad to hear it," Collins said quickly. Why must she be so talkative? Could she not see that he was anxious to be on his way?

"Longbourn?" one of the gentlemen behind him asked.

"Yes," Collins said, turning toward the young man.

"Mr. Oliver Lucas," he said with a bow. "My parents are particular friends of the Bennets."

"As are you." Collins thought to clamp his lips closed. Those words were not meant to be spoken. However, he did not close them in time, and more words spilled out behind them. "I mean, that is, it would stand to reason that you and your sisters are also particular friends of the Bennets, would it not? I believe my cousin Mary has been visited several times by Miss Maria. She is your sister, is she not? And Miss Lucas is a pleasure and seems quite well acquainted with my cousins Jane and Elizabeth." This time, he pressed his lips together. Mr. Lucas was looking at him with a quizzical expression.

"Yes, I guess you could say we are all particular friends of the Bennets."

There was a slyness to young Mr. Lucas's smile that did not sit well with Collins.

"And you are?" Mr. Lucas looked at him expectantly.

"Collins, Mr. William Collins."

"May I present my friend Mr. Joseph Goulding to you, Mr. Collins?"

Goulding? He had heard that name bandied about the sitting

room a time or two. And had he not met a Mrs. Goulding at church on Sunday? She was a sharp woman with a disapproving mien, if he recalled correctly, with two daughters trailing behind her and looking frightfully like their mother. Mr. Goulding did not appear to have inherited the critical air that hung around the females of his family. He seemed as jovial and perhaps just as roguish as his friend, Mr. Lucas. They were both dressed very well — nearly as well as Mr. Bingley.

"It is a pleasure to meet you," Collins remembered to say after a moment of awkward silence. "I was trying to remember if I had met you along with your mother at church Sunday last, but I do not believe I did."

"I was in London," the young man replied. "A friend was having a bit of a gathering."

Collins smiled. "Gatherings are always pleasant." He kept his smile in place despite the inane comment that had escaped his mouth. He turned and gathered his parcels. Departing this establishment was perhaps the best course of action.

"Ribbons and gloves?" The slant of Mr. Lucas's mouth was a trifle mocking.

"For my cousins," Collins replied.

"Bleeding the coffers before the passing of old Mr. Bennet in an attempt to secure the affections of those left behind?"

Mr. Goulding might not carry the appearance of a disparager as his mother and sisters did, but it seemed the trait had not altogether escaped him. Collins felt indignation pull him straighter as it settled between his shoulders and caused him to scowl.

"I fear you have misjudged me," he began as calmly as he could when feeling so affronted, but then, he had had practice at receiving ridicule, so the calmness was something a kin to a well-worn coat that slipped into place without much effort.

"So, you are not spending Longbourn's money?" Mr. Goulding shot his friend a derisive grin. "I am certain I heard you say to send the bill to Longbourn."

"It is simple and pure folly to speak to a subject when one does not hold all the facts," he replied with a smile. "Arrogance is not becoming, and as the scriptures say, it often precipitates a fall — a moment or longer of looking foolish." He gave a nod of his head and made to leave.

Mr. Goulding stepped in front of him. "You cannot call me a fool and walk away."

"I did not call you a fool," Collins corrected. "I said you were arrogant to assume that you know all the facts about my business and to declare judgment based on those assumptions. However, if you wish to be made a fool, I can oblige. These items that I hold are purchased with Longbourn's funds, just as you have said, and I have acknowledged. However, I do not purchase them on my behalf but on behalf of Mr. Bennet. He is ill, as you know, and cannot journey to town to buy these things for himself. There-fore, because he wishes to give his wife and daughters a surprise, he sent me in his stead." Collins squared his shoulders and grow-ing more somber, lowered his voice. "These are the request of a dying man, so that he might share his affection for his family and see their pleasure before it is no longer in his power to do so. Who am I to deny him such a thing?" He looked pointedly at Mr. Lucas. "I am no oaf."

Mr. Lucas's eyes grew the tiniest bit wide at the comment.

"If you wish to court Miss Mary," Collins continued, "I am certain her father would prefer you do it properly and not through clandestine letters." Good, the man looked completely out of sorts now.

"I will not share what I know with him unless it becomes necessary." He took a step closer to Mr. Lucas. "And Miss Mary has nothing to fear. I have no desire to marry her, no matter what her mother wishes. I am sure Mr. Goulding understands that. Mothers will sometimes push daughters forward, but that does not mean the gentleman to whom they are presented is a willing recipient or even a ready admirer of the young lady's charms. Miss Maria and Miss Mary seem pleasant, and I wish you both well. But, I would encourage you to seek them out in a more proper fashion than it appears you have in the past." He gave a bow of his head. "Good day, gentlemen. Do call on us at Longbourn some time."

And with that, he left the milliner's shop with a handful of parcels and a satisfied feeling in his breast. That was, he thought to himself as he made his way to the carriage, the first time he had ever spoken his mind so clearly to someone who had attempted to abuse him, and it felt very, very good.

~*~*~

"Come, come," Mr. Bennet called in response to the rap at his study door. He had begun insisting on spending a few hours in his study, lounging in a chair not far from the desk while Collins added numbers and asked questions as needed.

"Ah, my soon-to-be sons."

Collins looked up from the column of numbers he had just finished calculating. Mr. Bennet was smiling broadly and had placed his book on the table next to him.

"Five daughters and three sons," the elder gentleman muttered before sighing.

"Two," Collins said before he could help himself.

"Nay, I did not misspeak. I count you as a son." There was a gleam in the man's eye. "An heir is as good as a son, is it not?"

Collins shrugged.

"Do not tell me you do not wish to be my son?"

"Oh, no, no, I would never do that. You are far too good a man to be my father is all."

"Foolishness."

If Mr. Bennet's lips were not curled into a smile, Collins might have considered the somewhat stern tone he used to be a reprimand, but as it was, he could not think of it as anything more than a jovial disagreement. That was likely how he looked and sounded when he teased Kitty about being silly. It did sting a bit even though he knew it to be in jest.

"I see you have come to embrace wearing more than one colour," Bingley said as he turned one of the chairs in front of the desk so that from the angle in which he sat, he could converse easily with both Mr. Bennet and Collins.

"I am not so poor a student as to ignore the instructions of the master."

"The master?" Mr. Bennet looked curiously between Bingley and Collins.

"I have asked these gentlemen to help me with learning how to present myself," Collins explained. He had forgotten that Mr. Bennet did not know about that little agreement, and he did not particularly wish for the gentleman to know the particulars of why he had sought help.

Mr. Bennet smiled. "I will assume that it is not to impress me."

"No, sir." What else could he say? "I wish to look the part of a gentleman rather than a parson." That was true. He did wish to fit in with his neighbours.

"Well," Mr. Bennet said as he smoothed the blanket on his lap and steadfastly did not look at Collins, "I am certain Kitty will appreciate the effort."

Collins thought for a moment that his heart would either cease its job of ticking along or jump from his chest. The shock of such a comment left him in a state of utter confusion. Did one admit such a thing to the father of the lady one admired? Or did one remain silent? What he did know for certain, was that his face felt as if it was burning in the heat of a midsummer's day.

Chuckling, Mr. Bennet lifted his eyes to Collins and then shifted them to Bingley and Darcy. "As I said, three sons at some point. I have no doubt of your success, William."

His Christian name caused another stirring of uncertain emotions within Collins. He had never heard it said in such an amiable tone. His father had spoken it with indifference, spat it at him, followed it with a curse, yelled it, and, on occasion, snarled it. He had heard it used once or twice in an encouraging fashion from his tutor, but this declaration of Mr. Bennet's was one of complete trust and confidence. It was genuinely startling and excessively welcome.

Thankfully, he did not have to decide how one should respond to such a thing as the door opened just then, and Mr. Hill entered. "You have a caller, Mr. Collins," he said.

"He does?" Mr. Bennet replied. "Who might that be?"

"Mr. Lucas, sir."

"Oliver?"

"Yes, sir."

"I met him at the milliner's shop," Collins said as he rose from the desk. He hoped that the gentleman had only come to call and not to repay him for the somewhat harsh words which had been spoken before they had parted ways.

"You may ask him to join us," Mr. Bennet said as Collins reached the door.

"I will make mention of it," he assured Mr. Bennet. He was not certain that Mr. Lucas would wish to join them even if this was a friendly visit.

"Have you received the marriage articles?" Mr. Bennet asked Darcy as Collins closed the door.

It was only about two weeks until both Darcy and Bingley married their ladies. Mr. Bennet had insisted it be soon, for he wished to be in attendance. There would be no reading of the banns. It would all be done as quietly as one might without having Mrs. Bennet excessively put out. However, in deference to the fact that Mr. Darcy had just passed his period of mourning for his cousin, she had been surprisingly reasonable. The fact that Mr. Bingley had promised a ball to celebrate the arrival of the new year did help some.

"Mr. Lucas," Collins greeted and waved his hand toward the sitting room.

"I would prefer to speak to you in private." He was spinning his hat in his hand as he spoke.

"Of course. Will the dining room do?"

Mr. Lucas nodded somberly, but then a smile graced his lips as there was a rustle on the stairs behind Collins.

Turning, Collins saw Mary standing rooted to her spot on the stairs. Kitty and Lydia pushed past her and continued to the sitting room from which he could hear the high-pitched tone of Miss Bingley as the door opened and then closed.

"Do you wish for her to join us?" Collins whispered.

Mr. Lucas shook his head. "I will pay my respects to Mrs. Bennet in a moment," he replied without taking his eyes off Mary.

Collins knew that look, for he felt it every time Kitty was near. "Very well," Collins replied. "Then, shall we?" He motioned to the dining room.

"I wished to explain myself," Mr. Lucas said as the door to the room closed. "And to offer an apology."

"Then carry on."

Mr. Lucas blew out a breath. "First, I must apologize for calling you an oaf and for my friend's rude behaviour."

"You are forgiven for your words, but I do not see how you are responsible for your friend. A man can only be found guilty of his own actions, although I suppose, the association with fellows of ill repute can be held against a man." Collins's brow furrowed as he thought about that. "Yes, yes, I will forgive you for your choice of friend."

Mr. Lucas blinked. "Joseph is not all bad. He is just critical and does not always hold his tongue."

"Not all bad is not all good. But then none of us are without fault, are we?" He pressed his lips together as a few familiar passages of scripture came to mind, and a sermon began forming itself unbidden.

"You sound a lot like Miss Mary," Mr. Lucas said with a laugh.

"She is always breaking into some lecture on one subject or another."

"Indeed? She has spoken very few words to me. Not that I blame her. Her mother was excessively forward in her attempts at matching us."

The gentleman before him relaxed and smiled broadly. "That is Mrs. Bennet. She is well-meaning but misguided."

A pensive scowl settled on Collins's lips, and he nodded as he weighed the description. He did not think Mrs. Bennet's stratagems were ever approached from a place of ill will. She was not conniving, and she did seem very concerned that her children be happy. Her fault lay in allowing her daughters too much freedom. "I think I agree, though I have not known her so long as you have."

"My mother is similar," Mr. Lucas continued. "As you can imagine, if my mother or Mrs. Bennet were to hear of a possible courtship between Miss Mary and me, we would be thrust together and paraded to the front of the church before we were even certain of ourselves. We are both young. I am not yet finished with my studies, though I will be at the end of the next term. This is why Miss Mary and I have conducted our courtship in secret. Neither of us wished to be hurried into marriage without ample time to discover if we would suit."

Mr. Lucas's reason seemed sound, and though it still seemed wrong to Collins to have conducted any secret affair, it was understandable. "Is this why your friend does not openly proclaim his attachment to your sister?"

"You have met his mother," Mr. Lucas replied. "My mother and Mrs. Bennet are kittens compared to Mrs. Goulding. She wishes for him to marry well and from town. There would be great distress for many if it were to be made known that he wished to marry my sister." He shook his head. "It will eventually have to be told, but he had hoped that one of his sisters would make a good match and his mother would be somewhat mollified."

If there was one thing Collins knew well, it was how unpleasant an unhappy parent could be. "I can understand the reasons, but I struggle to condone the actions," he finally admitted.

"That is understandable," Mr. Lucas replied.

The young man seemed to be a very level-headed gentleman and rather likable.

"Do you love her? I know I am only her cousin, but I should like to know."

Mr. Lucas nodded. "I do."

"But not enough to endure your mother's raptures?"

"I had not considered it in such terms," Mr. Lucas admitted. He smiled sheepishly. "When said in such a fashion, I do appear to be rather weak, do I not?" He shook his head. "You are definitely not an oaf, but rather wise."

"Oh, I am not that. I am simply a man trained in the profession of the church and see things from a different perspective, I suppose."

"No, what you said in town and just now were wise words. I have been pondering your words since we parted ways."

"That is the duty of a parson. To impart words that cause his listeners to ponder."

"Then, you must have been a very good parson."

Collins smiled. "I had hoped one day to be, and my patroness did compliment me on my skills of oration as did my instructors at school. However, I had only just begun my position as a parson before coming to Longbourn." He moved toward the door. "I have not said a word to anyone about what I know, and I shall not. However, Mr. Bennet did tell me that I should invite you to join him, Mr. Darcy, Mr. Bingley, and myself in the study."

"I would rather see Mrs. Bennet," Mr. Lucas replied.

"You mean Miss Mary," Collins corrected.

Mr. Lucas chuckled. "Indeed, I do."

They stepped into the hall. "I would encourage you to at least inform Mr. Bennet of your desire regarding Miss Mary. I truly think he would be delighted to know that another of his daughters has found a match."

"I will consider it," Mr. Lucas replied.

Collins waited until Mr. Lucas had entered the sitting room before he made his way back to the study. That was twice in one day that he had managed a conversation with a gentleman as if they were equals or, his lips tilted in his familiar smirk, perhaps he had presented himself as more. Perhaps he was becoming what he wished to be – master of his own domain.

# Chapter 8

Using the candle he held in his hand, Collins lit a second one that was in the lamp on the table next to where Mr. Bennet had been sitting earlier that day. He looked around the room.

Mr. Bennet had told him he was to make this room his second refuge. His first was his bedchamber, of course. There he could lock himself away without there being much chance of being disturbed, but here, he was more accessible, and here is where Bingley had very firmly insisted he should read each evening.

Truth be told, Bingley had wished for him to sit with the others in the sitting room, but Darcy had pled his case and convinced Bingley that the study would be better for reviewing what needed to be learned.

Collins tipped his head and eyed the book on the desk. He wanted to go over it again. He was positive he could remember nearly everything Mr. Bennet had told him about the tenants listed in it. He glanced at the door. No one was with him; he could peek at it.

He crossed to the desk, placed his hand on the book, and just as he was about to lift the cover, shook his head and retreated to the chair near the lamp without the book. He did not want to have to tell Bingley or Darcy tomorrow afternoon that he had spent another evening studying, for both gentlemen had thought it best if he spent one evening consuming the novel he had promised Kitty he would read.

He sighed as he settled into his chair, and taking up his book, he placed it unopened in his lap while he pondered the lovely Miss Kitty Bennet and watched the shadows chase each other in the flickering dance of the candles' flames. Perhaps in the new year when Bingley had his ball, he would dance two sets with her. Perhaps by then, she would even be accepting of his addresses, or at least, by then, he would have learned enough from Darcy and Bingley to be able to present them. By spring, he might even find himself in a position to make her his wife. That thought could not be made without a smile finding its way to his lips.

"May I enter?"

*Evelina* clattered to the floor as Collins started at the sweet voice that called to him from the door.

"Your father is not here," he responded as he bent and retrieved the book.

"I know. I was just with him," Kitty said, "and then I saw the light under the door and thought it might be pleasant to sit in here if I am allowed."

Collins nodded. "If you leave the door open."

She smiled and pushed the door open just a bit further before crossing the room and pulling a chair from in front of her father's desk to where Collins was sitting.

"Allow me to help you." Collins jumped up from his seat.

"I can manage," she said with a pointed look.

"But it is not right. I should provide the service to you. It is what a gentleman does for a lady."

Her lovely lips puckered into a contained smile. "You have done as you ought. You offered your assistance, and I refused. It is likely I who has not done as is proper."

He stood beside his chair, waiting and feeling very useless and awkward as she arranged the chair as she wanted it.

"I am certain you did nothing improper," he muttered.

Even tugging a chair into place and twisting it this way and that, she moved with grace. How she managed to look so utterly enchanting while doing such a thing was a puzzle he would like to have the opportunity to ponder over and over again as he watched her do whatever it was she chose to do.

"You can be seated," she said with a laugh as she took her seat. "We are cousins. There is no need to be so formal, is there?"

His brow furrowed. Was there? They were cousins, but to him, she was more than just a relation. However, he could not tell her that. Not yet anyway. He was not ready. He still had lessons to learn. He only knew how to tie his cravat in two different knots, and his hair, according to Bingley, remained in need of attention. He ran his hand through that mop of brown on his head and shrugged.

"I suppose there is not. However, it is what I have always been taught, and it seems strange to do anything else." He settled into his chair once again. The candles' flames were still causing the shadows to dance, but he could not be persuaded to watch them when the object of his former imaginings sat so near.

"I suppose I can understand that," she said. "I am certain I should feel quite out of place if I were to visit your patroness. Lady Catherine, was it not?"

He nodded. "Yes, Lady Catherine de Bourgh. A wonderful

woman. Very gracious and so concerned with seeing that things were done as they ought to be done. She had overseen several improvements at the parsonage before I took up residence because she thought I would enjoy them. And I did."

"Is the parsonage a large house?" She pulled her feet up and tucked them under her as she turned toward him.

"No, not so very large but not precisely small. There were four bedrooms and two sitting rooms as well as a generous study. The study faced the garden on the side. I had thought to plant some vegetables in it. I understand that is what the former parson did, or I should say, had done for him. However, I had wanted to feel the accomplishment of seeing the work of my hands on the table during the winter. And I admit to finding great pleasure in watching the Lord's creation renewing itself through the seasons." He pressed his lips together. He was in danger of rambling on about things which would likely not interest her in the least. That was not the best way to make a good impression. What lady would wish to be tied to a gentleman who babbled on about trivial things as if they were the most important things in the world to one and all?

Kitty's elbows rested on the padded arm of the chair, and she was using them to prop up her chin as she listened to him. "What of flowers?" she asked when he paused. "Would you have planted flowers? I think there is nothing better than to have fresh flowers on the table in the sitting room, so that one can look upon them as she stitches or draws."

The corner of his mouth tipped up in a half smile. She seemed eager to hear what he had to say.

"There was a rose bush which Lady Catherine said produced

lovely white flowers as well as a couple of climbing plants which had been trained up and over an archway. I confess I had not thought to plant any flowers beyond those, but that might have been an oversight on my part."

"Mama has some lovely rose bushes. You remember we showed you where they were?"

He nodded. Mrs. Bennet had been excessively proud of those roses.

"There is a garden for vegetables near the kitchen," Kitty continued, "but Mama has not allowed me to plant anything there. She says it is Cook's domain, so I must satisfy myself with a few flowers in one bed in the garden."

There was a true hint of disappointment in her voice at having her desires to plant curtailed that was accompanied by a small pout. She was excessively charming.

"Do all of your sisters plant flowers with you?" he asked, not wanting this discussion to be at an end. He wanted to see her lips curl upward again and to see that enchanting animation in her eyes and features which always accompanied her speaking on a topic of interest. There was no mistaking what she liked or disliked. It was easily read in her expression, even when she attempted to hide it.

"No," her eyes sparkled in the glow of the candles. "Jane and I are the only ones who enjoy the activity. Lydia has tried to plant a few flowers, but she lacks the patience needed to help them along to maturity. She grows bored and forgets them. I usually tend to them for her, so we can have flowers in our room and because I would hate to see them die from neglect. Mary would rather plant trees, or so she says whenever Mama asks her to join us. And Elizabeth planted a group of peonies one year and has a small lilac bush. She prefers things that tend to themselves, for though she adores their colours and fragrance, she would rather spend her time wandering and gathering wildflowers than spend it in the garden. I do not see how anything can be better than tending to one's garden, but," she shrugged, "we are not all alike."

"Peonies," Collins muttered, "I do like those."

"They bloom for only a short time," Kitty cautioned. "You would need more than one group of peony plants in your garden if you wish to have a summer filled with beauty."

He allowed it to be true while silently he thought that a summer and a garden could only be truly beautiful if it contained her.

A few moments of silence stretched between them until Kitty lifted her head from where it rested on her hand and picked up the conversation once again. "I am certain Cook would not mind giving you a corner of the garden so you could grow a few things, and I would be happy to share all I know about growing flowers." She bit her lip as her brows furrowed. "That is if you wish. I am sorry you will have to leave your parsonage."

He pulled in a breath and let it out in a great sigh. He had been considering his removal from his parish. No one, save her, had even hinted that leaving his position would be anything more than routine.

"It is a bittersweet thing, leaving Hunsford. There is a portion of me who wishes to know if I would have made a good parson, if I would have been an instrument of blessing in the community and to Lady Catherine. I feel I would have been. I was heartily welcomed when I arrived, and my lady was always pleased with my sermons." He had hoped to finally have found in Hunsford a home and a place where he could grow and bloom just as the plants in a garden did when well-tended. However, "I dare say, the good Lord was not surprised by my change of residence and can use me for the same here, albeit not with sermons." He brows furrowed. How? He did not know.

"You have already been a blessing to my father," Kitty said as if she knew he was wondering how he could possibly be what he wished as the master of an estate when he had not studied to be one. "He said you are improving each day, and he does not give praise where praise is not due."

"Thank you," he said softly. "My welcome here has been most unexpected." His eyes grew wide. "Not that I did not expect a welcome, but to be thrust into a position of standing in the stead of your father while being little more than a stranger – no not thrust so much as gifted. Not that your father's illness was a gift, but his generosity and graciousness in teaching me..." He sighed and shook his head. He was a bumbling idiot at times.

"Does Longbourn feel like it could be your home?"

He searched her face. There was no sign of condemnation for his rambling incoherence. He nodded his head. "More than anywhere I have ever been."

A soft smile curled her lips and reached to her eyes. "I am glad of it. Everyone should feel at home somewhere in the world." She paused. "You feel at home even with Lydia and Mary being less than agreeable?"

He lifted a shoulder and let it fall. "It is not so very bad, and it is understandable. I shall just have to prove to them that I neither wish to toss anyone out into the hedgerows nor force anyone into a marriage she does not want."

"You are driving Lydia to distraction by not allowing her to argue with you. I think that is wise." A small giggle escaped her as she shifted in her chair and unfolded her legs.

"A soft answer turneth away wrath: but grievous words stir up anger."

Her brows furrowed in question.

"Proverbs fifteen verse one," he replied. "Solomon was the wisest man to ever have lived. The Lord gifted him with a special amount of wisdom, you know." He looked at her and received a small nod in reply. "He wrote that."

Silence filled the room.

"It's a book of poetry," he said. "Proverbs," he added when she gave him a quizzical look.

"Then perhaps I will read it."

"You should."

Again, the room fell into silence.

"I am keeping you from your reading," she said, picking up her book of verses.

"I do not mind. I have found our discussion to be quite delightful." And he wished it to continue. If only he could think of a topic to discuss. But he could not, so he opened his book to where he had marked his place with a small bit of the pink ribbon he had purchased with her in mind when he was in Meryton.

"How far are you?" she asked, looking up from her book.

"Letter thirteen."

"Which is that?" She closed her book and put it back on the table while leaning towards him to try to spy the words in his book.

"Evelina left off the last letter saying they were to go somewhere." He scanned the page. "A ridotto, and then they were to return to Howard Grove on Wednesday."

"Oh," she gasped. "The trouble she has at the ridotto!"

"Indeed? More than she has already had?"

Kitty nodded. "She falls into so many troublesome circumstances. I truly do not know how she bears it as she does!" She held out her hand. "Might I read it to you? I would ask you to read it to me, but do you not think it would be better to hear a young lady's letter read by a lady?"

There was no way he could argue such a thing. Perhaps he could have assured her that he would have read it in a higher tone, but to be perfectly honest, he would prefer to hear her read. He did so love to listen to her voice. Therefore, he took the ribbon from between the pages and passed her the book.

She shifted in her seat, gave her lips a quick moistening, and began.

*EVELINA IN CONTINUATION Tuesday, April 12. My dear Sir,*

*We came home from the ridotto[1] so late, or rather so early that it was not possible for me to write. Indeed, we did not go -you will be frightened to hear it-till past eleven o'clock: but nobody does. A terrible reverse of the order of nature! We sleep with the sun, and wake with the moon.[2]*

---

1. *ridotto: historical, An entertainment consisting of music, dancing, and sometimes gambling. Source: oxforddictionaries.com*
2. *from Evelina by Fanny Burney*

# Chapter 9

Kitty looked up as Darcy and Bingley passed the open door to the sitting room and proceed up the stairs instead of entering. They had been spending a great deal of time with Mr. Collins. She could not imagine what they were doing up there in his room or in the study or in her father's room, but whenever they arrived, they always went in search of Mr. Collins before they called on Jane or Elizabeth. To her, it seemed very peculiar.

She poked her needle through the fabric and pursed her lips. It would be much better if they were to go find Mr. Collins and bring him to the sitting room with them. She knew that he was intent on learning all he could about Longbourn, but she wished he would be just a little less attentive to his duty. She would not admit it to her sisters, but she wanted him to come sit next to her and read while she stitched. She could not explain it, but there was a comfort that she felt in his presence which she had not ever in all the seventeen years she had lived experienced anywhere else. She drew her needle back up through her fabric, completing the leaf on which she was working, and prepared to continue the stem of her vine.

The thought of how he got flustered and pressed his lips closed on his words brought a smile to her lips. He had so many thoughts to share when he forgot himself and allowed his words to flow freely. It was not all entertaining or even always something she understood, but she did like the way he would fold his arms and get that far away look in his eyes as if he were in some distant but wonderful place. And then, he would remember he was not wherever that was and would cease speaking, often abruptly. Lydia found it a great source of jokes, but Kitty did not.

"Miss Kitty, I see you have nearly finished your design." Captain Saunders took the place next to Kitty where she had hoped Mr. Collins would sit.

"I have. Do you like it?" She held up her work for his scrutiny. She doubted a captain in the militia was well-versed in the finer points of needlework, but since he had made mention of it, she thought to oblige him. "I shall soon be ready to put the front and back together. Will it not be the loveliest bag for spring?"

"Indeed, it will," he replied with a smile. "Nearly as lovely as the lady who carries it."

She smiled and ducked her head. He did know how to speak very pretty words even if they did not make her feel as at ease as Mr. Collins less pretty words did.

"It is a fine day," he continued. "The sun is warm for this time of year."

"Was your walk from town pleasant then?" His cheeks and nose were still rosy, and he rubbed his hands together, so she knew it was not altogether warm outside.

"Oh, very," he replied readily. "I had hoped, after we have had a moment to warm ourselves, to perhaps take a turn of the garden?"

"I had hoped we might have a chance for a more private conversation," he added upon seeing her look of contemplation.

"Oh." Kitty's heart thumped wildly at such a suggestion. He was not thinking of making some sort of offer, was he? He had been paying her marked attention, but they were merely friends, were they not?

"Do you not wish to walk with me?"

"No, that is not it." She busied herself with putting her stitching away so that she would not have to look at him. "I am just not sure I wish to go outside. I know it is sunny, but I am so comfortable here. The fire is warm, and the company is pleasant. Perhaps we could play cards," she suggested hopefully.

She did not like cards as much as Lydia did, but she preferred them to having to consider an offer of some sort from a dashing gentleman who was a delightful conversation partner and who made one look exceptionally good on his arm, but who did not stir her heart in any particularly wonderful fashion. He was not the one she wished to have at her side. He was not the one she wished to seek out when she wanted a quiet discussion. He was not the one who understood her and welcomed her as *her*. Captain Saunders welcomed her. He even sought her out, but he never made her feel as if she could be just herself. In his presence, she felt as if she needed to be like Lydia, ready with a playful quip or light giggle and a batting of eyelashes. While those things were enjoyable, they were also tiring.

"Yes, yes, cards would be acceptable. Whatever you wish shall be my command."

The words sounded gallant and caused her to smile, but they also felt a trifle flat.

"Lydia, we must play cards," she said.

Lydia, of course, nearly flew from her chair in her haste to see things arranged.

Just as the tables had been set, and Lydia had given directions as to where each person was to sit, the one gentleman Kitty had wished to join her finally entered the sitting room with Mr. Darcy and Mr. Bingley. She smiled at him, but he did not return her smile. How odd!

"Mr. Collins, would you care to play?" she asked, rising from her chair. "You may take my place."

"No, no," he said in a very serious tone. "I would not wish to keep you from your fun."

"But I do not mind. I can play the next round."

He shook his head and lifted the book he held. "I shall just read near the window. The light is very good for reading today."

"Very well." She attempted to keep the disappointment she felt out of her voice.

"You are very solicitous of your cousin," Captain Saunders whispered. "It does you credit. Not everyone is so kind to gentlemen such as he."

She blinked. "Such as he? I am not certain I understand your meaning."

The captain shared a smirk with Captain Denny as he shrugged. "I mean no offense, of course, but he is awkward. Very lacking in charm, you must agree. But, I do understand, he will one day be the one to decide how you live, so your gracious acceptance now will no doubt see you in good stead when the time comes."

Kitty attempted to keep her brows from being lost in her hairline, but her surprise and afront at such a comment was such that she could not. "I am certain I never considered such a thing!"

The captain patted her hand where it lay on the table. "Of course, you did not. You are too kind to think ill of anyone. It is just one of the many things I admire about you."

Kitty bit her lip and studied her cards, making sure to hold them with both hands so that he could not touch her as he had. It was a particularly unsettling feeling to have his hand on hers. It tingled at first like a little burst of excitement might, but then that sensation faded as quickly as it appeared and was replaced with a feeling of impropriety.

"You admire me?" she asked quietly.

"I do."

It was a simple reply that for a moment felt very good. She had never before had someone say he admired her in such a direct fashion.

"Very much," he added in a whisper. "That is what I had hoped to speak to you about in the garden."

She nodded but turned her attention to her cards as it was her turn to play.

"I have surprised you."

Again, she nodded. "I fear you have." Shocked, surprised, terrified, thrilled, confused...there were so many words that sprang to mind to describe what his words had done to her.

"It is not an unpleasant surprise, I hope," he added. "I had thought my attentions were obvious."

She swallowed. Had she been too stupid to see his admiration? His expression held no judgment.

"I had not..." She shook her head. She would not admit that

she had not been thinking. Instead, she would say, "No, it is not unpleasant, just surprising."

The afternoon of cards and small talk could not end soon enough. Her mind was in a jumble. Her heart was in no less coherent a state. Her nerves made her feel jumpy, and she struggled not to be cross. It was so very vexing to be admired by – her hand flew to her mouth, and she gasped – the wrong gentleman. The realization did little to help her heart stop its fluttering nor did it cause her nerves to retreat. What it did was cause her eyes to fill with tears when Captain Saunders asked her if she as well.

"I am well," she assured him. But she was not. "I was merely woolgathering. I am dreadfully ashamed to have been doing so instead of listening to the tale you were telling."

"You need not fret so much." His voice and the accompanying smile were soothing. "I am not offended. It happens to everyone at some point."

"But it should not have happened," she replied. It should not have, but she also knew she had been entirely powerless to keep such a thing from happening then and was just as unlikely to be able to keep it from happening again. Her mind wished to ponder nothing other than how Captain Saunders with all his pretty words and handsome features was inferior to an awkward, sometimes bumbling, gentleman who sat quietly by the window reading a book she had asked him to read even though he did not like novels.

"Truly, you take it too seriously. We all have minds that wander at times."

She rubbed the space between her eyebrows.

"You are not well," Captain Saunders declared.

She sighed. "My head is just the smallest bit sore, but I am certain it will not grow worse." It likely would unless he left, and she could escape to her room to think. However, that was not something one told a gentleman who had just declared his admiration for oneself.

"I have surprised you and not given you a moment to think."

She nodded and smiled sheepishly at him. His expression fell but only slightly.

"I would rather that my declaration be met with joy than with a headache, but I can also appreciate the need to consider even if I had not expected it."

"Thank you," she said softly. There was a pang of guilt at having caused him any disappointment. She was not the sort of lady to enjoy causing disappointment.

"If it is as sunny a day tomorrow as it is today, might you be willing to take a walk in the garden with me? Would that allow you enough time to consider?"

She lifted one shoulder and allowed it to drop. "I think that should be enough time."

It was not, but she did not know how else to answer.

Captain Saunders was not a poor choice. He had land and an acceptable income which would be his as soon as his time with the militia drew to an end. She would not want for anything if she were to become his wife. Her life would be comfortable. And he seemed as if he was a kind man who would show her respect and treat her well. Such an offer must be considered carefully, especially if no other offer seemed forthcoming.

And that was what she truly needed time to determine. She had one day – only one day — to discover if there was any hope of Mr.

Collins ever returning her admiration, and if not, then, she might do just as well to accept Captain Saunders.

Oh, how she hoped it would rain!

# Chapter 10

"What were you and Captain Saunders talking about so seriously?" Lydia asked after the officers had left and she and Kitty had gone up to dress for supper.

"It was nothing," Kitty prevaricated.

How could she tell Lydia that there was a handsome officer who seemed intent on pursuing her as more than a conversation partner while his friend flirted with Lydia? Such an admission would surely only result in squeals of delight and the loud declaration that Kitty was to be the happiest girl in all the land. This would likely be followed by a discussion of how if Captain Saunders was thinking of marrying, Captain Denny must be also, for talk of one wedding often led to another.

Still more difficult would be the task of telling Lydia that Captain Saunders's offer was not the one for which Kitty wished.

It was best to keep silent as long as possible.

Lydia looked at her skeptically. "You were talking in low tones about nothing?"

Kitty nodded. "He mentioned wishing to take a walk in the garden, but I really could not be moved from the comfort of the sitting room for any inducement."

"I could be," Lydia replied with a giggle.

"I could not be," Kitty replied as she sat to inspect her hair. It did not need a full restoration, but it was starting to grow unkept. A bit of attention was required, so she picked up the brush and began her work of smoothing here and repining there.

"I was quite glad Mr. Collins did not take your place at our table," Lydia said as she fastened her dress in the front. "I honestly was shocked that you would even offer such a thing! To be forced to entertain him for a full game! It really would have been just the thing to ruin a perfectly good afternoon."

"He is not so dreadful as you believe," Kitty retorted. "If you would but attempt to become acquainted with him, you might find yourself very much surprised at what you find."

Lydia huffed and came to stand next to the bench where Kitty sat. "Are you nearly finished?"

Kitty placed one last pin in her hair and moved to relinquish her place to Lydia but then, pausing, decided that a butterfly would be just the thing to likely capture the attention of Mr. Collins, so she remained in her place long enough to secure the comb in her hair. She only had a day, after all, to draw him out – if it were even possible for him to be drawn out. That thought caused her heart to ache in a most unusual and unwelcome fashion.

"Captain Saunders nearly held your hand," Lydia said as she sat down before the mirror on their shared dressing table. "How thrilling was it?"

Kitty shrugged.

"Did it send little prickles skittering up your arm?" Lydia pressed. "I have always found a handsome gentleman's touch to do just that."

"It did at first," Kitty replied as she got down on her knees to look under the bed for her missing slipper. "But then it just felt improper." She pulled out the wayward shoe and slipped it onto her foot.

"Improper?" Lydia spun on the bench to look at her sister.

"Yes," Kitty replied. "It was very odd, I assure you. Startling even."

She picked up the book of sermons she had been attempting to read. There were some interesting parts, but often, they made her eyes weary and her mind hurt as she attempted to decipher what was being said. Why a sermon writer could not just put their thoughts on paper in as entertaining a fashion as a novelist did, she did not know. Perhaps gentlemen who wrote sermons were too serious to have fun. Or perhaps it was because they were all old and stodgy. Whatever the reason, reading sermons was only something she would do to show Mr. Collins that she could be interested in what he liked just as he was demonstrating the same to her by reading *Evelina*.

"I wonder if Captain Saunders likes novels," she said from her perch on the bed where she waited for her sister.

"How could he not?" Lydia cried. "Any gentleman of sense would! I declare that if a gentleman does not find pleasure in a novel, he must be either intolerably stupid or dreadfully dull!"

"Mr. Bingley does not like to read," Kitty replied.

"Mr. Bingley is too pleasant to need to read."

Kitty's brow furrowed. Lydia did not always make sense.

"Are you still reading that dreadful book?" Lydia stood and approached Kitty.

"I am. Mr. Collins is reading a novel, so I am reading sermons."

Lydia snatched the book from Kitty.

"Lydia!" Kitty cried. "Look what you have done!" In her hand, she held one page of the book – and not even the whole page but only three-quarters of it.

"It is just a silly book of sermons." Lydia lifted her chin and tossed the book on the table next to the bed. "It is not as if it is a good book that many will wish to read."

Kitty scrambled off the bed and retrieved the book, smoothing out the pages that had been bent when Lydia tossed it. "Papa would be ashamed to see you treat any book as you have this one."

"It is not Papa's book."

Kitty clenched her jaw and drew a breath through her nose. "That is not the point. The point is that you have treated a book with disrespect and by extension its owner."

Lydia's mouth curled into a sly smile. "You are not going to tell Papa that I damaged Mr. Collins's book, are you?"

Kitty flipped through the pages as she considered if she would indeed tell Papa about Lydia's behavior. It was likely the right and proper thing to do, but she did not like it when Lydia was mad.

"Are you?" Lydia demanded.

Kitty squared her shoulders. "I am undecided."

Lydia's eyes grew wide.

"If you can be civil to Mr. Collins for the whole evening and all of tomorrow, I will not tell Papa."

Lydia huffed and crossed her arms. "It seems as if Mr. Collins is rather special to you," she said only turning toward the door as her sister opened it rather than moving to follow her. "You do not actually *like* Mr. Collins, do you? Is that why you have been sneaking into Papa's study? So you can be with him?"

Kitty drew a slow breath. That was it precisely, but it was also not something she felt she could or should tell Lydia. Lydia did not know how to keep to herself secrets that did not please her. Therefore, Kitty shook her head and said, "Of course not. I am just trying to make him feel welcome."

"He is no Captain Saunders." Lydia, who was smiling once more, crossed to the door.

"No, he is not," Kitty admitted. He was so much more.

~*~*~

Kitty peeked at Mr. Collins for the fourth time during dinner. He had spoken to her father for nearly the entire meal about some wall that needed repair and Mr. Doney, who was to be hired for the job, and what the expected expense would be as well as when it would be best to begin such a project in the spring. He had passed her several dishes of food and had replied in one or two words to any question she asked, but beyond that, he had completely ignored her.

She scowled at the last remaining piece of baked apple on her plate. Baked apples were a particular favorite of hers on most occasions, except when a gentleman was being so vexing! It really was beyond enough!

Elizabeth leaned close to Kitty. "Are you well?"

Kitty forced her lips into a smile and nodded.

"You were getting a headache earlier. Has it returned?" Elizabeth was studying her face very carefully and not looking at all convinced that Kitty was indeed well.

"I fear it never left," Kitty admitted, blinking at the unwelcome tears which gathered in her eyes. How could she be rid of a headache which was caused by a gentleman who wished to make an offer but from whom she had no desire to receive an offer when the one gentleman who could save her from having to consider the first gentleman would not pay her a bit of attention? Oh, even thinking about it made her head spin and ache nearly as much as her heart.

"I am not Jane," Elizabeth said softly, "but I do know how to listen."

Kitty pulled her lip between her teeth and glanced at Lydia.

"I understand," Elizabeth whispered. "After dinner is finished, we can read in the small drawing room next to Papa's study."

Kitty nodded her agreement. She would go collect her book of sermons as soon as dinner was over and join Elizabeth and most likely Jane in the small drawing room. If any of her sisters could help her with her problem, they could. Mary had no beau, nor did she seem interested in having one. Lydia was far too nonsensical about beaus to be of any use, and when you added to that her dislike of Mr. Collins, she would be quite the opposite of useful. But Elizabeth and Jane? They were both happily attached. They would surely have some good advice for her.

It was not two minutes after Kitty had swallowed that last morsel of apple when Elizabeth caught her father's eye, tipped her head toward the door, and her father dismissed them from the room.

"How do you do that?" Kitty asked Elizabeth as they climbed the stairs.

"Do what?"

"Talk to Papa without words?"

Elizabeth put an arm around Kitty's shoulders. "We know each other well, I suppose. That and Papa is very observant and had been watching you with concern for at least ten minutes before I asked to be allowed to leave."

"He was watching me?" Did he watch her often? She had never noticed.

Elizabeth nodded. "Now, do you wish to read in that drawing room or would you rather join Jane and me in our room?"

It was not an easy question to answer. If they were in Elizabeth's room, there was very little chance any other sister might stumble upon their conversation. However, if they went to the drawing room, she would be able to pass the study and perhaps see Mr. Collins.

"Pardon me." That very gentleman brushed by them.

"How will you be spending your evening?" Elizabeth asked him.

He stopped, turned toward her, and with brows furrowed replied that he intended to spend it in his room. "I have some ledgers to look over, and I am thinking of retiring early." He turned partially away from them and then back. "I also need to decide if I shall return to Hunsford for a short time to see to my things or not. The Earl and your father both wish to know."

"You are thinking of leaving?" Kitty asked.

He nodded. "Only for a short time. Not even long enough to be missed." He gave a small bow and scurried toward his room as if being chased by the devil.

If he were gone even one day, she would miss him. How could he say he would not be gone long enough to be missed?

"He has been acting very oddly today," Kitty muttered as she followed Elizabeth to her room.

"Do you not need your book?" Elizabeth asked with a teasing smile.

"Oh, yes, I do, though I truly doubt I shall be able to read a word."

Elizabeth's brows flicked up quickly, and she leaned toward her sister. "I do not plan to read, but if you have a book, Lydia will ask far fewer questions."

Kitty's eyes grew wide. "Oh, yes, yes, I understand." She hurried to her room, snatched up her book of sermons, and dashed to Elizabeth's room.

"Sit wherever you would like." Elizabeth was unpinning her hair. "I intend to make myself excessively comfortable on the bed. You are welcome to join me. I am certain Jane will."

"What will I do?" Jane asked as she entered the room.

"Join me on the bed for some conversation."

"With pleasure! And what shall we discuss tonight?" Jane asked eagerly.

"Gentlemen, I suspect," Elizabeth said with a small knowing smile for Kitty that caused Kitty's cheeks to flush.

"I do like discussing gentlemen," Jane said with a laugh.

"You are far too much like Mama at times, dear Sister," Elizabeth teased.

"Jane is nothing like Mama," Kitty said.

Elizabeth climbed onto the bed next to Jane and patted the spot next to her in invitation to Kitty. "Jane is very interested in seeing all her sisters well-matched, just as Mama is."

"You are?" Kitty's brows furrowed.

"Yes, indeed, I am. I am afraid I was in danger of pushing Elizabeth at Mr. Darcy if Lizzy had not come to her senses when she did."

"No!" Kitty gasped. Jane pushing anyone in the path of a gentleman seemed very unlike the Jane she knew.

Jane nodded. "I wanted her to be as happy as I was with Mr. Bingley, even if he had not yet offered for me. I knew he would."

"How did you know that?" Kitty relinquished her book to Elizabeth.

Jane shrugged. "He was so solicitous to me that I just knew."

"I did not know you read sermons," Elizabeth interrupted. "I thought it was only Mary who read these." She flipped open the cover. "William Collins?"

Kitty nodded. "He is reading *Evelina* because I suggested it, so I thought it only right that I read one of his books." Her lips puckered, and she sighed. "I do hope he is enjoying *Evelina* more than I am enjoying those." She shook her head. "They are dreadfully dull."

Elizabeth chuckled.

"They are so much better when they are spoken in church rather than read at one's leisure."

"Oh, I can imagine they are!" said Jane. "Why do you not ask Mr. Collins to read them to you? That might make them more bearable. He has, after all, taken orders, so he would know how best to deliver them."

Kitty rolled her eyes upward and shook her head, willing her frustration to not spill down her cheeks, but it would not listen. She swiped at her cheek.

"What is the matter?" Jane had her arms wrapped around Kitty in an instant.

"He has ignored me all evening, and if I cannot get him to like me, then I shall have to give him up and marry Captain Saunders."

She covered her face with her hands. "I do not want to marry Captain Saunders."

Jane squeezed her tight and rubbed her back. "Why would you have to marry Captain Saunders?"

Kitty sniffled and wiped her eyes with the palm of her hand. "Because he is going to ask me tomorrow."

"You do not have to accept an offer just because it is made," said Elizabeth.

"But what other offer will I ever receive?"

Jane sighed. "You are young and beautiful. Many gentlemen will call on you."

"I think the issue is not how many gentlemen will call, but which one, in particular, is currently paying her no attention," said Elizabeth.

"Oh!" Jane released Kitty somewhat and leaning back, looked at her. "You love Mr. Collins?"

Kitty made an indecisive sound and shrugged.

"If you are crying over him not speaking to you at dinner, you love him," said Jane, pulling Kitty back into her embrace. "And I do think he admires you."

"I am not certain he does," Kitty said between fresh tear that fell at the thought of him not admiring her. If this was what love felt like, she was not positive she wished to be in love. She had hoped love would be a warm, comforting feeling that occasionally caused one's heart to race. This, this feeling of utter wretchedness, was neither warm nor comforting.

"I suspect," Elizabeth said, taking Kitty's hand, "that he does not know how to express such a thing. He seems so nervous so often, does he not?"

Kitty nodded. He was very much like that little tomcat, Shadow, who poked his nose out hopefully when someone would enter the inn, but then would scurry away when any children, especially young boys, came too close.

"If you love him," Elizabeth continued, "you may have to tell him."

No. Kitty shook her head. No, she could not do that. She was not brave enough for that!

"Very well," Elizabeth said softly, "then you must, at least, make your admiration clear."

Kitty sighed. Had she not been attempting to do just that? She was certain he was not the sort of gentleman who would be swayed by coy smiles and fluttering lashes. How could she make him understand her admiration other than how she had attempted to make it known?

"Whatever you do," Jane said, "do not accept Captain Saunders's offer of anything. Not even a courtship. If you love Mr. Collins, you will be miserable with anyone else." She leaned back and looked at Kitty once again. "Promise me."

"I promise."

"No matter how disappointed you think your refusal will make Captain Saunders, you must refuse."

Kitty was uncertain she had ever heard Jane speak so adamantly.

"I do not like disappointing people either," Jane said in a much gentler, softer tone, as she squeezed Kitty tight once again. "We are the same that way. But tomorrow, you shall have to be Lizzy."

Kitty could not help but laugh along with Jane at such a thing while Elizabeth scowled and picked up the book of sermons.

"Oh, a page is torn."

"Lydia," said Kitty. "She dislikes Mr. Collins so much and for no reason. He is not what she thinks, but she refuses to see him for who he is."

"Does she know you like Mr. Collins?" Elizabeth asked.

Kitty shook her head. "She asked me before dinner if I did, but I said no."

"An unhappy Lydia is not pleasant," Jane muttered.

"Precisely," Kitty agreed. "If I knew Mr. Collins returned my affections, then I would have told her the truth, but I did not want to make things worse than they are for Mr. Collins." Kitty sighed. "You know he is determined to win her over. He told me so."

"Then, I would expect it to happen," said Elizabeth. "He seems to be very persuasive in his own soft and awkward way."

"He is quite wonderful, is he not?" Kitty asked quietly.

"Indeed, he is," Elizabeth replied. "And you should tell him."

Kitty shook her head. "I cannot."

"Do you remember Celia?" Elizabeth waited until Kitty nodded. "She and I were the best of friends." She smiled and looked off into the distance. "The trouble we caused Mama!" She laughed lightly.

"The last bit of trouble we caused was just before I went to Aunt Gardiner's house and Celia...well..." She drew a breath. "It was just before Celia died. We had been out wandering and come across a large puddle because it had been raining for three days. Celia dared me to jump over it. I told her that I would if she did, so she did. She leapt over it with ease. But when I made my attempt, she startled me by yelling something about a bird in its nest with babies. I landed in the middle of the puddle. My pride was hurt more than my backside, and I assure you, my backside was very sore.

"Mama was furious to have my skirts so soiled and refused to allow me to have dessert with my dinner as a result. I was angry with Celia for a full two days. I did not go to call on her. I did not even write her a note in our friends journal before retiring for the night each night as I always did. I left her one small, half-hearted note on the morning before I was to leave for town. She would keep the journal while I was gone, and I would write to her from town." Elizabeth paused and sighed. "I never got to write another note to her in that journal. It was destroyed in the accident, and her father burned it. I never apologized for being angry with her."

She turned to Kitty. "I have been thinking about Celia a great deal lately. In fact, I was just telling Mr. Darcy about her today when he called." She smiled and took up Kitty's hand again. "Do not let pride or fear or anything else keep you from telling those you love that you love them. Promise me?"

Kitty nodded.

"Good, now tell Jane when you first suspected you liked Mr. Collins as more than a cousin, for I am certain she is dying to know."

Jane picked up the pillow next to her and swatted a laughing Elizabeth with it. "As if I am the only one!" she cried.

After a few more minutes of laughter, all three girls calmed.

"I think I noticed something about him from the very first moment I met him, but I did not begin to suspect we could be good friends or possibly more until Papa sent me to help him find a book in the study."

# Chapter 11

Collins straightened his brown jacket and his simply-tied cravat before answering the knock at the door to his room.

"What are you wearing?" Bingley demanded as he entered the room.

Collins looked down at himself. "A brown suit of clothes." Was that not apparent?

Bingley scowled. "Let me rephrase." He shook his head and muttered. "You and Darcy. So literal." His left brow rose imperiously. "Why are you dressed all in brown?"

"I like brown. It suits me." Dull, unobtrusive, easily ignored.

Bingley folded his arms. "No, it does not. Brown with a touch of red in your waistcoat suits you much better."

Collins shrugged. "Perhaps tomorrow."

The statement was met with a sigh of resignation, or was it disappointment, from his tutor. It did not matter. In just a few hours, his failure would be complete. Kitty would be promised to another and would never be his. He had spent the majority of the night resigning himself to that fact. Last night was the only time in his life he wished he could drink as much as his father had.

"I am given to understand," said Darcy from the chair in which he reclined, "that you spent the full night in your chamber after steadfastly ignoring Miss Kitty during dinner." He shrugged when Collins turned to him in surprise. "I saw Elizabeth."

Collins shook his head and rolled his eyes toward the ceiling. Of course, that was why Elizabeth had questioned him last night. He should have known.

"I think I will go to Hunsford for a few days," he said, ignoring any implied question which Darcy's comments held. "It would be good to bid my farewells to the congregation in person. Has your uncle selected my replacement?"

Darcy nodded. "He has. The man is set to take up his post two days before Christmas." He unbuttoned his jacket and crossed his ankles. "Ignoring Miss Kitty was not what we discussed. You were to engage her in conversation during dinner and make yourself available in the study after."

"I am not Captain Saunders," Collins replied. "Now, shall we proceed to the study?"

"I do not have the pleasure of understanding your meaning," Darcy said, not moving from his relaxed position.

Collins walked first to the dressing table, then the window. Admitting his failure to himself last evening had been challenging. Admitting it to his friends, whom he admired greatly, was nearly impossible. It was not that he was necessarily a proud creature, but he was a man. And like any man whom he knew, he did not like to be found wanting. He shook his head. How many times had he been told he was wanting? Far too many to recall the exact number. He should find it much easier than he did, given all that practice.

"Saunders applied to Mr. Bennet for permission to present a courtship to Miss Kitty."

"I still do not see how that means you must forego the waistcoat with red in it," grumbled Bingley.

"A red coat, not a red waistcoat, would serve me better," Collins retorted.

"An offer does not mean an acceptance," Darcy inserted. "Elizabeth did not accept me the first time I presented my request."

"Precisely!" Bingley said, waving his hand toward Darcy. "Have you told Miss Kitty that you admire her?"

Collins swallowed. "That was not part of my instruction."

He looked anywhere but at Bingley or Darcy. He had never stood in opposition to any of his instructors — ever — in all of his life. He had never even attempted to oppose his father. He had been as accommodating as possible, even taking responsibility for failures that were not his own.

"It is now." Bingley stood directly before him with the red waistcoat in his hand. "Tell her you admire her or wear this, and do not go to Hunsford. Fight for her, man!"

Collins stared at the red waistcoat, then shook his head. "I do not know how to fight." His words were barely above a whisper.

"Then wear the waistcoat, and allow us to help you," said Darcy.

Collins paused at the offer. He was not sure that even Darcy could help him win Kitty at present, but his heart would not allow him to give up without one more attempt, so he nodded and shrugged out of his jacket.

Bingley looked exorbitantly pleased as he handed the preferred garment to Collins.

"You look presentable," Darcy said as Bingley was smoothing the back of Mr. Collins's jacket at the shoulders. "We are not adjusting the cravat," he warned his friend, who huffed but said nothing. "Shall we?" He held the door open.

"Where are we going?" Collins asked before moving toward the door. He had no desire to be anywhere near where Captain Saunders might be presenting his offer to Kitty.

"The study," Darcy replied. "But eventually, we will have to darken the door to the sitting room. There are some very pretty ladies within it who will be expecting us." He smiled broadly.

Collins felt an unwelcome pang of jealousy at Darcy's happiness. It was something he would likely never have. "We are not going there first?"

"Not even if that is what Bingley would prefer," Darcy replied with a chuckle as his friend once again huffed. "For an amiable fellow, he does enjoy pushing his friends beyond their limits. Never, and I do mean *never*, tell him you dislike dancing, for he will be as adamant about seeing you dance as he is about cravats and waistcoats."

Bingley shrugged. "I neither understand why anyone would not want to wear a dashing set of clothes nor how someone can dislike dancing."

"And so, he is determined to educate us unfortunates," Darcy muttered. "At least your wearing a red waistcoat does not require you to stand up for a set of dances with his sister."

"Did Miss Bingley join you today?" Collins asked. Caroline Bingley and her sister Louisa did not call very often. They usually made their appearance once per week, stayed for a quarter hour, and departed.

"Thankfully, no," Bingley replied. "My sisters are still not pleased to be adding the Bennets to our family, although I think that is due to the fact that Darcy has also joined himself to the Bennets."

Collins had heard several tales about the ambitions of Caroline Bingley. "She will attend the season?" he asked.

"As soon as possible," Bingley replied.

"She will do well," Collins added. "She is beautiful, and beauty is often all that is required." He gasped. "It is not that I am saying all she has to her credit is her beauty," he added.

Bingley laughed, obviously not offended in the least. "No, she has her fortune." He tipped his head and pushed the door to the study open. "And very little else," he muttered as Collins passed him.

"Surely, she possesses some good qualities," Collins said. "They are currently just well-hidden behind ambition," he added.

"You, my friend, are wise beyond your years," Bingley said with a chuckle.

"Mr. Lucas," Collins said in surprise as he realized that Mr. Bennet was not alone.

"Mr. Collins," the man replied with a small bow. "Mr. Bingley, Mr. Darcy."

"It seems our Mary is slyer than I thought possible." Mr. Bennet looked from one gentleman to another. "It also appears I am the last to know this."

"We were sworn to secrecy," Bingley said as he took a seat. "We were not supposed to know."

Mr. Bennet's head bobbed up and down. "That is understandable."

"And it was Mr. Collins who remonstrated me for my part in the affair," Mr. Lucas added. "He encouraged me to come to you."

Mr. Bennet smiled at Collins. "You shall do very well in my stead if you are willing to call out not only Mr. Lucas but also Mr. Goulding. Lucas is a fine chap, but Goulding is a bit of trouble. Too high in the step for my liking."

"Yes, sir," said Mr. Lucas in reply to the stern look he received from Mr. Bennet. "I will do my best to lead him right. Much as Mr. Collins has done for me. I thank you –"

Whatever else he was about to say was lost to the door of the study flying open and Mrs. Bennet entering with Kitty in tow and both Lydia and Mary close behind. "Mr. Bennet, you must make Kitty accept Captain Saunders."

"Must I?" The gentleman replied, looking past his wife to his daughter, who was shaking her head.

"Yes, you must!" Mrs. Bennet pushed Kitty forward. "An officer! She refused an officer!" The words were spoken as if refusing an officer were tantamount to refusing the king.

Collins watched Kitty. Her cheeks were understandably red, but instead of looking down in embarrassment, she held her chin high, and he could see her determination in her eyes.

"Am I to understand that you do not wish to eventually become the good captain's wife?" Her father asked her.

"I do not," she replied. "Not now, not ever."

Collins's heart skipped a beat. He had not yet failed. There was still a chance he could persuade her to like him if she were not attached to Captain Saunders.

"Have you heard a more ridiculous thing?" her mother cried. "What will she do if she does not marry the captain? It is not right that Mr. Collins will have to see to her care if there is never another offer! It is bad enough he will be stuck with Mary."

Mr. Bennet chuckled. "I do not think Mary will remain unmarried, will you, Mary?"

Mary stepped forward sheepishly. "No," she answered uneasily, looking at her father, then Mr. Lucas, and back to her father, who nodded, causing her to smile. "No, I believe I shall marry."

"Indeed?" Mrs. Bennet's brows rose with her voice. "Who shall marry you? You would not even attempt to win Mr. Collins."

Mary looked at Collins and smiled. It was the first time he had ever received anything other than a scowl from the lady.

"Mr. Collins does not want me, Mama," she said as if it were just a matter of routine to make such declarations, "but Mr. Lucas does."

Mrs. Bennet's mouth opened and closed and opened again as her hand flew to her heart. "Mr. Lucas?" she finally squeaked.

"Yes, my dear, I just gave the young man permission to present his offer, which it seems will be accepted with alacrity," Mr. Bennet replied.

"Oh."

Mrs. Bennet seemed completely and utterly lost for words, and for a moment, Collins feared she might swoon. He thought to move, take her arm, and lead her to chair, but since no one else, particularly not Mr. Bennet, seemed concerned, he did not. Instead, he stayed where he was and shifted his eyes back to Kitty. How she could withstand the mortification of having herself presented in such a fashion before so many, he could not fathom. She was apparently as strong as she was gentle.

"Now, Kitty, my dear," her father said, "was there a particular reason for your refusal of Captain Saunders? He seemed a respectable sort of fellow."

Kitty's chin rose just a touch higher. "He is a fine gentleman," she began.

"Who looks quite dashing in his uniform," her father added, causing Kitty to scowl.

"His uniform?" she cried. "Why must I accept someone simply because he wears a uniform? He will not wear it all his life, and then what am I to do when he is no longer dashing. There must be some commonality, some shared interest, and there is none."

"Those things come with time," Mrs. Bennet cajoled.

Kitty pulled her arm away from her mother. "I want to marry a gentleman whom I know shares my interests or is willing to at least explore them, and I will gladly do the same for him. I do not want to just be the lady on his arm, Mama." She turned her eyes toward Collins. "I want to be the lady sitting next to him in his study, reading or talking or just...sitting because he makes me feel at ease."

Was she speaking of wishing to marry him?

"But Captain Saunders is so handsome in his uniform," her mother tried once more.

Kitty huffed but did not turn her eyes away from Collins. Then, with a small stamp of her foot, she said, "I do not wish for an officer. I would rather marry a gentleman in a parson's frock or a well-worn brown jacket than any man in a uniform," before she left the room.

Collins looked down at his jacket – a well-worn brown jacket. The right side of his mouth tipped up in a small smirk. She wanted him.

"William," Mr. Bennet said softly, drawing Collins's attention. "Go get her, Son."

# Chapter 12

Lydia caught Kitty by the arm just as Collins reached the bottom of the stairs. He wanted to rush up the stairs himself just as Lydia had done, but he did not. Instead, he waited where he was, impatient to speak to Kitty, but not wanting to interrupt Lydia. The girl liked him so little as it was, there was no need to give her more reason for her dislike.

"You like Mr. Collins?" Lydia demanded of her sister.

Kitty turned, and seeing him at the bottom of the steps, smiled and shook her head. "No, I love him."

She loved him? Oh, he was a fortunate fellow! How? He did not care. That she loved him was his only thought.

"Love him?" Lydia cried. "But when I asked you last night you said you did not like him, that you were only being kind."

That was a good point. He had heard that as well when passing Kitty's door on his way to dinner. It was why he had been so confident that Kitty would accept Captain Saunders.

Kitty's head dipped. "I lied because you have been abominable to him, and I did not want to be the reason for your behaving even worse toward him."

Ah, so that was it. She was thinking of him even then. Lying might not be right, but her reason seemed noble.

Lydia gasped, clearly affronted by such a suggestion that she would behave as Kitty said. "If I knew you liked him, then I would have been pleasant."

To Collins, Kitty did not look as if she believed that. And for good reason, most likely.

"Truly," Lydia insisted. "If you love him and he loves you, then he would never turn Mama or me out of our home. You would not let him. Therefore, I would be free to be pleasant."

Kitty shook her head and took her sister's hands. "I would not have to stop him from turning you out of your home. He is good and kind and loving, Lydia. If you would just put away the foolish notion that he is here to steal your home, you would see it. He would never, never turn you out."

He had waited long enough.

"Not even if your sister had accepted Captain Saunders and left me to grow old and lonely without her." Collins climbed the few steps that stood between them.

Lydia's slowly turned toward him, eyes wide. "You would not?"

He shook his head. "You are my family, and I shall always care for you, even if you do not care for me."

Lydia's brows furrowed. "Truly?"

He nodded. "Even if you were disagreeable."

"No." Lydia shook her head. "No one is kind to disagreeable people."

"Mr. Collins is," Kitty said. "He has not been harsh with you at all. Not once, and you deserved to be spoken to crossly on several occasions."

The replying scowl Lydia wore did not hide the fact that she did not appreciate being reprimanded. She turned to him again.

"Do you love Kitty?"

A smile spread across his face of its own accord. "With all that I am."

"And you will not send me away?"

He shook his head. "Not until you marry, which shall not be for a few years."

Lydia gasped. "A few years? I shall marry sooner than that!"

"Only for the deepest of affection and respect," Kitty scolded. "It is not a thing to be rushed into."

Again, Lydia scowled. "You sound very much like Jane, and I do not wish to be scolded." She turned and with a flick of her head scampered down the stairs, leaving Kitty and Collins alone, or as alone as one might be while on the stairs in the middle of a busy home full of people.

"You love me?" Kitty asked shyly.

Collins moved up to stand next to her, then taking her hand, drew her down to sit beside him on the steps while he assured her that he did indeed love her.

"However, I never thought you would return my affections," he admitted.

"Why would you think that?" She lifted the hand that held hers and kissed it. "Are you well?" she asked when he did not answer her query.

"I have never been kissed before," he said softly.

Her eyes grew wide. "What? Never?"

He shook his head.

"Not even on your hand or your cheek?"

He could well imagine how something like that could cause her to be so shocked. Her family was not like his.

"My father was an unpleasant, angry man, who saw no need for such softness," he explained. "It would make his son less of a man to have such frivolous emotions such as love running rampant in his mind." He smiled at her soft gasp. "It is difficult to imagine when your father is as good as yours is, but those were the very words my father used when dismissing a maid, without a letter, who had come to comfort me after I fell and cut my leg. I was ten, and at that moment, I determined that I would never be like my father, not because I did not possess the ability to be as he was, but because I chose to be better." He shrugged. "I had to bear a great deal of reproof for being weak, for weakness is what my father called kindness."

"How horrible," Kitty held his hand to her heart and then, after a moment's pause, released it before leaning over to kiss him on the cheek. "You could never be like him. Your heart is too good."

His face grew warm both from the kiss and her words of praise.

"Why did you think I would never love you?" she asked.

"Because you are all that a young lady should be — kind, beautiful, gentle, graceful, and so at ease with everyone – and I am... Well, look at me. I am large and not at all handsome. And I speak too much."

"Only when you are nervous or when you forget to be nervous." She smoothed the hair from his forehead when he looked at her quizzically. "I like hearing you talk when you forget to be nervous. You look so happy when you do. I imagine that is how you must look when giving a sermon."

"I could not say." She liked listening to him ramble?

"And you are handsome," she said with a smile. "Your hair is just the right shade of brown, as are your eyes. They are not so dark as most, but rather unusual I should think, and perfectly suited to you."

"They are ordinary," he declared.

"Not to me," she said firmly, "and I do know a lot about how people look. I have not seen eyes so golden."

He was not at all certain he believed her, but he wanted to. Therefore, he allowed it to be so.

"I am still large and awkward, and I do not always know how to act."

"You perform beautifully," she replied, wrapping her arm around his and leaning into his side. "And I like tall gentlemen with broad shoulders. You are even taller and have broader shoulders than any of the officers I have met. It is quite a lovely distinction."

Again, he was not certain she was right, but he wanted her to be. Therefore, he allowed it to be so.

"I shall continue to tell you until you believe it," she said softly. "For it is true. I would never, ever lie to you. I could not, for it would break my heart to disappoint you."

He drew a slow deep breath and released it just as slowly. For two minutes, they sat in silence with her head leaning on his shoulder in a most comforting way. She accepted him as he was. He did not need to be anything more or less than what he had always been. However, he knew that with her at his side, he would always strive to be more and not less.

Finally, he broke the silence. "I cannot promise to ever be more than I am. I shall likely always speak too much. I do not know if I shall ever come to love novels as you do, but I shall attempt to like them. *Evelina* is very good, so it is entirely possible that I will come to love novels as much as poetry or sermons." He pressed his lips together. In the middle of making an offer of marriage was not the time to begin rambling.

However, she did not seem to mind as she was smiling up at him, waiting patiently, when he looked down at her.

"I can only promise," he continued, "to love you with every ounce of my strength until my dying breath if you will allow me to be your husband." He shook his head. "No, that is not right. I shall love you whether you marry me or not. I shall just be infinitely happier if you marry me and not someone else."

She looked at him silently, her clear blue as a deep lake on summer's day eyes filled with expectation.

His brows furrowed. Why was she not answering? Was this not where she was supposed to answer his question? His eyes grew wide. "Forgive me, I forgot the most important part. Will you marry me?"

"Yes."

It was one small word, spoken in a soft, sweet lilt, but it was filled with so much – love, acceptance, trust, understanding – so many things that had seemed just outside of his reach all his life until this moment.

He rose and pulled her to her feet. "I should tell you that I have not practiced hugging anyone, so I might be rather bad at it."

She giggled. "You cannot be bad at hugging."

"I might be. I did not think to ask Mr. Bingley or Mr. Darcy about this," he muttered. It was an oversight, perhaps, but not an intentional one. He had been so focused on just persuading her to like him that he had not considered anything beyond that. Marriage was his goal, but he had not thought he would be where he was so quickly.

She stepped up one step so that she was closer to being his height. "Just wrap your arms around me. Like this." She took his hands and drew them around her waist before she wrapped her arms around his neck. "You can pull me closer," she whispered.

"I have never kissed anyone," he whispered back, "but I should very much like to kiss you." Having her here in his arms was causing all sorts of new and unusual feelings and desires. It was delightful. She was so soft, and she smelled like flowers. He'd never be able to walk through a garden again without thinking of her and how she felt here in his arms. He pulled her closer as she had suggested, and his lips tipped into a smirk. It was a good suggestion. Closer was even better.

"Then kiss me," she said. "And I will not know if you are doing it well or badly for I have never kissed a gentleman."

His smirk grew into a smile. "That is very good to know." Tentatively, he bent his head and pressed his lips against hers. They were as soft as the rest of her. To his delight and surprise, he discovered that the Good Lord must have created him knowing how to kiss, for the thrill of that first touch seemed to take over his senses as he pressed her more firmly against him and claimed her mouth with all the passion that first thrill had aroused.

# Epilogue

One year, seven months, and two weeks after Collins's proposal had been accepted on the staircase on what he now referred to as a glorious December day, the flowers in Longbourn's garden were displaying their finest colours as the Bennet family walked its paths.

"Your roses are coming along nicely," Mrs. Bennet said as she came to stand next to Mr. Collins.

He had received as a wedding gift a small rose bush from Hunsford's garden by Lady Catherine, and it now bore lovely small white buds.

"They are nearly as good as mine," Mrs. Bennet added.

Collins smiled at his mother-in-law. "I should be honoured if they were ever half as good as yours, madame."

She had every right to be proud of her garden. Her roses were fragrant and robust, producing beautiful flowers which were excellent for cutting.

She giggled and swatted the words away. "You are a flatterer, Mr. Collins."

"No, madame, I am not. As the psalmist says, 'The Lord shall cut off all flattering lips,' and so I do not flatter. Your roses are the finest I have seen, and when mine are half as good as yours, in due time, I shall be honoured to be compared in such a fashion."

"I think you flatter," Mrs. Bennet repeated. "But not in a bad way, of course," she added. "You would never do that."

Collins had learned that while his mother-in-law was not the most astute of women, she had a heart that cared deeply for all her family, even him. She had welcomed him as a son most heartily just moments after she had left her husband's study on the day he had been fortunate enough to have secured Kitty's hand. She, even now, proudly presented him to one and all as her son.

"And a sly one he was. Loving my Kitty but not letting on a word. Not a single word," she would say. This would often be followed by a list of things he had accomplished since arriving at Longbourn – books he had read, tenants he had visited, improvements that were planned. She even proudly proclaimed his vegetables to be some of the best to have graced her table.

It had taken her some time to come to accept that a gentleman and master of an estate would wish to soil his hands with such a hobby as planting vegetables. However, he had assured her it was beneficial to knowing how best to keep crops producing and that knowledge would help the estate.

And it *had* been helpful in his education of how things grew and what needed to be done for best yields. The estate's income had increased – not substantially, but enough for him to be able to provide a very special gift for his wife on this her nineteenth birthday.

"Do not touch that!" Mrs. Bennet cried with alarm as a small hand reached toward the rosebush they had just been admiring. She crouched down. "It will poke you, Thomas. You mustn't touch your papa's roses. We shall find other flowers for you to pick for your mama." She scooped up her grandson and moved toward the lilac bush, declaring how much better picking some of those flowers would be as there were so many and not a thorn upon the bush.

Kitty wound her arm around her husband's and lay her head on his upper arm just below his shoulder. It was their favorite way to stroll through the garden. "What shall Mama do when there are two to claim her attention?" she asked.

"I suppose one day we shall discover that," Collins replied.

"Yes, one day in late December or early in the new year," Kitty said, causing her husband to stop mid-stride.

"You mean?"

Kitty nodded. "I do. I have felt the quickening."

"Oh, my love!" he cried, pulling her into his embrace and kissing her while paying no heed to the others who were in the garden with them. "Children are a heritage of the Lord," he said as he released her.

"And happy is the man that hath his quiver full of them," she replied with smile.

"You have been reading the Psalms again?"

"Oh, indeed, I have. They are very good. I only wish I had known that the scriptures contained such poetry when I was younger. I should have eagerly devoured them then as I do now."

"Are they as good as a novel?" he teased.

She bit her lip. "I cannot truthfully say I enjoy them more than a novel."

He pulled her close to him. "That is perfectly acceptable."

"They are far better than sermons — unless you are reading

them to me." She sighed. "I do like listening to you, even when my mind will no longer take heed of the meaning of the words."

"I am blessed," he murmured. Blessed seemed too small a word for how his fortune had been changed, but he could think of no better word, so he left his statement at that. That in and of itself was a blessing. His words no longer ran away with him as often as they used to, but then, he had never felt the security of belonging anywhere before he had come to Longbourn and married Kitty.

"It is time for cake and tea," Lydia informed them. "Make haste, for no one can eat until you get there, Kitty, since it is your birthday."

Lydia had changed and only for the better as far as Collins was concerned. He had worried that she might cause him much consternation with her love of gentlemen and flirting, but one short season in town had cured her of that. Unfortunately, it had come in the form of a disappointment in love. For that, he felt sorry. However, all was not lost. There was a young gentleman who had written to him just last week, requesting to be allowed to visit.

Bingley and Darcy had assured him that the gentleman in question was of good moral fabric and well set both with land and funds. So, Collins had only yesterday sent off the invitation for the young gentleman to visit. From what he had been able to gather from his wife as well as Jane, at whose house Lydia had stayed while in town in February, the admiration of Lydia for this gentleman was not small. Therefore, Collins was hopeful that there would soon be one final Bennet sister happily matched.

He held the chair for his wife as she took a seat at the table which had been laid out in the garden.

At another smaller table, four nursemaids sat with their young charges. One maid for each of the four babies. Bingley's daughter had found her footing early and was dancing at the end of her leading stings, while Darcy's daughter, as well as Mary's son, sat on their nurses' knees. Thomas Collins was still clutching a bouquet of lilac and tasting them now and again as his nursemaid rose and carried him to the table to present his mama with the well-slobbered gift. Then, he and his nurse returned to their table and waited — impatiently — to be allowed to eat cake.

Collins stood at the head of the table, his wife sat on his right, his mother-in-law sat one chair down on his left as an empty place had been left in honour of the man who had given life to the lady celebrating her birth.

Mr. Bennet had seen his four eldest daughters married and beginning their families before he had slipped from this world to the next one night the previous spring.

Collins looked at that chair and silently lifted his glass in salute as the others followed suit. Then after a sip of his wine, he cleared his throat and began the small speech he had prepared, albeit with a small adjustment having just heard Kitty's news.

"We gather today to celebrate the lady who is not just at my right hand but is my right hand, my completion, the helpmeet of God's provision. She is a loving daughter and sister, as well as an excellent wife and a mother who is a blessing to her children." He paused and smiled. "I say children instead of child, for, in December, Thomas will be joined by a sibling."

There was a great deal of cheering and congratulations that followed the statement. Mrs. Bennet found it necessary to consume a quantity of her wine to accept such excellent news.

When everyone had settled into silence again — save for the

children, who still waited for their cake — Collins began again. "I would like to ask you to lift your glasses in honour of this lovely lady, but first I must tell you why we are gathered here in this corner of the garden near the back of the house." He drew a breath. "It is on this spot that we shall, in time, be sitting inside a conservatory."

Kitty gasped, her hand flying to her mouth.

"My wife loves many things, and one of those is flowers. The Lord has prospered us, and I have commissioned the building of a conservatory, so she can grow flowers even when the garden has gone dormant. She and her family – each of you – have brought such joy to me and given me a life I never would have expected to have. I had a father, but I had no family until I arrived here at Longbourn. The growth which takes place in this conservatory – each new life – shall be a reminder to me of you all, but most particularly of my wife."

He raised his glass. "To my wife, Kitty Collins."

"To Kitty," the other repeated.

"And," Darcy said, rising, "to her husband, the Master of Longbourn."

"Here! Here!" cried Bingley, followed by a rousing reply from everyone gathered...

"To the Master of Longbourn."

# Assessing Mr. Darcy

*Will her brother's opinion keep her from finding true love?*

# Chapter 1

Elizabeth Bennet leaned against one of the oak trees that grew on the hill near the edge of Longbourn's property. Taking out her spyglass, she settled in to watch.

Overhead the brilliant reds, yellows, and oranges were still mixed with a few traces of green, and normally at this time of year, she would sit beneath one or another of these trees and attempt to paint their splendor. The feat usually ended with her applying paint to the leaves and pressing them on her paper. Her desire to capture beauty far outshone her ability. Her future home would not be filled with her own creations. Instead, she would have to rely on purchased paintings, or perhaps, she could convince her younger sister Kitty to produce a few pieces for her. Kitty was the most artistic of her four sisters.

Today, however, observing the leaves above was but a peripheral pleasure, for today, she had far more interesting things at which to peer. Netherfield had been let at last!

The grand home with its park that abutted this very edge of Longbourn's property was to welcome a young unmarried gentleman and his sisters. One sister, she had been told by her uncle was similar in age to her. It would be a pleasure to have another lady in the neighbourhood. She smiled. Especially a lady with a wealthy brother in want of a wife.

"What are you doing?"

Elizabeth jumped, nearly dropping her spyglass. "Why must you insist on startling me, William?"

William Bennet smirked. "Because it is so delightful to see you jump."

"It is because I can do sums better than you." Had Elizabeth's hair not been secured under her bonnet, it would have flipped quite satisfactorily as she turned her head.

"Yes, well, you inherited your father's keen mind, and I am stuck with my father's dull one." He stood next to her on her left and leaned against the tree trunk.

Elizabeth lifted the spyglass and looked toward Netherfield as her heart pricked her. Finally, after no more than two minutes of silence, she turned to him. "You have had Papa to guide you, and you have done well. I should not have been so cruel as to point out something with which you struggle. But you do vex me at times. I do not appreciate having the working of my heart tested on such a regular basis simply because you are light of foot."

He shrugged. "And I should not startle you, but we both know that I will continue to tease, and you will continue to retaliate with the one thing you do better than I."

Elizabeth's brows rose. "One thing?"

He laughed. "The one thing I will allow that you do better than me."

"I dance better than you."

"Very well. I will admit that you do two things better than me, but I will not admit to anything further. A brother must feel at least marginally superior to his younger sister."

Elizabeth allowed it to be. He was not her brother by birth. He had been born William Collins, a distant cousin to her father. However, even at birth, he had been far more important to her family than just some cousin. It did not matter that her father and his father had not spoken to one another in years. William Collins was the heir to Longbourn since her father had never produced a son.

It had been years — fifteen, to be precise — since William had arrived with his few bags and his poor manners and lack of learning on Longbourn's steps. His father had died, and since there was no nearer relation, and since he was the heir to Mr. Bennet's estate, the child had been delivered with all his worldly possessions to them, to be their son and brother.

He had been ten, and after six months of living with them, he had asked if he too could be a Bennet. Her father had willingly obliged, excessively pleased to have someone bear his name who would not be giving that name away before a parson in a marriage ceremony.

A carriage approaching Netherfield, brought Elizabeth back from her reverie, and she focused her glass to look as closely at it as she could. She could not see much detail, but the equipage did appear to be very fine, almost regal.

"A carriage," she said, handing the spyglass to William.

William adjusted the glass for his use and whistled. "This Bingley fellow is not shallow in the pockets, is he?"

"I dare say he is not," Elizabeth agreed. "Give the glass back when they have stopped. I want to see how the grooms and driver tend to their passengers."

William laughed. "You do not. You wish to see if Mr. Bingley is as handsome as he is rumoured to be." He looked through the glass once more. "There is a second carriage." He handed the glass to her. "You will want to see this one."

"Why?" she asked, positioning herself to be able to look at the second carriage.

"You will know when you see it."

"Oh, my!" She looked at William. "Does Mr. Bingley have two carriages, one that is lovely and another that could carry the Prince Regent?"

William shook his head. "I would venture a guess that he has not come alone."

"A friend?"

"That would be my assumption. A very wealthy guest."

"Do you suppose it is a gentleman?"

William laughed. "Yes. A single gentleman is not going to bring some fancy lady with him."

"Why not?" Elizabeth made a face at her brother. "He has sisters. It could be a friend of theirs."

She scowled at the look of disbelief on William's face. It was his way of questioning her ability to reason things, and she hated it. Not because it was a hideous face or anything like that, but because he never used that expression except when she had not thought things through properly. She despised being wrong.

He leaned near her ear as she watched the carriages approach the house. "He could be bringing his mistress. I hear many of the wealthy men from town have them."

"Oh, for heaven's sake, William! You must stop reading the society paper and listening to Lydia. And please refrain from speaking to me of such things. They really are reprehensible. Mary is not wrong about that."

Mary, the third eldest Bennet daughter, was a very serious sort of young woman who loved nothing better than to study books of etiquette and when she had none of those, she scoured sermons. Their father teased that if Mary did not marry, she would be the most sought-after governess in all the land, for her knowledge of how a young lady should or should not present herself was of superior quality.

Lydia, the youngest Bennet, was the opposite of everything Mary was. Lydia loved to laugh and found sport in most things. She was also fond of presenting herself as a less-than-proper young lady. Elizabeth wished her father would do more to correct such behaviour, but he seemed incapable of scolding Lydia as severely as she sometimes deserved. Lydia was the baby. Lydia was young. Lydia meant no harm.

Even William tolerated Lydia's behaviour more than he should, though he, at least, would scowl before chuckling at her antics.

"Do you see Mr. Bingley?"

Elizabeth pushed him away. Or more precisely she attempted to push him away from hanging over her shoulder. But William was a large fellow, sturdy, strong, and tall. She would have had just as much hope of pushing the oak over as she had of moving William if he did not wish to be moved, and at present, he did not wish to be moved.

"Not yet."

"I will have you know that I know more about town and in

what sorts of devious behavior some gentlemen participate than is found in the papers."

If Elizabeth were not so focused on not missing Mr. Bingley's arrival, she would have rolled her eyes. "Yes, I know. You learned many things at university. Not all of them useful."

He chuckled. "There you are wrong."

She turned toward him. "How is knowing about mistresses and cockfights and all the rest useful?"

"I have five sisters to see well-matched. You do not think I am going to house you all forever, do you?"

She swung her arm to her side and smacked him in the stomach with a satisfying thud.

He bent forward. "I meant to say you are all far too pretty to remain unattached."

"I thought so," Elizabeth replied. "Oh, the carriage doors are opening."

She watched as a gentleman helped a lady out of the first carriage and wrapped her arm around his. That must be the sister who was married and her husband. The gentleman who was likely Mr. Bingley exited next.

"What does he look like?"

"Very handsome." She held the glass out to William but did not let go of it. She still needed to see the other sister and whomever it was in that second coach.

William whistled.

"What?" Elizabeth pulled the glass back and looked.

"She's a beauty." There was a hint of admiration in William's voice that Elizabeth rarely heard.

"Prettier than Charlotte?"

"Yes. And stop trying to match me with your friend."

Elizabeth lifted and lowered one shoulder. "You cannot disagree that joining the prominence of our family with that of Sir Williams' would not be a good alliance."

"And are you going to marry for the advantage of the match?"

He knew perfectly well she was not. "I am not the heir. You have a duty to the estate."

"To sire a son as well as seeing that the tenants are well and my own domain does not crumble around me. That is my duty. That does not require me to marry for advantage, and if it did, Charlotte has very little money. Estates run best with funds, not titles and prestige."

Elizabeth shot him an annoyed look. "Do not forget you must take care of Mama. Charlotte gets on well with Mama, and Charlotte is very good with figures."

She knew that smirk he wore and prepared herself to hear something that would likely perturb her further.

"Yes, but I would prefer a figure like that," he pointed toward Netherfield, "and not like Miss Lucas's."

"Charlotte is pretty!"

"I did not say she was not. But she is two years older than me, and to be blunt, she dresses like a spinster."

"She does not! She likes greys and browns."

Elizabeth only received a huff in reply.

"Oh, my!" she said as the occupant of the second carriage climbed out of his equipage. "He is tall." And handsome.

"Who is?" William pulled the glass away from her. "I think I am taller."

"But not so handsome," Elizabeth teased.

"I should hope my sister does not find me overly handsome. Just handsome enough to recommend me to her friends – both the old and new ones. You are planning to be friendly to the new neighbours, are you not?"

Elizabeth shrugged. "If they are tolerable, yes."

"They are tolerable," William insisted.

"You have not met them."

"I have seen enough to know that I wish them to be tolerable. How about you? We are still hoping Mr. Bingley will suit for Jane, are we not?"

Elizabeth nodded. "Of course, it is best if the eldest marries first. And Jane is such a sweet girl. She deserves to be happy and," she grimaced, for she knew what teasing was to follow when she added the last word, "wealthy."

William laughed heartily.

"But only if she loves him, and he loves her. I would not see Jane in a loveless marriage for all the gold in the empire," Elizabeth added quickly, speaking above the continued laughter. "She should have an army of servants to make her life easy because she is the most caring of us all."

She swung her arm again and smacked him. It was the most effective way to get him to be serious. He may not have been born to her father, and he may not have the same quick wit, but William had adopted her father's sense of humor quite readily.

"You'll never snare a husband if they find out how violent you are, Lizzy Bennet." He rubbed his abdomen. "But I agree. Jane deserves the best. You all do. You have done so much for me."

Elizabeth wrapped her arm around his. "What have we done for you?" She nodded toward the path, and they began the long walk back to Longbourn House from the oak tree.

"You took me in. You allowed me to have your name, and you have accepted me as a brother. You never treated me as less than you."

Elizabeth squeezed his arm more tightly. "How else were we to treat you? We had no attic room in which to lock you."

He chuckled. "Yes, well, I know the word is not one we use often, but I love you and Jane and Mary and Kitty and Lydia and our parents. See, you allow me to call your mother and father my mother and father. Not everyone would do that."

Elizabeth smiled up at him before resting her head against his shoulder. "Find me a gentleman as tall as you so that my head will fit just below his shoulder just as it does on you."

"And you will assist me in finding a lady to my liking?"

"Is your liking Charlotte?"

"No."

Elizabeth sighed dramatically. "I suppose, if I must." She peeked up at him again. "Miss Bingley?"

"If she is not too dreadful or already attached to that tall, hand-some fellow." He nudged her with the arm she held. "If she is attached to the friend, do you think you could attempt to per-suade him to like you enough to not like her?"

"If I cannot, perhaps Lydia could," Elizabeth teased. Lydia was an expert at flirting.

"No."

Elizabeth looked up at him, her brow furrowed. He never spoke so firmly about Lydia. He was more likely to give Lydia what she wished than deny it.

"She is too young," he answered her unspoken question. "She should not be properly out until next year, and even then, she will be too young." He sighed. "Some of you must marry soon. I really cannot look out for all of you and keep Lydia from destruction."

"Destruction?" The word leapt from Elizabeth's lips.

"The militia will be arriving soon."

Ah! Now, William's position made sense to Elizabeth. Lydia loved any gentleman in a fine suit of clothes who carried himself in a gallant fashion. A uniform and a soldier's swagger would be an even more tempting treat.

He blew out a breath. "But enough of that. I am still a young man. Father has not departed, and there is hope that both you and Jane will soon be wed."

"Both Jane and me?"

"Do not sound so shocked. You did call the stranger handsome, did you not?"

"Not in so many words. I said he was more handsome than you. That is not the same as saying he is handsome."

"Then you do not find him handsome?"

Elizabeth pressed her lips together.

"No reply is the same as admitting I am right," William said.

"Why must you be so frustrating?"

"Because you are so good at sums," he teased. "Now, tell me. Do you find the stranger handsome? Should I appraise him and report to you when father and I call at Netherfield." He lowered his voice. "Do not tell Mother we intend to call. Father is enjoying his tease."

Elizabeth laughed. Her father was always enjoying a tease of her mother. "Very well. So long as you never reveal that I am amenable to receiving your report about the stranger."

"Not a word shall pass my lips."

He winked at her, and she hoped that his promise would be as sure as his promises to her usually were.

# Chapter 2

Fitzwilliam Darcy blew out a breath as he exited his carriage. The quiet portion of this stay was over. Solitude would not be easy to find while he was here, and he so loved solitude. He stretched and straightened his jacket. The house appeared in good repair, and the staff seemed eager to greet them. These were all good things. Bingley just might have done well with this decision.

It was not that his friend lacked sense; he just seemed to wish to see the good in a person or situation so greatly that anything negative could be forgotten far too easily.

"What did I tell you?" Charles Bingley approached him. "It is beautiful, is it not?"

Darcy nodded. "The exterior looks very good."

"The interior is equally as lovely," Bingley assured him. "And the décor is quite tasteful. I do not think you will find a thing of which to disapprove."

"We will see the stables later?"

Bingley chuckled. "Your horses will be well-tended. I do know how to care for cattle. I just do not know how to be the master of this." He waved his hand toward the house. "Now, come. We do not want to miss Caroline's opinions."

Darcy really did not care if he heard Caroline Bingley's opinions on this house or any other. Charles's twin sister was as critical as Charles was accepting.

"Oh, Mr. Darcy!" Caroline cried as he entered. "What do you think of my brother's folly? Such a grand home in such a desolate place. Did you see the high street? One hat maker – one! And I would venture a guess that the styles are not current."

"Hats can be ordered from town," Bingley replied. "As can many other things, and it is not more than a half-day's drive to London. Therefore, there is little about which to be concerned. Indeed, your being separated from your favourite shops might just allow me to preserve the inheritance Father left me."

"Charles, do be serious," Louisa interjected. "What sort of gentlemen might a lady such as Caroline find in this remote location?"

A small smile passed between the two sisters. Darcy knew exactly which gentleman they hoped to secure as Caroline's future mate. It was a choice of which he did not approve. No matter how pretty Caroline was or how much he liked her brother, he did not wish to marry her. She was not the sort of lady he desired – not that he had found such a lady in town, Derbyshire, or Kent.

"Most gentlemen have an estate that is not in the center of London," he said. "There may be one or two in Hertfordshire or nearby who would do quite well for Caroline." He turned away to look at a painting on the wall, so that he would not have to hide his smirk at the clucking and gasping that came from Bingley's sisters.

"Aye!" Bingley cried. "And Hurst has a townhouse from which you can conduct your search while in town."

Silently, Darcy thanked his friend for not pushing Caroline toward him.

"Are you going to remain here for the season?" Caroline asked in surprise. "How will you find a wife if you do?"

"I hear from the solicitor who arranged the lease of Netherfield that there is a family of five beautiful ladies three miles from my door." He pointed one way and then the other. "I am not certain in which direction you will find Long – something." His face scrunched. "Longburn?

"Born," Darcy muttered. "Longbourn." How many times had he heard the details of where Netherfield was located in relation to pretty ladies over the past week? It had to have been at least a dozen times. His cousin, Richard Fitzwilliam, had even expressed an interest in visiting just to see the spectacle of these renowned beauties of Hertfordshire. How Bingley had forgotten the name of the estate was beyond Darcy's capability to understand. He sighed. To be fair, the man had only mentioned the name of the estate twice.

"Right!" Bingley cried. "Longbourn! That is it!"

Bingley could not contain his smile, and Darcy knew that his friend's excitement at finally having leased an estate as his father had hoped he would was hampering the man's ability to think straight. He could not fault his friend for that.

"I do believe you promised me a tour on our arrival," Darcy suggested. "May I suggest we start with my room?" He turned to Caroline and Louisa. "You will excuse us, will you not? I am certain you will wish to refresh after your journey, and Charles will want my opinion on many things that will bore you."

"We will join you for dinner," Bingley added. Then turning

to the housekeeper, he said, "My sisters will also need a tour, of course, and if you could have some sort of refreshment sent to the study... I expect Mr. Darcy and I will begin our tour there after we have seen our rooms."

"The blue bedroom has been prepared for Mr. Darcy," Mrs. Nichols replied.

"It is the third door on the left?"

"Yes, sir. That is the one." The housekeeper then turned to the Hursts and Caroline and offered to show them to their rooms and have tea set out in the drawing room in half an hour's time.

"Handily done," Bingley commented as his sisters and brother-in-law left the room.

"Thank you," Darcy replied with a grin.

"I have had my fill of Caroline's displeasure in not being consulted about the leasing of this estate. The distance to town is not far unless, of course, you must travel it with an unhappy sister."

Darcy chuckled. "I can understand that. Georgiana is not so vocal as Caroline, but she is not backward in making her displeasure known. A trip from town to Derbyshire can be harrowing if she is put out with me – which she seems to be more and more often." Their recent trip from Ramsgate to London had been excruciating.

His aunt had assured him it was due to her age and that this stage would pass eventually or if not, his uncle had added, Georgiana would soon enough be *properly* wed, and then it would fall to someone else to weather her ups and downs. His sister's marrying, however, was not something Darcy wished to contemplate. He had come perilously close to losing her to a scoundrel recently, and his uncle and his aunt knew it. It was why she was staying with them currently while he was in Hertfordshire. Mrs. Annesley, her new companion, seemed better than the previous one, but neither Darcy nor his cousin Richard, who was co-guardian of Georgiana, wished to rely entirely on their own opinions. Therefore, Lord and Lady Matlock were enlisted to act as observers for the time being.

"I would like to take a ride around the estate at some point," Darcy said as they began their ascent of the stairs. "Tomorrow morning might be soon enough unless you care for an escape before dinner?"

Bingley chuckled. "We must inspect the stables, so a short ride would not be unwelcome." He smiled. "Especially if it is in the direction of Longbourn."

Darcy shook his head. "Wait until the father calls on you before you introduce yourself to any of his daughters."

"There are five daughters," Bingley continued as if Darcy had not tried to dissuade him from the topic. "We could be brothers if we were each to find one to our liking."

"We could be brothers if you would marry Georgiana as your sister wishes," Darcy whispered.

"Or if you married Caroline as my sister wishes," Bingley replied. "I think we both would desire to become brothers in a different fashion."

Darcy shrugged. "At least with you, I would not need to worry about Georgie."

"She has no interest in me," Bingley opened the door to the blue bedroom. "And I have no interest of that sort in her. I would prefer a more mature lady. One who is steady and calm – not that Georgiana is not those things, but she is young and..."

"Say no more," Darcy interrupted. "It is just now, after what happened in Ramsgate, that I find I would like to know she is being cared for by someone as honorable as you are, and since she seems to find me such a bore and rigid, you seemed the perfect sort of fellow."

Bingley clapped him on the shoulder. "Then I shall help you find another me for her when the time comes." His lips tipped into a crooked smile. "Not that finding another like me is going to be an easy task."

Darcy laughed. "No, I would have to agree. You are a unique creation, which is why if these fabled beauties are not to your liking, I would not be opposed to your considering Georgiana."

"If all my other options fail, I will give it some thought," Bingley assured him with a laugh. "Now, you will wish to know that my room is just four doors down the hall to the right."

"And Caroline's?"

"Do you plan on visiting it?" Bingley teased.

"I wish to avoid it," Darcy replied as he rang the bell for his man and began to strip off his travelling clothes.

"One door beyond mine," Bingley replied. "I tried to place you as far from her as I could without being too obvious in my intent." He lifted an eyebrow. "I am not the sort to push my sister at a friend."

"That is because your sister is of a marriageable age and not at all what your friend desires in a wife, and you know it. While I, on the other hand, think you and my sister would suit quite well once she is old enough. But," he held up a hand to stop Bingley's protest, "I will not push her at you. I will merely present her as an option and be happy for you if you should find another more fitting choice."

"Do you like it?"

Darcy turned to look at his friend. Confusion was written clearly in his expression. Did he like what?

"Netherfield," Bingley clarified without Darcy saying a word.

"What I have seen of it, yes."

Bingley's shoulders relaxed, and he smiled. "And the neighbourhood?"

"I have yet to meet anyone from the neighbourhood, but the town did not look so horrid as Caroline seemed to think."

"There is an assembly in two weeks. We should become acquainted with everyone by then," Bingley assured him with delight. Bingley was fond of social gatherings.

Darcy was not, and he groaned. "Everyone?"

Bingley's head bobbed up and down.

"Can I not just meet a few of the prominent men and then cast my judgment? Must I meet everyone?"

Bingley continued to nod. "And you must attend the assembly. I told them that you would."

Darcy's mouth dropped open. "You told them what? And who is them? You mentioned nothing about an assembly when you begged me to come here."

Bingley laughed. "I am not so daft as you might think, old man. What chance did I have of getting you to consent to come if I had told you?"

"None," Darcy grumbled.

"Precisely!" Bingley stood at the door. "*Them* refers to the solicitor, who is the uncle to the pretty young ladies, and Sir William.

I think you will like him, although he does ramble on about some things.”

If Bingley had noticed rambling enough to list it as a possible annoyance, then Darcy very much doubted he would like Sir William. He had turned to his valet to request his riding clothes but paused. “Wait. Did you just say that these ladies you hope we will find to our liking are the nieces of a country solicitor?”

Bingley shook his head. “Do you listen to yourself when you speak like that?”

“When I speak like what?”

Bingley lifted his chin and peered down his nose at Darcy while affecting a snobbish voice. “Did you say these ladies were related to a country solicitor? I should hope not. I would not wish for my clothing to be sullied with their presence.”

“I am not a prig,” Darcy defended.

“If you say so,” Bingley replied. “But you sound like one at times.”

The comment rankled. There were reasons for caution. “You should be looking to marry a gentleman’s daughter. You will be a gentleman and need a wife who is familiar with the rank.”

Bingley lifted an accusatory brow and shook his head as if disappointed. “Is it impossible for a solicitor to be related to a gentleman?” he asked.

Darcy’s brows knit in confusion. “Then they are gently bred ladies?”

Bingley nodded. “Longbourn is the name of an estate.” He tipped his head and smirked. “Had you forgotten they live at Longbourn, the estate next to mine.”

Darcy hated it when Bingley became testy in a one-who-knows-all sort of fashion, especially when it was when Darcy had made an error in reasoning. It was as if the man enjoyed pointing out Darcy's faults. He did not need Bingley to do that. He had his cousin Richard for that.

Bingley began to open the door. "I will meet you at the bottom of the stairs in a quarter hour. Perhaps we should begin by inspecting the side of the property that adjoins Longbourn's, so that you can see that it is a proper estate."

Darcy grabbed a cushion from the chair near him and hurled it at Bingley. He could hear Bingley laughing as the cushion hit the door and not its intended target.

"Shall I be ready to return to London at a moment's notice, sir?" his man asked.

Darcy shook his head. "No, not just yet. I think I can survive him for at least a while." He blew out a breath. "Even if it means attending an assembly."

"Very good, sir," his man replied. "The brown or tan breeches?"

"Tan." Fifteen minutes and then after some fortifying tea, he could be on his horse and gaining some sort of perspective on where he was and what troubles he might face during his stay at Netherfield. Nothing was so relaxing or refreshing to his mind as a ride. He sighed. Yes, a ride was just what he needed.

# Chapter 3

"Are they here?" Jane asked eagerly when Elizabeth and William had returned to Longbourn's garden.

Elizabeth nodded. "And Mr. Bingley is as handsome as Uncle said he was."

"And accompanied by an equally as handsome sister," William added.

Jane chuckled as she took Williams other arm to make a turn of the garden. "Mama will not be happy to hear that. She bemoans the number of young ladies in the neighbourhood as it is."

"She'll be happier when she hears that Mr. Bingley has brought a handsome and wealthy gentleman with him," William whispered. "And he has caught the eye of our sister," he added in an even lower tone.

"William!" Elizabeth cried. "You promised to not say a word."

"You were not going to tell Jane?" William scoffed.

Elizabeth lifted her chin and did not reply. Of course, she had intended to tell Jane. She told Jane everything, for Jane was not only her eldest sister but also one of her closest friends, much like William was.

"I will not mention it to Mother or Father," William's tone was apologetic. "I promise."

"And none of our other sisters," Elizabeth added.

"It will be yours and mine and Jane's secret," William assured her. "Will you forgive me for mentioning the handsome stranger to Jane?"

"He did not mean any harm, Lizzy, and he did not tell me anything you would not have told me eventually."

It was just like Jane to attempt to make things better. She seemed to have a greater need than most to see things returned to as peaceful a state as possible. Her constancy and tranquility were something which was knit into the very fiber of her being. She could not be parted from it, and it could not be parted from her. It was her nature, and that nature was both a balm to everyone she met and the basis upon which her beauty rested.

Elizabeth shrugged. She did not wish to be done being perturbed with William, but she knew she truly had very little reason to be overly put out. "So long as he says nothing – absolutely nothing – about my finding the gentleman who accompanied Mr. Bingley handsome, I think I can overlook this small breach of his promise."

"Not a word further will fall from my lips regarding your interest in that gentleman," William said.

"Then you are forgiven."

"Lady Lucas said that Mr. Bingley has promised to attend the assembly."

Elizabeth had not heard so much excitement in Jane's voice when speaking of an assembly before. "Are you so anxious to meet him?"

"I cannot lie," Jane whispered. "I am intrigued. There are no acceptable gentlemen left in the area for me to consider, and if

Papa will not send me to town for a season, I do not know where I will find a husband. Aunt and Uncle Gardiner do their best, but their soirees are not those bursting with landed gentry. And I do so wish to have an estate to call home and not just a fine house in town."

"No tradesmen for our Jane," William declared. "She is too fine a lady for that!"

"Indeed, she is," Elizabeth agreed while Jane shook her head and looked as displeased as Jane could muster when not truly put out.

"Did you walk far?" Jane asked.

"No, just to the knoll looking over Netherfield and back," Elizabeth replied. "Why?"

"I was wondering if perhaps after we have had tea with Mama and you have told her all you know..." Jane hesitated. "We could go riding."

"That is very forward of you," Elizabeth teased.

"I would just like to get a glimpse of him," Jane added. "All my hopes rest upon this Mr. Bingley, and Papa is still refusing to call on him."

"He has just arrived, Jane. Papa cannot call on him so soon."

"But will he call at all? He refuses to allow me to attend a season, and he tells Mama he will not call on the new neighbour. I am beginning to believe he wishes for me to never marry. Why else would he have refused Mr. Connor two years ago? He seemed a fine choice for a husband. He admired me, and I admired him."

"He was not what he seemed," William interjected.

"What do you mean?" Jane demanded.

"Mr. Connor and I attended school together. He had several

ladies he admired and at least one he had led to believe he was going to make an offer of marriage." He looked toward the house and led them in the opposite direction. "She and her child received a small pittance from him and then nothing. She had many suitors when he met her, but now, she has no husband. She lives with a relation somewhere is what I heard."

"Can it be true?" Elizabeth could not contain her surprise. Mr. Connor had never appeared to be anything less than a perfectly honorable gentleman.

"My sources of information are good. I am sorry. It is true."

"And you never told us?" Jane asked.

"Father did not wish to cause you more pain than he knew his refusal of Mr. Connor was going to cause." He looked at Elizabeth. "I promised not to say a word, so you must not tell him that I have told you. I would hate to disappoint him, but," he stepped away from them, removed his hat, and ran a hand through his hair, "how could I not reveal what I know when Jane questions our father's intentions?"

Jane's hand lay on her heart. "Mr. Connor was so bad?"

William nodded. "He was."

"And Papa would rather I think ill of him than know the truth and feel pain?"

William shrugged. "He would do anything to see you happy."

"And these two years I have thought he did not care for my happiness. I have been so critical in my mind of everything he has done. Far more critical than I should be."

Jane looked so miserable that Elizabeth immediately wrapped her arm around her sister's shoulders while doubting that Jane's version of critical was truly as horrid as Jane seemed to think it was.

"You told Papa about Mr. Connor?" Jane asked William.

"I did."

"Thank you," Jane whispered. "I would not have wished to be tied to such a man." She looked from one to the other of her companions. "Imagine my misery if I had accepted him!"

Jane's sorrow of a moment ago was sliding into anger. Anger was something Jane was as capable of showing as Elizabeth was at times, particularly when that anger was at the perfidy of another. Jane was calm and steady, but she also desired justice.

"You must assess Mr. Bingley," Jane said to William. "You must determine if I should like him or not. And his friend, too. I would not wish for Lizzy to fall for someone like Mr. Connor."

There was an urgency to the demand, and William looked sufficiently solemn as he agreed to be their protector from all sorts of unsavoury gentlemen.

"Do you still wish to go riding?" Elizabeth asked as they turned once again toward the house.

"Oh, most certainly!" Jane cried. "You are not the only curious creature, Lizzy."

~*~*~

"And his friend has a carriage that is finer than Mr. Bingley's, you say?" Mrs. Bennet fanned herself with her handkerchief at such wonderful news. "Did he appear single?"

Elizabeth looked at William. "Did he appear single to you?" How exactly did a gentleman appear single from such a distance?

"There was no lady on his arm, and he did not look overly old." William's head bobbed from side to side as he attempted to make a calculation. He made that gesture often when he was attempting to decide between two options. "I would venture he is not yet thirty."

"Is he handsome?" Mrs. Bennet's excitement was building. Elizabeth could hear it in her voice.

The right corner of William's mouth tipped upward, causing Elizabeth to catch her breath and pray that he would not mention her.

"I am perhaps not the best judge of such things, but I think he could be considered handsome even if he did not have such a fine carriage."

Mrs. Bennet turned to Elizabeth. "Did you think he was handsome?"

"I did. Both he and Mr. Bingley were very handsome from what I could see of them through my glass."

Mrs. Bennet clapped her hands. "Two daughters married. Jane shall have her pick and then..." she looked around the room at her daughters, "one of you shall have the other."

"Elizabeth shall have the other," William inserted. "She is the second eldest, and it is the natural order of things that the older sisters should marry before the younger ones. We would not want to see any of them on the shelf, and those who are closest to such a travesty should be put forward first."

Mrs. Bennet gasped. "You are right. You are very, very right. I had not thought of it so, but Elizabeth is not getting any younger."

Elizabeth's brows furrowed in displeasure at being referred to as nearly past her prime when she was only twenty.

"And she is the most likely to pose the most problem in making a match," her mother continued.

Elizabeth gasped.

"You are so stubborn," her mother replied. "You insist on stating your own opinion on things even when it disagrees with a perfectly acceptable gentleman's opinion. That is not the best recommendation to a man that you will be a biddable wife."

"Lizzy is anything but biddable," Lydia declared, causing Kitty to titter.

"I shall be perfectly biddable for a man of sense."

"For a man who has the good sense to see things as you do," Mary muttered.

Elizabeth arched a brow at her next youngest sister. "I do believe that is what I said."

"Oh, Elizabeth," her mother cried in exasperation. "You shall never marry with such an attitude. You are altogether too headstrong. A certain amount of stubbornness is an asset to a lady, but so much is untenable. Simply untenable. If only your father had agreed with me on that, you would be as mild as Jane."

"My dear," said Mr. Bennet from behind his book, "your second daughter's temperament is such that no matter how you might have attempted to make her pliable, there was no hope of her ever being as mild as Jane. You'd have better luck attempting to make Lydia as fond of propriety as Mary."

"Papa!" Lydia cried.

"You are not always proper," her father replied. "I really ought to confine you to your room and remove your allowance more for some of your actions, but unfortunately I seem unable to do so."

"Because she would wail far too much," Mary muttered.

Her father lifted a brow and gave her a reproving look.

"I am sorry," she said.

"You are forgiven, as well as correct. I do love peace as much as Jane." And with that, he turned his attention back to his book.

That was not, however, enough to end Mrs. Bennet's discussion of the matter.

"I still believe Lizzy could be more pliable."

"She does not wish it," Mr. Bennet said without lifting his eyes. "There will be a gentleman who will appreciate her keen mind and determined spirit."

"I am certain I have never heard of such a thing," Mrs. Bennet declared.

"You oppose me quite regularly, my dear, and I still have not turned you out."

Mrs. Bennet gasped.

"Nor would I," her husband continued. "I find I like you far too well to be without you."

"I should say you do," Mrs. Bennet agreed with a little smile.

The room fell silent for a moment as the clock on the table near their father's favourite chair ticked away the time.

"Will you call on him?" It was Mrs. Bennet who broke the silence.

"Call on whom?"

Elizabeth saw the way her father's lips twitched.

"Mr. Bingley, of course!" her mother replied with some force.

"But not the handsome stranger? Shall I wait until he has departed before I call?"

"Oh, Mr. Bennet, you vex me most severely. I am certain my nerves shall see me in an early grave."

"You are far too young to worry about that," her husband replied. "Your nerves shall likely outlive both you and me."

"Mr. Bennet! Do not speak of such things, for I do not wish to think about them." Her handkerchief fluttered in front of her face more rapidly.

"I shall call on them tomorrow," Mr. Bennet said softly, and then when his wife had looked his direction in delighted surprise, he winked at her before turning his eyes back to his book once more. "But only if I can have some peace until I do."

Mrs. Bennet immediately stood. "Kitty, Lydia, go find something to do in your room. Mary," she waved her hand, "never mind, you shall not make a peep because you have your book. Jane, Lizzy – "

"Might we go riding, Mama?" Jane asked.

"Yes, I think you must," she agreed. "And I shall see Cook about a dinner party." She turned to her husband. "You must invite them to dine with us."

"I will do no such thing."

"But your daughters." She clamped her lips closed as he raised a brow. "I shall speak to Cook to be prepared just in case you change your mind and wish to invite them to dine."

"I shall not change my mind," he replied.

Elizabeth knew he would change his mind eventually. Her father loved peace far too much to endure too many petitions from their mother.

"William will ride with us," Elizabeth said to her mother.

"Oh, that is an excellent idea." She followed them to the door, but then she turned back toward her husband. "Do you suppose you could ask what their favourite dessert might be?"

"I am not inviting them to dinner, nor am I inquiring after their likes and dislikes on such topics."

"But your daught—very well, I shall just plan on your favourite."

Their poor father. As much as her mother instructed Elizabeth on being pliable, she demonstrated quite the opposite. It was a rare discussion between her father and mother when they agreed on everything.

Jane wrapped her arm around Elizabeth's. "Come on. Before she decides she needs us to help her decide receipts." She pulled Elizabeth toward the stairs. "We will meet you at the stables, William." And with that, she dropped Elizabeth's arm and scampered up the stairs.

"She seems eager to be away," William said with a laugh.

"Indeed, she does," Elizabeth agreed before dashing up the stairs behind Jane. And who could blame her? There were handsome gentlemen just three miles away, and, to be perfectly honest, Elizabeth was just as curious to catch another glimpse of them as Jane was to get her first.

# Chapter 4

Darcy had found his tea with Bingley to be refreshing, but not so refreshing as the feel of the wind against one's person as he rode. At least, that is how Darcy saw it. He and Bingley had discussed the basics about which books were most important to look over first and what Bingley's hopes were in securing an estate like Netherfield. It was for Bingley as it was for many gentlemen.

Bingley wished to gain the prominence that such an estate would bring him as well as a place into which he could put some of his inheritance in such a fashion that it would continue to reap benefits well past when he departed this earth. Bingley was no fool. He was happy and amiable as well as obliging to a fault at times, but he was no fool once he put his mind to a matter. It would take some doing, but Darcy did not expect it would be overly long before Bingley understood the workings of an estate as well as any gentleman did. Darcy smiled wryly. Bingley had the added advantage that he was likely to gain the approval of all his neighbours with very little effort. That was how Bingley was. He liked people, and they liked him. It was an enviable quality.

"I see the knoll," Bingley circled back to where Darcy was riding at a slower pace. "There." He pointed to his left. "And that fence there must be the one of which the groom spoke. We are nearly at the end of Netherfield's lands in this direction. I shall have to ask him tomorrow for a marker of where it ends in the opposite direction."

"Do you truly care to know?" Darcy teased. "Are there pretty ladies at an estate in all four directions?"

Bingley laughed. "I wish there were, but I think the only pretty ladies that are near my estate are in this direction. Mr. Philips did not mention any others."

"Mr. Philips, *their uncle*, did not tell you about any other pretty ladies? How odd." Darcy's tone was sardonic.

Again, Bingley laughed. "You should be so lighthearted more often, for you are very good at it."

"I cannot be." Darcy's reply was quick. He found it incredibly difficult to relax with anyone he had not known for any length of time. And even then, there were those such as his aunt Catherine and Caroline around whom he could only marginally relax, though he had known them for years. Lady Catherine was just too demanding and always looking for things to reprove for him to be anything more than mostly at ease in her presence, and Caroline? Well, he was never truly at ease around any lady who was attempting to convince him to marry her.

"I think you could be if you tried," Bingley retorted.

Darcy shook his head. "To this point in my life, it has been impossible, and I do not see that changing any time soon."

"Very well," Bingley conceded. "I shall attempt to work on you, but I will not be utterly discouraged if I am not immediately successful. It shall be an offering of thanks for the help you are giving me with the estate."

"I think I would rather not receive your gratitude if it is to be given in such a fashion." Darcy drew his horse to a stop. In the field just beyond the fence, there were three riders – one gentleman and two ladies. "It seems we are in luck," he called to Bingley.

"What do you – Oh! Yes, indeed, we are!" Bingley replied as he noticed the riders.

"Do they have a brother?"

Bingley's face pinched. "I am not entirely certain. I believe I remember something about a cousin or brother or some such thing, but..."

"You were far too focused on the ladies to commit that bit of information to memory."

Bingley smiled sheepishly. "I was."

Darcy shook his head. It was just like his friend to put all other thoughts out of his head when discussion of a pretty lady was broached. It would be good for the man to marry if only so he could focus on what needed to be done instead of where a wife might be found. Maybe they would be fortunate, and they would find a steady and calm lady amongst the beauties of Longbourn. Then, Darcy could encourage a courtship while still retaining enough of Bingley's attention to guide him in setting himself up as master of his own domain.

"Shall we approach them?" Darcy asked.

Bingley drew to a halt and looked at his friend with concern. "You wish to meet strangers?"

"For you, I do."

"Not for yourself?" Bingley teased.

Darcy shook his head. "No, I am not eager to marry, but I know you are." He clucked to his horse as he turned him in the direction in which the fence ran. They would approach it slowly and at an angle so as not to look too eager. "You do realize that choosing one lady as a wife will mean not choosing every other lady, no matter how beautiful."

"Yes," Bingley answered tersely. "If you think so meanly of me, I am surprised you would think to offer your sister to me."

"I do not think meanly of you. I merely wished to judge your enthusiasm for marriage. You truly wish to marry? You are only four and twenty."

"And you are eight and twenty. I see no reason why my age should be a detriment to marrying if yours is not one to remaining unmarried. Yes, I know there are not many in our circles who wish to be married so young, but I have my inheritance, and I wish to settle into it as my father desired. Therefore, it would be best for me to take a wife, so that I can send Caroline to live with Hurst, and my wife can be hostess for you and my other guests."

"So you wish to marry to be rid of Caroline?" Darcy asked with a laugh.

"I do. You should consider it. If you were married, she could not fawn over you as she does now."

Darcy continued to laugh. "That is a worthy argument. I shall have to consider it if I ever find a lady who is to my liking."

"I would not be as fastidious as you for a kingdom!" Bingley declared. "Perfection is rarely found in human form." He smirked. "Except, of course, in the form of the great and noble Fitzwilliam Darcy."

Darcy's eyes narrowed. "I do not think of myself as perfect."

"No, but you do wear an air of superiority at times that suggests you do."

"I do not."

"You do."

"Pick a marker."

"The stile."

"It shall not be as satisfying as thrashing you at Gentleman Jacksons, but..." Darcy did not finish his sentence, opting instead to urge his horse into a gallop. It was a trick he had learned from his cousin, Richard, and had found particularly useful in beating Bingley in a race. The man was not only an expert at making friends, but he was also very good at selecting fast horses.

"It was not a fair race," Bingley grumbled as he reached the stile just behind Darcy.

"No, it was not, but it was excessively satisfying," Darcy replied with a wide grin.

"That was some show of horsemanship," the gentleman in the adjoining field called out.

Bingley doffed his hat and made a grand bow. "My thanks to you, sir."

"Mr. William Bennet," the man said as he approached Darcy and Bingley.

He was a large man, both in height and breadth, with a friendly countenance.

"Mr. Charles Bingley and my friend Mr. Fitzwilliam Darcy." Bingley motioned first to himself and then Darcy.

"Two of my sisters," William said as he motioned for the ladies with him to come forward. "Jane is the eldest and Elizabeth the next after her."

Darcy caught his breath. Uncle or no, Bingley's solicitor was not lying about the beauty of the ladies at Longbourn. Miss Bennet was the sort of lady the masters sought, which made Miss Elizabeth's beauty seem to pale in comparison but not to him. There was something enchanting about the set of her eyes and the slight disproportion of her features. It was *her* beauty, not that of her sister, which had caused his breath to hitch.

He touched his hat and gave a nod in greeting but said nothing. He could not. His tongue seemed to be stone. Thankfully, Bingley's tongue was as loose as ever.

"We were just inspecting this side of the property since a ride after being confined in a carriage seemed to be a most refreshing activity." He looked at Darcy and tipped his head toward the Bennets.

"Indeed, it is," Darcy managed to say.

"Elizabeth loves to ride nearly as much as she enjoys walking," William said. "Jane prefers riding, and I could not choose one over the other even if forced."

"Do you ride here often?" Bingley directed his question to Miss Bennet.

Darcy breathed a sigh of relief, strangely happy that Bingley had not selected Miss Elizabeth.

"Is something amiss, Mr. Darcy?" Elizabeth asked.

Darcy's eyes grew wide, and he shook his head. "No, why do you ask?"

"You were frowning."

"Was I?"

"You are doing it again."

"I am?"

Next to Darcy, Bingley chuckled. "You will have to excuse my friend. He often looks displeased when he is contemplating something. I assure you he is far more pleasant than he appears and often more civil than he sounds."

Darcy scowled at Bingley.

"That," Bingley said triumphantly, "is a truly displeased expression."

Darcy opened his mouth to hand Bingley a retort he well-deserved, but Elizabeth's laughter stopped him and caused his lips to curl in pleasure.

"I thank you for the demonstration, Mr. Bingley," Elizabeth said. "I shall now know the difference between when Mr. Darcy is pensive and when he is vexed."

Bingley, gallant, *helpful* friend that he was, nodded his acceptance of Elizabeth's thanks.

"If you spend enough time with us," Darcy said, arching a brow at his friend, "I am certain you will have ample practice distinguishing the two expressions since Bingley seems to enjoy vexing me. He is such a trying fellow. You have no idea how he tries one's nerves."

"I do not," Bingley retorted.

"Our mother says the same thing about our father," William interrupted.

"Our father intends to call on you tomorrow," Jane inserted.

"I shall look forward to his arrival," Bingley replied. "We do not wish to take you from your ride."

Darcy did not believe a word of it. Bingley looked absolutely smitten and in no rush to leave Miss Bennet.

"You are not," that lady replied with a small duck of her head. "We were only going to ride a bit further and then turn back. This respite has been quite pleasant."

"Indeed, it has been," Bingley replied with one of his charming smiles that he used when speaking to any particularly pretty young woman who had captured his fancy.

"Do you ride here often?" Darcy repeated Bingley's question from before, which had not yet been answered.

"Not so often as I wish," Jane replied. "However, we do take frequent walks along the path to the knoll. The aspect is quite lovely from there. William was thinking of building a bench under the oak tree, as it is Lizzy's favourite place to hide away with a book."

"Perhaps one day you can show me the aspect," Bingley offered. "However, I am not a great reader, so I shall not be carrying a book, although Darcy may bring one with him. And he is often looking for a quiet spot to read. I am afraid I am not overly good at providing such, and my sisters are even worse."

Darcy grimaced. "Indeed," he said dryly.

William laughed. "Sisters can be trying."

"Almost as much as brothers," Elizabeth retorted.

"Ah, but there is only one of me and five of you." William turned to Bingley and Darcy. "While they can be trying, I would not trade them for the world, for they are all delightful in their own way."

Darcy could hear the edge of a warning in the man's voice. Not one of the Bennet ladies would be left unprotected. Mr. William Bennet would see to that. It was a sentiment that Darcy could both sympathize with and respect. "I feel the same way about my sister."

He held William's gaze for a moment, earning himself a small nod of the man's head.

"We should return home and allow you to continue your inspection." William touched his hat. "Until tomorrow."

Darcy watched as the Bennets rode across the field.

"Miss Bennet is an angel," Bingley said.

"I would agree," Darcy replied as he nudged his horse forward. And her sister was a temptress, he thought, as he cast one more look at the retreating forms of the Bennets. He would be pleased to meet her father and explore her connections more fully. He shook his head. That was not a thought he had ever expected to have. However, if her connections were sound... Well, it might just be possible that he and Bingley could indeed be brothers.

# Chapter 5

"How was your ride?" Mr. Bennet asked that evening as the family sat down for dinner. "Mary said you rode in the direction of Netherfield." The right corner of his mouth was lifted in a small smirk, and there was a laugh lying just below his words.

"It was most interesting," Elizabeth replied. "Did you know that if you look at the knoll from a distance with your eyes squinched shut just so," she demonstrated the action, "the trees look almost as if they are made up of daubs and streaks of paints? I am certain even I could replicate it with little effort." She knew precisely what her father was asking, but, seeing as he seemed in a playful sort of mood, she thought to oblige him with a delectable piece of ridiculousness.

Her father chuckled as he passed William a bowl covered with a cloth. "And will you make an attempt?"

"I should say not!" her mother replied. "And you will not make that expression again, Elizabeth. You shall have lines and wrinkles before you are thirty if you continue to do so."

Elizabeth shared an amused look with her father. "Yes, Mama," she replied.

"Were the trees on the knoll all you saw?" her father asked.

"No, we met Mr. Bingley," Elizabeth replied, adding, "and his friend," over the squeal of delight from her mother.

"Was he handsome? Did he look rich?" Her mother clapped her hands. "Did he take notice of our Jane? She really is too beautiful to be poor."

"None of our daughters will be poor," Mr. Bennet assured her.

"Oh, what do you know of it?" Mrs. Bennet argued. "You rarely attend an assembly. There are so few men of acceptable means. What we need are what Mr. Bingley and his friend provide – wealthy men in want of a wife."

"I do believe that nearly all men are at one point or another in want of a wife whether they be wealthy or no." Mr. Bennet placed a thick piece of beef on his plate. "And what is acceptable to you and what is truly acceptable as far as fortune is concerned are not one and the same."

He smiled at his wife when she gasped at his words. "However, I will agree that our daughters are deserving of the richest men in the kingdom." He held up a finger. "But only if those men are as honorable as they are rich. No daughter of mine shall be given to someone with a healthy bank account but no heart. Nor shall I see them tied to a fool. Those, my lady, are my qualifications for any suitor for *any* of our daughters. No matter how dashing a gentleman might look in a uniform or what carriage he drives."

"But there are so few gentlemen from which to choose," Mrs. Bennet protested. "If we were to travel to Bath, we might do better."

"I dare say we would only find gouty men to marry there," Mary muttered.

"Oh, no!" her mother said with some force. "I have heard tell of many a handsome young man looking for a wife in the Assembly Rooms. Why just last week, Mrs. Goulding was telling me about some fellow who was desperate to marry, so that he could claim his inheritance," she put down her fork and knife and leaned toward the center of the table, "and I can tell you, his inheritance was substantial. Sub-stan-tial." She pronounced each syllable slowly and emphasised it with first a raised brow, then a pointed look, and finally, a vigorous nod of her head.

"As great as Mr. Bingley's?" Their father asked, turning the conversation back to what Elizabeth knew he wished to know.

"Why, yes, if what my sister says is true. Mrs. Goulding told her that this gentleman had nearly six a year. Six! Can you imagine? What fine clothes his wife must have!"

"He has no wife," her father replied. "You said so just a moment ago. Therefore, his wife does not have fine clothes."

Mrs. Bennet huffed in exasperation. "If he had a wife, her clothes would be very fine. Simply the best. They must be, you know, if she is to represent her husband as she ought."

"Did Mr. Bingley have fine clothes?" Mr. Bennet asked Elizabeth.

"He did. He was wearing a blue coat and black breeches with a hat to match. He looked very dapper. Would you not agree, Jane?"

Jane smiled down at her plate. "Indeed, I would."

"And he seemed to forget the rest of us were even there when he talked to Jane," Elizabeth added. "I dare say he is smitten."

"He is not," Jane refuted weakly.

"What think you, William?" her father asked around the food in his mouth. "Was Mr. Bingley smitten with our Jane, or is Elizabeth seeing only what she wishes to see?"

Elizabeth's eyes narrowed, and she shook her head. Her father enjoyed teasing her about how she liked to assess the character of strangers.

The clink and scratch of cutlery on plates ruled in the room while William swallowed his mouthful of food and washed it down with a sip of wine.

"Elizabeth might be correct. He did seem to single Jane out during our short conversation."

"Oh, I cannot believe you were so fortunate to meet him and on his first day!" Mrs. Bennet cried. "Lady Lucas was certain she would beat me to it and have Charlotte married first. Charlotte is a sweet girl, but she is no Jane." Mrs. Bennet beamed at her eldest daughter before taking a sip of her wine. "Although Charlotte may do very well for you, William."

Elizabeth bit back a giggle and shook her head as William leveled a glare at her instead of their mother.

"Yes, yes, there are few who can compare to Jane," Mr. Bennet said. "However, I should like to know what you thought of the man, William. Do I need to bother calling? Or will he do?"

Elizabeth pulled her lip between her teeth. She was excited for Jane. Mr. Bingley seemed just the sort of gentleman that would love Jane as she deserved. She held her breath for a moment, anxious to have William share his approval but seeing a look of question pass across his face. The expression caused her to remember Mr. Bingley's friend. Mr. Darcy was handsome, if a bit grave, but more than those things he was intriguing. He seemed to always be thinking as they were speaking. His thoughts would shadow his features, pulling at his brow, playing at his mouth, and then relaxing into indifference as whatever it was had been seemingly tucked away for the moment. It was very like what William was doing right now, although William was not so good at feigning indifference.

"It was a good first encounter," William said at last, "but I should be sorry to form an opinion on such a short acquaintance. If Mr. Bingley is as he appears, then, yes, he should do quite well for Jane if she will have him."

"Or if he will have her," Mary muttered.

"And why would he not have her?" Lydia asked. "Jane is the most beautiful of us all. She is even prettier than I am, though she is not taller." She lifted her chin and looked down her nose at Mary.

"I am only saying that a gentleman should be consulted as to his opinion on the matter of his marriage before his future lot is cast in the die," Mary replied. "We are speaking as if the whole of his life has been decided since Jane and Lizzy find him handsome, and he is capable of speaking to them. I just think it unwise to assume the end before the beginning."

"Mary! I do not know where you get these ideas." Mrs. Bennet shook her head. "Of course, he will want Jane. Every gentleman prefers a pretty wife to a plain one." She looked at her daughters one by one. "And none of you are to look as pretty as Jane until we have secured him." She shook her head at Lydia when she opened her mouth to speak. "I know it will be very hard for you, Lydia, but they shall do the same for you when it is your turn."

"They shall all be married before that," Mary muttered, earning her a glare from her youngest sister and a giggle from Kitty.

"If we might return to some sort of sense," Mr. Bennet said. "I am not assuming Mr. Bingley will wish to marry my Jane, though

I will find him immensely daft if he does not. I am only asking if he is a good prospect, and William has said that he might be. We shall call on him tomorrow, and then, I will add my voice to William's assessment."

"He seemed very amiable," Jane said softly as her cheeks glowed rosy.

"I shall remember that," her father replied with a wink and a smile. "I shall leave the house with the intention that I will like the man. Then, he has only to lose my good opinion rather than gain it. Will that be to your satisfaction, my dear?"

"Yes, Papa," Jane answered.

"What of his friend?" Mr. Bennet asked, looking at Elizabeth. "Am I supposed to be predisposed to like him as well?"

"I would prefer for you to make your own assessment," Elizabeth replied, though she did hope her father would find Mr. Darcy acceptable.

"You did not find him to your liking, then?"

"I did not say," Elizabeth replied. "You do not intend to meet him until tomorrow, so I do not wish to spoil your enjoyment."

"The impertinence!" her mother cried. "You shall never snare him with such saucy responses." She looked at her younger daughters. "Perhaps Kitty would be better?"

"No," William said sharply, causing everyone to turn their eyes toward him. He slowly put his knife down and took a roll from the covered bowl in front of him. "I mean to say, if Mr. Darcy is worthy of any of my sisters, then it will be Lizzy. He is a serious-looking sort of fellow."

"He has a nicer carriage than Mr. Bingley, who has four thousand a year!" Mrs. Bennet declared. "I do not see how he cannot be worthy of Lizzy."

Elizabeth watched William finger his knife rather than picking it up to put butter on his roll. His eyes were looking at nothing and everything. There was something he was not saying and did not wish to say.

"I was merely thinking of his character as Father said earlier. We must discover if these gentlemen will treat Jane and Lizzy as they deserve to be treated. I have seen many wealthy gents who showers his wife with money and clothes but neither affection nor respect."

"Oh, I have read stories of such in the paper," Lydia agreed. "What is his name? Kitty and I will look tonight."

Elizabeth wondered from Lydia's tone if her sister would be more pleased to find a tawdry story about Mr. Darcy than to not find one at all. Lydia loved a good story.

"Fitzwilliam Darcy," William replied. "I would not be at all surprised if he is mentioned somewhere in the society pages. His uncle is the Earl of Matlock, after all."

Elizabeth's eyes grew wide, and her mother looked as if she was about to faint away.

"An earl!" Mrs. Bennet exclaimed.

"Yes," William replied. "And men with as much money and connections such as Mr. Darcy has are rarely not in the society pages."

"How much does he have?" Mrs. Bennet asked.

"I have heard ten thousand a year."

Mrs. Bennet fell back in her chair and fanned herself with her handkerchief. "Ten thousand and an earl!"

"Yes," William muttered. "Which is why we need to proceed cautiously. Men of his standing are not always honorable."

He did not lift his eyes from the roll he was breaking into bits on his plate but not eating. There was definitely something he knew about Mr. Darcy that he was not saying. Elizabeth would not press him on it now, but later. She smiled to herself. Later, she would extract the truth from him.

# Chapter 6

Darcy picked at his sleeves, righting every supposed imperfection, while he stood at the window in the drawing room at Netherfield. He glanced at the clock in the corner. It was two minutes past the acceptable time for callers. Hopefully, Mr. Bennet would not be too late in calling. He wished for this interview to be over. His mind had played with the possibilities of how it could go several times last night and then again this morning.

"You seem anxious, Mr. Darcy." Caroline said as she came to stand next to him.

Darcy stepped one step away from her. She always insisted on standing closer to him than what he was comfortable with. However, she was right. He was anxious, and it was not her close proximity which was creating the anxiety. The source of his unease was another lady. He had spent a great deal of time pondering Miss Elizabeth Bennet last night. There was something about the animation of her features when she spoke that would not let him put her out of his mind. Her beauty, he was confident, he could eventually talk himself out of needing to admire, but her spirit was something that captivated him. He felt a deep, unsettling need to see her again. However, he was not going to tell Caroline such. Instead, he merely said what was likely obvious.

"I am just restless."

"We could take a turn of the garden," Caroline suggested. "Louisa would be happy to join us."

Darcy shook his head. "No, I will stay with your brother. He is expecting callers, and I wish to meet them."

Her brows rose. "Indeed?"

He could well understand the skepticism in her voice. He was not known for his enjoyment of meeting new people.

"There cannot be anyone worth meeting," Caroline continued in a tone much sweeter than her words. "It is the country, and a dreadful looking one at that."

"There is more to judging an area than the number of hat shops on the high street."

Darcy smiled. He couldn't help it. Bingley rarely used that tone of censure with his sister.

"Your brother is correct," Darcy added. "Meeting the prominent gentlemen in the area is an important part of the evaluation process."

"And one should do it with a proper attitude," Bingley added, still using his stern voice.

"You are not seriously thinking of remaining here long, are you?" Caroline asked.

"I signed papers for a year," Bingley replied. "I will be staying; whether you do or not is completely up to you. I shall house you as long as you can tolerate it, but an establishment can be set up for you if Hurst will not take you."

Caroline gasped. Her displeasure with being in Hertfordshire had grown last evening upon hearing her brother's effusive praise of Miss Bennet. Today, she seemed determined to sway her brother's opinion through Darcy. However, Darcy was not planning to be a willing party to her scheme.

"It is best to see the area in all seasons," Darcy agreed.

"You cannot mean to stay here as well?" Caroline cried.

Darcy shook head. "I am sure I will need to return to town for my sister, and eventually, I will need to make a journey to Pemberley. However, I will attempt to see this place for at least a portion of time during each of the seasons." And, if at all possible, he would spend a great deal of time in the area so that he could see Miss Elizabeth if her family proved to be acceptable, which brought him back to his current anxiety. He hoped with all that was within him that her father and brother were gentlemen with whom he might form a friendship.

"Are you well?" Caroline asked him.

He startled from his contemplations. "Why do you ask?"

"Your face fell just then as if something was troubling you."

"I was just thinking about all that I have to do," he prevaricated. It was not that at all. If he were to answer her honestly, he would have to admit that his desires as they pertained to Miss Elizabeth and her family were startling to him each time they overtook him – which had been many times since that meeting yesterday.

"We could invite Georgiana to join us," Caroline cooed. "That would surely give your mind some ease, and Louisa and I, some acceptable companionship."

"I am of half a mind to send you back to London on the first coach I find," Bingley snapped. "You know I do not wish to marry Georgiana any more than Darcy wishes to marry you."

Caroline sucked in a sharp breath at his words.

"Oh, do not look at me so," Bingley continued. "Darcy knows

full-well that you have set your cap at him, and yet he has not made a move to secure your affections."

"Charles," Louisa scolded. "You are too harsh."

Bingley turned toward his older sister. "She," he pointed at Caroline, "will not give this area or my decision an ounce of respect. She is set against it and determined to colour the whole experience with her displeasure. She has not even met Miss Bennet, with whom she might be able to form a friendship, yet she has dismissed the notion. I am not too harsh."

"You are a trifle sharp," Darcy interjected.

Bingley whirled to face him.

"I am not saying that what you said was incorrect. I have no desire to marry your sister. However, it might not have been said at the most appropriate time." He gave Caroline a small smile. "You are a beautiful, accomplished young woman. There is no deficit in you that causes me to reject you." He sighed. "I just do not believe we would suit, and..."

He shifted uneasily. He did not reveal much of his inner thoughts aloud very often, and when he did, it was never to Caroline Bingley. He sometimes shared them with Bingley and Richard, but beyond that, even his sister was not privy to many of his closely guarded views.

"I wish to marry for love." There he had said it. "I do not love you. Not in that way, at least. You are a friend and the sister of a friend, but, I apologize if this is too blunt, that is all. And no, I do not see that changing."

He placed a hand on her arm as he saw the tears gathering in her eyes. "Believe me, there is no deficiency in you. My affections are just not engaged."

She lifted her chin. "I understand." She turned to her brother. "I will return to greet your guests, but I find I must get some air. Louisa!"

Mrs. Hurst rose quickly from her spot on the sofa near her husband and escorted her sister out of the room.

"I shall be returning to London before the season," Hurst said from behind the paper he was reading. "I shall take Caroline with me." He lowered the paper for a moment and looked at Darcy. "That was well done, sir. Neither she nor her sister has listened one jot to my opinion on the subject of her being the mistress of Pemberley. They shall have to give it some credence now."

Darcy sighed. He had known that at some point he might have to dash Caroline's hopes, but he had hoped that some other gentleman would catch her fancy and the issue would take care of itself.

"You wish to marry for love," Bingley said with a grin.

Darcy nodded. "As you know. However, I do apologize for causing your sister pain."

"She is the cause of her own pain," Bingley retorted. "I just hope she can accept your words and begin to look for a husband in earnest."

"I doubt she is completely daft," Darcy replied.

"You'd be surprised," Hurst muttered from behind his paper, causing Bingley to laugh and Darcy to shake his head and grin.

~*~*~

"Mr. Bennet, Mr. William Bennet," Bingley rose from his seat and greeted the gentlemen as they entered the drawing room half an hour later.

Darcy had finally relaxed enough to sit in a chair and participate in a discussion about the fields they had seen on their morning ride. Now, however, as the gentlemen he had eagerly anticipated entered the room, his nerves once again rose to an uncomfortable pitch. He tugged his sleeves straight and fidgeted with the buttons on his waistcoat. At this moment, he would very much like to take Caroline up on her offer to walk around the garden. He doubted, though, that Mr. Bennet and his son would be disposed to accepting such a suggestion, and Bingley, no doubt, would be equally as unwilling a participant since the tea he had ordered was just being brought into the room. Therefore, Darcy would take his seat and endure the discomfort of remaining motionless. He was certain that it would have been better to meet these gentlemen in the field with a gun, a few dogs, and the chance of securing a pheasant dinner. Calls in the drawing rooms were, in his opinion, made the best use of by gentlemen when courting lady.

"I understand my eldest daughters came upon you while riding yesterday," Mr. Bennet said as soon as he settled onto a settee. "I believe William made all the proper introductions."

"Indeed, he did," Bingley assured him. "It was a delightful surprise to meet some of my new neighbours so soon upon my arrival."

Though Darcy's eyes were on Mr. Bennet, he could also see that William Bennet was studying him carefully. He shifted his eyes to the young man and made note of the small scowl he wore.

"Have you spent much time in the country?" Mr. Bennet was asking Bingley when Darcy turned his attention back to the conversation.

"I have spent a considerable amount of time at Pemberley, but this is the first time that I will be officially residing somewhere other than in a town. My father's business was in manufacturing, so we lived in Manchester. In fact, his sister and her husband are still there."

"My brother Gardiner is in trade," Mr. Bennet answered with a smile. "He does right well, I can tell you that. He has as fine a home as can be found near Cheapside and warehouses that are never idle."

Darcy tipped his head to the side, and one eyebrow rose as he contemplated how his relations might react to such ties should he decide to pursue Miss Elizabeth. Lady Catherine would never be satisfied with any choice he made that was not of her own choosing, but Lord Matlock? Well, there were political advantages to having some connections in trade. "What sort of things does he store in his warehouses?"

"Mainly textiles, although he is not opposed to accepting a shipment of spices, tea, or any other good with a healthy profit margin." The right side of Mr. Bennet's mouth tipped up, and a sparkle, not unlike the one Darcy had seen in Elizabeth's eyes, settled into her father's eyes. "Gardiner inherited most of the intelligence in his family."

"Indeed?" Darcy's brows rose.

"He is the most sensible one of the three. Did you meet Mrs. Philips?" Mr. Bennet asked Bingley.

He nodded.

"She is nice but a bit flighty, is she not?"

Bingley shrugged. "I really could not say."

Mr. Bennet laughed. "Very well, I will not force you to be impolite. I shall take on that task myself. I can tell you, having been married to her sister for these past twenty-three years, that Mrs.

Philips is indeed flighty and as good at carrying a tale as the society papers in the *Times*. My wife is very similar. Gardiner, however, cares not one jot for gossip that cannot benefit his business and has a head for numbers that is matched by few. I assure you he is the most sensible of the three."

"He sounds an interesting sort of chap," Bingley commented.

"That he is. My eldest daughters are favourites of him and his wife, while my youngest are favourites of Mrs. Philips. I know of what I speak when comparing sensibilities."

Darcy was not altogether sure he enjoyed hearing a gentleman speak so of his family on so short an acquaintance.

"It is best if you know the particulars before you are subjected to my wife's schemes."

Ah. That made sense.

"Is she a matchmaker?" Darcy asked.

"Only if a gentleman meets her qualifications," Mr. Bennet said with a chuckle, "and if her sister's intelligence is accurate, I believe both of you have enough qualifications to your names to be worthy of her daughters."

A fortune hunter? Darcy had met enough of those in his seasons.

"Do not look so frightened, Mr. Darcy. I assure you, you will not be trapped in some unscrupulous scheme. Mrs. Bennet's daughters are to be prized, which is something on which I do not disagree with my wife. But unlike my wife, whose main goal is to see her daughters well-settled without a worry for their financial care – and who can blame a mother for wishing such for her children – my desires for them extend to their emotional well being."

"My sisters will not marry without love and respect," William inserted with a curiously pointed look for Darcy. He had seemed a very pleasant sort of fellow yesterday. Darcy was uncertain what had transpired between then and now to cause him to be so skeptical.

"I wish the same for my sister," Darcy replied. "My cousin, Colonel Fitzwilliam, and I are her guardians now that my parents are no longer with us," he added.

"How old is she?" William asked.

"Not yet sixteen."

"The same age as my Lydia," Mr. Bennet said. "It can be a trying age. I should know since I have endured it four times already. I wish you well with your task, sir."

"Thank you. I hope to succeed with it."

Mr. Bennet tipped his head. "You sound unsure of yourself."

"I have had a setback as of late," Darcy replied.

"I hope it was nothing too serious."

Darcy blew out a breath. "The trouble was discovered in time."

"Does she travel with you?" William asked.

Darcy shook his head. "My aunt thought it best for her to remain in town and continue her lessons."

"Lady Matlock?"

"You know of my connections?" Darcy replied to William. The fact that William knew Darcy was related to Lord Matlock and still looked at him with suspicion rather than just promoting his sister spoke well of the man to Darcy. It seemed William was adamantly truthful about his sisters not marrying for anything other than love and respect.

"Several of them," William replied.

There was a lifting of one brow that accompanied a pointed

look which spoke of the young man knowing something that Darcy should realize was not a recommendation of his character.

"I should be interested to hear all you know at some point." Darcy rose as Caroline and Louisa entered the room with Hurst and were introduced. He chuckled to himself as he realized he would no longer be the object of the younger Bennet's scrutiny. Caroline would have that pleasure.

"We do not wish to overstay our welcome," Mr. Bennet said after a few minutes of small talk with the ladies. "I will extend an invitation to you all to call on us at Longbourn, but I will do it with the warning that my wife will attempt to discover your favorite dishes and will insist that you join us for dinner."

Again, the right corner of his mouth tipped up, and his eyes twinkled. "She wished for me to make the invitation myself, but she will get far more pleasure extending it to you herself, so I refused her pleas. I will, however, inform you that she is the best hostess in the area, and our cook is excellent. You will not be disappointed, should you choose to accept her offer."

He handed his teacup to Bingley and pushed up from the settee. "William and I will look forward to seeing you in the future as well. In fact, William will be riding out tomorrow morning. I suspect you are the sort who enjoys an early morning ride as much as he does."

"Indeed, we do," Bingley agreed eagerly.

"He will be riding alone," Mr. Bennet cautioned with a grin.

"As will we," Bingley replied, "although if I am with Darcy, and he is with me, we are not truly alone, are we?"

Mr. Bennet joined Bingley in a hearty laugh.

He took his hat from the butler. "It has been a joy to meet you, and I do not say that to most. In fact, if I were to be honest, I try my best to avoid meeting new people – old ones, too." He winked. "I prefer books."

He gave his farewells to the Hursts and Caroline and was gone, William following closely behind him.

Darcy looked at the clock. Fifteen minutes almost to the second. It was possible that he might be able to like Mr. Bennet. The man was short on calls and, according to his own account, a lover of books. He released a sigh. Now, if only he could figure out what it was that the younger Bennet held against him.

# Chapter 7

Placing her bonnet on the table near the door and beginning to unfasten her pelisse upon returning from her walk the next day, Elizabeth smiled as she saw Jane descending the stairs. For once, she would not have to break her fast alone.

"Did you see William?" Jane asked eagerly.

Elizabeth chuckled. "No. Nor did I see Mr. Bingley or Mr. Darcy."

Jane sighed. "Do you think they will call on us? Papa told them they may."

"I was there," Elizabeth reminded her sister.

Their poor father had been thoroughly questioned by their mother about the house, both Mr. Bingley's and Mr. Darcy's clothes, the demeanor of both gentlemen, and the type of china in which the tea was served, as well as about Mr. Bingley's other guests. Mr. Bennet had borne it as patiently as a gentleman might until he had answered each question twice. Upon the third presentation of a question regarding if the butler seemed pleased to be serving his new master, Mr. Bennet told his wife that she might gather all the information she needed the following day as he was certain that Mr. Bingley would be calling on Longbourn since Mr. Bennet had given him leave to do so.

"But are you not eager to see them again?" Jane wrapped an arm around Elizabeth's and went with her to the breakfast room.

"Perhaps not so eager as you," Elizabeth teased.

"Is he not perfect? His features are so animated when he speaks, and his hair is just the most divine mix of sunshine and sunset."

"Jane!" Elizabeth said with a laugh. "You sound more like Lydia than yourself."

Jane sighed as she took her seat. "He is just so handsome and amiable."

Elizabeth could not deny that. Mr. Bingley appeared to be all that a young man should be – handsome, pleasant, and rich. She smiled. Even she sounded a bit like her youngest sister.

"Good morning, Papa," she said as her father entered to gather his cup of tea and a plate of toast and jam before burying himself in his book room for a morning of reading in relative silence.

"Good morning, Lizzy, Jane." He poured his tea into his cup and looked up at Jane with a smirk. "Has William returned from his ride?"

"No, and Elizabeth did not see him," Jane replied in a very sincere and concerned tone.

Mr. Bennet drew out his watch, looked at it, glanced at the clock on the mantle, and with a shrug, returned the watch to his pocket. "It is only early yet. However, when he does return, I wish to speak with him first."

Jane pulled a lip between her teeth and nodded while her father chuckled.

"I shall not keep him long. I only wish to know something about a field." He placed a second piece of toast, smeared with jam, on his plate and prepared to exit the room. "I would expect him in no more than an hour. I know how he likes to eat his break-fast before the sun is too high in the sky."

An hour later, Jane paced from the window to her seat in the sitting room, sat for a moment, and then paced back to the window. "It has been an hour," she said to Elizabeth. "He should be here by now."

"He is likely just enjoying himself. He does not have other gen-tlemen to ride with every day," Elizabeth replied.

"Oh, but he will be hungry," Mrs. Bennet added. "I always tell him to take an apple or a biscuit with him, but he refuses. And now he shall faint of hunger, and Longbourn will be without an heir. I am certain I could never be at ease seeing Longbourn given to some stranger."

"Mama, he shall not perish from hunger after one day," Eliza-beth said.

"One never knows," Mrs. Bennet argued. "He will be weak, and if he should perchance get his feet wet, he will not be strong enough to fight off the illness that will arise and then after an excruciating period of fever during which we shall attempt to make him at ease — but it will be impossible — he shall gasp his last and leave us to another."

"Mama!" Elizabeth cried.

"We could go look for him," Jane sat on the edge of her chair, looking excessively excited. "We could take an apple with us."

Mrs. Bennet's hand flew to her heart. "Oh, you are so good, Jane." She turned to Elizabeth. "Why did you not think of that?"

"Because I do not believe William is in any grave danger. He is only a few minutes later than expected."

Mrs. Bennet pursed her lips and shook her head. "Go with your sister. I cannot have both William and Jane missing. Surely if you are with her, there is little chance that anything ill will befall her."

"Do you not care if Lizzy does not return?" Mary asked.

"Whatever would possess you to ask such a thing?" her mother demanded. "Of course, I shall be devastated if Elizabeth does not return, but one must realize that of all my daughters, Jane is the most beautiful and likely the one to ensure that if something happens to William, I and any remaining unwed children, of which you may be one, will be well-cared-for should the worst befall your father."

Elizabeth was not certain if she should be insulted by her mother words or simply pleased that, should she not return, she would be missed. She did not stay in the room long enough to hear the argument that was about to erupt between Mary and their mother. Mama would likely be calling for her salts soon enough as she would talk herself into flutters. Instead, Elizabeth hurried up to her room behind Jane and prepared to set out to find her missing brother.

~*~*~

"When you marry Mr. Bingley," Elizabeth began when she and Jane had ridden far enough from the stables to not be heard by anyone, "you shall have to invite Mary to visit you in town. I am certain Mr. Bingley will not always remain at Netherfield, and if we do not wish to have Papa driven to an early grave due to the incessant arguing between Mama and Mary, we must see Mary well-matched soon."

Jane giggled. "They have been bickering a great deal lately."

"I think it is the way Mama critiques everything Mary does. It is always wanting in some way. She is not so lively as Lydia, she is not so accomplished as Mama expects her to be, and she is not so beautiful as you – not that any of us is."

Jane gasped.

"You know it is true, Jane. Not one of us can compare to you in beauty. Although Lydia does come close, she does not have your sweet spirit."

Jane shook her head. "Kitty. Kitty is far prettier than I am."

"Kitty?" Elizabeth's voice was filled with incredulity.

"Yes, Kitty." Jane replied. "When she is not following Lydia's advice and just dresses herself as she wishes, she is pretty, and in a year or two she will be the one all the young men will be seeking." Jane smiled broadly at Elizabeth. "That should make Lydia excessively perturbed!"

"Our poor father!" Elizabeth cried as both she and Jane dissolved into laughter for a moment. They both knew that Lydia expected to be the one to step into Jane's place when Jane married. It did not matter to Lydia that she was the youngest. She was only second in her mind to Jane.

"Mr. Crenshaw," Jane said when they had sobered.

"What do you mean?"

"I will not have to find a husband for Mary. Mr. Crenshaw has been paying her particular attention at assemblies for the last year, and he always appears to be very happy to see her if we happen to meet him in Meryton."

Elizabeth's brow furrowed as she thought. Mr. Crenshaw had been polite in every meeting, and he had asked both her and Mary as well as Jane to dance. "Are you certain he has singled her out?"

Jane nodded. "Watch him at the next assembly. He will ask us each to dance, but he will not be as animated dancing with us as he will be with Mary. And, if you watch him when he is not dancing, you will see that he is often looking in her direction."

"Truly?"

Jane nodded.

Elizabeth had not paused to notice such things at assemblies. She had been so busy looking for possible matches for Jane that she had not once thought about Mary. She would have to make an effort to be more attentive at the next assembly.

"He is very nice," she said after a moment of silent contemplation.

"And pleasing to the eye," Jane added with a smirk.

"True," Elizabeth agreed. Mr. Crenshaw was not tall and dashing, but he was not short either. And his features reminded her of those that a sculptor might chisel out of marble. He was neither portly nor thin, and she had to admit he always smelled rather nice.

"That, along with the fact that his farm does very well, will make him a most acceptable choice for Mary. She shall want for nothing." Jane looked at Elizabeth. "And even William approves of him. I asked — last night as I was thinking about the assembly and remembered Mr. Crenshaw." She sighed. "It will be the most perfect assembly ever if Mr. Bingley asks me to dance."

Elizabeth chuckled. "It will be indeed."

"And Mr. Darcy will ask you."

"If William allows it," Elizabeth muttered.

"Whatever do you mean?"

"Have you not noticed how uneasy William seems when he speaks of Mr. Darcy?"

Jane shook her head.

"Well, I have, and I have been determined to ask him about it. However, I still have not had the opportunity to do so. There must be something about Mr. Darcy of which William knows and does not approve. Perhaps I should not even like him."

"But how can you not?" Jane cried. "He is very handsome and rich – very, very rich!"

"Yet, if his character is wanting," Elizabeth refuted. She drew her horse to a stop. "This is the field Papa said William was going to, is it not?"

Jane looked in all directions. "I believe so."

"And yet he is not here."

"Mr. Jones," Jane called to a man who was plucking fruit from a tree in the orchard that stood next to the field in which they rode."

"Aye, miss," the gentleman climbed down from his ladder and came to stand by the stone wall that enclosed the orchard. He wiped his brow with a handkerchief and then replaced his hat. "How might I be of service?"

"Have you seen William?" Jane asked.

"Aye," the man glanced at the sky, "some time ago now. He and I and the two gents with him had a good discussion about the piece of wall in need of repair. Those boards will not hold back the cattle for long, especially after the winter does her work."

"I am certain Father will have it repaired before the trees are flowering in the spring," Jane replied with a smile.

"I do not doubt it, miss. Your father is a good man, but there are only so many hands to complete so much work."

"True, but my father adores jam on his toast – damson jam in particular – so I dare say, you shall be first on his list of things to be seen to."

"A good jam is a pleasure. That's for certain," Mr. Jones agreed with a chuckle. "I like it right well myself."

"How is the baby?" Jane asked.

"He's a joy, miss. Fat and pink, he is. He'll be in church this Sunday."

"I am glad to hear it," Jane said.

"As am I," Elizabeth added.

"Those gents will be there as well. The tall one – Mr. Darcy – said he'd be pleased to meet my Zachary. They both seemed very nice sorts of fellows." He removed his hat once again and dried his brow. "They and the young Mr. Bennet were headed toward Oakham Mount, though I think the young Mr. Bennet was talking about only going as far as the wood."

"Thank you, Mr. Jones." Jane dipped her head, an action that was met with a small bow from Mr. Jones before he returned to his work.

"Do you wish to go to the wood first or Oakham Mount?" Elizabeth asked.

"It seems silly to go to Oakham Mount before the wood if William was talking of going there, do you not think?"

Elizabeth nodded, and the two turned toward the wood that stood between Longbourn and Oakham Mount.

# Chapter 8

Darcy turned quickly toward William. "What did you say?"

"That militia is due to arrive in Meryton soon," William replied.

"Who is their colonel?" Normally, the arrival of a regiment in an area caused little concern to Darcy beyond what was standard. The increase in men in an area always came with some inherent tribulations if those men were to be of the rowdy sort, and then there was the ever-present issue of providing accommodations as needed as well as food and supplies. However, this time Darcy had a reason for increased concern.

William shrugged. "Forster, I believe, is what Sir William said when he called last, and if anyone knows the happenings of Meryton better than the gossips, it's Sir William Lucas."

Darcy had heard a rumor that Wickham had attached himself to some militia. He would have to ask his cousin to see if Richard knew under whose command Wickham would be.

"Do you know this Colonel Forster?" William asked.

Darcy shook his head. "But my cousin might."

"The town will be less serene once they arrive," Bingley commented. He stopped and picked up a rock to toss into the stream beside which they were walking. Upon getting to the shade of the woods with its low hanging branches, they had decided that dismounting and leading their horses would be the best way to proceed, and then, William had suggested they water their mounts at this stream.

"As will be Longbourn's sitting room," William muttered.

"Do you provide lodging?" Darcy asked.

William shook his head. "That would be ill-advised considering the number of sisters I have," he replied with a laugh. "The officers will find their way to our house well enough, however." He shook his head again. "And my mother and youngest sisters will welcome them with great delight."

"Ah," Darcy commented. "A gentleman in a smart red coat can turn a head or two – at least, that is what my cousin says."

"He is most certainly right!" William said.

"Do all of your sisters prefer red coats to other colours?" Bingley asked.

William chuckled. "Not all. Lydia certainly, Kitty most likely, but the others are looking for more than a smart jacket."

Darcy stopped and stood for a moment at the edge of the stream. What a trial it must be to have five sisters for whom to care. He had found his one sister enough of a trial, and Bingley's two sisters were forever giving him trouble. Five! To see all five well-matched and wed!

"I believe one of my sisters was impressed by a blue coat the other day," William added with an amused look for Bingley, who grinned in response.

"It is a fine coat. Cost me a good deal, but it is as long in value as it is in good looks."

"Bingley is as much enamoured with fashion as is his sister. However, he is more frugal," Darcy teased. He was finding it easy to be relaxed the longer they moved through the countryside together.

"And does your sister have any preference for coats?" William asked, keeping his eyes directed forward, though Darcy noticed the poor fellow's ears growing red.

"Whichever one Darcy might be wearing," Bingley responded with a laugh.

"Is that how it is?" William asked.

"No!" Darcy exclaimed. "That is not how it is." He did not want the brother of the lady he wished to know better to think he already belonged to another.

"It is how Caroline would wish it," Bingley replied.

Darcy glared at Bingley until he caught his eye, then he tipped his head toward William. Had he not been listening last evening when Darcy had been telling him how William Bennet seemed to admire Caroline?

Bingley's eyes grew wide, and he stumbled. "She has no hope of securing Darcy," Bingley added hastily. "His affections lie elsewhere."

"You are betrothed."

Darcy blinked. It was not a question but a statement as if William knew that it was a fact. "No, I am not."

"Not to Miss Bingley," William agreed.

"Not to anyone," Darcy refuted.

"No one?" William asked.

Darcy shook his head. "Why would you think I am?"

William shrugged. "Just a rumour I heard, although the source seemed good enough to be believed."

Fallen leaves crunched under boots and hooves.

"Have you met any of my relations?" Darcy asked. There was a hoped-for betrothal about which only those close to the family would know, but he did not think any of them would speak of it, save, perhaps, for his Aunt Catherine.

"No," William replied.

Darcy's chest constricted as realization dawned on him. There was one other person who might bandy about the supposed betrothal. He looked up through the leaves at the sky. The sun was climbing higher in the clear blue beyond the trees' canopy. "It is growing late."

Bingley pulled out his watch. "It is not so very late." He snapped the timepiece closed and tucked it back into his pocket.

"Late enough," Darcy retorted. "By the time we have returned, I will be far beyond hungry."

Bingley looked at him skeptically as well he should. Darcy always ate something before going for a ride, and he had just indulged in some wild berries. Darcy shook his head and hoped Bingley would not press the issue. If William Bennet was a friend or even an acquaintance of George Wickham, Darcy wanted nothing to do with either William or any member of his family.

"If you insist." Bingley's look of disbelief remained in place. "But we might come across more berries."

"I would rather have a cup of tea and a piece of toast." Far away from any of Wickham's associates. Darcy stepped to turn back in the direction from which they had come. However, his foot found some damp leaves covering a rock and slid off of the rock. His ankle twisted as his foot slipped, and down he went.

"Oh, do not move." A feminine voice called as Darcy attempted to rise.

His right hip, having made contact with the rock when he landed, smarted more than his pride and that combined with the ache in his ankle gave him incentive to not refute the instructions. He cursed his boot, the leaves, and that blasted rock for keeping him from his escape and instead, throwing him in front of the very lady he was hoping to forget once he returned to Netherfield.

William helped first Elizabeth and then Jane from their horses.

"What have you done to poor Mr. Darcy?" Elizabeth teased her brother. "Did he say something not to your liking?"

"It was simply wet leaves," Darcy answered. "I am certain in a moment, as soon as I have recovered my breath, I shall be well and able as ever to return to Netherfield."

"Longbourn is closer," Elizabeth said, as she motioned for William to do something.

Darcy's eyes grew wide as William knelt at his feet and placed his hands on Darcy's ankle.

"I know the boot has likely saved you any serious injury," William said apologetically. "However, if I do not assure my sisters that you are well, one of them will likely take on the task of examining your ankle in my stead." He shot a displeased look at Elizabeth, who pressed her lips together to keep from smiling.

Darcy willingly allowed William to prod and poke his ankle before bending it this way and that. He did not wish for Miss Elizabeth to conduct such an evaluation. She was distracting enough just standing there.

Darcy blew out a breath when William moved to stand up. "As I said, all is well."

Elizabeth crossed her arms. "Then I should like to see you stand on it."

"Do you not believe I can?" Darcy questioned.

"You nearly hid your discomfort," she answered. "Longbourn is closer," she added.

"I can ride my horse. There is no need to walk, so it makes little difference whether I stop at Longbourn or continue to Netherfield."

"The surgeon can be summoned faster from Longbourn than Netherfield, and the longer you let that foot hang at the side of your horse, the more swollen it will become."

"Are you always so argumentative?" Darcy snapped. His foot was throbbing, and she was correct. He did not know which was worse.

"Only when speaking to someone with little sense," Elizabeth retorted. "Do as you will, but I do hope you do not mind having your boot cut off our foot. It seems a waste to ruin such a nice piece of leather."

"We could remove the boot now," Bingley suggested.

"No!" Darcy growled. "Just help me onto my horse."

"Come, Jane," Elizabeth said. "Give William the apple." She was already mounting her horse with William's help.

It seemed to Darcy that William was always ready to bend to his sister's will, and Miss Elizabeth with the fine eyes? Well, she was nothing more than a harridan in a pretty package. Bingley could call at Longbourn if he wished, but Darcy would not be setting one foot outside of Netherfield, not that he could at present even if he wished to do so. Blasted leaves! He gritted his teeth as he placed his weight on his foot and managed to hoist himself onto his horse.

"We will send someone for the surgeon," Miss Bennet assured Mr. Bingley before following Elizabeth.

"You do not need to see me home," Darcy said to William.

William shook his head. "You almost convinced me."

"I beg your pardon?" Darcy asked.

"I thought perhaps my source was painting you with a cruel brush as you did not appear to be as cold as he described. However, I see I am wrong."

"Your source is a liar," Darcy snapped.

"I had thought so as he did tend to be very good at changing a story to suit the crowd around him, but what kind-hearted gentleman rejects the help of a lady who is thinking only of his wellbeing? He does not. An arrogant one does." He clucked to his horse and rode a distance away before turning and stopping to look back. "I cannot stop you from calling at Longbourn, but I shall not be recommending either of you to my sisters or my father."

"Well done," Bingley grumbled. "And no, I shall not be marrying your sister just because you have ruined my chances with Miss Bennet."

Darcy nudged his horse forward. "I do not want to be examined in the home of a stranger," Darcy called after him. "How is that wrong?"

Bingley said nothing. He just galloped away.

"Blasted leaves," Darcy muttered as he urged his horse to go faster while concentrating on keeping his foot from getting jostled too much.

~*~*~

Darcy leaned back on propped up pillows and looked around his room – the room in which he would pass many hours over the next day or two. The surgeon had assured him that the ankle was only sprained and with a few days of rest would be well on its way back to full strength.

"Your writing things, sir." Darcy's valet placed a small desk on the bed.

Darcy placed it across his legs and unfolded the slope before sliding the drawer that ran the length of the top open and preparing his pen and ink for writing. Withdrawing a sheet of paper from its drawer, he began his letter to his cousin.

He had half a mind to tell his man to prepare for travel and be gone from here, but his conscience would not allow him to forget his promise to his friend. He blew out an exasperated breath. He also could not drive from his mind the face of Elizabeth Bennet.

He paused in his writing. She had been correct. His foot had swollen a good deal before he had gotten to Netherfield. In fact, he had considered stopping at Longbourn so that he could remove his boot. Thankfully, his valet had been insistent that it could be pulled from his person rather than cut. It had not been a pleasant extraction, but the boot had been saved.

"Mr. Darcy."

His man was back.

"Miss Bingley is without and would like to know if there is anything you require. She has even volunteered to read to you if needed."

Darcy's brows raised. Bingley must be more than a trifle angry at him, or Caroline would never have made it so far as his door. He shook his head.

"I am certain you can procure whatever might be needed, and

as I have not injured my eyes or my head, I am capable of reading to myself."

"I shall tell her, sir."

"I will, however, be in need of having my meals brought up on a tray," he called after his man, and then turned his attention back to his letter. He disliked using only half a sheet, but there was not much to tell his cousin. He had shared that the ladies at Longbourn were as beautiful as they were fabled to be, that he had injured his ankle, that Netherfield seemed a fine, solid house, and that he had reason to believe the younger Mr. Bennet was an associate of Wickham. He followed that assertion with his request for information about which militia Wickham had joined. That was all that was needed. Therefore, whether half a sheet of words or a full sheet written twice over, this paper was going to be folded and sent.

Darcy secured all of his supplies in his desk and moved it to the side of the bed. He would have his man see that letter sent express as soon as possible. With a sigh, he picked up the book he had been reading from the table next to the bed.

"Blasted leaves," he muttered as he prepared to pass a few of the long, lonely hours before him with some poetry.

# Chapter 9

Jane glared at Elizabeth from across the sitting room. She had not spoken one word to her since they left the wood. Jane was not one to raise her voice and allow her anger to spill forth in unguarded words when she was put out. No. She usually became a wall of silence – firm and impenetrable until she was prepared to have a discussion with whoever had offended her.

Such silence accompanied by that glare was more than Elizabeth's guilt-ridden heart could withstand. She very much disliked it when Jane was angry with her. She needed to right the wrong that stood between them. However, she knew Jane would not air her grievances in front of their mother and sisters. Therefore, Elizabeth rose from her place and returned her stitching to the basket on the table. "I am going for a walk in the garden." She looked at Jane. "Would you like to join me?"

The eyebrow over Jane's left eye arched.

"Please," Elizabeth said softly.

"She has had too much sun as it is," Mrs. Bennet declared. "We cannot risk her turning brown."

"Please," Elizabeth mouthed.

Jane's eyes narrowed, and her lips pursed before she sighed. "I will wear my wide-brimmed bonnet," Jane assured her mother. "The one I wear to tend the flowers."

"Just the same, stay in the shade as much as possible," their mother called after them. "A gentleman does not want a wife who looks as if she had been put to sea."

Jane took her hat from the hook on the wall near the door at the rear of the house.

"Forgive me," Elizabeth said as soon as their feet had reached the garden path. "I should not have argued."

"No, you should not have," Jane agreed. "When will you learn to hold your tongue?"

Elizabeth sighed. "Not soon enough, I am afraid."

Gaining Jane's forgiveness was only the first step in setting things to right. Elizabeth knew she also needed to speak to William, whom she had seen circling the garden from the window in the sitting room. While Jane might offer her forgiveness — grudgingly though it currently appeared to be — forgiveness between sisters was not enough to undo the wrong that Elizabeth's propensity to argue had created.

"Let me talk to William. There must be something we can do to fix this mess I have created. Mr. Darcy's response to my insistence was not so very unusual. I am certain any gentleman would have been less than polite when his foot was injured. I should have considered that."

Jane wrapped her arm around Elizabeth's, a sure sign that her anger was fading. "I cannot believe William wishes to cut ties with both Mr. Darcy and Mr. Bingley over a few cross words."

"I do not believe he truly will once he has had time for his anger to cool," Elizabeth said hopefully.

"He is very protective of us," Jane cautioned. "He may not change his mind."

It was a possibility that Elizabeth had considered. William could be stubborn to a fault at times, especially when it came to family and how they should be treated. While it was an endearing trait of his that he cared so much for his sisters, there were moments when it did become a hindrance – such as now.

"Even if he does not change his mind," Elizabeth assured Jane, "I will find a way for you to see Mr. Bingley, even if I have to walk to Netherfield myself and apologize to Mr. Darcy."

"You would do that for me?"

Elizabeth nodded. "I would do just about anything for you, my dear sister, even humiliating myself by begging forgiveness from a gentleman who should be seeking it from me."

Jane laughed lightly. "You are too good."

"I am not, and you know it. That is why our brother is stomping around the garden. Be careful of the rose bushes," she called to William, who was swatting at the trees and bushes with his walking stick as he moved along the path.

"I would not dare harm them," William called back. "And, I am not going to change my mind, Lizzy." He straightened his shoulders and lifted his chin. "No matter how pathetic Jane might attempt to look. Those gentlemen are not the sort that deserve my sisters."

"Everyone spits an angry word at one time or another," Elizabeth replied as they approached him. "And I am very good at provoking such words." She smiled at William.

He sighed and shook his head. "You are a proficient at it, but it is more than that. They are just not the sort of gentlemen with whom I would like to see my sisters."

Oh! He was infuriating at times!

"What is it then?" Elizabeth asked. "You cannot just declare someone unfit to marry without reason. You know I will not just accept your decree without proof."

William scowled at the veracity of such a statement.

"You have not liked Mr. Darcy since you heard his name," Elizabeth continued. "You were cautious about him as if you knew something about him when discussing it with Father at dinner on the day we met them. Yet, Lydia has not found anything unflattering in the papers tied to his name, so what is it that you are not saying?"

William held Elizabeth's gaze for a long, silent, stubborn minute. "Very well," he finally said. "I have heard that he is not as he appears, but gossip is not right."

"Neither is sending away a perfectly amiable and handsome gentleman, whom I like very much, for no apparent reason," Jane said firmly. "I do not wish to die a beautiful spinster, William – at least, not without knowing why it must be so."

William handed her his handkerchief. "There is no need for tears."

"There is when you are three and twenty and not allowed to marry anyone!" Jane cried with a stamp of her foot – a rare display of temper for her.

William turned away from them, walking three paces forward and then returning. That he did not wish to say anything was evident in his every feature, yet he could not look at Jane dabbing her eyes with his handkerchief without shaking his head and beginning an explanation. "Mr. Darcy was supposed to install his father's godson as the rector of a valuable living. It was written in his father's will. Yet, when the position fell open, Mr. Darcy refused to do as his father had instructed, and now, because Mr. Darcy is an arrogant – " he cleared his throat, "man..."

Elizabeth was certain that was not the word William had wanted to use.

"...there is a man who is having to shift his way through the world when he should be preaching sermons and stirring the fire in the hearth of his parsonage."

"Could there not be a reason for Mr. Darcy's refusal?" Elizabeth asked.

William turned toward her. "This same man told me Mr. Darcy is betrothed, and yet, today, when I asked him, he denied it."

"Perhaps because he is not betrothed," Elizabeth argued. It was very unusual for William to believe one person over another so adamantly. Had he even paused to consider that Mr. Darcy might know more about his being betrothed than someone else? Whatever other bits of information William had heard about Mr. Darcy must be colouring his judgment.

"You are very argumentative, Lizzy Bennet," William spat.

"Only when I am speaking to those who are refusing to use the good sense the Lord gave them!"

"No, not only then. Any time you think you are right – which is nearly always." William crossed his arms and glared at her.

Elizabeth pulled herself straight. Was there no one who was willing to sort this thing out? How difficult could it be to set things to right? "You will not discover the truth for your sister?" She motioned to Jane.

"I know the truth, and it is that Mr. Darcy is a cold man and any friend of his is not to be trusted."

Elizabeth rolled her eyes and huffed. He only knew what he thought was the truth. Truly, William could be as stubborn and set in his ways as their mother! "One angry exchange? Is that all the evidence you have?"

William did not reply.

"I thought so." She held his gaze. He could glare at her as long as he liked. She would not be driven away by a look of displeasure when she knew she was right, and he needed to reconsider his position.

"I did not say Mr. Bingley could not call," he finally said.

"No, but you will likely sway Papa, and then what does it matter. I shall die an old maid." Jane wiped her eyes once again as she looked upward in an attempt not to let any more tears fall.

"You will not," Elizabeth said, wrapping an arm around Jane's shoulders. "*I* will not allow it to happen."

"And I shall not say a word to Father unless asked," William added. Tears from any of his sisters were his weakness. "At least, I will not say a word about Mr. Bingley that is. I may tell him about Mr. Darcy."

Elizabeth arched a brow.

"He is not what you think he is. I have only told you a portion," William replied.

"And who is this gentleman who has told you these things? Is he a man of high morals? Is his reputation so far beyond reproach that you would risk our sister's happiness?" Elizabeth could not say why she was so determined to hold to the idea that William was wrong about Mr. Darcy. Perhaps it was because Mr. Darcy was handsome, or perhaps it was because his eyes had spoken of sincerity when they had first met. She had seen the way he pondered things before speaking. He was not a gentleman to act brashly. There must be some other explanation for the living not to be bestowed as intended. There just must be.

"Mr. Darcy's actions today confirm the truth of what I have heard," William retorted.

Elizabeth shook her head. Mr. Darcy had spoken crossly, but that did not mean he was always cross or cold. However, she knew that trying to reason with William just now was likely futile. Therefore, with an "if you say so" that clearly spoke of her disbelief, she and Jane left him and completed their turn of the garden before returning to the house – Jane to her room where she could wallow in misery undisturbed, and Elizabeth to her father's study.

~*~*~

"My Lizzy," he greeted her with a smile as she entered. "How might I be of service?"

Elizabeth settled into one of a pair of leather chairs in front of his desk. "I was wondering. Is it possible for a will to be ignored?"

"What do you mean?" Her father leaned forward. "Are you planning to contest my will?"

There was a teasing turn to his lips.

"Of course not!" Elizabeth replied. "I was just wondering about if someone were to leave, say, a set of dishes to his friend's niece and upon this someone's demise, the heir read the will but did not like this friend or his niece. Could he refuse to give the dishes to the niece?"

"Does the niece know about the bequeathing of the dishes?"

Elizabeth nodded.

"Then, I believe, she, or the agent acting on her behalf, would have grounds to protest, and the will would need to be executed as written. A will is a binding legal document. What it says must be carried out."

That was exactly what Elizabeth had thought. She only wished to be assured that she was thinking correctly.

"Was there anything else?"

She shook her head. "No."

"Then may I ask why you are inquiring after wills?"

Elizabeth had known he would be curious about that. "William and I were having a discussion about someone who has not done as instructed by his father's will, and I was certain that the will would have to be followed."

"Did he not give someone a set of dishes?" Her father's lips were still curled in amusement.

"No, it was a valuable living."

Her father's eyebrows rose, and his expression became serious. "Was a protest launched on this gentleman's behalf?'

Elizabeth scowled. She should have thought to ask William that. "I do not know."

Mr. Bennet leaned back. "If no protest was mounted, then I would be asking why it was not."

"Do you mean there could be a reason for the court to deny the gentleman his inheritance?" Again, she chided herself for not having thought of that in time to make mention of it to William.

"Why else would someone not attempt to gain what was rightfully his?" her father asked.

"I do not know," she answered honestly. There had to be a reason both for why Mr. Darcy had not given that man, whoever it was, the living and for why the man had not pursued the matter through the courts of law. Who would walk away from something that would provide him with the means to live, and quite comfortably, without at least attempting to pursue the matter in court? Of course, William had not said the case had not been taken to court, but if it had been and this man had not been installed in the living, then it would mean he had been denied by the court for some reason.

"It is then possible for a court to rule against a man attempting to claim his inheritance?" she asked.

"If there are conditions which must be met," her father replied.

"It is all very interesting and complex," Elizabeth muttered.

"Indeed, it is. That is why your uncle enjoys his work as he does. There is much to study, and your uncle has a keen wit, even if his wife does not."

Elizabeth chuckled.

"Of course, I should not jest but merely be thankful that a gentleman's intelligence is not judged by that of his wife."

"Papa!"

He winked at her. "I did not say I did not love your mother. However, she does drive me to distraction at times." He picked up the book he had discarded on his desk when Elizabeth had entered his study. "Was there anything else?"

"No, Papa. I think I know all I need to know."

"Was William right or wrong?" Her father called to her before she could close the door.

She poked her head around the door. "He was wrong, Papa." Very, very wrong.

# Chapter 10

"Hurry," Elizabeth called to Jane as they walked out early on the Monday morning after the incident in the woods. "I do not wish to miss seeing Mr. Bingley go to the stables."

"Why could we not just go riding where you say he went on Saturday?" Jane called back.

"Because," Elizabeth stopped and waited for Jane to catch up with her, "Mr. Bingley might not take the same path every single day, and if we were to request our horses, we would likely have to explain to William why we did not wish to ride with him."

"Will he not think it strange for us to be walking in the field?"

"He will not ride in the field today. He has gone to Meryton to see the blacksmith."

"Then I do not understand why we could not ride. It is not like we would be interested in visiting the blacksmith," Jane retorted.

She had a point. William would not expect them to join him on such an errand. When she was young, Elizabeth had enjoyed going to the blacksmith shop with her father and brother to see the fire and the glowing metal. However, she had long ago outgrown such a fascination.

"I thought it best to avoid William altogether," Elizabeth said.

"Mr. Bingley has not yet called at Longbourn, and it is William's fault."

There, she had put voice to her anger. How William could keep Jane from an advantageous match such as Mr. Bingley posed, based on nothing more than mere gossip, Elizabeth could not fathom. For each of the past two evenings, she had subjected herself to poring over society pages with Lydia to make certain there was no mention of Mr. Darcy and secretly hoping that some bit of news about him might appear that would cause some doubt in the mind of her brother. However, the exercise had been for naught. There was nothing in the papers that could be remotely tied to Mr. Darcy – neither good nor bad. And yet, William seemed unrelenting in his position.

Their mother was beside herself with curiosity and had made several pleas to Mr. Bennet to call once again on Mr. Bingley and invite him to dinner. How were her daughters to make fine matches if he would not extend himself for them?

Each time Mrs. Bennet said such a thing, Elizabeth would skewer William with a pointed look to which he would only reply with a raised brow and an expression of being superior in his opinions. It was maddening. Elizabeth wanted to rail at him, but she would not, for she knew if she attempted to sway him in such a fashion in front of their parents, he would find it necessary to make his disapproval of both Mr. Darcy and Mr. Bingley known. As of yet, he had not shared what he knew with their father. Elizabeth knew he had not since she had asked him yesterday morning and again today when she saw him in passing in the upstairs hallway.

"He will relent with time," Jane said.

"He might," Elizabeth admitted, although she doubted it to be true, "but how long will that be? Will it be before Mrs. Long presents her daughter to Mr. Bingley? Or before Sir William invites him to dinner so he can meet Charlotte and Maria? We cannot risk such things, for although none can compare to you, how shall he ever know that unless he has spent time with you?"

"I do not like sneaking around."

"Who would be angry with us for staging a serendipitous meeting with Mr. Bingley on our walk?" Elizabeth asked. "Papa would chuckle, and Mama would be more than pleased to learn of such a scheme. It is only William who does not wish to see you well-matched."

Jane grasped Elizabeth's arm before she could lift her spyglass to her eye. "I do not wish to be the cause of a rift between you and William. You have been more than brother and sister. You have been friends. I do not wish to see that end."

Elizabeth shrugged. The thought pained her heart. She did consider William to be a friend and confidant. They had shared many secrets over the years. Even when he was at school, he had written to her about his friends and their antics – well, at least, some of them. She doubted he had told her everything since he had not mentioned hearing tales about Mr. Darcy. "He is wrong, Jane. I know he is. I asked Papa about the will. The living could not be refused simply because Mr. Darcy did not wish to give it to this person William met. If he will not listen to reason, then it is not you nor I who have caused a division. It is him and his unbending opinion."

Jane sighed. There was a sad resignation to the sound.

"We can make things right," Elizabeth assured her. "But to do so, we must talk to Mr. Bingley."

Those were the words that Jane needed to hear.

Elizabeth lifted her glass and scanned Netherfield's grounds.

Putting things right was something of which Jane could approve – even if doing so required a bit of subterfuge.

"He is halfway to the stables," Elizabeth said. "We will know if we are in luck shortly." She settled against the trunk of the tree and continued to watch the stables to see in which way Mr. Bingley would ride. With any luck, it would be toward the knoll and then to the left just as his route had been on Saturday.

As fortune would have it, Mr. Bingley appeared to be a creature of habit, and Elizabeth and Jane descended the knoll with plenty of time to slow their breathing and look at ease when he saw them.

Elizabeth lifted her hand and waved to him.

"He is not going to stop," Jane whispered.

"He will," Elizabeth whispered back as she waved a second time.

Mr. Bingley tipped his hat, and for a moment Elizabeth thought he would just ride on as Jane had said. However, he did not.

"Good morning, Mr. Bingley," Elizabeth said brightly as he drew near. "We are pleased to see you." She poked Jane with her elbow.

"Indeed, we are," Jane added.

"It is a pleasure to see you as well," Bingley replied.

Elizabeth noted how his eyes moved quickly from her to Jane and remained there. Jane ducked her head and smiled. She could box William's ears for keeping Jane and Mr. Bingley apart!

"There is a stile just over here," Elizabeth motioned toward the knoll. "I wish to speak with you."

Bingley's eyes shifted back to her. "You wished to speak to me?"

Elizabeth nodded. "About your friend."

He huffed.

"Please," Elizabeth entreated. "Is Mr. Darcy well?" she asked cautiously. It seemed as if Mr. Bingley was angry with his friend and the indifferent shrug that accompanied his words suggested she was correct.

"He is, although he has been confined to his room for these two days."

"Will he be able to leave his room soon?" Jane asked.

Bingley smiled at her. "I believe he will be."

"Oh, I am glad," Jane replied.

Bingley swung down from his horse and walked the animal toward the stile where he secured him before crossing to where they stood waiting.

"I must thank you for sending the surgeon so quickly. I have yet to know the area well, although I did venture into Meryton on Saturday."

"How did you like it?" Jane asked.

"It is a fine town full of the friendliest sorts of people. Sir William has invited us to dine with him once Darcy is able to join us."

"Sir William is a delight," Jane said.

"Charlotte – Miss Lucas — is our particular friend," Elizabeth added as she shared a did-I-not-say-as-much look with Jane.

"But we did not ask you to join us to speak of our friends," Jane added quickly.

"No, according to Miss Elizabeth, you wished to know about my friend."

There as a decided note of bitterness in the word friend that caused Elizabeth to raise a brow. "We had hoped that you would call," she began.

Mr. Bingley's eyes fluttered, and shock suffused his features. "You did?"

"We did," Jane answered, again dipping her head and smiling.

"I thought I was not welcome." His brow was furrowed, and he shook his head slightly as if bewildered.

"I would welcome you."

Elizabeth wanted to shout and wrap her sister in an embrace for being so brave as to admit such a thing, for Jane was circumspect to a fault at times.

"You would?" Bingley could not contain the smile that spread across his face. "That is very good news."

"Indeed, it is," Elizabeth agreed quietly. A match between Jane and Mr. Bingley seemed almost assured if they could only sway William's opinion.

She waited patiently for a full minute as Mr. Bingley and Jane just looked at each other. Then, after coughing lightly, she said, "About Mr. Darcy."

"What do you wish to know?" Bingley asked eagerly, extending an arm to each of them.

"Is he betrothed?" Jane asked.

Bingley laughed. "No. Nor does he have much hope of ever becoming betrothed."

"Why would you say that?" Jane asked in surprise.

"Because he is too adept at offending," Bingley replied.

"Then he is cruel and cold?" Jane could not hide her horror at such a thought.

"No, no. He is just..." Bingley sought for the word.

"Ill-at-ease?" Elizabeth offered.

"Yes, yes! That is it precisely." He turned toward her. "I do not think I have ever met someone who has noticed that about my friend."

"Lizzy is very astute," Jane said.

"I would have to agree," Bingley replied. "Was there anything else you wished to know about Darcy?"

"Perhaps we could sit down," Elizabeth suggested.

Bingley agreed that it was a good idea and soon they were seated on the rise of the knoll.

"Our brother has not told me all he has heard about Mr. Darcy." Elizabeth smoothed her skirt over the top of her boots. "However, he has mentioned something about a will not being honoured."

"So, it was Wickham," Bingley muttered. He shook his head. "The will was honoured."

"Then, there was a reason for the living to not be given to this Wickham?" Elizabeth asked.

Bingley nodded. "He refused it, and Darcy paid him three thousand pounds in lieu of the living so that he could study the law. However, Wickham found that such study did not suit him, and when the living fell open, he came looking to claim it."

"But he had refused it," Jane said.

"Darcy reminded him of that fact. I am uncertain that Darcy will appreciate my sharing all of this with you, but since you asked." Bingley stretched out his legs and leaned back on his arms, looking for all the world as if he did not particularly care if Mr. Darcy would be happy with him or not. "Mr. Wickham was not in a favourable state of living at the time and was not pleased to be refused. He abused Darcy most severely and eventually retaliated in the cruelest fashion he could. That, I cannot tell you about other than to say Wickham's plan was designed to inflict the most pain possible to Darcy."

Elizabeth leaned toward Bingley. "Mr. Wickham was given three thousand pounds and was then shortly thereafter in need of money?"

Bingley nodded. "I should not likely say this to ladies, and I would not except to answer your question, but his proclivities are expensive."

"William did say he had played cards with him," Jane said.

"That is one of his vices," Bingley agreed. "As I understand it, his mother was a spendthrift, and I imagine he has inherited some of her traits in that area."

"Will Mr. Darcy be receiving callers soon?" Elizabeth asked, allowing the topic of Mr. Wickham to drop, although she had to admit to herself that she was curious to learn more. However, that was not the point of this discussion. This discussion was to promote her sister and to make it possible for Mr. Bingley to call on Jane without fear of being rejected by any of the men in her family.

Bingley looked at her in surprise. "I could not say with any certainty. May I ask why you wish to know?"

"I owe him an apology. I was demanding. It is a fault I own."

"He was rude," Bingley retorted.

"I am not saying he was not," Elizabeth replied. "I am only saying I was not right. Neither of us was shown to best advantage in that exchange. I should have considered the fact that he was injured more carefully and thought better of his comfort."

"You were thinking of his comfort. Riding to Netherfield did cause him a great deal of discomfort and swelling as you said it would."

"I am sorry to be correct," Elizabeth said, and she meant it. She had sprained an ankle more than once in her formative years as she tried to keep up with an older and larger brother. "However, I did not consider the comfort of his spirit. I would be very thankful if you would tell him of my sorrow in causing him discomfort."

Bingley smiled. "I suppose that will mean speaking to him." He shifted his position. "I will admit to being rather put out with him over his actions."

Elizabeth smiled. "I had thought you were."

"Did you?"

She nodded. "You did not seem willing to speak about him at first."

Bingley laughed. "Your sister is correct. You are most astute."

"Not always," Elizabeth assured him. "Will you call on us?"

"I do not know if that is wise."

"Our brother needs to see that you are as amiable as you appear," Elizabeth argued, "He would never promote any gentleman who was given to vice or who would in any way disrespect his family. Nor would he willingly accept a friend of such a gentleman. Therefore, you must call on us to show him that what he believes about Mr. Darcy cannot be true."

"And you would like me to call?" he asked Jane.

"Very much," she replied. This time, her head did not dip, but she did still smile and blush.

"Then I shall," he rose from the ground and extended a hand to

Elizabeth first and then Jane to help them rise. "Today. I shall call today."

Elizabeth placed a hand on his arm as he turned to take his leave. "If you can think of any way to help us sway our brother's opinion of your friend…"

"I will give it some thought."

Elizabeth drew a breath and with her heart racing added, "I…" but then faltered. She was uncertain if she could be a brave as Jane had been. Jane, at least, had some evidence before her that Mr. Bingley would not be opposed to her declaration of interest. Elizabeth had nothing but the harsh words of an injured gentleman to propel her forward, but she knew she must not waiver. Mr. Bingley was looking at her, waiting patiently for her to continue.

"I should like very much for it to be possible for your friend to call at Longbourn, so that I might get to know more about him." She pushed the words out of her mouth before her brain had a chance to stop her.

Mr. Bingley smiled. "Then, I shall consider even more carefully how to sway your brother's opinion. And," he leaned a little bit closer to her and lowered his voice, "Darcy will definitely not approve of my saying this, but he shall be delighted to hear you would welcome him."

Elizabeth pulled the right corner of her bottom lip between her teeth to keep from smiling too broadly.

"Truly?" Jane's voice was filled with poorly masked excitement.

"Truly." Bingley touched his hat and gave a small bow. "Until this afternoon," he said before turning and walking back to his horse.

Jane waited until he had tipped his hat to them and ridden away before she wrapped her arms around Elizabeth with a little squeal of delight. "Oh, your plan was brilliant!"

"Now it is brilliant? Earlier you did not seem to think it was."

"I was wrong," Jane said as they began their journey home. "Mama will be so delighted to have him call."

Yes, Mrs. Bennet would be pleased to have Mr. Bingley call at Longbourn, but not nearly so much as Jane or Elizabeth. For their happy futures appeared to not be outside the realm of possibilities – despite one foolish and stubborn older brother.

# Chapter 11

Darcy descended the grand staircase at Netherfield slowly, one painful step at a time. His ankle was improving but placing weight on it was still difficult. Limping around a room with quick steps on a sore ankle as he had done for the past two days was not so bad as attempting to walk down a flight of stairs.

"Are you going somewhere?" Bingley, still dressed in his riding clothes, leaned against the wall at the bottom of the stairs.

How Darcy wished he could have gone for a ride this morning. He was so dreadfully tired of being confined to the house. He had had his fill of his room. However, to venture out of it meant being tended to by Louisa and Caroline, and Caroline seemed just as determined as ever to attempt to sway his mind in her direction. Riding would mean he would be free of both of Bingley's sisters, but it also meant his ankle would be jostled more than it should be. He had no desire to repeat having his boot become lodged on his foot due to swelling. Therefore, he had come to a decision. He was going...

"Home," Darcy replied.

"To town or Pemberley?"

"Town. I should l like to see my sister."

Bingley nodded. "Will you, at least, have tea with me before you leave?"

"Not unless you wish it." The man had not visited him in two days, and it was obvious from his expression that he was still not happy with Darcy. There was no way Darcy was going to impose on his friend if he was not welcome to do so.

"I do," Bingley replied, a small smile tipping his lips, giving away the fact that he was not as put out with Darcy as he pretended. "I do not wish for you to leave."

Darcy blew out a breath as he completed his journey to the bottom of the staircase and lowered himself onto the second step to rest his ankle before he proceeded any further.

"It still hurts?" Bingley nodded to Darcy's foot.

Darcy nodded. "It is not so strong as I would like it to be. I think it best to have my physician look at it when I am in town. Now that swelling has receded somewhat, he may see something that was missed before."

"You are determined to leave then?"

Again, Darcy nodded. "My remaining will only hinder any chance you have of securing Miss Bennet." He looked up at Bingley. "I did not do you harm intentionally, and I apologize for my temper."

Bingley extended a hand to Darcy. "Come. Have tea with me. I would like to speak with you."

Darcy looked at Bingley warily. "You would?" He allowed Bingley to help him rise from where he was seated.

"I would." He took Darcy by the arm. "Lean on me if you need to."

"Thank you," Darcy replied and did just that. He leaned his

weight partially on his friend as they moved down the hall to a small withdrawing room behind the larger sitting room.

"Caroline does not like this room," Bingley whispered. "So, I have made it my own. It has only one smallish window and is therefore too dark for her liking. However, I do not mind the lack of sunshine so very much, especially if it brings with it a lack of sisters. I was about to eat some breakfast in here where it is free of female complaints when I was informed that your coach was being readied for travel." He locked the door behind him. "I want to make certain my sister does not interrupt me for I would like to eat in peace," he explained.

Bingley seated himself at a small round table that stood with four chairs near the window at the far end of the narrow room. There was a grouping of three cushioned chairs near the hearth and a ladder-backed chair near the door next to a cabinet which held a decanter and glasses. On the wall across from the fireplace, was a low bookcase with glass doors. Those pieces of furniture and a few paintings were the extents of the décor in the room. It was a very pleasant room. With the lamp lit, Darcy imagined this would be an excellent place to while away some hours with a book.

Darcy carefully took his place at the table. He was slowly learning how to sit down gracefully without causing his ankle too much discomfort. He was still a bit awkward, but not so awkward as he had been just yesterday morning.

"I saw Miss Bennet and Miss Elizabeth while I was riding today," Bingley began as he poured tea for himself and Darcy.

"You did?" Darcy asked in surprise.

The left side of Bingley's lips tipped up, and his brows flicked upward and back down quickly. "I did. They were waiting for me."

Darcy added sugar to his cup. "It was not an accidental meeting?"

Bingley shook his head. "No, Miss Elizabeth wished to speak to me and arranged it so that she could. I am not entirely certain how she knew I would be riding where I was, but she and her sister were waiting and called to me to join them."

"Her brother must not know of this meeting," Darcy grumbled.

"You are correct. He does not." Bingley took a bite of his scone, following it with a bit of tea. "She asked about you."

"Who asked about me?"

"Miss Elizabeth."

Darcy could not help the small smile that crept onto his lips. Whether or not he had a hope of ever discovering if they would suit, he still found the information that she had inquired after him to be pleasing.

"She wanted to know if you are well enough for callers."

Darcy held his cup suspended in the air almost to his lips. "Is she thinking of calling on me?" What sort of lady called on a gentleman? It was supposed to be the other way around.

"She wishes to apologize."

Bingley's brows rose over an accusatory look, and Darcy sighed. "You are right, again. She is not the one who should apologize."

"I should say not," Bingley replied.

"Have you forgiven me?"

Bingley shrugged and nodded. "Tentatively, yes. However, if I never succeed with Miss Bennet, I retain my right to be put out with you." He held up a finger. "Which will mean that I will push you and Caroline together as much as necessary to have my regret somewhat mollified by your discomfort."

Darcy chuckled. "You are an evil man."

Bingley smiled broadly. "Far more evil than you imagine since I know that there is a pretty young lady to whom you need to apologize who would like nothing better than to have you call on her."

The sounds of the house, the ticking of a clock, the footsteps that scurried through the corridors, the nattering of the Bingley sisters as they descended the grand staircase faded into nothingness as the sound of the rhythmic thumping of Darcy's heart resounded in his ears. Miss Elizabeth wished for him to call on her? It could not be. He had been rude to her. She was not supposed to welcome him after he behaved as he had. If he were she, he would not wish to see him. He took two swallows of his tea and slowly returned his cup to the table as the sound of his heart diminished, and the room and Bingley came back into his consciousness.

"I do not deserve her," Darcy whispered. "She is too good."

No matter who might be associated with her brother, Darcy had not been able to talk himself out of wishing to know more about Elizabeth. She drew him as none other had ever done. That fact, mixed with not wishing to be confined to a house with Bingley's sisters and not wanting to remain where he was unwelcome, had been part of why he had planned to leave. To be near to someone so fascinating yet denied access to her presence for more than a few moments, if at all, was too torturous to contemplate. However, if he were in London, at least then, she would be too far away for him to regret not being able to call oh her as he wished with the intentions he could never make known or have accepted.

"You are correct," Bingley replied rather harshly. "She wished for me to convey her sorrow in having caused you discomfort. She said she should have considered your comfort of spirit – or some such thing." He placed his cup on the table and leaned toward Darcy. "You must pursue her even if you are not at this moment worthy of her." He held Darcy's gaze. "She understands you."

Darcy shook his head. No one understood him. Not at first. Sometimes not even after a long acquaintance.

"I know of what I speak," Bingley retorted. "When I told her you were not betrothed – because Miss Bennet had asked — and that you were likely never to become betrothed, Miss Bennet asked the reason. I told her that one of your many talents is in offending."

Darcy scowled at Bingley, but sadly, he was right. Darcy often found himself offending someone.

"While I was attempting to explain that you were not a heartless beast who offends because he gains pleasure from it, Miss Elizabeth suggested it was because you were ill-at-ease." Bingley's brows rose as he gave Darcy a pointed look. "Who, besides me, Richard, and Georgiana, realize that truth about you?"

"No one. Maybe my uncle."

Bingley nodded. "And Miss Elizabeth Bennet." He took a sip from his cup. "Marry her. There is likely not another woman in all of England who will understand that about you and still wish to have you call on her after you have been rude."

"That is a bit harsh," Darcy muttered. "True, but harsh."

Bingley popped the last of his scone in his mouth. "I am calling at Longbourn today. May I tell her that you will be riding tomorrow near the knoll?"

Darcy shrugged and nodded. "Yes?" He could risk the loss of a boot for such a reason, could he not?

"Capital decision," Bingley replied. "Shall I inform the staff that you are not departing?"

"Right. Yes." Darcy moved to stand up, but Bingley stopped him.

"Allow me to pull the bell. I told them some about Wickham," he added after ringing the bell.

"You did what?" Darcy asked.

"I told them about Wickham and the living he refused. Apparently, Mr. William Bennet has heard Wickham's tale of how he was mistreated by you. Miss Elizabeth, however, had deciphered that there must be a reason for the will to be ignored." Bingley looked at Darcy pointedly once again. "I repeat. Marry her."

Darcy chuckled and shook his head. "Did you tell them anything further about him?"

"I told them that he is given to vice and not to be trusted," Bingley replied. "But I did not tell them about Georgiana." He sighed. "Their brother is as protective of them as you are of your sister. He would not allow Wickham near them, nor will he welcome any gentleman who would disrespect his family in any way. Likewise, he will not accept the friend of such a gentleman. Therefore, it is imperative that we find a way to demonstrate to him that you are not the sort of gentleman to treat any of Bennet's family meanly. And that is why Miss Elizabeth was adamant that I call and do my part to show myself worthy of Miss Bennet – who, by the by, said she would welcome my attention."

"Congratulations," Darcy replied, and then after a moment to ponder Bingley's words, during which he considered his friend married to the sister of the only lady who had, to this point in his life, captured his attention as none other had ever done, he added, "Do not play with her emotions."

Bingley scowled at him. "I would not."

"No, I do not think you would, but you must appear to be above such since if you are found wanting, then I shall also be found wanting, seeing as I am your friend. That is, of course, if we can prove to the younger Mr. Bennet that I am not as reprehensible as my actions have accused me of being."

Bingley grinned. "You do not wish to be found wanting?"

Darcy shook his head. "I think your advice is excellent. I believe I must marry Miss Elizabeth."

Bingley laughed heartily at that. "I was beginning to wonder if there would ever be a day when I would hear you single out a lady." He filled his cup again. "No need to rush," he said. "We must attempt to come up with a way to secure the affections of the lady's brother, so that you and I will be free to pursue our happiness with his sisters."

~*~*~

Later that day, Darcy looked up from his book when Bingley entered the drawing room at Netherfield after his call at Longbourn.

"Caroline is not allowed to call at Longbourn in the future," he said, dropping into a chair next to Darcy.

"I do not see why I cannot," Caroline said with a smirk.

"Because you were rude, and I am attempting to make a good impression on Miss Bennet and her family. Telling Mrs. Bennet how her room is only half the size of some drawing room you sat in once to drink tea with some..." he pressed his lips together, obviously changing his mind on the word he was about to use, "ladies from the ton is not how one ingratiates herself to her neighbors. Nor should one tell a young lady such as Miss Lydia that the ribbon she is using to trim her hat is just like the one you saw last season." He glowered at his sister. "She seemed very flattered to have your attention until you condemned her fashion sense as already been done!"

"The call did not go well?" Darcy asked, attempting to thwart the upcoming argument, but it was to no avail. Caroline would have her say.

"I have no desire to become friends with *these* people, and you could do much better than Miss Bennet. Oh, she is a sweet girl to be sure and so pretty, but seriously Charles, what can she do for you?"

"Run my home! She is a gentleman's daughter and as such has first-hand knowledge about the workings of an estate and how one who is mistress of an estate should behave."

Caroline snorted. "I doubt her mother has taught her very well." She shared a look with Louisa. "Mrs. Bennet is not, how shall I say it?" She waved her hand in a circular fashion. "She is no wit."

Louisa bit her lip and looked at Bingley uneasily. "She does not seem to be, but we have only just met her."

Caroline huffed. "You know as well as I that she is not a glowing example of a gentlewoman, but then, she was not born to be one."

"Neither were you," Darcy said sharply, drawing the attention of everyone in the room. He never enjoyed one of Caroline's arguments with her brother. However, hearing her condemn the Bennets provoked him to the point that he could not remain silent.

"I may have been wrong before when I said there was no deficit in you which would cause me to reject you. You know very well how I regard ladies of the ton who are catty and cruel. I apparently did not realize that you were one of them."

Caroline gasped.

"You could be mistress of Longbourn," Charles inserted. "Then you could show Mrs. Bennet how a tradesman's daughter is supposed to run an estate. The young Mr. Bennet had a difficult time looking at anything else in the room save you. You could do far worse."

"And I could do better!" Caroline cried.

Bingley shrugged. "Perhaps."

"I could," Caroline insisted.

"You could," Darcy agreed. "However, I do not see how you will ever be happy with such a mean spirit. A gentleman of any status will have to interact with those who are not of his sphere as well as those just entering his sphere. He cannot afford to be petty and demeaning if he truly wishes to establish himself well and be respected. And if a gentleman cannot afford such behaviour, neither can his wife. You have seen just as many troubled marriages as I have. Being a demanding sort of lady and prone to the ridicule of others does not bode well for a peaceful marriage."

"Well said," Mr. Hurst said.

"Longbourn is not a horrid estate," Louisa added. "Everything was tidy. That sitting room did get excellent light, and from what I could see of the garden, it must be spectacular when in full bloom."

"I did not like it," Caroline replied.

"You are well within your rights to not like what others might,"

Mr. Hurst said. "However, those opinions should be kept to one's self and only delved into with caution when necessary to disclose them. For instance, I found the drapery to be too garish, but I am not the one deciding on the décor, and to be truthful, they were not out of place."

Charles expelled a great breath. "I know you are not pleased to be here, Caroline, but could you please be reasonable and accept the fact that I like it here and I like Miss Bennet? There is no need to demonstrate your superior fashion sense or schooling. It will be evident and better appreciated if you do not point it out."

"Miss Bennet?" There was a pleading tone to Caroline's voice.

"Yes, I prefer Miss Bennet to Miss Darcy — or to any other lady for that matter."

"You will not be moved?" Caroline asked.

The shake of Bingley's head was met by a resigned sigh. How many times had Darcy witnessed these two argue over something? Caroline would petulantly pursue her brother to change his mind until it became clear that he would not be moved. Then, and only then, did she resign herself to the idea – albeit unhappily.

"I will not be marrying Georgiana, and Darcy will not be marrying you. Therefore, you should begin searching for another, and you could start with Mr. William Bennet. He seems very upstanding."

"I have no hope?" The question to Darcy was small and quiet.

"I am sorry, but no," Darcy replied.

Caroline sighed again and pushed up from her chair. "Then, I see no need to stay here if I can neither move Charles or impress you. I am a very accomplished lady."

"I know," Darcy replied. "And some gentleman will be happy to have you for his wife, but that gentleman is not me."

She shrugged and moved to the door of the drawing room where she stopped and turned toward them once again. "I apologize for being less than civil, Charles. I shall attempt to display myself to better advantage and make our sojourn in this backwater as pleasant as possible."

"I am happy to hear it, but Darcy'll not marry you even if you are pleasant."

She huffed. "I was not attempting to sway him."

"You were not?" Hurst asked with a laugh.

Caroline paused a moment too long before replying in the negative to Mr. Hurst for either him or her brother to believe her answer.

"Give him up," Charles said.

Caroline lifted her chin and shot him a hateful look before saying, "I already have," and leaving the room.

"Miss Elizabeth will be walking near the knoll tomorrow morning," Bingley said to Darcy.

"Oh ho!" Mr. Hurst cried. "You'll want to prepare your sister for that disappointment," he said to his wife.

Darcy shook his head and glared at Bingley. "We are even," he growled.

Bingley laughed. "As long as I succeed with Miss Bennet."

"No, even if you do not," Darcy retorted. Then, he turned to Mrs. Hurst. "It is as your husband suspects, so it would be best for Caroline to treat Miss Elizabeth with respect and kindness should she wish to keep my acquaintance."

# Chapter 12

Elizabeth paced along the fence from the stile to the bottom of the knoll just down and to the right of the tree she liked to sit under. She glanced up at the sky. The sun was shining, and the clouds were nearly white. There was only a hint of grey in them. The day should be a dry one.

She opened her book and attempted to make her mind focus on the words. She had brought it with her even though she had not intended to read today. To leave without it and go toward her favorite reading place might have caused some to be curious – William in particular. He had been just leaving for the stables when she had descended the stairs with her pelisse and bonnet on.

She snapped the book closed. It was no use. All she could think about was Mr. Darcy. He had plagued her dreams all night. Hopefully, he would be receptive to her apology and willing to help her convince her brother that neither he nor Mr. Bingley was reprehensible.

"Miss Elizabeth."

Elizabeth spun from her contemplation of the trees and her dreams, where the man presently calling to her had at one point forgiven her and another, ridiculed her for her demanding nature. Her heart thumped loudly as she moved toward the stile.

"Good morning!" she called to him. "I am delighted to see you are able to ride. Mr. Bingley said you had found your confinement to be trying." She kept a smile on her face and her tone light. Even as her stomach tumbled nervously.

"It was excessively trying," he said as he swung down from his horse.

Elizabeth bit her lip to keep from telling him to be careful as he winced while putting weight on his ankle. "Can you make it over the stile? We can sit in the shade." She motioned to her right.

"I think I can manage it," he replied. "It cannot be any more difficult than descending a set of stairs or mounting a horse. It is amazing the movements upon which we rely and about which we do not think until some portion of our person is incapacitated in some fashion."

"You can lean on me if you need." Elizabeth pressed her lips together. She had told herself she would not try to direct him in any fashion today, but it was much harder than she had imagined it would be. And she had considered that it would be difficult.

He smiled. "It is healing, so I think I can manage. However, when we must rise from our places later, I may require assistance."

Elizabeth expelled the breath she has been holding.

"Before you say what I suspect you are going to say," Darcy said as they walked the few feet to where she and Jane had sat with Bingley just the other day. "I must insist that it is not you who needs to beg forgiveness. My behavior was reprehensible."

"You were injured," she replied. "We can all become cantankerous when in pain. We can sit here. Do you need help?"

He shook his head. "No, I think I can drop onto the ground under my own power, though it will not be gracefully done." And it was not.

"Are you well?" she asked in response to the groan he uttered.

"I am." He stretched out his injured leg but kept his other leg bent. "An injury does not excuse my lack of patience."

She shrugged. "It is not an excuse. It is a reason. There is a difference, Mr. Darcy. One attempts to brush something away as if it should be overlooked completely while the other is given in hopes of making a situation or action understandable. I should have considered your injury when proffering my advice –"

"Which was sound, by the way," Darcy inserted. "I nearly lost my boot."

"Could we begin again? Neither of us showed ourselves to best advantage."

He shook his head, and Elizabeth's heart clenched at the thought of their not being able to reconcile the ill behaviour displayed at their last meeting.

"I would prefer," he said, "to continue as we have been, for I would have you know that I can be dour and disapproving at times. It is a fault I willingly own, and I do not wish to present myself to you as anything that I am not." He removed his hat and placed it on the ground next to him. "I would rather begin by knowing you are an intelligent lady who is not put off by my occasional fits of spleen. I think whatever relationship we might foster will be better for the transparency. It is one of the things I despise about the season – there are so few who are what they appear."

Relief that he was not going to send her on her way but would rather be friends spread across Elizabeth's face. "You may come to regret such a request," she teased. "I can assure you that I have many faults of temper, and one of them is my insistence that I know the best way to do things, and another is my tendency to express my annoyance when others do not immediately agree."

Darcy chuckled. "We are much alike then. Am I forgiven?"

She nodded. "Am I?"

"Without a moment's hesitation," he replied. He shifted so that he could see her more fully as she sat beside him.

Oh, he was handsome! From where she had seen him on his horse on their first meeting and then on the ground in the woods, she had thought him very attractive, but now that he was here, so close to her with his hat removed and looking very relaxed, he was even more appealing.

"I understand Mr. Bingley told you somewhat about Mr. Wickham."

"Yes, he did," she said, pulling her eyes away from the cut of his jawline and blushing.

"Is your brother a good friend of Mr. Wickham?"

Elizabeth shook her head and shrugged. "I do not believe he is. He had never mentioned him before I questioned him about his opinion of you. Indeed, he did not mention his name even then. I dare say, Mr. Wickham is no more than a passing acquaintance."

"I am glad to hear it."

His broad shoulders rose and lowered as he drew a deep breath and expelled it. "It was not entirely my injury that made me cross that day in the wood. I had just discovered that your brother knew Wickham."

He shook his head and looked past her, a pained expression settling into his eyes. "Your brother asked me if I was betrothed but said he had not met any of my family. There was only one other person of whom I could think who would know such information."

"Mr. Wickham?"

Darcy nodded. "He was a childhood friend."

"What happened?" Her hand flew to cover her mouth. "I apologize. It is not my place to know."

His smile was soft and reassuring. "I would like for you to know every last thing there is to know about me, and I would like to know the same about you if you are willing to be so open."

Her lips parted of their own accord as her brow furrowed. Was he saying what she thought he was saying?

"Yes," he replied to her unspoken question. "I think you and I would suit each other very well, and I would like to explore the possibility of our compatibility not just as friends but as future mates."

For a full three deafening thuds of her heart, Elizabeth could not find anything more to say than "oh."

"Would you be willing to consider me as more than a friend?"

After having only met twice – with one of those times being nothing more than an argument — he wished to court her? "Do you always make such hasty decisions, Mr. Darcy?

He chuckled. "No. I rarely do anything in haste. However, you and your enchanting eyes and smile have not given me a moment of peace since we met. I find I am as anxious to know about you as a man is for a drink of water in the desert. I cannot explain it. I just know that I must discover all I can about you."

"You are certain you wish this?"

He nodded.

"I apologize for my hesitance, but I am not the sort of lady whom gentlemen trip over one another to call on."

"Then, they are fools. Will you?"

She laughed. "Yes. I would consider it an honour to enter into such an arrangement." She could feel the heat of embarrassment climbing onto her cheeks. "I must admit that I have found myself fascinated by you."

"You have? How so?"

"You think deeply."

"I do, but how do you know that?"

The surprise in his tone caused her to smile. "There is a small twitch of your eyes or lips and a pause before you speak. You looked very pensive on our first meeting."

"Bingley said you were astute."

How she wished that were always true, but she knew that she often leapt to conclusions and held to her beliefs about a person or situation to be true, even when they were not. In that way, she and William were alike, and she could see very clearly at this moment how that tendency was harmful. "I wish it were always true. I do attempt to decipher character, but I am not always correct."

"No one is," he replied. "I have made some grievous errors in that regard." He plucked a blade of grass and ran it back and forth between his fingers. "I wish to tell you something, but I confess to being fearful." He blew out a breath. "However, I have promised to reveal myself to you as fully as I can."

"You do not have to tell me if it is painful." How wrong her brother was about this gentleman! He was not cold or cruel. He might be irascible at times, but Mr. Darcy was not unfeeling.

"I feel I must, but before I do, I must beg you not to speak of this to anyone as doing so might harm someone who is very dear to me."

Her heart clenched at the look on his face. What he was willing to tell her was excruciating, and she could not deny the honour of being so trusted. "Of course, I will not say a word."

"Thank you," he said with a small smile before finding some spot beyond her at which to look and proceeding to tear the blade of grass in his hands to shreds as he told her about his sister, Georgiana's, narrow escape from a life of misery at the hands of Mr. Wickham.

"We, my cousin and I, were both mistaken in the character of Georgiana's companion, Mrs. Younge. We had no idea that she was an associate of Wickham." He sighed. "That is why I was so cross when I discovered your brother's acquaintance with Wickham. I thought I had once again misjudged someone's character, and I feared that if I were correct about your brother, it would mean never being able to know you. It was as if Wickham was attempting to tear yet another thing away from me. He claimed my father's affections, nearly robbed me of my sister, and then, when I finally met a lady who captured my interest and, I feared, my heart, he was there again."

Elizabeth brushed a tear from her cheek. "I do not know what to say," she muttered.

He turned his attention back to her and immediately fished in his pocket for his handkerchief. "I did not mean to distress you."

She shook her head. "You must not apologize for telling me about Mr. Wickham. If my brother knew, he would never give a word the man told him a second thought. I will not tell him," she added quickly when she noted the look of concern in Darcy's eyes. "I have given you my word. I am just assuring you that my brother would never be friends with such a man."

For a few moments, the sound of the breeze rustling dry leaves and a bird chirping were all that could be heard as they sat in companionable silence. It was strange to Elizabeth how right it seemed to be sitting here with him, bearing a small portion of his cares. She glanced at him. His head was tipped back slightly as he watched the clouds. She would not be opposed to being his wife. In fact, the thought was rather intoxicating, much like the small smile that curved his lips, for he seemed to be precisely the sort of gentleman who would best suit her. He willingly owned his faults, cared deeply for his sister, and had presented himself to her in a very direct fashion. All of those things spoke to a strength and nobility of character that made the idea of being married to him something to be sought happily without a moment's pause to worry about her future happiness. With him, she just knew that she would be happy. She smiled and shook her head. It was just as he had said – it was a realization that defied understanding.

"My brother is not really my brother," she said breaking the silence.

"I beg your pardon?" Darcy turned toward her.

"I do not have any grievous tales to share, but you should know that William is a distant cousin and heir to Longbourn, whose father died when he was ten, and he was sent to live with us. He has since become more of a brother than a cousin. In fact, he and I have been good friends nearly from his arrival."

"It is not easy to lose a parent whether you are young or old."

She chided herself. He had just told her he was the guardian of his younger sister. He would not be her guardian if his parents lived. "How long have your parents been gone?" she asked quietly.

"My mother died when I was but a boy and my father just five years ago." He smiled at her. "Too old to be taken in by a loving family. Your brother is fortunate."

She returned his smile. "He is, and if we can convince him that you are not the ogre you appeared, then.." she swallowed the fear that rose in her throat. If Jane could be brave, she reminded herself, surely, she could be as well. "One day, perhaps you could also become part of our family?"

Any fear that might have fluttered in her stomach was dashed away by the bright grin that overtook his face. "I would like that very much." He shifted his position. "As much as I would like to sit here all day with you, I fear it is not a good idea. For one, my stomach is about to become very boisterous, and for another, your brother might come looking for you. That would not aid us in our quest to sway his opinion."

Elizabeth pushed up to her feet, straightened her skirts, and blushed when she realizes she was the subject of Mr. Darcy's close scrutiny. She held out her hand to him. "Try not to topple me," she teased. "I should like to be able to dance every set at the assembly, and I fear there might not be enough time to heal if I should injure myself."

"I would not dream of causing you pain," he replied lightly as he took her hand and pushed up from his position, using only his strong leg as much as he could. "If my ankle is better by then, perhaps I will be fortunate enough to claim one of your sets?"

"Oh, two sets would set Mama up proudly," Elizabeth replied with a laugh. "It will also likely shock her unless we have been able to move our meetings from clandestine locations to more standard surroundings for a gentleman to call on a lady."

He tucked her hand in the crook of his arm as they walked the short distance to where his horse was enjoying a wildflower. "With your permission, I would like to accompany my friend when he calls on your sister."

"I would like that very much, but William will not be welcoming."

"I know, and I cannot blame him. I would be far from welcoming to anyone who called on Georgiana after treating her as I treated you – especially if I believed him to be as Wickham has painted me to be." He lifted her hand to his lips before crossing the stile. "We will sway him. We must."

Elizabeth stood at the stile for an extended period of time after Darcy rode away. He liked her. The handsome new neighbour's much more handsome friend liked her. She shook her head. It was wonderfully unbelievable. Finally, when she could see him no longer, she retrieved her book and returned to Longbourn.

# Chapter 13

For two days, Darcy endured the glares and huffs of William Bennet as he sat with Elizabeth in the sitting room at Longbourn. Each day, he had also enjoyed a few glare-free moments in Elizabeth's company as he would stop at the knoll each morning where she was waiting for him. He had learned a good deal about her in a short time.

Her mother was not the source of Elizabeth's intelligence. Caroline had been correct about Mrs. Bennet not being a wit. However, he could see that in her strange and loud way, she was a caring mother, intent upon seeing her daughters married. In that way, she was no different from any of the mothers, as well as many of the father and brothers, of the ton. They all wanted to see their sisters and daughters married and married well. He could not fault Mrs. Bennet for that desire. He did struggle with enjoying her boisterous nature, but then, he struggled with that trait in all people.

Elizabeth had been raised in a good household. It may have been wanting in some ways – such as exposure to the masters – but it was not lacking in love. That was clearly evident. Mr. Bennet, while not always present and often quiet when he was in company, had quick eyes. He might look as if he were reading a paper, but Darcy had seen the man silently watching both him and Bingley. Thankfully, Elizabeth's father, unlike his son, wore a pleasant expression when observing and had not told either him or Bingley that they could not call. If William had spoken to his father about anything that Wickham had told him, it did not appear that it was something which would hinder Darcy's acceptance when he finally approached the gentleman about a proper courtship and marriage.

On the third day after Darcy and Elizabeth had come to their understanding at the bottom of the knoll, Darcy found himself and Bingley invited to dine at Longbourn. Happily, he dressed in his best suit of clothes and entered the carriage. He and Bingley intended to arrive early so that they could speak privately with Mr. Bennet before they ate.

"Are you certain before dinner is the best time?" Bingley asked.

"No," Darcy admitted. "But I should like to have the interview over with before our evening begins, no matter the outcome."

"We could be asked to leave." Bingley fidgeted with his sleeves as he sat in Darcy's carriage. The Hursts and Caroline would arrive later in Bingley's carriage.

Darcy nodded. He did not need to be reminded of the fact that he might be unsuccessful. He had no fear about his acceptance from Elizabeth. She had given that to him this morning. He smiled as he remembered holding her in his arms and the softness of her lips against his own.

"You look far too happy for the situation," Bingley muttered.

"I am attempting to think about pleasant things," Darcy replied.

"Such as?" Bingley prompted with an air of skepticism.

"A pair of fine eyes," Darcy replied with a smile.

Bingley chuckled.

"And soft lips," Darcy added.

Bingley's eyes grew wide. "You have kissed her?"

Darcy shrugged. "I did not say that I have."

"Out with it." Bingley bumped Darcy's uninjured foot with his.

"It was this morning when I asked her if she would allow me to speak to her father even though her brother has not relented in his position, and after she had given me permission to do so, she also gave me permission to kiss her," Darcy said.

Bingley shook his head and chuckled. "I never expected you to beat me to it."

"You intend to kiss Miss Elizabeth?" Darcy teased.

"Obviously not!" Bingley said with a laugh. "You have gained the acceptance of a lady before I have even asked."

"We cannot all be so decisive," Darcy quipped.

Bingley continued to chuckle. "I hope then that we are successful with her father, or you will be plagued by the memory of that kiss far more than I will be distressed about never having gotten one from Miss Bennet."

Darcy drew and released a breath. Whether he was successful or not, that kiss was likely to plague him until he could claim another. "We must succeed" was all he said before the carriage fell into silence for the short distance that remained of their three-mile journey from Netherfield to Longbourn.

"Is the master available?" Darcy asked Mr. Hill when he opened the door to them.

The elderly servant's lips curled up in a small smile, and the skin around his eyes crinkled with delight. "He is in his study. I will inquire if he is willing to see you, Mr. Darcy."

"And Mr. Bingley," Bingley added.

"And Mr. Bingley," Mr. Hill amended. "Wait here, I will return shortly."

"Perhaps we should have waited," Darcy muttered as the urge to flee suddenly took hold of him. The fear of his petition being denied settled into his stomach and caused his heart to race.

"It is far too late to decide that now," Bingley chided.

"I know," Darcy said as he tugged at his jacket. "We will succeed."

"Of course, we will," Bingley assured him, although to Darcy it did not sound as if Bingley were very sure of their success.

"Oh, Mr. Darcy, Mr. Bingley," Mrs. Bennet said as she descended the stairs, "why are you standing here instead of sitting within?"

"We were waiting on Mr. Hill," Bingley answered.

"Waiting on Mr. Hill? For what?" Mrs. Bennet asked. "Hill," she said as the servant approached them, "why are these men waiting for you?"

"The master will see you," Mr. Hill said to Darcy and Bingley.

Mrs. Bennet gasped. "You wish to see Mr. Bennet?"

"Yes, ma'am," Bingley answered.

"Indeed, we do," Darcy added.

"Well! Do not let me detain you!" she cried in delight and moved toward the sitting room. "Perhaps we will have a bottle of claret with our dinner?" she asked, turning back toward them when she was just outside the sitting room.

"Perhaps," Darcy replied with a tight smile while he hoped that there would be a happy reason for imbibing.

Darcy's heart thumped loudly with each of the few steps to Mr.

Bennet's study. He paused only a moment to pull in a fortifying breath and to remind himself of his need to succeed before entering the room.

"Gentlemen," Mr. Bennet waved them to the chairs before his desk, "Mr. Hill informs me that you wish to speak to me."

"We do," Darcy said as he took his seat. The room felt very warm at present even with only the presence of a few glowing embers in the grate.

"I will assume it is about my daughters."

Darcy silently thanked the Lord for allowing the gentleman to broach the subject, so that he did not have to. "Yes, sir. I would like to marry Miss Elizabeth."

Bingley looked at him with wide eyes, and for good reason. Marry was not the word that was supposed to have come out of his mouth. It was supposed to be court.

"I mean to say, I should like permission to court Miss Elizabeth with the intent of eventually marrying her." Darcy rubbed his hands on his breeches and forced his lungs to fill with air.

Mr. Bennet chuckled. "I assume you have never done this before?"

Darcy's brow furrowed. Why would he have done this before? Offering to court and marry someone was not something a gentleman did on a regular basis, was it?

Mr. Bennet continued to chuckle. "I am teasing you, Mr. Darcy. These requests are not easy for any of us to make." He turned his eyes toward Bingley, who gulped.

"I would like to court Miss Bennet," Bingley said.

"To what end?"

Bingley blinked.

"Do you also wish permission to marry her?" Mr. Bennet asked.

To Darcy, it looked as if the man was enjoying their discomfort far too much. Of course, he was not about to point that out.

Bingley nodded eagerly. "Of course. Yes. I would like to marry her if that is her wish after we have come to know each other better."

"Is there any reason I should deny either of you?"

Darcy began to shake his head but then stopped. "There is one reason."

Again, Bingley turned wide eyes to him.

"Your son will not approve of either of us. I was rude to Miss Elizabeth when she came upon me after I had injured myself."

Mr. Bennet's brow furrowed. "She has welcomed you since, so I am going to assume that either you have been forgiven or your rudeness was not such that it angered her. For I know my daughter is not one to allow rudeness to pass without some exchange of words."

"You are correct," Darcy said. "She has forgiven me, but..."

"William has not."

"No, he has not, but for reasons that go beyond my behaviour on that morning in the wood."

Mr. Bennet's head tipped, and he studied Darcy with curiosity. "What reasons might he have? I know he has not seemed welcoming of you since he learned your name."

Darcy blew out a breath. "He has been told some things about me that are not true. However, the person who shared these lies with him is convincingly charming, and then when I replied crossly to Miss Elizabeth, Mr. William Bennet took that as proof that what he had heard was correct."

Mr. Bennet's head bobbed up and down slowly. "Would this have anything to do with a will not being executed as written?"

"Yes, sir."

"That explains why Lizzy was asking me about wills." He sighed. "She seemed very determined to prove your innocence. I think you will have no trouble convincing her to accept you." He grimaced. "However, her brother will be more challenging. I thought I had met the most obstinate child when Elizabeth was born, but then William arrived." He shook his head. "He is exceptionally hard to move at times – especially if he thinks his family, Lizzy in particular, has been injured. His opinion once lost is most challenging to restore."

"I understand. I am the same."

Mr. Bennet chuckled. "That is good to know. Such obstinacy will stand you in good stead when dealing with Elizabeth." He smiled. "You both have my permission to present your offers to my daughters, and I will make my son aware of the fact that I find no reason to prevent you. Of course, I will expect a call regarding all the financial particulars once you have come to the point."

"Thank you," Bingley said happily.

"Yes, thank you, sir," Darcy said. "Both for your permission and believing me to be as I appear – for I assure you I am."

Mr. Bennet stood. "My Lizzy would not defend you so strongly if you were anything other than honorable. She saw the error in the tale she had been told and ferreted out the information she needed to be assured that her opinion of you was correct. Therefore, it is not I but Elizabeth who deserves your thanks on that front. However, since she is not here, I will take it." He chuckled and moved around his desk.

"I think I will wait to tell my wife the good news," he said. "She will be overjoyed, of course, but her joy can become excessive."

"She met us in the entry," Bingley said.

Mr. Bennet sighed. "Then there is no hope for you now. I suggest you speak to my daughters directly or the whole business shall be decided and proclaimed by their mother."

And they did just as he said, securing their ladies during a stroll in the garden before dinner.

As it turned out, dinner was a somewhat painful experience for Darcy. Mrs. Bennet was overjoyed just as her husband had said she would be, and William seethed with anger exactly as Darcy had expected he would.

Thankfully, William had kept his opinions to himself for the entire evening and did not created a scene or put voice to his displeasure while in company. However, as Darcy was leaving, William had approached him, which was why Darcy now stood at the edge of the field near the knoll as the sun was rising, waiting for William to appear for their appointment.

Darcy sliced the air with his foil and shuffled through a position or two. His foot was hurting, but not so much that it made him concerned about having a great disadvantage. What did concern him regarding disadvantages was William's reach. Darcy was certain that the younger Mr. Bennet's arms were longer than his, which would make it far easier for him to land his points.

"This is ridiculous," Bingley said.

"I agree," Darcy replied. "But he demanded satisfaction for having his wishes ignored. It will change nothing. It will only make him feel he has gotten redress."

"He believes lies!" Bingley fairly shouted. "And he is challenging you to defend your honour without bothering to ask you about what he has heard!"

Darcy sighed. "I realize what he is doing and that it is foolish, but I also believe he will be more willing to listen after he has expended some of his anger."

"At your expense!"

Darcy nodded, and Bingley paced a circuit near the fence, muttering to himself about foolishness and how the weather was growing decidedly more chilled each morning.

It was only about five minutes later that William Bennet arrived with Mr. Bennet.

"I would not allow him to find another to stand with him," Mr. Bennet explained. "I have no desire to have this foolishness broadcast far and wide." He leveled a glare at his son.

"He is not what he seems," William replied.

"So you have said, repeatedly. However, I have yet to learn if you have discussed that with him." Mr. Bennet replied.

"No, he has not," Bingley answered.

"Good morning, Mr. Bingley. I can see you are as pleased as I am to be here."

"Indeed." Bingley crossed his arms and scowled at William.

"Shall we begin?" Darcy asked.

"I applaud your ability to be so calm," Mr. Bennet said to Darcy.

Darcy only smiled grimly. His calmness was a façade. Within, he was incensed that William Bennet was so stubborn as to act before thinking. That quality did not recommend him to Darcy. He could understand the man's need to protect his sisters, but he could not comprehend doing so in such an ignorant fashion.

Mr. Bennet chuckled at Darcy's response and nodded his understanding. "Let me amend that. I applaud your control."

Bingley stepped between Darcy and William. "You will cede the field when you have been hit three times." He raised a brow and glared at William. "He is injured, and I'll not let him suffer for longer than that."

William gave a nod of his head. And then, when Bingley had stepped back, the duel began.

"What are you doing?" Elizabeth shouted from the top of the knoll before running down to where her father was.

"William feels he was injured in some fashion because Mr. Darcy dared to pursue you after William had told him he was not welcome."

"And you condone this?" she asked her father in surprise.

He shook his head. "I did not want him bringing anyone else into the situation, so I insisted that I be the one to attend him and see that things were done fairly."

"You!" Elizabeth turned on William, who had stopped his match with Darcy and was standing, waiting to resume. "You would question our father's decision? You would question my ability to choose wisely?" She spat the questions at her brother as she advanced toward him. "How could you?"

"He has fooled you," William replied.

"The only fool is you!" Elizabeth cried. "You have no support of your beliefs other than a few cross words spoken by an injured man."

"I know what I have heard," William ground out. "I have no desire to see you tied to such a man as I have heard Mr. Darcy to be."

"I have already accepted him."

"It can be undone." William pulled himself straight.

"You are being ridiculous!" Elizabeth threw her hands up in exasperation.

"That is precisely what I said," Bingley agreed.

"I am being as I should be," William shot back. "I am trying to protect you just as you asked me to."

"Stop!" Elizabeth brushed tears from her cheek. "Just stop."

Darcy longed to go to her, to comfort her, but he also knew that in so doing, he would only provoke her brother further.

"I will stop if you will undo what you have done."

Elizabeth gasped and looked from her brother to her father and back.

"William," Mr. Bennet said sharply, "consider carefully what you are asking. I have given my permission. I see no reason to refuse a man like Mr. Darcy."

William looked nowhere but at Elizabeth. "What is your answer?"

"You are truly asking me to chose between you and Mr. Darcy?" William nodded.

Elizabeth shook her head.

Darcy forced himself to stay where he was instead of thrashing William as he deserved. If he were ever to win over Elizabeth's brother, it would not be with force or apparently logic.

"I love you," Elizabeth's eyes shifted from William to Darcy. "Both of you." She held Darcy's gaze for a heartbeat or two before she shrugged sadly and turned back to her brother. "But," she wiped tears from her face with the palm of her hand, "I choose him. I choose Mr. Darcy."

For the briefest of moments, Darcy wanted to shout his victory to the sky. Elizabeth loved him enough to choose him above her brother. However, in a flash as powerful and quick as lightning, his elation was dashed to grief for he knew what he had to do. "No."

All eyes turned toward him.

"I cannot allow it." He moved toward Elizabeth. "I will not take you from your brother no matter how dear you are to me. I would be no better than Wickham if I did. He has always taken what he wanted without regard for those around him." He shook his head. "No that is not true. He has taken what he wanted where I am concerned while relishing in the pain it caused me."

Elizabeth shook her head. Her tears increasing and tearing at Darcy's heart.

Mr. Bennet stepped over to where he was. "But in refusing Elizabeth's choice are you not allowing the stories this Wickham has told to take her from you?"

Darcy swallowed against the tears he could feel threatening and nodded. "But I will not be what he is. He nearly claimed my sister this past summer, and my desolation would have been complete. I cannot be the source of such pain for another."

"But what of Elizabeth?" Mr. Bennet asked softly.

That was a touch too far for Darcy's composure. "I will," his voice cracked, and a tear escaped down his cheek. "Wait for her," he finished in a whisper. "For as long as it takes." He bowed to William and Mr. Bennet, pressed a kiss to Elizabeth's hand and quickly found his horse and took his leave before either his resolve crumbled, or he made an utter fool of himself by weeping.

# Chapter 14

Through her tears, Elizabeth watched Mr. Darcy, followed by Mr. Bingley, go. Her father wrapped her in his arms.

"I thought there was little danger in your brother meeting with Mr. Darcy, or I would have forbidden it."

Elizabeth had no words. All she was capable of doing at present was shaking her head. It was not his fault that Mr. Darcy had left her.

"Come," he said gently. "You may ride my horse, and I will walk beside you."

"No," she managed to force from her lips.

"You cannot stay here," said William.

She pushed away from her father and turned toward her brother. "Do not speak to me!" She blew out a breath. "Ever," she added. "I did not choose you, nor will I ever. And I will not return to the house with you!" Fury such as she had never felt rose within her. How could he be so stupid as to not see that Mr. Darcy was a perfectly honorable gentleman?

"Lizzy," her father said softly, "you will eventually have to speak to William."

She shook her head.

Mr. Bennet sighed. "I will send Jane to you. You will be under your tree?"

Elizabeth nodded.

"I do not want Jane to have to wander hither and yon trying to find you," he cautioned.

"I will be where you said." She drew a sleeve of her pelisse across her eyes in an attempt to dry her tears, not that, at this moment, she thought they would ever stop flowing.

"Will you accept both my handkerchief and that of your brother?" Mr. Bennet held out his handkerchief to her as William withdrew his from his pocket.

Gratefully, Elizabeth took the piece of cloth from her father but hesitated before accepting William's. She did not wish to even touch something which belonged to him at present, but she did have need of something to dry her eyes and nose. She murmured a thank you and turned to leave them and go to her tree.

"Lizzy," William called after her. She could hear his concern for her in his voice, and despite her anger, it pricked her heart.

"Do not speak to me," she threw the words over her shoulder. Then she stopped. She would not listen to him, but he could listen to her. Perhaps now he would be more willing to do so. "You know nothing of him! Nothing! When you know about him. When you can tell me all you know about him which you have heard from his own lips – not from the lips of another profligate schemer – " she smiled at his look of shock at her choice of words. "—only then, will I allow you to speak to me."

And with those words, she turned away once more and made her way to where she could attempt to gain control of her sorrow. She could not return to the house and her mother as she was right now. She would need to gather some semblance of fortitude before facing her mother's concerned coddling.

She sank down under the tree, heedless of her gown or pelisse. Not much seemed worthy of consideration presently. She pulled her knees up and rested her forehead on them as she allowed herself to fully indulge in the misery of her heart. She berated William for his actions for several minutes until her anger was spent. Then she turned her thoughts to Mr. Darcy.

She lifted her head and looked toward Netherfield. "I love you," she whispered. She had not known it until she had been met with William's demand. She had known she admired Mr. Darcy and that she longed to know more about him. She had known that she wished for him to take her hand and, she smiled through her tears, she had known when he kissed her that she would like to have him do so again. But in the instant when she had to choose between giving him up and remaining as she had always been or stepping away from the familiar confines of her family to be at his side, she had come to realize just what it was that drew her to him. It was not his wealth or his handsome features. It was him – his heart, his character, the way he smiled when he saw her, the ease with which they entered into intimate conversation – it was who he would be even if all his riches were removed and his features, disfigured. And she had known that she could not give him up any more than she could hand William her own heart.

How such a love had developed in so short a time was beyond her comprehension. But then, it did not matter how it happened. It only mattered that it had and now it been torn from her.

She buried her head in her arms which still rested on her knees and wept without thinking for a few moments. Then, determined that she would not be a complete watering pot when Jane arrived, she lifted her head, dried her tears, and attempted to keep more from spilling as she replayed the events of the morning in her head. She had been so excited to see Mr. Darcy when she had left the house, and then... The sound of metal clashing with metal and the sight of her brother and Mr. Darcy engaged in battle had frightened her.

"Elizabeth?" Jane touched her shoulder to alert her sister to her presence before carefully taking a seat next to her on the ground. She wrapped her arms around Elizabeth's shoulders. "Papa told me what happened."

"When will I learn to hold my tongue?" Elizabeth shook her head. "If I had remained silent..."

"Shhh," Jane cooed. "What has been done is done. We cannot alter that now."

"I love him, Jane. I love him most ardently."

Jane squeezed her close.

"This is my fault. If I had not allowed my anger to overcome me, William would not have said what he did, and Mr. Darcy would not have left me."

"William was wrong," Jane said firmly. "I will not excuse your actions, but I will also not allow you to bear all of this on yourself. You may have been demanding, and you may have spoken in anger. However, none of that would have happened if William had been reasonable."

Jane always had a way of framing a picture as it should be when Elizabeth was beginning to scramble the pieces and create scenarios that were less than accurate as her mind spun in its distress and struggled to right whatever cart had been upset.

"Papa said that Mr. Darcy has not given you up completely." Jane drew and released a deep breath. In it, Elizabeth could hear the weight of concern Jane bore. "We have only to hope William will regain his senses soon, and I think he will."

"He is so stubborn," Elizabeth refuted.

"As are you," Jane said as she smoothed Elizabeth's hair behind her ear on the far side of her head where Jane's arm rested around her sister's shoulders. "He was greatly shaken when I saw him. I have never seen him so."

Elizabeth shrugged as if she did not care, even though she did. Her heart hurt because of the fracture that had occurred between her and her brother.

"Give him some time. He is not without sense. He will see reason. Papa will make certain he does."

Elizabeth sighed. She hoped it was true.

Jane removed her arm from around her sister, wrapping it instead around Elizabeth's arm and snuggling into her side. It was often how they would sit and tell stories to one another at night when they were younger. They still did it now, though not so often.

"Do you remember when William first arrived?" Jane asked.

Elizabeth nodded. "He was so big, and he scowled so much."

Jane laughed. "That is what you said. You looked up at him and said, 'you are very tall' which you followed with 'why do you not smile?'"

"And Papa explained to me what it meant for someone to die."

Jane nodded. "And you decided it was your duty to see William smile. The torment you caused him with your questions! 'Do you like apples, William? They are a very cheery fruit. Do you like horses, William? I like riding with Papa. Would you like to have my kitten? She is very good at catching mice and at snuggling with me when I am afraid of the thunder.'"

Elizabeth laughed. "I was a trying child, was I not?"

"Excessively," Jane agreed. "And yet, you became the sister William loves best. No matter how you teased him about his incorrect sums or how often you followed him around when he had told you to stay home." She laughed softly again. "Do you remember falling in the stream? I think you were about eight, were you not?"

Elizabeth nodded. "I was, and that water was not warm."

"You had been told to stay home, but you wished to fish with William and his friends, who thought it great fun to challenge you to stand on a rock in the middle of the stream."

"On one foot," Elizabeth added.

"And you did it for about five seconds before falling into the water."

"William fished me out and wrapped me in his jacket."

"And proceeded to earn himself a black eye and a bloody nose venting his displeasure on his friends because they had caused you harm," Jane finished the story quietly. "He loves you. He acted foolishly, but he did it because it was you. He did not challenge Mr. Bingley."

Elizabeth dried her eyes again. She knew it was true. William was a determined protector of all his sisters, but he was downright immovable when it was anything that threatened her. When she was ill, it was he who would sit beside her bed reading or who would fetch tea and broth as needed. He had held her hand when the surgeon had stitched up the gash on her leg from another of her escapades when she had been following him without his per-mission. She could still see the ashen sheen of his face as she bit her lip to keep from crying out with each poke. He had made her look at him when her curiosity begged her to watch the gruesome work of the surgeon. And he had, after he had seen she was well, emptied the contents of his stomach.

"He means well, Lizzy."

"I know," Elizabeth admitted. "But he is wrong."

Jane rested her head on Elizabeth's shoulder. "And he will move the heavens above to correct his wrong for he will not be parted from you for anything in the world."

Elizabeth hoped with all her heart that it was true, for though she longed to see Mr. Darcy again and eventually be his wife, she knew that she would never be truly happy if it came at the expense of an irreparable breach between her and her brother.

They sat in silence for some time. Elizabeth's tears had finally stopped – or nearly had. There were a few that insisted on filling her eyes whenever she would think of either William or Mr. Darcy.

"Are you ready to go home?" Jane asked.

Elizabeth nodded. "I believe I am."

Jane rose first and helped Elizabeth up.

"What does Mama know?" Elizabeth asked as they began the walk back to Longbourn.

"She heard everything Papa told me, and she has instructed that a bath be waiting for you as well as a cup of tea and a piece of toast."

"Am I to be confined to my bed?"

Jane nodded her head. "You know Mama. She would take to her

bed, and therefore, it is expected that you will as well. However, that will likely be for the best, as you will not need to see William, nor will you have to hear Mama's moans over the situation, for I am certain I will be assigned to your care."

Elizabeth smiled. "I am sorry to be such a burden to you."

"You are never a burden, my dearest sister."

"Unless I have angered William and caused Mr. Bingley not to be allowed to call," Elizabeth teased.

"Well, yes, there is that," Jane agreed with a small laugh. "Perhaps that should be how we pass our time – teaching you how to hold your tongue." She pulled Elizabeth close. "I own that it is a fault and needs correction, but I love you just as you are, you know."

"I know, and I love you. However, I do not think I will need much instruction. If I can remember this day and the way my heart hurts for those I love, it will be enough."

"He loves you. Mr. Darcy, that is," Jane said. "Papa told me before I left to come to you about how he promised to wait for you and that he cried." She sighed. "You must admit that that is very romantic."

"Jane!"

"I know, the rest of the story is not pleasant, but to be loved so dearly." She sighed again. "I almost wish William had challenged Mr. Bingley."

"You do not," Elizabeth said with a laugh. Jane could be just as given to fanciful notions as Lydia at times.

Jane shrugged. "Perhaps I do not, but I would adore having a gentleman be so moved at the thought of losing me even for a short time."

Elizabeth shook her head. "You are impossible at times," she chided playfully, but she would not have Jane any other way, and she was excessively thankful for such a whimsical conversation that would put her in better spirits before she was to face her mother's sighs and lamentations before being tucked into bed.

# Chapter 15

For two days, Darcy hid himself away in his room. The first day, he was accompanied by a bottle from Bingley's wine cellar. It had imparted the numbing stupor he sought for a time. He had felt blissfully separated from the real world and its woes until he awoke the next morning. Then, just as he knew it would, the world crashed in upon him in loud, nauseating waves, pounding at his head, and churning his stomach.

On the third day, Darcy arose and prepared himself for the day. He would not wallow in misery for another day. Elizabeth was not lost to him forever, just for now, and his friend had need of his advice about accounts and crops and other such things. He would find a purpose – something into which he could throw himself, and in so doing, he hoped to be able to weather the time between now and when the younger Mr. Bennet finally located his senses and welcomed him with something a touch friendlier than a fencing foil.

"Good morning," Caroline greeted as Darcy entered the breakfast room. "I trust you are feeling much improved today."

He gave her a small smile. "I am, thank you." He poured some tea and took a seat.

"I visited Longbourn yesterday," Caroline continued.

Darcy took a sip of his tea and braced himself for what he assumed would be another attempt to sway him to her cause now that she knew Miss Elizabeth was not to be his for some time since Bingley had shared with her all that had happened.

"I called on Mr. William Bennet."

Darcy lifted a brow, curious to know why she had called on the gentleman.

"He was not home."

"Indeed?"

She nodded. "He left Longbourn the same day he met with you in the field."

"Why did you call on him?" Darcy was interested in the fact that Mr. William Bennet had not been home, but at the moment, he was more interested in why Caroline would be calling on him in the first place.

"To prove that my cap is no longer set at you." She lifted her chin and held his gaze.

"And it is set at Mr. William Bennet?" Darcy asked in confusion.

"Oh, goodness, no!" She laughed and then stopped suddenly as if captured by a thought. "I suppose he might not be so bad a catch." Her head tipped to the side as if she were considering the idea for the first time. "He is tall and, though not particularly handsome, he is not dreadful to look upon." She shrugged. "Many ties between families is often better than just one."

"You will have to explain that," Darcy said, lowering his cup and reaching for a scone. The cook at Netherfield was no slouch. Her work was delightful, and her scones were quickly becoming Darcy's favourites.

"You shall marry his sister. Charles will marry his other sister. And then, if I marry him, we shall all be tied together in several different strands. A nice tight knot."

"You would marry him just to complete some knot of relations?" Darcy was still not certain he followed her logic.

Caroline shrugged again. "I would prefer not to, I believe, now that I have spoken about it. I do not think I could manage to keep my composure if I were to be too tightly tied to either Mrs. Bennet or her youngest daughters. I am not disparaging. I am simply declaring we do not get on well. Not to mentions, there is a noticeable lack of shops in Meryton."

Darcy nodded. He could not see Caroline tolerating Mrs. Bennet or a lack of shopping for any extended period of time.

"Then why did you call on him?" Darcy asked.

"I wished to share with him what I knew of Mr. Wickham. Mr. Wickham did attempt to flirt with me when we first met him, but I was too cunning to be drawn in."

"He did?"

She smiled at him and nodded. "Some gentlemen find both me and my inheritance attractive."

"I have never said you were unattractive," Darcy countered.

"No, you have not, but then you have not fallen for my charms either." She refilled her cup and settled back in her chair. "I thought if I could convince him of Mr. Wickham's rakish ways, I could perhaps do you a service." Her gaze fell to study the contents of her cup. "You are a friend, and even if that is all you shall ever be, I do not wish to see you suffer as you must have been – indeed, as you likely still are."

"I thank you for your kindness," he said. He would overlook the small amount of pleasure that seemed to fill her voice as she spoke of his suffering. He had disappointed her, and such feelings of satisfaction that the person who had disappointed you was suffering somewhat of the pain that he had caused were not unusual. He was thankful that she had been able to rise above those vengeful feeling to attempt to help him. If she had acted so thoughtfully more often, perhaps he would have considered her more closely. He paused before indulging in another bite of his scone. "I am still not choosing you."

She shrugged. "I know, but one cannot fault a lady for the attempt." When she smirked, she looked very much like her twin. "Truly," she continued, "I have given you up. I am not so foolish as to attempt to come between you and Miss Elizabeth. Truly."

"Thank you."

"Mr. Darcy."

Darcy looked up at the butler.

"When you are finished, sir, you have a visitor."

Darcy's brows furrowed. "Who might that be?"

"Mr. William Bennet, sir."

Darcy could not contain his look of surprise. He expected the young man to come to his senses at some point, but he had not thought it would be so soon. He had seemed more reticent in personality than to easily capitulate.

"Will you see him, sir? He was concerned you would not."

With good reason. "As soon as I have finished, I will join him in the front drawing room."

"Very good, sir. I am certain he will be most appreciative."

"You are not rushing?" Caroline asked as Darcy settled back

into his chair to enjoy the last of his tea and scone at a leisurely pace.

"I think allowing him to cool his heels for a while might be best."

This reply was met with an approving smile.

"Would you like to join me for this?" he asked Caroline when he had finished his last morsel of food and drained his second cup of tea.

She sighed. "I do enjoy a good spat, but no. I will allow you the privacy you deserve."

He thanked her and went to find Mr. William Bennet.

"Mr. Darcy." William shot to his feet when Darcy entered the room.

"Mr. Ben –" Darcy's greeting stopped abruptly as he took in the condition of the gentleman before him. William appeared to be wearing the same clothes he had been wearing on the morning of their appointment, and they were exceedingly rumpled. However, that was not what arrested Darcy's words. No, that honour went to the state of the man's face. His right eye was nearly swollen closed, and his lower lip was two times the size it should be with a nasty gash held together by two stitches near the right corner of his mouth.

"Please forgive my appearance and my early call." He fiddled with what remained of his hat. "But I knew that if I were to go home first, Mother would not allow me to leave once she saw me."

"I can see why." Darcy motioned for him to retake his seat, which he did.

"I have been to town." He paused and looked at his hat. "I should have gone to town before now."

"I apologize, but I do not understand."

William blew out a breath and rose from his seat. "My father died when I was ten. That is when I came to live at Longbourn."

"I know. Your sister told me."

He paced in front of the windows behind the chair where he had been sitting. "What she likely did not tell you is that I thought I would never again have a reason to smile. I thought that my world had come to an end. My father was no pillar of exemplary behavior, but he was my father. He had told me about his unreasonable cousin and his wife who only had daughters. He had thought it humorous that they would be at my mercy when I came into my inheritance. I had no reason to not believe what he had told me about them, and so, I arrived at Longbourn expecting to be reviled and treated poorly."

"But you were not."

He shook his head. "No, I was welcomed with great comforting arms and by one impish young lady determined to see me smile." His lips attempted to tip up into a smile, though it was difficult with the lower one being so swollen. "Lizzy latched onto me and followed me around like a lost pup might do someone who fed it." He shook his head. "She was a lovely little bothersome shadow."

"And she stole your heart."

William nodded. "I would do nearly anything to protect any of the Bennets, but for Lizzy, I would do so much more. And I confess that desire clouded my judgment of you. For that, I must apologize."

Darcy gave him a small nod of his head. He could understand that sentiment. He was much the same when it came to those he loved.

William took his seat once again. "I went to town in search of Wickham. I now have in my possession nearly the full, truthful story of your relationship. There was a portion he would not tell me, no matter how much I insisted. He only said he could not because it would put his life in danger." Again, his lips attempted to tip into a smile. "More danger than it was in as I was asking him. I guess he knew I would not hang to know a secret." He met Darcy's eyes and held them with a knowing look. "I assume it is about your sister, and I will ask no further."

"Thank you, and it is. She was not ruined, but it was close."

William shook his head. "I have been an unmitigated arse."

"I will not refute that," Darcy agreed.

William chuckled. "You could not. Your character would not allow you to lie in such a fashion." He shifted uneasily. "I know I have no right to ask this, but there is something that I would very much like for you to do for me."

Darcy's brows rose. The fellow expected a favor?

"Elizabeth refuses to speak to me or even see me, and not without justification, as I have said, I was an arse. However, I do believe she might forgive me for my stupidity more easily if you were to accompany me to Longbourn." He blew out a breath. "There is no gentleman of more noble character with whom I would see her, for I know that from what I have heard, you will protect her as fiercely as I would, and that is all I have ever hoped for her to find in a husband."

Darcy smiled. "I would be delighted to be of service to you in such a fashion."

"Mr. Darcy."

Darcy turned to the butler.

"Your cousin and sister are here to see you, but I told then you were occupied."

"We are finished, are we not?" Darcy asked William. "I was about to ride out with Mr. Bennet, but I believe I can welcome my cousin and sister first while my horse is readied."

"Of course," William muttered as he fidgeted with his hat once again.

Darcy rose along with William and made all the proper introductions when Richard and Georgiana entered the room.

A sound as if the wind had been knocked out of him emanated from William, causing him to be only able to stammer a greeting and Darcy to chuckle. It was similar to how Darcy had felt when first introduced to William's sister. A Bingley William might not be, but anyone who would take Wickham in hand – quite literally – as William had for his sister was not a man Darcy would brush aside – even if that gentleman had caused a great deal of distress with his foolishness.

"You will have to excuse Mr. Bennet's appearance." Darcy motioned for them all to be seated. "He has just come from extracting his displeasure on a fellow whose lies caused his sister some grief."

Richard, who had been looking at William, turned quickly to Darcy with a questioning look.

"Colonel, Miss Darcy!" Bingley cried as he entered the room. "Good heavens what happened to you?" he said as he took in the appearance of William. "This is not Darcy's doing, is it?"

Darcy laughed. "No. I have not laid one finger on Mr. Bennet."

"Though he would be well within his rights if he did," William added.

"I am confused," Georgiana said. "Why would my brother wish to harm Mr. Bennet?"

William blew out a breath and shook his head. "Because I was a fool and listened to a tale about your brother that was not true. However, I chose to believe it and was less than willing to allow him to be accepted by my sister."

Georgiana's eyes grew wide. "I beg your pardon? My brother has made an offer to someone?"

"I have," Darcy answered. Joy swelling in his heart at the admission.

"You have?" Richard nearly shouted.

"Yes, I have and so has Bingley," Darcy replied, attempting to shift some of the attention from himself.

"Both of you?" Richard began to laugh. "I had heard tell that there were some beauties in the area, but so soon?"

"They are the most beautiful ladies in Hertfordshire," William's voice held a decided edge to it.

Darcy chuckled silently. Not even a colonel would be tolerated to even hint at disrespecting William's sisters.

"He does not exaggerate," Bingley replied.

"Well, I am happy for you, but I thought that I was needed to convince someone of Darcy's worth."

"That would be me," William said. "I need no further convincing. I believe I know all I need to know." He rubbed the area below his swollen lip. "I had a discussion with the fellow who lied to me, and after some *persuasion*, he told me the truth."

Richard leaned back, folded his arms, and smiled approvingly at William. "I do hope the other fellow looks at least as damaged as you do."

William's lips curled into a smile as best they could and said, "I have very few injuries comparatively."

To which Richard responded by calling William a fine fellow. Then he shook his head. "Then I am unneeded? There is nothing with which you require my assistance."

"Oh, no!" William said quickly. "There is an assembly next week, and there seems to never be enough gentlemen to dance with the ladies." He shrugged. "And I would like for once not to have to listen to my sisters complain about being left standing and not being able to dance every set."

"An assembly, you say?" Richard rubbed his chin. "I do like to dance, and since it is a country assembly, we might even allow Georgiana to attend, mightn't we?" He looked at Darcy hopefully.

"She is not out yet," Darcy answered.

"But it is a country assembly, and your betrothed will be there, will she not?"

"Yes," William replied, "and her four sisters. Three of whom have not yet been spoken for."

"You would throw your sisters at him, yet refuse Darcy?" Bingley asked.

"I have heard everything I need to know about Colonel Fitzwilliam," William replied with a smirk. "The fellow I spoke to and who blackened my eye has a healthy fear of the man, and that is a good enough recommendation for me."

"He should fear me," Richard muttered.

"Who?" Georgiana asked. "You all seem to know who this fellow is, and I would like to know."

"No," Darcy answered. "You would not."

"I am certain I would," she replied.

Darcy shook his head.

"He is not worth your notice," William replied. "A total scoundrel."

"Aye," Bingley agreed. "That he is." He clapped his hands together. "Have you been shown to your rooms?"

"No," Georgiana answered.

"Then, that must be done." Bingley turned to Darcy. "Shall we make it a grand party which calls at Longbourn today?"

Darcy smiled and clapped William on the shoulder. "We are going to Longbourn now. Apparently, William would like my help in persuading his sister to speak to him."

Bingley laughed. "As if she will notice more than you." He waved toward the door. "While Darcy is off courting his lady, allow me to make you comfortable by directing you to your rooms."

"Shall we?" Darcy asked William. "You might not be anxious to see your sister, but I will not lie. I am."

Darcy gathered his hat and coat, and then, the two men stepped out into the bright light of the day, both happy to be on their way to Longbourn. One hopeful to be forgiven, and the other to put his short agonizing wait to an end.

# Chapter 16

Elizabeth knocked on the door to her father's study before opening it. "You wished to see me?"

"No," her father replied with a smile. "But William does, and I did not expect you to come if I told you that." He rose from his chair and crossed the room. "I think I shall go torment your mother's nerves for a while." He stopped in front of her and took her by the shoulders. "You are not to leave this room until this is settled." His lips curled up on one side in a small smirk. "And I have no doubt that it will be settled soon." He kissed her cheek and left the room.

"Lizzy?" William, who had been sitting in front of his father's desk, rose and turned toward her.

Elizabeth gasped, and her hand flew to her mouth. Whatever sharp welcome she had thought to give him died on her lips.

"I have heard the whole ugly truth – or as much of it as I could extract – from Mr. Wickham. I know you said I should hear it from Mr. Darcy, but..." he stopped talking and looked at the floor.

"But what?" Elizabeth questioned as she crossed to him. She gently touched his eye. "Does it hurt?"

"Not as much as my lip or my heart." He took her hand.

"Why did you not go to Mr. Darcy?" Elizabeth asked again.

"Because he was not the cause of my blindness to reason. Mr. Wickham was, and since I could not thrash myself for having caused you pain, I thought I might be able to thrash him and receive my just dues in the process."

"William!" Elizabeth scolded. "When will you stop censuring and calling out every gentleman who appears to do me harm? You did call him out, did you not?"

William nodded. "But, instead of swords, we met with only our hands as weapons, and not in a field. We met at a club where gentlemen tend to do this sort of thing for sport."

"You men are a funny lot," Elizabeth muttered.

"I will never stop protecting you, Lizzy," he added. "At least not until that responsibility falls on another." He sighed and dropped her hand. "I do not feel worthy of your forgiveness. I have been an utter fool." He shook his head and rolled his eyes upward. "Likely the greatest fool in all of England."

"You were foolish," Elizabeth agreed. "But, you know the truth about Mr. Darcy now?"

"Mostly. Wickham would not tell me part of why he was attempting to tarnish Darcy's name, but I know about his dissipate behaviour and his refusal of the living, as well as his attempt to later claim it. You were correct. There were reasons for the refusal. I should have bowed to your greater abilities to reason things, but I was so determined to make certain you were not tying yourself to someone of questionable character that I convinced myself you were only protesting because he was handsome and rich." He grimaced as she glared at him. "Yes, that was ill-thought-out."

"Indeed."

He should know better than to think so of her. She had often told him and Jane that she would not marry any gentleman whom she did not feel she could respect, or whom she thought would not respect her. Admiration was longed for, of course, and wealth could not be ignored, but it was the character of a gentleman which would recommend him most strongly to her.

"All my thinking was rather faulty." He was looking at the floor once again. "And I should be very sorry if such foolishness has created a breach of a permanent nature between us."

"You hurt me." Elizabeth placed a hand on his cheek, causing him to look at her. "Not just by separating me from Mr. Darcy, whom I love, but by not valuing my judgment."

He leaned his cheek into her hand as a tear slid from his swollen eye. "I know. I have buffeted myself in spirit most severely for two days for that."

"You will not do it again?"

He sighed. "I shall attempt not to, but I cannot promise success."

"It is good enough." She removed her hand from his cheek and opened her arms to him in invitation. "You are forgiven."

He wrapped her in his large arms, crushing her against him, and thanked her over and over.

"I was not certain if you would forgive me," he said when he released her. "So, I brought something with me that might help ensure my success."

She looked around the room, but she did not see any gifts.

"It is not in here," he said. "He is in the garden, waiting to see you."

Her hand flew to her heart as a smile spread across her face. "He? Mr. Darcy? Is Mr. Darcy here?"

William nodded his head. "I went to beg his forgiveness before I came home. I was fearful that Mother would not allow me out of her sight once she saw me."

"Has she seen you?"

"No, I came through the servant's entrance, and I intend to wash and put on fresh clothes before she does."

Elizabeth chuckled. "That will help you some, but not completely." Their mother was not one to take an injury to any of her children with any amount of composure. A wound to one of her children was always the most severe of that sort she had ever seen.

"I have already obtained all the potions and tinctures she will require," he added. "Now, while I sneak upstairs to make myself somewhat presentable to our mother, you should escape to the garden."

Elizabeth threw her arms around him. "Though you are a fool at times, I could not ask for a better brother. I love you and am so happy I will not have to be parted from you, for I would still choose Mr. Darcy."

He squeezed her tightly and then released her. "I am glad to hear it. I should not want any of my sisters to choose me over their husbands. Now, go. And when you are done in the garden, if you could distract Mother with Mr. Darcy, I would appreciate it greatly. She will be more forgiving of my stupidity if she knows I have made amends in such a fashion."

Elizabeth tipped her head. "Perhaps I will, or perhaps I will send Mr. Darcy home, so that you can suffer as you should."

"You said you forgave me," he reminded her.

"Yes, and I will not withdraw that, but there are consequences to all actions, are there not?"

"Please, Lizzy," he begged.

She said not a word in reply, choosing instead to only smile and shrug before leaving the room. She was happy to have their relationship restored, and she was nearly positive she would invite Mr. Darcy in just so she could have him near for longer. However, she was not above enjoying making her brother feel uneasy for just a while longer.

~*~*~

*Mr. Darcy was waiting for her.*

The thought made her smile as she put on her pelisse, and it caused her breath to catch as she saw him, pacing a circuit at the far end of the garden nearest the servant's entrance. It was a portion of the garden that could not be seen from the sitting room. William must have either been hiding Mr. Darcy from their mother, or he wished to give her a private place to be reunited with Mr. Darcy. Whatever his motivation might have been, she was glad that Mr. Darcy was here where they could speak in private.

He turned toward her just at that moment, and a beautiful smile spread across his face. A smile that was just for her and because of her. Jane was right. It was very romantic to have a gentleman respond to you in such a demonstrative fashion.

"It has been a long two days," he said as she approached him.

"It has," she agreed.

He extended his arm to her. "Would you care to take a turn around the garden?"

She placed her hand on his arm but shook her head. "There is a bench to our right. I would rather sit there." There she would be guaranteed of not being interrupted by some sister being sent out by their mother to act as a chaperone.

"If that is what you prefer." He led her down the short path to the bench. "I was surprised to see your brother this morning. I had thought it would be longer before he came to see me."

Elizabeth allowed him to pull her close as they sat down. "I was surprised as well, though I should not be, I suppose."

"He cares for you very much," Darcy said, putting words to Elizabeth's thoughts.

"He does."

"He is not the only one who cares for you," Darcy lifted her fingers and kissed them. "Will you still have me? Even after I walked away from you?"

"You have no need to apologize," she chided. "Your actions were beyond reproach. I, on the other hand, was once again demanding and that caused the whole ordeal. William would not have made his demand as he did if I had not provoked him. Of course, I would not have provoked him if he had not challenged you, so the beginnings of the wrong lie with him. However, I am still at fault."

He placed a finger on her lips. "Will you still have me?"

She nodded, and he removed his finger from her lips. "If you will still have me."

"I cannot imagine living without your demanding person at my side. Two days without you was enough." He wrapped an arm around her and pulled her closer to him. "I love you, Elizabeth. I do not know how you stole my heart so quickly, but you have.

And I do not want it back. Keep it and care for it for now and always."

She rested her head against his shoulder right above where she could hear his heart beating. It was a wonderful, reassuring sound. "Seeing as you have my heart, it seems only proper that I keep yours in return." She took his free hand and held it between both of hers. "I love you, though, like you, I do not know how it happened so quickly, but this closeness we share feels as if it has always been."

"Perhaps that is how it is supposed to be."

"Perhaps," she agreed.

They sat as they were, her head resting against his shoulder while she held his hand, for several minutes.

"William is hoping I will invite you in so that Mama will be too happy to be put out with him. She was very displeased when Papa told her about him challenging you and demanding I chose you or him."

Darcy laughed. "I can imagine any mother would be upset with a son for driving away a suitor."

"Seeing us well-married is my mother's sole goal in life aside from having her dinner parties spoken about for longer than her sister's ever are."

"I shall remember that and praise her when I can. It is best for a gentleman to keep his mother-in-law happy, or so my father said."

Elizabeth giggled. She would enjoy continuing to learn about him. "Well, then, I suppose I must invite you in and not just because I do not wish to have you ever leave me again."

They rose reluctantly from the comfort of their secluded spot in the garden.

"I am not returning you to the house without a kiss and a promise that you will not suffer me to wait too long before we marry." He wrapped her in his embrace.

"I had hoped you would kiss me," she admitted, tipping her face up to look at him and meet his lips as they descended to hers.

There would be three months to wait for the wedding, but as Darcy and Elizabeth waited, this corner of the garden, as well as Elizabeth's favourite tree on the knoll, would know many of their secrets and witness many ardent kisses such as this one. And with each meeting, whether it was on the knoll, in a drawing room, or on a dance floor, Elizabeth would find herself delighted by the love that she found and was constantly reminded of as she began the lifelong pleasure of learning about the man who held her now.

William would be sorry to see her leave Longbourn. However, in a year's time, he would find his way to London to spend a season with the sister he loved best in all the world while he sought to prove himself worthy of a brother's good opinion while hoping that brother would prove to be far less foolish than he had been while assessing Mr. Darcy.

# Before You Go

If you enjoyed this book, be sure to let others know by leaving a review.

~*~*~

Want to know when the next Leenie book will be available? You can always know what's new with my books by subscribing to my mailing list.

(There will, of course, be a thank you gift for joining because I think my readers are awesome!)

Book News from Leenie Brown

(bit.ly/LeenieBBookNews)

~*~*~

Turn the page to read an excerpt of another one of Leenie's books

[*Below is the prologue to Choices, A Pride and Prejudice Variation Series. Each of the four romantic tales found in this series is a result of one father choosing to ensure that his two eldest daughters ended up happily married. Mr. Bennet had no idea the chain of events that the scheming, which follows this conversation with his friend Sir William, would set in motion.*]

## October 1811

*Not handsome enough but with fine eyes?* Mr. Bennet chuckled to himself as he tucked himself away in the corner of the drawing room at Lucas Lodge. From here he could keep an eye on his daughters and listen to various conversations as people moved from place to place. Most of them would, at one point or another, pass through the door near him to the room beyond where there was a table laid out with various forms of refreshment.

He chuckled again as he repeated Mr. Darcy's comment to Miss Bingley to himself. Fine eyes, indeed! His Lizzy possessed the most expressive eyes of any lady Mr. Bennet had ever met. One look let you know quite clearly what she was thinking.

"Fine eyes," he muttered. It was as he had suspected when he had first met Mr. Darcy — Elizabeth would make him a fine wife. It had not taken long for that reserved and well-educated gentleman to fall under the spell of a lady whose mind was just as astute as his own. Not handsome enough? The man must have been in some foul mood to have spoken so harshly and, he added with some force to himself, wrongly. Elizabeth was not Jane, but she was by no means lacking in beauty.

But that was the fly in the ointment. Elizabeth had heard the slight Mr. Darcy had made at the assembly and taken such a strong disliking to the man. Mr. Bennet sighed and shook his head. He knew that bringing the two together would be quite the undertaking — excessively difficult but utterly necessary if he wished to see Elizabeth well-matched and happy. Mr. Darcy was, in every way that Mr. Bennet could determine, the gentleman who was his daughter's equal.

"I tried to arrange a dance between them," said Sir William as he handed his long-time friend a glass of lemonade. "But, she is quite set against him, it seems."

"I saw," Mr. Bennet replied. "And then I heard him mention her fine eyes."

"Indeed?"

Bennet nodded. "Miss Bingley is quite put out by the comment. I do not envy his position of having an unhappy woman yapping at his elbow." He raised his eyebrows and smirked as he took a sip of his drink.

Sir William lifted his glass in salute. "Hear, hear. I have had it happen a time or two in the past eight and twenty years myself. There is nothing quite like the continual complaining of a disgruntled woman robed in supposed humour to try one's nerves."

"He is a patient one. I am sure I could not abide Miss Bingley's comments so graciously as he." Mr. Bennet shifted in his chair. "It is a good sign, for if he can tolerate Miss Bingley in a fit of pique, he should be able to handle my Lizzy."

"Aye, he should, but Lizzy's tongue and mind are a bit sharper. And her opinions are not so easily swayed." There was a hint of caution in Sir William's voice.

Mr. Bennet knew that his friend agreed with him about Mr. Darcy and Elizabeth making a fine match. That had not, however, stopped Sir William from voicing his concern, repeatedly, that Elizabeth could not be swayed from her current dislike of the gentleman.

"She will come around, although," Mr. Bennet drew out the word and lowered his voice, "that may not happen until after they are married."

Sir William laughed. "Exactly how do you propose we get her to marry him when she does not like him? Surely, you would not suggest a compromise?"

Mr. Bennet tapped his finger against the side of his glass. "I would do almost anything to assure the happiness of my Lizzy, even if it meant bearing her anger and forcing her hand."

He watched Elizabeth, who was talking intently to her dear friend, Charlotte Lucas. He smiled as she sneaked a third glance at Mr. Darcy. If Mr. Bennet was not mistaken, and he rarely was when it came to understanding Elizabeth, she was fascinated by the man from Derbyshire. It was a fascination that he was certain was foreign to her.

"I pray it does not come to it, but if a compromise is necessary, can I count on your assistance?"

Sir William studied his friend and then Elizabeth for a moment. "You are convinced she will be happy?"

"Completely."

Sir William sighed. It was a sound of resignation and the same one he always made when he was about to bow to Mr. Bennet's wishes.

"Then, my friend," he said, "I will happily assist you with whatever you need."

Leenie Brown has always been a girl with an active imagination, which, while growing up, was both an asset, providing many hours of fun as she played out stories, and a liability, when her older sister and aunt would tell her frightening tales. At one time, they had her convinced Dracula lived in the trunk at the end of the bed she slept in when visiting her grandparents!

Although it has been years since she cowered in her bed in her grandparents' basement, she still has an imagination which occasionally runs away with her, and she feeds it now as she did then — by reading!

Her heroes, when growing up, were authors, and the worlds they painted with words were (and still are) her favourite playgrounds! Now, as an adult, she spends much of her time in the Regency world, playing with the characters from her favourite Jane Austen novels and those of her own creation.

When she is not traipsing down a trail in an attempt to keep up with her imagination, Leenie resides in the beautiful province of Nova Scotia with her two sons and her very own Mr. Brown (a wonderful mix of all the best of Darcy, Bingley, and Edmund with a healthy dose of the teasing Mr. Tilney and just a dash of the scolding Mr. Knightley).

# Connect with Leenie

E-mail:

*LeenieBrownAuthor@gmail.com*

*Facebook:*

www.facebook.com/LeenieBrownAuthor

*Blog:*

*leeniebrown.com*

Patreon:

https://www.patreon.com/LeenieBrown

**Subscribe to Leenie's Mailing List:**

Book News from Leenie Brown

(bit.ly/LeenieBBookNews)